Forbidden Fairytale: The Complete Trilogy

Forbidden Fairytale:
The Complete Trilogy

First Edition

Yanet Platt

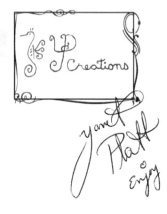

Forbidden Fairytale: The Complete Trilogy by Yanet Platt

First Edition

Fantasy, Fiction

YP Creations

North Aurora, Illinois

ISBN: 978-1-6671-5932-4

Imprint: Lulu.com

Book Design by Yanet Platt

Self-Published through

www.Lulu.com

Printed in the United States

City of Trinafin

Introductions

1

I am here at this moment to tell you a story that started out forbidden but true. A legend turned into an external existence of beauty and forbidden love. And if you are here reading this, then alas you have found a rare piece of the ancient times that were lost between the ages of time. Treasure this story as you are about to embark on an unforgettable journey that leads you through my enchanted life. This is my story of my forbidden fairytale...

My story begins on an ordinary morning here in the city of fairies called Whisperia. A city that is deep within the tropics of the rain forest where we live in harmony with the creatures of the lands. The fairies that live far within the city stay high among the treetops in wooden carved homes that are covered with enchanted flowers. Those flowers give the city an exhilarating aroma that quenches your heart. The city itself appears to be one with the jungle as majestic waterfalls drizzle over the lands sending enchanting rainbows soaring everywhere.

The lands below our city contain many creatures that push our imagination into oblivious. One of those creatures that are pure at heart, are the unicorns. They release a shimmering white glow from their coat that is very intense and soothing, when they want to be seen. Their coat is as white as a snowflake and as soft as a single feather. Their lullabies are what I love most about them. Their songs echo soft vibrations throughout the domain. Their dark brown eyes are the size of a walnut shell, but their vision is grander than our own. Their copper horn twists tightly upward giving them a powerful appearance. I have been told that the older and wiser they are, the longer and thicker their horn will be.

I do enjoy unicorn back riding at night though as we race among their kind letting only the moonlight guide our footsteps. The gentle unicorns' presence has always been here within our city. I have learned though that only the pure at heart are allowed to ride with them. Even the senators' race amongst them, although they do love to braid the unicorns' mane on every full moon. I try not to laugh at them especially when they have twigs and flowers sticking out from the top of their heads.

One of my favorite creatures that I would have loved to been able to see, was the fierce dragons. They existed here many centuries ago as I was told that they were evil creatures that had no respect for any living being that roamed the domain. The dragons would devour them whole only to spit out their bones, disgusting the thought isn't it. Dragons would fly over the moonlight to find the concealed locations of the delicate unicorns' in hiding. They said that their souls were filled with treachery and powerful black magic. The fire that was spewed from their throats would crisp everything it consumed. And their teeth were sharper than any sword or arrow made by magic or by hand. Their leathery skin was harder than any stone, but smooth to the touch as silk fabric. Their scales glistened in the rays of the tremendous sun. I would have loved to have been able to see, touch, or even ride one for that matter. I admit that would have been a terrifying time, but still nonetheless, it would have been breathtaking to witness.

A legend that is also told with the dragons is one of a forbidden city. A city that lies far within the south of Whisperia way out near the ocean, a city called Trinafin. Their castle is told to be more enormous and superior than any other castle combined. Within Trinafin lurked creatures that were more evil than the dragons themselves. They would scout the lands looking for anything that moved on the ground so they could torture. This is perhaps why we live above in the treetops, except our castle though. Their black magic was so treacherous that the dragons themselves would dread the creatures. That also could be why they obeyed their every command. No one knows what the creatures actually looked like for it was told that they always wore hooded cloaks. It was also told that if you ever did encounter one, that tears of blood would flow from your delicate eyes. But if this were true, then we fairies would live in constant fear.

So enough discussing about legends let's continue on about a city that is in this time; a tremendous city that lies northeast of Whisperia called Urinia. That city is built within and from the mountains. All of the walls and ceilings are built from its stone. Tunnels and bridges are carved out from the mountains that lead the way from home to home and to the city. Urinia also has many small rivers and ponds streaming throughout the land. In which small beaches seem to be everywhere as well as for the sand! Their streams also make grand water slides. You sit on a gigantic leaf as you are carried throughout the streams upward and downward. I am exhilarated when I am allowed to travel to the city on days when I am not needed, or when I simply sneak out of the castle.

Well, on the edge of the city of Whisperia there is a massive castle that stands miles long and wide, a castle in which I call my home. It is built from a deep gray stone that keeps us warm at night and cool during the day. Also very interesting enough, there is no glass in the windows of the castle. We fairies prefer to allow the gentle breezes to come in and soothe our skin. Sometimes servants fly in and out of the windows from time to time. They move faster that way taking the short cuts through them. But the windows themselves are enchanted from preventing bugs, animals and rain from coming in. Moss also covers half of the castle which gives shade to most of the windows.

So, before the sun rose I got up to get dressed in the mist of the morning. I took off my white silky nightgown and hung it on the corner of the canopy bed. I slipped into my working dress for the day. It is a silky sapphire blue fabric with golden laces around the front to tie. Gold sequins flow from the top of my back to the bottom of the dress. The dress does drag a little from the back giving it a small train appearance. It is not a very fancy dress you see. I am a servant in this castle, but not exactly. I am neither servant nor royalty but I have been raised here as both, for I do not know where or who my parents are.

I was told since I can remember that a week after the disappearance of Queen Lily I was found in the king and queens' bedroom. I was wrapped in an ordinary brown cloth made of soft cotton. King Duralos was furious thinking that I was abandoned by one of the servants. He asked everyone in the castle but they all denied me. So the king decided to hold a week of adoption. If no one wanted me then the queens' main maiden, Trathina, would raise me under the watchful eye of the king. The first day finally came for my adoption. The whole kingdom arrived; even fairies from Urinia came. As Trathina placed me in the crib that stood near the head throne I started to release a dim glow. At that very moment I was receiving my wings. Everyone was curious on what my wings would reveal, for they usually resemble your parents. Just as I was receiving them a bright purple lightning bolt struck across the sky, sending blinding light everywhere for a brief moment. Once that moment was over and shortly after they saw my wings, no one wanted to adopt me.

My wings you see, are extremely wider and taller than any other fairy in the lands. I also have something that no one else does, golden feathers. They line the edges of my wings. I also have different hues of blue flowing within my wings creating unique lines and curves that blended together. They are quite unique but exceptionally embarrassing. I am the only fairy with such wings. I feel out of place but I keep them tucked in most of the time. Fairies that stay within the castle though, have gotten accustom to my wings since I started to live here. They don't glare or treat me differently like the fairies in the city do. Perhaps that is why I don't usually leave the castle. Everything is here anyway, so I do enjoy living here in the castle in peace.

One more exotic and unusual thing about me is that I have a crystal diamond on my navel. I do not understand its reasoning on why it is there, but I do know that once again I am the only one with such a thing. The only interesting thing about the diamond is that it changes colors with my mood. It does burn a little when I get distressed or upset. Therefore I choose not to reveal my stomach as many girl fairies do in the city. Trathina is the only one that honestly knows it is there. That is another reason why I choose to stay within the castle walls.

Well then, Trathina, my nanny you could say, has told me the story of the day of my adoption. You could say she acts like my mother even though I know she isn't. Trathina is a bit taller than me, mostly everyone is though for I am only 5'1. Her wings are colored a silky white with light lavender swirls in it. Her skin is a soft pale pinky hue with rosy cheeks that stand out. She has midnight black hair that reaches her lower back. Trathina always has it tied behind her head though, she never has it lose. I have heard that she is very old, but for fairies age is only a number. For we never appear nor feel our real age.

As I walked over to the nightstand a golden goblet filled with berries awaited me. Trathina enjoys spoiling me now and then with an early snack. I took the goblet in my grasp and placed my right hand over the top. A white light shone from my palm as the berries started to melt and thicken. I was forming the berries into a smoothie, that way it would stay fresh. You know, I don't believe that I possess much magic but sometimes, I am told otherwise.

A warm breeze came into the bedroom from the balcony door. I walked over onto the balcony to see the grand view of our castle and jungle. The suns' rays just started to pour in sending splashes of color everywhere within my room. I stretched high in the air fluttering my wings letting only the tips of my toes touch the ground lightly. The tender breeze ran its fingers through my brown and golden streaked hair.

Suddenly a soft purring came from behind me. I turned my chestnut brown eyes toward the fireplace. An exotic snow leopard rested by the warm orange flames that still burned slightly from last night, her name is Snowfire. She has a pure white coat with black splotches everywhere. Her eyes are a dark green color with a lighter hue in the middle. She gave a long stretch and a yawn as she quickly fell back to sleep.

Trathina has told me that once I started living within the castle Snowfire appeared roaming around the castle. As she found my room Snowfire would not leave my presence. The servants could not remove her from my sight, no one really understood why. They all stopped trying to remove her after they saw that she meant me no harm. We became friends since that moment and she has been snuggled by my side ever since. She was a cub at the time when we first met. Perhaps she too lost her family somehow. Snowfire grew attached to me as I did to her.

Snowfire suddenly jolted up with her ears twitching all about and ran to the wooden door of my room. Her eyes started to glow brightly in the shadows.

"Who could be coming so early this morning?" I asked her.

Suddenly the door abruptly flung open and Trathina came barging in with a grin from ear to ear. She never knocks before she comes in, never. "Good morning my lady, there's lots to do today don't you think!"

"And what is there to do so early this morning that will be different than any other day?"

Trathina went over to the bed and started to make it ignoring my question. After she finished tucking in the corners of my soft cotton quilt she sat down on the bed. She crossed one leg over the other and stared at me with a blank look and replied, "After your lesson with the swords you will need to go to the fabric rooms. There the servants will start crafting your gown for the ball. You do realize that moment is already this weekend."

I sighed in deeply as I walked away from the balcony and headed to the fireplace. I placed my golden goblet down on the marble mantel as I turned to Trathina and half exaggerated, "Of course I do realize that it is this weekend, and I am extremely overjoyed to get that done right away."

I tried to give her a cheerful and excited expression but I'm sure that's not quite what she saw. She saw upon my face a forced smile. Trathina crossed her arms and scrunched her eyebrows together at me. She questioned, "You really aren't thrilled to go are you?"

I couldn't lie to her, it would not be fair to her. I admitted, "Trathina, I am eager to start working on the gown honestly I am, but the actual ball is what I'm not looking forward too." Trathina's face quickly saddened. She got up from the bed and walked slowly over by my side near the fireplace. I really didn't feel like doing anything differently on this day. But I still gave in to her guilty and depressed appearance. I sighed deeply and surrendered to her plans. "Alright-alright, what are your plans for me today besides my work in the gardens and class?"

A wide grin spread upon her face. She straightened her back and pushed her shoulders back. "You will have a special breakfast this morning with King Duralos. After breakfast you'll have the company of Prince Cethios, alone for dessert."

I stepped back a bit from her as she stated those words. I was taken off guard and confused. I asked, "Why would King Duralos want to eat breakfast alone, with me?" I started to ponder on the thought that the king never ate alone, especially with me. His advisors or other fairies that helped him with his duties always accompanied him. My eyes opened wide in fright. The only reason the king would eat alone with me was when I did something wrong and he wanted to scornfully interrogate my decision making skills. I quickly tried to recall all the recent things I had done wrong. I then remembered about the small incident in the kitchen. I didn't purposely cause that small fire, it wasn't my fault. Besides, I am rarely allowed to go into the kitchens and when I do, I can't help it if I am a little accident-prone and cause miniscule fires here or there. I demanded, "I'm going to get scolded at aren't I? You would tell me what I did wrong before I meet with the king right? And wait-wait, you do know that Cethios never eats alone, right?"

Trathina gently placed her warm hand on my shoulder completely ignoring my response, yet again. Delicate tears flooded her fragile eyes. She gave me an immense hug. I mean, did I miss something? After a brief moment passed by she let me go. She wiped the tears from her eyes and half assures me, "You will be going through so much this week. Now, don't hesitate to ask me for advice, or if you need an ear to listen to you. I am here for you. Whatever it is you need."

I started to confess, "Since you mentioned it I..."

But, she quickly interrupted me and boasted, "Now then we must make haste lots to do!"

I rolled my eyes and sighed. She was always on a land of her very own, not wanting to know the truth that surrounded her. Trathina hurried for the door and slammed it behind her, of course. A few seconds later the door swung opened with Trathina behind it once more. She asked me from the doorway, "Are you having your hair in that manner, you know um, all over in a messy untamed way."

I couldn't believe she said that to me. She squinted her eyes at me as if she was trying to see me from a distance. I simply shrugged and answered, "I could comb it down or tie it up. But I thought I could go for the wild look today."

She frowned at my sarcasm, but she still left with a slam of the door. It would be nice if for once she didn't slam that poor door. I mean, what did that door ever do to her?

Walking over to my dresser I sat down on the cushioned chair. I gazed over to the mirror glumly to see my reflection looking glum as well. I'm not sure how I expected to see myself in but I did look a bit horrid. My hair didn't help either for it was a bit messy.

Snowfire trotted over from her spot near the fireplace where she waited patiently until Trathina was officially gone. She sat near my side as she placed her furry chin onto my lap. I whispered to her, "I'll still pull my hair up, but you know she'll still hate it either or."

I turned and continued to stare at my reflection as I started to ponder on how I dreaded this very moment. I knew this day would one day come. You see, King Duralos wanted me to marry Prince Cethios, Prince of Urinia. Honestly that land probably belonged to King Duralos anyway. But, I'm not sure if he's just being ignorant about it, or simply chooses to avoid that land. He wants me to be taken care of I'm sure but I didn't want that. Zethron, the kings' advisor, would always push the idea on King Duralos.

Zethron has always hated me since I can remember. He enjoys making my day turn into a total nightmare. He is a sinister fairy who is filled with evil. Even his wings appear dreadfully evil. They are filled with several shades of gray and black. Also there are small circles in them as if small eyes are staring right into your very soul. His wings come down to four points at the bottom, giving them a look of two claws. His hair is as black as night and slicked back. Zethron also has a large hooked nose that flows downward toward his chin. His eyes are also almost colored a solid black that give his appearance a more defining and frightening look.

12

Zethron always wants to know where I am, keeping an eye on my every move. It becomes extremely annoying when there are servants who stalk my every movement around the castle. He would tell the king that in my life I shouldn't be able to have a soul mate. He would also contradict his words and say that Cethios is my soul mate in life and love, if any of that even makes sense. It is very disturbing knowing that I shall never be able to meet someone who really was meant for me, someone who wants to be with me and will love me for who I truly am. I'm always telling King Duralos that Zethron is full of treacherous evil and hatred and that we should send him away but, he dismays my every word. Trathina is the only one that secretly agrees with me about him.

I suddenly looked down at Snowfire and I started to chuckle. She was licking her nose uncontrollably. I complained to her, "I'm hungry too. I just thought I could delay time or..." Snowfire shook her head at me as if replying no to me. I sighed, "Alright let's go."

I stood up from my chair and slowly shuffled toward the door. Snowfire was behind me pushing my legs to go faster. As I opened the door Snowfire zoomed out pasted me rushing towards the kitchens. But before I closed the door I gave a quick glance around my room for one last time. I knew I wouldn't be seeing my room in that same peaceful way again, for the day of the ball comes dreadfully near, and I will then after that be engaged to Prince Cethios. Then from that moment on I will be in mourning, for one day after that will be my wedding day.

Breakfast or Dessert

2

As I walked down the corridor, I pondered about Cethios. He was a completely rude, selfish and inconsiderate fairy. Cethios is a tall skinny yet muscular fairy with black hair that is always cut short and spiked up or combed back. His light brown eyes have a splash of green right in the center. Cethios does not appear super muscular but he isn't weak. Do not under estimate that fairy that's for sure. He isn't a gentleman, in which you'd think he would be, being a prince and all. He only thinks of himself and his good looks. With that, Cethios thinks he can win any girl fairy over with that. The prince is not trustworthy and he's extremely unfaithful. I see him with a different fairy almost every day! His wings appear just as untrustworthy, for they are black with small plum circles within them. Hideous and weird I like to say.

As I was lost in concentration, I touched the cool walls and headed to the kitchens. Cooler breezes came in through the windows that relaxed my heart even more than the walls alone. Tall bronze twin doors with silver circles all over them now stood in front of me. They were cracked open a bit so I figured Snowfire had made her way inside.

Walking into the kitchens and looking up, I saw all the fairy chefs fluttering around preparing breakfast for everyone in the castle. Pots, pans, spoons and ingredients were all hovering around in the air. Suddenly flour sprinkled from above and onto my hair and shoulders. A caring voice shouted out from above, "So sorry my lady, my hands are extra buttery today!"

I chuckled as I rubbed my hands over my head and dusted my shoulders. I laughed, "That's okay Trajean!"

Trajean is the head chef of the castle. He makes the best honey cakes ever! His blonde curly hair hid behind a hairnet as he wiped his forehead with his sleeve. The other chefs around him were fluttering about making pancakes, omelets, sugared hams and much more.

This kitchen, and every other kitchen in the castle were colossal rooms extending upwards with multiple levels within it. It appeared as one kitchen if you were standing. But if you flew up a bit there was another kitchen on top of that equipped with all the same appliances. Another and another continued upward, there were five kitchens in this room. It does make it a lot easier to cook and prepare so much food in a little amount of time. It appears as a mirage that flows upward on a hot and humid day. There are also small islands that float in the middle of every kitchen that holds all of the ingredients. It is very entertaining to watch all the chefs' zigzagging through kitchen to kitchen preparing all of the meals.

On top of the ovens are gray and red bricks. The ovens themselves are a dark cherry wood with silver lining on the edges of every doorknob. I understand that wood burns up but gray marble lines the inside of the ovens. That same marble lies on top of the ovens as a counter top. And a steel bar hangs over that where the pots and pans hang from.

The kitchen itself has magnificent jungle carvings on parts of the walls and on the ceiling. Leaves and vines are the main patterns in this kitchen though. You really come to appreciate the craftsmanship in the detailed work when you stop and look at the art work instead of just taking a glimpse.

Trathina was already taking the cakes out of the oven when I arrived. Her hands were already glowing a bright white which meant that the pan was extremely hot. The magic that she was using prevented her from burning her hands. She replied without looking up, "The Honey cake that Trajean made for you is now ready. It has extra essence of oranges, extra moist just for my lady!"

"Thank you Trathina, and thank you Trajean." I glanced over to see him smile and give me a small bow. He then continued his cooking. I cleared my throat and replied to Trathina, "So, where do I start?" I took a small white apron that was hanging from the small island in front of me and I started to tie it around my waist.

Trathina on the other hand started to cut the cake in slices with an edged knife. They made the slices of cake look like slices of oranges. She started to spread orange cream over the slices of cake as she continued to ignore me. Trathina replied without looking up yet again, "King Duralos has been waiting to speak to you. He has already started his breakfast. Why don't you go and join him?"

I looked over to the second eating room to my right. All the servants were already starting to eat and to enjoy their meal. My stomach curled in as I became nervous. I replied a small lie to Trathina, "I already know what he is going to talk to me about. Can't I just eat breakfast with the others and join the king afterwards?"

15

Trathina walked towards me then around me, she untied my apron and slipped it off of me. "Now-now, don't be bashful. Go get some utensils and be on your way."

I grunted from her request as she gave me a small push towards the other side of the kitchen. As I headed towards the drawers where the utensils were a female chef was leaning against them. She handed me some utensils already wrapped in a blue cloth as she flushed a bright pink color. She softly asked, "Will the king be talking to you about Prince Cethios today? He is a handsome one, don't you think?"

My jaw dropped in shock. I wanted to scream and slap some sense into her but I held it in. Everyone thought he was such a great guy. Why was I the only one who knew better? I was the only one that saw him for what he truly was, a fraud! Trathina flew over to us with a grin on her face and replied, "That will be all thank you Kaleen. The second breakfast room still needs some preparing." Kaleen gave a small bow and left on her way over to the second eating room.

I turned to Trathina and responded, "Handsome yes, but hideous on the inside."

Trathina turned towards me and placed her hands on her hips as she grunted with disagreement. "Proper fairy women do not use those kinds of words. Besides, I believe Cethios is properly mannered, a good fairy gentleman. Annoying he may be if you count on when he speaks his mind. He speaks the truth from his heart. Great knowledge he has, yes indeed."

I couldn't help but to extend a huge smirk across my face. "Knowledge, is that what we are calling it now a days? Here I thought it was simply called ignorance or stupidity." I chuckled a bit as I wiped my eyes.

Trathina on the hand didn't seem so amused. She replied irritably, "Azalea, at least Cethios thinks before he speaks. You on the other hand can learn from that!"

I rolled my eyes away from her looking over to the second eating room. I took in a deep breath and walked toward the counter. I took the plate of cake and a goblet of berry juice. I opened my wings and flew out of the kitchen slowly. I didn't want to storm out in front of Trathina, or worse have King Duralos think I was upset at him.

As I flew out into the eating room King Duralos continued his meal as he glanced up briefly. I placed my goblet and plate on the mat next to him. The main table is long enough to fit twelve fairies comfortably. King Duralos sat at the front end of the table. I gave a small bow as I replied softly, "Good morning 'Your Majesty'. I do hope you have enjoyed your breakfast so far."

He was finishing stuffing his mouth with strawberries. King Duralos' complexion is a soft peachy hue with light chestnut brown eyes. His hair is wavy and light brown that is cut short and reaches up to his shoulders. He is a bit taller than I am and he's also very slender. The kings' wings are a forest green color with blue swirls over them. King Duralos was dressed in dark emerald hues, contrasting to his wings. The king replied after he gulped his food, "Ah Azalea good-good, join me here for breakfast."

I sat down and looked around for Zethron. Usually, he was attached to the kings' hip! "Where's Zethron 'Your Majesty'? Is he not joining us for breakfast today?"

"Nope, he's too busy preparing for the ball. He will be in the gardens all day perfecting everything though. Usual he wouldn't want those responsibilities, but nonetheless someone has to do it." He stuff his mouth with food as he continued to talk, "Well, we are here this morning to talk about you. We must discuss a situation that will affect the rest of your days."

I bit my bottom lip as my palm became sweaty. I hesitated but replied slowly, "And what situation is that 'Your Highness'?"

He pushed his meal aside with his delicate hand, as his plate was now empty. The concern in his eyes made me clench my teeth together. Well, at least I know he wasn't going to yell at me. "Azalea, you and Cethios get along quite well yes?"

I inhaled a deep breath. I started to feel dizzy. I replied, "Cethios is in a world of his own and...."

"Yes-yes but, he cares for you. He really does I can feel it, and you need someone like that in your life. He has these certain plans for you, we have discussed them recently."

I jerked back as he said those words. Yeah, plans to tie my wings together and push me off a cliff perhaps! I hesitated but asked cautiously,

17

"Plans? What kind of plans does he have for me? And why wouldn't he just tell me himself?"

King Duralos' face went from pink to a pale white. It seemed as if he was very uneasy about the conversation we were about to discuss. He replied with concern, "He just wants to take care of you. He has discussed them with me first as a sign of respect toward my crown."

I felt the room start to spin. My eyes seemed to dim my view of sight. I believe the news shocked me to a point where I forgot to breathe! I couldn't believe that King Duralos couldn't see that Cethios just wanted the crown for himself! I responded, "I don't understand why would he want me? I am just a servant. He has so many fairies lining up beside him. Don't tell me you don't see them fluttering around him at every waking moment. All they hope is that he'll choose them to be his princess; they'll do anything for him. They'll even give up their right wing just to have Cethios choose them."

"Is that jealousy I hear in your voice my lady? Are you afraid of challenging those other fairies to a duel?"

He chuckled as he spoke, but I quickly answered, "'Your Highness' first of all, if I do take any of those girls to a duel I would win within seconds. This obviously is before they even figure out how to properly hold a sword. Secondly, why should I throw myself at Cethios and humiliate myself even more than what these wings of mine don't already do! He chooses to flirt with all those other maidens. I shouldn't have to challenge anyone if he truly prefers to be with me."

The king continued to chuckle to himself as he ignored me. It seemed as if I was talking to the mist in the air that surrounded me. The king chuckled yet again, "You can catch good fairy gentleman if you present yourself with your wings open. Good fairy gentleman, like Cethios."

I lost my patience and half exploded, "You mean only Cethios! 'Your Highness', Cethios doesn't want me because he loves me. I don't think he even knows the true meaning of the word. I'm still just not understanding why he wants me?" King Duralos suddenly gave me a solemn look. I knew I wasn't going to get anywhere with this situation. I became mortified as I realized that nothing I said was going to change his mind. I was dreading this moment since the day they introduced Cethios to me as Prince of Urinia. Then it really hit me, I dreaded the truth of what this was leading to. I hesitated but cautiously asked, "Wait 'Your

18

Highness', are you implying that I wed Cethios? Is this seriously what is in stored for my future?"

King Duralos seemed to ponder my question as if he didn't know exactly how to answer me. The expression on his face though revealed everything. "If Cethios asked for your hand in marriage, you would say...."

I didn't even let him finish his sentence as I interrupted him. "No! I would tell him a definite no!" I turned myself from him as I slowly started to poke at my cake. I was so upset I didn't want to look at the king any longer. I honestly wanted to run away from this situation as fast and as far as I possible could.

But the king replied to me in a gentle voice, "Why would you reject his offer? He is a good man that sees you no harm."

I gulped my food as I pushed my plate away from me. I could hardly believe that he truly meant me no harm. Cethios loves to trip me while my hands are full with things, among other things that he does to humiliate me. He simply tells me it humors him. Great soul mate he'll make. I asked the king as calmly as I could, "Do you honestly think he'll be faithful to me if I do marry him? Or do you even think he'll truly love me or appreciate me?"

I'm guessing my questions disturbed him a bit as I noticed his face start to turn a bright red. "Azalea, you are like a daughter to me. Cethios has asked for your hand in marriage." As he continued to speck his voice kept getting louder and louder. "He will propose to you at the end of the ball and you will accept his offer!"

My mouth dropped to the floor in shock. I couldn't believe this is really how it was going to be. I somehow still managed to gather by breath as I continued to ask, "I don't honestly have a choice, do I? Is that truly my fate in life? Do you think that is what I honestly deserve?"

King Duralos whispered, "Fate, Fate?" My worst fear suddenly happened, he started to yell at me with full force. "You should be worried about your future not your fate! I will not always be able to protect you. Do you honestly think that you will forever be in this title that you are in now? You have to take up more responsibilities than you will ever imagine! You must be prepared for these upcoming events. You should be more concern for these fairies in the city not just only your fate! Do not pretend or appear to be selfish!"

I couldn't help it, I shouted back at him. "Selfish I am not! Does fate not represent the future? Besides, I have different feelings about my life, about myself that I cannot explain. Things are emerging from the darkness of the night and they are materializing in my dreams, things that I cannot answer!" The king now calmed down as he looked at me intensely. I continued more softly, "I have these strange dreams and they seem to be coming to me more and more, as my coming of age nears. They are warning me or telling me about something. They seem to be intensifying as the nights go by. But I only remember momentarily when I wake up. Then, as the sun reaches my room it vanishes in the mist of the morning. I am left with anxiety and heavy breathing. I understand they're about my life and it's about me being somewhere else, someone else. I am living a different life. I wake up glowing in my skin and it worries me. I am worried because I cannot answer the questions that my subconscious mind is giving me."

Tiny beads of sweat formed on the side of my forehead. I haven't told anyone about these rude awakenings. The king sighed deeply. Hopefully I calmed him down a bit. King Duralos asked with concern, "Explain to me a bit more about these dreams in which you are having."

I felt out of breath as the words were stuck in my throat. I felt ashamed feeling speechless, but I continued, "Dreams of worlds and creatures that I know do not exist. Dreams of hope, love, hatred, sadness and…." I glanced at King Duralos who was now listening intensively. I had to tell him the truth of how I felt even though I knew he would become upset. I replied as quickly as I could, "And that I marry someone else. I can't remember his face but it's very important to me, to my life and for my life. My soul mate is out there and I can feel it in my very skin. It's not Cethios that for sure and I plan to find him one day."

The king stood from his chair, wings up too! He was furious with a deep passion inside him that even his knuckles turned a burning red. "You will do no such thing! You will do so to marry Cethios, this is my command to you! You shall not deny nor refuse his hand! I rule this land and you're in it! On the day of the ball, you will accept his proposal. Do not force me to force you in shackles on your wedding day!"

He stared at me with anger in his eyes as he suddenly went white in the face. It seemed as if death was standing next to his side. He seemed to fear one of two things. One, was the deep sorrow in my brown eyes, which I doubt. Or two, for that very moment a single tear rolled down my cheek. It sparkled with a shimmering golden hue. It shone brightly as it left my face and onto the ground below. I was confused by his reaction. It seemed as if he had realized his worst fear.

He then turned from me and slowly walked around to the back of his chair as he folded down his wings. He gripped the chair tightly with a blank look. He seemed as if he didn't know what to do, say or how to react. It made me wonder what he was thinking about. His eyes were full of tears as he replied softly, "I'm so sorry Azalea I really am. I just want what's best for you, in case I am ever to leave these lands. I must go now and have some time to myself, to ponder this moment. Stay, finish your breakfast." I stood up and gave a small bow as he left the room as a sign of respect that I have for him. Before he exited the eating room, he held the doors open and begged, "Talk to Cethios yes?"

I couldn't refuse him any longer, for I knew I wouldn't be able to win. "Yes 'Your Highness' I will."

King Duralos smiled and gave a gentle nod of his head. He closed the door with a soft bang. I sat back down as I was now all alone in the room. The day had already become humid and dry, but I felt cold on the inside. From the corner of my eye, I could see Trathina coming out from the kitchen slowly. She was caring a tray with goblets of different sizes and colors. Once she was at my side she asked in a soft whisper, "Milk, tea or juice my lady? I have all different kinds of juices."

I took the cloth from her tray and wiped my face. "Trathina, now I am being forced to marry Cethios without a choice, against my will."

"Maybe it's for the best my lady. Think of it as once you are a princess, queen in waiting, think of all the fairies you can help, all of the good you have been so longing to do. Now, please cheer up, Prince Cethios is on his way here. Just make the best of it."

I nodded as Trathina took my old goblet and replaced it with a new one. She went into the kitchen without any more words to say. As the kitchen doors continued to swing Snowfire stuck her head out and stopped them. She happily trotted her way over by my side. When Snowfire reached me, she placed her head on my lap and started to purr softly. Her purr seemed to vibrate a soothing melody into my skin. Snowfire always knew when I needed her and how to comfort me. I took a piece of the leftover honey cake and gave it to her as she quickly chewed it happily. I too started to eat for I didn't want to eat in the company of Cethios.

Snowfire turned her head toward the doors on the opposite side of the eating room to my right. Her eyes started to glow a dark red. I knew at that moment that Cethios was coming through those doors, she hated him too. Cethios did come in seconds later with two fairies, one flying on each of his arms as they giggled and laughed.

Both of the girls that came in with him have orange wings with black spots all over. Their bottom wings seem as if they were not connected to their top wings. Their clothes needless to say, looked as if they couldn't get any smaller. Both of the girls were wearing light orange tops with skirts that had splotches of green and blue everywhere. The fairies had white shimmering glitter all over their faces. Honestly, the only thing I was jealous about was that they were showing their navel. But of course, they had nothing on their navel. I call those girls temporaries, because once Cethios is bored of them, he gets new ones. Once Cethios made his way over to me, he raised his eyebrows and asked, "Good morning Azalea, did you enjoy your breakfast?" He had a huge smirk on his face.

I knew Cethios already knew that the king and I discussed that horrible plan of his. Actually, forced me is more like it but I didn't want Cethios to see that I was bothered by it. It would only satisfy him knowing that I was upset. I replied in my best happy voice ever, "Good morning Cethios, yes I did enjoy my breakfast. Thank you for asking."

I could tell that he was not content with my response. He replied with arrogance, "Azalea, do not take that formal tongue of yours with me. Take your place and address me as Prince Cethios. I don't have that title just for nothing. You need to learn and mind your manners."

I rolled my eyes around as he stood there with his nose in the air. Of course, arrogance was shoved so high and hard in his head. All he wanted to do was try to embarrass me in front of his air headed fairies. As usual his companions giggled at his comment. One of the fairies that was with him leaned over to him and smugly replied, "Oh don't be so rude to this poor servant 'Your Highness'. She obviously has lost her tongue, improper manners. They just don't educate poor girls like that anymore."

I wonder if she really understood what she had just said. She seemed so ditzy. Cethios laughed along with the other fairies. After a brief moment Cethios chuckled to them, "Why ladies, this servant is none other than the infamous Azalea, the king's adopted daughter." My eye twitched a bit at his words. But of course, the girls turned in shock and gawked at me as if I was some interesting creature they have never seen before. Yet, they still had that facial expression as if they thought they were still better than I was. But infamous, what was his suggestion by calling me that? Perhaps he was simply jealous of the thought that I was actually quite well known throughout the land and he wasn't. Cethios headed for the other side of the table and extended his arm out. "Sit my ladies and join me for breakfast."

As they sat down some chefs came out from the kitchens with trays hovering next to them. They went over and placed the food in front of them. I on the other hand took my plate and goblet and stood up to leave. Snowfire gave a high-pitched snarl at Cethios and the girls. The two girls jumped up a bit scared from Snowfire's growl. I laughed hysterically on the inside! I gave a small curtsy and started to walk towards the kitchen. Snowfire made it safely there, I on the other hand didn't. Cethios shouted over to me, "And where do you think you're going?"

I froze as I gritted my teeth. I knew he just had to embarrass me even more before I left the room. I spun around slowly and replied, "To the kitchen 'Your Highness'. I must get going on my chores for the day." I dreaded using those words. I knew that phrase only filled his head with more arrogance. But I didn't want him embarrassing me even more in front of the girls. I wanted to get out from his presence and fast! I also didn't want him going to King Duralos and blabbing a lie or something else.

He replied arrogantly, "Good, go get some desserts for me and my beautiful guests."

The girls giggled and blushed from what Cethios had said. It just burned me on the inside knowing that he was going to be my groom to be! Even the stone on my stomach burned. I held in my anger as I replied as calmly as I could, "Why you haven't even finished your breakfast yet, why should I?"

Oh, good one, I couldn't believe I said that but, I just had too! Cethios looked up at me with his cheeks full of food. He gave a loud gulp from his food as he seemed upset. He forced a smile and replied, "Azalea do you think I am rude to you?"

I just stared at him with my mouth slightly gawked open. What was I supposed to say to that? I couldn't tell him the truth, or could I? I would actually enjoy that. "Sometimes, usually, all the time if you want me to be honest with you. We are supposed to have an honest relationship from now on, am I right?"

"Has King Duralos spoken to you about this weekend and for what awaits for you in that moment?"

"Yes, he has spoken to me about…."

Cethios interrupted me as he quickly replied, "Do you then accept those terms in which he has spoken to you about, about my proposal?" My mouth dropped open in shock as well as the two girls. I didn't know what to say, I couldn't believe he was telling me this in front of those girls. I mean, this announcement wasn't ready for the public just yet. And by the look of the girls' faces, they weren't going to keep this a secret! Cethios glanced over to each of the girls, jerking his head to one side. "May you excuse me my ladies? I must have some privacy to speak to this, enchanting fairy of mine."

Enchanting? Oh, was he talking about me now? It was a bit of a shock to me as well as the two fairy girls as they glanced at each other with shock and jealousy on their faces. They still both stood up and replied at the same time, "Of course, anything for our prince."

They walked over to the other side of the eating room where they first entered. They stood by the door with their hands behind their backs. The eating room was large enough that where they stood, they wouldn't be able to hear anything coming from the table. Or so I thought. Cethios extended his arm to me and replied as seductively as he could, "Please, come and sit next to me. I promise I won't bite."

I grunted; he wouldn't bite. But I'm sure he'd probably gnaw on my skin! I sighed deeply as I slowly walked over and sat down next to him. I still held on to the plate and goblet though, I mean where else was I supposed to put it. Besides, I wasn't honestly sure whether I really wanted to sit down or not. I think I was still baffled at the whole enchanting thing. Cethios then asked softly as he desperately tried to gaze into my eyes, "Azalea, how long have I known you now?"

"Since I can remember, probably since birth."

"Well, you may or may not believe me, but I really do care about you. I say this from the bottom of my heart."

I chuckled almost hysterically, "Oh really, I would have believed you centuries ago but now, no. Besides, how many times have you told that to one of your other fairies?"

I couldn't keep this in any longer, I was going to explode. It's better to tell him now than later when it would be already too late. But all Cethios could do was give me this corky smile. He replied softly, "Azalea, those girls are like decoration on a cake. I need their support one day. I will be king and I, I can't have them objecting me, can I? The day of the ball only has one reason, I am to find a bride. Young beautiful fairies will be coming from all over the city. It's all part of the excitement, but at the end of the day, I will be choosing you."

"Do I attract you because I am the only fairy that is not attracted to you? Or should I say, you don't want someone who objects you, and I do, and that burns you doesn't it? You want to imprison me for the fact that I will resent you. A queen must be obligated to his king and you want to enslave that fact. You are afraid that I will bring an uprising against you if I do not wed you."

Cethios chuckled to himself as if he was trying to hide his true reaction to my outburst. He half heartily chuckled, "My lady, where do you get these ideas from? You have such a free mind. Well don't worry, I will be choosing you that night."

"Is it then my free mind that frightens you? You want to control it. You're terrified on what I can do with it, aren't you? I will fight you; I do hope you realize that fact. I will resent you."

Cethios moved uncomfortably in his seat. I knew I angered him, but I will not lie to him any longer. He must know what he is getting himself into. Cethios placed his hand on his chin and replied cautiously and slowly, "We have known each other since you were born. I know the stars in your eyes and I know what drives your dreams, hopes, and passion. I will not purposely hurt you. I give you my word as a man. The fairies in this city and their future are in your decision to make. You are the only one that cares for them. I want to make you my queen to support you. All these other fairies just want the treasure, and you, you don't care for any of that. I can make this happen if you trust me. I adore you and I want to be by your side, to be your king. I want to support the decisions that you make for these fairies. You are a very powerful fairy, I know you are and, you are the only one who can make things happen for the fairy people. And then maybe at the end of our time, I want to share it with you. You are my treasure in the golden sand. Once the arrangements are made, it's only you who will be by my side. I will share my life only with you."

Cethios reached out and placed his hand on my arm. I flinched but for some reason I didn't move away. I wasn't sure whether or not he was being honest with his words. I mean, did I really have a choice to deny his hand anyway? He continued, "I care for you, and I hope one day soon, you will care for me too, as well as trust me. My heart will be yours that night and forever after that."

Should I honestly believe him, I mean come on. For some strange reason I wanted to though. Was he really going to change for me? The whole time he spoke to me though his eyes never left mine. Cethios never flinched nor sweated. Either he was telling the truth or he was a great liar. I was extremely nervous the whole time he spoke to me. I replied to him in a low whisper, "Why do you then treat me the way you do. You weren't always so heartless. When we were younger, we were these inseparable best friends for eternity. You were different before, but then you left me. For about one century you spent your life in Urinia. When you came back though, you were completely different. It was as if I was staring at someone else. A dark creature with took your soul. And your eyes, they don't gleam the way they used to. I'm not sure what's in you now, but I know the Cethios I knew then is not in there now. You should know you can't hide the truth from me forever."

Cethios turned his face away from me as he dazed off towards the window and softly clenched his other hand into a fist. It seemed as if he was pondering my words. Sadness and regret seemed to fill his eyes momentarily. But then his expression quickly went to arrogance as if he regained himself and unclenched his fist. He replied carefully, "Please Azalea, I do apologize for everything I have done to you. I do hope that one day you could forgive me. Also, call me Cethios."

All I could do was stare into the empty space that surrounded me. I was so unsure of this situation. I didn't know how to respond, but deep down I knew I had to say something. "Okay, Cethios, do you honestly mean those words that you said to me? Are you willing to give me your word against all creations? Are you going to be faithful to me always? And, no other fairy will ever come between our trust? Will you cherish and protect all other of everything that is mine?"

Cethios looked at me without blinking and leaned over closer to me. I felt fuzzy and light headed, he never looked at me that way before. He then picked up my hand and kissed it. Goosebumps formed all over my arms as he gently replied, "My lady, my Azalea, my heart and trust will be yours to keep. So is my wild soul in which the heavens created just for you. My admiration is everywhere for you, and I do desire your trust. I ask thee again as I will ask thee the night of the ball, do you accept my proposal?"

I was confused here. I was seeing a side of him I haven't seen in a very long time. He was pouring his heart to me and I didn't know how to respond. Part of me still wanted to punch him hard in the face. But still I never dreamed of this kind of proposal, this was not romantic at all. And all I could do was stutter from the shock at his weird change of heart, "I um, I...." I turned my head slightly towards the kitchen door. I could feel the presence of Trathina and probably all of the other chefs and servants at that moment on the other side of the kitchen door. They were all pressing their bodies against the door and the walls trying to hear our conversation, shame on them. I replied to Cethios, "Let me go and get some dessert for us. I will give you my answer on the day of the ball."

"Wait-wait, dessert?" Cethios asked. I turned to look directly within his eyes. I wanted to know if he would send me away. Would he truly rather be with me instead of those girls? Cethios glanced at the fairies by the door, then back to me. He whispered, "Yes, our dessert. Go get us one of those scrumptious pies. You know which one is my favorite."

I stood up and gave him a small curtsy and headed for the kitchen. As I entered the kitchen though, chefs, servants, and Trathina all jumped away from the walls and pretended to be busy talking. They were all caught in the act. Trathina asked with a bashful pink face as if she didn't know what was going on. "So how did it go with Prince Cethios? Did he pronounce his love and respect for you?"

I hated to admit she was partially right. Perhaps I did see him in a wrongful eye all these days. Or I didn't even give him a chance really. I looked up to see everyone staring at me with enormous grins on their faces. I half shouted to everyone, "Alright, alright, everyone can go back to work. My life isn't an open book to read you know."

Every nosy fairy sighed sadly and went on their way. They were saddened by the fact that I did not reveal anything to them. I stood there and waited till all fairies were gone except Trathina. I replied to her, "May I please have some berry pie?"

With a smile on her face, she quickly took off flying towards the icebox in the third level kitchen. When she flew back down, she had one pie and only one fork. She handed it to me and replied, "Go and feed him some pie. It could be a romantic moment for the both of you. And after,

27

perhaps you can spend the day with him and get to know him better. Give him a chance. Oh, ask him to go with you to your sword swinging lessons. You both can teach each other a trick or two. I heard he's unbeatable."

"But should I believe in what he said. Should I trust him?"

Trathina sighed deeply to my question as she answered, "Did he not give you his word? Is that not enough for you? Azalea, do not make me think that he is too good for you." Trathina placed her hand on my shoulder and continued with great concern, "There could be love and boundless trust there, if you learn to let it in. There might even be a happily ever after." She then turned and left toward the door that led to the hallway. She was disappointed in me as I turned my gaze away from her. But before Trathina left she replied, "I'll excuse you from your chores from this day forward, if you so choose it."

I didn't even get a chance to reply to her. As for when I glanced back towards her, she was already gone. I was now alone in the kitchen with Snowfire whom now was sitting on the island counter eating some kind of left over. I pondered about what just happened in the eating room and with Trathina. I felt as if my head was going to burst with madness. I mean, if only Cethios would get rid of those stupid fairies. Then perhaps I could be sort of all right with this arranged wedding!

Walking over to the door that led to Cethios I stopped in front of it. I balanced the pie in my left hand then slowly placed my right hand over the doors. I closed my eyes for I wanted to see what was happening in the room before I entered. I have been forbidden from spying on anyone, I am the only one that actually possesses that magic. Stumbled upon it by accident really, when I was younger I did it a lot! I couldn't help it, but I was alone in the kitchen at the moment. Well besides Snowfire but I hardly think she'll tell anyone.

My palm started to let out a low white glow. The vision of the next room started to appear in my mind. I saw and heard…

Both fairies were already standing next to Cethios rubbing his shoulders. One replied, "Cethios did you really mean what you said to that hideous servant? And what about us, are you honestly going to be only for her? Will you forget about us?"

The other fairy added, "Yes don't you love us anymore?"

"Ladies-ladies." Cethios replied, "Do not worry, love is not an action nor a feeling. It's a word that describes something that is desired, but isn't real."

One fairy answered, "You told her she had your heart and your word."

Cethios chuckled to himself, "She cannot decide nor command what I do with the outer parts of my body. My body has a burning desire for passion."

Then one jealous fairy flew in front of him and with took him by the chin as she kissed him passionately.

I filled up with so much anger my palm started to sweat. My whole body grew numb with hate. I felt so deceived, betrayed and ignorant for believing in him. My hand slipped from the door suddenly. I instantly lost my connection. I wanted to take my shoe off and beat him with it! I am on a verge on marrying a complete jerk. My future now seemed hopeless. If only I could flee this kingdom and never return again. I wiped my sore eyes to see Snowfire still on the counter top. Her eyes burned with red flames as her low growl sent vibrations throughout the kitchens' air.

"Snowfire were you snooping in my mind? Shame on you." Well, I was sort of doing the same thing. Who was I to judge? I took a step closer to Snowfire and replied, "You stay here and out of trouble. In fact, go wait for me in the sword swinging room or in the gardens. Go!"

She gave a small growl and jumped off the counter with a powerful leap and darted out of the kitchen. I wiped my face and chest with a nearby cloth. I raised my right hand over my body and slowly moved it down. I re-prepared my hair and body removing sweat of anger and stress off my body. I still rubbed my eyes for a brief moment. I knew he would never change for me, ever.

As I forced a smile on my face, I pushed the door and went into the eating room. The ditzy girls were back by the door as if they had never left that very spot. Their massive grins made me want to fly over there and beat it off of them. Walking over to Cethios I still kept the pie in my hands as I tried to stay relaxed. I stood there next to him and replied as happily as I could, "Cethios, here is your pie as you wished."

I continued to hold the pie as Cethios rubbed his hands together. "Why thank you Azalea, yum, that does smell delicious." I cut out a small piece with the fork. He closed his eyes and opened his mouth. Cethios had some nerve, I couldn't believe he thought he could get away with something like that. I knew what he wanted me to do but I had something else in mind. I lifted the pie up and slammed it on his face with a plop! You can't blame me; he did have his mouth open. "You fluttering clutch!" Cethios screamed out. The other fairies came rushing over to his side.

I then slowly enjoyed the pie from the fork. "Yum, your right Cethios, this is delicious." I replied to him. I tossed the fork at his chest.

Cethios stood up wiping his eyes trying to take the pie off his face as he shouted, "What do you think you were doing!?"

I licked my fingertips to rid myself from the rest of the pie that landed on them. I replied to him, "Why, I gave you your pie. Isn't that what you wanted? You did have your mouth open, didn't you? I'm so sorry, did I miss?" I started laughing out loud. I opened my wings as wide as I could as I startled the other fairies. I flew out of the room still laughing. I left the fairies to clean up their prince. I on the other hand was still upset from the fact that he thought he could fool me. Besides, I was late for my sword swinging class and I had to rush over. Oh well, the prince did get his just dessert after all.

Fate in the Sword Swinging Room

3

I was still soaring through the air as I pushed my way through the doors of the sword swinging room. I landed on my toes just a few feet in front of from them. I inhaled deep breaths as I looked back at the doors. They were swinging back and forth as they started to slow their sway.

The room itself had a sweet aroma of lilies and roses. The floors were made of a soft blue cushion that covered the entire room. On the wall where the doors stand are mirrors that covered its entirety. In front of the door to the far left are cabinets filled with swords and awards. To the right of the room against the corner sits a small table with burgundy silk roses in a stumpy forest green vase. A door lays blended in with the mirrors at the very edge of the room. Although, no one but James and I know it exists there.

James was now standing in the middle of the room with his arms crossed over his chest. James is a tall slender fairy with grayish white hair. His silver glasses usually hang almost at the tip of his nose as his light blue eyes usually peer over the top rim. His delicate eyes remind me of the morning sky. James appears to be extremely weak but in reality he is swift, cunning and impossible to beat in a duel. His wings are a dull gray with bits of silver within. James is the head trainer in swords. He always tells me that strength is only the compassion of your mind, in which it conquers over your ability to give back in a physical reaction. James replied over to me, "My dear Azalea, what upsets you this morning?"

I started to pull my hair away from my face as I answered him calmly, "Why do you refer to me as upset?"

He walked over closer to me and glimpsed at the doors as they finally stopped swinging. "Since when do you come in here flying? Besides, my doors have now become swinging doors rather than sliding ones."

"I'm so sorry James." I honestly was still upset from breakfast. I went up to the doors and placed my right hand upon one of them. Light blue light shone from my palm as the doors glowed with that same light. The edges of the doors that were cracked started to mend together. The pieces of the wood swirled themselves together slowly as if they were dancing a slow ballet. I let go of the door as I started to check the edges.

After that, I walked over to the sword cases where James was already awaiting me. He was taking two swords out from one of the cases and examining the sharpness of them. We only practice with dull enchanted swords for our safety.

I glanced over to a sword in which was locked up in its own case. The sword is magnificent in its own beauty of appreciation. It is long, slender and made of a silver metal. It has gold lining on the edges of the sword. The handle has pink and blue stones shaped as diamonds and hearts. The handle itself curves downward slightly that contours to the curve of your hand. It also has gold lining with silver glitter over the handle.

James looked over to me and sighed out, "Ah, Queen Lily's sword." James now stood behind me with a smile on his face.

That sword I have loved and admired from afar since I can remember. I turned around and asked him, "James, when will the time come when I am able to fight with this sword?"

He placed his hand on his chin to ponder my question. He replied with a thought, "I will share a secret with you if you promise to share it with no one." I spun around quickly and looked at him with my eyes widen, as his were as well. He handed me a sword as he took off into the middle of the floor. He started preparing for my lesson of the day. James placed the sword gentle to his forehead then to the ground. He positioned himself then signaled for me to take my place in front of him. He replied with a smile, "This weekend embraces a special event for you, does it not?"

I looked down at the sword as I gripped it tightly within my grasp, this weekend was not special to me at all. I was still very much upset with the thought from breakfast. I then did something you should never do. I went up to James and gave my first swing in anger. He ducked and lifted his sword in the air to block my hit. "Fighting in anger is always upsetting to me. You of all should understand that when you fight with anger, you shall and will always be defeated. Anger will not conquer your goals. You know better, come we spar as you tell me what grieves you." Our swords collided as we ducked, dodged and continued to swing the swords. Beads of sweat started to drip down the side of my forehead moments later after we started. "Azalea what disturbs you? Since when do you glow of sweat during the first hour of your lesson?"

I started my story as we continued to spar. "Well, today King Duralos told me that I must marry Cethios, that I have no choice in love, none whatsoever. I must marry an inconsiderate fairy. My so called prince will not be faithful, nor can he be trusted. He will not love me, I guarantee you. And in the end, I will be used and left to be wasted away to nothing. Why does he want me? Me, out of all the fairies he can handle. I don't understand, to make me miserable perhaps. I will never be able to find my true soul mate. My soul will be cursed, starting with this weekend at the ball."

James gave a quick blow in which I blocked, but in return he spun downward and curved his leg out as he quickly placed it between my knees. He pushed my knee forward in which of course caused me to fall down on my back. I gave a short scream as I fell hard onto to the cushioned floor. James now stood up and held the tip of his blade to my neck. By this time I was breathing hard and trying to catch my breath. James replied breathlessly, "Is that why you came storming into my room of tranquility?" His face turned slightly red with hints of anger in his voice. I did honestly feel bad at that moment for angering him. And even though James was upset briefly, he still helped me up to my feet.

I felt dizzy as the room continued to spin circles around me. I took in deep breaths as I tried to control my breathing. I replied to him between breaths, "You know, for being an ancient fairy that you are, you are difficult to defeat…did I disturb you before I barged in? Were you meditating in serenity? I truly am sorry if I disturbed you."

James dabbed his forehead with his gray hanker chief. "No-no, one must have their own unique entrance. You just have um, your own unusual way."

I pointed the tip of my sword to James. "So, are you going to tell me that secret of yours?"

James moved my sword away and pointed to the small table in the corner. He replied softly, "Come, lets' have some lemon tea before you leave for the day."

I opened my wings and fluttered over in front of him as he was already walking over to the table. I hovered in front of him with my arms crossed. "Are you deliberately trying to distract me from remembering that you have a secret to tell me?"

"I'm offering my lady some tea in generosity, you shouldn't reject my offer. It is delicious for your heart and soul." My expression from being upset went to calmness. I surrendered and landed on my feet as we walked over to the small table. On the table stood two small white tea cups, each with a slice of lemon inside. A silver tea pot hovered over from where the mirrored door stood, it hovered in midair until James with took it. He poured some in each cup as he replied, "Now, I will not be able to reveal all to you today, the soldiers will be coming soon for their daily training."

"But why do you train soldiers? Who does the king plan to fight with?"

"My dear, so many questions so little time to explain your place with fate."

I was lost in his words. I looked down at my teacup. It had pink flowers designed on it. James' cup had royal blue flowers on it. Warm mist escaped our teacups as it flowed around the table. I swirled my fingers within the mist then placed my pointer finger in the cup. Long ice cubes shaped like small lemon slices appeared inside the cup. I with took the misty water from the air and reformed it as ice into my cup. I do prefer chilled tea, not warm. I asked James, "What do you refer by, my place with fate?"

"Azalea, do you remember how we first meet?"

A smile and a small chuckle came upon me as I remembered that day. I was very young and was playing hide and seek with Trathina and some other servants. I stumbled into this room and fell in love with the swords and the mirrors. As I pressed my body into the corner mirror I fell through. Once inside I stood up and dusted myself only to be in shock at what I saw. The room was filled with greenery as if it was a secluded jungle. The ceiling seemed iridescent in hues of blue. A small waterfall drizzled over some grey stones as it fell into a small pond in the middle of the room. Hovering over the water in a meditating position was a fairy with his eyes closed. I shouted over to him, "Good morning, my name is Azalea! What's yours?"

His concentration was disturbed as he splashed into the pond below. Running over to apologize I too jumped into the pond. I'm not sure why, perhaps I thought that I needed to save him. So, drenched with water James simply smiled and with took me by the hand. He didn't seem upset at all. We walked over to some pinky azaleas by his garden. I started to smell the sweet flowers as he replied, "My lady, these flowers just bloomed about a century ago….You came into this world to save us all, and today and always I will try to save you."

I didn't know what that meant but James assured me that one-day, I would understand. Since that day he has been training me with the swords three times a week. James continued to sip his tea as he finally replied, "You are now at an age where you are able to accept the understanding of this extended knowledge that I will share with you. Except it and take it in with wisdom and apply it to your heart. Ask me no questions for I will only reveal answers to you."

I interrupted him, "How will I know which answers go to which questions, if the understanding is beyond reasoning to my questions?"

James raised his hand as his palm gave a dim white glow. He was meaning for me to stop talking, of course. James continued to sip his tea and continued, "Secrets will reveal themselves to you at a slow pace, but surely one day you will know. Follow your instincts no matter if at the time, it is the wrong thing or the right thing to do. But follow it nonetheless without hesitation. Accept yourself for who you really are for the truth lies within your very skin. Death will one day kiss you softly upon your rosy cheeks, but it will not inherit your soul. Make your decisions cautiously and wisely. There will be days which darkness will surround you. You shall not surrender to this torture, I forbid you to give up. Your magic is greater than you see content with, dig deep into your mind to find your utopia, for there it shall be. But on this day you have come to an age where your sight and instinct becomes acceptance. Your wisdom has intensified since your training started with me. The good I have seen you do for these fairies in this city and for nature itself, gives you strength in your heart. Now I give you my blessing, your future lies beneath your wings. Follow that voice inside you that speaks the truth. Trust what you see within your eyes and your heart. There will be a day when all of this will be clear to you or, perhaps day by day. You will know what you need to do for your future and your fate. Being said that take this knowledge and don't ponder much over it, you have too much on your mind already." James sipped his tea some more and took in a deep breath. He let it out slowly as he reached over and placed his warm hands on mine. Squeezing my hands gently James replied, "Now the big secret is that yes that day has come. You will carry Queen Lily's sword on the day of the ball."

I tried to play it cool but failed, the immense smile on my face gave me away. I wanted to scream, shout and jump all around but, the seriousness on James' face made me not. "Thank you James." I still stood up and gave him an immense hug squeezing him softly.

As I let go he replied to me, "Now go, the soldiers will be arriving soon. And, one more thing Azalea." He leaned closer and whispered, "On the day of the ball no matter what happens, take that sword with you and carry it at all times. Never let it out of your sight."

I was confused. I was going to ask him what he meant by that but as I turned, soldiers started coming in through the door. I walked away from James and headed for the door. Still, I looked back as James gave a small bow before the soldiers that now stood in front of him.

Before I headed out I stopped to look at Queen Lily's sword once more. A soldier with glorious green eyes came up by my side. It was Fendric, James' head student of the class. He replied to me, "Beautiful isn't it."

I smiled and replied, "Yes, that sword is beautiful."

Fendric gave me a confused look with a raised eyebrow as he with took my hand and answered, "No, I meant the reflection of my lady Azalea."

Looking behind the sword there was a mirror as I saw my reflection staring back. I gave a small bashful smile and glanced back to James, whom was already starting his lessons. Fendric gave me a warm smile as he softly kissed my hand and then released it. I was speechless momentarily, but as I regained myself I replied softly, "Thank you but, I must be on my way. I am needed in the gardens this day and at this moment."

I gave a small bow, turned and headed toward the doors. I glanced back to see Fendric still warmly smiling at me as I walked away. I turned back and giggled to myself as I headed out of the room. And this time I remembered to slide the doors.

The Surprise Gift

4

I slowly walked over to the gardens in the back of the castle. It was my favorite place to go and favorite obligation to do, attending to the flowers. The flowers themselves have grand personalities. Their petals form small mouths, and let me tell you they tell the finest stories in the lands. They would actually give me history lessons from time to time about the ancient plants and herb that we use now a days. Their stories of the past are amazing as well, stories of the king and queen and their time before them. They do only tell me when no one is around though. If Zethron found out that I was learning about the past he would tell the king to discipline me with more chores. I would be scrubbing floor for weeks!

Well then, the flowers seemed to form their own city behind the castle. It usually takes me a month or so to serve all of the flowers. After that month I simple start all over to the beginning. We do have some of the most exquisite exotic plants around.

I started to attend to some purple roses when suddenly my breath was taken from me. Zethron was positioned behind my shadow sending shivers onto my skin. I with took a green spray bottle as I turned around. I pretended I did not realize he was there. I gave a small shriek. He raised his nose in the air and replied arrogantly, "Good afternoon Azalea, late to your chores today?"

"Why Zethron, you know I have practice with James in the early morning today. Besides, I spoke with King Duralos during breakfast. That threw my schedule off for the whole day." I paused as I gave him a confused look and continued, "Why would that be any of your concern?"

A massive smile stretch across his face as he asked, "So you have spoken with the king. Excellent, so what was your response to his request?"

I walked sideways away from his presence to the other flowers. I squirted them with the water bottle as they cheered lightly. I replied to him without looking his way, "Why, you of all fairies should understand that when something is discussed in private with the king, it remains in secrecy unless the king himself tells you."

From the corner of my eye I saw that he scrunched his nose in with anger. He leaned over and took the water bottle from my grasp. Ignoring him I waved my glowing hand over this wilted blue rose in the ground. It lifted out of the ground and into a brown clay pot I had nearby. I started to pour dirt into the pot when the rose started squealing, "No-no-no-no-no-no-no!" With its delicate leaves it started pushing the dirt out of the pot. It also tried to climb out of the pot with its roots.

I leaned over and whispered to it, "You are sick. I need to move you to a shadier spot before you wilt even more. Go ahead and stay in, I'll bring you plenty of cool water. I'll bring back once you are well, I promise."

The blue rose turned its head toward me and whimpered. But then replied, "Ok-ok-ok-ok-ok-ok-ok." The rose settled in as it started to pull the dirt towards the center of itself.

"That's better isn't it." I whispered to the rose as I kissed it gently on its head.

Zethron probably started to get annoyed as he leaned towards my ear and replied as softy and as calmly as he could, "My lady, my presence would have been but there were certain situations that needed my attending too and…" I turned around to look at him as he suddenly placed his left hand around my neck. He squeezed my neck tightly as he turned my head slightly to the side. He continued, "And if I find out that you denied the princes' proposal, or plan to corrupt it, your fate will diminish within my grasp. Your soft whispers will come to a complete end."

I shifted my neck as Zethron released his tightening grasp. I looked into his eyes without fear and replied, "Is that a threat of anger, or are you uncertain of your securities?"

Zethron leaned back and slowly walked away snickering to himself. As I started to take in a huge sigh of relief I heard rustling behind me. Beruchium, the main gardener stuck his head through the bushes behind me. "My lady, is everything alright?" Beruchium is a tall dark brown skinned fairy. He has brown wavy hair with dark green eyes. His wings are also a green and brown color as if they were camouflaged with the land. Beruchium is able to change his wing colors from time to time to blend in with his surroundings. Sort of like a chameleon.

I rubbed my neck slowly with my fingertips as I answered, "Yes thank you but, what is so important that Zethron needed attending to here in the gardens? He despises coming out here."

Beruchium bit his bottom lip as he poked his head back into the bushes. I saw him fly over the hedge and over to my side. Once he landed he glanced around to see if anyone was around. Once content he whispered, "Well, the king has told us that on the day of the ball the prince will propose to a fairy and make her his bride. The next day the wedding will take place but…" He looked around and spoke even quieter, "Between you and me, Zethron has casted a spell away from the castle. I'm not sure on what though? Just in case she makes a run for it. A spell that will stop her in her place, unable to move if she tries to escapes. Do you know whom he will be choosing?"

I felt the stone on my stomach set a flame. I became extremely infuriated. How could the king not tell me that my wedding day to Cethios would be the next day! I wanted to scream from the top of my brains. This treatment was unfair, I was being set up! I clenched my teeth anyway and tried to give Beruchium a confused look. I didn't want him to realize that it was me who was going to be Cethios' princess. But just before I was able to reply to him he said, "Are you hoping he will ask you? You know you could do a lot better than him. Don't go off and be frustrated with me. But he knows you loath him. So therefore he wouldn't ask you, am I right?" Beruchium saw that my expression saddened, for only if he knew. He replied, "My lady, did I upset you? I hope I did not, for that was not my intent."

I rubbed my face slowly with my fingers. I didn't want to ponder my fate any longer. I replied to him with a forced smile, "No, that really is the best thing I have heard all day today, really."

Beruchium smiled intensely as he responded, "Well then, come follow me. I have a surprise gift for you. It is hidden behind the castle. Will you join me?"

I wondered what the gift would be. I really didn't want to be present here on this day any longer. I turned my gaze towards the castle and then glanced to where Zethron disappeared into. I didn't want him to see that I was going to take off. I wouldn't want to be followed by one of his servants or worse, get Beruchium in trouble. But without any further hesitation, I replied in a whisper, "Let's go."

With an enormous grin on his face we left. We crossed the gardens heading south. I saw all the other gardener fairies smiling and waving contently. As we reached the edge of the castle premises the tall stone wall stood in front of us. Beruchium gave a small jump up as he flew above the castle wall. I'm not sure what he was doing or where he was going. I was afraid to ask him as I realized we were leaving the grounds to keep heading south. All of the told legends happened in the south. I froze as I looked up to Beruchium and as he shouted down to me, "My lady, are you up for an adventure!? It might take all day!"

I looked down at my toes as I wriggled them. I wasn't wearing any shoes and I wasn't sure how the jungle floor might be to my bare feet. I rubbed my right hand on my toes as small black shoes appeared on both of them. I glanced back at the castle one more time as I took off into the air toward Beruchium. I flew in front of him as I asked, "Are you not needed in the gardens today?"

He shrugged with a laugh in his voice, "My business is settled here for the day. Come it'll be fun." As I looked south into the jungle then down onto the ground below my feet, my stomach curled. I have never been so high up in the air before, flying this high was nearly forbidden for me. I placed my hands on my face as Beruchium laughed at me. His laughter was probably because my face had started to turn green from the high altitude. Beruchium took off as he landed between a pair of trees, I followed him down. He replied as we landed, "Now, follow and listen to the rustle of my feet and the echo of my voice. When the jungle gets to dense and you are unable to see, listen to your inner voice. Also very important, tuck in your wings at all times! Promise me you will not have them open. For the jungle will grab you and tear at you. Promise me no matter how terrified and frightened you are."

I gave him a concerned and confused look. I wasn't sure if he was trying to tell me about today or if he was warning me about the future. But what would I be doing outside the castle walls anyway? I nodded and promised him. Fear struck through my veins though not knowing what he was meaning by, but oh well what could I have done? As I pondered on what he wanted to show me, we continued to head south into the oblivious. I trusted him very well though so I did not question him. Beruchium also taught me the ways of the lands since I could remember.

After what seemed like many hours later, the air started to get thinner and thinner as the jungle got thicker and thicker. The vines and branches of the trees pulled on my dress and my wings, even though I had them tucked in all the way into my skin. The whispers of the jungle started to pound on my subconscious mind. I did at times close my eyes and follow Beruchium by sound only but, I kept tripping over low trunks and branches. My vision started to blur as I only kept seeing the same greenery over and over. My feet started to ache with the intensity of the burning sun. And just as the pain in my body couldn't take any more, Beruchium stopped in his tracks. He leaned over to me and whispered, "We have arrived my lady. Close your eyes and take my hands." I did as he said before the exhaustion almost with took my skin. Suddenly the sweet aroma of passion flowers came to me with the essence of water lilies. The air felt cool and moist against my skin as I opened my wings slowly, stretching them to my full advantage. I felt as if I were in utopia! Relaxation filled my soul as Beruchium replied, "Go ahead and open them."

I opened my eyes to see an enchanting ecstasy of wonder. We were standing in a clearing with beautiful wild flowers covering the edges of it. In the middle of the clearing sat a small pond with a small island in it. Water lilies covered to top of the water as in the water itself, were varieties of coy fish swimming about. On the island was a small gazebo big enough to fit about twenty fairies. There were a few vines with pink flowers that draped the inside and out. Carvings of leopards formed on the top of the gazebo ceiling. A small waterfall drizzled over the gazebo sending the rest of the water landing in the small pond below. The sun gave light in the perfect angle that sent a magnificent rainbow soaring above the whole clearing. A butterfly caught my eyes as I realized that millions of them were fluttering from flower to flower.

I flew over to the inside of the gazebo as water drenched me for a brief moment. I shouted over to Beruchium, "Beruchium, this is beautiful!"

He flew over to me and landed inside the gazebo by my side. He shook a little from the water as he smiled widely and replied, "It is yours my lady."

I turned to Beruchium in shock as I whispered a bit, "What did you say?"

Beruchium again replied, "It is yours, a gift from the other gardeners and from me, for our lady."

"But what is this treasure for, why?"

He walked around feeling the wood and how smooth it felt. He replied with a smile, "Well, you are coming to your age of wisdom and, your coming of age nears within these days. So, we thought that when your day comes to wed, it could be here. It's for you and your true love, or perhaps just a sanctuary. It is a gift for our lady."

"But how am I supposed to find this place again though? I don't even remember how we got here, half of the time I had my eyes closed. And that's if I didn't trip over something."

Beruchium walked over to me and placed his hand over my heart as he replied, "Follow your inner voice and it shall guide you here, always."

I smiled at him as I took his hand within mine and gently squeezed it. "Thank you so much." I released his hand and started to walk around and take in deep breaths of my surroundings. We spent quite some time here, having a few snacks from the surrounding berry bushes, taking a few sips of cool water from the fall and looking over all of the exquisite work and the outside area. The coy fish were absolutely stunning. This place was truly an amazing treasure.

After what seemed like quite some time, I looked over to my right as I suddenly realized that the sun was starting to set. "Beruchium, we must get going to the castle before they realize that I am missing."

Beruchium slowly walked over to me ignoring my comment and took both of my hands within his. He whispered, "Azalea, will you cherish it forever?"

The security in his eyes made me forget that I had to reach the castle soon. But I replied to him with a warm smile, "I promise, I will cherish this very spot and keep it within the heart of my soul. I promise you that I shall wed my true love in this very spot."

Content with my answer he released my hands and bowed. We started to head back to the castle, but before we left I took one last glance at my wonderful gift. Never have I felt so grateful for receiving such a grand treasure. In fact, I don't think I have ever received anything like this before. This was the best gift ever!

Heading home we flew above the treetops for no one would be able to see us flying in the dark. I tried to hold in my fear of heights as much as possible. We arrived at the castle gardens where the main fountain stood. There were small lantern globes hovering in the air giving the garden an ancient appearance. Pink and blue lights swirled in the water fountain. I flew up over the fountain as I dunked my feet into the water to cool them down. My magic now disappeared off of my sore feet. They were now bare once more. Beruchium gave me another small bow and then left on his way.

Being almost completely dark I too took advantage of the situation. I flew around the castle and up into my rooms' balcony. I enchanted the balcony doors to forbid anything or anyone from entering my room, for usually I sleep with the doors open. A thin glittery mist fell from the top of the doors as it disappeared down onto the moonlights reflection on the floor.

I walked over to the folding wall to change for the night. Suddenly a low growling noise came from my bed. There laid Snowfire with her eyes glowing a bright deep violet color. I walked over to her as she turned her head away from me. "Snowfire don't be upset with me. I'm sorry I didn't take you with me. We left in a hurry, sort of. Besides, you go places without me too. I know you leave at night sometimes or you disappear throughout the day. You don't see me getting upset at you do you? Who knows where you go?"

She gave a small shrug as her eyes went back to a deep green color. She rolled over as she started to let out a gentle purr. Wow, and just like that she was already asleep. She must have been exhausted as well.

I walked back over to the folded wall to finish changing. I then plopped into my bed as I too was soon fast asleep. It was going to be a pleasant night. Or so I thought it would be.

Rude Awakening

5

My dream came to me like a soft whisper in the shadows of the night. All I could see was darkness until from afar a light blue mist started to appear. The figure of a fairy came closer and closer into view. The figure was of a woman fairy. Her skin was a light brown tint, with peachy cheeks. Her dark chocolate hair flowed just above her mid back. She was wearing a golden dress that seemed to sparkle in a silver hue. She started to smile as her wings started to appear behind her. They had blue spots with purple lines down the middle. It gave the appearance of lightning bolts on her wings. And of course she had golden feathers on the edges of her wings, like me. A brief thought came into my mind, perhaps I was seeing my mother. She started to speak softly to me, "My sweet daughter Azalea, no matter which else on the day of your moment, gaze into the moonlight to the south. Follow your inner heart into the night sky above. Remember I am always with you, look deep inside yourself to find..."

Her face suddenly went from joy to grief, as it finally fell in horror. A razor-sharp sword suddenly wedged out from her mid chest. The tip dripped blood that had a golden shimmer to it. A golden tear fled her eye as she released a high pitched scream that echoed in my ears....

Suddenly I awoke and shot up straight in my bed as I held onto my ears. The echo of her scream still seemed to bounce around within my ears. Sweat dripped down from all over my body. I felt as if I was having some kind of panic attack. My chest ached as if it was me who was stabbed. It was extremely hard for me to breathe. I looked over to Snowfire who was snuggled over by the fireplace. I had to tell her my dream before I forgot any detail. I whispered over to her, "Snowfire." She gave a small twitch, purred softly then scooted herself closer to the fire. I shouted over to her, "Snowfire!"

She released a small yelp then looked over to me. I moved my hands trying to signal for her to come over. She gave a small stretch then with one leap she landed onto the bed. I tugged on her ear softly for I wanted her to listen to me. I described the dream to her. She sat there attentively listening to every word I said. She seemed to be concern with what I was describing to her. I was taking in deep breaths for my mind started to spin and my heart started to pound faster. By the end of my telling I had my hands on my forehead. "Snowfire stay and sleep here with me here until I fall asleep."

Snowfire nodded and rubbed her head on mine. She let out small purrs as she comfortably laid down next to me. I took my blanket and pulled a small thread from the corner. As I whipped it in the air it transformed into another soft blanket. It flowed in the air and down onto her. After I tuck in my snow leopard friend I started to rest and be tranquil. The warmth of her body soothed my worries. Then for some reason I looked out onto my balcony and into the night sky. But instead of just stars I also saw a creature of some sort fluttering about far away near the stars. I couldn't make it out so I closed my eyes and fell asleep. I shrugged it off for I knew the more sleep I had the better.

And before I knew it the week had flown by and the weekend was here. For the next morning was now the day of the grand ball. The day I have been dreading for centuries. No matter what I did, I could not have stopped this day from coming, the starting day of my arranged marriage.

The Room of No-Existence

6

I awoke by the rustling of my curtains being stirred about. Trathina was pushing the curtains from the balcony doors to the side and tying them together. Trathina shouted over to me, "Wake up my lady, today is the day of your new beginning! Wake up, on Cethios orders you were left to sleep in, and now it's already midday!"

Great I thought, perhaps he did that on purpose to keep me out of his way this morning. I still wanted to just stay in bed for the rest of my life! Suddenly there was a knock on the door as Trathina quickly rushed over to it. I rolled over and started to stretch as I saw two servants flying in. One servant carried towels while the other servant carried a tray with fruit, bread and a goblet of water. Both servant fairies were wearing tan gowns as their bright pink wings fluttered. The servants, whom I now recognized, were Razyna and Priniza. They were twin fairies who were about the same age as I am. They were tall with wavy curly light brown hair. They also had bright light blue eyes. You could say they were identical but, one had a birthmark shaped as a butterfly on her right shoulder, which was Razyna. We would all do the same castle chores together. You could say that we are very good friends.

Razyna flew over with the tray of food and placed it on my lap as she replied, "Breakfast in bed, 'Your Highness'."

She gave a small curtsy but I stopped her as I raised my hand up. My palm gave a white dim glow as I implied to her, "Razyna, please do not rephrase me as, 'Your Highness', out of all the crazy things that are going to start taking place today. To you and your sister I am just Azalea."

She blushed and replied, "Upon Cethios' wishes, he demanded that your title is 'Your Highness', 'Your Highness'."

I looked over to Trathina who was taking clothes from the closet and reorganizing it with Priniza. I glanced back to Razyna and whispered, "Obviously I'm sure you know by now that I am the one who will wed Cethios." She nodded as I continued, "And I'm letting you know, that I am being forced against my will. But what can I do? Well then, by my demands call me Azalea. Cethios may take away my freedom, but he will not take away my friends."

"But you will be queen one day and I simply will only be...."

I interrupted her as I pushed aside the tray, stood up and grabbed her hands. "It was only a few hours ago that I too shared the same chores as you. It was only a few hours ago that I too did the cleaning. We have both shed tears and sweat from the burdens of these castle chores. I am none better than you. You will always remain one of my good friends no matter what happens. Now I'll ask you once more, call me by the name you have always known and called me by. I'd like to keep it that way."

After giving Razyna a huge hug she smiled and flew over by her sister and Trathina. Trathina and Priniza were coming out of the closet carrying a simple silver long gown. I on the other hand sat back down and started to stuff my face with as much food as possible. I knew I wouldn't be able to eat later on this day. Trathina walked over to me as she replied, "Now we must make hast. You will be going somewhere different, somewhere special where you shall bathe and change."

I stood up with the tray as Priniza tried to take the tray from me. I replied to her, "No thanks, I will be taking the tray down myself."

Trathina over heard what I said as she in return remarked, "Oh no you don't, from this day forward you will be treated like royalty. You will act like royalty because you will be royalty."

I looked at Priniza as I slowly handed her the tray. I whispered to her, "I'm so sorry."

She blushed and replied, "No my lady, that is what I am here for now." Priniza gave a curtsy and left the room with the tray.

I turned to Trathina as I was now frustrated. She was still near my dresser gathering hair items. I walked over to her and protested, "Trathina, I do not wish to be treated differently. I am none better than any of these servants here in this castle. How can I go from one day scrubbing the floors of the castle to the next day being a princess?"

Trathina eyed me with anger in her eyes as she fumed, "Well the other servants are not going to wed Cethios are they? They will not be queen; they will not have the responsibility of ruling this land and the fairies within it! You will be treated differently and you will accept it! Now let's go to the bathing room before it gets even later!" I bit my bottom lip to her response. There wasn't much to say anymore. Anything I would say would just upset her even more. Trathina and Razyna headed for the door. I on the other hand inhaled a deep breath and waited briefly, then I started to follow them. I slowly closed the door behind me and hurried to catch up.

As we zigzagged through the castle halls they started to become less and less familiar. I was never aware that this part of the castle existed. We walked through halls and staircases that I didn't even realize were there. You could tell that the way we were heading had not been walked through in ages. Dust and some thick silver webbing covered parts of the walls, figures and statues. Huge colorful paintings and grey stone statues of fairies stood along the walls. I didn't even recognize any of them. Finally after endless trailing through the forgotten halls, we came to a halt in front of an enormous picture that was painted with heavy oils.

The painting was of a small waterfall that had two unicorns standing to the far left of it. Next to the unicorns was a gigantic brown boulder, while a mermaid sat on a small rock in the middle of this pond where the water from the fall landed in. The mermaid seemed to be part tiger fish, sea dragon and half fairy. It appeared as if she was washing her hair or running her fingers through it. An enormous willow tree sat on the edge of the pond to the right of the water fall.

Trathina replied, "No one knows of this location except for me, and now Razyna and you. This room is of no existence. This was Queen Lily's special room. If she would have known you, I know she would have wanted to share it with you." I felt such honor after Trathina said those words to me. She continued, "Only those who carry the blood of royalty may open this door but, I have been working on a chant that I hope might open this door today. I have been working on it since..." Trathina's voice started to trail off and seemed to be slowing down. I turned to look at the painting for my hearing went completely silent.

Suddenly the willow tree started shimmering and swaying as if wind was brushing gently through the vines. The rustling of the movement from the tree suddenly came to my ears like a whisper of echoes, then louder and louder. The sounds of the leaves buzzed in my ears. Suddenly I could hear and see the unicorns snorting and running around. They were galloping around and jumping off the boulder. It appeared as if the painting was coming to life in front of my very eyes. The waterfall started to flow and the mermaid started to move as well. The noise of it all fluttered in my ears. I was not understanding what was happening in front of me and to me!

The mermaid seemed to be enjoying her sun bathing when she suddenly turned and looked directly at me as chills flooded over my skin. I could feel my body stiffen as the mermaid started to squint her eyes at me. It seemed as if she was trying to see who I was. Then as if she suddenly recognized me, she began to wave frantically and enthusiastically. Her laughter rang with intensity within my ears. The mermaid started to point downward as if she was trying to tell me something. I didn't know what she was trying to point to. I slowly moved my gaze to the bottom of the painting.

On the frame appeared a medium sized silver maple leaf. It started to shine a bright light. Smaller leaves started to appear around the bigger leaf. They started to circle the leaf as they moved faster and faster around it. I became dizzy with the motion and curiosity with took me. I couldn't help myself as I slowly and cautiously reached out to it. I could hear the mermaid cheering. Then, I touched it with my fingertip. It felt smooth and furry all at the same time. Suddenly a shock of vibrations engulfed my entire body. I shivered as the intensity flowed through my veins. Suddenly the painting in front of me started to melt away. I stepped back in shock as I watched the painting drip its colors all over the floor. A dark wooden door finally reveled itself.

Trathina's voice came back into my hearing as she started to cheer slightly, "You see, I knew there was a trick in getting this opened. I knew I could figure it out!" She opened the door as Razyna walked in first. I on the other hand was still in shock of what just happened. Trathina asked me with concern, "Are you alright my lady?"

I suddenly became aware of my surroundings. I don't think anyone else saw what I just did. I didn't want to tell Trathina, perhaps she would think that I was losing it! Still shaken up from it I replied as smoothly as I could, "Oh yes, I'm okay, I was just mesmerized by you trying to open the door."

"Why thank you, I have been practicing. Alright then, come on let's go in." We walked in together and I was astonished at what I saw before me. It made me appreciate our enchantments and magic even more. There was a miniature oasis in the room like James' but bigger. Exotic and colorful birds of all sorts were flying all over the place from tree to tree. Rainbows seemed to cover the entire sky with their impressive enchantments. Butterflies fluttered by the ground in between all of the flowers as if they were dancing within the mist of some certain rhythm. I closed my eyes momentarily and inhaled the wonderful aroma of sweetness.

I walked over to the pond in the middle of the room as the waterfall drizzled over it. There was a light foggy mist over the water. It was iridescent in color as it swayed over the pond. I placed my hands between the sand and the water, it felt extremely warm. Behind me Trathina was taking her shoes off and walking over to me. I on the other hand usually wore sandals but today I was bare footed, thank goodness. She replied, "Go ahead and jump in and strip down. Now, I know you would love to stay a while here but, our time today is limited immensely. We must get ready for the ball for your grand entrance awaits you!"

Trathina thought she would be sneaky and she tried to push me in. Luckily, I saw her before she could strike. I flew up and over to the side as she tripped and fell in. But just before I could laugh at the moment, Trathina grabbed my hand and took me with her. Slosh! Razyna laughed hysterically on the shore while I laughed in the water. Trathina wasn't so ecstatic about it though. She struggled to get out of the water as she tripping a few times on her way up to the beginning of the shore. As she started to wring her clothes she replied with annoyance, "Alright, funs over, go and take your bath. I'll just dry off over here."

I continued to laugh as I swam to the center of the pond. I quickly stripped off my clothes and threw them on a small boulder nearby. Blue and purple bubbles appeared as I just dunked my head in and scrubbed it. I scrubbed my body with a sponge that I with took from the bottom floor of the pond.

After a brief moment just before I almost finished, lavender and orange lights started to swirl around me. Faster and faster, they swirled until suddenly out popped up some small sea horses. They were curvy from their backs to their tail with a long mouth that stuck out. Their stomachs pushed outward with small pointed scales all along their backs. One squirted water at me as they all giggled at each other. There were about twelve of them floating in front of me. Then they started to talk among themselves and to me, "Good evening Azalea, so sweet of you to join us on this lovely evening."

"Oh yes, we finally meet the beautiful Azalea."

"So awful to have met you this way though."

"But to see you is so grand though, it is."

"Oh yes, will you come back and visit us again?"

"Do say you will."

"Shame to have not been able to see you grow up though."

"Terrible, we'd thought we'd never see you again, ever!"

"I think she has her mothers' eyes; don't you think Lavender?"

"Oh Sunbloom, I see much more resemblance than you could ever imagine!"

"Do you think we have offended you?"

"We wouldn't want to do that!"

"Hey-hey, why did the dragon have no enemies?"

"Why-why?"

"Because he ate them all!"

All the seahorses laughed out loud and continued, "Well, wonderful to have spoken with you."

"We do love you, but we do have to go."

"Come back soon and visit us!" And just like that they were all gone under the water, just as unique as they appeared. I didn't understand anything they were saying. They confused me. I hardly got a chance to say anything. I swam over to the small waterfall as the water coming down had soapy bubbles within it. I quickly finished my bath and swam back to shore.

Before I got out four red and purple butterflies were holding up a white cottony towel for me. They wrapped me in it and kissed me on the cheek. For a brief moment my body shone as the towel turned into the silver dress that Trathina brought, and my body was completely dried. Two other pink butterflies came up to me as one landed on my head. My hair quickly dried as they started to curl it and prepare it with pins and a small tiara. Razyna came over with small diamonds in her hands as she carefully placed them in my hair. One of the butterflies flew over to her and smacked her on the hand. I laughed as the butterfly replied to Razyna, "No-no-no-no! Me-me-me-me!"

Other pink butterflies came over and took the diamonds from Razyna as she replied to me, "Gosh, they are feisty little ones don't you think?"

I nodded to her as we both just laughed. I looked over to Trathina who was handing bobby pins to the butterflies. I replied to her half sarcastically, "Trathina, the sea horses in the pond, they are um, really friendly."

Trathina started laughing, "Oh Azalea, there are some in there but, they do not know how to talk. Though, I would see the queen laughing to herself sometimes. She would tell me that they made her laugh by doing tricks but, not talking. Perhaps you hallucinated such a thing. There is much pressure on your mind at this moment." Trathina placed her hands on my forehead then onto my checks.

You could see the butterflies were getting upset as their colors intensified. One pushed Trathina's hand away shouting disapprovingly, "No-no-no, you smudge make up! Stop touching!"

Trathina eyed me cautiously as if she suspected something, but what? One of the butterflies placed their little delicate feet on my eye to close it and place make-up on it. I could hear the butterfly curse a little as I felt it wipe away the liner and start over. I told Trathina I was fine but, when I opened my eyes, she still looked concerned.

After the butterflies were done, we bid them farewell and our thanks. They flew off into the flowers near the pond. After we headed out through the same door we came in from. I stalled for a brief moment at the doorway as I glanced over to the pond. I wondered; did I imagine that whole conversation of the sea horses? Was it all my imagination? Perhaps I was hallucinating from stress. It couldn't be real, could it?

As we exited and closed the door behind us I turned back to see the painting reappear the same way it melted away. I don't think anyone else cared that the painting reappeared back onto the door. But as we started heading away from the hall I looked back once more to see that same mermaid frantically waving goodbye.

The Betrayal and the Finding

7

Moments later as we reached the halls that I was able to recognize, I asked Trathina if I would be able to walk to my room alone. She agreed to it only because she still had other arrangement to finish before my grand entrance. I asked Razyna if she could join her as well. I sort of wanted to visit James alone before I went to my room. I knew if I would have asked Trathina she would have declined my request in visiting him. I wanted to ask James about the mermaid in the painting and the seahorses. Perhaps he knew something about it that I did not.

As I got closer to the sword swinging room I heard swords colliding with great force. I stood next to the door and placed my right hand on the wall as my palm started to glow. The vision of what was happening inside suddenly came into my mind...

I saw James sword fighting with Cethios. They were both breathing hard with beads of heavy sweat dripping from their foreheads. Cethios gave a hard impact to James' sword in which sent him stumbling back almost falling down. James quickly opened his wings to catch the air around him so he wouldn't fall to the floor. Cethios snickered, "You are way over your head old man. Your ancient magic and spells cannot help you any longer."

James replied breathlessly, "You do not understand with what and whom, you are dealing with. You cannot control her no matter how much magic you possess!"

Cethios struck James again with another swift hit, but James stopped it with a quick flick of his sword. James started to spin with the speed of a lightning bolt. He then spun right under Cethios feet as he dove feet first under him. As he went under, James did a back flip as he landed on his feet behind Cethios. James swung his sword under Cethios feet knocking him down. Cethios laughed on the floor as he flew upward and landed back to his feet. He chuckled to himself and replied, "You are powerless and foolish! These stories and these training lessons, they must stop between you and Azalea. You give her ideas of rebelling, strength and wisdom with the sword that she does not need to know. You will do so for the safety of your life. You must command her and imply to her, that this marriage is the right decision for her to make."

James wiped his forehead with his sleeve and pushed his silver glasses up closer to his eyes. "Azalea is the cleverest fairy I know, and the only one for that matter. Her decisions come solemnly from within her. I do not make her decisions and neither should you. You cannot contain the fire that burns deep within her soul. You will never imprison her."

With rage in his eyes, Cethios flew forward knocking James into the mirror behind him. The mirror behind him seemed to crack in millions of places but it did not shatter onto the floor. Cethios now held his sword against James' throat as he shoved him more into the wall. Cethios leaned over to his ear and whispered, "I will and can take you out from Azalea's life. I will rid myself of you, if you do not come to understand that your allegiance lies with me. I will ask thee one last time, where do your decisions lie upon?"

James turned his gaze toward the wall where I stood behind. It seemed as if he was looking directly at me, or if he knew I was standing there listening and watching. He gave a stiff gulp as he gasped between his teeth, "Between you and Azalea, nothing will ever come to an existence. Her destiny must be fulfilled and her hatred for you will only grow stronger, each and every single day. You do not understand the power of destiny. Your life's desires will crumble at your feet."

Cethios started to breathe harder and harder as he then swung his swords' blade across James' delicate neck. Cethios stepped back and watched as James fell to his knees holding dearly to his precious neck. Cethios replied with satisfaction, "It would be my pleasure to watch you die and fade away into just a memory, but I have a ball to attend to and a fairy to screw over."

Just before I lost my grip against the wall, I saw Cethios start to fix his suit and his hair. I was glowing in my skin with deep anger. But it quickly turned to panic as I frantically glanced around for somewhere to hide. I knew Cethios was on his way out, and if I didn't move or hide somewhere fast, Cethios would find me here and who knows what he would do to me! I looked up to see a huge lion statue above the hall. I opened my wings and flew up behind it. I tucked in my wings as much as I possibly could. I was able to blend in my wings to my back making it become one with my skin as if I had no wings at all but, a small strand of feathers would still remain.

Just then, Cethios casually walked out of the room as if he was extremely proud of himself. I listened for his footsteps to diminish down the hall before I moved. I flew down in a rush as I slammed into the doors knocking them onto the floor. I landed in front of them as I turned quickly raising my right palm and shouted, "You must seal, you must heal. No one shall enter under my will, let this now be fulfilled!"

A bright blue light suddenly immerged from my palm. The light engulfed the air around the doorway as a gush of wind passed me to the doors. The doors that were on the floor in front me swiftly moved up and replaced themselves back on as they turned a deep red color. They seemed to be pulsing with a rhythm as if lava was streaming over them with furry.

I turned over and ran toward James who was now on the floor gasping for air and for his life. When I reached him golden tears flooded my eyes, as I saw the state he was in. Blood started to seep onto the floor beneath him. I cried through sobs, "Oh James, I am so sorry I didn't come in. I could of..."

He placed the tip of his finger to his bottom lip as he whispered, "We haven't, got much time. Place your hands, on my neck." I did as he asked as I was starting to shake uncontrollable from the shock. The thick warm blood oozed between my fingers as I tried to keep the blood from spilling out. James gurgled, "Believe in yourself, you are the chosen one. You must reach deep inside of yourself...unleash the magic that has been contained...then....you must....you must..."

I wasn't sure what James was trying to tell me! "James! I don't understand, James! Don't leave me! James!" I suddenly started to hear his heart beat. It seemed as if it was pulsing loudly in the room. His beats were getting slower and slower. I wasn't sure what I could do or what I was supposed to do? I pushed harder on his throat.

James now started to close his eyes as he whispered, "Azalea..."

Rage started to flow in my veins as they pulsed with furry. I was angry with myself for not coming in to help. I was even angrier that Cethios would even do such a thing. There were so many secrets that were concealed before my eyes that I could not unlock. Even more, depressed that I knew I had no idea where or who my true family was. And now, James my only true friend who was like my family was disappearing away within my fingertips. And there was nothing that I could do but only watch in horror.

With all this anger that boiled inside me I suddenly felt a rush of energy bursting through my blood and veins. Both of my palms started to glow a bright red as they became a white golden hue. I could feel warm energy infusing with my skin as the light from my palm started to glow brighter and brighter. I started to scream from the top of my lungs as the light engulfed us and the entire room. I had no idea what was happening to James or me. All I could do was scream from the hot and heavy madness that bombarded my very skin and my subconscious mind. I screamed with all of my might, "James!"

After that moment I guess I must have blacked out, for I remember nothing at all. Although, I do recall hearing James' soft whisper within my ears, "It is and shall be done. Your powers are no longer suppressed or hidden by your subconscious mind. You are capable of releasing this stamina that flows from your heart and to your soul. You are our destiny, our future, as your enchantments now flow freely within your veins."

Trust

8

I opened my delicate eyes only to find myself lying on the canopy bed in my room. The sweet aroma of lavender and roses filled within my lungs. I sat up slowly as I looked around to see my room covered with different varieties of flowers. Great I thought, Cethios is now sucking up to me after he just attempted to kill James. I suddenly remembered, James! I looked down at my gown to see no traces of blood anywhere on it. I was confused, was it a dream? I could still feel my heart trying to pound out of my chest. I looked at my palms as they still released a small white glow as they still felt warm. They still pulsed with energy from the moments that had passed a few seconds ago. Right then I knew I hadn't dreamt what just happened.

I rolled over to the edge as my feet touched the floor. The floor seemed silky and squishy between my toes. I looked down to see that red and white rose petals covered the entire floor. I thought to myself again, oh yeah, Cethios is trying to get on my good side.

I looked over to the folding wall and there hanging on it was this beautiful gold and silver dress with lace and beads all along the front and on the train. I got up and tiptoed around the petals and over to the dress to get a closer look. As I got closer I saw that the beads were from real diamonds and pearls. I was in complete shock. The servants in the fabric room did such great work!

I then noticed Queen Lily's sword hanging next to the dress. I touched it softly with my fingertips as I trembled slightly. I was so excited that this day had finally come, the day that I can have Queen Lily's sword within my grasp. As I admired the sword I heard a loud bang as my rooms' door hit the wall. Yup, Trathina just walked into the room. "Good you're already here! I thought you were going to take the long way to your room. But nonetheless you are here. James told me he just saw you walk in."

I couldn't help myself, I half heartily shouted at her, "James! You saw him, is he alright? When did you last see him?"

Trathina of course laughed at my questions. "Of course just seconds ago. He rushed passed me though, he seemed out of breath. But he said you were in your room."

I contemplated on he brought me up here and how? Where would he be going in such a hurry? Did I really help save his life?

Razyna and Priniza walked in through the door as Trathina quickly replied to them, "We must make hast, this gown may take some time getting on and we don't have much time either. The guests have already started to arrive."

They all huffed trying to lift the dress and place it on me. It felt as if it weighed a ton with that long train behind it! About an hour later or so after much preparing, I was all ready for the ball. I replied to everyone thoughtfully, "Thank you all so much for helping me on this day. But before we go, may I have a moment to myself to gather my thoughts. I would like to catch my breath as well."

Trathina and the servants gave a small bow and walked out of the room. She closed the door softly behind her, for the first time ever I might add. I waited until I heard their footsteps vanish from my hearing. I slowly walked over to the balcony and placed my hands on the edge. I closed my eyes tightly to hold in the tears that wanted to burst out. This was happening way too fast for me. But the cool soft breeze helped as it brushed gently against my face.

I opened my eyes to only stare at the bright blue moon. I started to wish upon it, hoping I could find an escape from this day, from this night. I started to wish harder, wishing that I knew my parents. I wanted to know just who I really was. I looked above the moon to see the brightest star. Perhaps I could wish upon it. I could wish for something to happen, anything to happen, an adventure, a reason, an explanation, and of course true love. I closed my eyes to wish upon this very moment, but when I opened them, I only found myself in the same spot that I started out in.

I looked down to let a tear roll from my eye and down my cheek. As I watched it fall and land on the floor it seemed to splatter with golden glitter everywhere onto the floor. That's odd I thought, how could one single tear produce so much water? The glitter turned into a bright light as a golden butterfly emerged from it. All I could do was just stared at it, I mean what could I do I was in shock? It flew up over to me and flew quickly around me. The butterfly then took off into the sky toward the moon as I watched it fly off. Suddenly something else caught my eye. I whispered under my breath, "No, it can't be."

It was the same creature from the other night. But I didn't acknowledge it because I thought it was a part of my dreams. The creature was soaring gracefully below the milky stars. It seemed enormous even from the distance that I was watching it from. I could tell this creature was very grand. I had to get a better look of this I just had too. I grabbed my dress and with all my might lifted it up and flew out of my balcony and onto the roof. I landed and sat there attentively watching it. It dived into the trees below then up again into the starry night. As it came into the moonlight heading south, it gave me a clear view of the creature. Yes, a dragon! I knew I wasn't imagining anything on the night of one of my rude awakenings. I still jerked a little in my skin just knowing there was a dragon out there. Regrettably though, I knew that after tonight I wouldn't be able to leave Whisperia to go see or find the creature, an adventure.

I opened my wings to their full extent as I stood. I wanted to soar high in the air with the dragon. My heart ached for that adventure to join the dragon. I lifted my arms as my wings fluttered a bit. But then…
"Azalea? My lady, are you in here?"

Trathina! She entered my room, she had come back to get me to go to the ball. For a brief moment I had forgotten about this night and my grief. If she found out that I flew out onto my balcony roof, she would be furious. She'd probably think I was trying to make a break for it. I probably will be chained to the floor and to my room forever after that, unable to even open my wings ever again!

I flew up higher so my dress wouldn't drag over the edge of the balcony roof. I still just had to lean over to see where specifically Trathina was standing in the room. I suddenly gave a small shriek as I quickly placed my hands over my mouth and sat straight up. She was now on the balcony looking around and out onto the lands below. I was hoping with all my might that she didn't look up over onto the rooftop. I closed my eyes tightly for perhaps if I couldn't see her, she couldn't see me!

Just as she started to leave, my shoe started to slip off! Great, what more could go wrong on this night? Yup, I had to think it, it started to sprinkle. Well at least it wasn't pouring rain right? Oh why wouldn't she just leave! Finally after a couple of minutes she left slamming the door behind her. And as the door echoed its bang so did the clank of my shoe hitting the ground. Thankfully it all happened at the same time.

I closed my eyes tightly hopping that she didn't hear or noticed the other bang. Before I entered back into my room, I looked back into the starry night to see nothing. Disappointed I flew down to the balcony and placed my shoe back on my foot. I ran for the door, I knew I had to get to the entrance hall and fast before Trathina did. I held onto the door handle tightly before I opened it. I glistened with anxiety, I was hoping that she wasn't standing in the hall. I wouldn't know what to do or what to tell her if I saw her. My stomach curled in as I got more nervous.

I opened the door slowly to find an empty hall, thank goodness. After that I ran! I ran to the main hall entrance as fast as I could. The clanks of my shoes echoed throughout the halls. I was just hopping no one would hear me or even care to look. I struggled with my dress for I had to hold it up so I wouldn't step on it as I ran. As I reached the huge wooden doors, I opened them with a loud clash!

I was in quick amazement as I entered. There before me in the hall stood a gorgeous white unicorn with silver flowers and lace in its hair. It stood on a red silk carpet leading from where I stood to the entrance of the grand hall. The carpet itself had a variety of colored petals over it. Luckily only the unicorn was in the entrance hall and not with Trathina. I walked up to him and chuckled. I always thought that unicorns looked funny with gunk in their hair. Suddenly Trathina barged in through the side doors. "Where have you been Azalea? I have been searching high and low for you!"

"I wanted to come here alone. I took the long way through the servants' hall, being that after tonight I wouldn't be able to see the beautiful wood work carvings in those halls again." Oh good one, I couldn't believe I thought of that at the last second. I smiled at her with pride.

Trathina gave a sigh of relief as she walked over to me. Trathina stood there calmly fixing the unicorns' hair from the other side of me. She slowly replied, "Azalea, I know from this moment on your life will take a big turn. I understand that you are very nervous and excited. But, you know that I have always looked after you, as a daughter. I did sort of raise you since you were a young baby. So remember, no matter what happens, just know that I love you." A tear rolled from her cheek as she wiped it away quickly and continued, "Know that I am and have been proud of you, of this decision that you have made. Cethios is a good man, truly he is, give him a chance to prove himself. I know you won't do anything stupid or ignorant on this day. No offence."

I chuckled, "Really none taken."

Trathina glanced toward the doors then back to me and continued, "You know, that is why we are here alone. Cethios demanded for guards to be here, you know in case you decided to run away or something. But, I told him that you are wiser than he knows. I know you will do the right thing."

Great more guilt was now placed upon me even more. I honestly did want to run away as fast as I could and as far as I could. She gave me a warm smile then turned and walked toward the doors she came in from. Just before she left through the doors she threw white and golden glitter up into the air and replied, "Good luck, and wait until you here the trumpets!" Trathina left with the slam of the doors.

I inhaled a deep breath in and slowly let it out. I felt as if my world had just ended. Suddenly and unexpectedly, a deep voice replied, "Well thank goodness she's gone. I'd thought she'd never leave!"

I froze as I looked around, no one was here just me and the unicorn! "Hello?" I asked. Well, what more could I ask? I had no idea who I was replying to?

The voice replied once more, "Don't be afraid my love, you have spent your years with me running wild underneath the moonlight. Now don't be in shock that I am now coming forward. Besides this day is extremely important. This is the day that will forever change the future. Your fate awaits you. Now, do you accept your path?"

I turned my gaze to the unicorn as I stepped back confused and realized, "Mirage, is that you?"

"Who else would it be? Now come, we don't have much time! Are you prepared to leave tonight, this very second my love?"

I placed my hands on my hips as I replied, "Yes, I am ready but, all these centuries I spent night by night riding with you, you listened to my hopes, my dreams and my fears and, why didn't you ever answer me? Or at least acknowledge that I was talking to you." Mirage stepped closer and nudged me in the shoulder. I stammered, "Hey are you ignoring me?"

He stomped his foot loudly and shouted, "Azalea! All your questions will be answered. Remember what James told you, remember!"

"Of course I remember, don't you think his words are not burning against my subconscious mind? But what about Trathina's words just now? Do they not matter either?"

"Azalea we don't have much time! We must go!"

I looked at the doors. I thought that once I enter through those doors my free will, will be lost forever. I need to know the truth about what was and is out there. I have nothing here for me, no family and no reasoning. As I gave him a big hug all I could see was the dragons' image soaring high within the stars in my mind. "I need to know what secrets lie in my life and beyond. Where we go I don't care or know but most importantly, yes, I accept my path."

"Finally my love, that's what I have been waiting to hear!" Mirage leaped over my dress' tail with his powerful hind legs. He then slashed the long train that weighed me down with his mighty horn. I spun around and leaped on his back and with a loud bang we clashed through the opposite doors. Just in time I thought as the trumpets started to blow behind us. Into the empty hallways of the castle we went. The footsteps of Mirage running rapidly echoed throughout the castle. Luckily no-one was in sight, for they were all at the ball.

Finally after it seemed as if the halls were never ending, we rushed through the main doors and out of the castle. Mirage gave a loud neigh as he stood on his hind legs for a brief moment. We then dashed toward the back of the castle heading south. I just realized where we were heading too. I shouted over to Mirage, "Are we heading south to where the dragon was?"

His laughter vibrated through the air and through my skin as I could barely hear him. We were riding so fast that the wind rustled over my ears. Mirage shouted, "No matter what happens my love, keep running south! No matter what happens you must trust me and your inner guide!"

Just before Mirage leaped over the castle wall, I saw Beruchium. He cheered with his hands waving in the air, "Go-go, don't look back my lady. Go!"

Mirage took one huge leap over the wall and landed gracefully onto the ground. After that we kept racing with the wind and under the moonlight for quite some time. As I kept looking back, the castle kept getting smaller and smaller, until finally diminishing before my very eyes. He was running so fast at times I couldn't even keep my eyes opened. "This feels so exhilarating!" I shouted over to Mirage. My heart was pounding with the speed of light. I have never before felt so free! We have never ran this fast before. At times we only galloped but never this fast. We ran past trees and streams so fast that it seemed as if we just merged in with the land.

I was enjoying this feeling of freedom within my grasp when suddenly, Mirage came to a screeching halt. The sudden stop sent me off into the air. I opened my wings to catch the air so I wouldn't go any further. I flew over to him as he was on the ground still breathing hard from the running. He shouted between breaths, "Go! Go! Zethron has set a spell to stop my hooves from moving once we were found missing! Go my love! Go before he finds us both! GO!"

I just remembered what Beruchium had told me before. I shouted to Mirage, "I can't leave you here, Zethron will find you!"

"No! You must go, do not worry about me. It's you that they want. Go, before it's too late and this would have been all for nothing, GO!"

I hesitated briefly as warm tears swelled in my eyes. I rushed over to Mirage as I bent down and kiss him on the forehead. I whispered to him, "I will not disappoint you." I then shot straight up above the trees and started to fly south as fast as I could. I only lasted an hour or so, but before long I fell to the earth below from exhaustion. I am not accustom to flying so what else could I do? So I started to run with all my might. I jump over logs and rocks. I ducked below branches and twigs and splashed through streams. I fell twice but just as fast and hard as I fell, that is just how fast and hard I got up, with even more determination than before. Bruises and scrapes now cover my legs and arms as they burned with agony. Pain crept within my body but I refused to let it win. I continued to push harder towards the south, far away from Whisperia as I could even though my wings and dress were torn almost to shreds.

Much, much hours later morning started to approach me. I guess I ran all night like the speed of sound not looking back and regretting nothing. I came to a clearing as I now stood on top of a huge waterfall. I moved forward and looked down to see that it was a long deep drop. I wanted to fly down but I was too weak with exhaustion, among other things, unable to even move. The cool mist of the water felt good against my skin, it eased the pressure of the pain. The sun started to rise to my left as my body began to warm. I was catching my breath as I pondered on what I had just accomplished. I worried, where will I stay, what will I eat and how will I find the dragon?

Just then, rumble-rumble-rumble…. I heard a long low noise behind me. Once again I thought too soon, perhaps it has already found me. I slowly turned around being cautious as I was now standing at the edge of the cliff. The trees that were a couple feet away from me started to tremble. I tried to look onto the jungle floor but I was unable to see anything, it was extremely dense. I whispered under my breath, "Oh no." I knew it must have been the creature that was trembling the jungle trees, and suddenly a massive green and silver head came out from the rustle of the jungle. "Dragon." I whispered under my breath. Fear and fatigue ran through my blood vessels as I was unable to move. It had silver spikes all along the back of it head and neck. Its green scales glistened from the suns' morning rays. Its dark green eye came closer and closer. I wasn't able to step back for I knew I would fall over the cliff and into the watery rocks below. The dragon jerked its head back and then slowly forward again. The creature started to reveal its rows of sharp teeth as it snorted a small blue flame out from its nostril. I couldn't move as it came closer and closer until…

"Ahhhh!" I had lost my footing and was now falling over the waterfall to the sharp edged rocks below. I screamed on my way down as I realized I was unable to open my torn wings. I suddenly saw the dragon take off from the cliff soaring over to me. Its massive body came closer and closer to me, jaws wide open until…black.

I am not sure what happened as I blacked out from the fall, exhaustion and fright. I am not sure what got to me first, the jagged rocks below or the razor-sharp rows of teeth from the dragon.

The Plan

9

Meanwhile right after Trathina had left me alone with Mirage…

The Grand hall was filled with fairies from the city of Whisperia and Urinia. All the women fairies were dressed in gorgeous gowns of all designs and color. While the men fairies were dressed in proper dark suits. King Duralos raised his hand as the musicians stopped playing. Everyone stopped and gazed their attention to the head throne where Cethios and King Duralos were standing next to. The king started his speech, "I will now be announcing the bride to be of Prince Cethios. This fairy is well known to some of us. She has been there for the city through the hardship of sorrow and through the joyous moments. Her glow brightens up our world as her uniqueness stands her out. Her love, compassion and dedication for the fairies of this city, makes her perfect for this positions in which she will resign in. Our Prince of Urinia has chosen…" As the king raised his hand up some of the girl fairies started running their fingers through their hair or fixing their dress. The king continued, "Our enchanting, Azalea!"

The crowd cheered as some looked disappointed and upset. Prince Cethios walked closer to the king as within his palm was lying a small golden pillow. And on the pillow itself, was a small tiara of pearls and blue jewels. Cethios was still winking and throwing kisses to some girls within the crowd. As the crowd parted though, a red velvet carpet was reveled with white and pink rose petals on it. It led from the head throne to the entrance of the grand hall. King Duralos and Cethios walked forward off of the head throne as Cethios raised his hand. The crowd became silent. He replied, "Open the doors to reveal the love in my life and my future bride!"

As the crowd cheered the grand doors opened slowly. It revealed an empty hall with only the end of my dress in the middle of the floor. Everyone went silent once more, but not from being told but from the shock that I wasn't there. King Duralos went white in the face with grief. Zethron on the other hand, who was now standing behind the throne chair, turned red with anger. Cethios mumbled under his breath, "I knew it."

Cethios turned toward Zethron as he just nodded and disappeared behind the curtains. King Duralos cleared his throat as he announced, "My fellow fairies, it seems as if we have a shy bride to be."

Trathina just then barged in through the side doors, but as if someone had pushed her right through them. Her hair seemed stressed out as small amounts of her hair was flowing to the side. The crowd turned at her direction as she replied, "Ladies and gentlemen, my fair fairies, Azalea has left to her room. She was feeling ill and light headed from all of the excitement. She excuses herself as I apologize on her behalf. If you forgive her, she would like to lie in bed for the remainder of the night, to rest her nervousness. Please, let us continue the excitement and celebrations of the evening as she wishes."

Cethios glare turned into a forced smile. He replied, "Well then, tell my blushing princess to get some rest. I will visit her later on tonight. Send her the best lavender oils to ease the tension." Trathina finally caught her breath as she gave a small smile and bowed. She slowly walked back and closed the door behind her. Cethios opened his wings and replied, "Let's continue this grand evening and please, allow me a brief moment to visit my future bride and I shall return shortly for the festivities."

As the chattering, music and dancing continued Cethios exited through the grand doors. He closed them with a soft bang as he walked up to Zethron, who was already awaiting him. Cethios replied, "Send the guards after her. Have them scout the lands and the palace, leave no insignificant pebble unturned. She must be found tonight!"

Zethron scrunched his nose in as he agreed, "Yes, we mustn't let her ruin our plans. Trathina can no longer interfere in this. We must keep a watchful eye on her though. Send a guard to keep watch over her at all times. Trathina mustn't leave this castle. And as for James and that cat of hers…"

"Zethron 'Your Highness', James has been taken care of." Zethron raised an eyebrow in content as Cethios continued, "But we couldn't find her leopard."

Zethron expression went from content to anger as he replied with a red face, "We must find them both! But, Azalea did accept your proposal, didn't she?"

Cethios took in a deep breath in and out slowly. He rubbed his hands over his face and through his hair. He answered, "She never said yes, but she never said no either."

They both stood there pondering briefly on their circumstances. Then Zethron appeared content as if he had come up with a brilliant plan. Zethron stepped closer to Cethios as he whispered, "We shall tell the king that she did accept your proposal. That she was kidnapped by those freaks in the south and could still be alive. I can guarantee you, that is where she is headed. We can therefore, finally rid ourselves from those creatures in the south. We will take their lands and claim it as our own, as well as their glorious castle." He paused with a superior smile as he continued, "Perhaps these turn of events could become prosperous for us. This could be better than we have hoped for. And once we find her, before anyone else, after she proves her worth, we'll just kill her ourselves!" They both drowned in each other's laughter of evil. Moments later, Zethron replied, "Now, let's quickly go find that unicorn of hers before someone else reaches him. She could very well still be with him if we make hast." This, was sadly only the beginning of Zethron's horrendous plan.

Red Rain

10

Zethron and Cethios stepped out in front of the castle doors. They both kept their hands in their pockets as they lifted their noses to sniff the air. Zethron bent down to the ground and placed his right hand upon it. As his hand started to glowed he replied softly, "What we cannot see is hidden, so it shall not be forbidden. Reveal to me the footprints, of that unicorn prince."

Bright yellow hove prints appeared on the ground as they both smirked at each other. They headed south following the hove prints extremely close. After about a few hours or so they finally reached Mirage, who was still breathing fast on the ground. Mirage being unable to move rolled his delicate blue eyes toward Zethron and Cethios. Mirage replied to them, "Your too late, Azalea is free from your evil grasp! You will never be able to conquer her free spirit!"

Cethios bent down near the unicorns' head and replied as calmly as he could, "Where is she heading to?" Mirage attempted to get up, but couldn't. His whole body was under Zethron's control. Zethron laughed to himself as he saw that his spell still ran through Mirage's blood stream, a spell that he conjured days before this very moment. "Well?" Replied Cethios urgently, "My patience is running out."

Mirage finally catching his breath replied, "I will never reveal anything to you. You are not my master, we respond to no-one for that matter! No-one, but yet only one!"

Cethios leaned closer and tugged on his ear, "And that better be me. Now I shall ask you once more. Where is Azalea? Or, your life will cease to exist."

Zethron leaned over and added, "I will send your immortal soul to the demons of the underworld if you do not answer correctly."

Mirage now slowed his breath down to almost nothing, then answered in almost of a whisper, "Where I will be sent to is a place of glory. Your place is beyond description of pure evil. And, to answer your question fool, no. I will not answer anything to you. If I die your life will be cursed, filled with treacheries. As soon one day your plans, your doing will be revealed to your…"

At that moment just before Mirage could finish, Zethron drove his sword into Mirage's chest and into his heart. Cethios stood up and looked at Zethron confused as he shouted, "What have you done? I didn't want this creature's life to end! Do you realize that you have condemned your soul for all eternity?"

"This creature's life is not something worth pondering over. There is nothing mystical nor magical about these creatures! What matters most here is that we find Azalea!" Zethron quickly pulled his sword out of Mirage and placed the tip of his sword under Cethios' neck. Zethron replied through his teeth, "Cursed we are not Cethios, neither doomed nor forgiven. You are in this with me whether you want to or not now! You are not going to ruin my…"

He paused as a drop of red water fell from the sky and landed on his arm, then another and another. Suddenly like a gush of wind it started to pour. It was raining thick red blood as it was mixed within the pure water droplets. Cethios placed his hands over his face and ran it through his hair. He looked at his hands in anger as he shouted, "Zethron you fool, you have cursed us both! There is no turning back now! Your words and your doing will come back upon us both one day! It is raining blood from the sky of immortal life! Do you completely understand what you have done?"

They both glared at each other as the droplets continued to fall from the open sky. Zethron and Cethios then turned away from Mirage and started to run toward the castle. It seemed as if they were running in slow motion for they could not escape their doing.

The blood continued to pour for the rest of the night in that very spot. For an immortal soul was taken from vitality. Such a thing should never happen to such a captivating creature, especially that of a magical creature. As the unicorn prince Mirage, laid still with no life in his enchanting jungle.

The Deceiver

11

The next morning the day after the ball, King Duralos was sitting in the eating room alone. The sadness on his face seemed like sorrow on a gloomy rainy day, even though it was a beautiful day outside. Slices of mangos with blueberries and oats were in a small green bowl in front of him. His appetite didn't seem much to follow through today, for he felt as if he had lost his daughter. The memories of her joy and happiness filled the air around him, even her accident prone laughter. But without Azalea around he felt emptiness and bitter cold inside his heart.

As King Duralos poked at his food with a small fork Trathina and Zethron came in from the kitchen doors. They both walked slowly over to the king. Zethron sat down next to King Duralos as Trathina continued to stand. King Duralos looked up at them and replied, "Sit, please Trathina. Any word on where Azalea might be?"

Zethron leaned in closer to the king as he replied, "Your Highness', we have some vital news that we have received. But do brace yourself for the news may seem raw." The king gulped as Zethron continued, "Someone has kidnapped her."

Not having any more strength left in him, the king whispered, "Why? Why would someone want to kidnap her? I simply cannot comprehend their reasoning on doing so." King Duralos turned to look at Trathina who had a blank expression on her face.

Zethron continued, "Your Majesty', the creatures from the south took her. They want a war. It is said that they grew restless with their deceitful ways. They want to take over our land and destroy our kind. This is their way of starting this treacherous plan. But we can avoid such circumstances. If Prince Cethios takes his honorable place in this kingdom of Whisperia, then perhaps he can convince the creatures to release her without a tragedy. It was Azalea's wish to see Prince Cethios as king. We can get her back without them torturing her or even worst, killing her."

Zethron's words cut deeply into King Duralos as he suddenly was filled with rage. King Duralos half shouted, "Zethron, I am king of this land and I rule here! Azalea was not a princess of this land. Her words do not rule over unless they have gone through me! If Prince Cethios wishes, he can marry some other fairy and become king of Urinia, and not of Whisperia. Our bargain if you have not forgotten, was to give Cethios this land if only he was to marry Azalea. If only she accepted his proposal for that matter! Now, you once told me that Azalea did want Cethios. Her disappearance shall not go unnoticed. If he truly loves her, he must go and find her and save her himself! Only, if only he truly loves her, if not the reason being for my kingdom. If that being true, he must marry someone else and leave this land. That is all the words that I shall give you! Go, leave me and go tell your prince this message. I wish to see no-one no more for the remainder of this day."

Zethron tried to conceal his anger but the color and expression on his face reveled all. Zethron stood up and gave a small bow and replied, "As you wish, 'Your Highness'."

Zethron motioned to Trathina to leave with him, but the king turned quickly and with took her hand. "No-no, not you Trathina, I must speak to you alone."

Zethron's expression of death sent fear down Trathina's very own skin, for he feared that she would speak of something that should not be said. Trathina gazed her eyes onto the floor as she sat down next to King Duralos. She was trying to hide the fear in her eyes, not from King Duralos but from Zethron. Zethron gave his bow again and made his way out of the eating room as he cautiously closed the doors. King Duralos whispered over to Trathina as they both leaned in closer to each other, "Trathina?"

"Yes, 'Your Majesty'?" She answered with a quivering voice.

"Trathina do not worry. I blame you not so do not burden yourself. I understand you of all fairies wanted to see Azalea wed Cethios. But if you have any, any information at all, you must tell me." He sighed deeply as he continued, "Did she speak to you before her disappearance?"

Trathina's eyes widened as beads of sweat started to appear on her forehead. "Yes, I spoke with her for a brief moment in the hall." Her eyes jolted to the doors where Zethron had exited from.

The king replied, "Trathina, if you know anything at all please be honest with me. Is it true that those creatures from the south kidnapped her? Or did she simply run away on her own free will?"

Trathina's eyes were still on the doors until finally she turned her gaze to King Duralos. She trembled in slight fear as she replied, "Yes, it is true. For when I left her in the grand hall entrance she was eager to be presented as Cethios' bride to be. Her kidnapper..."

King Duralos interrupted her, "How do you know she was taken?"

Trathina gulped hard once more as she replied, "The unicorn that was with her told a guard before he died, that a creature took them both against their will. They were heading south of the jungle when suddenly the creature only took Azalea and then slashed the unicorn. The unicorn survived for about an hour or so, just enough time as the guards arrived. For when they found him, he was already taking his last breaths."

They both were silent until the king sighed, "I wonder if the creature knew that the unicorn was Prince Mirage." Trathina's eyes widened in fear, perhaps for she did not know that it was Mirage that had died, one of Azalea's good friend. The king continued, "Did Prince Mirage give a description of the creature?" Trathina only shook her head without giving any words. A tear fled from King Duralos' eye as he quickly wiped it away. He replied, "Find her my lady and bring her home, we will find these traitors. And as for Cethios, send him after her. It must be his honor to bring her home."

Tears now fled from Trathina's eyes as well. She stood up and gave a small bow as she replied, "Yes, 'Your Majesty'."

Trathina left the eating room from the same doors she entered from. Before she left she gave the king one last small bow, in respect and for his grief. The king once more sat alone in the eating room. He continued to stare and poke at his breakfast, as early morning had turned to mid-day.

Still Alive

12

I wasn't sure where I was or even if I had any of my body parts. Was I still intact? Every part of my body felt so sore, even my nose! Warmth though kept embracing my body over and over, in a constant pattern. I was slowly waking up as the constant warmth started to annoy me. I became extremely nervous for I was afraid to open my eyes. I wouldn't really know where I would be. I opened my eyes cautiously as I was looking up. I was in an enormous burgundy barn. I did feel more at ease knowing I wasn't in a dragons' stomach!

There were piles of thick hay all over the place, even on the second level, sort of like an open attic. There were small yellow birds that darted in and out from this massive hole in the ceiling. Having no ceiling is sort of pointless I think. There were small windows on the sides of the barn that were left wide open. Perhaps to let the cool breezes come in because it was extremely muggy in here.

Just then that same green and silver dragon from the jungle stood in front of me. It was hovering its enormous head over my body. I panicked as I screamed from the pit of my stomach, "What do you want from me!?"

I stood up quickly and drew my sword. Thank goodness it was still hanging on the side of my torn dress. The dragon stepped back a bit and snorted. It was huge with spikes descending from its head to the tip of its tail. Four thin spikes stuck out from the tip of the tail as well. Dark green scales covered its entirety with silver tints on the edges of them. Small whiskers came out from the edges of its cheeks that flowed outward from the corner of its face. It also had small whiskers coming out from of the top of its eyebrows. Just then a deep voice came from behind the dragon, "Calm down and take it easy. He's not going to hurt you."

Out stepped a tall fairy looking man. His black pants appeared worn and faded from the bottom. As his white shirt appeared to be slightly pressed, but the sleeves were pulled up away from his wrists and scrunched on his upper arm. He had dark brownish hair that was combed back and that curled a bit from the bottom of his head. Extremely handsome he was, oh yeah. His brown almond color eyes melted my heart. I couldn't help but to shiver in my skin and to stutter my words. "How, how, do you, do you know that?"

The dragon stepped closer and to my surprise replied, "I'm not going to eat you if that's what you think. When I found you, you just looked extremely frightened that's all. I just thought from the kindness of my own heart, I would bring you somewhere safe."

"Safe?" I laughed hysterically, I felt as if I was losing it. A talking dragon, how common really is that? I replied, "How am I being safe here?"

The dragon snorted black smoke out of its nostril and all over my body as it replied, "Some sort of appreciation you have. And, you smell!"

Insulted, I tried to open my wings to fly back a bit. But I struggled to open my wings. I looked back to find them bandaged up, as well as my right ankle and left wrist. The fairy looking man drew his sword as he stepped back too and replied, "You can at least put your sword down in some sort of appreciative way. I did only wrap up your wounds, even though I have never mended up wings before. But it's the thought that counts. So, where exactly did you come from?"

I was confused by his words. What did he mean by not mending up wings before, was he not a fairy himself? And where was I that he did not know what wings looked like? Also, everyone knows who I am, so why didn't he recognize who I was? "I am a fairy from the City of Whisperia. I am a maiden in the castle. And you?"

He bit his bottom lip, as he seemed to be observing me. He squinted his eyes as he chuckled, "You seem to be very well dressed to be only a maiden in the castle. Sure your dress is torn from here and there but…" I raised my sword higher as he sighed and continued, "I am an elf here in this city, the City of Trinafin. But this castle of yours, is there more of your kind?"

I looked around baffled, was he serious? I asked, "Beside the point, how long have I been here?"

"Awake standing there or asleep unconscious?"

My mouth dropped in utter shock. Did the elf think he was funny or was he trying to be annoying? I rolled my eyes still holding my sword as I asked again, "Please, I would like to know how long I have been here. I do have a right to know."

The elf shrugged his shoulders, "Alright, you have been here for about a week. Some hit to the head you had."

A week! I felt even more nauseated as I replied, "Perhaps this dragon dropped me on his way here! I shouldn't have been out for a week."

The dragon once more snorted out black smoke that drenched me. I closed my eyes as his puff of air sent my hair flying upward. The dragon responded, "I knew it! I told you she smelled funny and she's unappreciative! I cannot believe she thinks I dropped her!"

The elf stepped closer to me seeming completely unaware of my anxiety of being a week out. He eyed me cautiously, as if studying me. He replied softly, "Here I thought your kind had no existence."

How dare he! "Existence? You are an elf. I have never heard of such a thing. Perhaps you are the creatures that we fairies grew to fear. You, you put down your sword first and tell your dragon to step back. I am skillfully trained to fight and I am not afraid to do so."

The elf started to laugh almost hysterically at my response. Through chuckles he replied, "It is you who feels threatened. Do you really expect for me to place down my sword first?" His eyebrows narrowed as his chuckled subsided. He stepped closer and continued, "You fairy, place down your sword and I, I promise you that Cetus won't eat you."

The dragon stepped back as if horror had struck him deeply. I mumbled, "That creature of yours has a name?"

The dragon, Cetus, raised his head high in the air and replied in a high soft voice, "No-no-no don't you put me in the middle of this. That's not what I am here for!" Cetus leaped up into the air as if he was suspended momentarily in midair. He moved his massive wings up and down once as he sent huge gusts of wind everywhere. And in another blink of an eye he flew out from the enormous gap in the ceiling of the barn.

The elf raised one eyebrow up and murmured under his breath, "Coward."

I then leaped forward towards him in attack. Clash! Our swords bashed together as he blocked my swing. It was so severe that blue sparks flew sideways from the swords at first blow. The elf laughed once more as if I was entertaining him. He responded, "Do you think a fairy can match the strength of an elf, especially that of a woman."

75

"Do not underestimate my strength elf. I have been taught by the very best in my city."

We dashed again and again as we both blocked each other's hit. I jumped on a barrel as he swung his sword under my feet. I jumped up and flipped forward in midair and over to the other side. He spun around and said, "Quite the over achiever you must have been. And my name is Xanthus, not elf!" We continued to fight and jump around barrels of hay and water as Xanthus replied breathless, "It is a shame to say that those bandages and my effort is being wasted away. You know, having me cut them off with my sword and all!"

"Ha, are you introducing yourself to me or do you think I'll grow soft?"

I swung my sword harder than ever as I knocked him off of his feet and onto the floor below. I started to give a small cheer as he then counter acted and swung his foot under my feet. I fell to my back as he quickly stood up and placed his sword to my stomach. He replied half breathlessly, "I just thought you would want to know the name of the elf who defeated you."

"You wouldn't defeat me, besides my name is Azalea."

"You call that a name?"

"And yours?" I tried to get up but he swung his sword sideways to prevent me from succeeding. I then spun around the opposite way to get up as he swung his sword that way as well. We both succeeded as I now stood up with my sword pointing toward him, and my dress seeming to cling to my body. His side blows tore my dress to pieces as now my stomach was reveled, as did my gem.

He paused momentarily as all he could do was stare at it. Xanthus looked up to me confused and asked, "Are we made of stone as well?"

I couldn't believe he just said that to me. I had to knock him down and fast so perhaps I could maybe make a run for it. I then thought of James and the move he did while fighting Cethios. I looked at Xanthus as I started to spin and just like that I slid under his feet and flipped over behind him. It gave me a chance to push him and to cut his shirt into pieces. I left him without sleeves and perfect cuts of diagonals on his shirt. I laughed, I couldn't help it. I honestly didn't want to hurt him. Xanthus being un-amused, spun around and pushed me hard into the wall behind me. I gave a small gasp. He had the side of his sword to my throat as he whispered near my ear, "Laughter doesn't seem to come to the defeated anymore, does it?"

I kicked his arm with my knee as hard as I could. I moved my face sideways allowing the sword to fly upwards. He quickly with took the sword in midair, as I was able to move away from the wall. We both had each other at our wills and had our swords tip against each other's neck. We both were breathing hard trying to catch our breaths. Sweat glistened on my body as well as Xanthus' as we were both extremely exhausted. Me especially, I was completely sore all over from the night that I ran away.

Just as we were about to start once more, a loud clash of breaking glass came from the entrance of the barn. I turned my head slightly to see an elf woman standing there next to the broken glass. Xanthus turned his head as well as he replied painting, "Nylina, what are you doing here?"

The woman was in complete shock as her mouth gawked open. She was a short and cubby elf with curly brown hair. She had her hair sort of tied behind her head but small curls seemed to escape that. Her eyes were a hazel tone as her skin was a smooth tan. She replied, "What am I doing? I came to bring a refreshing drink to our guest. Cetus told me that she finally was awake but heavens! What are you doing to her?" She grabbed parts of her maroon dress and ran over to me as she shuffled her feet. With one flick of her hand the sword that Xanthus had moved away from my neck. She turned to Xanthus and grunted, "Put that sword away before you poke your eye out!"

He raised his eyebrow as he did as she asked. Nylina came closer to me as she started to brush my dress off. She took the sword away from my hand as she then saw the gem on my stomach. She dazed off, as she only seemed to stare at it. I know it was weird to have that but, they both didn't have to stare at it the way that they did. I cleared my throat, "Um, may I have that back. It is sort of important to me."

She quickly looked at the sword as if she had realized something, "Is this yours?"

She looked at me blankly as I replied, "No, it was given to me as a gift. It was our Queens' sword. I simple appreciated it and its beauty and therefore I was allowed to…"

Nylina raised her hand and replied, "There's no need for an explanation. Here, you put your sword away. Now, it's getting late, let's all go and eat some breakfast before it is too late for it. And, we can introduce ourselves properly."

She turned to Xanthus as if there was no more to say as she glared at him in a disapproving way. But he replied through small chuckles, "She started the fight. I merle kept her entertained. Besides I was only trying to help her, heal her wounds for that matter. I can't help that she's so scared and defensive."

I turned to glare at him as he just shrugged his shoulders at me. Nylina took me by the hands and said, "Now whatever it may be we'll get this settled over breakfast." We all walked over to the door. Nylina leaned over the broken pieces and waved her left hand over it. It slowly seemed to reverse itself to form a cup of juice on a small silver tray. It all landed in her hand as she replied, "A cup of strawberry water my lady?"

"Why thank you." I could only stare at the cup. That was amazing and at the same time weird. How was she able to reverse that, so that the dirt and pebbles did not stay in the water? I looked into the cup and swirled it around making sure that there was no dirt in it. As we headed out the doors Xanthus continued to stay near me. I don't think he fully trusted me that quickly as Nylina determined to. I stuck my right pinky finger in the cup as it glowed for a brief moment. I took my pinky out of the water as the tip of my finger was colored with a green hue.

Xanthus gave me a confused look, perhaps thinking I was weird or something. He asked, "What was that for?"

I looked at him with my eyes wide open. I had to think of something fast! "I, I was testing the temperature of the water?"

Confused Xanthus asked, "Why would strawberry water be hot in the first place?"

All I could do was simply stare at him blankly as he rolled his eyes and walked ahead of me. I couldn't think of anything fast enough to tell him. For if only he knew the truth. What I was really doing was checking to see if there was any poison in it. If there was my pinky would have come out red and stinging for that matter. James taught me how to do that once. I sighed as I ponder about him. I really hoped he was doing alright and was in a safe place.

I stared to sip the water in content, it was quite refreshing after not having anything to drink in quite some time. Suddenly I turned my gaze towards the sky. As I looked up complete shock with took my heart. I was astonished with awe at what I saw with my very own eyes.

Nylina's Story

13

As I looked up into the turquoise sky, a single golden tear rolled down my check from astonishment. Awe and amazement had taken my delicate heart, Dragons! There were about twenty or so of them flying in the sky. They seemed to come in different varieties of colors and sizes. The dragons were diving and swirling up in the air as their scales glistened in the sunlight's' rays. The dragons' colors were from a light orange to a deep dark burgundy hue. They appeared so massive even though they were so far away. Then this one dragon that was white with golden trimmed scales caught my eye. It looked so graceful as if it were dancing in the air.

Suddenly a red dragon let out this gigantic bellow roar as dark blue fire came out from its throat. I dropped my cup of water in shock and gave out a small scream. The cup seemed to shatter into millions of pieces as the shattering noise echoed within my ears. I looked over to Xanthus, whom now had stopped and spun back around to look at what had happened. He gave me a disappointed look as I just scrunched my eyes together and shook my head at him. Nylina walked over to me and placed her hand on my shoulder as she gently replied, "Oh don't worry my lady. Accidents happen, it's alright." Nylina bent down a bit and once more reversed the broken pieces back to their original form. "Here you go, good as new. No really it's clean."

I took the cup from her slowly as once again I looked into the cup. I still found it amazing on how she did that. A bit embarrassed I blushed and replied, "Thank you, I'm so sorry it's just that the dragons, they startled me that's all. Especially, when one of them breathed out that fire."

Xanthus gave a half smile as he rudely asked, "Are all the fairies from your city this clumsy or have you really never seen a dragon sneeze before?"

Nylina turned to Xanthus as she could only shake her head in disappointment at him. And all Xanthus could do was shrug his shoulders at her. I flashed a half crooked smile, I really didn't know what to say. But I did want to honestly walk up to Xanthus and hit him across his face. I told Nylina, "No really, where I am from we were told that dragons did not exist. That they went extinct centuries ago."

Nylina was the only one that looked shocked. Xanthus on the other hand didn't look so convinced. Nylina seemed extremely upset for some reason. She turned and quickly replied over to Xanthus, "Xanthus, be a dear and go help get breakfast prepared. Set an extra setting for Azalea, she must be starving! Then we can make sure we are all properly introduced. Oh and tell the king to clear a part of his day. This fairy would like to speak to him in private after breakfast."

My face went blank as my mouth dropped. Why would she say or even do such a thing like that without even asking me? Xanthus of course quickly gave a small bow then gave a high pitched whistle. Cetus came diving out of the crowded sky heading straight toward Xanthus. And just before Cetus hit the ground, he curved his body upward with the wind. Xanthus grabbed his dragons' front paw and flipped over onto his back. And for a brief moment just before Xanthus left our eyes met, as if time had stopped momentarily just for us.

Suddenly as if time had continued, off they went into the sky with a gust of powerful wind. But of course the wind seemed to only blow Nylina's hair up. As for me, it blew me off my feet and onto the ground below. I gave a small scream as I hit the hard cool floor below my feet. I quickly stood up just as fast as I fell, hoping that Nylina didn't see. But she did see as I saw her try to cover her giggle. "You'll get accustom to the gusts. Now, I have arranged for you to speak to the king and..."

I interrupted her, "But why, I just got here, well actually just woke up is more like it. But..."

"My lady, if you owned your own castle and if some guests just arrived; in which they probably will be sleeping in one of your rooms. Wouldn't you want to know whom it was?"

She did have a point. I can't go back to Whisperia now. I do need a place to stay and perhaps sleep. Cethios is probably furious for what I did to him. I wouldn't be surprised if he placed me in the dungeons! I looked at Nylina in the eyes as I apologized, "I'm sorry you're right. I do thank you for allowing a complete stranger to come into your castle, and for inviting me to join in for breakfast."

She glanced at the stone on my belly as she mumbled under her breath, "Not being a complete stranger as you think." I looked at her confused for I quite didn't understand what she meant. She started to quicken her pace as we headed towards the castle. After a brief moment of

81

silence Nylina asked, "Now my lady about the dragons, is it true that no one has honestly told you the truth about them? Have you not been taught?"

"Taught? We were restricted from even trying to discover anything about them. In our city, I was told that they would feed on fairies and devour them whole."

Nylina burst out laughing as if I had told her something hilarious. I stared at her in shock. She took one glance at me then quickly stopped. She replied half chuckling, "My dear, I am so sorry that you were told such lies. The truth is that dragons are actually gentle creatures. I mean if persisted or angered then you know, that is a different story, but. Well I think you will be safe here. Dragons do eat the creatures of the land though but definitely not fairies or elves. Sometimes they would even prefer to eat from the sea. They'll dive in and out from the ocean, really quite interesting to watch."

We started to get closer to the castle as the stone peaks started to come into view. I thought to myself, what role did Xanthus have in this castle? I wondered what the name of the king was. I had so many questions and I didn't know what, whom or when? "Nylina, would you be able to tell me the names of everyone whom I will be joining for breakfast?"

She opened her eyes in grief as is realizing the true situation, "Oh where are my manners! Well of course you know my name is Nylina. I am the main maid in this castle. The kings' name is Alcander. The queens, bless her soul, is Whistalyn. Her soul passed away centuries ago and…"

"Do you mind me asking how?"

Nylina bit her bottom lip and answered, "About a year after Morpheus was born, Morpheus is the prince. We found Queen Whistalyn in her bedroom. She was peacefully sleeping still holding Morpheus in her arms. She just couldn't wake up though." A couple of tears fled her eyes but she wiped them away just before anymore could escape. She sucked in a deep breath and slowly exhaled. She continued, "It is very sad but, she still remains hidden somewhere in a castle. We keep her because she still breathes. We can only hope and leave her to sleep undisturbed. None of our spells were able to wake her, none. Hence why we believe her soul is lost, but perhaps one day, she will come back."

Nylina seemed to stare off into space as we continued to arrive closer to the castle. I noticed that this discussion disturbed her so I thought I could change the subject. "So what does Xanthus do in this castle?"

Her eyes lit up once more with happiness. "Ah yes, he is Prince Morpheus' best friend. Yup, Xanthus, he is my son." I slightly spit out my water as I was in shock to hear that. But Nylina continued her story. "Xanthus' father travels all over the seas. He writes to him about once a year. So for him that's quite often."

I interrupted her, "How does he travel around in the water?"

Nylina looked up into the sky as she squinted her eyes. "He travels with his dragon in the air, then by boat while at sea. Dragons are excellent swimmers. Ah yes-yes continue. Well then, Cetus and Orion sleep in the barn that we were just in. And the kings' dragon, Atrigo, he sleeps in a different barn. But you know the barn really isn't their home because the world is their home." Nylina took in a deep breath as she continued, "And to the south of us is the ocean. The mermaids make their home there with all the other creatures of the sea."

I replied half hesitantly, "Mermaids? But I thought..."

Nylina started to laugh at me as she replied, "Mermaids exist as well you know. I know you thought dragons and elves were just a myth too but, here we are aren't we?"

I actually thought mermaids only existed in Urinia but, oh well I didn't want to push her good mood. I think she thought she was on a role. I wouldn't want to start explaining half of my life to her. Perhaps not just yet I think.

We started to reach the castle as its rustic appearance reminded me of my castle back home. I started to feel home sick as my stomach curled in a little. I thought that the elf castle looked more ancient though. Perhaps our waterfalls kept it looking more alive. In which also perhaps that is why they didn't have moss covering the outer walls. Their castle did seem even more enormous than ours. It seemed as if they had more rooms to spare. "Nylina this castle is amazing!"

She giggled at my amazement and replied, "You should see the city itself. Mm the food is exceptionally delicious."

I gave a smile as I laughed inside of myself. She seemed so distracted in her own world for a moment. She probably was still thinking of the cities' food because she was still licking her bottom lip.

As we entered the castle some of the servants seemed to stare at me briefly. But Nylina gave them a firm clearing of her throat. I also noticed that their ceilings weren't so high. Perhaps they don't need that much space, without wings high ceilings would be pointless I guess.

They also seemed to have more painting of everything and anything. The paintings were of creatures in the jungle I have never seen before and of elf women and men. We passed this one small painting of a mermaid in a small pool of water as an elf woman sat in the pool with her. As I looked closer I realized that she was the same mermaid from the painting that led to Queen Lily's hidden room. I stopped Nylina as I asked, "Nylina, who is that mermaid in that painting?"

Nylina stopped and looked at the painting with me as she replied with a smile, "That is the sorceress mermaid, her name is Falin. Also next to her in the water is Queen Whistalyn."

I still glanced a bit as Nylina simply smiled then continued forward. I was wondering that, perhaps that explains why that painting came to life, the mermaid was a sorceress! But why did she appear to me?

As we continued to walk through the castle I thought it was weird that they didn't have any statues of any creatures, as we do in our castle. There seemed to be more furniture as well. We continued to walk through the castle as we finally came to a halt in front of these huge brick doors. Nylina turned to me and asked, "Are you ready?"

I gave a confident smile but when I looked down I grunted. I looked at Nylina, who seemed as if she had no idea at what I was grunting about. I responded, "I do look a bit hideous. Is there anything you can do or that I can do before we enter?"

"Oh heavens I forgot. Well the beauty specialist is here before your very eyes!" She waved her hands over me and recited, "What is torn here and there, go ahead and mend in care. Dirt and grime run away, make her beauty if you may."

And just like that my torn dress became whole again. The small threads mended together as if they were stitching themselves together. My hair, being all over the place combed itself back. I could feel small tugs on my wings as they too mended together. It felt amazing being able to flutter my wings again without pain.

Nylina clapped her hands as I glowed for a brief moment. Nylina pulled out a small mirror from her pocket and a small piece of a lavender flower. She crumbled the lavender flower in her hands as it became a small pile of purple glitter. She softly blew it all over me. I started to cough as I saw the glitter melt on my skin. She handed me the mirror as she replied, "What do you think? The lavender melts work great and they even last up to ten hours! But we will get you cleaned up later on. We won't leave you this way all day."

I took the mirror from her as I looked into it. Wow, I was amazed. She did a heck of a job. It seemed as if I had just left my room on the day of the ball, and that was a week ago! "This is amazing, thank you Nylina."

She took the mirror as I handed it back to her. She quickly replied, "Great thanks here we go!" And without even taking in a breath or finishing her sentence, she opened the doors.

Breakfast

14

I wasn't mentally prepared when she opened the doors so suddenly. I probably had the blankest look upon my face. I didn't know what to expect. Nylina shouted over to everyone in the room, "Good morning everyone, so what's for breakfast?"

Nylina walked with a quick pace as she headed over to the table. Once she arrived there she immediately sat down and started to stuff green grapes in her mouth. I on the other hand walked slowly towards the table. What was I supposed to do, she just left me there! I immediately noticed that their table was a lot smaller than ours. Our table in Whisperia was so much longer that you could barely see who was sitting on the other end. But theirs seemed to be so much closer to everyone. It was also made from a deeper cheery colored tree as you could still see the dark tree veins. The table seemed to only sit about eight!

The king gave a small gentle cough while looking at Nylina. She turned red for a brief moment as she spoke with the grapes in the side of her mouth. "Oh where are my manners! Everyone this is Azalea from...um...a ways from here." She tried to smile but the grapes in her cheeks forced her to give a crooked smile.

The king rolled his eyes at her as he replied, "Forgive her my lady, her thoughts are more focused on the food. Well, I am King Alcander. To the right of me is my son Morpheus and to the right of him is Xanthus. And to the left of me is Nylina, whom I am sure she gave a proper introduction of herself." I turned to Nylina whom tried once again to smile but she was already eating something else. The king continued, "We are pleased to meet you and to have you here to join us for breakfast. Now please sit down, you must be exhausted and hungry."

Yeah, his introduction was more proper than Nylina's. They all sat down as I sat down as well with them. The only one who was already sitting down was Nylina, whom now seemed to be just about done eating.

The king was a thin elf with a soft concern upon his face. He appeared extremely young as if age had not touched his very skin. White or gray hair had no trace anywhere. His eyes were a light chestnut brown with a hint of dark blue, as if the night sky was somewhere among his eyes.

Morpheus looked similar to Xanthus but he appeared to have more meat on his bones. Yes a bit chubbier. His hair was longer than Xanthus, but his was tied behind his head. His eyes had more hazel to them than brown. He was extremely handsome as well.

Two elf women dressed in white and tan came out with carts as they placed more food on the table. The food looked different than I had ever seen. It did all smell so delicious though. As soon as the servants left, everyone started to take food from here and there. Portions of the food hovered up from its original plate and onto their clean plate to eat. They just pointed as the bits of food rose up. Oh great, now what was I supposed to do? There were no utensils! The only one I had was the one next to my plate! It appeared to be some sort of buffet of some sort. Well, I did the only thing I knew best, stare. Yup, I mean what's a fairy to do? I just watched the food travel from plate to plate. Nylina leaned over to me as she replied, "My dear is your appetite lost?"

I looked around for I wasn't sure on what to say, I was not accustom to this. Usually in Whisperia you would be served just one plate. Or at least I was. And even if I attempted to hover some food onto my plate, I wouldn't know how to do it. I whispered over to Nylina, "What is on this table besides the fruit and breads?"

The king chuckled as he overheard me. Nylina responded, "There's three milk pancakes, stuffed crepes, vanilla french toast, brown sugared ham and..."

My eyes widened, "Nylina, I'm so sorry I can't...I'm not accustom to this...I..."

The king interrupted me and replied, "That is no problem my lady. Just reach over and eat what you truly enjoy. I will not be offended."

I gave a sigh of relief as I reached over and took a slice of what seemed to be some sort of cake. I took a small bite from my utensil, yum banana walnut cake. I hadn't had that for quite some time. I grabbed my goblet that first was empty. Abruptly to my surprise it filled up with some sort of brown liquid. "Do you like our goblets?" The king asked as he continued, "They fill up with what your desire of thirst is for the moment. It senses your deepest craving through the sensitivity of your fingertips."

"Interesting."

"Well, go ahead and take a sip." The king gave me a secured smile.

I looked into the cup once more but, what would I crave for that is this dark brown color? I got nervous, should I test it for poison? I don't think the king would want to poison me in front of all the elves, would he? Oh well I took a sip anyway. As the liquid rained over my tongue and down my throat, I received chills all over my skin. The flavor, I couldn't remember it but it was sensual. Suddenly, it came to me. "Chocolate, I haven't had this in centuries. This was right before the king made it forbidden. He said it was so delicious that it became sinful to eat."

The king replied, "Intelligent spell isn't it. Xanthus came up with it." Seemingly satisfied the king continued to eat. I glanced over to Xanthus who seemed to be content with himself. I on the other hand continued to eat, I was starving!

After we were done eating the servants came to remove the plates. I still felt odd not being the one who would pick them up. After the table was cleared we all stood up. King Alcander took one last sip from his goblet before he surrendered it to a servant. He replied, "Azalea and I will be going to the Gardens of Vinalin for a few moments. When we are finished with our discussion, Azalea will need a tour of our castle and perhaps our city."

Morpheus walked over to me and with took my hand, held it carefully then kissed it. He sent chills down my spine, such courtesy. I flipped my wings open unconsciously as I almost knocked over Xanthus. The bandages fell off and landed softly onto the floor. I uncontrollably giggled, I couldn't help it. Morpheus looked into my eyes as he replied, "My lady Azalea, I would enjoy the honor to escort you around the castle. Our moments together I can guarantee you will be quite pleasant. Oh, what beauty of light reflects upon your glowing skin."

I fluttered my wings as he once again kissed my hand. "Um, why thank you Morpheus." I replied with a pleasant smile. Morpheus gave a small bow as he left out the doors with Nylina by his side giggling. As I turned around to Xanthus I almost knocked him down yet again with my wings. Suddenly two small feathers from my wings fell off as they flew by his nose and slowly sailed to the ground. I tucked in my wings as I replied to Xanthus, "I'm sorry did miss; I mean, did I hit you?"

Xanthus raised one eyebrow as King Alcander seemed to tilt his head toward me. Xanthus scrunched his face for he seemed as if he didn't want to talk to me. But nonetheless he replied, "If you'd wish, I could show you around the grounds. But I am sure you would rather have the company of the prince by your side."

How arrogant to think that I would want such a thing. "I'm sure you are mistaken, not everyone prefers a prince by their side." I replied over to Xanthus, as the king seemed to nod at my reply. Xanthus gave me an expression as if he was confused with something. But he still gave a small bow and left the room.

King Alcander turned to me and replied, "At the end of our discussion, you could simple reply to me whom you'd rather prefer to accompany you around the castle. Now my dear, shall we visit the peaceful Gardens of Vinalin?"

I slowly nodded my head as we started to head out of the eating room toward the gardens outside. I gave a hard gulp for I knew I had to tell him the truth of my situation. I wondered if he would turn me in or if he would understand? I know Cethios would kill me if he got his hands on me. I mean, he already tried to kill James. Actually he thinks he did! Who knows whom else he tried or did kill? Even if he wouldn't, I would still have to marry him against my wishes and will. I felt so deserted and alone for that brief moment. I didn't know what to expect from this king. What else was I to do?

We finally reached these half glass and half-wooden doors. We pushed the doors slowly and made our way out into the gardens as the bright orange sun shone brightly in our eyes…

The Secret in the Gardens of Vinalin

15

There were millions of flowers from all sorts of colors and types. I have never seen so many exquisite flowers before. Miniature waterfalls fell from small bronze rocks that lead to small streams with bright yellow and orange corral fish. The sweet aroma of sweet pea flowers filled my lungs. We walked slowly until we came to a small clearing made of red stone. The king replied, "So, there is a story you must tell me, I do have all day. No short cuts, details are what make a story very interesting. So please go ahead and begin. I have great hearing so whispering will not affect my ears. But please do refrain yourself from doing so." He walked slowly with his hands behind his back.

I on the other hand took in a deep breath and slowly asked, "King Alcander, before I begin, may I trust you with the words that I will be exhaling?"

King Alcander stopped walking as he turned his body slightly toward me. "I will not deceive you Azalea. You need not to hide the truth, for only the truth will release any darkness that may surround your heart, and allow it to become free. Lies will keep you trapped within your skin. Let me ask thee, are you seeking sanctuary from a murder?"

I opened my eyes wide. "No, my goodness no!"

"Are you a thief?"

"No-no, I am not dishonest nor a fraud. I am only a servant of my castle of Whisperia. I run from no given judgment!"

The king smiled at my outburst as if he was content with my reaction. He continued, "Now, doesn't that perceive satisfying from inside? I fear neither your words nor your actions. For fear itself is only the lack of self-confidence that flows inside your heart. And evil could over turn your self-esteem as it over takes your mind entirely, one not so full of life. And rage is filled with unanswered questions of an un-assured heart. So indeed, honesty is in your eyes that I can see. Love flutters within your wings with the warmth of your smile. So Azalea, you should not fear your words, fear what words you choose to hide. But understand the truth, for I then shall only give you warmth and shelter. But I must know the reasoning of your presence in my city."

A smile came upon my face for when he finished, I knew I was able to trust him. Only those who speak from their inner souls in that manner may be trusted. "Your Highness', I know a sword trainer whom also spoke from the wisdom of an ancient heart."

"And are you able to place your trust him?"

"I am."

"Then perhaps that story of yours will flow more smother, yes?"

I laughed a bit, "Yes of course." I stared up at the sky only to see that same white and golden dragon soaring by. And for some strange reason, I felt such great comfort. I closed my eyes briefly as great security filled my open heart. I opened my chestnut brown eyes as I started, "I am a servant in the castle of Whisperia. The only difference is that I was adopted by the king, after they found me abandoned in the bedroom of the queen. I can assure you that I am not treated like royalty. I do share the same days with those of the servants. I do take classes though here and there, training with the swords and all. My bedroom is separated from the rest of the servants. I used to get made fun of, a lot. You see I am the only fairy in my city with feathers on the edges of my wings. And the prince of this other city, Urinia, he wanted to wed me since I was adopted through royalty. His main concern was to overthrow my adopted father and take over the kingdom, land, jewels, and treasure. I was being forced against my will to marry that inconsiderate jerk. I just, I couldn't do it 'Your Highness'. I care for those fairies and under his unfaithful rule, he would make them suffer. So, the night of our announced engagement he tried to murder James. James is my mentor and, you can say like a father figure to me as well. After I saved him, I think, and after I was prepared for the announcing, I ran. I ran away from that moment and that night as fast as I could, and I did not look back. I have so many unanswered questions about my true life, about my real parents, about who I really am inside. Questions that I cannot answer on my own. And under his marriage, imprisonment is more like it. I, I would have no choice but to obey his ruling. I wouldn't be surprised if he was planning my death as we speak. I, I..." I couldn't help it, I was out of breath as I gave soft inhales by the end of my story. By this time also, I had found a small stone bench that I sat on.

King Alcander came over and sat next to me as he replied softly, "Well if there is anything I can help you with, or if you need anything to answer your questions, or just time to think things over, your reasoning and secret is safe with me. Now the real question is, do you think they will come looking for you?"

I stopped to ponder the thought. I would hope not but you never know. I replied softly, "All of the fairies within my city are much afraid to enter the south. They are afraid of the mysteries and dragons, but on the other hand we were told that they do not exist. So hopefully Cethios will not come looking for me."

"Cethios?"

"Yes, that is the princes' name. Um, King Alcander, would you give me away?"

The king pondered my question momentarily. He forced his eyebrows together as he answered, "Did I not grant you shelter? Shelter you seek then safety you shall receive. But you must realize that you cannot remain hidden forever. I do trust in destiny and in fate. You see I believe that Cetus found you for a good reason. And I see a glow around you that describes your destiny. And I, I see that it lies here. Besides, both of the boys have grown a liking to your presence. They would fight over the duty to keep watch over you and attempt to heal your wings over the past few days." A warm fuzzy smile came upon my face as I realized that, they liked me and they cared. The king asked, "So Azalea, whom would you prefer as your company for the day?"

There was not much to think about, I already had my answer. "Prince Morpheus must be occupied. I'm sure he wouldn't want to spend the day with a servant. He probably would prefer a princess or…"

King Alcander interrupted me as he laughed, "Actually, he is looking for a potential mate. Most girl elves do follow him such, but he knows better. Servant or princess, anyone can catch his eye whomever has a pure heart, but no one has captured his heart just yet."

I didn't want to say it but I couldn't help myself. I had to ask. "And Xanthus, 'Your Highness', has anyone caught his heart?"

King Alcander smiled widely for I think that he suspected that I would want to know more about him. The king replied, "Ah yes Xanthus, no. No one has caught his heart just yet. He still is on his own, perhaps waiting for that special someone as well."

I pondered, they were both handsome except Xanthus had an attitude that interested me. But then again, I never had a chance to choose anything. I really wanted to know more about the castle and the lands. If I went with Morpheus I'd be too shy to ask anything. And Xanthus, I'm not sure but… "'Your Highness', is Xanthus free for the day?"

The king looked confused as he turned toward me and asked, "Really, are you sure? You wouldn't want Prince Morpheus to accompany you instead? His heart could be yours if you'd wish?"

I bit my bottom lip as I looked up into the sky at the dragons frolicking in the air. I wanted an adventure and, I don't think the prince would want to take me on a dragon ride. "Thank you but, having the princes' love and having him all to yourself is not always what is on the mind of every girl. Not this one that's for sure. If it's' alright with you, and if Xanthus doesn't mind."

The king stood up and nodded. He replied, "I am surprised by your decision but, nonetheless very well." King Alcander gave a wave of his hand to a servant elf that was in the gardens a few feet from us. The servant walked slowly up to the king. The servant gave a small bow as the king replied to him, "Azalea wishes the company of Xanthus. Tell him she will await for him here, Thank you." The servant gave another bow as he was off on his way. I stood as the king with took my hands and held it between his warm tender hands. "I must go and tend to some duties now. Xanthus will be here shortly to give you a tour and to show you to your quarters for the night. Do try to catch up with Morpheus later, yes?"

"Perhaps."

The king nodded in content and left. I now stood alone in the clearing as I sat back down on the stone bench. I started to look around as I noticed that most of the flowers around me were azaleas with some sweet pea flowers. What an ironic coincidence I thought. I took in deep breaths of my surroundings. I finally in all of my centuries felt safe and relaxed. My muscles have felt so sore, for I hadn't been able to relax them like this for ages.

The Tour and the Gift

16

In the mist of all of the enchanting flowers, I saw Xanthus making his way over to where I was sitting. I stood up quickly and brushed away at my dress a bit. As soon as Xanthus was about five feet away from where I stood, he replied, "I am surprised you would want to spend the day with the one who defeated you this morning."

"Well, aren't we filled with pride? Let me refresh your memory, I allowed you to defeat me. Therefore, I didn't want you to be embarrassed to the fact that a lady defeated you. Besides, I knew I would need your accompany later on anyway. I just wouldn't want you escorting me around in crutches."

Xanthus chuckled to my response as he replied, "Shall we continue onward to see the castle? And after towards the end of the tour, Nylina has set aside a bathing room just for you."

We started to walk around the castle toward the front as I replied, "You know that bathing room does sound extremely soothing and comforting right about now."

Xanthus snorted, "Soothing? The bath is really what is needed for you."

I started to laugh to myself. I couldn't believe that he thought it was I that needed it. I mean, has he looked in a mirror lately? I did spend a week in a dragons' barn though. I mean, couldn't they have taken me to a nice warm bed instead of a bed made of hay?

We entered the castle in the front through these huge wooden doors. As we entered, I saw two grand staircases, one on each side of the entrance room. They were made of a deep cherry wooden tree. Bright silver lined the banister as did to the edges of the steps. The floor itself seemed to be made of some kind of beautiful light ivory marble. All of the colors came together beautifully.

I noticed that in the middle of the ceiling was a huge colorful crystal chandelier. As we started to ascend the stairs I looked down below to the floor to see the chandeliers reflective light. But I realized that the colors were swirling around and darting here and there. I wondered what was wrong, was I hallucinating or something? I looked straight in front of me to see the chandelier. We had almost reached to the top of the floor. We were standing in the middle of the staircase and just about eye level to the chandelier. To my surprise instead of seeing small dangling crystals I saw small flying crystal dragons. They seemed to dart around in only that area. So that far away it appeared ordinary. But up close it was very extraordinary.

I stopped and leaned over the banister to get a better look. It was so exquisite I had to stop and take a long look at it. I slowly stretched out my hand hoping one would fly over to me. Surprisingly one did! A small green crystal dragon flew slowly over to me. It landed on my palm for it was no bigger than my hand. I noticed that it was clear on the outside. But on the inside, it was just like a diamond, filled with ravishing color.

"Magnificent aren't they." Xanthus replied as he walked down next to my side.

"Yes, they are quite exquisite."

Xanthus slowly placed his right hand under my hand where the crystal dragon was standing on. The little dragon let out a small low pitch roar as it spread it wings out. Xanthus replied, "It is made from a bendable crystal found deep within the mountains. It is placed under an enchantment so then, the crystal itself thinks it is a dragon. Be gentle though, I have broken about three or four in my days. They are extremely delicate and fragile. But it is very strange that…"

"What would be strange about this?"

"Strange that one came out and flew over to you."

"And what is wrong with that?"

"They only…um, they only come out to those who are worthy to see the beauty inside of them, the small crystal diamond that lies inside." Xanthus quickly let go of my hand as the dragon was on its way back to the middle of the chandelier.

I turned to him and asked, "Worthy? You're just jealous because it flew over to me, and not to you. Stop being so envious, it's bad for your heart." I slipped passed him and continued up the staircase. As I reached the top, I saw that he was still standing where I left him. He was just staring off at the crystal dragons, he appeared to be confused and pondering something immensely. I shouted over to him, "Are you still upset about the little crystal dragon? Look, if you want, I can fly over there and catch one for you. Are you listening to me or ignoring me? Xanthus?"

He turned and eyed me for a brief moment. He then turned his gaze towards the steps and continued up the staircase. He walked over to me as if confronting me with something he was upset with. He quietly asked, "You say you are a servant in your castle. And yet here you are wearing an exquisite gown with diamonds and pearls almost covering its entirety. A servant to your word, do you say?" He took a step back from me.

What was he trying to get at, that he did not believe me? I replied to him sternly, "Look, you may or may not trust in what I say. But I do say this to you, yes, I am a servant of my castle, I am nothing more than that. Besides, I have nothing to prove to you so believe me if you wish or not. My situation is none of your concern. This dress is not that of a princess, and not mine I assure you, but I did not steal it if that is your assumption. Why would you question me when I only speak the truth of what I have been told, of what I have grown to believe? What good would come from lying anyway?"

Xanthus came closer to me as his eyes met mine, he then eyed my stomach then back into my eyes. He asked, "You honestly don't know who your parents are or who you really are, do you?"

I stepped closer to him as I replied in a whisper, "No I don't know, but if you did would you tell me? Why would you want to keep the truth from someone in which has no clue to her past? Someone who deserves to honestly know whom she really is? You do not know how it feels knowing that your whole life could have been different or better just by knowing your true identity. You have no idea how it feels waking up in the middle of the night, knowing that you are completely alone and deserted within the land that you live in. You feel this emptiness inside, that for some reason you cannot answer nor complete, and you have no control over anything to find the truth nor any idea on where to start… Besides, were you eves dropping on my conversation that I had with the king?"

Xanthus bit his bottom lip as his gaze quickly left mine. He replied, "I do apologize, you are right it is none of my concern. Shall we continue the tour then? There is much to see."

He tried to pass me but I quickly with took his arm. "I don't want to continue this if you do not have faith in me. Do you really question who I am? I mean, I don't even know who I truly am, I have nothing but only just my name." I let go of his arm as I glanced around, not really knowing what I could do. Why would he not believe in me? I wanted him to trust me as I wanted to trust him.

Xanthus sighed as he with took my hands and replied, "I truly am sorry for my rudeness and my questioning about who you are. I assure you I was just filled with a bit of envy that's all. If I hurt you, I truly am sorry. Please let's continue. I am sure there are a few rooms in this castle that will make you feel better." He tugged me along by the hand for a few moments as he then released it. The first few rooms were sort of interesting. There was this one sewing room that had so many types of fabrics. They were sorted from designs and colors. The walls themselves seemed to be covered with all the fabrics.

There was an exotic bird room that I really enjoyed. I have never seen so many different varieties of birds. We hand feed some of them as Xanthus told me nothing but stories, and I as well to him. I felt as if we were connecting in some way as the day continued. There were so many rooms that I didn't even know existed.

We approached this huge door that seemed to be made of a dark brown tree bark. As we entered, I was in complete awe. There was this gigantic tree right in the middle of the room. It had huge thick branches that were spread all over the room and into smaller rooms all over. The rooms seemed to be holes that were carved out into the wall. There were small steps that were carved in the tree and branches.

As we got closer, I saw that the rooms were full of books that covered the entire walls. Each room was filled with different subjects in them. History of the elves, arts, science, nature and the depths of the sea are just to name a few. As we climbed the steps, I leaned over to see that it still had the same bark of the tree on the sides. I was in amazement. Moments later we came to this isolated room in the far back after much climbing. Xanthus turned to me and replied, "I think this room will become one of your favorites."

I stared at the books as I tried not to look down, for only a small thick thread of rope prevented us from falling off the side. I still felt a bit queasy but I mean, what do I have to worry about I could just fly down. But still the thought of falling made my head spin. I concentrated on the books as I reached for this dark emerald colored book. It had a small blue baby dragon on it. I ran my fingertips over the books' cover, it felt as if it had some type of rough scaly skin on it. It read, The Legend of the Dragon.

Xanthus responded, "If you'd like, you can take it with you. I know you don't understand much about them so I figured perhaps, now you would know more. I know you'll appreciate it. That's if you read it."

"I will, I'm not just going to stare at it you know. Besides, are you giving me a gift?"

Xanthus turned red as he quickly answered, "No, I'd thought I could save some of my breath instead of me explaining so much to you. I'd thought you could just read it at your own pace. I don't know if fairies are fast learners or slow learners."

I laughed, "We're not slow learners if that's what you're assuming." I held the book tightly to my chest. I knew he was giving me a gift even though he didn't want to admit it. I continued, "Thank you, I shall cherish it them."

We continued onward as I saw many other rooms and paintings along the way. Xanthus enthusiastically told me stories about each and every one, as I listened intensively. Their history seemed so complicated. I didn't even know so much had happened. We were only taught about the present time.

We spent the whole afternoon drifting through the castle engulfed in each other's conversations. Just before the sun started to set, we approached this door that appeared to be made out of soap. It had different sizes of bubbles forming and popping all over it. Xanthus cleared his throat, "Behind these doors awaits your change and bath. Do you need me to call a servant or two?"

"I think I can manage on my own but, is there a lock behind this door?"

Xanthus raised his eyebrow as he asked, "What for?"

I smirked as I replied, "I wouldn't want someone to barge in you know. Seeing things, they don't deserve to see or need to see. Or probably have never seen before."

He scrunched his face in confusion as I quickly entered to room and then closed the door behind me. I waved my glowing right hand over the door as a small blue light appeared before me. It quickly turned into a lock made of marble. Suddenly I heard Xanthus muffled voice behind the door. I think he just understood what I told him.

"Well, it's not like I want to see anything anyway!"

I pretended I didn't hear him as I giggled softly. I heard him grunt and walk away. I giggled some more as I turned around. I was in awe once more. There before me was a colossal water fountain in the middle of the room. As the water splashed from the top it landed on three huge green petals. It was made of this black and green stone and marble. From the top of the sprout came out colorful bubbles that floated around everywhere in the room. On the water surface of the bottom dish were red rose petals all over. The support between the two dishes were swirled and made of green stone. It was completely amazing.

To the left was a tri-fold wall made of some bamboo plant. Next to it was a small wooden table where some towels laid. Hung on the tri-wall itself was a gorgeous simple silver gown. As I walked closer to it, I saw there was a tray with some soup and a golden goblet. I quickly ate and enjoyed the potato soup and some grape juice. You got to love that goblet that fills itself!

After I walked over to the fountain and dipped my foot into it. It was extremely warm! I shed that evil gown that Cethios gave me and stepped into the small pool. I sank in as I found out that it was a couple of feet deep. As I sat down the water just reached my neck. I dunked my head in as I just started to relax.

Suddenly I heard small high-pitched laugher. It grew louder and louder as I glanced up to the top of the fountain. Suddenly out squirted colorful butterflies from the top of the sprout, with the constant bubbles that were already coming out. They flew down as they swirled around me giggling and laughing. Finally, one stopped on my finger as I raised my other hand to shake its small hand. It replied, "Good evening my lady. We are here to make you sparkle and shine. So please-please, sit back and relax. Do not - do not interfere in our grand work. We will do the rest."

It gave a small bow as it took off with the rest of the other butterflies. Some scrubbed and rinsed my hair, while others did a pedicure on my hands and feet. Just as they were done some butterflies curled my hair up with pins while others stuck small white dandelions in my hair. It all happened so fast as if it was a rapid blur. Finally, about an hour later the same butterfly once again stopped and landed on my finger. It replied panting, "Well, what were you doing, running around in the mud? Well then, finally your skin is sun kissed. Please, do not come back scrubbed in mud! No-no-no-no-no! Shame on you, now shoo!"

It threw me a kiss and just like that it was gone with the other butterflies back inside the sprout. I couldn't believe it, the butterflies here in this city were just as nippy and impatience as the ones back in Whisperia! The only thing that surprised me was what a great job they did on my hands and feet. They looked great; I was impressed! I finally got out and got dressed. The gown felt simply soft and sinful against my skin. I did take a couple of pins out from my hair. My head hurts a bit when my hair is placed so tightly up.

I walked up to the door and unlocked it as I slowly exited. I entered the hall to find it empty. Perhaps Xanthus went to go get something to eat. I walked forward a bit only to find myself tripping, falling and landing face first onto the floor. I lifted my head to see a small white string with yellow bells in front of me and in back as they started to jingle. I stood up as the string and bells disappeared slowly. Suddenly I heard a muffled thunder sound as I looked up. There above me was a small black cloud as it started to gently let out snow. The small white fluffy flakes melted on my skin as their coolness sent shivers down my spine. What a trick Xanthus left for me as moments later the cloud disappeared. All I could do was shake my head and laugh. Softly I heard footsteps behind me as I turned around to see Xanthus coming down from the other hall. He too had changed and bathed. Xanthus replied, "Shall we continue on, now that that awful odor is officially gone."

"You know, you shouldn't talk about yourself that way. I could say it for you if you like?"

Xanthus stepped back as he raised his eyebrow and replied, "Wow, did you think of that all by yourself? Did you hurt yourself or do you feel proud of your accomplishment?"

"I don't think I would consider myself arrogant. But you on the other hand are a different definition of that. The only thing I am asking for is respect and…"

"Respect? If I do recall on the first moment that we had together, you challenged me by raising your sword and then not placing it down. I understand that you are a guest in this city but,"

I interrupted him as he did to me. "Well, I was unsure of your priority. I simply didn't know if you were a friend or foe?"

"Would a foe take the time to bandage and try to heal your wounds? Besides, I was the one who took a chance. I was helping

100

someone who I truly didn't know who they were and what their intentions were."

I took in a deep breath in and let it out slowly. My chest started to burn I was in a confrontation that I didn't know how to handle. I knew I wasn't going to win this conversation for his remarks were just as smart and challenging as mine. I slowly rubbed my hands over my face and hair. I took out a white dandelion from my hair as I looked at it and jolted my eyes around the hall. Great, I knew I had to apologize to him. I replied, "Xanthus look I; I have been through a lot the last couple of days. I have my reasons to be alert and responsive. I do want to apologize for, well I understand that…"

Xanthus chuckled as he responded, "Okay, okay, don't hurt yourself trying to apologize." I gave him a shocked look. Here I am trying to apologize and he was stilling being difficult! Xanthus continued though, "Alright, I think we both were a bit hostile. I apologize as well. But this day has ended and much has happened. Now let me show you to your room and tomorrow we shall continue the tour of the city, if you wish."

I nodded my head and followed him through halls and crocked stairways that twisted and turned. I thought I was going to get sick. We were silent the whole way. I didn't know what to say to him anyway. I felt ashamed in a way, but I did have my reasoning as well.

We finally stopped in front of this huge green door. It appeared to be covered in different sizes of vines. But there was this one thick vine that seemed to have fur on it. It was curved throughout the door as it was lying on top of the other smaller vines. Xanthus gestured at my hand. "May I?"

I shrugged and simply gave him my right hand. He placed his hand gently on top of mine as he placed his pointer finger as well on top. He shifted my hand to the bottom of the furry vine. He slowly placed my fingertip onto the vine as we followed its curvature up the door. Xanthus then let go of my hand as he blushed. He cleared his throat, "This door will now only open to your touch."

We both stepped back as the door started to rumble and shake. The vines on the door started to slither away towards the edge. After it was all over it revealed a plain green door. I reached for the knob and opened it. I peered inside as I saw it was just as big as the eating room. A huge canopy bed with white silk stood in the middle of the room. Carvings of animals and trees were on the walls. As I stepped in, I sort of sank down. The floor seemed to be made of some sort of soft pillow. I could have even slept on the floor! Xanthus replied, "Will this do for you? Or do you prefer…"

"No-no, this is just as grand as a room of a royalty. I wouldn't ask for any other room. Thank you." Xanthus smiled and bowed as he started to leave. Just before he closed the door I exclaimed, "Xanthus wait!" He stopped and turned around still holding on to the knob. I asked, "Will you, I mean if you're not occupied. Will you give me that tour of the city tomorrow?"

Xanthus bit his bottom lip and looked down onto the floor for a brief moment. He replied, "Are you sure you wouldn't want Prince Morpheus to show you around. Perhaps he wouldn't offend you so much as much as I do." I walked closer to him as he jotted his eyes over into mine. He whispered under his breath, "Wow."

I gazed at him as our eyes stayed focus on each other. I replied, "If you prefer not to, I would completely understand."

Xanthus questioned, "Are you certain this is who, I mean, what you want?"

I twirled my fingers together as I became nervous. "Yes and, may I ask you for a favor? If it's not too much to ask for?" Xanthus nodded as I asked, "May I have a guard at the door for safety? Or..."

Xanthus interrupted, "My lady, do not fear. You are the only one who can open this door once it is closed. But if you'd feel safer, I will slumber in the room next door. Just give a shout if you need me or anything."

"Thank you, and please do call me Azalea."

Xanthus nodded and closed the door slowly. I went over to the bed and laid down into its softness. As I was looking up, I realized that there was no ceiling! I gasped, how was this supposed to be safe? Just then a thick purple lightning bolt shot through the sky, with smaller ones coming from the side. I placed my hands over my mouth as I shrieked. I didn't want Xanthus to hear me and get worried. I also wouldn't want him to think I was petrified. He would have probably loved knowing that I was though.

It then started to pour really hard and fast. I placed my hands over my face as I waited for the water to hit my body. I waited, and waited and nothing. But I did hear the rain hitting and bouncing off of something. I opened my eyes slowly to see the rain bouncing and dripping over something. I realized that the ceiling was made of some see through form and I wasn't going to get wet.

I became at ease watching the multi-colored lightning bolts shoot across the sky. Hearing the rumble of the thunder calmed me down as well. Moments later I found myself falling fast asleep listening to the raindrops. I was peacefully sleeping until my dreams awoke me.

Not so Rude Awakening

17

A woman with long wavy brown hair was lying down on a magenta colored silk bed. Bright scarlet silk hung from the beds' canopy as it started to sway with the breeze. The elf woman was breathing slowing as she slept with her baby by her side. As they snuggled close to each other a red arrow suddenly was shot into the woman's arm. It sank deep into her skin as it melted away. Suddenly another arrow shot into her arm as it glowed a bright blue. A familiar voice replied, "Over rule this magic that was placed within your veins, sleep under this slumber, for on this day it shall rain. The day will come when you shall rise, it shall be to everyone's surprise. The poison that you feel, shall soon slowly heal. You shall await, until the day comes for all to be revealed."

Her body shone with a bright blue hue as it calmly pulsed into a dull white. As the light slowly stopped the image started to fade from my grasp. As I left my subconscious mind, I started to awaken.

I opened my eyes to find all the sparkling stars above me, and a great deal of warmth coming from my side. I turned my head slowly to see where the warmth was coming from. I suddenly gave a low soft scream. "Snowfire!"

She was purring away lightly as if nothing was wrong as she cuddled by my side. I felt much safer than ever before. But how did she get in I thought? Was she already in here before I came in? Perhaps the door doesn't work against sneaky snow leopards. I started to ponder after I was filled with joy. I hoped Cethios would never find Snowfire or me here. I wouldn't want to put these elves in danger.

I placed my arm around Snowfire, kissed her and hugged her tightly. I again started to peacefully fall asleep. I wondered why I had dreamt that dream. And what did it mean, what did it symbolize? Was the elf woman I dreamt of the queen? I wasn't sure what I was supposed to learn from that but, I quickly closed my eyes yet once more. I soon fell asleep with the warm comfort of Snowfire by my side.

Snowfire and a Confrontation

18

A soft knock came to the door. I shot straight up to find Snowfire gone. "Azalea my lady may I come in?" Nylina was knocking on the other side of the door.

It took me a while too completely figure out where I was. I replied, "Yes come in." I continued to rub my eyes as I looked over to the door. Why wasn't she coming in?

She replied, "May you open the door? Remember only you can open it. I am helpless at the other end at the moment."

I quickly jumped out of bed and rushed over to the door. "Sorry, I forgot about its enchantment." I opened the door cautiously though.

Nylina came trotting in with a tray of breakfast floating aside her. In her hands was a beautiful blue velvet dress. She replied, "Sorry about that, did I wake you? Xanthus insisted that I come and wake you. He said you'd probably sleep all day. Besides you might miss breakfast. Oh and I brought you a change of clothes." She walked over to the bed as she started to stare at it. She cleared her throat and half-heartedly shouted at it, "Where are your manners? Go ahead and make yourself!"

The bed suddenly started to make itself as it tugged up the sheets. It even fluffed its pillows. When the bed was done, Nylina placed the dress slowly and carefully on top of the bed. She then took the tray from midair and placed it onto the bed. She walked over to the door as she replied, "When you are ready, Xanthus will be awaiting for you downstairs. Oh, and if you get lost simply walk up to a painting and ask, where am I? A map of the castle shall appear with a small circle on it. The circle will imply where you are." She smiled and started to leave.

I quickly replied to her, "Nylina."

"Yes my lady."

"Thank you, thank you for everything."

Nylina turned red and gave a small bow. She left as she closed the door slowly behind her. You know, I kind of like that door. It would prevent Trathina from barging in the way she usually did. I did hope she was doing all right.

I made my way over to the bed as I looked to see what was on the tray. There was a white bowl with circled bread that was covered in dark brown glaze with strawberries. Next to it was a tall glass of what looked to be lemonade. There was a thin slice of lemon hanging from the glass. Strange to eat for breakfast but, I shrugged my shoulders and ate it anyway.

After I was done I quickly dressed myself, for I didn't want to keep Xanthus waiting for long. I twirled my right pointer finger around as the laces in front and in back tied themselves together. I looked around wondering if I had dreamt that Snowfire was next to me. I looked over to the balcony door to see that it was left opened. Funny, I don't remember leaving the doors opened. A cool breeze started to sway in when I heard a low rumbling noise. A small dark shadow started to appear on the other side. "Snowfire, is that you?"

The low rumbling noise continued as I started to fear on what might be making that noise. Suddenly it pounced on me! It knocked me down as it started to lick my delicate face. "Yuck Snowfire!" I gave her an immense hug. "I am so glad that you found me. I was afraid I was never going to see you again. Wait, does anyone know you are here?"

Snowfire hopped off of my lap as she shook her head in a no reply. I quickly described my journey to her from the moment I left with Mirage to this very moment. Of course, Snowfire sat there listening intensively to every word I said. As I finished I replied, "So I am on my way downstairs to meet with Xanthus." I placed my hands on her cheeks as I rubbed my head on hers. I replied to her as she nuzzled my chin, "Thank you for always being there for me. Please look after me today just in case, because I know you will anyway."

Snowfire gave me a small lick on my nose. I tugged on her ear as I whispered, "I love you with all of my heart." I then took off out of the room, of course letting her out first. I made my way down to the front curving staircase. I did ask a couple of paintings for directions on my way down. You know those maps should be called, you are right here. They worked great!

As I reached the front hall I saw that Xanthus was standing next to Morpheus. They were talking to each other as if their conversation was very intense. They were both talking in a very low voice, seeming as if they didn't want anyone to hear a word. As I got to the bottom they both

106

smiled at me as if they were hiding something. Morpheus quickly took my right hand and kissed it. "Good morning my lady, I'm hoping that your slumber was very pleasant and comfortable."

Of course I was breathless, this guy was hot! For a brief moment, I forgot to breathe. "Yes um, thank you."

Morpheus continued, "Xanthus and I are both very willing to show you around our grand city today. But I thought perhaps, you'd like a prince to escort you today. A royal tour I thought. May I ask you whose company you'd grant on this exquisite day?"

I looked at them both confused as Morpheus released my hand. What were they trying to do? I thought I asked Xanthus to company me today. Perhaps he was still upset with me, or simply he just didn't want to? But, for some reason Xanthus appeared to be very nervous. He wasn't even looking at me or looking up. Was he doing this on purpose? Morpheus on the other hand had great eyes as well as great eye contact. Morpheus replied smugly, "My lady, I understand that you are a servant within your castle but, you don't necessarily have to have a servant tour. You can be with a prince even though you are not a princess. I would enjoy this day with the warmth of your smile."

My goodness! Why was everyone trying to force Morpheus on me! Even he was pressing himself on me. But he was handsome and light on the eyes. I slowly sighed a deep breath out as Xanthus was still not looking at me. I replied, "If you don't mind…" I turned to Xanthus whom now looked at me in the eyes. "Xanthus would you mind if…"

Xanthus quickly interrupted me, "If you'd prefer Morpheus to show you around our city."

I frowned, what was his issue? I hesitated momentarily but responded, "No, if you don't mind, if you would be able to take me. That's if you don't have other things to attend to." A small crooked smile came upon Xanthus face as he tried to hide it. I turned to Morpheus and asked, "I do apologize for any inconvenience. Another day perhaps?"

Morpheus nodded and responded, "Till another day." He gave a small bow and left the grand hall.

I waited until Morpheus left then I walked up to Xanthus and demanded, "Look, if you don't want to take me…"

Xanthus interrupted, "I just thought you'd prefer a princes' escort."

I just about lost it, "Why does everyone think that I need a prince in my life? And for what, to have an empty cold castle and to hold emotionless jewels and gold? A treasure that cannot love back is no treasure at all. Do not assume that you know who is right for me. A princes' love is not what I sought after."

Xanthus crooked smile came upon his face once more. But this time he did not try to hide it. He replied, "Feel better?"

I was baffled, "What do you mean if I feel better? You're the one that gave me that confusing confrontation."

"Nothing about that was confusing to me, besides are you prepared to have a servant escort you?"

I half shouted, "No." Xanthus looked startled by my answer. He looked at me confused as I replied, "I am prepared for a tour giving by the one and only, Xanthus."

He smiled as he lifted his arm up a bit, just enough for me to slip my arm around his. We then walked outside through the grand doors together, chuckling and arm in arm.

The City and the Enchanted Pendant

19

As the sunlight spread its warm waves over us, I saw an immense dragon sitting before us. It was Cetus with a small black saddle on his back. Cetus chuckled as he gave a bow, "Good morning, I will be your travel support for the day. And don't worry my lady, I already ate for the day. Yup, nice and full."

I got closer to him as I shouted, "Good morning Cetus to you too, and thank you!"

He was so enormous that he almost covered the sun! I was barley the size of his foot! Xanthus stepped over to my side as Cetus replied to me, "I'm not deaf. I can actually hear better than elves, and probably better than fairies too!"

Xanthus laughed at me as I was in shock. I was just trying to be proper by saying hello. How was I supposed to know they could hear all the way up there? Xanthus asked, "Are you prepared to go now?"

"Wait, are we seriously going on, on…on Cetus?"

"Of course, how else would we be able to reach the city? If we go on foot it could take days." I looked over to Cetus who appeared to be blushing. Xanthus replied half sarcastically, "It's just like flying for you. But much higher I'd imagine. You're not, I mean…you're not afraid are you, of heights?"

"Of course not!" I stammered. I hated to admit to him that I was a bit afraid. I had never flown to that height before. Cetus lifted his claw as I jumped on it, and flew over to his back. I crossed my legs and sat sideways on the saddle.

Xanthus followed but he seemed to climb more. He sat behind me giving me a strange look. He replied, "You do know that you probably might fall off sitting that way."

I turned back and tried to glare at him but the sun caught my eye. I replied, "You're enjoying this aren't you?"

Xanthus laughed, "Wouldn't want to see you fly off that's all!"

Cetus gave a low growl at Xanthus as I hoisted my dress up a bit and swung my left leg over to the other side of the saddle and Xanthus scooted forward. I gripped the rope tightly that was around Cetus' neck. Cetus puffed out a small black smoke at Xanthus. I couldn't help but laugh. Cetus replied, "Xanthus, be a gentleman would ya, geeze. Don't worry my lady, I won't fly so fast."

I was impressed. "Why thank you Cetus. At least someone here cares about me."

Xanthus still didn't move as Cetus stretched out his neck again toward him. Xanthus finally gave in and scooted even closer to me as he rolled his eyes. He placed one arm around me as the other hand held on to Cetus' reigns.

With one high pitched whistle, we were up into the clouds. It all happened so fast as the ground seemed to quickly leave my fragile sight. I screamed as I sank back into Xanthus. Of course, he laughed at me. I hated having him know that yes, I was afraid of heights. My eyes were very tightly closed. I felt the cool and warm mists around me change and swirl around my body. Xanthus sort of shouted over to me, "Open your eyes Azalea, you're missing the magnificent view!" I could barely hear him with all the gusts of wind brushing against my ears. Xanthus pulled the reigns around his back as he placed his hands on my arms. He shouted, "Open them, you'll love seeing this I promise!"

I had my hands over my face. I was petrified! I couldn't look. Xanthus slowly moved my hands from my face as he held me tightly around the waist. I still had my eyes closed though. I shouted back to him, "I'm sorry I just can't!" I felt Cetus take a dive as my stomach swooped up. I couldn't help it, I screamed.

Even though the wind was rushing past my ears, I could still hear Xanthus laughing at me. He shouted, "Just open them! Just once have faith in me! I won't let you fall I promise you that!"

I clenched my teeth and opened my eyes slowly. I was amazed at what I saw. We were cutting through the clouds as if they were balls of small feathers. The clouds seemed to be weightless mists of vapor. The small cotton balls of clouds seemed to appear, and disappear. I fell in love with the sky. About an hour passed by as we flew in the air and as I enjoyed the warmth of Xanthus.

The city started to come into view as we started to see the tips of the city houses. They were all different shapes and sizes. As we got closer Cetus started to dive down toward the city. And yes, that strange feeling jumped into my stomach. But this time I didn't scream, I just held my breath instead.

We landed with a heavy thud in a clearing, I quickly jumped off and landed on my hands and knees. I tried to focus my mind on my stomach but, I couldn't stop breathing so hard. I almost passed out as I kept losing some of my sight. The flight was amazing don't get me wrong. But it did take a lot out of me. Everything was still spinning so fast I couldn't seem to get up. All I could do was feel my head pounding. Xanthus on the other hand jumped off without any worry. He replied to Cetus, "I'll give a whistle if we need you."

Cetus gave a thunderous roar and like a gust of wind, he took off into the air. The wind made my hair fly forward over my head. Yes, I was still on the floor. I was trying to situate my breathing. Xanthus glanced around, as he didn't see me anywhere. Then he looked down as he saw me on the floor. He crossed his arms and chuckled a bit to himself as he replied, "If you'd like, I could give you a tour of the ground too."

"I just lost my footing that's all."

Xanthus scrunched over and placed his hands on his knees. He replied near my ear, "Do you need a hand standing up?"

I opened my wings and flew to my feet. I ran my fingers through my hair and tried to fix it. I steadied my breaths and responded, "No thanks, I got it myself."

He smiled to himself as we started to head towards the city. As we got closer the city actually looked bigger than it appeared. The market places were made so that they were in front of the homes of the elf living within it. It was pretty intense seeing the city so squished together like that. The homes and markets were made of some kind or red and brown brick. Probably that way when the dragons breathe their fire, the city wouldn't go up in flames. Per say a fireproof city. Vast amounts of willow trees dropped over most of the markets here and there. It seemed as if they were the doors to some places. Different sizes of tables were also in front with the things that they were selling.

The elves that worked the markets lived behind it, in their homes. They seemed to be content with themselves and their small businesses. The city was also categorized in sections. So, first were the crafts, stones, swords and fabrics. After that were the herbs, jewels, books, and magic crafts. And at the very end, which was Nylina's favorite, was the food.

We stopped at about every single market hut that there was to see. Xanthus described many stories about almost every single hut. When we reached the section of the swords, he smiled enthusiastically as he shared his thoughts with me. He replied as we entered the small hut. "Some of these swords I have made myself. I have designed some for certain elves to fit their specific needs. Every sword that I have made is designed around their hands. You see, everyone's hand is shapes differently and are unique. Some are delicate and some are stronger. Therefore, everyone needs a different amount of weight placed at the handle. That is how you make a sword become personally yours."

Xanthus showed me swords that were long, short, wide and thin. Some had gems and jewels, while others just had metal and wood. They all had delicate details in the handles. Some of the blades even had gold or silver lining on the edges of them. You could tell that Xanthus loved to do this. He even showed me a place where he would come to work on them and practice. He even tried to give me a lesson on how they are made. I never knew they were so much work. Xanthus really was dedicated on the swords, I was impressed.

As we reached the herbs, Xanthus described to me the powers of each plant in detail. Xanthus tried to make sure he didn't miss one. Some were to heal, give strength, give courage and much, much more. I never knew there were so many types of plants that were growing in the jungle.

The day passed on and got later and later. Our conversations seemed to intensify deeply. We both shared the same feelings and similar stories. I wanted to believe that we were getting closer. But I wasn't sure if perhaps it was in the air.

As we reached the magic crafts a mysterious woman approached us. She was wearing a long green hooded cloak. Her hands appeared fragile and delicate. You could barely see her face. She stopped in front of us as she replied, "Good afternoon, I have these two beautiful pendants that I have crafted with my own hands. They are free to my first customers if you answer my riddle correctly."

I smiled at Xanthus as he simply rolled his eyes at me. I gave him a nudge as I replied, "Come on what do we have to lose?"

"I'm sure a few gold coins."

I frowned at Xanthus as I looked at the woman. I replied to her, "We would love to answer your riddle. But I do not feel comfortable taking these pendants from you just by answering a riddle." I had bought some beautiful silk pink fabric earlier. I really liked it but at the moment I couldn't figure out a use for it. I did think that perhaps I would be able to use some of it as a silk nightgown, but I replied to the woman, "Here, take this even if I answer wrong or right."

The woman seemed to smile as her hood fell off of her head. It revealed her beautiful timeless face. She had curly orange hair that flowed behind her ears. She also had clear light blue eyes. But something about her appeared familiar but, I couldn't put my finger on it. She replied, "You are very kind to offer this to me even if you answer incorrectly. Are you sure you are willing to give this up without a sure gift in return?" I nodded to the woman as her grin widened even more. She replied, "I knew I had picked the right couple for this."

Xanthus quickly flushed red with embarrassment as he tried to answer the woman but she quickly asked her riddle. "If a baby wolf was born into a family of four, three girls and one male, how would he know which one is his mother? And when the little cub grows up how will he know that his father remained faithful?"

I smiled shyly as Xanthus appeared confused. I replied to the woman, "That's quite simple."

The woman appeared unsure as she replied, "Oh really? Explain."

"Well, once the cub is born all he has to do is recognize the male and the head female wolf, his mother. Once he knows the two leaders of the pack, he finds a mother and two sisters. You see, because wolves' mate for life. That means he remained faithful. Their love, you can say is binding to each other."

The woman gave a slight cheer as she reached in her pocket and took out two silver pendants with their own chains. The pendants were both silver little keys. The top of them were shaped as a heart as within the middle was another heart that was made from small stones. One side was silver as the other side was golden. The woman replied as she handed one to Xanthus and one to me, "When these two are placed together, they will unlock anything your heart desires. Once the faithfulness is gone between you two, they will disintegrate into the misty beyond in which they came from. They represent your hearts and your faith in each other."

We glanced at each other not knowing what the woman was meaning by her words. But as we looked back to face the woman, she had vanished within the crowd. Xanthus looked at me confused and replied, "Are you going to keep yours?"

"Of course, it was a gift from…"

"From a strange woman. Do you even understand what she was telling us?"

"I'm not sure?" I shrugged my shoulders as I placed my charm over my head and onto my neck.

I looked over to Xanthus as he shrugged his shoulders and replied, "Do you really expect me to put this on?"

"Yes, it was a gift. Sure, we don't know who it was from but, she seemed warm and kind hearted. I'm sure she meant us no harm. Besides, these are like some sort of beautiful souvenir, I have one and you have one."

I glanced at Xanthus excitedly as he appeared unsure. Xanthus saw that I started to appear saddened after he didn't respond to my excitement. He rolled his eyes and replied, "Alright, here, you place it on me." I smiled gleefully as I took the charm from him and placed it over his head and around his neck. Both pendants seemed to give off a small glow for a brief moment as it then dulled down. Xanthus questioned, "What do you think that was about?"

"I'm not sure, perhaps it meant the reflection of the mist that surrounds us on this day. Or it just caught the reflection of the sun." I glanced back at my pendant as Xanthus tucked his into his shirt. I'm sure he was just trying to keep it safe. I on the other hand left it out. I kind of thought it was beautiful and exquisite.

We were confused for a moment, but we simply continued on our way as we finally got to the markets of the food. The aromas of different varieties made my stomach curl in. I wanted to try everything! We ate so much by the end of the afternoon, I thought I was going to burst through my dress!

We arrived to this market that had different sizes of coconuts hanging from the ceiling. They seemed to be hanging from small strands of different colored ribbons. Xanthus ordered and bought a medium size coconut that was tied with a white ribbon. After, we headed for some shade under a willow tree by the cities' gardens. I asked Xanthus, "I'm not understanding, why were they all different shapes with different ribbons on them?"

Xanthus replied, "They are enhanced with a chant that keeps them frozen on the inside. Each shape holds a different amount inside. Each ribbon stands for a different flavor." As I sat down by the willow tree, Xanthus sat down next to me as well. He opened the coconut by placing his forefinger on the top. It seemed to split right down the center. Xanthus replied, "It has frozen cream inside. I have chosen a vanilla flavor, is that alright?"

I shrugged my shoulders, "I guess. I don't know what that is anyway."

Xanthus handed me a small wooden spoon. I scooped up some of the cold cream and ate some. As soon as I did, it sent chills down my spine as I closed my eyes enjoying the sensation. "This is really good."

Xanthus smiled at me as we continued to share the cold cream. As we reached the end, I bit my bottom lip. I wanted more but, I was too full anyway to even fit any more. I gazed over to Xanthus whom was now staring at me. He asked softly, "Azalea, did you enjoy your day with me today?"

"Yes I did, I wish it wouldn't end. But wouldn't you say the same?"

Xanthus leaned over closer to me as he half breathed, "Did you really mean that?"

I leaned back a bit and replied, "I wish I didn't say it in that way though, by the way you're looking at me. But, I'd rather not deny how I feel. I am not a deceiver if that's what you're going to get at. I would forbid that you would lie to me as well. If...if..."

He leaned closer to me as my heart started to beat faster and faster. I felt dizzy and nauseous as the willow tree made a low soft humming rhythm, and because I knew what he was about to do. Suddenly, he kissed me softly as he placed his top lip above mine. He placed his hands on the side of my face as our mesmerizing kiss intensified. I melted into the mist of the air, butterflies flew within my stomach. What else could I say, this was my first kiss. A moment later we parted as his eyes darted into mine, I honestly didn't want him to stop. He gazed onto the floor. He replied with a small shake of his head, "I um, I shouldn't have, I apologize for my, I wasn't…"

I interrupted him feeling more awkward than I should, "I don't accept your apology. I have no regret on what we just did…unless you do? I mean, is what just happened, forbidden?"

Xanthus turned and placed his hands gently on mine. He asked, "Why would you even ask that?"

"Why would you even apologize for kissing me? Let's be honest, this will never be real. It would be a forbidden fairytale. Tell me, when have you heard a love story with an elf and a fairy?" I glanced down, what was I supposed to tell him? I mean, did he want me or not? I was confused on what was going on. I couldn't even look at Xanthus, I thought I had embarrassed myself enough.

Suddenly Xanthus looked around and jumped to his feet. He turned to me as he extended his arm out to me. "Why this one of course." I looked at him confused as I could only shake my head. I looked at him as I gave him my hand to stand up. Our eyes met again as he replied, "Azalea, may I take you somewhere? Away from the city?"

I looked around toward the city. Where was it that he wanted to take me? "I guess…"

Xanthus' smile sent small goose bumps all over my skin. I haven't seen Xanthus with so much confidence. We both walked out from under the willow tree as Xanthus gave a sharp whistle. And just like that we were gone, high above the clouds into the bright empty space of earth on Cetus. Cetus soared slowly just barley embracing the air around us. I assume he could still sense that I was afraid. I shouted out to Xanthus, "Where are we going?"

"May I trust you?"

"As the stars trust the night to keep them reflecting their glow of…" I didn't get to finish my sentence as he softly kissed me once more embracing my face in his hands. Cetus dove for the ground as I held tightly onto Xanthus.

A horizon of water and land suddenly came into view. As we neared the edge, the smell of salty water tickled my nose. And as Cetus pounced on the floor, I jumped off and this time landing on my toes. I looked around to see that we were near these huge caves and waterfalls. I saw the beginning of the ocean as my heart sank in awe. I always wanted to see this view and finally, it came true. Small blue sea creatures jumped in and out of the blue water. They really were not so far away from us.

Xanthus gave a small bow to Cetus as he replied to him, "I will not be needing any other favors from you for the rest of the day, thank you. We shall enjoy a quiet walk back."

Cetus snorted a small blue fire bolt out of his nose. "Yeah okay, sure you will." Cetus chuckled with such sarcasm as he took off straight into the air like a lightning bolt. He landed with a loud splash into the ocean. In the distance a small laughter echoed.

I walked to Xanthus and asked, "What was that all about?"

He shrugged his shoulders and replied, "Who knows with that dragon. Come, I want to show you something."

We both ventured off over the rocks and small pools of water. We were heading toward a small waterfall that appeared quite dull, as it had no breathtaking rainbows soaring above it. But I didn't ask any questions nor did I care. I followed Xanthus as we were hand in hand.

Purest Thought

20

We reached the miniature caverns that appeared to be very ordinary. I realized that we were standing in the middle of many other enchanting waterfalls. It gave me such a feeling of freedom and of a sensational bliss that glowed inside my skin. The light mist from the falls felt cool against the humid air that embraced us.

We started to climb over a vast number of rocks to reach the small waterfall, well I did more flying than climbing. The waterfalls that lay before us made me realize just how small we really are in this world. Compared to everything else, we were only a tiny memory in the vast caves and waterfalls. Xanthus replied to me, "Welcome to the Waterfalls of Aqualyn. They are enchanted waterfalls filled with mystery and wonder. I come here to get away from it all. You know, come to think about things in life, about situations in life."

I stumbled over to him as I almost slipped on a rock that was covered with a limitless amount of moss. I replied to him, "Does anyone know of this enchanting location? Or is this your own personal place of serenity?"

"Some mermaids, Cetus and I, and now you. I doubt though that you will be able to find it once more though on your own."

"And why would that be?"

Xanthus laughed to himself as he jumped over some rocks to come closer to me. He replied, "Half of the time, well actually the whole time we flew here, you had your eyes closed, and tightly I might add to that."

I was in shock; how could he say that lie! I had my eyes opened momentarily for about a quarter of the way here. I bent down and placed my right hand over some water that drizzled over some rocks. The water and my hand glowed a light blue for a brief second as out came a small ball of water. It swirled and continued to glow over my hand as I then pulled my hand back and released it toward Xanthus. It ended up hitting him right on the chest. It splashed all over his clothes and face as I started to laugh out loud. Xanthus quickly bent down and formed a water ball as well. He chucked it right onto my face as he laughed hysterically. Then, it was war!

We spent several minutes bombarding each other with water balls. I never had so much fun in my life! Finally, just before we were both out of breath Xanthus replied with his hands on his knees, "Before night approaches us and over whelms us, would you like to venture into the caverns to see more?"

I tried to situate my breathing as I replied, "Sure, I'd love too!"

Xanthus started to head left of the falls as I followed him. We stood in front of this tiny waterfall where a huge rock stood next to it. There wasn't a cave behind the fall, there was just a very large boulder sitting next to it. Xanthus said, "All you see is this rock but..." He took me by the hand as we continued to follow the rocks' side. The opening seemed to get narrower and narrower as another rock to the right of us was closing in on us. I wanted to turn back as I started to feel secluded, but I continued to follow, I trusted him. We now were standing in a place where rock seemed to be all around us. There looked like there was no way in or out. As my breathing started to become a bit heavy Xanthus replied, "Help me push this boulder."

I laughed half-sarcastically, "You're kidding right?" I stared at him blankly as he just smiled at me. He started to push the rock. Oh well I guess, what do I have to lose? I shrugged my shoulders, took a deep breath and started to help him push. Suddenly the rock started to move in slowly as warm water started to pour down and drench our bodies.

The floor below us dropped as we both screamed and fell down below into a black abyss. We landed in a small puddle of water, sort of like a small pond. As we stood, Xanthus clapped his hands as the rock above us closed shut. I wanted to scream as I felt the air get dense. Just before I panicked bright green light started to glow below our feet, just before the darkness engulfed us. The light reveled an underground chamber of some sort. The rock in front of us slowly diminished as a small subterraneous passage now lay in front of us.

Suddenly the floor below us started to sink as I now no longer felt the ground below my feet. I felt as if I was going to go insane, where was he taking me? We started to swim through the tunnel towards the other side. As we swam, I started to quickly get extremely tired and out of breath. I mean come on, I have only swum a couple of times in Urinia, but not for more than a couple of minutes. I called out to Xanthus, who now was ahead of me, "Wait Xanthus, I can't, wait..."

To my horror I started to sink! I couldn't move my sore body any longer. I closed my eyes under the warm water. I admit it, I was terrified! But before long I felt someone tugging on me, and hard! I came above the water as I gasped for air. I was holding on to Xanthus neck as I laid on his back. He swam to this shore in the cave as he struggled to reach it with me on top of him. When we reached the white sand, I was still gasping for air. We both laid on the cool beach with our eyes closed. Xanthus replied breathlessly, "You sure are an extremely heavy fairy. Aren't your wings supposed to be the strongest part of your body?"

Breathlessly I replied, "First of all, my wings are for air not water. And, and secondly, did you just call me extremely heavy! I am average height and weight, everyone else is just abnormal!"

Xanthus laughed as we both still were taking in deep breaths. Once again, he replied breathlessly, "Welcome to the Caves of Esmera."

I started to look around but it appeared blurry from my sight. It seemed as if small brightly colored lights flickered before my eyes. I tried to concentrate and focus, and as I did, I gasped! "Xanthus where did you bring me, this is amazing! I got the chills all over my skin and, it is really-really warm in here!" I stood up slowly as I still stumbled a bit. Xanthus on the other hand still remained on the floor trying to situate his breathing. It was dim as a sunset but bright as the wondrous stars above. There were hundreds of jewels and gems of all sorts on the walls, they seemed to cover the entire cave! There were emeralds, diamonds, rubies, sapphires and many other precious stones! They were all so gorgeous with different shapes and sizes. I was in complete awe of where I stood.

"This is beautiful. Never have I seen such a precious treasure before. And let me tell you I have seen the treasure of Whisperia. But this, this is more precious than all of that combined. I am seeing it with my own eyes and I still don't believe it!" My words seemed to echo and bounce along the walls of the cave. It was completely secluded. There was no light except for the gems twinkling and glowing. There seemed to be no way out or in. I walked forward a bit as I stretched my wings open to their fullest. I felt so relaxed on the inside as well as out.

I flew up a bit towards the ceiling, as I wanted to get a closer look around. I went up to this one turquoise gem that seemed to glow a bit brighter than the ones around it. It was the shape of a diamond but, there seemed to be a part broken off at the bottom. I slowly moved my fingertips towards it. I had this odd urge to touch it. The stone on my stomach started to feel strange.

As I placed my fingertips on it, an electric shock seemed to flow freely through my veins. I quickly let go as I suddenly started to receive an image in my subconscious mind. It was a beautiful woman fairy, the same one from my dreams. She had the enchanting golden feathers that surrounded her wings. She was gentle holding a small infant in her arms. She smiled greatly as she kissed the infant on the forehead. The woman started to sing a sweet melody as the soothing lullaby was sent straight into my heart. The image in my mind started to diminish as the fairy woman softly replied, "I'll love you always, my sweet baby Azalea."

Then nothing, the image was gone. I opened my eyes only to see the broken gem glowing brightly. I was completely motionless as I wondered if, the other part of that gem was the very same one that now remained on my stomach. Confused by what had just happened, I took in a deep breath and shook it off.

I flew over to Xanthus who was now only sitting up on the white sand. I sat next to him as he replied to me, "Do you love it? If you promise to adore it and cherish it always, it could be yours?"

"And how could you make that happen?" He opened his eyes wide at my comment, and simply shrugged his shoulders and raised one eyebrow up. He seemed confused for a bit as I simply shrugged my shoulders at him. We both looked around in silence for quite some moments. I guess we were both enjoying the magnificent view of the gems. Then I wondered and asked, "Xanthus, do you know any ancient stories, an elf story, a legend perhaps? Will you tell me one?"

He leaned back with a smile and gazed deeply into my eyes. I received chills once more, but this time it wasn't the caves' beauty, for it was from the way Xanthus gazed into my eyes. I stared back and waited intently for him to start. He gave a small sigh as he seemed to give in. He started, "Alright, I know this one legend that was told but, I don't quite remember now who told it to me. It is said that an age of time will come that will be filled with peace. It will come between two nations that have been parted for millions of centuries. These two nations will combine and have a grand king and queen, whom all will respect with all their might. But before the powerful king and queen come, there will be a time of grief and sorrow. A time filled with bloodshed, death and evil. This darkness will dampen the lands that we live in. The magical powers of the two combined though will be greater than anyone alone can ever conjure. As well as by themselves, they possess an immense magic that is so deep and unimaginable. The peace of the new king and queen will sweep across the lands. Forever after that will their greatness rule."

I thought about his words and pondered. I asked him, "Xanthus, do you think that, this century could be that era? Do you think that we could be a part of that legend? Perhaps, a forbidden fairytale even?"

"I'm not sure, you and I are different but..." He shrugged his shoulder at me and as he gazed into the gems around us. Now that would be a great adventure I thought. For me to be a part of something important like that would feel so meaningful to me in my empty life at the moment. It would be challenging and precious.

Moments later I stood up as I started to gaze around at some of the exquisite gems again. Xanthus on the other hand continued to sit as he seemed to ponder something immensely. He remained quietly until he stood up and replied to me, "Azalea, you had an opportunity to be with a prince and become a wealthy princess. Yet you turned it down, twice."

I rushed over to him in flight as I replied, "I knew it! You were listening to the conversation that I had with King Alcander, weren't you!"

"I wasn't listening! I just simple over heard. I can't help it that your voice is very loud." He turned and walked away from me as he continued, "Why did you then?"

I crossed my arms and turned my head away from him. Why would he want to know, why did he even care? "Why does this bother you so much that you just must know my reasoning?"

Xanthus walked over closer to me and asked, "I guess I'm just curious. I just want to know why you did though. Do you not want to be with a prince, would that be horrible if you did?"

I sighed and responded to him as I opened my wings even wider, "Well I guess, I just don't want to be forced to love someone who I hardly know. I don't want to be forced to marry someone just because of their title and what comes with it. If I am going to spend the rest of my centuries with this person, it should be because of love and passion. It should be because we share the same interests, because we share one common passion. It should be because we want to be committed to each other, and not because we have to or because it was arranged before us."

Xanthus came closer to me as he placed his hands on my arms. He gazed deeply into my eyes and whispered, "Why are you are asking for a forbidden fairytale love?"

"Why can't I have one?" I looked down as I dropped my wings. He touched my face gently with his fingertips as he then dragged them slowly down my neck and towards the middle of my chest. Suddenly my dress seemed to melt away on my skin as it turned into a sexy blue lingerie. It still appeared to be my dress with lace around the front, and now I was revealing my stomach, stone and legs! I was in shock. I knew what was on his mind that very second! Low warm mist started to appear on the ground. I looked into his eyes as I opened my wings and flew up and back away from him. I asked him as I crossed my arms across my chest, "So let me ask you this, what are your intentions at this very second, honestly?"

The smirk on his face was hypnotic, he chuckled, "Why simply nothing. I know it's extremely late and therefore, I know we won't be making it back to the castle on this night. I thought you would appreciate a cooler silk, seeing that you are, glowing and, mesmerizing and..."

"And you think you would get something else in return somehow just because we are trapped in here for the rest of the night. I assure you that is not the intentions that are in my mind. I swear, that is not going to happen."

I flew up a bit higher as he replied, "You swear it do you? Well, would I need to get a rope to haul you down here then, to see those intentions come true?"

"You sure do!" I remained there in midair as suddenly Xanthus bent down and took a lace from his boot. I saw him twiddle with it for a few moments, as the lace started to appear to grow. Sure enough I saw him start to swing the rope around over his head. I chuckled to myself. I didn't think he would honestly try to haul me down. I started to fly higher up the cave but then, the thick rope suddenly wrapped around my ankle. I chuckled to myself and tried with all my might to fly higher up but I couldn't. As he tugged me down, I tried to struggle free. He laughed to himself, as I'm sure he found this very amusing.

I bent down and tried to remove the rope around my ankle as suddenly another rope looped around both of my wrists. I let out a small chuckle of laughter. Finally, I reached the ground as the rope still remained around my ankle and wrists. Xanthus pulled me close to him as I rambled with nervousness and joy, "I do hope that you realize that this is going to be

123

difficult really for you. I honestly have never done this before and, you should realize that you are receiving someone who doesn't know how, and has never, or what to…"

Xanthus tugged on my hands as he placed my tied wrists around his neck. He replied, "And what makes you think that I have done this before either? I am unknowing as much as you are. I have chosen to be this way and remain this way until the right day came when, when I could be with you, when I found you."

I wondered what he meant by that? I really was tired of pondering everyone's words. I looked behind him as a dark purple velvety bed appeared with smooth silk that drenched over the canopy. Xanthus bent over and grabbed my legs as he carried me over to the bed. He slammed me down onto the beds softness as he too fell down, on top of me, with a plop. The rope that was around me started to melt away as it shrunk back into a bootlace. The lace laid on the bed next to me as Xanthus simply brushed it off of the bed. He replied, "I do want to tell you Azalea, that I admire your courage and bravery for leaving your city and your security, and wanting to search for your true happiness. Even though you did not know what or who you were going to run into. But I need to ask you this, will you accept this night? Will you accept me for who I truly am? No matter what the outcome is?"

I placed my hands on the side of his face as I replied with a sigh, "Of course, I honestly knew what I was getting myself into when we entered this cave. Why else would I honestly be here? I am here because I want to be, I am doing this because I want to." Xanthus started to kiss my ear softly as I continued, "Are you trying to seduce me now that you have me here?"

Xanthus chuckled, "If I continue will it work?"

We continued to kiss softly as he rubbed his hand over my stomach. He slowly sat up still half on top of me as he sighed in a deep breath. It was if he was preparing himself for something. He took his shirt off and as he did, I gasped. I finally saw him without his shirt on. Yeah, he looked deliciously hot without his shirt but that was not what I was gasping about. There within his navel was the same stone that I had on my stomach. I reached over and ran my fingertips over it slowly. I was confused, was that what he meant when he said he waited to be with someone, until he met me? Xanthus sighed as he glanced down at his stone, "I'm not sure when I received it or how I even got it. As far as I know it has always been there. I didn't understand why its reasoning existed until the day I saw you, and when I saw yours, I was in shock to see it. Does this change anything between us? Is it wrong that I did not tell you sooner?"

I took in a deep breath and sighed out, "So, are we connected in some mysterious way? I mean, did you know of me, did you know I existed?"

"No, I just assumed that there had to be some vital reasoning behind it being there. I assumed that there was someone destined for me out there. I just never knew who?"

I started to think over his words as I quickly asked, "The day we met, when you saw my stone, did you know that exact moment?"

Xanthus shook his head, "I'm not quite sure, I don't think I realized the significance of its importance that very moment. I was too busy trying to defend myself."

I chuckled a bit. I started to think if we are supposed to be alike in some way. But then, why do I have golden feathers on my wings? I asked him, "So we both have the same stones but, where do you think my feathered wings come in part?"

Xanthus smiled to himself as he replied in a whisper, "I'm not sure, perhaps you're part bird." I smacked him on the arm as he laughed. I did not find that humorous, even though Xanthus thought it was. He asked me through chuckles, "So I have a question for you. Do you trust me entirely?"

I assured him, "Why wouldn't I, again, I wouldn't be here if I didn't. Do you trust me? I mean, are we going to share a part of our lives together after this night?"

Xanthus looked at me as he slowly bit his bottom lip softly. He leaned over and whispered in my ear, "I was planning for a binding eternity if that was alright with you? Besides, you are asking for a forbidden fairytale love, are you not?"

I looked at him bashfully as I smiled shyly. I didn't know what to say to that. But I did have to ask, "So honestly, is this your first time?"

Xanthus rolled his eyes, "If you promise not to dwell on it, yes, yes it is. If you want, you can go shout it out to the whole city while we're at it."

A smile came upon my face as I saw him roll his eyes once more, as if a bit embarrassed. I replied softly, "I'll only tell a part of it. And don't worry I have not either, and you know I can honestly keep a secret because this one time..." He interrupted me by kissing me passionately, perhaps to shut me up. Perhaps he knew that I would keep on talking if he would have let me. I wasn't trying to stall or anything. He was talking to me too. Perhaps he was trying to stall a bit as well.

The gems around us seemed to blur and brighten. Misty blue fog appeared all around us as it seemed to come from the ground below. Our romance continued throughout the night as our physical love became one. That night, our passion intensified.

Xanthus kissed my chest with his soft lips, then whispered in my ear, "I love you with all of my heart, I truly do love you. Will you promise too always be mine?"

Through breaths I answered, "I shall bind myself to you if you bind yourself to me."

"Always yes."

On this night we continued to share our love with every precious moment that passed us by. On this night every breath taking second was filled with only the purest thoughts...

Outside the cave

As the night continued and as the stars seemed to glow brightly above, a small blue light shone from the cave that Xanthus and Azalea were in. Suddenly for a brief moment a mild quake shook the earth. It shook from the cave through Trinafin, Whisperia and even Urinia. It awoke some but mostly everyone slept through the quake. Not knowing of what had just become of the fairy and the elf.

The Turn Around

21

I awoke to feel warmness drenching the back of my neck over and over. The lights from the gems in the cave still seemed to glow immensely. I rolled over to find Xanthus still sleeping next to me. I slowly placed my palm on his face as I thought, I didn't want to be anywhere else but here. As I snuggled closer to him, I thought of what went on last night as a smile came to my face. I unfortunately then started to think about what I needed to do about my future, about my situation in Whisperia.

"Azalea? Are you awake?" Xanthus whispered to me as he started to stretch his sore muscles.

I replied, "Yes but, is today now what was supposed to be tomorrow. So then what was last night now is yesterday?"

I think I confused him as he raised one eyebrow at me and replied, "If you are referring by if we have entered a new day, then yes it is morning."

I moved up a bit as I laid myself partially on his chest. I rubbed my hand over his chest as he kissed me softly on the forehead. I looked up over into his eyes, "Should we be heading back soon?" I didn't want this moment to end but I knew we had to get back.

Xanthus sighed, "Yes, eventually. But this time we can take the other exit of the cave, instead of having to exit the way we came in. The other way actually leads to a rocky road above the cave." Xanthus chuckled to himself, as he knew he had just confused me. But I thought to myself, what other exit or entrance could there be? Xanthus explained, "Come I'll show you."

He got up and handed me my clothes from the other side of the bed. My lingerie though was now back to the dress that I had on before. He helped put on my dress as he tied the back lace and as I tied the front. Xanthus slowly ran his fingers through my hair as he slowly gave me a kiss. I still blushed slightly even though it wasn't our first kiss anymore. I couldn't help it! The way he kissed me and gazed into my eyes will forever make me melt! I then loosely tied my hair up. Behind us, the bed slowly started to diminish into the smooth white sand below our feet.

Xanthus walked over to the back wall as he placed his right hand over it. He recited, "Cave of mighty might, take this stone of height, and make a soaring flight." The cave stated to tremble as light brown dust fell from the walls and ceiling.

I shouted over the loud rumble, "What's going on, what did you do?" The noise was so loud I couldn't even hear his reply. I fell over from the shaking earth of the cave. I remembered, oh yeah why can't I just fly up? So I did. Suddenly from the far left of the cave stairs started to appear from the rocky wall. Moments later the trembling of the earth ended I asked Xanthus, "And how long did it take you to figure that out?"

He shrugged his shoulders. "I'm not sure, I just made it up once, when I first found this place. I couldn't find a way out so I just conjured it."

"Xanthus, I must ask you, I see that you enjoy venturing out into these adventures places constantly but, where is this place you call home? You know, a place for you to go and rest after all of this is over?"

Xanthus took in a deep breath and held it in. He squinted his eyes as if he didn't know how to answer me. He finally exhaled as he asked, "Do you miss your city?"

Was he serious? "Of course I do. It's where I grew up, where I got my integrity and understandings. I would go back if it wasn't for my situation. I know I must go back one day and deal with the responsibilities of..."

I didn't even get to finish as Xanthus rudely interrupted me, "Of getting married to your prince. That's accepting your responsibilities, now that your quest has been set out and conquered, as of last night. Now you may go back as a more skilled fairy."

My mouth dropped in shock. "No, it's not like that at all! How could you even say that to me?" Xanthus ignored me as he started to climb the stairs as he held onto the wall. I opened my wings and flew over next to his side as he continued to walk. I hesitated but replied suddenly, "I left to find answers to my questions. I left to be free of the enslavement that was going to be my destiny. I left to find love. I left and found you! Does that not matter to you anymore?"

"But your responsibility is to wed Cethios is it not? You said so yourself that you need to confront your responsibilities!"

"Ugh! What is your uncertainty this morning? And please do not mention his repulsive name!"

Xanthus grunted, "Perfect, you already know how to give orders."

"Why is this upsetting you? I'm not understanding, yes I do have to face it one day but I'm not marring him. Wait, are you upset because you have some sort of commitment of your very own? You have your our own responsibilities and now you're trying to take it out on me."

He suddenly stopped as I was flying behind him and as I slammed into his back. I didn't know he was going to stop so quickly. I landed on the steps as he turned to face me and half angrily shouted, "You have no idea on how much pressure I must deal with continuously, about commitment and responsibility that I too have to face with one day!" He turned frustrated and continued up the steps.

What was his problem? I looked up to see a small opening at the top of the cave. I grabbed my dress and lifted it up a bit and hurried up the steps. As we exited the cave I flew in front of Xanthus as the cave shut with a loud bang! I shouted over to him, "Xanthus!"

He shouted back, "What!"

I landed in front of him and answered him, "Explain to me this commitment or confrontation that you have. You have heard mine and I was hoping that you would help me confront it, as I would you. Do you not have faith in me, in us? What happened to your words of trust and of being together? Or was that said to me only so you would be able to have a night of continuous pleasure?"

Xanthus widened his eyes as I suddenly felt hot and steamy breath upon my neck and back. My hair flew forward in front of my face. A deep voice boomed behind my body as it sent vibrations through my skin. "You stayed here all night with the fairy?"

I turned my body slowly around to find Cetus sitting there behind me. Xanthus stepped forward to his dragon. "Cetus stop. I have enough to deal with as it is. Just take us to the castle immediately."

Cetus hesitated, "But…"

Xanthus placed his hands on Cetus hips and jumped over to his arm, then onto his back. Xanthus sat there gazing forward not replying anything at all.

Was that it though? I have never felt so used and betrayed before. Perhaps I would have been better off with Cethios. I wasn't sure what I could do at the moment? I turned around and faced the peaceful ocean. I couldn't find the strength to look at either of them anymore. He was hiding something like everyone else, but why? And why must everyone have something to hide? I couldn't hold it in any longer, golden tears fled my eyes as I cried softly to myself. I made sure though not to turn and face Xanthus or Cetus. I didn't want either of them to see that I was crying.

"Are you going to get on?" Xanthus asked me. But, all I could do was shake my head no and place my hands on my face. Xanthus demanded to Cetus, "Let's go!" Cetus hesitated momentarily as he jerked his head back. Xanthus shouted once more to Cetus. "Go, onward to the castle!"

Cetus opened his wings and started to flap them. He hovered a little off of the land as he suddenly stretched his neck over to my ear. For at that brief moment, time stood still all around us. Cetus whispered to me, "One of your questions will be answered after our departure. Look to your left away from the sky, and you'll find a part of your heart. For I truly know what lies inside you."

After he finished time seemed to continue once more. The mighty dragon gave a loud roar as a stream of blue fire escaped his throat. Within a couple of blinks from my wet eyes, they were gone. I continued to stare out into the deep blue ocean.

I looked down at my feet, for I suddenly felt as if I was stepping on something very furry. There by my toes stood colorful flowers that seemed to have fur on them. I stepped back as I realized that those flowers weren't there when I first stepped over here. Seconds later loud rhythmic humming started to grow from the flowers. A multiple of beautiful hummingbirds emerged from the flowers, as if they had made up that mirage of flowers. They flew around me humming tones of softness.

As the humming birds suddenly turned and flew to the left of me, I continued to gaze at them as they slowly disappeared and nothing remained but the marvelous blue sky. I then saw something gleaming in the sunlight as a soft roar echoed in my ears. I continued to stand there as an enormous white dragon caught my eyes. That dragon was the one that I have been seeing throughout the entire time I have been here. It landed with a loud thud as it shook the earth gently below me.

The dragon had snowy white scales with golden adjacent here and there. Its sharp claws and spikes also glimmered in the mornings' sunlight.

The dragon gave another roar, but this time it was louder and fiercer than ever. I did nothing but stand there and gaze into the eyes of the dragon. I was confused in my heart at that very moment. I wasn't sure if I should run away or stay there frozen. The creature bent its' head close to mine as it revealed its razor sharp teeth.

It strangely and suddenly gave a low growling purr. The dragons' enormous eyes met mine…wait a second! I could tell those eyes from anywhere. I was in complete shock as all I could do was stand there motionless. I just realized who was standing in front of me!

Golden Dragon

22

I threw my whole body on the snout of the dragon and gave it an enormous hug! I took in a deep breath as I sank into the scales of the creature. I let out a small scream of delight! I was exhilarated to find out that it was her. "Oh Snowfire, I am so lost I don't know what to do in this mysterious puzzle of life anymore. And what piece do I belong to and, and…" I stayed there until my heavy breathing became slow once more, I was emotionally distraught. Moments later I opened my wings and landed sitting on the floor. "Snowfire tell me, I know you can respond to me so don't try to hide it any longer. So finally for this brief moment, I will listen to you."

She sat down onto the floor next to me as she shook her body intensively. She replied, "Yes, I'm truly a dragon in my true form. I can change my appearance, as you know into a snow leopard. All dragons can actually morph into a different creature. Convenience really, just to keep our existence alive. This keeps evil creatures from hunting down our existence. They wouldn't know if they were killing a dragon or a regular creature. It also explains why really one big meal every month or two keeps us sustained. But, when I was hatched I was given to you as a gift from your mother. I was told I am to always guard you, protect you and of course love you as well. You are just as old as I am. This means I am extremely young and you are, well young. I never revealed myself to you because of certain situations that I didn't understand at the time, but I soon forgot. But I'm truly sorry I did not reveal myself to you sooner. And as for your mother I'm sorry, I only knew what she looked like. I don't know anything else about her. As for Cethios, we left just before the raid happened and…"

"Wait-wait! A raid?"

"Well, Cethios put out a search for you and me. So James…"

I stood up in shock, wings up and all. "James! Is he alright? Do you know that last I left him Cethios had, had…" I started to space out thinking about what I had seen. How all that blood just drenched everything, spreading everywhere slowly seeping onto the floor, oozing between my fingers.

Snowfire started to purr softly as she could sense that I was starting to weaken with the thought. She purred, "Calm down Azalea, James escaped with my help. We both fled the city with Beruchium's help actually. Luckily for him Zethron thinks he's as dumb as a tumbleweed! So therefore I know he is out of harm's way."

I pondered her words for a bit. Perhaps Cethios is looking for me right now. Even though Xanthus was upset with me and I him, I still didn't want him involved, or anyone else for that matter. I asked Snowfire, "Where's James right now?"

Snowfire snorted small blue fireballs out of her nostrils. "Hum, I am not sure. He jumped off of my back as we neared the city. But Azalea, that's not what's important right now. What's important is that Cethios will find you, and these elves well, they are and will be in danger. Before I met with James in the gardens, I overheard Cethios declaring war!"

I stepped back from her and stared off into the ocean. I didn't know that this was going to form. But I knew I had to do something and fast! I took in a deep breath as I let the air around me smoother my skin. I gathered my thoughts and opened my wings. I flew over and onto Snowfire's back. I shouted to her, "Hurry, we must warn the king!"

With a sonic boom effect we were off into the open sky above. We headed for Trinafin's castle. This time courage and bravery filled my veins as I, I had my eyes opened for the whole time that I soared with Snowfire. The wind rustled my hair as my band fell off of head. My hair moved freely with the ravenous wind. I needed to become fierce and stronger, war was approaching us and I could not hide any longer.

I tucked in my wings as I placed my glowing hands on Snowfire. They glowed a bright golden color. And as I leaned to the right so did Snowfire. I leaned forward and she flew faster. I realized that I was steering Snowfire! With this new magic that I now discovered inside me, I still allowed Snowfire to get us to the castle on her own. Trees pasted us in blurs of heavy mists. I did feel slightly faint for some times but, I continued to swallow my fear as I kept my eyes opened. I did also notice that Snowfire flew faster than Cetus…

The True Prince

23

We landed suddenly with a loud thud in the front of the castle doors. I jumped off of Snowfire as her distinctive dragon figure melted away into her snow leopard shape. "I'll fit in the castle a lot better that way." Snowfire replied.

I chuckled to her, "Your right, your big hips wouldn't be able to fit through any of the doors."

We both chuckled and laughed as suddenly she gasped, "Hey!"

With a smile on my face and with much determination we both ran through the hallways of the castle. I tried to remember where the grand hallway was as I started to run faster. We finally got to the hall as we crashed through the doors. I was able to catch a glimpse of Xanthus and Morpheus as they exiting the grand hall on the other side. Two large leopards followed behind them as they left, one was black and the other one was orange. The door slammed loudly behind them leaving King Alcander alone in the hall. I ran up to him breathlessly, "'Your Highness', I…"

I gave a small bow as the king replied to me, "Azalea my lady, thank goodness you are alright. Come, Xanthus said he last left you with Snowfire by the ocean."

"Wait, he knew about Snowfire? And, why wouldn't I be alright?" I didn't understand the meaning of his words. Why would he say that in that way?

He stretched out his arm to me as his eyes filled with concern. "My lady, we have received a letter this morning from your king and from Prince Cethios. He has found you here in this city and he wishes that you be returned to your kingdom, where you can reclaim your place. If we decline your freedom, as they say, they will declare war against our kind."

I exclaimed, "No you can't, I mean you mustn't I, I…"

The king raised his hand as if to silence me. He replied, "My lady, Xanthus and I have sent forth a letter with a mighty dragon, who needless to say, was not content about the situation. But the letter resigns in that you shall not return to wed Prince Cethios. If a war is what he wants then a war is what he shall receive. We have concluded that Cethios probably told your king that we have you captured against your own will. But, one of our hidden guards said that they saw a fairy gentleman in the markets yesterday. They said he was concealing his identity with a heavy cloak. But they knew it was a fairy for within a brief moment a brisk wind threw off his hooded cloak. It revealed his face and what appeared to be wings underneath. Perhaps it was Cethios."

My heart started to beat faster and faster as he spoke. I wondered if he saw Xanthus and I at the markets or worse, if he saw us kiss. I started to feel lightheaded as I sat down in a nearby chair that stood at the head of the hall. I asked the king, "Do you think he was following us?"

King Alcander sat next to me in his throne. He gave a deep sigh and replied, "I'm not quite sure but we have set a war date in the letter that we sent out. And well my lady, we have set that date as early as next week."

I rubbed my shaking hands hard over my forehead as it pounded immensely. "War? Why are we going to war? Especially over me 'Your Highness'."

"I honestly think that Cethios is using you to his advantage, using you as an excuse to attack my city. But also the prince insisted in fighting for you and your freedom against Prince Cethios." He paused for a brief moment as he continued, "Azalea, the prince, well my son, he does love you immensely. Even though he will not admit it to me. But I can see the passion in his eyes, this passion that he has for you. He doesn't want to lose you now that he has found you. This was his idea to go forth with war. He wants to find Cethios and destroy him. He replied that your safety and freedom is what matters the most. He wants to be by your side and would like to see only himself with you. Azalea, you both share something that is unique and should not be forgotten nor lost. You should know why he is going to war. He will be leading the armed men, for when he returns in victory, if it is to be so, he wants to seek your hand in marriage."

Marriage! I was in shock! How could Morpheus think that I am the prize for victory? "I'm sorry 'Your Highness' but I am not some trophy of war. I do not accept your sons' proposal. Please do not force him on me either. I do not want to be forced into this. It is true love and freedom that I seek not your sons' wealth or love. Even though I have been giving this opportunity many times, I shall not accept it. I still prefer a pheasant to a prince. I truly am sorry."

The king turned a mixed colors of embarrassment or of anger, I wasn't sure. The king replied softly, "I am not understanding my lady?"

I stood up from my seat and stepped back a bit from the king. I did feel bad and I didn't want to upset or disrespect the king, even though they were going to war for me. I replied to him, "'Your Highness', since the day I met Xanthus I knew there was something more there, something different. Yes, we spent the whole day together yesterday and we fell in love. Or at least I thought we did. Look, do forgive me 'Your Highness' but I must deny Prince Morpheus' hand in that arrangement." I gave him a small bow as I turned and started to leave. But behind me King Alcander started to laugh and hysterically I might add. I stopped and turned once more to face him and to see him laughing. I walked back up to him as I half shouted almost angrily, "'Your Highness', I do apologize but my words are not a matter of laughter."

The king replied as he still continued to laugh, "No-no, I just seemed to forget that you don't know. Neither does anyone else in this city, well perhaps they do right now. You are going to find this really amusing."

I stood there as I crossed my hands over my chest. "Try me 'Your Highness'."

The king saw that I was not laughing with him. He cleared his throat as he stopped his laughter. He still had the sense in smiling a bit though. He replied, "The situation is that you did fall in love with the prince. It is the situation that you are in love with my son. You see, my son is Xanthus."

My mouth dropped in shock. My sight seemed to grow dimmer and dimmer. Then yup, I fell over and hit the ground below me with a loud thud. The king rushed over to me as he stumbled off of his throne. He bent down over me and asked with great concern, "Are you alright my lady? Azalea?"

It seemed as if the room was empty with no air to breathe. No air for my lungs to grasp, it was suddenly really difficult to breathe. Although, I was still somehow able to reply to the king, "So, they switched places, ages ago. Xanthus is truly the prince and Morpheus is, his friend, servant elf?"

The king shrugged his shoulders and raised one eyebrow. Now at that very moment I did see Xanthus in him. He replied, "They switched places when they were younger. They came to me and asked. I had no reasoning not to agree. You could say at one point when they were younger, they did appear quite identical. But Xanthus didn't want the title of prince until he found someone who appreciated him for him. And Morpheus, he honestly could care less."

I suddenly stood up angrily as I opened my wings wide. I startle the king a bit as he almost fell over. Yeah, I get that a lot. "So, he lied to me?"

"Well perhaps that's not quite the right term to recall it by. They both are making their speech in the city as we speak. They are proclaiming the truth about the war and about seeking forgiveness for their misleading gestures. Perhaps you can still make it there in time to hear it from his lips and not mine."

I gave the king another small bow and thanked him. I then dashed out of the hall with Snowfire right beside me. As we reached outside of the castle Snowfire leaped into the air as she instantly regained her dragon figure. I too jumped into the air and landed onto her back. The air around me brushed its smooth hands all around my delicate skin.

I leaned forward gentle as my hands glowed. We zoomed through the wind with such lightning speed. And before long we started to approach the city as it started to appear between the trees. And yet once more, we neared the enchanting city of Trinafin.

The Demand

24

Snowfire gave a thunderous roar as I jumped off of her. I landed on the soft ground on my hand and knee, with my wings opened wide. I was filled with much rage and endless confusions. I stood up and ran toward the city as Snowfire took off back into the weightless air.

As I reached the crowded city I was surrounded with different types of emotions from the elves. Some were filled with anger and shock while others were filled with happiness and relief. The crowd parted as I walked toward Morpheus and Xanthus, whom were giving their speech at the front of the city. The crowd seemed as if I was some type of disease they didn't want to catch. They parted as I walked slowly towards the front. I stood a few feet before them as I closed my wings and blended them into my skin as best as I possibly could. Morpheus continued his speech, "We must fight to regain our freedom and peace as one nation once more. These fairies will hold us to our will and show us no mercy if we do not show them our courage and bravery. I understand that for some of you this will be difficult. I do understand that some of you who stand here today still remember a gentle friend who still remains in that other kingdom. We must fight to regain that strength that we once shared. We can live among each other once more without the fear of one another. We must rely on the decision of our king and prince. Your prince shall lead us to victory, the uniting of our kingdoms. But forgiveness is what we seek before we go to this war. Forgive us, for Xanthus and I have switch places on you many centuries ago. I have been posing as the prince but, only under the guidance of Xanthus. Do not judge us on this day, our sorrow is within your hands. Xanthus wanted to find someone to appreciate and love his flesh and not merely his crown. He approached me with such a burden to take his place for the mere time. I, well I could not turn down my best friends' offer. But with this war we shall conquer the fear of..."

As Morpheus continued I glanced at Xanthus who was eyeing every elf with such authority and sophistication. Until that is, when his eyes met mine, they filled with sadness and regret. Xanthus started to approach me as I widened my eyes with grief. What was I to do? I wasn't sure if he really wanted to be near me at this very moment in front of all these elves. They probably were all filled with mixed feeling about fairies at this very moment.

Anger started to fill my skin when I thought about how he treated me so. I turned around and started to run towards the uncharted jungle. I didn't want to face Xanthus just yet. I ran out of the crowd as fast as I could run. By this time Snowfire was now sitting on the outside of the crowd. I suddenly ran past her. She only turned her head towards me and watched me run past her. As she turned her head forward she saw that Xanthus was running after me. He shouted, "Azalea! Wait Azalea!"

Snowfire saw Xanthus heading closer and closer as she sent out a loud roar with tremendous burning flames of fire. Xanthus dodged the fiery shot. Just as Snowfire was about to attempt another one, Xanthus stood right in front of her. He held his hands tightly together as he quickly rushed them toward the sky then towards Snowfire. He shouted, "Glacier flame!" As his palms glowed an icy blue, a small ivory colored snowflake emerged from his palm and floated toward Snowfire. She laughed with a roar as once more she shot burning pulsing fire from her throat. But as soon as the fire touched the tiny snowflake though, her fiery breath quickly turned into millions of snowflakes. Snowfire quickly shut her snout as it turned blue. She bent her head back and whimpered as black smoke sizzled out of her nostrils. Xanthus replied under his breath, "Cool down."

He continued to run after me. As branches and twigs tugged on me, I frantically looked around for a place to hide. I started to hear Xanthus catching up to me as his muffles came closer and closer. I stopped running by a nearby tree to catch my breath when suddenly a loud thud came from above me. I looked up to see a huge net fall and engulf me whole. I screamed as it snagged me and pummeled me into the treetops up above into the air. I hung there in the netting breathlessly and confused on what had just happened.

Xanthus finally caught up as I saw him a few feet below. He was breathing hard as he bent over and placed his hands on his knees. He looked up as he started to smile and laugh breathlessly to himself. He replied, "I knew those things would come in handy one day."

"I am so relieved that you find this humorous." I replied as I struggled and tugged around the netting to see if I could free myself from the horrible contraption.

Xanthus continued, "It's not every day I catch something so exquisite. But you know, all of the other smart creatures usually sense it, and they somehow maneuver around it."

"I was distracted by your ignorance that all! Beside the point, are you now calling me ignorant? First yesterday it was heavy, now today it's ignorant? Great just great, I wonder what you're going to call me tomorrow?"

Xanthus still chuckled, "I'm in luck, there is a tomorrow with you. And I'd better be careful; it seems I caught a feisty one today! Besides you just called me ignorant. Does that not count on my behalf? Also, you are always placing incorrect and deceiving words in my mouth."

"You have some nerve to come over here with that kind of attitude, like nothing is wrong. When the truth is that the real deceiver is you! How can you so easily dismay what happened this morning!"

Xanthus stood there with his hands calmly at his side, seeming so relaxed. He replied, "If you would calmly let me explain the situation…"

"Well obviously you didn't want to talk then, what difference does it matter this very second! Perhaps the letter from Cethios, is that what coincidentally changed your mind to give me an explanation? Go on, it's not like I have somewhere to go at this very moment. It's not like I can go anywhere anyway, but for you I'll just hang out here for a bit!" Xanthus cleared his throat, but before he could reply I replied, "Are you going to give me a speech? Because I'm really getting tired of speeches that have no answer in them whatsoever!"

Xanthus threw his hands up into the air as he grunted, "What would you have me say that won't upset you even more?" I hung there swaying quietly after he said that. He was sort of right though, I didn't give him a chance to say anything. He was already under a lot of pressure as it was and I guess I wasn't helping either. But I really didn't want to hear anything from him. He replied with a smirk, "You know, having you hanging there helplessly is sort of interesting."

"Ugh, would you just get me down!"

"I'm not quite sure I would want to let out such a rare and savage creature back into the lands. It could be very dangerous."

"Ahhhh! Would you please just get me down?" I screamed at the tops of my lungs. This was becoming extremely frustrating.

Xanthus clapped his hands together once as the netting got loose. I of course fell to the ground with a scream and a thud! He could have at least cushioned my fall. Xanthus came rushing over to me as he suddenly sat on me, forcing my hands to the side. Sitting pretty much on my chest, he made it impossible for me to even move! He replied, "Now my lady, you can choose to accept my apology or not. I didn't want to spend an eternity with someone who pretended to love and appreciate me. I for one thought you would understand that. Besides no one wanted to accept me knowing that I was not going to give them jewels or a castle. Once they thought I was a servant no one wanted anything to do with me, or fall in love with me for that matter. But you, you thought differently of that situation. And no matter what the outcome was, you still wanted to be with me. Even if it was only me you ended up with. Also…"

I interrupted him, "I'm sorry. I don't associate to liars or to deceivers." I tried to turn my head to face away from him but, being in the position I was in I just rolled my eyes away.

Xanthus replied, "Did I ever tell you that I wasn't the prince, in those words? I still do proclaim my love for you. Will you forgive me when I tell the city that it is I that fell in love with the fairy? Then would you forgive me?"

I bit my bottom lip softly trying to think quickly in what to say. I finally replied, "You know, it is extremely difficult to answer you when you are cutting off my circulation of air."

"Yes but you still have enough air in you to reply."

Hot breath suddenly started to pour all over us. As Xanthus' hair started to fly forward he turned around to see who it was. Morpheus sat behind us while he sat on his dragon. His dragon was black and green and just as huge as Cetus. Morpheus' dragon stood up as he gave a small bow and as he replied, "Good afternoon my lady, a thousand apologizes if I have frightened you. My name is Orion, I am dragon to Morpheus. It is such a pleasure to have finally met you."

Orion stretched out his neck around Xanthus who still remained on top of me. Orion continued, "Well, not under these circumstances but, still such a warm pleasure. I'd kiss your delicate hand but I'd fear that I would crumble it within my grasp."

Wow, Orion was extremely polite and proper. Xanthus finally stood up off of me and helped me up. I gave him a little shove, as I was still upset with him. I brushed my dress off as I ran my fingers through my hair. I turned to Xanthus and replied, "Morpheus' dragon is a lot more proper than yours."

Xanthus simply shrugged his shoulders, "He's a baby what can I do?"

A small puff of black smoke suddenly embraced Xanthus from behind. Cetus was standing behind him now. Xanthus turned around with his mouth opened as if he wanted to reply something, but nothing came out. To the left of me the trees started to vibrate with a rhythm as Snowfire popped her head through the brisling trees. Cetus jumped back and gave a small high-pitched squeal. We all chuckled as Snowfire replied, "Did I startle you? I didn't really mean to."

Cetus replied as he shot a blue flame from his snout, "Of course not!" Cetus sat down as he looked away. I guess he was a bit embarrassed and frightened by it.

Morpheus jumped off of Orion and walked over to Xanthus and I. Morpheus replied, "They took it, and accepted my words with much respect. The men are starting to prepare for battle as some willingly know the long journey will be fierce. Some know they will not be returning for the painful journey home after it is all over. We shall as well prepare, the week ahead still remains with strive and grand courage. Azalea, you will remain within the castle walls where Nylina can keep an eye on you and...."

I interrupted him, "Excuse me? I am going to this battle as well. I am not a child and I don't need to be watched."

Morpheus stepped closer, "I cannot have you go and have your life at risk under my hands."

"I will not be under your hands. Besides you are not the prince, therefore you cannot hand out orders. I have been trained by the best trainer in our city since I can remember!"

"You shall not go and that's final!"

"I will not take orders from you! You have no authority over me!"

Morpheus and I were about to go head on when Xanthus stepped between us. Xanthus took me by the hands and moved me away from Morpheus. I angrily stuck out my tongue at Morpheus. Xanthus replied to me, "Maybe it is best if you stay. I would not be able to bear the thought of your injuries or, or even worse, death. War is no place for a woman who…"

I interrupted him, "Excuse me? You think that I won't be able to take it? You think I am weak, because I am a woman. Well that is where you are completely wrong!"

"No! Ugh, do not make this difficult for me. You will and shall remain here. If Cethios finds you I cannot bear the thought of, of…" Xanthus looked away from me as he took in a deep breath and walked over to the dragons. He rubbed his hands over his face. I could tell he was really upset and was going through a lot of stress.

Snowfire replied to him, "We can fight Xanthus we can help. I have seen Azalea fight myself. She is better than any other fairy man in our city."

Xanthus turned toward us as I could tell that anger and sorrow filled his eyes. He knew I wasn't going to let him trap me here. I think his worst fear was knowing that I wasn't going to let him tell me what to do. And just before Xanthus was going to speak an elf busted through the trees that were in front of us. The elf exclaimed, "'Your Highness', your help is needed within the city immediately!"

Xanthus nodded as the elf gave a short bow and left back in the same direction he came from. Xanthus placed his hands on his hips as he sadly looked down. He looked over to Morpheus who still was upset with me. Xanthus shook his head slightly as if he didn't know what to do. He turned to me and replied softly, "Azalea, we will not discuss this later this situation ends here. You will remain here at the castle. Do not place me in the position where I am forced to have guards at your door. Morpheus, take Snowfire to the city barn for the remainder of the preparation. Orion, take Azalea back to the castle and see to it that she does not escape your sight. I will be gathering the dragons and preparing more swords. War approaches us as we speak, we cannot linger any longer."

I looked away from Xanthus as I whispered under my breath, "Great, here I thought there was a great difference between Xanthus and Cethios. But now I only see that they both want to imprison me against my own will."

Xanthus looked at me as if he wanted to reply to it. I knew he had heard me. I didn't whisper my words that low. Xanthus seemed as if he wanted to run to me and embrace me in his arms but, he simply clenched his fists tightly and gazed away from me. Xanthus and Morpheus then both jumped on the dragons and went off into the air up above leaving Orion and me in the clearing. As I watched them fly away I noticed that Xanthus didn't even glance back to see me.

Orion stepped closer to me as I leaned onto his leg. I felt helpless, I really did want to help. This wasn't Xanthus' fight against Cethios it was mine! I sat down by Orion's warm belly. I couldn't even move for I had no strength left in me. I was filled with so many mixed emotions. This demand was not fair at all. I was now once again unsure on what I was supposed to do. Orion replied, "My lady, please forgive me but, an order is an order, and the castle is where I must take you. It is only for your safety. Xanthus just doesn't want to lose you. He loves you dearly." Orion spoke softly as I tucked my body more into his belly.

"Orion please, may we remain here a few moments longer? Please keep me company here in peace, I don't want to be alone."

Orion nodded as he laid his head down next to me and started to purr. His vibrations were being sent through my skin as a soothing melody. As afternoon went on to evening I was spaced out of thought. I stayed there until I couldn't think any longer. My stomach stone burned with the intensity of the sun as anger continued to run through my veins.

Eventually the day turned to night as I fell asleep against Orion. He placed me in his hands carefully as he took off slowly into the air. The warmth of his flesh kept me in a deep slumber that I could not awake from. He hovered over my room as he placed me in bed. The ceiling spread like silk, then shut itself after I was inside. Orion hovered over my room then disappeared into the mystified night. My depression and the warm scales of Orion left me in a deep sleep for three days leading to the day before the elves left for the war.

The Escape

25

"Azalea, Azalea! Wake up Azalea!"

I awoke to the sound of someone rudely screaming in my ear. I rolled over to my side to see Snowfire as her snow leopard form and extremely angry. She was staring at me right in my face. Her eyes were burning with a scarlet color hue. I grunted to her, "What can I do for you on this day? Because there seems to be nothing I can do for anyone else."

Snowfire let out a thunderous roar as she pounced on my body. I screamed out and jumped straight up. I yelled at Snowfire, "What will you have me do?"

"So you ran away once. And now that it is really important, you won't do it! What I don't understand is, why is it so hard for you to do it again! I thought you would let no one get in your way, no one!"

I yelled back, "There are guards at my door and probably under my balcony door as well, isn't there?"

Snowfire turned her head from me as she grunted, "Yes."

"So unless you have a plan, there is no possible way we can escape!"

Snowfire pounced off of the bed with one leap and ran with full speed toward the door. She pressed her soft delicate ear against the door with her eyes closed. I asked sarcastically her, "What are you doing?"

"Shhh!" She shushed me I couldn't believe it. This whole situation was out of control! I lay back down as I started to fall back asleep. Suddenly Snowfire jumped on me and shouted, "Listen, James is out there! I know it, he doesn't want you to just sit here and do nothing!"

I shot straight back up from the bed and asked, "James is here? Where is he exactly?"

"I found him a day ago, preparing to fight with the elves. He asked about you, he wanted me to tell you this… you have come into this world to save us all, and today and always, I will try to save you. Does that mean anything to you?"

I stared out onto the balcony window as the curtains swayed back and forth slowly with the wind. Snowfire had a right to tell me that. Here I was doing nothing, while James was out there trying to save everyone else and me. Well, it is finally my turn to save him. If Cethios found him, he would surely kill him and this time wait until his life energy would leave him. I closed my eyes tightly. Snowfire was right, I could not stay here locked up any longer. I belong there, in the moment of war! I need to confront Cethios, and only me!

I quickly jumped to my feet and tried to make it to the small closet on my left but, of course I tripped over the bed sheets! With a loud thud I fell onto the floor, well I did eventually make it to the closet.

Inside the closet hung beautiful colorful dresses of all types, fancy and casual. Below the dresses on the floor was an old bamboo chest, I bent over and opened it slowly. Inside were old worn clothes, probably from Xanthus and Morpheus when they were, um younger. Well, I sized them up a bit and it seemed like they would fit me. Also right on top of the clothes in the bamboo chest was Queen Lily's sword. I took it out slowly and held it tightly in my grasp. Seeing the stones sparkle and glow filled me with courage and strength.

I quickly changed into the clothes. I pulled my hair back and tied it up in a loose bun. I then tied the sword around my waist with a small black belt. My stomach seemed to feel weird at that exact moment. As I bent over and lifted the shirt on my stomach, I saw that my stone was glowing a deep lavender color hue. I shrugged my shoulder not knowing what it meant. I walked over to Snowfire who lied on the bed with her chin on her paws. I asked her, "Do you know exactly where James is right now?"

Snowfire shrugged and replied, "Perhaps somewhere between the tent carriages, but today and tonight the soldiers will move ahead and all day tomorrow as well. Then tomorrow night they'll set up the tents before the day of the war."

I crossed my hands across my chest as I pondered on how exactly I was going to join them without being noticed. I replied to Snowfire, "I'm going to need a horse to ride on. But I can't go to war without you. But if they see you like that or your dragon form, I'm sure we will be noticed."

Suddenly, Snowfire leaped off of the bed with one leap once again as she landed onto the floor right in front of me. She started to pull her body back as if she was stretching. Then right before my eyes, I gasped.

Snowfire morphed herself into a beautiful white horse. I could believe it! I whispered under my breath, "Incredible." I was speechless as her short horsehair formed back into long leopard fur.

Snowfire replied as she shook her whole body, "I'm sorry, it does usually last for a couple of hours or sometimes even just one day or night. I will need a couple of hours after to recover."

I gave her an enormous hug, I couldn't believe she tried that for me. I replied to her, "All we need now is a plan. How are we going to escape those guards?"

Snowfire purred softly, "Well, James has already set up a diversion. The two guards at the door will soon be called to aid a very old elf with his tents. After they leave we only have about a minute or two to escape this room, before the two other servants come to replace them."

I bit my bottom lip softly as I walked slowly towards the balcony window. I pushed the curtains back as I saw the sun was just about setting behind the trees. I stretched my hands out toward the misty air. The mist appeared to swivel around my glowing white hands. I rushed over to the bed as the mist started to swirl all over my body. The air lifted up my hair as it sent chills over my skin. I knelt on the pillows that were on the bed. I placed my left hand on my check and my right on the head pillow. My hands glowed a bright lavender color as I felt my stomach start to burn! I closed my eyes tightly and concentrated as I with took the mist around me.

Suddenly a soft ghostly image of myself started to appear on the bed. I was replicating my image as if I was still sleeping. The covers started to take on a form as if my body was in there. Heavy beads of sweat started to bead down my back and forehead. After a few brief moments, there laid an exact replica of myself in the bed. I let go of the pillow and my face as I sank slowly onto the floor. I tried to control my breathing, as my breaths were very heavy. I exhausted my energy just a bit. Snowfire replied to me as she pushed me up off of the floor with her head, "That really looks like a living replica of you! Great work!"

I stood up slowly as I held onto the wooden post of the bed. I placed my hands on my head to stop the pounding and the feeling of nausea. I breathlessly replied to Snowfire, "Thanks. I used to do that to Trathina when I would go off with the unicorns at night. Also, when I would go to Urinia for a day to relax."

"How long does this replication usually last?"

"Hopefully long enough, about two days if the mist doesn't start fading away. Perhaps we'll be halfway in the mountains or the valley by then."

Finally when the room stopped spinning before me, I flew over to the door. I placed my right hand over the door as I closed my eyes. The image of who and what was happening outside my door appeared in my mind. Two tall heavy built elf men stood by the door. They were wearing their arrows and bow on their backs. They had their swords tied around their waist as well. Their armor wasn't much but, it was enough I guess. They looked prepared for war! Finally after a few minutes of waiting, a tall and thin servant with deep brown eyes came to them, "Your assistance is needed outside of the castle, after that you may return to your post. One of the armed men outside said that it shall only take a moment. Some servants will arrive shortly after you leave, until you both return. The elf soldier demanded that it was very urgent."

The servant turned and left. The two armed elves looked at each other as if they did not believe the servant. They looked at the door, and then slowly yet quickly left down the hall. I whispered to Snowfire, "I don't think they believed it, but they left anyway. We must hurry now, let's go!" I opened the door cautiously and looked around. I exited as quietly as I could as I shut the door softly behind me. I flew up towards the ceiling and made my way to the front of the castle. I was hoping no one would look up. Before I entered the grand staircase my heart started to pound rapidly through my chest. I felt as if my heart was beating too loudly, and that perhaps someone would hear it.

I finally reached the grand hall as I carefully hid behind a pillar at the top of the grand staircase. I looked toward the entrance as I slowly glanced down. There by the grand doors stood Xanthus, Morpheus, King Alcander and Nylina. The king replied to Nylina, "While we are gone keep an eye on Azalea. Make sure you don't lose her out of your sight. You will take my command while I am away. I am trusting you to keep that fairy safe."

I felt guilt, for I knew as soon as they found out I was gone, Nylina was going to be in trouble. But I had to go! They all wore concerned faces, except for Xanthus. He appeared more upset than the others. As they exited Morpheus glanced up toward the pillar where I was hiding. I swiftly moved behind it, I was hoping dearly that he didn't see me. Hopefully he was glancing up at the chandelier of dragons. Oh, I hope one didn't fly over to me and reveal my hiding spot!

I waited until I heard them leave the grand hall. I leaned over carefully as I started to see Nylina make her way up the curving staircase. I had to fly around the pillar to the other side over the balcony. I leaned over the edge and gulped hard. I felt as if my heart was going to pound out of my throat! I slowly moved on the other side of the pillar over the edge holding onto the cool pillar. I fluttered my wings as quietly and shortly as I could. I didn't want Nylina to spot me because of my extensive wings!

I moved over just in time as Nylina reached the top of the stairs. I quickly flew down and as I called out to Snowfire. I gave a small whistle as she leaped down the curved staircase and over to me. I quickly and quietly opened the doors as I headed outside, glancing up over to the staircase. I didn't want anyone to spot me on my way out of the castle. I had made it this far and I didn't want it to get spoiled. But nothing in my whole life would have prepared me for what I saw with my own chestnut brown eyes. My tender breath was taken from my own dear soft lips.

The Preparation

26

Millions of elves walked next to castle as they headed toward the north. Each elf was distracted with their own dwellings. Some were packing their things on their horses or wagons, while others were preparing their armor and swords. Thank goodness to that I thought to myself. That way everyone would be too busy to even notice me.

I spotted an elf not so far from me who was preparing his horse. I walked over cautiously and quickly and with took a cloak that he had lying on his horse. I wanted something to cover up my wings better. I took a helmet from his horse as well. I felt bad as for when I was done he looked around the floor to see if he dropped them. I of course, ran quickly away into the crowd to blend in.

The black hooded cotton cloak was long enough to cover my wings. As for the helmet, it was silver with a long piece that came down onto the face. It covered my nose really. I stuffed as much of my hair as possible into the helmet to conceal as much as I could. The silver reflection of the helmet did give way to the heat outside and was extremely cool on the inside. I looked around not really knowing what to do, so I only walked along a carriage filled with swords for the moment.

As we entered the jungle day became night. The sky was filled with white stars that shone brightly up above us all. That was though, when you glimpsed them between the treetops. I did scout the front for a bit looking to find Xanthus or James. But I was unable to find either of them, not even the king! As the night went on I could feel my legs weaken and becoming sore, I was getting beat tired. I looked around to see if any of the elf men felt the same but, they seemed as if they could go on forever! And just before I almost dropped to the floor I heard a soft voice come from behind me, "Do you need a lift my lady? Are you completely tired of walking?"

I turned around to see that it was Snowfire morphed as a beautiful white horse. I gave her an immense hug as I asked, "Where were you when we exited the castle hours ago?"

"I'm sorry, I had to hide in a carriage filled with some smelly old tents. I didn't want to be seen until it got dark enough to leap out and transform. That way I have more hours for me and more hours for you to sleep. That is while I am morphed as a horse."

I gave a small leap as I jumped onto her back. I did feel guilty though, for I was about to fall fast asleep. I looked around once again as I finally saw some elves sleeping on their horses. Good, I didn't feel as bad anymore.

A couple of elves still walked with their right hands glowing in front of them. They were holding out an energy globe of light that hovered over their palm. That guided their path throughout the jungle. I then quickly descended into a deep slumber on Snowfire. I did sleep quite comfortable than I expected.

Hours later as the morning sun lightly touched my soft face, I awoke. I quickly jumped off of Snowfire and gave a big long stretch. I felt quite uncomfortable for I wasn't able to stretch my wings, still it was good enough. I noticed that Snowfire's hair was starting to get longer and softer. I quickly gave her a kiss as I replied to her, "Go on and get some rest before someone discovers you or me. Thank you, I'll see you later on in the day."

She gave a small neigh as she started to make her way away from the elves and me. She headed into the uncharted jungle as a nearby elf saw and suddenly asked me, "Where is your horse going?"

I tried not to panic. In my best manly voice I replied, "She has to use a rest area. She is a very shy horse and doesn't want to disrespect anyone."

The elf shrugged at my comment and continued on his way. I gave a sigh of relief as he didn't ask me any more questions. We all continued to walk through the morning and through the mid-afternoon as well.

A soldier elf came by just as we were almost entering the evening. He was handing out some sort of drinks to the soldiers in what appeared to be a cup made of a large green leaf. I took one cup from him and thanked him. Inside the cup was a thick blue liquid drink. I didn't even know what I was about to drink. I was staring at those around me as they all seemed to enjoy the drink. It even seemed to energize some of the elves that were walking. I thought, it could be some sort of smoothie that gives you energy. So, I drank it anyway. After I was done I did feel quite revitalized and full. It was as if I had a complete meal filled with what I needed to survive for a few more days. It was delicious and it even tasted like blueberries, and I didn't even want more! I looked around to see what they elves were doing with their small cups. I didn't want to just toss it on the ground. One nearby soldier elf leaned over to me and replied, "Just let go of it. It will do the rest on its own. Did you not have one yesterday before we headed out?"

That would have made sense to have one of these before, it would have made the trip more manageable. But yet I simply shook my head as the shoulder elf frowned and shrugged. I didn't want to have to explain anything to him. Thankfully he continued on his way. Although, I was still confused by his words but I still did as he said. I opened my hand and released the cup from my grasp. As I let the cup sit on my palm it started to float up into the air above me. I watched it float up into the sky and transform back to its original shape. The leaf had attached itself back onto the branch of the nearest tree it found. The tree started to sway back and forth. I looked around into the other trees as I noticed that almost all of the trees were swaying back and forth. It was as if they were thanking us for giving them their leaves back as they all swayed to some sort of rhythm.

As we reached the beginning of the evening, the valley started to come into view. I thought to myself, that must be The Valley of Melinatha. All of the war legends ever told consisted within that vast valley of mountains and hills. As we neared them, fear started to strike inside my stomach. I think deep down in me, I wasn't really ready for war.

We suddenly came to a halt near the edge of the mountains. Finally after much searching I saw King Alcander rise onto some crates. I froze for I knew Xanthus and Morpheus would probably be nearby. I didn't want either of them to spot me. King Alcander spoke, "We make our final camp here before we ride off to war. Tomorrow we shall fight for our rights to remain in peace with this kingdom as well as with theirs. We will finally rid ourselves from their evil prince that poisons the blood of his followers and as he threatens our existence. We shall fight for our lives and for our city. We shall not see the day that our beloved Trinafin turns into ruins. It shall not become a memory, we shall not become a memory, nor shall we allow our castle or us to become a legend. We will move on and become one kingdom of unity. For we elves do not cease to exist or vanish into the mists of the night without a fight!"

Everyone cheered and clapped at King Duralos' words. His wisdom and bravery spread into the hearts and minds of all others that stood before him. I too was filled with courage and pride. His words were short, but filled with feelings and hope. I wanted to cheer with everyone else but, I was sure my voice might be recognized from one of the surrounding elves.

152

Immediately after that all of the elves started to prepare for the night's rest. I on the other hand quickly set out into the crowd. I wanted to move myself away from the front, and also out of the eyes of the king. Elves here and there set up mini campsite with small fires. Others prepared the fires while others prepared a good night meal. Other elves started to open the tents with thick yellow rope. I couldn't just stand here and do nothing, I thought. Everyone was doing something except me. I finally pulled up my courage and helped some elves with their tents. While I held the rope tightly, some other elf hammered it down into the ground with metal pipes. I spent the rest of the evening and night doing just that. I helped pull the ropes making sure that about every tent was pulled properly and securely.

Finally, when it was just about pitched black outside, everyone was finished and started to go into their tents. I walked over to a hovering energy light globe that hung in mid-air as I took a look at my throbbing hands. Pain shot through them deeply, especially in my palms. I saw that they were filled with cuts, scrapes and blood as they pulsed and burned. I bent down and tore a bit of fabric from my pant leg. With the fabric I carefully tried to wrap up my hands. I think I did a horrid job, for I could not stop trembling in agony.

After I finished I fumbled around trying to find a place to sleep comfortably in. I didn't want to sleep in a tent with other elves for I'm sure they would notice something different immediately. Besides, just about all of the tents were filled to their capacity.

As I searched for a vacant one my depravation was finally catching up with me. I was cold and sore as I finally stopped between two large tents. I stood there trying to regain my strength from walking all day and from helping with the tents. I didn't even know where I was anymore and I didn't even care. And just before I passed out, someone caught me in midair. That someone replied with such affection, "My lady Azalea, you should be in a warm tent drinking tea with some of your favorite honey cake."

I turned around to see that it was James. I cried, "James, you're all right!" I threw myself on him as I hugged him extremely tight, I wasn't expecting to find him within all this commotion. I did notice that he had a long thick scar under his chin on his neck. I didn't want to ask about it, for I knew how he got that scar. All I really cared about was that he was alright.

He whispered to me softly, "Come, let's go inside and get all warmed up shall we."

As we entered his tent I was amazed at how many colorful pillows and blankets there were. They all looked so fluffy and comfortable. I just wanted to lie down on one of them and not get up for a century or two. We headed for a small coffee table in the middle of the tent. I noticed that there were two sets of warm tea and two small pieces of cake out. I don't usually drink his tea warm but today it was extremely acceptable. I sat down and drank the tea as I slowly felt the warmness engulf my delicate body. I replied to James, who started to sit next to me. "Why are there two sets of tea and cake on this table?"

James sat next to me as he smiled warmly and replied, "I knew you were coming." James started to shake his head as he saw that my palms were wrapped up. He took my hands as I held them up in the air, palms up. He held out his hands above mine as the poor wrapping slowly came off from my hands. Once again he shook his head in dismay. He wrapped them up carefully and better than I did. His wrapping actually stayed in place. James replied to me as I slowly took small bites of the cake. "You should go and visit the tent that is next to mine."

I swallowed my cake down with the tea as I gulped loudly, "That tent is a lot bigger than yours. Are you sure you're not sending me over to see the king?"

"I assure you I am not." He sipped his tea carefully with a smile on his face. As he finished he continued, "You know, your journey is just at its beginning. Always remember that your guidance is your heart that lies deep within your soul. Do not let anyone tell you differently, ever. After you leave my tent, you must become braver than ever. You must fill yourself with more courage as well. Never hesitate your decisions that you will and shall make after this moment. Trust those whom you think least of, when the timing is right and calls for it. Follow through and do as you will. Let no one stand in your path of destiny. Remember reach for the stars above you, for they too conceal energy, and always reach deep inside of yourself."

James placed his fingertips onto his lips and kissed them softly. When he let go a small puff of pink shaped lips came out and over to me. The small puff smothered my face with kisses as it soon diminished into the air. I chuckled silently as I thought to myself, I have to try that same spell one-day. I stood up and gave James a small bow in respect in gratitude.

154

Before I left the tent I replied to him, "It is an honor to fight next to you, by your side. I wouldn't want this to be any other way. Thank you for everything that you have ever done for me."

Just before I left James shouted over, "And my lady Azalea, these tents are sound proof from the inside!"

Wide-eyed I still smiled and left. I wonder what he was meaning by that, oh well. I cautiously walked over to the tent as I just remembered that James never told me whom I was going to see. I stood there at the entrance glancing over and seeing just how really big this tent was. I stared at the entrance as I got nervous. Oh well, I can't stay out here forever.

The Map of Surveillance and the Promise

27

As I slowly pushed aside the fabric I looked around in amazement as awe with took my breaths. There were about three levels in the tent. The floors were made of oak wood as inside it appeared to be some kind of porch. The edges of the levels also had wooden banisters to hold onto, as so you wouldn't fall over to the next level. On the stairs and banister there was dark emerald green ivy that wrapped around it. On the ceiling and walls there were dark blue and black silk that draped over it all. It all hung sort of low.

In the middle of the first floor was a medium sized table. On it appeared to be some small piece of land, like a third dimensional map. As I walked around it, I saw that it was an exact replica of the Valley of Melinatha. And to my surprise I saw that it also had the campsite of the elves and fairies as well! I leaned over and squinted my eyes to see small white figures walking around.

I realized it was a live view when I saw King Duralos walking around near this one tent. It appeared he had on a silk robe and was talking with another fairy, a tall thin fairy that I could not recognize. I leaned closer as fear filled within me, I realized that he was talking to Cethios!

I took off my helmet and placed it on the floor. I wanted to get a better look at the map. I wanted to touch it; I was curious on what it was made of. Just then from one of the floors above someone called out to me, "Azalea?" I looked up in shock for I forgot for a brief moment that I was not by myself in the tent. It was Morpheus! He asked half angrily, "What are you doing here? Is, is that my old clothes you are wearing?"

He walked down from the wooden steps and over to me. I attempted to bargain with him, "Look Morpheus, I am here to fight with the others, I'm here to help. I am not going to just sit in an empty castle and hope for the best."

"If Xanthus finds you..."

"Then please don't tell him. I know he will not understand if he finds out that I am here but, I am not leaving. This is my fight too." As Morpheus neared me, I could tell he was upset with me. I quickly leaned back just before he with took my arm. My hands glowed a light red as I reached for my sword and took it out quickly. I held it against his chest as I replied, "Either you make me go back by force, or you help me. I'm prepared and willing to fight you to rightfully stay here where I belong. I would rather have you help me instead though. Make your choice, and make it quickly."

Morpheus stared at me as he shook his head in frustration. Finally, as he saw that I was not going to stand down he sighed and gave in. He lightly pushed the sword away as he backed away. He then lifted his finger up as if telling me to wait. He took off running up the stairs to the third floor. After hearing him fumble around over a few things he finally came back down and over to me. He was holding a sling with a bow and arrows. They appeared to be very thin and fragile. As he neared me, I placed my sword back around my waist and into its casing. He held it out towards me as he replied, "Take this, it's my mothers. Unfortunately, I did see you hiding behind the pillar just before we left the castle. I sort of knew you weren't going to stay there. So therefore, I brought these for you, to bring you good luck for tomorrow. I doubt my mother will be using them any time soon. Don't worry, they're a lot stronger than you think, unbreakable actually."

Darn, I knew he saw me back at the castle. I took it from him as I gave him a big hug, "Thank you for not forcing me to go back, and for your understanding. I will take these with honor."

Morpheus quickly started to reply to me as he lightly pushed me towards the entrance. "Now hurry, I can take you to a nearby empty tent where you can stay for the rest of the night undisturbed. You might still have a chance to stay and fight before Xanthus sees you and…"

Well, it was already too late, Xanthus had just walked in through the entrance. Morpheus and I both came to a screeching halt so we wouldn't bump into him. We both became nervous for when he saw me, anger filled his deep almond brown eyes. Xanthus attempted to hold in his anger the best he could and replied softly, "Morpheus, what is she doing here?"

Morpheus stood there in shock and speechless as he raised his arms up. He didn't know what to do nor what to say to Xanthus. Morpheus replied with a shout as he turned his gaze away from Xanthus, "What 'Your Majesty'! You hear that, the king needs my assistance. I'll be heading out then. Don't worry about me I'll retrieve to another tent that I know is…"

All Xanthus could do was glare at Morpheus. I just understood what James said about the tents being sound proof. There was no way Morpheus actually heard the king from the inside. But Morpheus quickly made his way out through the entrance as he gave me a pity look. I knew he really wanted to help me. Xanthus still glared at Morpheus as he exited.

Xanthus turned his gaze slowly towards me. I felt oddly nervous. I mean, I had never seen Xanthus so angry before, I thought he was going to explode! Xanthus replied in a calm soft voice as he glanced at the things I was holding, "What are those?"

I looked down at the bow and arrow that Morpheus gave me. I wanted to make up a lie but I knew he wouldn't believe me. Also, it was already too late to try and hide them behind my back. What could I tell him, he already saw them. I whispered softly as I gulped hard, "They are um, a gift from Morpheus. They are for the battle, for tomorrow."

His face turned red as he exploded! "You will do no such thing. Do you completely understand how much danger you are placing yourself in? I am risking everything for you! And you think I'm just going to allow you to fight tomorrow? You are going to be sent back to the castle immediately where you will remain safe!"

"I am not a child nor do you have command over me! You are neither my father nor my partner in life to tell me what I can and can't do! This is my fight, not yours!"

Xanthus took a step closer to me and continued, "When a fairy threatens my race and my city it becomes my problem and my right to fight. It isn't always about you!"

"I am not leaving here or you to fight by yourself!"

Xanthus started half laughing as if he was losing it as he ran his fingers through his hair. In a calmer voice he replied, "I will not stand the sight of seeing my future wife whom I love with all the breath that lies within me, being killed by a dull sword, a sharpen arrow, or even worse, by Cethios himself."

We both stood still as Xanthus breaths started to thicken and as tears filled his eyes. I didn't know how to react as I just realized his words. Shock was filled inside of me. Here I thought he was angry with me. But the sadness in his eyes said otherwise. I walked over to him slowly as I placed my hands on his arms. I still didn't know how to respond as I saw a silver tears flow down his cheeks, weird I thought. But instinctively I reached for them and wiped them away with my hands. Xanthus reached for my hands and held them on his face as he whispered, "I am fighting for your freedom from this compromise that lies before you. I am fighting for your love, so that I may ask for your hand without it being forced upon you. So that you may have me, if it is still what your heart desires, if I still remain your pursuit in true love."

I leaned in closer to him and whispered back, "I am not leaving you, aren't they my people as well? You shall not rid of me on this day nor on any other day. No words that you say shall change my thoughts or decision. You need to understand that I will not and shall not be ruled over. My decisions and actions are of my own will. My place is here and you need to understand that. I shall not hide in the shadows of darkness any longer." Xanthus then kissed me passionately and hard as he leaned harder into me. I rubbed my hands on his back softly as I quickly stopped. Pain shot through my palms as they still burned. After we parted I leaned over and grabbed the arrows and bow off of my shoulder. I asked Xanthus, "Now, if it's not too late, may you give me a quick lesson on these."

Xanthus half smiled as he took the arrows and bow from me. We both walked over to the second floor of the tent. He gave me a different bow and arrow as he placed the other ones on a nearby chair. He replied, "The ones Morpheus gave you have a unique enchantment on them. When you see your target and have that image placed in your mind, you will never miss. The arrow, once it hits its target, will retrieve itself back to the casing. Therefore, you never run out of arrows."

I nodded and asked, "Is that why I am practicing with an ordinary bow and arrow?"

Xanthus laughed as he replied, "Yes but you need to know how to shoot an arrow first, don't you?" He placed the bow in one hand of mine, the arrow went between my fingers and his. He guided my hand as I pulled the arrow back. We aimed at a small blanket on the wall above the entrance. As we let go of the arrow, I gave a small shout. The arrow flew and landed onto the third dimensional map in the middle of the room.

Xanthus took the bow from my hand and let it fall onto the floor. As he took me by the hands, he looked very confused. He started to unwrap the bandages from my hands, as I of course had a look of small painful agony and embarrassment. They burned intensely; I honestly didn't want him to see them. Once he finished unwrapping them, he seemed so disappointed. Xanthus replied softly, "What is this? How did this happen to you? And most of all what were you doing?"

I moved my hands away from him as I turned around. I didn't want him to think that I wouldn't be able to handle a battle. I already had blood and cuts on me and I only put up some measly little tents! I didn't want to tell him, but I did. "I was helping some of the elves with the ropes. I was helping them put up the tents. I couldn't just stand there and do nothing. I wanted to help."

"You didn't think to place a glove spell on your hands. That way you'd still have your strength but you wouldn't be able to hurt your hands."

I really didn't think about that at that moment. You would think I would since I always helped Trathina take the cakes out from the ovens. We would just place a protection spell from the heat. Figures you know, you always think of great things after it already happens.

He walked around me and faced me once more. He took my wrists and placed my palms facing up. He placed his palms onto mine as his hands started to glow a bright red light. My hands started to burn. I tried to move away but it was as if my body was frozen in place. I closed my eyes tightly to concentrate the pain only in my hands but it seemed to shoot all over my body.

Moments later as I let out a deep breath the immense pain had diminish. I opened my eyes to see Xanthus rubbing my palms and fingers. He started to give them small kisses as he gazed into my eyes. Was he trying to seduce me again? My hands and palms seemed as if nothing had ever happened to them. I gazed yet again into his eyes as he gazed into mine. Butterflies seemed to flutter briefly in my stomach. I took a deep breath as I asked him, "How were you able to do that?"

As I asked, I saw that for a brief moment Xanthus appeared to be out of breath and out of energy. It seemed as if he was very weary, but yet quickly regain it back within seconds as he replied, "What I did was, I transferred some of my excising strength and vitality into you, therefore giving you enough energy to heal your wounds."

With that being said he smiled and jumped off of the banister and over to the first floor. Perhaps that was his way of reassuring me that he was really alright. I smiled to myself as he did that. I on the other hand took the stairs to get to the first floor of course. He was on his way to retrieve the arrow. As he reached it he stopped and gazed onto the fairy camp on the other side of the mountain. I walked over to him as I too started to gaze off into the little white figures. I asked him, "So how can this be conjured?"

Xanthus placed his right hand on his chin, "Well, the image is brought to us by a unique seeing cloud that hovers above us as we speak. The figures are made of a watery substance that is found within the air that surrounds us, also the substance that is found within the trees. It is formed by the different types of energy that we release through our skin. This way, this helps us see if the enemy is cheating. If they start to ascend into the valley an alarm will go off. This way we may sleep comfortably. We wouldn't have to worry about an ambush in the mist of our slumber. This, this is the map of surveillance. It was given to us from our ancient ancestors." As he spoke, I kept my gaze on Cethios. I was watching him pace about in front of a couple of tents. Xanthus disrupted my gaze upon Cethios as he asked, "Azalea?"

"Yes?"

"Azalea if you found Cethios in this, would you reveal him to me?"

I started to move my gaze away from Cethios as if I was looking around for him. If Cethios wanted death to come to me by his sword, then death shall come to him by my sword first! I responded to Xanthus, "Well, this figure ahead of the camp is King Duralos. He is my stepfather whom I respectfully love as a biological father. Please see to it that no harm comes his way."

Xanthus nodded as he started to eye me curiously. He asked, "And Cethios?"

I didn't want him to think I was protecting him so I quickly responded, "No I don't see him. Perhaps he is within a tent somewhere but, I cannot find him."

Xanthus looked down, he seemed as if he didn't trust my words. He walked over to the entrance as he waved his hand over it. The fabric had now turned into a wooden door. Xanthus asked with a sigh, "Do you have a tent to rest in?"

"No, I don't, but I'm not going to ask you if I can stay here in this one either. I know you don't want me to stay."

"And why do you think that?"

"Am I wrong?"

Xanthus stood there by the door as he pondered momentarily. He replied, "No you're not. But you see that is going to be the difference between you and me. I will never be dishonest with you. You told me once that you have nothing to hide, but I guess I cannot trust your words any longer, now can I?"

"I don't have anything to hide. Would you feel better if I did tell you which one of those figures is Cethios? And for what, so you could leave this very moment and try to kill him yourself in the mist of the night in the darkness of his evil? I am not ignorant nor am I concealing him if that's what you think. I am protecting you from the horrendous rage that burns deep inside of you this very moment. You want to go off and kill him this very second with stupidity, but it honestly seems as if you want some sort of revenge. But why I don't really know. When the time comes tomorrow before battle when you are not alone, when you are rested and prepared to fight properly instead of foolishly, then yes at that moment I shall reveal to you who Cethios is. Am I wrong about that as well?"

Xanthus stood tensely as he balled his fists tightly in his palms as his hands glowed a soft white. He was looking down at the floor for I knew I was right and he just didn't want to look at me in the eyes, or admit it. Xanthus angrily replied, "Are you purposely invading my thoughts?"

"Am I wrong?"

Xanthus released his fists as he seemed to finally relax moments later as he gave in. He walked over to me and placed his hands on my arms. He replied, "No, you are not wrong. I do not protest on your respond on not revealing him to me. But do promise me this, you will always remain honest with me and faithful."

He gazed into my eyes deeply as tears seemed to slowly fill them once more. I replied to him, "I promise. I give you my word and all of my will, if you give me yours. I will be yours to keep forever, if only I may keep you."

Xanthus leaned over close to me as his lips softly brushed against mine. My heart started to beat rapidly as my breaths became deeper. He whispered, "I promise."

As he kissed me softly, I started to get a bit dizzy as weakness from sleep deprivation started to take control of me. Xanthus caught me just before I slipped away. He carried me up to the third floor as he placed me onto the soft bed. It felt like a bed made of softness just for me as I melted into the feathery silk covers. Before slumber with took me I felt the warmth of Xanthus by my side.

Before my dreams with took me I heard Xanthus whisper into my ear, "I shall love you always Azalea."

Moments later just as I felt Xanthus kiss me upon the forehead, I feel asleep. But nothing, nothing, would prepare me for what lied ahead of me. For if only I knew what fate lied ahead for everyone and me, the fate that lied within the mornings' phenomenal sunrise.

Krynton

28

Meanwhile on the other side of the Valley of Melinatha, the fairies prepared themselves for a long and excruciating battle…

King Duralos paced slowly in his tent walking back and forth with his hands behind his back. Stress and concern drenched his delicate face. He was wearing his jeweled crown that shone with desirable rubies. He wore his black velvet pants with his burgundy robe that seemed to elegantly glide with every soft movement as he turned.

His surroundings were also highly decorated as well with an exquisite charm. It seemed as if he still remained in his castle of Whisperia, in his glorious room. An immense cherry oak sleigh bed stood in the middle of his tent. Small paintings of his families' generation hung on the tent walls. The frames of the paintings were all made of a rich gold and stoned with jewels. Velvety beige and ruby colored blankets lay behind the paintings giving the tent a warmer appeal. It appeared as if the king had taken some of his treasure along for the battle as well. His armor though, was nowhere in sight. For the king was not planning to attend the war, but rather watch from the sidelines as a coward, hoping someone would simply bring his Azalea to him, so he may head back home quickly with her.

Just then a tall muscular fairy walked inside the kings' enormous tent. His dirty blonde hair was short and comb back. His clothes seemed to be ironed and pressed with such care that no wrinkle was in sight. He walked in holding his armor as he started to put it on himself. He asked the king as he placed his helmet under his arm, "You wanted to see me 'Your Highness'?"

"Ah yes Fendric, how are the soldiers doing?"

Fendric's dark emerald eyes burned with a dark and horrendous evil. For if only King Duralos knew his true identity, then perhaps he would have not appointed him head leader of the fairy soldiers. He replied to the king, "The soldiers are prepared to fight vigorously with strength. Courage flows within their veins as we speak. They are prepared to conquer the other side, the land of the elves."

King Duralos gave a small sigh of dismay at Fendric's words. The king finally stopped pacing as he stopped in front of Fendric. King Duralos replied, "We are not here to conquer any lands that do not belong to us. We are here to fight for Azalea's freedom from the elves' enslavement. We must bring her back to Whisperia unharmed."

"Your Highness', the elves are here to fight in a horrendous battle, they are filled with a sinister evil that scorches in their blood. They are not here to negotiate your daughters' life nor is she their concern. They are here only to destroy us and rid themselves of our kind, to vanquish us from existence."

The kings' eyes filled with fury with the words that escaped Fendric's lips. King Duralos shouted in anger, "If you want to send your soldiers, our people to death then you have no soul! I send my people to defend themselves to protect our rightful lands. Death I wish it not. But Azalea is among them on this night and shall remain captured until we free her tomorrow. And I know of this because I have faith! Once you find her bring her home along with the rest of my people!" Fendric's smooth face turned a deep burgundy color as he was filled with embarrassment. He walked a bit back as he gave a small bow. He started to leave the tent as the king stopped him before he could. The king replied to Fendric in a low voice, "Fendric, make sure she is not harmed by anyone. Take down anyone in your path just to bring her home unharmed."

Fendric smiled with a dark evil smirk that King Duralos had now noticed. But it was too late by now to do anything. So the king in response did nothing. Fendric replied, "As you wish 'Your Highness'." He exited the kings' tent as he quickly started to maneuver around the other tents. But before long Fendric now stood in the back of the campsite as he neared a pitch-black tent. It was just as colossal as the kings' tent. It was large enough to fit at least fifty fairies comfortably.

Suddenly Cethios exited the tent with a huge grin on his face as his nose soared in the air. Cethios whispered, "So, how is our king?"

Fendric quickly replied, "Still determined to find Azalea. Still considers that we are here for her."

Cethios reached into his left pant pocket. He took out a small black square mirror. He pressed his scrawny pointer finger on the front of it three times. The mirrors clear image became clouded as bright purple lightning bolts' shot across it quickly. It started to slowly clear as a ghostly image emerged within it glassy surface. It gradually cleared from its blurry shadow. It began to reveal a faint image in motion, as the hazy figures suddenly became clear. It was Azalea and Xanthus walking together in the marketplace in the city of Trinafin. They were happily walking side by side admiring the scenery and enjoying each other's company. The wind blew softly through Azalea's hair as Xanthus briefly brushed his hand gentle on Azalea's blushing cheek. Cethios replied in a low whisper, "These two are the ones we are truly after. Destroy the elf, bring the fairy to me alive."

Cethios curled his smooth lips up in a humble smile. Fendric replied confused, "Why is her life such an importance, 'Your Highness'?"

Cethios rubbed his thumb over the smooth glass mirror as the image of Azalea suddenly froze on only her soft delicate face. The feelings that he had for her were sort of mingled. He despised her with as much passion that flowed in his blood, unwillingly. But yet within his own soft breaths he still wanted to protect her, he loved her. Cethios closed his eyes momentarily as he then opened them slowly. He replied softly, "Her life has no importance. What is important though is that she is brought to me alive and unharmed. Her fate with me is none of your concern. But what is your concern, is that we leave before sunrise to get a head start."

Cethios paused as he cautiously started to look around. He seemed preoccupied with his own worries about something as he checked each side of his tent. Finally after being satisfied he walked back up to Fendric. Cethios whispered to him, "Now prepare yourself, and there after you must prepare the horses. They must not be disturbed by this tonight and tomorrow."

Fendric confusedly asked, "Disturbed of what?"

With that being said an enormous jet black and charcoal colored dragon landed next to Cethios. It landed with a loud thud as the earth below them trembled. Fendric stumbled over as he quickly tried to regain his balance. The dragons' claws on his paws were thicker than any other dragons. They were also sharper than any other sword ever crafted. His spikes on his head and the ones that flowed down his spine, ending at his tail twisted slightly as if jagged with sharpness. The massive dragon stood there with such grace and arrogance. The dragon appeared to be filled with as much evil and hatred as Cethios. For the eyes of the dragon revealed all. Fendric the head leader of the soldiers shook with slight fear as for he himself had never seen a dragon before in his life.

Cethios introduced the dragon as his very own, "This is my dragon Krynton. Quickly inform the other soldier. Dawn approaches us and your night is filled with a plethora of work. Go, for daylight shall be filled with elf blood and fairy victory approaches. Do not fail me, if your work is

166

prosperous on this night, I shall reward you with an admirable gift at sunrise."

Fendric smirked with pride as he gave a small bow. He left with such quickness as he hopped on a nearby black horse and took off into the darkness. Krynton gave out a low and eerie roar as it ended with a sinister laugh. The corrupted dragon replied, "I have no such patience and I am already craving sweet delicate elf blood."

Cethios patted Kryntons' enormous foot as the dragon dug his claws into the soft green earth below. Cethios was as tall as his back paw for this dragon was surely a massive one. Cethios smirked at his response as he replied, "We must wait patiently, surprising the enemy is always precious and must not be revealed too early. You must rest for the few hours that we have left. Build up your strength before our voyage is journeyed out."

Cethios slowly sucked in the delicate air that surrounded him through his nose. He walked back into his tent as this time Krynton gave out a thunderous roar. The dragons' mighty bellow seemed to echo throughout the surrounding tents. The elves themselves had no idea that they, the fairies had twin evil dragons on their side, anxiously awaiting the war.

Hours passed on as now the sky had swirled with crimson and majestic lavender hues. It was going to be a blistering hot and humid day. And now this moment daylight broke and the fairies started to head off toward The Valley of Melinatha. Each of them had determination and were off to brave the unknown. For each fairy was eager to have an elf at the end of their sword.

Tender Moment

29

I awoke softly to find myself alone in the warm soft bed and in the tent. The sound of trumpets blowing brought my subconscious mind to focus. As I rolled over to stretch my sore muscles I found a small bundle of lavender flowers. They were tied together with a thin pink-laced ribbon. I picked them up carefully and placed them on the tip of my nose. The sensual aroma relaxed my heart and throbbing headache.

As I gave another long stretch I started to hear the soldiers outside rustling around and shouting. That's weird, I thought that James said these tents were sound proof? I sat up and glance over to the tents' entrance to find it open. I wonder if Xanthus meant to leave it open. I quickly jumped to my feet and gave another quick stretch of my wings, I knew that throughout the day they would be blended tightly into my skin. That way no one would know it was me, only my feathers would give me away. Especially if Cethios found me throughout the crowd, I would be in endless trouble with Xanthus. I changed into some clothes that I found nearby on a small stool. Probably Morpheus' old pair of clothes that he brought for me. I tied Queen Lily's precious sword around my waist and I latched on the sling of arrows and bow behind my back. I reached over and with took the helmet. It was the same one I had worn yesterday. I wanted to conceal my face from Cethios or the king if I ran into either of them in the valley.

I stood onto the banister and jumped off. I flew down to the entrance of the tent with a swoop as I still had my wings visible. I reached the bottom near the door as I tucked my wings under the clothes. And just as I exited the tent shrunk behind me to the size of a large pinecone. I gave a small shriek as it almost took me with it. I was mortified as I was caught off guard. I turned around with my jaw hanging low as I saw James standing by the tent as his hands glowed with a mist of white. James replied with a chuckle, "Thank goodness you came out of there just at the right moment."

"What would have happened to me if I didn't?"

James seemed to ponder my question as he slowly replied, "Well, I would have been able to reverse the enchantment, eventually." He calmly walked over to another tent and did the same to that one. It too also shrunk to the size of a large pinecone. I started to glance around him as I saw a few stragglers behind quickly rushing over to the Valley of Melinatha. I'm sure by now all of the others were probably already there. Although, a few shorter and skinner elves were picking up the pinecones and magically hanging them to the branches of trees. It seemed as if they were part of the tree! James replied over to me, as he didn't even glance back to look at me. "You see, this way we don't have to waste much time clearing out the site. That way the tents are already prepared if we need them to come back to. And they are greatly concealed from our enemy."

I walked up to James as he started to give orders to a nearby elf. I walked over to him cautiously. He was acting very peculiar. I asked him, "James, why are you behaving strangely? Xanthus, he is already out there isn't he? He's out there in the front lines without me, isn't he?"

James appeared nervous for the first time ever. I have never seen him like this before in all of my ages of knowing him. He started to bite his trembling bottom lip. He pushed his glasses up his nose with his fingertips. He replied softly, "Well, it was up to Xanthus to either wake you to head out to war or, leave you at the back of it. I was given direct orders from Xanthus, although, I'm not quite sure he knew who I was really but, eventually he will nonetheless. My direct order was to stall you. I quite agreed and without hesitation stayed behind for a while. But, I don't think I am doing a good job at it, am I?"

I stood there in shock with my mouth slightly opened. How could he do that to me? I replied to James, "Why does he think he is allowed to do that to me? Leaving me here alone expecting me to fight from the sidelines like a coward?"

I turned away from James as I gave a sharp high-pitched whistle. Just before I ended my whistle Snowfire came bursting through the trees in her breathtaking white horse figure. She was running toward me with lightning speed. Just before it seemed she was going to run into me I jumped up and with took her reigns. I landed on her saddle, we were both on our way to join the battle when suddenly I tugged hard on Snowfire's leather reigns. I made her jump and turn around as we galloped toward James. I stopped in front of him as I jumped off of Snowfire. I gave him an immense hug as I held him as tightly as I could. I whispered to him, "James, no matter what happens on this day, I will forever remember that you were always there for me, no matter what my situation was. And...today and always I shall try to save you."

I swear tears wanted to escape his tender eyes but, I am sure he held them in with all his strength. I knew I couldn't keep this tender moment to last long, but it will last forever in my heart. I regrettably knew that I needed to concentrate on getting back towards the battle. I gave James one more massive hug as this time I felt him giving me one in return. A moment later I walked back to Snowfire and jumped on her back as we galloped toward the war.

The Capture and the Misfortune

30

As Snowfire raced through the heavy crowd of soldiers, hot sweat started to drip down the side of my forehead. The helmet that I was wearing was not helping any longer. It felt hotter and more humid than ever with all the heat coming from the soldiers that I was rushing by. My heart throbbed in my throat as if it was going to pound right through my skin! I felt the despair and anxiety coming from the soldier elves that surrounded me. My vision started to blur just before we reached the top of Melinatha. Snowfire started to jolt around as she ran. I could feel her begin to tense up.

As we finally reached the top, I looked down to see the vast open Valley of Melinatha. Next to that I saw the Great Plains of Oasia. The ones just before you enter the jungles of Whisperia. Both sides, the elves and the fairies, had already formed a strong thick line of soldiers.

On the fairy side Cethios sat on a pitched-black horse. Although the odd thing was that his horse also wore a helmet and body armor. Another odd thing about that was that there were spikes coming out from the armor. Strange to see such a sight, but Cethios still galloped proudly with that horse around the front of the line of soldiers. He shouted words of courage and misleading hope to every fairy that listened to him.

As I moved my gaze down the line, I saw another fairy galloping, also with a horse that was pitched black with armor on it. He didn't seem familiar to me at first but when I squinted my sight harder, I realized just who that was. It was a fairy who was always in the top grade levels in James' teachings and lessons; it was Fendric! James trusted him, but I guess Cethios' poisonous words had seeped into his vein as well as the other soldiers.

I moved my gaze even further down and looked all around but, I failed to locate King Duralos. On the elf side Morpheus and Xanthus were also galloping around giving words of bravery, faith, courage and hope. King Alcander sat on his horse behind the lines holding the flag of the elves. Just then Cethios blew a golden horn as they started to charge forward quickly. Xanthus and Morpheus gave a loud shout as they too started to charge. Both sides had swords in the air as well as arrows, ready to shoot into the air towards the other. Just before they collided, on the elf side some of the horses quickly leaped into the air as they morphed into dragons. The shriek and squeals of the fairies horror dwelled in my ears, my heart broke.

I suddenly gave Snowfire a hard kick as we descended down the valley toward war. Suddenly Snowfire came to a halt as she neighed loudly and jumped up and kicked her front legs high into the air. She was startled by something, but what? I looked up just in time to see Cethios' and Fendric's horses morph into enormous black dragons. I held onto Snowfire's reigns so tightly that they pulsed with heat and sweat. I stared in amazement to see two twin dragons on the fairy side. I realized my fears as I saw them dive toward the ground and chomp on soldier elves. Their screams echoed within my heart; my breath became heavy.

As we raced with intensity, we finally reached the inside valley as I reached for my bow and arrow that hung behind me. I pulled back an arrow and released it with all my might into a fairy that was pounding his sword against the elf's sword. Just then at that very moment a single golden tear fled from my right eye as I saw the arrow bolt into the chest of the fairy. The arrow came out from the other side of the fairy as it boomeranged back to the case on my back. The fairy fell to his knees and fell onto the floor without life. I turned my head around to my back to see the arrowhead drip with the deep red blood of the fairy. I closed my eyes tightly for a brief moment, as for I knew, I had just destroyed a life. Even though the soldiers followed Cethios and were filled with hatred, they were still a part of my heart, a fairy.

I opened my eyes as I continued to shoot arrows and fight with my sword from above Snowfire. The soldiers all really looked the same between fairies and elves. The only difference was that the elves wore a clear silver armor and the fairies wore a deep golden armor. And as the morning now had turned to midday, I started to feel lightheaded as the constant fighting had started to take its toll.

As I stepped aside to take a breather, I looked up into the sky to see two dragons that were being taken down by arrows. Their thunderous roars echoed throughout the soldiers as it also trembled the earth a bit. I took another deep breath as I looked higher into the sky. There almost right above me I saw Xanthus, Morpheus, Cethios and Fendric all fighting with their swords and dragons. Their dragons kicked, clawed and spewed fire among one another. Each one was trying to conquer the other.

Suddenly, I saw Xanthus fall of off Cetus as Cethios' dragon chomped on Cetus' bloody and sore neck. Poor Cetus gave out a powerful roar in agonizing pain. Fendric and his dragon started to dive towards Xanthus, as he was now vulnerable, just falling through the air and down to the earth below. Morpheus and Orion were too far away to save or even try to help him. I panicked, I shouted to Snowfire, "Snowfire! The air is where we are needed, now!"

She looked up and saw Xanthus falling down to his doom. Immediately she jumped into the air and morphed into her fierce dragon form. We headed toward Xanthus as she flew up as fast as she could. Snowfire spewed burning blue fire toward Fendric's dragon as she roared with might. She shouted over to me, "Hold on Azalea! Hold on!"

She flipped around in the air and clawed at Fendric's dragon as she sent them flipping upside down and briefly making them lose their concentration. They stumbled in midair momentarily. That gave us just enough time to fly towards Xanthus. I reached out my arms so he could grab them and that I could try to grab him.

As he did I screamed from the pain that shot through my arms as he tugged on them. Snowfire flipped right side up as Xanthus now stood on Snowfire's back. He then slid down her tail and just before he reached the tip he leaped over onto Fendric's dragon, who was now next to us.

He seemed to catch Fendric by surprise. I don't think that Fendric thought Xanthus was going to do that. Xanthus drove his sword with all his strength into Fendric's chest, right through his sturdy armor. He then kicked Fendric, the head leader of the fairies, off of his powerful dragon on towards the lands below.

Swiftly, Orion and Cetus came bursting through the clouds roaring as Xanthus jumped back onto Cetus. The two fierce dragons clawed and bit Fendric's dragon, sending him fall to the soft ground below. Orion and Cetus dove towards the ground after him. I replied to Snowfire as we sat there in midair momentarily watching, "I can't help feeling miserable, knowing that Fendric's life has ended. I'm not sure if he truly deserved it or not. On the other hand, Xanthus fought so bravely and courageously."

Snowfire snorted an orange fire ball with heavy black smoke from her scaly nostrils as she replied, "I believe Fendric's life was already doomed since he seemed to follow Cethios around on his free time. But, you'd think Xanthus would at least thank us for saving him and all."

We hung there feeling the gentle breeze momentarily as we watched the battle below us. I started to look around as I asked Snowfire confused, "Where's Cethios and his dragon?"

Before Snowfire even had a chance to answer me we felt a hard tug from behind. Cethios' dragon chomped on Snowfire's tail as he then pulled and flung us towards the opposite side of the sky. We both screamed as the air rushed loudly passed us. Snowfire regained her balance in the air. We searched around for Cethios as we saw him and his dragon diving towards the ground. We too dove toward the ground right behind them.

By the time we reached the ground Xanthus was already sword fighting with Cethios. I jumped off of Snowfire as I too started to sword fight with some nearby fairy soldiers. Just as I was nearing them both, I saw Cethios drive his sword into Xanthus unprotected left arm. Xanthus shouted with great pain and agony. I saw a sinister smile spread upon Cethios' face, for he knew that he was just about to rid himself from him. I had just finished fighting with a soldier as I quickly rushed over.

Cethios raised his sharp sword up into the air to deliver the final blow to destroy Xanthus, but I quickly intervened as my sword collided with his. Luminous blue and red sparks flew everywhere. My swings and hits were just as hard and strong as Cethios' were. I saw the anger filling his eyes towards me, he knew I had interrupted his moment of glory. I was delaying Cethios' fight with Xanthus, as he quickly healed his arm. Just enough time to close the wound and to keep it from bleeding, and for having some more time to regain some strength back.

Suddenly I fell to the ground as I tripped over a body that lied on the floor lifeless. As I hit the ground, I swung my right foot under Cethios foot, sending him helplessly to the ground as well. Cethios though, quickly jumped to his feet as he slashed his sword at me but I quickly rolled over. And just before he swung once more Xanthus collided his sword with his. He had taken my place in fighting with Cethios. I had to catch my breath as well, and thank goodness I did. I don't know how much more I am going to take of this.

As I stood and looked away momentarily to my right, I saw James fighting with a fairy. He was just about to fall onto the ground and to his doom. I quickly with took my bow and reached for an arrow. I shot it across the land with such speed towards the fairy that almost defeated James. As the arrow succeeded its target, the heavy fairy fell to the dirty ground below. James turned to me as he gave a short bow in gratitude.

I was about to turn back around toward Xanthus as a heavy sword hit me across the head. The blow sent my silver helmet off of my sore head and into the crowd of fighting soldiers. I frantically started to look for the helmet on the ground as I suddenly heard a breathless voice from behind me, "Azalea?"

My heart started to beat with great intensity as it started to ache as well. I desperately tried to figure out what to say or do but, I came up with nothing. Cethios now knew it was me who stood in front of him. There was no hiding from him any longer. I replied breathlessly as I turned around slowly to face him, "Cethios."

I lifted my gaze up into the air as I saw an arrow flying by me. I quickly reached up and with took it from its destination, as I spun in the air and dug it into his arm. As he shouted in pain, I focused behind him as I saw Xanthus. At that very moment he knew just who Cethios was. He had realized as well that the fairy he was so desperately trying to destroy, was Cethios.

Just as Xanthus was going to strike at Cethios from behind, two huge fairy soldiers intervened him. They seemed to be pushing Xanthus further away from Cethios and me. Cethios' eyes burned with anger as he pulled the arrow out from his arm and crumbled it within his palm. He threw the arrow pieces onto the floor as if it was nothing but dust. I took my sword and held it in front of me, I had the sharp tip pointing directly at him. Cethios replied to me with anger and exasperation, "Do you understand, do you completely comprehend, what you have put me through?"

He started to walk towards me slowly as my swords' tip still remained in front of him, pointing at his throat now. I replied to him, "Cethios, I am not yours to keep nor will I ever want to be yours. I will deny you till the day I take my last breath."

Cethios replied as he cracked his neck, "That shall and will be arranged."

Our swords collided with a loud clash! I looked behind him as I saw Xanthus desperately trying to free himself from the two fairy elves. You could tell he was trying to make his way over to me. I could hear Xanthus shouting over to me as his voice started to fade away in the distance. Either it was because he was falling behind, or it was because of my loud heartbeats that vibrated in my ears. Yes, fear was now chilling

175

over my skin. Cethios shouted, "You will come with me, even if it means by force!"

Our swords collided again and again. It seemed as if it was never going to end. His blows and attacks seemed harder and faster than ever this time. I knew rage and anger filled his actions as it freely flowed within his veins. His constant hits were now wearing me off as the daily fighting was adding to my weary.

My sight started to blur once again, but this time I couldn't focus it back. I tried with my might not to lose my consciousness. My breaths started to get heavier and heavier as I knew, that he knew I was now weakening. A grin appeared on his face for he knew I was about to fail. I couldn't keep up with him any longer. The strength in me burned as I desperately struggled not to give up.

Cethios quickly spun around behind me. He grabbed my stomach tightly as he pressed my back against his chest. He placed the sharp edge of his sword under my chin. My gaze once more moved toward Xanthus as he had just finished killing both soldiers. Cethios gave a low short whistle over to Xanthus. As he looked up and saw, his eyes widened with fear and despair. Xanthus started to shout, "Azalea! No, Azalea!"

Cethios then gave the sharpest whistle, which forced my eyes to close tightly and made my ears give sight of burgundy blood. It even made Xanthus stop as he placed his hands over his ears. Krynton suddenly appeared behind us as Cethios jumped up into the air and onto his back, dragging me along as well still with his sword under my chin. Cethios nodded off to Xanthus as he replied, "Farewell 'Your Highness', till another day."

With a gust of wind Cethios' dragon was up into the open sky, as my scream seemed to echo throughout the Valley of Melinthia. I noticed we were heading towards the north just as I passed out from exhausting. And as Xanthus quickly tried whistling for his dragon, neither Orion nor Cetus were anywhere to be found, for they too were off laying somewhere in the battlefield, injured and incoherent. For Cethios' dragon Krynton, was too fierce and too powerful for them both.

War lasted just before sundown, as on the ground the elves had won the war but it was in the air that the fairy dragon, Krynton, had won. Morpheus raced over to Xanthus who was just simply standing there, gazing onto the floor just as it started to rain. Xanthus felt helpless and ashamed, for he knew there was nothing at that moment he could do to save Azalea.

Silver lightning bolts shot across the darken sky as water dripped down Xanthus forehead. Once Morpheus reached Xanthus he demanded, "Xanthus, you must come quickly."

And as if returning from a deep trance, Xanthus shook his head, turned and followed Morpheus through the trampled bodies. Moments later they both reached a familiar face. The soldier sat wounded next to another lifeless soldier; it was Fendric. Morpheus replied to Xanthus, "He says his name is Fendric. He is the leader of the fairy soldiers, and Cethios' partner in war. Perhaps he might know some knowledge as to where Cethios has taken Azalea."

Xanthus bent over near Fendric as he placed his arms on his knees. He replied to him, "One of my soldiers has planted a wondrous herb in your blood stream. It shall and will inch you away from death, thus leaving us with much time for excruciating torture. So, you will answer my questions. First, where is he taking her?"

Fendric tried to laugh but just gagged and choked on his own blood. Xanthus stood up as he placed his foot on Fendric's chest. Xanthus replied, "I show no mercy towards those who stand in my way. There is still must time before death wishes to take you."

Xanthus pressed harder on Fendric's chest as he gagged some more. Finally, Fendric replied, "Alright, alright! He wants her."

"For what?"

"I'm not sure for what honestly. He always simply stated that he needed her alive, I swear that is all I know. He was planning to take her to, to Urinia."

Xanthus hesitated for a moment, but briefly asked, "Where's that city?"

Fendric tried to take in a deep breath but could not, his collapsing lungs denied him that pleasure. Xanthus, feeling some sort of hesitation released some of the pressure on Fendric's chest, thus allowing him to reply softly through muffled tears, "It is, it is farther north, northeast of Whisperia. A city that, that from the sky it appears to be many rocks, near the mountains... Please, please let me go in peace now. Forgive me, forgive me, I honestly meant Azalea no harm...forgive me."

Xanthus released his foot off of Fendric's chest as the fairy soldier finally took his last breath. Alas, he finally closed his eyes. James suddenly came rushing over to them as he gazed down at Fendric. James frowned, "I thought it was him, perhaps I wanted to deny the truth from own eyes. He was the brightest and wisest fairy in my class. I can see now that Cethios' poison reached him first. I did not succeed in saving him."

They all stood there speechless, not really knowing what to say to one another, especially Xanthus. They were all drenched in blood, sweat, mud and water as it continued to pour down on them. Suddenly red lights started to shine off of the dead bodies as their energy was now being dispersed into the land around them. All of the red lights seemed to glisten in the rain and under the moonlight. The bodies themselves started to disappear slowly, as they faded away into a ghostly figure, then into nothing.

Hundreds of elf soldiers started to head back to the campsite over the valley. They were all wanting to go back to Trinafin in peace. But an elf soldier came rushing over to Xanthus with a sword in his hands. He handed it to Xanthus as James replied regrettably, "Azalea's sword."

Xanthus looked at them as sadness filled his eyes. For a brief moment he closed his eyes tightly as he grasped the sword closely to his chest. For when he opened them, courage and anger flowed within them. Xanthus replied softly, "To Urinia they have taken my love, to Urinia we must now travel to."

A small smile came upon James and Morpheus' face as they all started to head towards the campsite. Just as Xanthus reached the top of the Valley of Melinatha he turned and gazed towards the North. He stood there holding Azalea's sword tightly in his hands and to his chest. That very moment a single tear fell from his eye, but this was no ordinary tear. For his tear glistened with a pure silver hue that glowed throughout all of the rain.

When a journey seems to end, another one begins. The dirt path you take might be cluttered with despair and hardship. But nonetheless you must always follow it. For you never truly know where your destiny might take you. This path might be long or short, or perhaps just too rough on your bare feet. Either or you must follow your dreams, hopes, passion and most of all love. For if you don't, you will always question the journey and wonder where it could have led you to. For not ever knowing could be worse than taking the rocky road alone. But for now, I leave you with this as I do say…

To Urinia is where they have taken me, then to Urinia is where we shall and must journey too…

City of Urinia

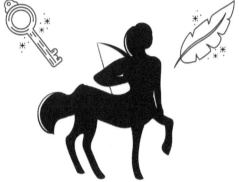

The Enchantment

1

An elegantly tall woman with a green hooded cloak walked carefully yet swiftly through the uncharted jungle. She carried something of value that was wrapped in a brown cloth dearly to her chest. The woman, with extreme paranoia, constantly looked behind her right shoulder as she stopped behind massive trees every so often. She stopped and concentrated on the surrounding sounds; she was listening for footsteps. She was concerned, for she wanted no one to be following her.

Hearing nothing to be suspicious of, the hooded woman finally stopped and relaxed her tense muscles as she leaned onto a tree for support. She concentrated on slowing down her deep breaths as she glanced down into her arms. With a delicate hand, she slightly unwrapped the treasure that stirred slowly in her arms. It revealed a baby girl dressed in a velvet green robe. The baby slept comfortable in her mother's protective arms.

The woman kissed the baby on her nose softly as she then covered her treasure yet again. She held the infant close to her heart as she closed her eyes tightly. The hooded woman's image started to dim slightly as she opened her golden lined-feathered wings. Her vivid body started to diminish like a mist of vapor. The woman now being invisible flew up into the cloudless sky above her. Once the cool air touched her delicate face she flew south high above the uncharted jungle.

The morning's crimson shimmering rays broke through the horizon as she continued her flight. She flew with determination all throughout morning and continued on throughout the afternoon, and as the day entered into evening the woman finally reached the ocean's shoreline. Her image reappeared as her beautiful infant was still sound asleep within her loving arms.

Once the woman landed near the Waterfalls of Aqualyn she entered a small cave nearby that appeared to be lifeless. She carefully walked in until she reached a dead end with barely any light left coming in to guide her. She then knocked on the stone in front of her four times with a small rhythm. The rock suddenly started to rumble as a small door appeared within the stone. The woman quickly entered as the door suddenly vanished behind her. She embraced the darkness with a deep inhale. But before the darkness overwhelmed her, she lifted her right palm, as an energy globe of light appeared hovering over her palm. The glowing globe lit her way throughout the small tunnel that lay before her.

Once she reached the end, she entered an enormous room within the cave. In the cave itself, were millions of jewels and gems that glistened and sparkled all over the entire caves' wall. The jewels themselves seem to light the entire room as they glowed brightly under their own light.

In the cave stood another hooded woman with her infant baby also wrapped in the same brown fabric that the other woman had. The second woman that entered the cave with the golden lined feathered wings removed the hood of her cloak. She was a beautiful fairy with long dark chocolate straight hair. She had a couple of golden streaks in her hair that matched the color of her exquisite wings. She cleared her throat slightly and introduced herself, "Good evening, I am Lily and this enchanting infant of mine is my daughter Azalea."

The first woman that was already in the cave removed the blue hood from her cloak. She was a beautiful elf woman with light brown wavy hair. Her hair was sort of combed back in a low ponytail with strands of curls here and there. The elf woman cleared her throat as well as she replied, "Good evening to you, this is my son Xanthus, and I, I am Whistalyn."

They both smiled and bowed as a sign of respect for one another. Suddenly an opening from the edge of the cave where the shore and water meet surged as it flowed slowly towards the center of the cave. From the water came a small blue stone table that quickly appeared before them. Then from the shoreline of the cave a tall mermaid appeared. She looked as if she was part tiger fish, sea dragon and part fairy. Once she emerged, she sat on the white sand as a wave of water pushed her up into the air about four feet high. She fixed her long hair as she carefully rose from the ground. Moments later her fins transformed to legs as they still resembled green scales. She slowly approached the stone table with a small bag clutched within her hands that appeared to be made out of dark green seaweed. Once she reached the stone table, she pushed her long orange hair behind her ears.

Without a single word she quickly started to place colorful stones, seashells and starfish on top of the stone table from her seaweed bag. The starfish, once placed upon the stone table, stood and started to move the colorful rocks around. They took the seashells and stones within their tiny hands. Moments later two small circles were formed from the seashells and stones. The mermaid then took out two small blue water balls out from her now empty seaweed bag. They were the size of a small melon. Inside each of the water balls appeared to be small air bubbles that swirled with every touch. The enchanting mermaid placed the water balls onto the stone table. The starfish picked up the water balls and gently placed them in the middle of each circle they had formed. Once the star fish had finished and were satisfied with the placement of everything, they laid down next to the small stone circles as if they were lifeless. Once they were still the mermaid hummed a soft melody, opened her mouth slightly with a grin, then as if speaking for the first-time above water with a small gulp of air she replied, "Good evening, thank you for joining me here on this most memorable night. My name is Falin, enchantress of the underwater lands. I am here today because I have summoned you both here. I am here to fulfill my wishes as well as yours upon demand and bargain. By bargain, for me to give them something of mine but for you to give them your life, if it so calls forth. On demand, because your kind depends on this unity, to continue on living and from vanishing from within the mist of time. You both must prevent everything, but only allow their lives to connect and intertwine for the future of us all. Now, come forth and place your child on the small water beds that I have made, so we may begin this enchantment, and prophecy."

The two women with their child walked forth as they each looked at each other with confusion and immense concern. Falin gave a comforting smile as her eyes gleamed with delight. She slowly stretched out her scaly arm forward. Falin once more seemed to take in a breath of air and continued, "There's no need to worry, these beds of water are quite comfortable I may say. Your child will feel as if they are sleeping on a feathery cloud of silk."

Whistalyn and Lily both took in a deep breath and, with slight hesitation did as she asked. They carefully placed their loving child upon the ball of water. The ball cushioned their delicate bodies as both babies giggled softly with delight. Satisfaction swelled within Falin as she spoke, "Shall we now begin then? Please look around the Caves of Esmera and choose a jewel for your child as a symbol of this great power that they shall inherit on this night. Choose carefully though, for once touched by your fingertips only that stone shall emerge from its desired resting place. For only two today, shall be released from Esmera's grasp. Once chosen come back forth and place that jewel next to your beloved child."

The fairy and the elf both nodded in agreement and took off towards the caves' wall. Whistalyn carefully inspected the wall filled with gems that glistened. While Lily on the other hand took off flying towards the caves ceiling as she too inspected the gems carefully. Moments later after much consideration they each were satisfied and had chosen a gem.

On their return Falin was concentrating as she slowly placed sweet smelling oils on the babies' foreheads, hands and toes. She then took out a blue jar from her seemingly empty seaweed bag. The jar was curved on the top and round on the bottom. Falin slowly opened the jar as lavender smoke emerged. She whiffed the sweet aroma near her nose as she carefully lifted the jar over each baby. She dropped one droplet on their foreheads, no more and no less. As she carefully placed the jar down next to her, Whistalyn and Lily slowly placed the gem that they had chosen near their infant.

Each gem's inner core swirled with mesmerizing iridescent color. It also seemed to pulse to its own rhythm. The starfish that were on the stone table undisturbed were now up and stretching as if awakening from an endless dream. The two starfish went to each gem that the women had chosen for their infants and picked them up. Suddenly they switched places taking Azalea's chosen gem to Xanthus and Xanthus' gem to Azalea. Both mothers were concerned and confused but they refused to move or comment. They trusted the mermaid and they did not reply a single word.

As the starfish carefully climbed onto the water ball they irrevocably placed the gem onto each of the babies' belly button. Falin replied with another deep breath, "Now, by switching the desired jewel that you have each chosen for your own child, shall help bring them to each other's arms with acceptance and subconsciously with desire." Falin paused briefly as her face expression went solemn, "You two are aware that their fates are in your hands starting this very vital moment?"

Lily and Whistalyn both turned to face each other momentary, as they both then turned to faced Falin once more. Determination filled their smiles as Lily was the first to speak. She replied tenderly, "I am fully aware of my daughters' fate and how my decisions affect her future. She will grow to be more than who she truly is. I am here today to accept everything that is above my heart, and to change my fate with her destiny."

Whistalyn glanced at her son as she bit her bottom lip slowly. Proudness glistened within her eyes as she replied, "I too accept and understand this commitment that they will grow to share together. It is my responsibility to raise my son as a gentleman and to have the intuition to accept his path with Azalea, honorably, respectfully and with love."

Both mothers turned to each other and embraced briefly with their backs to Falin. Falin herself seemed to be content with their response and with her own self. Grand joy filled the mermaid as she once more reached into her seaweed bag and extracted a handful of snowy iridescent glitter. The glitter pummeled out from her scaly fingers onto the floor and stone table. She then opened her fist gently and blew the magnificent glitter all over the babies. The baby elf and the baby fairy smiled joyously as they peacefully continued with their slumber, not knowing that their lives had just been intertwined together with fate and love. Falin cleared her throat slightly, "Now, from this moment on the destiny of your loved ones will be within your fingertips. If you do not preserve their fate, our dedication on this night will be wasted. Our future will not be extinguished of this hatred if you both fail to commit their prophecy we have set. You shall go and prevent this dusty path of hatred to continue and clear a new path with their destiny. Now, go and cherish and adore your beloved child."

Once Falin had finished speaking lavender mist filled the cave and the air around them. A bright creamy light suddenly engulfed them; it all quickly diminished within the mist after a few moments. The spell had been complete and there was no turning back. The two mothers carefully picked up their babies and kissed them on their foreheads and hugged them tightly. Lily turned to Whistalyn as she replied, "Thank you for agreeing to this arrangement. This is for our future and to our future we do owe."

Whistalyn gave a grand smile as she replied in return, "Yes we do. But I do have one question for you. When shall we introduce them to each other?"

Lily seemed to ponder her question briefly, but then quickly responded, "Well, if it is alright with you, I was hoping to introduce them to each other after she learns how to properly withhold herself as a young girl. Perhaps they could grow up together with respect for one another first as trusted friends. Therefore, when she reaches her coming of age, they will find love towards each other on their own."

Whistalyn smiled with acceptance, "Yes that shall be wise, so their adventures and love grow as the centuries pass by."

Once that being said they both glanced back to Falin as if waiting for her response. Falin spoke with great pleasure, "Now that we have settled with that, we shall…"

Just before she could finish her thoughts, The Caves of Esmera started to quake and tremble slightly. Falin quickly raised her hands up as they glowed a bright crimson as small flames danced within her fingertips. Lily quickly hugged her baby close to her chest as she vanished within the mist. Whistalyn on the other hand rolled her eyes in slight frustration and spoke sympathetically, "Please, there is no need to take precautions. I have told and summoned my most trusted friend and future nanny of my son, to be here on this memorable night. She truly should have been here much earlier but, I am sure she was simply caught up with important matters in the castle."

Falin's hands still remained up in the air as they burned with great intensity. Moments later from the other side of the cave an elf woman named Nylina came swimming up towards the shoreline in her blue cloak. As she stumbled upon the white sand she replied breathlessly, "Did I miss it? Is it truly over?"

As she slowly started to walk over towards them, Falin leaned over to Whistalyn and whispered, "Are you most certain you can trust this elf with this guarded information? Our lives are held within this secret?"

Whistalyn smiled with certainty as she replied, "Oh yes, I trust her with my life. I would not have this any other way without her knowing."

Once Nylina approached them she gave a small shake, as if she received the chills upon her skin. Briefly after that she was completely dry as if never stepping afoot upon water. She replied through chattering teeth, "Phew, that water is a bit cold. I do hope neither of you entered that way." Nylina walked up to Whistalyn as she gently kissed baby Xanthus on the forehead. Falin hesitantly lowered her glowing hands as their light seemed to diminish. Lily on the other hand, slowly reappeared just as simply as when she disappeared. Nylina turned and saw Lily reappear as she cried out with delight, "Oh how amazing! Here I thought it was only myth that fairies could disappear but, it's only royal blood in women though am I correct? How precious, is this your daughter Azalea? She looks very beautiful. May I give her a kiss?"

Lily gripped her daughter tightly within her grasp for she did not budge. She seemed unsure of the moment as she quickly glanced at Whistalyn. Whistalyn simply gave a small nod and a warm smile. Being a bit reassured that everything would be all right, Lily took in a deep sigh and let it out slowly, "I'm so sorry. Do forgive me for being so reserve. I am just not able to trust anyone at this very moment. I used to trust Azalea's future nanny but well, you see, she is seeing someone that I just don't approve of.. He's changing her and…" Lily glanced from Nylina to Whistalyn whom still had warm smiles upon their faces. Lily once again sighed deeply as she then continued, "And well, if you Whistalyn trust her with your very own life then, I say to you Nylina, good evening. This is my daughter Azalea. And yes, you may give her a kiss."

Nylina smiled greatly as she then bent over and gave baby Azalea a gentle kiss upon the forehead. Nylina placed her delicate hand upon Lily's arm. Nylina tenderly replied, "You know, despite the rumors that are thrown here and there about fairies, you are quite beautiful."

Lily blushed slightly with embarrassment, "Thank you, thank you to you both. You as well, elves are quite beautiful themselves."

Nylina blushed in return as well as she walked over to Whistalyn. Falin smiled with satisfaction as she took in one of those small deep breaths, "Now, shall we bring out their chosen guardians?"

Both the elves and the fairy nodded their heads in agreement. Suddenly from the shoreline behind them, came two enormous octopuses. They arose from the water as their skin changed in color, as if trying to blend in with the caves mystifying twilight. Both of the octopuses were caring an enormous egg, the size of a massive watermelon. They rolled their slithery slimy tentacles over to Falin. Once next to her they each carefully gave her the egg. The popping noise of their suction cups releasing the eggshell echoed within the cave walls. Falin placed each egg near the empty water balls. The eggs themselves seemed to flow with a bright blue and purple hue as if the waves of the ocean splashed upon the shell itself.

Moments later the eggs started to glow dimly as suddenly the egg next to Lily started to crack and rumble. A large crack spread all over the egg as from the bottom a small white dragon leg popped out, then a small tail. The baby dragon shattered the eggshell into millions of pieces. The white scales of the dragon glistened under the caves' lights as its emerald eyes glowed brightly. Lily questioned, "Will this dragon be hers'?"

Falin nodded, "Yes it shall, you must name her now though."

Lily looked carefully at the dragon as it suddenly started to suck on its tail. The baby dragon curled on its back as it started to rock itself to sleep. Lily giggled to herself as she looked upon the snowy white scales of the dragon. Lily replied, "Well it appears as if I have two babies to look after. But her name shall be…" Just before she could reply the name of the dragon, the dragon started to make a small gagging noise. Suddenly the dragon sneezed sending a small stream of burning red fire across the cave. The dragons' eyes glanced over to Lily as if embarrassed. The baby dragon rubbed its nose with her claw as she then continued to suck on her tail. Lily laughed, "Well my mind has been changed. I shall make it easier for us all, her name shall be Snowfire."

Falin nodded with acceptance as she turned her gaze to Whistalyn. Whistalyn bit her bottom lip confused as she laid her eyes upon the un-hatched egg. There was neither a crack upon the shell or any stirring about. The egg stood completely still on the stone table. Whistalyn turned towards Nylina whom simply shrugged her shoulders. She gave a small sigh as a smile suddenly spread upon her face. Whistalyn whispered, "I shall name, um…"

Whistalyn glanced over to Falin with confusion and asked, "Is my child's' dragon a he or a she?"

Falin laughed with much delight as if Whistalyn's question was humorous. Moments later after she saw that neither Nylina nor Whistalyn were joining her, she dimmed her laughter. Falin cleared her throat and replied with a chuckle, "Why, the dragon is a he of course."

Whistalyn nodded as she turned her gaze back towards the egg. It still did not stir or crack. Whistalyn leaned over to the egg and replied, "Alright there little one, I shall name you Cetus, Cetus, for bravery."

They all stared at the egg with curiosity as nothing happened. Falin on the other hand ran her scaly fingers through her hair. She replied half heartily, "Perhaps this mighty dragon is still sleeping, perhaps, if you reply a bit louder?"

Whistalyn and Nylina both stepped closer to the egg. Nylina watched the color swirl on the eggs shell as she shrugged her shoulders yet once more. Whistalyn replied louder and filled with more confidence, "I shall name this dragon Cetus for bravery!"

They all leaned closer to the unstirred egg. Suddenly, it started to stir. They stepped back just in time as the eggshell burst and flew all over the cave. The eggshell pieces quickly diminished within the mist as Snowfire's did. Now there before them sat a baby green dragon with deep bright green colored eyes. The dragon sat there cuddling his tail as his eyes widened as if with fear. His delicate baby eyes quickly shifted between everyone over and over. Suddenly the little dragons' eyes started to fill with tears. Just as everyone started to awe, Cetus started to cry. Tears fled his eyes as small bubbles came out of his nose and popped.

Nylina leaned over and picked up Cetus as he trembled slightly. She bent over and with took a small piece of thread from her sock, then flung it within the air as it turned into a small blanket. The new pieces swirled together quickly and neatly. She covered the sniffling dragon and kissed him on the head. Cetus, the little dragon now cuddled into Nylina as she replied, "Don't worry, I'll work on him. I'm sure there's a mighty dragon somewhere inside."

They all chuckled with enjoyment. Moments later Falin replied, "Go now, and succeed in this prophecy. Let it be fulfilled."

Everyone gave a small bow and their thanks. Suddenly the cave trembled for a brief moment as stairs appeared in the back of the caves wall. Whistalyn held her baby close as Nylina held Cetus. They walked towards the stairs and then started to climb them. Lily wrapped her baby more comfortably as she gazed over at Snowfire. Snowfire purred softly as she opened her wings and gave them a long stretched. She started to flap them as she flew up a bit. She ended up flopping sideways in the air a bit but, moments later she got the hang of flying. Lily smiled contently as she replied to Snowfire, "Well then, you look like you're going to be a strong one. Will you be able to keep up?"

Snowfire purred once more and nodded as Lily opened her beautiful wings. She flew up a bit as they both took off towards the top of the cave where an opening now was. Snowfire flew quickly and smoothly next to Lily.

Just before the elves and the fairy exited Falin shouted over to them, "Much caution to you all, for if word gets out of this mighty night, there might be those who want to stop this prophecy, or want to corrupt it. Go with much secrecy and care, and introduce your wondrous child to your grand city."

After they exited, the cave trembled slightly as the opening closed with a soft bang. Falin now sat there alone beside the two octopuses that still sat next to her side. She waved her hand over the stone table as the starfish came to life yet once more. They quickly gathered the stones, shells and water balls into a neat pile. Just as Falin started to place her things into her seaweed bag something from above caught her eye. She glanced up to see a single golden feather sailing down towards the stone table. Falin

189

stretched her arm out and with took the feather from midair. The softness of the feather seemed to comfort Falin's fingers. She gave a small smile as she turned to her two pet octopuses. She replied to them, "You know, this is going to be a very interesting era."

Her two pets nodded as they headed for the caves' shoreline. Falin as well headed for the white sand. Her scaly legs once again became fins as she dove headfirst into the water. Briefly after they vanished the stone table disappeared with the mist of the cave. For the enchanting spell was now set upon them.

But little did they know that an evil presence was near, an evil presence that was on his way near the City of Whisperia to stop Lily from reaching her castle. To find a way to stop the prophecy or, to simply twist it around to fit his desired prophecy...

****

Surrender

2

I awoke feeling sick to my stomach, but I continued to keep my eyes closed. My whole body felt as if it was still trembling with exhaustion. But moments later as the cool breeze continued to brush my face; I gathered up my courage and opened them. I could only see the buttery clouds passing me by, and I could also only see part of Krynton's leg, which meant we were still flying high above the earth. I didn't have much strength left in me to even attempt to sit up or even to maintain keeping my eyes open. I did get a chance to lean my head back a bit before I closed my eyes again. Fear struck within my heart as goose bumps instantly covered my skin, I saw Cethios flying Krynton. I'm not sure why but, perhaps I had foolishly hoped that it would have only been Krynton and I, although that would be an absurd assumption.

More horror flowed through my veins as I didn't know where I would end up at or what was going to happen to me. Would I survive? Would I have the strength to fight back and escape? I would have loved to just drop myself off of Krynton but, Cethios would probably catch me again or worse, just let me fall to my doom. I was still extremely weary from the battle to even attempt to fly down to safety. I honestly had no idea where he was taking me, oblivious to everything.

As I opened my eyes again momentarily, I gazed back over to see Cethios' face once more. I couldn't tell if he himself was weary from the horrendous battle we just fought, or if the wind was causing his eyes to swell. Either way, I closed my eyes involuntarily, seeing the entire clouds blur by was making me even more nauseous.

Suddenly a familiar scent forced me to open my eyes before I surrendered to my subconscious mind. Slight relief washed over me as I saw the grand view of Urinia and her vast mountain. That was really the only thing that soothed my inner soul, knowing just where we were heading too. Perhaps that was why Cethios appeared so drained. We had traveled days to reach Urinia, and I'm not sure if Cethios had camped out or had Krynton fly straight through. But just before I blanked out, deep sorrow and agony filled my heart, I wondered, if I'd ever see my beloved Xanthus ever again....

The next time I opened my eyes I had enough energy in me to keep them opened. I found myself standing in a dark dungeon with my wrists shackled and my arms hanging above my head. I glanced down to see that my ankles were also in shackles and chained to the wall. In the distance I could hear something dripping in consistency. I glanced around the room as the sense of death filled the dense air. Around me along the walls, were empty shackles that hung. Far to the left of me was a tall wooden door with enormous spikes coming out from it as a small wooden table sat next to the door. On top of that table seemed to be other shackles but with spikes coming out from the inside of it. There also seemed to be a whip near the door with spikes coming out of the leather strips. On the floor about a couple of feet from me, I spotted a chastity belt with spikes on the outside of it. Then I thought, oh my goodness, why does everything have to have spikes on it! What was Cethios planning to do with me!? What kind of dungeon was this? Granite I've never been in one, but still!

To my far right was a warm fireplace made of a dark black stone with a sword case nearby. The swords themselves seemed to be worn out and chipped. If perhaps I could just reach one, then maybe I might have a chance in escaping. But my chains were so close to the wall that I couldn't even lean forward. I glanced around more carefully now that my eyes adjusted to the low light. I wanted to see if there was anyone else here in the dungeon with me. But sadly, and thankfully, I was all alone in the eerie silence. The only noise that was trembling through my ears was the dripping water and the crackling of the fire. But I had no idea on where that dripping noise was coming from.

Moments later after I was completely sure I was alone I attempted to escape from my shackles and chains. I tried to squeeze my hands from the shackles but they were too tight against my skin. It was as if I was wearing some type of bracelet that merged onto my skin. The same went for the ones on my ankles. I gave a deep sigh as I started to feel dizzy. The thought of me not being able to escape kept lurking within my mind. Moments later I can honestly say that I gave up on that first attempt. Now, I tried to pull the chain links off of the wall or at least off of the shackles. But nothing I was doing was working. I was simply exhausting myself.

Alright, I'll just try to conjure up something to help myself out. But I didn't even know what to try or where to start! I closed my eyes and concentrated on the shackles. I concentrated on expanding the metal so I can therefore try to slip my hands out. My palms started to glow a low dim white light, but suddenly they started to burn. My white light turned to a low red light as my whole body felt hot! Nothing was happening, why wasn't I able to use my magic? I tried concentrating harder and reaching deeper, this time only thinking about unlocking the locks.

But suddenly a small black rain cloud formed from out of nowhere above my head. Bright yellow lightning bolts shot from within the cloud. I gave a low shriek as it started to rain on me with an extreme pulse. The cool water drenched my entire body. The only thing that the rain did was cool me down from becoming even hotter. Moments later though, it stopped raining as the little black rain cloud started to vanish with the mist. It probably finished its entire water density on me.

Just then the wooden door slowly cracked open and then slammed shut. I glanced up to see Cethios coming down the steps and making his way over to me. He walked arrogantly smirking to himself as his hands rested in his pockets. His hair was combed back and off to the side instead of spiked up. He was wearing some type of black pants and a white shirt that was opened a bit from his chest.

As he neared me, I tried not to appear mortified or appear to be trembling with fear. I wanted to appear strong and confident but honestly, that's probably not what he saw. He now stood in front of me as I just wanted to stretch out and kick him. But the chains were not long enough to allow me to do so. Cethios half chuckled, "You know, I never honestly really wanted to see you like this. It is an awful shame how horribly attracted you look right now though. But who knows how you'll look after all of the cruelty is done. That is, if you don't comply with my every word." He continued to smirk to himself as his gaze fell all over my body with his hands still in his pockets.

I retorted to him in the best confident voice I could give, "I'm not afraid of you Cethios. Fear is not what you'll see in my eyes nor shall you find defeat."

"Perhaps mortification then? You know you really aren't as brave as you think you are. Also, just to get this settled, those shackles that you are wearing are enchanted, magic proof you could say. So don't bother wasting your precious magic or effort attempting to escape them or me. I can't have you being completely exhausted before I even begin to have my way with you."

"Why do you enjoy torturing me so much? I…"

"Torturing?"

I gulped louder than I anticipated as that word escaped him. Perhaps I should have chosen a different word to say. Or perhaps I should have not said anything at all. Cethios' eyes lit up though when he replied that word. My skin crawled as a slight tremor vibrated through me. I wondered what he was thinking about.

Suddenly he started to look around the dungeon, and just as it appeared he was going to walk away, wham! He back slapped me across the face. I screamed in horror as the pain shot through my delicate skin. I shouted to him, "What was that for?! I deserve nothing from you, nothing!"

Cethios scrunched his nose in and frowned. I on the other hand tried to regain my eye sight, for it went slightly fuzzy after the slap. I licked the corner of my mouth, ugh! I tasted rusty iron; it was my blood. To my regret though, I'm sure this is only just a bit of what's yet to come. Cethios replied through gritted teeth, "That's for abandoning me on the day of our announcement at the ball."

"Awe, are you still wounded from that day? Besides, you could have had anyone you wanted. Anyone at all! Why are you being so devoted to me? You were finally rid of the one fairy who would rise against you. I probably wouldn't have ever returned yet, you still brought me back. Why?"

Without hesitation Cethios back hand slapped me again as I screamed from the top of my lungs, more with anger than in pain. His laughter echoed throughout the dungeon as if I was amusing him. And why was no one coming from hearing me scream? Did anyone hear me? Or did they simply dismay it? Cethios chuckled, "You still haven't figured it out yet have you? Aren't you supposed to be smarter than me? I can't believe even after you left to find you precious answers, you still can't piece together the pieces of who you are?"

This time, I simply hung there motionless staring at him with rage. I didn't want to answer him. I was truthfully afraid that he was going to back slap me again. I replied nothing as he stood there smirking at me rubbing his hands together. Good, I hoped it hurt him more from hitting me but, I probably doubt it. Finally, after I gathered up my courage, I replied softly to him, "If you are going to kill me, why are you having me endure all of this?"

Cethios laughed as if I had told him something hilarious. Was he going insane? All that was left was for him to foam at the mouth. He chuckled through breaths, "Why no, I need you alive. Zethron wanted you killed off after I was finished but…"   As he said those words horror struck deep within my chest, I swear my heart was stuttering to a halt.

I interrupted him, "Why? I still can't understand? What have I done that is so wrong besides being born?"

"That's just it though, don't you see, that's the whole secret isn't it. The queen gives birth to a beautiful infant girl, and just before she announces it, she disappears. Alas, surprisingly a child girl is found in the queen and kings' bedroom. Do you still not comprehend? You are that girl Azalea; you are her daughter. Being born is exactly what went wrong. You see, I need to marry a princess to become a king and, only you can give me that. That is why I need you. You see, your mother bestowed all her trust in me as a child and I, I was to watch over you. Unfortunately, I never knew what truly happened to her, but…"

Then, for a brief moment his breaths became deeper and slower. It seemed as if he had spaced out momentarily, as if he cared about her and me, as if he did have a heart. It seemed as if he was concerned with something but he couldn't seem to connect the pieces together. But seconds later as if he received some evil tremor of epiphany, he leaned closer to me. I gritted my teeth and closed my eyes tightly. I was waiting for another slap or something more, but nothing came.

I felt something tugging on my side and on my stomach. I opened my eyes slightly and cautiously. What was he doing? I gazed down to see that he was actually unbuckling all of my buttons, rope and equipment that I still had on from the day of the war. He tossed everything onto the floor next to me as he only left me with my brown shirt and my black pants. My heart raced as it seemed it was going to pound right out of my chest. Faster and faster my heart went as I had no idea on what Cethios was doing or going to do.

Just as I thought my chest was going to explode with my deep breaths Cethios leaned over to my ear and shushed me. The sensation of his cool breath over my ear sent waves of treacherous sensation over my skin. I shook slightly as he gently placed his hands on my hips. He whispered, "Relax Azalea, this shouldn't take long."

Cethios' soft lips came in contact with my neck as he kissed me softly. He rubbed his face slowly upon mine dragging his nose up my collar bone. Willing and unwilling chills shivered up and down my spine as I glowed with frustration. He then bent over towards my stomach as he lifted my shirt revealing my stone within my navel. It seemed to glow a lavender hue as I glistened with sweat of hatred. He then twisted my shirt and tucked it in over the top as it stayed revealing my abdominal. He rubbed his fingertips slowly and gently over my stomach as he then kissed it.

Cethios reached into his left pocket as he with took a small clear crystal. It seemed as if it was chipped off from somewhere. Suddenly realization hit me as I knew it was a stone from The Caves of Esmera! But how could he have gotten one out from the walls? How did he even know how to get into the caves? Perhaps I was over thinking this. He could have got it from somewhere else, someone else, anywhere else.

He held it up close to my navel as both stones now glowed a lavender hue. Right then I knew that it did come from the Caves of Esmera. But how did he come to it? Unexpectedly Cethios stood as an enormous grin spread across his face. He leaned closer to me as our lips brushed against each other. I turned my head away from him. I wasn't just going to let him kiss me! His soft ragged breath sent another wave of traitorous shivers up my skin as he whispered brushing his lips upon my ear lobe, "Now, I shall only ask you once and only once, you need to speak these words, I need to hear these words. Did you sleep with that elf?"

He leaned away from me as if studying my reaction as he locked his eyes within mine. I wanted to gulp my saliva down but if I did, I would sound guilt! In which honestly, I was but, I wasn't going to tell Cethios that. I didn't know what to tell him? I mean, if I did try to lie would he tell? And why was he wanting to know in the first place? He shouted and startled me as I jumped within my shackles, "Did you sleep with that elf!?"

"I thought you were only going to ask once?" I just had to play it smart didn't I? Of course, wham! Cethios yet again back slapped me across the face. This time he sent some of my blood flying across the floor. My mouth dripped with blood as golden tears filled and regrettably fled my eyes. But this time I did not scream. I mean, what was the point if no one was going to come to my aid, right? Moments later though as I regained my subconscious mind from the blow and the tears that fled my eyes were gone, I half sobbed, "Why is this so important to you, for you? What difference does it make if I did or if I didn't?"

Cethios cupped his hand over my chin as he lifted my head up slightly. He replied with caution as if sighing, "I still can't believe you are not comprehending this. Azalea, let me ask you, does that elf of yours, does he have a stone as well?"

"No." I did it, I lied. And I was sort of content with myself in doing so.

Cethios let go of my face as he ran his hands roughly through his hair in frustration. I hung there helplessly. Cethios paced around in front of me. It seemed as if he was pondering something intensely, or was simply confused about something. He was debating with himself whether or not he wanted to speak. Finally, he stopped in front of me as he placed his hands on his hips. He replied as calmly as he could, "You see, I'm not sure if anyone has told you about a legend, a legend of two nations coming together to unite all. And let me start by saying that, if you first sleep with another that doesn't have a stone like yours then, that first man shall inherit all of your powers and magic, therefore making him invincible and immortal. Therefore, my question to you really isn't whether or not he has a stone but, if you have slept with him. We also can't have both gem carriers getting it on and becoming immortals, can we? So, I am going to assume he does have a gem but, did you sleep with him?"

I brought up my strength to stay courageous as now I completely understood that I had to lie to him, for the sake of Xanthus' life and mine. I must give him a convincing act though, for if not, I'm sure he'd kill us both. Perhaps I can delay my fate with him or at least come up with something else. But also, I couldn't believe that all of these centuries I have been the daughter of Queen Lily. She was my mother, and I, I was a princess?

All this new information fluttered in my head like a mad wind on a stormy night. So then, did that mean that Xanthus and I were now, immortals? If all of this was true though, I still couldn't chance it by having these enchanted shackles. And by me having these shackles on, does that chance Xanthus' immortality and mine? I can't give Cethios the slightest thought though that I could already be immortal, or Xanthus for that matter. Also, what I have feared of, of me marrying someone not because of love but because of only the crown, was now really happing to me, but not just the crown itself, my immortality. And Cethios was doing it to me! I then gathered my courage with a deep breath and replied, "You're wrong, he doesn't have a stone like me and I didn't sleep with him or anyone for that matter. But I shall not be conquered over. Beside the point Cethios, why are you telling me all of this? I now know that I am a princess and that I have a higher authority over you and..."

Cethios chuckled at my response, "First of all my lady, before you get all of your hopes up, no one knows that you are a princess, just you, me and Zethron. Besides, no one will believe you anyways. You see in all truths now; I need you so I can inherit your magic and your immortality. Then…"

"You'll kill me." Cethios once again laughed at my comment, I swear he was going mad. He was behaving as if what I had said was ridiculously hilarious! I also was afraid he was laughing because it was true. Hopefully he would have a heart somewhere in there and not kill me. I wasn't sure of anything anymore.

He cleared his throat after he finished and snorted, "Regretfully no, you see Azalea, deep down, and I mean deep down, I really do care about you. You could even say that I love, love…"

"Then why do you have me chained up like a criminal and keep slapping the hell out of me!"

Wham! He back slapped me yet again across the other side of my face. I sort of knew he was going to. But the horrendous pain shot through my eye sockets all the way to my toes! I swear I even felt my eyes fly out of my head for a brief moment, I swear. My head pounded with such intensity. I shook my head slightly in attempts to regain my eye sight; it was starting to go blurry. By this time though more blood was now dripping out of my mouth and nose. My face felt bruised as I could feel it starting to swell up. I could barely stay conscious and awake as each time he hit me they were getting stronger and stronger. I honestly felt as if I wanted to just give up and slip into consciousness with the mist of the day. Cethios growled, "I'm trusting you with this because you see; there is a good side of me that wants you to trust me. I am trusting you not to reply or repeat this to anyone else, until the timing is right. Can I trust you?" He came closer to me yet again as he gently placed his warm hand upon my cheek. He brushed his soft lips against my lips just barely grazing them. I no longer had the strength left in me to deny him. He whispered in my ear, "I cannot save your life from Zethron if you don't cooperate with me. He will kill you without a doubt and hesitation. You must trust me if you want to continue on with your life. Or, if you ever want to see your beloved Xanthus again."

I leaned back away from him as I pressed my back onto the wall. He was truly surprising me. Why was he telling me this? This was all so unexpected. And most of all, how did he know Xanthus' name? Cethios still held his hand upon my cheek as I slightly turned my face into his palm. I brushed my lips against his skin as I whispered, "Do not attempt or try to blackmail me, for it shall not work. I can take care of my life all on my own without anyone's help. I need not to place my trust on you."

"Really? You can take care of your life all your own you say. Just like your handling your life now?"

Just then the sound of heavy footsteps started to ascend from stairs outside of the dungeon door in the distance. Cethios quickly dropped his hand and took a step away from me. He turned his head towards the sound briefly, as he then turned his gaze back to me. Our eyes locked as he quickly whispered in anguish, "That's Zethron, and if you don't trust me I cannot guarantee that your life will be spared from his wrath."

"Why should I?"

"Please stop your stubbornness and don't be stupid. Just do it!" Just as the door opened Cethios back slapped me again, hopefully for the final time. But surprisingly this time it wasn't so forceful as the other times. I hung there as my hair covered my face and as my head hung slightly down. I didn't want to see any of their faces. Also, I tried to appear lifeless and blanked out. But that wasn't very hard to do, for I was already exhausted and drained out from Cethios.

I overheard Zethron reply to Cethios, "Cethios, have you been torturing this poor girl?"

Cethios forcefully chuckled, "Have to get the answers out of her one way or another, right?"

"Well then, I can see that I have taught you well. Does she still suppress her own individual magic?"

Cethios release a sinister laugh, "Of course she does. She is too weak and too foolish to have done anything anyway. Besides, I held the stone that you gave me to hers and…"

Without hesitation Zethron interrupted, "Did it glow intensely with the force of its magic?"

"Yes it did."

Zethron carefully made his way over to me as he walked all around me, as if inspecting me. I had my eyes opened slightly so I could at least figure out where he was. I heard Zethron reply with amusement, "Is she out of consciousness?"

Cethios, a little too quickly answered, "Yes she is."

From what I could see Zethron turned towards Cethios and eyed him suspiciously. Cethios stood there full of confidents and reassurance. Would Zethron see right through him? Would he tell that I really wasn't unconscious?

Zethron scrunched his nose in with disgust. I feared for that exact second, Zethron didn't believe him. At that moment I knew, no matter how much I didn't want to, I had to trust Cethios. Zethron then turned and walked over to the fireplace. He with took a long sword from a small case next to the fire. He then did what I had hoped he wouldn't do. He drove the sword into the fireplace. The wood cracked and fell over the sword as it started to glow a bright cherry red.

Panic swelled deep inside my skin for I had a hunch on what he was planning on doing, but I refused to let that idea sink into my mind. Also, what could I do that wouldn't put me or Cethios in danger. More for me though I thought. But I wasn't sure a hundred percent why he was heating up the sword. Whatever he was thinking couldn't be good. I started to become nervous. With all the strength I had left I mustered up to control my shaking the best I could. Then, what made matters worse; I started to feel small beads of sweat trickling down my forehead and the back of my neck.

I slightly turned my gaze towards Cethios as he seemed perfectly calm with his hands in his pockets as he glared at Zethron. Moments later Zethron walked over to me as he stopped right in front of me with the glowing sword. Cethios asked as if un-amused, "What is that supposed to be for?"

Zethron smirked to himself as he snickered, "Well, you did say she was unconscious did you not? If she really is out, then she shouldn't feel a thing. That is until she wakes up. Also, if she truly is unconscious, then her heart beats and blood flow should be sluggish. Therefore, she shouldn't bleed to death. Since she's unconscious then, her body should be able to clot the wound before she wakes."

"Do you not trust my words?"

Zethron laughed, "You will learn to trust no one."

Cethios glanced away from him as he seemed to fill with deep rage and disappointment. He replied to Zethron through gritted teeth, "You should be able to trust me. Especially after all I have done for you."

Zethron gazed upon Cethios with even more disgust than before. He then turned to me and drove the sword into my right side. He then removed it as he tore it out. I have never in my life tried so hard at something like I did at that moment. But this was that time where my life depended on it, I mean really depended on it. I held in the scream that wanted to tear its way out of my throat. I held in my flinches and tremors that shook my body from the horrendous pain that quickly started to spread my entirety. I started to feel my heart race in my chest as it rushed as much blood as it could to the existing gash in my side.

Zethron threw the sword next to my side as blood dripped off of it. I tried not to shiver as a sharp bitter cold now started to sweep over my skin. I could sense that death was nearly upon me. Through my drumming ears I faintly overheard Zethron reply to Cethios, "Do what you need to do with her, then kill her. We have no need for her after."

Just as Zethron attempted to leave, Cethios stood in his path stopping him. Cethios replied quickly, "I want to keep her."

I could tell Zethron was disgusted as he grunted, "Fine, but she will remain in those enchanted shackles after you inherit her immortality forever after. She will also remain chambered in your quarters. And if I ever find out that you have set her free, it shall be your energy that leaves you. Do not have me regret this decision and this very moment."

Being content Cethios stepped aside from Zethron's path as they remained glaring at one other. Zethron then stepped aside and continued his way out of the dungeon. Cethios watched Zethron leave as he waited for his footsteps to descend. He then raised his right palm up towards the door as his hand glowed a deep red. The door suddenly barricaded itself shut as it too glowed with a burgundy hue.

Suddenly Cethios rushed over to me with deep regret and grief in his eyes. Something I had never seen before. But when he reached me, I was already trembling with great force in pain and with coldness, I couldn't contain it any longer. Golden tears fled my eyes as I could faintly see some tears escape Cethios' eyes as well. He placed his hands on my face as he shouted, "Azalea! Azalea stay awake! Do not close your eyes, Azalea!"

Suddenly I felt this great numbness conquering my entire body. I slowly whispered to Cethios, "I'm going to die here, aren't I?"

With an anguish voice Cethios replied, "I'm not going to let that happen. I made a promise and I intent to keep it!" Cethios pressed his left hand on my back wound and his right hand on the front wound. He pressed gently in attempts to stop the blood from escaping even more, warm blood seeped through his fingers as it dripped down my side and onto the floor. Delicate words escaped Cethios' lips as he whispered, "Oh no Azalea."

Tears fled his eyes as he placed his head on my shoulder and pressed harder. I could tell he didn't seem to know what to do as he was giving up hope. I could feel his body start to slightly shake. I gave a low sigh as I saw my hands start to give off a low dim pink light. I barely whispered to Cethios, "Cethios, my hands. I can't feel your warmth any longer…"

Cethios turned his head as he gazed upon my dimming glowing palms. Was this it, was I dying? Suddenly I heard Cethios half shout in frustration, "No! You're not leaving me."

Suddenly I faintly saw Cethios hands start to glow a deep red glow. Then unexpectedly, he forcefully slammed me onto the wall behind me as he pressed his body onto mine, and hard. His lips were on mine, kissed me passionately as I slowly started to feel his warm lips upon mine. I felt strange as warmth quickly over took my skin. I started to feel my heart beat faster and faster as it seemed to jump with life. The uncontrollable sensation I was feeling for Cethios came rising up within me. The numbness of death was no longer lingering within my veins.

Moments later as we continued our passionate kiss of fury, I realized exactly what Cethios was doing. He was transferring some of his energy and vitality to me. My side, where Zethron had driven the sword, was burning intensely as I could feel the wound starting to close. I felt it singe and tingle with very unusual vibrations.

I could feel Cethios pouring himself into me as he now rubbed my back slowly as we continued to kiss. I now had some warmth and feeling back in my arms and fingers. You know, he didn't really have to save me but, he did. I guess somewhere deep inside him, somewhere deep down, was the old Cethios that I once knew.

Moments later as if there was some type of miniature sonic boom effect, he pushed himself off and away from me. He stumbled over his feet

202

as he placed his hands upon his knees as he breathed heavily. Heavy beads of sweat dripped down his forehead and back. I too felt light headed and a bit dizzy as we both momentarily concentrated on trying to situate our breaths and control what was sizzling inside us.

Much later after the room stopped spinning for me, and probably for Cethios as well, he stood with his hands resigning on his hips. I could still tell though that he was still trying to calm down his breathing, for he was taking in slow deep breaths. I replied breathlessly to him, "You, you saved my life. Why? Why would you do that for me?"

Cethios simply stood there with his face flushed. He seemed blank as if he honestly didn't know what to say to me. Did he really care or perhaps love me in that deep cold heart of his? I wondered if he received any of my warmth and love. I mean, was there some good hidden somewhere in there? As I pondered all of this I gazed into his eyes as I did not falter my sight upon him. He ran his fingers over his face and through his hair as he wiped the tears from my sight. He replied softly but firmly, "You, you shall tell no one of this. No one! No one must know of what I have done for you. I, I..."

"You gave me a part of your strength, your magic, so I wouldn't be taken by death. You saved me from becoming a memory, a precious memory that resides somewhere in you. You gave me a part of you so that I, so that I could have the strength to mend the damage that was done upon me. But, if only I could mend the damage that was done upon you. You lie to others Cethios, but you shall not lie to me any longer, and I shall not lie to you. I saw a piece of you, a piece that no one knows about, about when you were here in Urinia. I saw, I felt the sadness that, that you felt. A memory I almost became but, a memory from you is what I inherited. A question that I hope, you will answer one day. I know what it's like to wonder, to ponder the question, who are your true parents? Cethios, why couldn't you have just come to me? I would have understood. I thought we could tell each other anything. But you can't hide from me any longer Cethios, you just can't. I now know part of what created this monster that you so desperately try to show. But what I am confused about is, is on what you have just done for me. I thought only love was able to..."

Cethios interrupted me as he sighed, "Azalea, you do not comprehend what you saw." With his abilities back under control, Cethios bent over and picked up the sword that Zethron threw next to me. It still glowed a faint cherry red as he held it in his grasp. He then held the swords tip to my neck as he replied cautiously, "Do not make me regret what I have done for you. I simply ask you that you tell no one of this moment that pasted us. It is a part of me that I should have never given to you but, nonetheless unwilling it was given to you. A promise I have made and a promise I intent on keeping. That is what I promised your mother. Understanding is what you and I shall both receive one day but for now, a promise I shall ask you to keep. Tell no one of this moment of what you saw and what I did for you. And I, I promise you one day you shall have one of your precious questions answered. Do we have a deal?"

I gazed my eyes down to the glowing sword as I quickly pondered his bargain. Would he stay true to his word? And what promise did he make my mother? Also, what question was he going to answer? I had to trust him, I just had to. I didn't want to but I honestly had no other options at the moment. As I gazed back to Cethios' eyes from the sword, I could tell that he was deeply concerned on me keeping what I saw to myself a secret. I took in a deep breath as I now had my breaths back to normal. I once more locked my gaze with Cethios' as I replied softly, "Alright Cethios, we have a deal."

Cethios tightened his grasp on the sword as he then slashed the chains that held my ankles and wrist to the wall. As I fell to the floor onto my hands and knees, I took in deep breaths into my sore body. My skin was no longer cramping in the same stiffen position chained to the wall. I tilted my head up slightly as I saw Cethios still holding the swords' tip towards my neck. Just because he saved me from dying didn't mean he wouldn't still harm me. I wasn't going to risk that thought.

I stood up slowly as I realized that the shackles still resided upon my wrists and ankles. Which meant I was powerless and sadly, I knew it. I sighed for I knew what I had to do, but I regretfully didn't want to say it. I bit my bottom lip as I replied to Cethios, "So what's next? What shall you have me do?"

A huge grin spread on his face from ear to ear. He replied with humor, "Oh Azalea, you don't know how long I have been waiting to hear you say that. Now, you shall bend at my will."

True Friend

3

Meanwhile in the city of Trinafin millions of elf soldiers were returning home from the vigorous battle. Some soldiers limped with pride and satisfaction just on the thought that they were home safely and alive. While others were unharmed, still proud of the battle they had just won. They all felt a kind of peace among each other as they walked side by side, for their city was safe from becoming over ruled by evil. Their purpose for leaving and protecting their existence had proven victorious. Most of the soldiers though still carried their swords, bows, and helmets. For their things proved evidence of a hardship and prosperous battle.

In the castle of Trinafin Xanthus burst through the doors as King Alcander, Morpheus and James followed behind. Xanthus quickly turned to them and replied breathlessly, "So, who will be joining me on the quest to Urinia?"

Everyone glimpsed at each other with guilt and sadness. Most of them were still feeling the grief and hardship of the horrendous battle from which they had just came from. King Alcander walked up to Xanthus as he placed his delicate hand upon his shoulder. Seeming as if there was no more breath left in him, he replied to Xanthus, "My son, I grieve in sadness for I will not be joining you in your journey. My place is here amongst my people. They will need my guidance after the hardship of the battle. Your time will come when you will inherit the throne as king, and your guidance and rule will be needed. But for now, you must follow your own heart. Go to her, she needs you as much as I know you need her. Go, I shall be there with you, but in your heart."

Sadness filled Xanthus' eyes but he knew the truth, his father would not be joining him for his responsibilities were with the elves of Trinafin. Xanthus nodded and replied nothing to his father, for no words could describe what he felt deep within his heart. But within King Alcander's eyes and his mighty hug to his son, said it all to Xanthus. For sometimes actions are stronger than words. Moments after that James stepped forward and replied to Xanthus, "I will be joining you to Urinia. But do understand that once there I must leave you to venture out in my own quest. There's still much to do that goes unnoticed."

Xanthus nodded with content to James' reply. At least he knew he had someone guiding him to Urinia. To lead the quest to his adored Azalea. Briefly after that Xanthus turned to Morpheus, whom in return sighed in uncertainty, Xanthus replied to him, "And you, will you be joining me on this journey?"

Morpheus appeared nervous as he quickly started to jolt his eyes around the entrance hall. King Alcander glanced at them both as he with took in a deep sigh. He knew that this situation was between them both and also, he wanted to rest before he went to address his people about the battle they had just won. He gave a small nod of his head as he simply turned and started to walk toward a door that was near the staircase. He opened the door, stepped inside and closed the door with a soft bang that seemed to echo throughout the hall.

Morpheus glanced over to James as if he was waiting for him to say the right words. But in turn James gave a small bow and replied, "I will await outside, therefore, your conversation will remain in a comfortable privacy." That was not what Morpheus wanted to hear. But just before James left outside he turned towards him and replied, "Morpheus, I do have an understanding that you shall answer with your heart. Do not let fear inherit your decision. For you see, fear is only the imagination that was created upon thought of doubt that perhaps may possibly never come true. Overcome that fear, and courage shall never doubt you."

James turned back to Xanthus as he bowed once more. He left with a smile upon his face and exited the hall through the front doors. With that being said Morpheus knew that James knew he was filled with fear. Fear and doubt of the journey that they were about to embark upon. Morpheus took a deep breath yet again as he tried not to allow his grief to appear through his eyes. He turned to Xanthus and replied with concern, "Xanthus, this isn't going to be like one of your usual quests is it?"

Xanthus could only shake his head no, for his words escaped him as he himself could not imagine what they would encounter as they venture to Urinia. Morpheus continued, "There isn't going to be your usual satisfying wonder at the end of the journey, is there?"

Once again Xanthus shrugged his shoulders and shook his head, unsure himself at what may come. Moments later though Xanthus found the words that had been lurking behind his tongue. He replied, "Perhaps there is after all of this is over. I'm not sure myself what we are going to find out there or, how long it shall take us."

They both stood there speechless and motionless. Neither knew what the right thing to say or do was. Their uncertainty was the same, but yet in other ways different. Xanthus was uncertain on what exactly they were going to encounter or even if they would be able to find Urinia or Azalea. Morpheus was uncertain on if he wanted to go off and venture into this at all. Would they make it? Would they even survive if there was another battle awaiting them?

Moments later after much silence from them both, Xanthus glanced down to his side. He noticed that he still had Azalea's sword tied to his side next to his own sword. He untied it as he held on to the handle tightly between his fingertips. Xanthus glanced back to Morpheus as tears so desperately tried to flood his eyes. He replied through a tight sob, "I cannot guarantee you that this journey will be secure or even safe. What honestly lies ahead of me, I truly don't know. The only thing I am sure of is that Azalea needs me, and I shall not abandon nor falter her. I ask you as my true friend, to be here for me."

Morpheus leaned over and placed his hand on Xanthus' shoulder. A single silver tear had succeeded as it fled Xanthus' eye and as it now made its way down his cheek. Sadly, more tears seemed to be on their way as Xanthus could barely try to keep them in any much longer. Xanthus sobbed through breaths, "Please. I'm not sure if we are walking into an ambush in Urinia or not. But what I do fear though, is what Cethios is doing or could have already done to my beloved Azalea. I fear that I will be too late or that I shall never find her or hear her laughter ever again. And I, I have been here, and I have done nothing."

"Do you blame yourself that Cethios took her in the first place?"

Xanthus took a step back from Morpheus as he inhaled a deep breath. He did blame himself as he thought that perhaps if he had kept her inside of the tent that day, she'd still be safe. Or perhaps, if he fought faster he could have reached her in time. Much more reasons and excuses fluttered his head as it seemed to pound with sadness and furry. Morpheus grumbled, "You cannot blame yourself for that day, for that moment. If you keep that pain within your heart, it will drive you mad even when so you do find her."

Xanthus glanced away from Morpheus as he tied Azalea's sword back onto his belt. He ran his sore fingers over his wet face and hair. He turned his gaze towards the chandelier as he thought of the day when a crystal dragon flew out to Azalea. Suddenly that same delicate crystal dragon was making its way over to him this very second. Xanthus extended his arm with his palm up as the crystal dragon landed smoothly.

Xanthus gazed at it as confusion filled his head. The mighty crystal dragon let out a small roar as it then jumped off of his palm. It almost crashed onto the floor as it quickly lifted its wings just in time. It slowly and carefree flew back with the rest of the crystal dragons.

He gazed at the chandelier as he seemed to ponder his thoughts even more. But in turn even though he was upset at himself he knew Morpheus was right. He couldn't let that rage consume him. Xanthus grunted, "Morpheus look, I shall ask you no more. I am leaving within moments after I gather a couple of things I need for the journey. I am hoping though to see you out there with Orion. If not, well then I hope one day you and I shall meet again."

With that being said he quickly left the grand entrance leaving Morpheus all alone in the hall. Morpheus continued to ponder with his thoughts on whether he should leave or not. He walked slowly under the chandelier. He was confused deep down in his heart. He wanted to be there for his friend but yet, fear played a small role in his heart. For he feared what he might encounter on his way to Urinia or what was in Urinia. Uncertainty filled him greatly as he turned his gaze towards the chandelier. The vibrant colors of the chandelier dragons swirled around him as he could only just stand there, as if in a deep trance. He pondered the thought if he should join Xanthus to the great oblivious.

A horrendous thought suddenly unburied itself from his mind. What if they were walking into a trap? What if Cethios had this all planned out? Could their very lives be at stake just to save Azalea's?

Suddenly his subconscious mind was brought back to reality as he heard a slight roar right by his right ear. Startled, he turned to see what that specifically was as he saw a small blue crystal dragon soaring by his head. Morpheus opened both his palms as the little delicate dragon landed right into his hands. It gave another small roar as it seemed to smile at him. It stretched its wings as it then took off with the rest of the crystal dragons.

He stood there confused at the thought for he was once told that they only come out to those who are worthy of their touch. Only those worthy to see the diamond that lies within the center of the dragon, only royal blood he thought. He stood there confused at that thought and on the thought of his future and fate. He stood there with much to ponder over, if he rightly was a true friend.

Fearless

4

Xanthus was out in the barn with Cetus and another enchanting dragon. The other dragon was just as enormous as Cetus. She was brightly colored an almond hue with copper adjacent on the edges of her scales. Her name was Kaya and she was James' dragon. Kaya stood there as pride and great courage seemed to flow within her and around her.

Xanthus was quickly pacing between them both as he checked the straps of the saddles. He wanted to be sure that they were tight and secure for the journey. He seemed exhausted as he ran back and forth between them. Moments later as he finally seemed content with the saddles he sat down on a barrel to catch his breath.

As he had a few moments to himself he glanced over to a small hay pile on the side of the barn under a small window. Briefly he gave a long low sigh, for he remembered when he first laid his eyes upon Azalea, and how he mended her wounds. She was still unconscious at that time, when he glanced at her beauty. He remembered how he so desperately tried his best to mend her wings, ankle and wrist, and how they fought with their swords together. For a brief second, more tears filled his delicate sore eyes. But he denied them the freedom of leaving and falling down his face. A small smile cracked upon his face as he remembered how Azalea had sliced his shirt in diagonals.

Just before he could remember any more, James walked into the barn. As he walked small pots and baskets filled with food and supplies floated behind him. Xanthus stood and seemed confused as he replied sternly, "I don't think that we will be needing so much food for the journey. We can just hunt for it if we really need it."

James laughed at his remark, "My dear Xanthus, you have not traveled into the lands of Urinia, the city after crossing The Great River of Anusuma, have you? There will be nothing to drink nor to hunt until you reach the city. Preparing yourself for a light journey will reveal to be foolish. Let me ask you. Have you ever experienced a deep quench from your inner soul, screaming through your severely parched lips? So parched that your skin and throat become so brittle that your own surrounding existence becomes a mirage?"

Xanthus stood there confused in slight discomfort. He shook his head as he replied hesitantly, "No, no I have not."

"Do you then still question my methods of packing?"

Xanthus shook slightly as chills spread down his skin; for he had never experienced the dry humidity of the desert environment before. He gulped hard and nodded with appreciation, "Shall I tie some of that to Cetus?"

James smiled and nodded to Xanthus' question. James replied with authority, "Once in the city of Urinia you can trade some of your coins that I shall give you for food or supplies. If you take your coins I'm sure they will question on the where about from which you got them from, just to be on the safe side."

After that being said they quickly finished preparing their things and their dragons. Moments later after they were satisfied with their packing, they exited the barn only to see that the sun was starting to set behind the world. The day had pushed itself ahead as the night started to approach the sky. And as they both jumped onto their dragons they heard a thunderous roar behind them. It was Morpheus and Orion, and by the look of it they too seemed packed for a long journey. Xanthus glanced at him momentarily without saying a word as he turned his gaze towards James, who needless to say was smiling uncontrollably. Xanthus turned back to Morpheus and replied, "It seems as if you are packed for an excruciating journey."

"Yes I have, with James' help. I think I am very well prepared."

"You don't have to venture with us Morpheus. This is not an obligation for you."

"Obligation?" As Morpheus replied that word back, Xanthus had realized what he had just said.

Xanthus took in a deep breath as he replied without even glancing up, "Look, you know that's not what I meant. I just…"

Morpheus quickly interrupted him, "You don't have to explain anything to me. Xanthus, I am here because you have never abandoned me in the decisions that I have chosen to follow at times. No matter how much fear over comes my soul I must learn to conquer it, so I can therefore achieve my goals and that way, I am stronger on the inside. Fear is only my subconscious mind that fears for my wellbeing. But I assure you, I will not let fear itself come between my actions and my thoughts." Morpheus smiled with pride as he finished. And deep down inside of Xanthus was the overjoyed thought that he would be joining them.

Xanthus suddenly frowned as he glanced back at James, who once again was beaming with pride and a heavy smile. Xanthus mumbled to James, "And I'm sure Morpheus came up with that all on his own, without any of your help."

James gripped Kaya's reins tighter between his fingers as he replied shyly, "I simply only give advice, I give no orders. I share my knowledge with others but, it is in them themselves who choose to follow it or not. You can never control anyone else's decision but merely your own. Persuasion is deeply within the mist of one's own judged words."

Xanthus gazed at James as he continued to grin. He then sighed and looked into the sky as he replied to them both, "Alright then, the days will only continue to flow, they will not stop for us therefore we must be off. James, will you guide us and lead us there?"

James bowed his head with gratification, "It shall be an honor to take the lead."

With that being said their dragons took off with one mighty leap into the misty air. And just as they entered the majestic sky it seemed to open up to its milky galaxy, filled with wondrous stars.

Faith from Within

5

Two nights had pasted since they ventured off as they flew without sleep and now entered the third day. They had already crossed over The Valley of Melinatha and The Great Plains of Oasia. They were now nearing the castle of Whisperia as dawn started to approach them. James and Kaya were a bit in the lead as the rest flew behind. James' energy globe started to dim as the sun's rays now poured over them. James slowed down as he shouted to Xanthus and Morpheus. "We should truly sleep during the day. For the night is when we really need to be alert!"

Xanthus himself could barely keep his eyes open. He shouted back to James, "Very well, but only for a couple of hours, after I insist we pursue on!"

They descended down as they landed near a dense part of the jungle. They quickly jumped off as their dragons checked for any other fairies or elves that were in the area. Once they were certain it was only them, they prepared for camp and a short nap. Their dragons quickly morphed into their animal form. Orion and Cetus morphed into leopards as Kaya morphed into a magnificent wolf. All three creatures took off together scouting the lands for food. Morpheus started chopping wood down for a fire as Xanthus set up a small table with food. On the other side James started setting up a small tent. Within minutes everyone was enjoying a satisfying meal of banana bread, cinnamon bacon and energizing blueberry tea. After they were satisfied with their portions they placed their belongings back into their packs.

Morpheus decided to take up his spare time by venturing out around the area. Xanthus quickly fell asleep by the fire as James decided to meditate nearby. About two hours later Xanthus was awoken by Morpheus, who was vigorously shaking him. Morpheus softly whispered, "Wake up, there's something I think you need to see."

Xanthus quickly and quietly got up and placed his boots upon his feet. They both glanced over to James who was still peacefully meditating by the fire. Morpheus whispered as he pointed to James, "Should we advise him?"

They glanced back towards each other as they simply shrugged their shoulders. They left quickly without making any sound. But as soon as they vanished between the jungles' leaves, James opened his eyes with a wide grin.

Xanthus followed Morpheus as he noticed that the jungle surrounding their skin was getting denser and thicker. They jumped over wide rotting logs, dodged thick branches and pushed away heavy vines. It was moments later that the air around them started to smother their breaths. And just before the heavy humidity almost forced them to cease their breathing, they reached a clearing.

Once in the clearing the air around them was very light and sweet. Surrounding the clearing were beautiful pink and blue flowers of different sorts. Small ruby colored hummingbirds jolted around the flowers as their humming soothed their inner hearts. In the middle of the clearing was a vast gazebo with pink flowered vines hanging from the inside the ceiling. Surrounding the gazebo was a small pond with large orange corral fish jumping enthusiastically over small pearl white water lilies. A soothing waterfall fell over the top that drizzled over the gazebo as the water in turn bounced off of the ceiling and fell into the pond below. They were in awe as Morpheus insisted with a whisper, "That's not all of it, come, follow me inside."

They both headed over to the gazebo as they jumped from stone to stone that was in the pond that lead to the entrance. Once they entered water drenched them as it also drenched the entry way. Once inside they saw all of the magnificent carvings of creatures on the ceiling and posts. As they pushed aside some of the flowered vines, they came upon some things that hung from it. There intertwined in the vines were three golden feathers. Xanthus stopped in front of the vine as he carefully freed the feathers from the vine. He held them within his fingers as if they were something of delicacy. Morpheus stepped closer to him, "You know, those feathers are not just from any creature. They have some sort of shimmering glitter to them. You know whose those are from, don't you?"

Xanthus remained speechless as all he could do was hold the feathers delicately in his hands. He replied softly, "Of course, I could tell whose feathers these are with my eyes closed." With a sad look upon his face he whispered under his breath, "Azalea."

Suddenly someone stepped through the water into the front entrance of the gazebo. The two elves quickly drew their swords and were prepared to fight. But briefly after they did, they realized it was only James. Xanthus quickly replied, "James you startled us. We thought you were still meditating by the fire."

"I was, that is, until I realized just where we exactly were."

Xanthus and Morpheus placed their swords back onto their sides as they continued to look around. Morpheus replied to them both, "I want to take a closer look at our surrounding area outside. Give a shout if you need me." Xanthus nodded as Morpheus quickly took off through the fall. Moments later you heard a loud splash nearby and shouts of laughter. He had indeed jumped in the pond to cool off.

Xanthus on the other hand smiled to himself, but deep inside he knew he couldn't join him. He was still grieving from the loss of losing his love, Azalea, to Cethios. He forbade himself from enjoying the surrounding area. Xanthus glanced at James whom was inspecting the hanging vines from the ceiling. Xanthus slowly walked up to him as he handed him the feathers. James took them in his hands slowly as he sighed, "Ah, you have found some of Azalea's feathers."

Xanthus seemed confused as James gave him back the feathers. He glanced around and asked James, "What is this place?"

"This, this is the gift that the gardeners made and then gave to Azalea. It was a gift for her coming of age. I heard though that it was well crafted, and I can see that words don't do it justice. Well, such a finding we have stumbled upon, don't you agree?"

"So we are near Whisperia then?" James seemed to ignore Xanthus' question as he turned slowly and walked up to a banister and looked upon its craftsmanship. Xanthus was confused as he stared at James. He wondered if he had heard his question or was simply ignoring him. Xanthus cautiously walked up to James, whom was now sitting on the banister and glancing around. Xanthus replied more firmly to him, "James, how much further to Urinia? I fear that I will not reach her in time. I'm afraid that I will never again see her smile or hear her laughter again. James, how much further? How many more days must I endure wondering if she's alive!" Tears seemed to swell in Xanthus' eyes as he took in deep breaths and attempted to settle the shaking his body was starting.

James on the other hand turned to Xanthus as if he did not hear a word he said. He gripped the banister and leaped off as he landed in front of Xanthus. James reached out towards Xanthus' hands and gently closed them as Xanthus held on tightly to Azalea's feathers. Xanthus' breaths seemed to come easier as he slowly took in deep breaths and as his body ceased in shaking. Moments later James let go of Xanthus' hands as he replied with certainty, "Faith, faith in love, faith from deep within your heart. Your faithful desperation for her keeps her alive. She can sense your determination and that, that faith gives her the strength to carry on and rejoice the new day that arrives with the sunrise."

James opened his wings and gave a small bow. He then flew out of the gazebo and left Xanthus alone. He left him alone with his thoughts. And as he stood there trying to situate his breaths once more all he could do was stare at the feathers within his hands. Moments later he completely opened his palms and let the golden feathers sail off out of his hands. The three feathers soared out of the gazebo and up into the air above.

Urinia

6

The two elves and the fairy ventured off towards Urinia as perseverance pushed them. They soared above the cotton clouds as mist still swept through them. And as the day passed Xanthus grew more restless and discouraged.

As the afternoon drifted on they came upon a flock of Pegasus soaring weightlessly through the air. They formed the shape of an arrow head as they flew. A small pink baby Pegasus flew with the head leader, probably its father. The other Pegasus' were a pure white with hues of pastel pink here and there. As the three dragons flew by the enchanted Pegasus, they did not even seem bothered by that fact. Morpheus was confused and shouted over to James, "James, why are the Pegasus not bothered by the dragons? Wouldn't they feel threatened by them?"

But before James could reply Cetus answered, "Well, the Pegasus themselves understand that, as an enchanted creature we share a unique bond that can never be replicated from any other creature. We do not adapt, the world adapts to us. A respect as well that we share under the guiding sun and the moon. Throughout the ages of the stars we have always respected one another, as have our ancestors."

James had an enormous grin that spread from ear to ear as Xanthus appeared shocked. Cetus had never before spoken to anyone like that before, not even to him like that! Surprised Xanthus replied, "Quite well spoken Cetus, didn't know you had it in you."

Cetus snorted an orange fire ball out of his snout as he turned towards Kaya and then back towards Xanthus. Cetus gracefully answered, "We are in the presence of a lady Xanthus; respectfully all must be well spoken."

They all chuckled to themselves as Xanthus chuckled to his dragon, "Are you attempting to impress our new companion, Kaya?"

Cetus snorted yet another orange ball of flame out of his snout and protested, "I'm not trying to impress anyone. I'm just being respectful and honest."

They all burst out with laughter yet again as they knew, Cetus had feelings of love towards Kaya. Perhaps Cetus thought to himself that they will one day be a couple. Kaya on the other hand turned her head slightly away from them all. But only James could see her true reason for turning, she was blushing slightly.

Moments later they dove for the ground as they glided under the clouds. To their surprise below them was no more jungle. But instead, there was bright orange sand with enormous green cactuses with bright brown thick thorns sticking out from them. The cactus plant seemed to cover the entire terrain. There wasn't a good enough clearing anywhere to set up camp or even land. They were all shocked at the sight. James shouted over the breeze, "Just what I was afraid of! We have no other option but to fly over this. Urinia is perhaps about another midday ahead of us. We should arrive just before night fall. We can rest for the night beside the mountains and enter Urinia just before day break!"

Unfortunately, with slight hesitation but without an option they all agreed to continue on. You see, for the past couple of nights they had persisted on without rest with the idea on arriving in Urinia as fast as they could. Fatigue was catching up with them, and resting for the night sounded mesmerizing.

As the day had finally pasted on and as evening was approaching, their spirits lifted slightly with the thought in resting. The sun was slowly diminishing behind a vast mountain that laid before them, a mountain whose tip couldn't be seen. The tip of course disappeared behind milky white clouds.

They arrived near a small oasis by the mountain as they landed near an enormous boulder. They glanced around as the oasis seemed to be enough coverage for them all. Xanthus and Morpheus started to prepare themselves for a night's rest, while James on the other hand did not take the tents out to prepare. He in turn replied, "We shall be safe for the night under these stars. There is no need for tents tonight. The oasis shall be our safety and will protect us from any other presence but ourselves."

Morpheus and Xanthus both glanced at each other with concern. They sort of didn't agree to that fact but, they trusted James and knew he would not put them in harm's way. They agreed with James then continued to prepare for the night. And after a satisfying dinner they took their sleeping blankets and laid next to their dragons. But within moments after night fall drenched the land, the unsettling silence overwhelmed the two elves. Morpheus whispered over to James, "If you say we are near the city, why aren't we hearing noises from it? Why is everything so still?" James seemed to ignore Morpheus as he started to fall fast asleep near Kaya's warm belly. Morpheus glanced over to Xanthus, whom in return simply shrugged his shoulders. Morpheus turned his gaze back over to James who was awake, slowly fluffing his pillow and blanket.

Without glancing over to the two elves James whispered, "You both will see in the morning. For now let us just rest." With that being said he was quickly off in slumber, fast asleep by his dragons' belly. Morpheus and Xanthus glanced at each other confused. Why was James so comfortable near the mist of the enemy? Once again they shrugged off the thought of being captured as for they trusted James. They too suddenly were overwhelmed by slumber and fell fast asleep near the warmth of their dragons' belly and under the glorious stars above.

Hours later just as the sun started to peak over the horizon Xanthus awoke. He gave a long stretch for his slumber for the night was more than satisfying. As he glanced around he quickly realized that Kaya and James were gone. He jumped to his feet and rushed over to wake Morpheus. As Xanthus pushed him slightly, Morpheus gave a small twitch. He awoke from his slumber sluggishly as he tried to draw his sword. But Xanthus quickly placed his hand over his mouth to keep him from making any noise. Xanthus gave a jerk of his neck towards where James would have been sleeping. Morpheus glanced and quickly realized that he was gone. They both quickly and quietly gathered their things and tied it back upon their dragons' sides. They with took tan bandages and small blades from their packs and started to tie them upon their lower back and ankles.

Once they were done Orion and Cetus morphed into their leopard form. The packs that hung on their sides as well shrunk size. Once finished they started to track James' and Kaya's footprints. Within moments though, they cornered the footprints near the entrance of a small cave. But strangely the cave ended abruptly, not even a couple of feet deep. Confused by the footprints Morpheus replied, "Xanthus, I'm not understanding this. His footprints and Kaya's end right in front of this wall, but…"

Xanthus seemed to study his surrounding, just where the footprints had ended. The idea hit Xanthus like a rush of air as he understood what he needed to do. Then to Morpheus' surprise, he started to push the wall in front of him. Morpheus stared at him with astonishment and asked, "Have you gone mad? Xanthus, what do you think you are doing?"

Still concentrated in his pushing Xanthus replied breathlessly, "Well, if you push this rock near The Caves of Esmera it will…" Xanthus glanced up to see Morpheus smirking at him. It was as if he was laughing at him in mockery. Xanthus quickly took in a deep breath and let it out with a sigh, "Would you just help me push, you can mock me later I promise."

Morpheus still laughing at the ridiculous thought started to push. Moments later after much pushing, nothing had happened with the wall. They were both exhausted and breathless as they both simple turned around to lean on the wall with their backs. Suddenly as they did, the floor in front of them concaved inward as a deep long curved hole opened before them. It also appeared as if water was gushing down it. It was as if it was some sort of slide. Morpheus and Xanthus glanced at each other exhausted and confused. They shrugged their shoulders, what else could they do, so they dove in. What did they have to loose right?

Within seconds they were sliding down this wild rapid as Morpheus shouted with amusement, of course he would. Xanthus on the other hand shouted with horror. They twisted and curved for a few good moments or so as they ended up splashing next to an enormous blue tent. And just as quickly as they landed on warm sand, that's how quickly they stood. They were completely drenched as water continued to briefly gush out of their pockets. And as they turned they noticed that James was standing right in front of them with a white towel around his neck. His hair was wet and combed back as his clothes seemed to just barely be dry. James smiled at them, "Good, you found the way in all by yourselves. I knew you boys would. Did Orion and Cetus follow?"

With that being said Orion and Cetus came out of the same sprout as water gushed out. They toppled over themselves as they coughed and panted. James, of course, found it amusing as he gazed over to Xanthus. Xanthus frowned, "Well truthfully, it seemed as if you had left us there. We had no choice but to find our way ourselves. Were you even planning on coming back to look for us?"

"Of course I was. Why would you doubt me now? One mustn't wake the un-woken in slumber of their mists, especially those who haven't slumbered in days. Entering into a battle that is unexpected with exhaustion and grief upon them will never succeed in their moment of time, when it is extensively important upon their life and the lives of others, especially the life of the one that you love." Xanthus and Morpheus both glanced at each other confused, yet again. James noticed that they were not following his dialect. He shrugged his shoulders and sighed, "Yes-yes, I was coming

219

back for you both. I have set up a tent for you both anticipating your arrival. I have clean dry clothes for you both and there is breakfast prepared."

They thanked him and entered the tent; which seemed to have another opening farther in the back. In the front where they entered was a small table with bread and bacon. They quickly changed and went over to the table to enjoy breakfast. They also tried this juice that James called Milk of Rum. They had a bit of it but, they ended up switching to just water. Once finished they walked over to the other opening of the tent as their leopards followed. Once outside they were in shock, for there before them sat the vast city of Urinia. For they were actually above it sort of speak, they were on top of the mountainside.

Down below them they could see that the city had multiple springs and small rivers throughout the land. From afar it appeared to have gigantic water slides all over the land as a few fairies were riding within them. The fairies were riding on these gigantic leaves through the streams and seemed to be enjoying the rapids. Small willow trees also seemed to cover the land with what seemed to be palm trees as well. Small markets were spread all over unorganized over the land. The markets themselves were small huts that seemed to be made out of some type of bamboo. The food was next to the jewel huts as also the fabrics were next to the herbs. It appeared to Xanthus and Morpheus as if it was a complete mess and unorganized. It seemed as if the jungle had collided with water and sand. Though bright colorful fish jumped with joy in and out of the water from stream to stream. On the edge there were small caves that seemed to lead to another side of the mountain that appeared to be more chaos. With slight frustration Xanthus replied over to James, "Do these fairies really enjoy living like this? It is chaos, absolute chaos down there."

James chuckled with amusement, "Well honestly, your beloved Azalea enjoys coming here. But one can only withstand about a week or two of this crazy madness. You enjoy the great food, the sun, the sand, but then you simply go back home after you can't take any more of it. Come back after a year or so and do it all over again."

Xanthus was astonished that these fairies would live like this. On the other hand James appeared excited and anxious to get down to the city. Then without hesitation James went back into the tent and grabbed a few more things. As he exited the tent it shrunk before their eyes. James handed Xanthus and Morpheus each a brown parchment that was folded many times. He replied to the two elves, "Those are your maps of the castle. The castle itself is a bit further down. You see that mountain to the far left, the one that appears to have holes, that's it! Well, I bid thee good luck, and do be very cautious. I must tend to other circumstances that need my attention; then, I shall find you and join you much later."

With that being said he and Kaya walked up to a nearby palm tree. James pulled on the bark as a part of it seemed to simply come off. As it did the tree seemed to instantly grow another piece. James set it on the floor and stood upon it as Kaya sat promptly behind him. He opened his wings as he and Kaya took off gliding down the sand towards the city.

Ghostly Hand Print

7

The two fearless elves, Morpheus and Xanthus, started to head towards the enchanted castle of Urinia. They walked swiftly in the scorching sand around the city. For they feared that if they entered the city itself, that they themselves might become distracted with all of the exhibits or even worse, become discovered by Cethios or his soldiers.

As it seemed like hours later they finally reached the back of the castle where it seemed to be deserted. For they were in luck, there was no one in sight. But they did find it strange though that there were no soldiers. For you would think that they would cover the entire castle in protection, it just seemed too easy. But perhaps Cethios thought that they would never enter the city without their dragons, or perhaps even on their own for that matter.

As they cautiously stood under a low window near an enormous willow tree, Xanthus withdrew his map from his left pocket. He grunted slightly and replied regrettably, "Unfortunately, we're going to have to split up, James suggested that it would be best. I honestly think it's quite foolish but, he did imply that being alone would be unexpected and successful in finding Azalea. He also implied that once inside, it still remained as if we were on untouched lands."

Morpheus seemed confused as he quickly asked with a raised brow, "What do you think he means by that?"

Xanthus shrugged and grunted once more, "I'm not honestly quite sure myself but, let's do try to meet back here at this location just before the sunsets, if either of us has found Azalea." At that moment Xanthus had spaced out in his own world. He truly hoped he hadn't been too late on saving the fairy that had taken his heart. For without her, he felt an empty and bitter coldness inside him. Without her warm smile and laughter, life seemed meaningless.

After a brief moment had passed him, Morpheus patted him on the shoulder reassuringly, "She will be alright you know, she's stronger than you think."

Xanthus wiped his stressed face as he replied with softness, "I do hope she has not lost her will to go on, or have the idea of doubt conquer her. I hope she doesn't start to consider that I am not coming for her. I wish she knew that I am coming to free her, and that I love her."

Morpheus patted him on the shoulder once more as he replied with confidence, "You need not worry, I know deep inside her subconscious mind and her heart, that she knows we are here for her, that you will never lose faith nor determination to have her back in your arms."

Just as Morpheus finished, two grand leopards came gliding down the sand dunes towards them, it was Cetus and Orion. Cetus quickly replied once he neared them with a growl, "So you expect us to just sit here and wait for nothing while you both risk your lives in there!"

Xanthus and Morpheus quickly both chimed in, "Yes!"

Both of the leopards were taken back by the comment as they growled deeply in disappointment. They had never before been left behind on anything adventure. But as much as they didn't want to admit it, the two elves were better off alone. They would risk them becoming discovered if they had joined. I mean, not very many fairies in Urinia had leopards by their sides.

Once the two leopards took shade and coverage near a bush, the two elves quickly started to prepare themselves under two opened windows. They both removed some rope from one of their side bags and left it to hang low from their side. They both searched the sandy terrain for a small rock. Once they succeeded they quickly enchanted it with a spell. An enchantment that once the rock landed inside, it would seal itself to the ground. The rock would be able to withstand any amount of weight that was placed upon it, and not move from its destined spot it rested upon.

Xanthus chucked his rock with the rope into one of the windows nearby. He waited momentarily then tugged on the rope to make sure it was secure. Xanthus turned his gaze towards Morpheus as he waited for him to throw his. Morpheus took in a deep breath as he threw his rock and rope into a higher window above him. But instead of landing softly on the ground, you heard a loud clash of something probably worth value shattering on the floor. The shattering lasted for about a minute or so, perhaps many things worth of value collided together and fell onto the floor.

Morpheus quickly wiggled the rope as the rock came back falling towards him. He caught the rock with one hand as his face turned cherry red with embarrassment. Xanthus shook his head with grief as he replied, "Perhaps you should try another window?"

Morpheus nodded in agreement as he replied in a low voice, "I think you're right, I'll just keep walking down a bit and… Yeah…" Morpheus was still quite red in the face. He was hoping dearly that he hadn't shattered their chance of not being discovered. He quickly started to walk a bit more around the back of the castle, still staying close to the wall just in case anyone became suspicious of the shattering glass. Xanthus on the other hand, climbed his rope and landed quickly and safely inside before anyone could even tell that someone had entered.

After about a few minutes of brief walking Morpheus spotted a window near the ground. He peered inside and made sure no one was in sight. He threw the rock back to its' sandy ground and quickly placed the rope back in his side pocket. He quickly enchanted the rope to become smaller so therefore it could fit in his pocket. He cautiously opened the window a bit more so he could fit as he swiftly jumped in. As he landed he glanced around the room to make sure it was safe.

The room appeared to be an ordinary bedroom but, something didn't feel quite right. There was a huge canopy bed to the left of him with brown and blue sheets made of what appeared to be heavy cotton. Triangle shaped pillows of different dimensions took up a quarter of the bed. To the right was a large vanity made of what seemed to be bamboo. As a small couch made of brown suede sat next to it.

Everything seemed as normal as could be but, there was something in the back of his mind that was telling him otherwise. He cautiously walked up to the bed and raised his left hand to rest it upon the banister of the canopy bed, and to catch his breath. But when he reached up and out for it, his hand went right through it.

He gasped as he stood back in bewilderment. He tried to carefully grab it once more as yet again, his whole hand went right through it. As panic turned into deep fear he cautiously made his way over to the door. Something was seriously wrong here and he wasn't going to stick around any longer to find out. When he reached for the knob he was surprised to find that his hand didn't slip through but, he was disappointed that it was locked. As agonizing pain grieved him even more, he knew that if he stayed in the room he would be caught for sure. If the bed was simply a distraction of the eyes, perhaps the whole room was as well. That would mean that there wouldn't be anywhere for him to hide.

He extended his right palm over the door knob as his palm started to glow a deep blue hue. He replied in a low whisper, "Swiftly and slowly unlock this door, I wish to be here no more."

The lock of the door seemed to glow a bright red as three small blue flames seemed to escape it. Slowly it diminished to its original dull silver. Morpheus waited momentarily as he carefully placed his hand on the knob. He wasn't planning on burning his hand off. And once it seemed cool, he crossed his fingers and tried to open the knob once more. But unfortunately it still remained lock. "This is insane." Morpheus whispered to himself. How could a door be locked from the outside instead of inside, and enchanted for that matter? Nothing seemed to be worth hiding in here, so what were they trying to keep from escaping out? He slowly placed his ear against the door as he surprisingly heard muffled voices from the other side. More grief filled his heart as he started to feel light headed with the confusion and the fear that yes, he might just be discovered. He whispered under his breath, "I seriously hope that Xanthus is having better luck than I am."

He turned around and glanced at the room once more. It felt pointless trying to examine or even look around for something useful to use, if in truth all of the things that stood in front of him were not existent. What was the point of this room? Still Morpheus took in a deep sigh and tried to ponder on a plan to get out. He glanced back at the window, perhaps he could leave the same way he came in and find another window to climb in. But to his deep surprise he found it shut and higher off of the ground. Morpheus grunted to himself and sighed as he closed his eyes in despair. He replied in a bit of frustration, "Nothing in this room is particularly real, reveal to me what I can feel."

As he extended his right hand forward he opened his eyes slowly. Everything started to lightly dim slowly before his eyes. All of the furniture started to glow as if it was a ghostly image. The only thing that did not dim though was one of the blue triangle pillows that layered the bed.

He stood there confused for a bit not really knowing what he should and must do. He slowly walked through the bed over to the pillow as the mist of the ghostly image of the bed swirled around his body. He picked up the pillow and started to examine it. He wasn't sure if there was a trick to this room or not. Was the pillow a key of some sort, it just seemed just like an ordinary object. But of course he thought too soon, for it seemed to prick his right palm. As he gave a low pitched shout he released the pillow from his grasp as it plopped onto the floor. Morpheus gave the pillow a small kick as he tried to make himself feel better under his whispered words of cursing. He held his right palm dearly to his chest as it throbbed with pain from the deep prick.

Suddenly on the wall in front of him where the bed seemed to rest, appeared an image of a ghostly hand print. Morpheus stared at it curiously as he glanced back to his pulsing and bloody hand. He shrugged his shoulders as he replied to himself, "What do I got to lose?"

He bravely walked over to the glowing hand print on the wall and placed his hand upon it. Brief pain shot through his palm as it vibrated all throughout his nerves. Moments past as he was able to free his palm from the wall and as it surprisingly grieved him no more. As he gazed upon his palm he saw that there seemed to be no sign of him ever having been pricked, or ever being drenched in blood. His right palm appeared as normal as ever.

For a moment he pondered on the thought if perhaps he had imagined the whole thing. But as he glanced back up upon the ghostly hand print on the wall, he saw that there within the glow still remained some of his blood. Seconds within that the blood quickly took on a motion as it started to swirl freely within it, as if it flowed with the mist of the morning before the sun reached the sky.

Moments later the wall started to shake a bit as a door suddenly appeared before him to the right of the glowing hand print. The door opened slowly on its own revealing a dark and gloomy hall as water fell freely along the walls. Morpheus drew his sword as he cautiously stepped inside. Though once he stepped a foot inside, the walls seemed to illuminate and glisten in bright colors as they swirled underneath the falling water. He continued to move forward as the door behind him slowly swung closed. He turned and glanced at the door as he gave a hard dry gulp down his throat in uncertainty. It was too late for him to turn back anyway even if he had changed his mind. He gave a quick twitch of his nerves as he turned around and continued down the lighted corridor.

As it seemed to twist and turn he ascended up small stone steps as the sound of his footsteps echoed and vibrated through the wet walls. He touched the cool falling water with his fingertips as he slowly ran them behind his sore neck. Finally after it seemed like an hour later he approached a cherry wooden door with a small bamboo knob. He cautiously opened the door with his sword drawn as he had no idea on what to expect on the other side.

As he entered the room warm water fell over the doorway as it suddenly drenched over his body. Once inside the door quickly slammed shut behind him entrapping him in the unknown room. He gazed around as he was left in complete awe. It was as if he was inside an untouched secluded oasis. But there was a small dresser and chairs that appeared to be made of bamboo and giant leaves. Small palm trees stuck out of the sandy ground as they appeared to cover the rooms' entirety. There also seemed to be a small pond to his right as a small water fall drizzled over a small boulder and into the pond. On the floor bright yellow sand seemed to cover the entire room as it seemed endless. Morpheus wanted to take his shoes off and enjoy the serenity feeling in the room but, yet again he felt this strange feeling about the room. This room was secluded off for a reason and he wanted to find out why if he could.

The smell of sweet water lilies filled the air as the aroma smothered his lungs. Morpheus placed his sword back to his side as he started to gaze around the room. To his far left were these enormous balcony windows with bright golden curtains that seemed to sway in a soft dance. Perhaps the doors were left slightly opened to let in small breezes.

As he got closer, on the other side of the balcony doors inside the room appeared to be an enormous wooden canopy bed. The turquoise curtains from the canopy bed swayed back and forth with a faster sway that they blocked his view. But he was still able to see that there was someone lying asleep on the bed. She appeared beautiful in her slumber as the soft waves in her hair moved gently with the breeze. As he continued to approach her, he noticed that the enchanting girl had severe bruises on her legs and arms. Her silky tan and blue dress was torn to shreds from the bottom, as well as near her stomach.

He moved the curtain from the canopy bed to get a better view of the girl. He gasped slowly within his chest as he saw an exquisite gem within her navel, as well as an enormous scar from her belly all the way to her back side. He carefully reached over and ran his warm fingertips over the girls' scar and gem. He moved his gaze over the beaten body as he also noticed that the girls' wrists and ankles were in some sort of shackles. "This is unbelievable."

Morpheus whispered under his breath. Moments later after examining the body he moved his gaze up towards her face. He wanted to see who it was that laid before him so badly beaten. As he did though, he stepped back in horror. The first thing that shocked him was that she had an enormous black eye on her left. It was puffed with a black and blue hue.

As for her lips, on the right was a small cut in a slit with dried blood. And finally the last reason that had him in horror, was due to the fact that he dearly knew the girl that laid before him in slumber. He softly whispered under his breath, "Oh no, Azalea."

Being Free

8

"Azalea, Azalea... Azalea!" I heard someone constantly calling my name, as if attempting to bring me back from the oblivious.

I was in a comfortable slumber after much pain and torture that I endured. I didn't want to leave my state of mind, for I feared that if I woke up, it would be Cethios. I feared that he would be wanting to wake me up and torture me some more or worse, for him to finally take me. I replied softly, "Cethios please, I've told you everything I know, I swear. Please leave me alone today. I honestly can't take anymore."

The voice continued, "Azalea, wake up! It's me Morpheus! Wake up Azalea!" I slowly opened my eyes as to my surprise; I did see Morpheus standing in front of me! Was I hallucinating or hearing things? Morpheus stared upon me with disbelief and slight anger. He asked with great concern, "What happened to you, are you alright? What did Cethios do to you?" Morpheus sat on the edge of the bed next to me as he slowly rubbed my scar on my stomach. I could feel his warm fingertips running over the scar that Zethron had given me when he drove that sword into me. I felt his soft fingertips glide over my stomach and over my stone that was on my belly button within the deps of my navel. He whispered through slow breaths, "So, the legends are true."

I felt him gently run his fingertips over the side of my lips and twitched slightly as he touched the cut that stung. Now more so I was concentrating on waking up. I replied to Morpheus, "Morpheus, is that really you? Am I dreaming? How did you find me?"

As I was finally able to open my eyes completely and, have the strength to keep them opened, I saw him looking at me confused. He leaned over towards my feet as he applied pressure onto my legs. I gave a low scream as pain shot through my entire body. I was now starting to feel the old pain resurrecting and spreading through my entire veins and skin. Morpheus replied with concern, "Did Cethios really do this to you?"

I tried to get up and lean forward but, the shackles around my wrists and ankles were held down by chains as my hands laid over my head on the pillow. I carefully licked my dry parched lips as I replied to Morpheus, "Well, from what I can remember, Cethios saved my life from

229

Zethron but, once he brought me here, I... I didn't let him, I wouldn't let him. So we fought, I fought back and then he chained me down and he left me here." I started to bring my subconscious back in focus as I continued, "And, and he will come back. Morpheus we need to hurry. You need to help me escape before he... Wait, you are here to help me escape right?"

"No Azalea, I'm here to just stare at you."

"Well, that is what you are doing right now."

Morpheus grunted, "Shish! Do accept my apology for simply spacing out momentarily. You know, realizing that your childhood stories are actually true, can be a bit traumatizing once coming to the fact that, all of it can really be truth." Before he jumped off of the bed he waived his right hand over my stomach. My clothes started to quickly stitch itself and connect as one whole dress once more.

And just as Morpheus jumped off of the bed Cethios came walking into the room. As the water drenched all over his body Morpheus ducked under the bed. Whew, just in time. Thankfully Cethios didn't see him, I hope. Cethios ran his fingers through his wet hair and chuckled slightly, "Why, I can see that I came in just in time. My princess is now awake."

"Damn you Cethios, you will pay for what you've done to me!"

Cethios continued to chuckle to himself, "Why Azalea, I haven't even done half of what I have planned for you my sweet. Till then, damnation will just have to wait." He came walking slowly over to me as he slipped his shirt off. He flexed his muscles as he untied his sword and tossed it onto a bamboo bench. He carefully took off his boots and socks and left them by the bed. I stared at Cethios' body as I shivered and as my heart began to race. Okay, what was Morpheus waiting for? For him to be completely naked! My deep ragged breaths were going to give away my uncontrollable nerves that subconsciously shook in a natural reaction towards Cethios. This was frustrating indefinitely.

Cethios approached the bed from the other side from where Morpheus ducked from. I once again desperately tried to squeeze my wrists from the shackles but, I couldn't. They seemed to be glued to my wrists and ankles! Cethios started to empty his pockets as he placed everything down on a small bamboo table near the bed. Within these contents were a set of keys and a small crystal gem.

Then after, he unbuckled his belt slowly yet carefully as he slid it off of the loops of his pants. He leaned onto the bed as his fingers caressed my side slowly. He slightly lifted my waist up and as he looped his belt around it. Then briefly he appeared confused. I think he noticed that my stomach wasn't showing anymore. I hoped he wouldn't figure it out. But thankfully he shrugged it off and climbed fully onto the bed from the bottom. He started to kiss my ankle slowly as he brushed his soft hands and his lips up to my thigh. He was starting to rub his hands slowly all over me, caressing just about every inch of me. He kissed my stomach slowly working his way up to my neck. I was sweating from anxiety, fear, and my stupid body's instant reaction for lust.

A small yet recognizable whisper of a moan escaped my lips; stupid instant reaction. I bit my lips hoping with all of my might that Cethios did not hear me, but my dread was confirmed when his lips twitched up in a small twinge of a satisfied smile. I grunted in slight frustration, what in the world was Morpheus waiting for! Cethios kissed and caressed my ear softly as chills spread like wild fire over my skin, curse them. Cethios' soft deep breaths blew passed my ear as he whispered in a soft moan, "Are you ready for the most memorable day in your pathetic life?"

I gathered what courage I had left and half begged, "Why Cethios, why are you doing this? You don't have to do this."

"Oh but I must. Don't worry so much, by this time tomorrow you will feel a lot different about me." As Cethios now laid completely on top of my sore body gently kissing my neck, grief struck my heart, I feared that Morpheus had left me all alone. But yet, thankfully before I could dwell on that thought I felt someone grab my right ankle and tug on it. Suddenly Cethios stopped and turned his gazed over into my eyes with a different concern. He asked questionably, "Did you hear that?"

I felt my left ankle being roughly tugged. Gratification filled me immensely as I quickly realized that Morpheus had grabbed the keys from the table. He was now unlocking the chains from my ankles. Cethios on the other hand seemed to be concentrating deeply on the sound. He started to slowly turn his body and his head towards where Morpheus was. Oh great! What was I to do? I knew I had to distract him somehow so Morpheus wouldn't get caught before he was done. So, I did the only thing I could think of in doing. I leaned up towards his face and dragged my lips across his cheek towards his ear. He turned back towards me confused still

231

as I then placed my lips upon his and kissed him. I dreaded it but, I had to distract him long enough, what else could I do?

As we parted he smiled a bit, strangely enough I actually thought I saw him blush. He let out a deep sigh quickly as he shook his head slightly, as if attempting to clear his thoughts. But he quickly turned his head to the side as his expressions changed. Once again he replied but with more seriousness in his voice, "I'm sorry, did you hear that?"

I smiled and confessed, "Yeah, that's the sound of your body hitting the wall."

He quickly appeared disorientated and surprised but I wasted no time, I lifted my free leg up and kicked him as hard as I could off of me. I sent him flying across the room as he slammed into the wall in front of me. He landed on the floor unconscious momentarily. Morpheus jumped onto the bed almost on top of me. As he unlocked my right hand from the chain I stressed out, "Well that sure took you long enough!"

"Hey, I was aiming for the element of surprise and aiming for the keys!"

As I saw Cethios get up from the floor I shouted, "Morpheus!"

And before he could answer he spun around and wham! Cethios had punched him right in the face sending him off of the bed and onto the floor with a loud thud. Cethios came closer to me and wham! I got a piece of his wrath too as he slapped me in the face! I screamed from the pain that shot through my eye socket! I mean, come on, what did I do to deserve that! Cethios un-looped the belt from my waist as he quickly tied it back into his pants. Cethios quickly reached for his sword just as Morpheus came to and stood up off of the floor with his sword at hand. As their swords pointed to each other Cethios snorted, "So, this is the grand Xanthus that stands before me."

I wondered if Cethios had heard me call out to Morpheus, perhaps his ears were still ringing at the time from me sending him across the room. Morpheus shrugged his shoulders, "Perhaps."

Suddenly they both thrashed their swords together as they collided with bright blue sparks. Morpheus now stood in front of my bed as he back flipped up into the air and onto the bed. He tossed me the keys as he jumped up in the air avoiding a swing from Cethios. He jumped forward and flipped over Cethios' head and landed right behind him. They continued to fight as Morpheus shouted over to me, "Quickly now, we haven't got much time!"

As they continued back and forth with the swords I frantically tried to unlock the last chain from my left hand. Moments later, I was free! Well, not exactly from the original skin tight shackles to my wrist and ankles but, I wasn't chained to the bed. I jumped from the bed and made my way cautiously over to Morpheus, avoiding the swings.

Then I remembered something, I started to frantically look around the room. Morpheus shouted over to me, "What are you doing? What are you looking for!"

"My mothers' sword, I can't remember where I last left it!"

Morpheus stood there for a brief second motionless and breathless. He asked confused, "Your mother?"

Cethios caught him off guard as he thrashed his sword onto Morpheus' blade. That blow sent him stumbling over as I caught him from falling. I asked him as I helped him up, "What's your plan? You do have a plan right?"

Morpheus now stood in front of me as he replied through ragged breaths and with a smile, "Well, I'm sort of making this up as we go along."

"What, are you kidding me! Cethios will eventually overwhelm you!"

Morpheus frowned, "Well thanks for the confidence booster. You really know how to motivate someone."

I ignored him as I tried to open my wings, realizing in frustration that they were still tied together. Suddenly Cethios gave a sharp whistle. I knew at that exact moment who he was calling. And as I glanced behind me I saw that I was standing right in front of the balcony doors. I whispered under my breath, "Oh no…"

Suddenly both of the doors swung wide open as a gust of wind started to pull me out onto the balcony. I couldn't fight it. So, I started to scream, "Morpheus help me!"

The pressure of the wind was so strong it dragged and pulled me without my feet even lifting off of the floor! As the wind rustled all around me I fought to keep my eyes opened to see what was going on with the fight. I couldn't see who at the moment was having the upper hand. Finally within seconds I managed to open my eyes, and I saw Cethios was charging straight for me. I knew I should have just kept my eyes closed.

He grabbed me by my waist as we both fell off of the balcony. And as we fell to the earth below my heart sank into my stomach. So I did the best thing I could think of at that very second besides panicking. I screamed. I screamed with such intensity, that it echoed throughout the whole mountain side.

The Racing Rapids

9

I saw to my horror that we were both falling quickly down to the sand below us. But suddenly Krynton came out of nowhere as we roughly landed onto him. I glanced back up to the balcony where Morpheus now stood and appeared extremely disappointment. Cethios saluted off towards him and shouted sarcastically, "Well that was entertaining, till another day!"

Once Cethios replied those words I saw Morpheus start to cheer and jump around. He then disappeared off into the room. Okay so, what was he so happy about? Here I was still in danger flying over the city in Cethios' grasp, with my wings still tied together might I add.

But just then, an enormous dragon knocked into us. It almost knocked me right out of Cethios' grasp. Needless to say I leaned into Cethios' chest as he dove higher into the milky clouds above us. I hated being so fearful of flying so high up. And with the sound of air rushing past my ears, I thought I heard Cethios laughing. Honestly, what did Cethios find hilarious? The other dragon spewed fire upon us as I felt the heat above me. Great, I swear my eyebrows had just singed off!

Krynton started to swirl around, diving and dodging this other dragon. I started to feel queasy and sick to my stomach, so obviously I had my eyes tightly closed. I wasn't sure how much more of this I was going to be able to handle. And for a brief moment as we spun upside down I dearly clung onto Cethios. I mean, I didn't want to fall off you know. Suddenly I heard Krynton roaring in horrendous pain. I couldn't believe it; this other dragon was perhaps winning. I slowly opened my eyes to see this other dragon. Carefully I took in slow breaths easing my stomach, hoping I wouldn't get sick. I focused my vision on attempting to locate this other dragon and not see the clouds blurring by.

Just then from behind us I heard a familiar voice that made my heart jump. "Let her go Cethios! And I shall spare the life of your dragon!" Xanthus! I spun around to see Xanthus on Cetus and I uncontrollably gawked at Cetus. Cetus appeared so much stronger and more muscular; he had grown since I had last seen him. I'm sure Xanthus must be so proud of him. And yet, my heart took a stabbing pain as I hope where every

Snowfire was, I pray that she would be safe. How much I missed her. And just as I felt a void in my heart from being a part from her, one part was being filled, it was seeing Xanthus. I felt so relieved to see him, for I truly thought I was never going to lay my eyes upon him again. And even though my heart was jumping with satisfaction, my skin curled slightly as I saw that Xanthus appeared to be filled with much rage. I had never before seen him that way, I can honestly say I was quite afraid.

Cetus flew over Krynton with his jaws wide open. Krynton on the other hand tried to swing around and hit Cetus with his spiked tail, but missed. Cetus' jaws landed right on Krynton's neck. Cethios' dragon jolted frantically with pain. His movements ended up tossing me out of Cethios' grasp. I ended up sliding down Krynton's back and down his tail. I held on as dearly as I could to one of his spikes as I shouted in horror. I couldn't hold on so tight, his spikes would have cut my hands up if I would had gripped it intensely. Cethios turned over to see me holding on as he laughed sinisterly.

Xanthus quickly jumped off of his saddle and slip down Cetus' back and over to the tip of his tail. Cetus dove towards my direction as Cethios shouted, "Then you shall have her in pieces!"

Krynton shook his tail vigorously as I slipped off. I screamed through the buttery clouds as I fell to my doom below. I saw Xanthus jump off of Cetus' tail just in time before Krynton locked his jaws within in it. I focused my attention on Xanthus as I saw him drop something as he soared in the air towards me; it was my mothers' sword. Krynton dove for the sword as all I could do was watch Cethios take off with it.

I started to spin out of control in the air as I frantically attempted to free my own wings. Phew, I was getting more and more nauseated as the ground was approaching fast. But thankfully, Xanthus finally caught up with me. I saw him take out a dagger from his ankle boot as he slashed the rope around my wings. We spun in the air as I now clung onto him as I laid on his back and as I wrapped my arms tightly around his chest. I felt him holding onto my arms as I squeezed him, immensely.

Then I heard the unthinkable, yup, he was laughing, uncontrollably I might add. I couldn't believe him, here I was completely petrified of falling to our doom and all he could do was laugh? I just simply waited for the ground to stop our fall but, this swinging feeling in my stomach suggested otherwise. Xanthus shouted over to me, "Your eyes better not be closed, my love!"

My heart soared with my stomach at the sound of him calling me my love. How much I yearned to hear his voice, to feel his skin touching mine, the warmth of his smile. I hesitated briefly as I continued to forcefully maintain my eyes closed. I couldn't open them. I shouted back, "I'm so sorry, I can't! I'm afraid to look!"

"Open them, but no matter what you do, do not let me go! For this time, you have me!"

Hesitant at first, but nonetheless I opened them. We were soaring through the air as my wings glided over the soothing warm air that smothered our skin. We slowly soared towards the ground as the trees passed below us. We approached this long clear blue stream as Xanthus shouted, "Do you know where we are heading too?"

I glanced around trying to find some form that could remind me as to where we were at or at least where we were heading too. I glanced down and noticed a small stream; a stream that branched out from The Great River of Anusuma. And within this stream I noticed that some of the rocks were twinkling with blue around it. As if they gave off their own energy. These rocks though, were enchanted with a spell to constantly keep these waters always warm and the fish, alive and healthy. A deep spell set by the centaurs. I glanced further up as I saw small twinkling lights between the trees.

Yes, I thought to myself! We were heading to the city called Magnesio, the city of the centaurs. I screamed out with delight, "Yes I do! I actually know where we are heading to! It's alright- were going to be alright!" I knew they will give us safe sanctuary since Cethios will probably be looking for us.

I started to feel Xanthus' heart beats quicken as he replied, "You do realize that we are heading towards that stream that leads to a waterfall, right?"

"No-No, those are the cities express ways. They're like some sort of slides but, of water. No-no, I know exactly where we are!" Then for once, I was laughing with enthusiasm as Xanthus was shouting in regrettable horror. I shouted to him, "This is going to be fun! Just keep your arms to your sides, everything is going to be alright. I'm going to close my wings! Are you ready?"

Xanthus shouted, "No-no-no-no!" Oh well, I did it anyway, if I didn't act fast we were going to miss our opportune moment in doing so.

We darted down quickly as we landed in the warm water with a loud splash! Once in though a gigantic leaf submerged from below us. Xanthus gasped for air as he held onto the leaf. I did as well, we slowly drifted down stream as Xanthus gasped for air, "Why did you do that for?"

"Get on the leaf and I'll show you how this works!" I think I was more excited about this than Xanthus. But regardless Xanthus climbed up on the leaf frowning as a back support formed right behind him. I climbed in after him as I sat down in front of him. The leafs' steam in front of us curved forward to form some type of holding bar. I excitedly exclaimed to Xanthus, "This water way leads us around the city to another nearby city where I know we can find shelter for the night. Then in the morning we can go back."

With frustration Xanthus grabbed my shoulders and turned me around to face him. He half shouted in my face, "What! You plan on going back inside that castle after I finally have you safe with me? You think I am going to just allow that?"

I shoved my wrists at him, "I am unable to reach my powers whatsoever with these on. Not including the ones I have around my ankles! And until I get these off, I will remain under Cethios' control and wrath! I am his, and will bend to his will with these on, are you ok with that?"

"But..." He couldn't even attempt to finish as his face went blank. It seemed as if he stopped being responsive.

I waved my hand in front of his face, "But what Xanthus?" I turned to face what was in front of me, I needed to see what consumed his thoughts; I needed to see what he was staring at. A smile spread upon my face. The wild rapids were fast approaching, I enjoyed this entrance to the city of Magnesio. This, was going to be exhilarating. I exclaimed, "Xanthus hold on!"

We fell down the first fall as we were thrown about here and there through the rapids. The warm water splashed upon us. It was a force that was heart pounding and exhilarating. I had to admit, I was enjoying this. But, I don't think Xanthus felt the same way.

After it seemed liked eternity, it finally became calm. Moments later we floated towards a small beach as our leaf boat melted back into the streams' floor. The sun beside us melted into the trees beneath the earth. As I swam slowly up to the sand I replied breathlessly to Xanthus, "Wasn't that exciting?"

Xanthus slumped over onto the sand as he shook his head. He was still trying to situate his breathing, "You call that fun?"

I laughed at his comment as I leaned over him in the sand. I ran my hand through his wet hair pushing it back off of his forehead. I traced the tips of my fingers slowly down his cheeks as he grabbed my fingers and slowly placed them upon his lips as he kissed them. My heart continued to race but, it wasn't due to the rapids, it was the intense moment I was having with Xanthus. I slowed my breaths as I gazed into his mesmerizing eyes that soothed my heart. Xanthus raised his hand as he placed his warm palm upon my cheek. His thumb slowly rubbed the bottom of my lip as I hungered for his kiss.

I slowly started to lean towards him, but before I could get any closer my wrists and ankles started to burn immensely. I turned from Xanthus and sat upright and glanced down at the shackles, just in time to see them start to turn a cherry red. Suddenly you could see the bright red start to flow through my veins. Something was being spread into my body as it burned and pulsed with intensity. I couldn't believe Cethios was doing this to me! Why? Why!

I stood and stumbled a bit backwards, why I decided to stand surprised me. You would have thought I would have continued to sit but, something urged me towards the city of Urinia, something surged through me. I started to feel light headed as blue wisps floated within my vision. I glanced over to see Xanthus, he walked over to me and took my hands in his. He suddenly grasped the urgency in my eyes as he saw the red poison flowing freely through me. I tried to reply to him, to tell him what was happening but, I was only able to whisper his name, "Xanthus…"

My eye sight seemed to dim as I saw the concern and horror in Xanthus' eyes. Just then I felt the stinging hot pain swell within me as I blanked out almost lifeless, lifeless in Xanthus' warm embrace.

The Silver Fern Emblem

10

Xanthus slowly placed me on the cool sand as he desperately tried to wake me. Realization hit him in an awestruck pain as he knew his attempts were meaningless. There was nothing he could do to wake me. Therefore, he recognized that he himself had to find shelter and safety for the night. Xanthus glanced to the East where small lights appeared between the trees. And as night now over took the earth he knew he had no choice. He had to venture off towards the lights and towards the unknown. But what he did not know was that, it was the city of centaurs, the city named Magnesio. Xanthus replied under his voice, "I sure hope they are friend and not foe."

Xanthus picked me up and held me close to his chest. He carried me over to the city as icy wind started to smoother our delicate skin. Once he entered the forest though, humid air rushed passed us. What Xanthus didn't know was that there was an enchantment in the forest, to keep it warm at night and cool during the day.

Xanthus carefully placed me down right under a willow tree as the shackles on my skin continued to pulse with a fiery hue. Stress and concern laid upon Xanthus' face as he kissed my forehead softly. He whispered, "I shall not abandon you, I will return for you once it is safe. I love you."

He then left with hast as he cautiously approached the lights. But within moments he was able to see small huts made of sand, leaves and branches. There were quite a few of them spread out disorderly. Small fires hovered in the air about a foot off of the ground between the huts. It seemed absurd to think that there would be some sort of order, all off Urinia seemed chaotic.

Just then, two centaurs exited a tent as they walked side by side, conversing amongst themselves. Their bodies were that of a strong fierce horse, with powerful hind legs. Where a neck and head should have been of a horse was a body of that of an elf, from waist up. The male centaur only had a sling around his chest as a bow and arrows flung behind him. His hair was cut short just above his ears as it flowed in the breeze.

As for the female, brown soft fur covered her chest just like the rest of her horse trait. As for the rest of her upper body, it was delicate tan skin. Her blonde hair flowed with the warmth of the breeze just above her waist. Both of their horse parts were that of a chocolate colored horse with black splotched here and there.

As Xanthus hid behind some bushes he could see that both of the centaurs came to a halt about ten feet from where he was. They jolted about and neighed loudly as they turned and galloped to the opposite direction. Xanthus pondered if they had seen or, oddly enough, smelled him. And just before Xanthus was able to move from his spot he heard hooves stomping right by his side. He stood and slowly turned around as he was astonished.

He was already completely surrounded by centaur soldiers with their arrows pointing directly at him. He took in a deep breath as he nervously tried to figure out what he was going to say. Honestly, he was speechless and dumbfounded on how quickly and quietly he was surrounded. Xanthus took in another deep breath and replied with hope, "This night truly is remarkable, wouldn't you agree, under the circumstances that I... I humbly come only to negotiate a safe venture. As I, I am unarmed and truly come to you with only the thoughts of peace."

A mighty onyx coated centaur slowly stepped forward from the crowd of soldiers. He bowed slightly and replied, "Good evening to you sir, remarkable the night is indeed, but as well as your courage. I am Prince Melancton of Magnesio, and I do believe though that you are trespassing on my land and, it seems that you are attempting to enter my city."

Xanthus glanced around as deep down he knew that he needed their help. Also, that it would be impossible and foolish to try to fight all these soldier centaurs alone. He returned the slight bow and gulped hard, "I do apologize with my utter most sincerity for any inconvenience that I may have caused. But, I honestly mean no harm to anyone. I am here desperately in need of help, and for a secure place to rest just for the night."

Prince Melancton snorted and stomped his right hove impatiently. Suddenly another centaur with the same onyx coat but with white spots pushed her way through the crowd of soldier centaurs. Her long black hair flowed with the breeze as a lilac stuck out from her hair. She gasped as she pushed some of the arrows away from Xanthus, as if in disgust. The girl centaur neighed in frustration and replied to the prince, "Father, I have become aware of this situation that you were so desperately trying to forbid me from. But if this elf implies that he means us no harm, then so be it. If his true intentions were the worst, don't you think he'd come with more of his kind. Or don't you think he would have done something else by now?"

Prince Melancton snorted and neighed loudly as the soldiers placed their arrows back into their cases on their backs. Xanthus gave in a huge sigh of relief as Prince Melancton continued, "You need to forgive my daughter Narcissa. She is very bold but, her curiosity one day will deceive her." Narcissa bent her head down low as her father replied directly to her, "You must now go back to where you belong. I will see to it that our guest is well taken care of."

She bent her head down even lower as she gave a low neigh. She then turned around and galloped away from the forest to the huts. As Xanthus let out a short quick breath, he was relieved to see that some of the soldier centaurs started to gallop away. Xanthus replied to the prince, "I am most grateful for your generosity to a stranger but, I do ask for one special request if I may." The mighty prince stood tall as he crossed his arms across his chest. Xanthus continued, "My lady is very ill and needs immediate attention. I left her in the entrance of your city under one of your willow trees. She…"

Prince Melancton raised his hand up silencing Xanthus shortly as he replied to four of the nearby soldiers, "You, brave knights, keepers of Magnesio, go forth and retrieve this maiden in need. Take her to Hypathia's tent." Without hesitation he continued as he turned back his attentions to Xanthus, "Hypathia is our knowledgeable herbalist. She would know exactly what your maiden needs. Therefore we can heal her the best way we can. Now follow me, I shall guide you to your hut for the nights rest. It will be near Hypathia's so you can stay close to your maiden."

Xanthus gave a small bow as he started to follow the prince. It didn't seem like the prince was one for patience or hesitation. Xanthus pondered if the mighty centaur was the ruler of this land, for you would think a king would have confronted him and not send his son to see what the situation was at hand. Xanthus asked, "If you do not mind me asking your highness, you say you are the prince of this land but, is there a king or simply your mighty rule?"

The prince neighed in amusement, "No-no, I am only Prince Melancton of Magnesio. My city needs no king. Our true king is an ancient one, an elf nonetheless. He, Magnesio, bestowed this land to our kind when the earth was yet but a child. He has since moved on with his beloved, traveled far in the East and has never returned. So the responsibility has laid upon us to take care of these lands. Therefore only the bravest, wisest and sometimes oldest may lead our kind onward. That is where I come to place, after my time has come to a close, I shall choose one whom I think, shall lead our kind forward. That of course in my mind, will be my daughters' son, if she ever has one. I shall teach him the ways of the centaurs and he will inherit the responsibilities of his kind."

Xanthus nodded and asked cautiously, "So you will bestow an obligation upon him to rule and not allow him to choose whether he would want to live a different life?"

"It is not an obligation. It is his honored duty, his destiny is to lead his kind. It is bestowed to him as a gift. For the gods above know that he will lead his kind to great victory. It is a fate that is…" Prince Melancton glanced down upon Xanthus whom appeared to be pondering with great concern and sadness. The prince asked, "Are we discussing the destiny of my future grandson or are we discussing the fate that lies somewhere upon your path?"

Xanthus remained quiet with his hands behind his back as they continued to walk. For truly at this moment he did not want to reveal whom he was, Prince Xanthus future heir of Trinafin. The thought suddenly occurred to Prince Melancton as he asked, "I do apologize but, I do not think I ever caught your name."

Xanthus bit his bottom lip hesitantly; there was no shame or wrong allowing the prince of centaurs to know just who he was. Prince Melancton had already offered him and Azalea sanctuary, what could go wrong. But just as Xanthus opened his mouth to reply, a soldier centaur came rushing over to Prince Melancton. The soldier appeared distressed as he whispered quickly and quite quietly a few things into the princes' ear. Prince Melancton nodded with sadness as he then clapped his mighty hands together. Suddenly two other centaur soldiers came out from behind Xanthus and over took him ever so effortlessly as they tied his hands behind his back. The prince replied regretfully, "Take him to see Hypathia."

Xanthus attempted to free himself as he shouted, "What have I done? Wait! What have I done!" As they carried Xanthus, whom continued to struggle, you were able to spot an immense difference in their strength. Xanthus appeared fragile and breakable under the centaurs' grasp.

Moments later they pushed Xanthus into a small warm hut. The inside was lined with some type of dark fur as a small fire hovered just about a foot off of the ground within the center. Small shelves filled the hut as on the shelves themselves, were a plethora of books and small bottles with herbs within them. By the fire sat a beautiful white centaur as her long

243

white layered hair flowed behind her back as small strands fell upon her face. Her chestnut brown eyes glared at the fire as a small pot hovered over the flames. Next to her lying down on a small brown cot, covered in blankets, was Azalea.

Azalea was glowing a light brown all over her body as a light ivory mist swirled around her, smothering her skin. The blankets seem to cover her entire body up to her chest but, her legs and stomach were not.

Once Xanthus' eyes fell upon his love, Azalea, it was if his world had collapsed above him. Xanthus automatically exclaimed, "What have you done to her! No, Azalea!" Xanthus struggled to free himself even more so with great intensity as anger flustered within his skin.

The centaur woman, Hypathia, pointed to another cot on the other side of the hut. Hypathia hissed with slight anger, "Place him on the cot face down, and remove his shirt."

Xanthus' eyes widen in fear as he shouted, "What! No! You must tell me what I have done wrong!" He continued to struggle as they placed him face down on the cot, not so gently I might add. One soldier centaur tore Xanthus' shirt off and threw it in the fire. The flames consumed his shirt within seconds. Xanthus turned his head to face Hypathia as he saw that she was slowly raising a small segmented leaf from a Silver Fern from the pot. It emerged glistening with an emerald hue as it hovered within the air emerging from the pot on its own. It also glowed with a fascinating cherry red hue around it.

The piece of the Silver Fern started to slowly hover its way towards Xanthus. The centaur woman smiled with a twinge of evil delight and anticipation. Xanthus slowed his struggling as he watched the fern piece slowly start to hover over his back. In that exact moment he knew what was about to occur. He finally stopped his attempts to free himself from the centaurs' grasp, for he knew the inedible was coming and there was no use in struggling any longer. It was pointless in trying to escape. He closed his eyes tightly, grasped the cot firmly within his grasp and clenched his teeth.

Suddenly through gritted teeth he grunted fiercely as he attempted to hold in the agonizing discomfort that desperately wanted to escape his throat. But within seconds the inevitable finally occurred, he couldn't hold on to his strength any longer, he shouted in horrendous pain as the scorching Silver Fern embraced his delicate skin on his back. His skin burned with pain from where the piece had landed on. Though within seconds, agonizing pain shot through his whole body as he suddenly blacked out from the excruciating torture from the enchanted Silver Fern.

The last thing that Xanthus saw was Azalea sleeping peacefully, as he desperately hoped that everything was going to be alright. He wanted everything to be alright, especially Azalea's safety. For Xanthus himself did not realize just what type of magic was being bestowed into his veins, as he blacked out from the pain. And now, and forever always, that piece of the Silver Fern was permanently tattooed on his back.

Denentro

11

As I slowly opened my eyes I found a tall handsome centaur man with curly brown hair and emerald colored eyes staring right at me. I felt a bit nauseated and sore all over. I tried to concentrate on who was staring right at me, my eye sight was still sort of fuzzy. Then it came to me, "Denentro!"

I jumped to my feet and gave him an immense hug. But just as fast as I stood, that's how fast I almost fell over. Denentro quickly caught me within his strong grasp, for I was still a bit dizzy. You see, Denentro was one of my good friends since I was very young.........

It was a foggy night and I was riding on Mirage through the forest. I got lost within the mist as I thought I was galloping towards Whisperia. But in reality I kept racing North East of the city. I suddenly overheard whispers carried by the wind as I came to a halt. I shouted out into the mist, "Who goes there? Show yourself! Or you shall face my wrath me in a duel!"

I was scared and frightened to the fact that one, I only had my training sword with me, and secondly, I was alone. I still withdrew my sword from above Mirage as a faint figure appeared through the mist. Once I saw him I dropped my sword. I dismounted Mirage as I slowly and carefully walked over to him. I gave a low bow as I stared in astonishment. Beruchium had once told me about them, how he wondered whether or not they had gone into hiding or just vanished from existence. But at that moment one was now standing right before my eyes.

I replied in a low tone, "Please do so, and accept my apology. I mean no harm to a creature of a respectable enchantment. My name is Azalea, and I come from the city of Whisperia."

Denentro gave a low neigh as he stepped closer. He gazed upon my wings and stared at my golden feathers. He smiled and replied softly, "Indeed, I can see that you have lost your way. The city of Whisperia is about an hour or so away from here. My name is Denentro; I too have ventured afar from my city, in an imperative quest."

"And what is it you are looking for, in this imperative quest of yours?"

Denentro stepped forward and gently placed his hands upon my shoulders, as if lifting me up from my bow. Once I stood on my own I was able to clearly see who he was. He gazed into my eyes as he replied, "To find a friend."

And since that moment on we have been just that. He would come to that exact location where we first meet, and I would then travel to his city. We sort of kept it a secret for I'm sure Zethron would have not allowed it. Mirage would come to the gardens and find Beruchium and he would just know what he was trying to say. Beruchium was more than just a trainer, more than just a teacher, he was my friend. I sighed uncontrollably as I pondered about my friend, I do hope that he was alright at this very moment.

Denentro though, since that very moment has taught me the ways of the peaceful centaurs and their magic. We are actually around the same age, as regretfully I have also found out that he is Narcissa's cousin.........

As I gave him another immense hug I replied to him, "I'm so glad you are here. I wasn't sure if you'd be out of the city on one of your expeditions. But I can clearly see that luck was on my side today. How have you been, it's been too long."

"Indeed it has, I was in another abandon city on an exploration when word came to me by the earth. I was told that you were seen in Urinia. So, I came forth as fast as I could. I hoped you'd stop by and see me but, I can see other circumstances brought you to me on this night." He took a step sideways as he pointed aside me. There on a small brown cot, whom appeared to be passed out, was Xanthus. I closed my eyes briefly as my body felt numb, what have they done to him? Denentro replied, "I have heard of certain situations between the two of you. But what I ask of you is this, tell me in your own words of these endeavors. I want to hear them from your own lips, and not his."

Xanthus laid there unconscious and faced down on the cot with his hands behind his bare back. I forced my tingling legs to move forward as I slowly walked up to Xanthus. I asked Denentro, "Why are his hands tied behind his back? Is that, oh no, Denentro, is that the Enchanting Silver Fern piece tattooed on his back?"

247

I carefully, through fumbling fingers, started to untie the rope from his wrists. Once freed, I carefully pushed his arms off of his back on laid them next to his side. I ran my trembling hands gently over his back as I rubbed his tensed muscles. Denentro walked over to me as he handed me a small bowl with ice water in it, as well as a small light auburn towel. Denentro replied, "Here Azalea, take this. It shall sooth his muscles."

I took the bowl and towel from him with slow deep breaths as I attempted to situate my shakiness. I sat next to Xanthus as I dipped the towel into the iced water. I slowly rubbed the cool towel on his back. I bit my bottom lip gently in frustration, he didn't deserve this. He had done nothing wrong. Poor Xanthus, he gave a low soft moan as the cool towel touched his skin. I asked Denentro, trying not to sound too angry, "Why was this placed on him, did you not take his word."

Denentro frowned in sorrow and in regrettable guilt. I could see the apologetic look swirling in his eyes. He sighed, "Whether or not they did or did not, this was by choice of Hypathia. Her truth spell was embedded into him. Once he lost consciousness, and once his honest words started to escape his lips, I had arrived. If I was here a few moments sooner I would have been able to intervene but, I arrived seconds too late. His subconscious mind with the spell, reveled the truth of his actions and thoughts."

I choose to ignore him momentarily. I mean, I know what spell was placed on him and what it does but, poor Xanthus. He endured horrendous pain as the magic swept into his blood stream. But I mean then again, I trust these centaurs, and I was out of it. I was out under Cethios' wrath and unable to speak or do anything myself. Stupid shackles. I'm sure Hypathia was doing what she thought was right, and being cautious.

I continued to dip the towel into the bowl and rub it on Xanthus' back. Denentro neighed softly as he replied with concern, "Azalea, we need to talk. Please join me outside for a brief moment will you." I guess I appeared frustrated as I still continued to ignore him. What can I say? I was still struck with pain knowing that my love had to go through this horrendous discomfort. He continued, "You used to confide everything to me. What difference does it make now? He has already told us everything. He is Prince Xanthus, heir of Trinafin. He is not here to harm any of us. He has told us about the same gem you have, and that he shares one of the same. He has told us his thoughts about the legends he was told as a child, and how he has implications, and it involves you two. And let's not leave out the part where you two have mated in the Caves of Esmera. That was too well detailed for my taste. I needed not to hear about your endeavors of pleasures, although Hypathia did get a kick out of it."

My mouth automatically dropped open in shock and in embarrassment. I could feel the heat rising to my face as I blushed regrettably. He chuckled briefly but continued, "Also, he replied that he is trying to free you from Cethios' grasp. Now, I don't know about you but, to me that sounds like a lot for just a couple of months. Now, I would love to hear your side of the story. Especially since Xanthus does not know what specifically happened between you and Cethios. What happened to our old friend? Have I been gone that long?"

I gulped hard, "Well, the only thing left to say is that..."

"Is that the legends are true. And that we have much to discuss in such little time that we have. But, I do not know about those shackles that are bestowed upon you."

"Did Xanthus tell you about these as well?"

Denentro laughed, "No, I can visibly see that they are upon your ankles and wrists." I gazed upon them and sighed with a half-smile. I guess I did have much to tell him. Denentro replied, "Come, the prince shall be alright. He should be waking up any moment now anyway. Come, please, let me also explain what herbs Hypathia has given you, and what herbs you can continue to take. Therefore, we can dull the magic that Cethios is inflicting on you with those shackles. Therefore, his deadly magic cannot inherit your delicate skin."

I nodded. I turned from Denentro momentarily as I bent over and slowly kissed Xanthus' back. I placed my forehead to his briefly; please don't wake up in anger, I thought. I couldn't bear the thought of him becoming angry at the centaurs or worst, with me.

As I stood I realized the words that Denentro had said. I remembered James' prediction, on how he foretold that death will one day kiss my cheeks but would not inherit my soul. I smiled to myself knowing that I had cheated death, twice now. I followed Denentro out of the hut but, I stopped at the door and glanced back at Xanthus. Denentro slowly took my hand carefully within his as he replied, "Come, do not worry about him so, he shall be alright. I'm sure he is going to wake up in resentment anyway for the fact that we did that to him. But, we just had to know; for once my kind found you in the state you were in, my kind just didn't know if he had done that to you."

I nodded, "Thank you, I do appreciate it very much. I quite agree, I'm sure he's also going to be enraged once he finds out that- that Silver Fern piece is permanently tattooed on his back."

We both chuckled together as we exited the hut. I started to unravel my story to him about what had happened in my life since that day I had spoken with King Duralos. But as I got to the part where Mirage had taken me out of the castle, I of course asked, "By the way, have you seen him? I've been meaning to thank him for..."

Denentro's eyes almost instantly glazed up as his expression sadden. He replied softly, "You haven't been back to Whisperia since that day, have you?" I shook my head in a solemn no as grief crawled over my very skin, what was he meaning by his words? I was not understanding. He softly whispered the worst news I had ever heard, "Prince Mirage died that day; he was slain hours later by Zethron himself. I arrived just moments after he removed his sword, moments to see him and Cethios run off; just as the cursed rain of immortal life fell upon them both."

I fell to the floor and released a low scream as golden tears flowed down my cheeks. My hands uncontrollably found their way through my hair making their way down to the side of my neck. I rubbed the back of my neck, soothing myself I rocked back and forth. I stuttered between short breaths, "Why... I could have prevented... I could have stopped it or... Saved him... He didn't have to sacrifice anything for... I loved him..."

As I continued to cry the clouds above us opened up their gates and started to pour. It rained in memory of Mirage's life for the spirits above knew I was mourning one of their own. Denentro gave a low neigh as he sat next to me and placed his warm arms around me. I sank into his strong smooth chest as the overwhelming feelings overcame me. I cried as I mourned the death of one of my beloved friends.

Mirage knew all along about the spell, the spell that was placed upon him if he ran away from the castle. He knew his life was doomed if he did. And yet, even after all of that he still took me away from the castle. He still placed my life first before his. He saved mine knowing his was going to be taken from him. He ended his life to keep my life on its path to its destiny.

Conflict

12

Xanthus opened his eyes as he automatically placed his hands on his pounding forehead. He released a low moan as his whole body ached with pain, especially his back. He sat up as he rolled his neck around and stretched his back. He glanced over to the cot where Azalea had laid but, he saw that she was gone.

He stood slowly and wobbled a bit, his intentions were to find his love and head out back to the city of Urinia. He groaned, he also had to find Morpheus and James. What a night. He glanced down and frowned, and he had to find himself a shirt. As he started to head out of the hut Narcissa came walking in slowly. She was carrying a small cup with ice in it. Narcissa attempted not to stare at Xanthus' bare chest but failed, she eyes him shyly, "I brought you some ice to chew on, to ease your pain. I want to apologize for what was brought upon you. If I was here, I would have been able to prevent the spell and the…"

Xanthus glanced around not really seeming interested in Narcissa. He interrupted her, "That's great thanks, where's Azalea?"

Narcissa seemed startled once that name escaped his lips. She neighed softly agitated, "Azalea? That was the maiden who was with you?" Narcissa appeared to fluster with anger momentarily as within moments she composed herself and forced a smile upon her face. She placed the cup of ice down as Xanthus was not even interested quite the least in taking it. Narcissa with took a nearby shirt that was left for him and held it in her grasp. She held it out for Xanthus to take. He hesitated, this gesture seemed more than just handing over a shirt. Xanthus grunted he needed the shirt nonetheless, so he quickly took it. He shoved his arms though the sleeves and started to button it up. Narcissa remained staring at him as she silently burned with furry. She was extremely jealous of Azalea and she wanted to take everything she had for herself. Narcissa neighed lowly as she asked Xanthus, "Does Azalea have your entire heart?"

Xanthus rolled his eyes. He snorted, "Of course, she is my…"

"Is she your true maiden, your fiancée?" Narcissa stood in front of Xanthus and locked her eyes with Xanthus'. She slowly ran her fingers over Xanthus' shoulders and down his chest.

Xanthus stared blankly at her, compelled by some sort of ancient magic, holding his gaze, igniting his senses. Knowing what was happening, Xanthus forced his eyes to blink as he shook his head, receiving an epiphany and realization. He had to get out and away from this centaur. He pushed her fingers aside. Narcissa continued to try to seduce him as he replied to her, "She is not my fiancée, not yet, but…"

"There is no but, either she is or isn't. Hmm, why don't you just sit back down and relax. Allow me to heighten your senses beyond incredible measures." She leaned closer to Xanthus to kiss him as she closed her eyes.

Xanthus on the other hand glanced around the room confused. What was this centaur trying to pull? Was she truly serious, did she not know who he was? Why was she so desperately trying to throw herself at him? Xanthus leaned back away from her as he carefully grabbed her shoulders and pushed her lightly away. He replied, "Narcissa, I'm flattered but, this is not going to happen…"

Narcissa opened her eyes bewildered and distraught. No one has ever denied her wants before. She was hurt, "Why? What's the problem? She isn't your princess!"

"You're right, she's not my princess. But, I do plan on making her my queen, my wife, one day."

Narcissa neighed loudly in rage, she took a step back and stomped her hove, almost like a child. Xanthus raised an eyebrow up in disbelief, this centaur was impossible! Xanthus smirked to himself, he needed to go find Azalea. He glanced once more at Narcissa then slowly walked around her as he exited the hut. He left Narcissa alone in the hut to fester up whatever emotions she was feeling.

He now stood outside of the hut as he immediately located Azalea. She was sitting by a small hoovering fire with a male centaur. Xanthus stood there watching them, talking, laughing and enjoying each other's company. Suddenly goosebumps over took his skin as he heard Narcissa behind him reply almost in a soft baby voice, "You see, she doesn't truly love you. How easily does she dismay your suffering as she spends her time with someone else."

Xanthus turned to her and smiled and hissed through his teeth, "That is where you are wrong."

*****

I looked up to see Xanthus walking over to Denentro and myself. And as I stood so did Denentro. I replied to Xanthus once he was in hearing distance, "Xanthus are you alright? I was about to go into the hut in a few moments and…"

Xanthus quickly glared over at Denentro, it was as if he was jealous of some sort. He rolled his eyes back to me as he raised an eyebrow and interrupted me, "Who's this?"

"Xanthus, this is one of my good friends. His name is Denentro."

Denentro walked up to Xanthus as he gave a low bow. Denentro replied, "It is a pleasure to meet the heir of Trinafin. Please, do take my place next to Azalea. I must excuse myself; I have a few things to tend to before I venture out. Daylight approaches very soon, truly it was a pleasure." Denentro bowed yet again as he turned and gave me a warm smile.

He galloped away as I walked up closer to Xanthus and replied, "There is a hut up ahead where we can get some supplies before we head out. We will be traveling back up to Urinia through the waterways with a raft that Hypathia has for us. Once there we can try to ambush Cethios alone and have him release these shackles. But we must make hast and try to find Morpheus before…"

Xanthus interrupted me as he eyed me cautiously, "So, what were you and that centaur talking about?"

My mouth dropped in frustration, was he not listening to me? As I looked at him blankly I wondered if he was even concerned about Morpheus. Why was he more interested in Denentro and me? There was something wrong with him. I crossed my hands over my chest as I asked, "Why does that matter right now? That is not what is important. What's important is…"

Xanthus clenched his fists tightly by his side and interrupted me, "Azalea, I shall only ask you once more, what were you both talking about?"

I was lost within his words. Why was this bothering him so much? Was he not concerned with Morpheus' safety right now? Cethios knew Morpheus was running around the castle! But just then, I figured out why he was so flustered with jealously and filled with anger. I saw Narcissa's

253

shadow behind him as she came into view. She probably manipulated his mind a bit with the ancient magic of the centaurs. Of course she would. She placed her hand upon Xanthus' shoulder and replied with sarcasm, "Oh no, are you both arguing? Tisk-Tisk, what a shame to ruin such a relationship over something so pathetic. Well, what I mean to say is, did I interrupt something of importance?"

Xanthus pushed Narcissa's hand away as he rolled his shoulder as if freeing it from her grasp. Xanthus shook his head and ran his hands through his hair, he closed his eyes and took in a deep breath. He was mentally fighting her manipulation. I turned my attention to Narcissa as I gave her a stern look, "Why Narcissa, what not a pleasure in seeing you again. Still roaming the lands manipulating others to care for you instead of allowing free will to take its place. Afraid no one will?"

Narcissa glared at me as she stomped her hoof. She neighed lowly as she opened her mouth to reply but, I interrupted her before she could, "Narcissa save your breath, it's not meaningful to me." I turned my stern glare to Xanthus and continued, "So, here is the true reason why you are upset with me... Your heart has doubt, somewhere. It doesn't have to be massive, but, it's barely enough. That is why you can be slightly manipulated by Narcissa's ancient magic. She's in your mind, confusing it. Xanthus my love, did I not give you my word in always remaining honest and faithful to you? Are my words and love meaningless to you, do they mean nothing? How can you so easily dismay my trust and commitment to you? How can you forget my promise to you? How can you forget our binding to each other in The Caves of Esmera? It breaks my heart how easily you can dismay it."

Xanthus eyes welded up in regret. He tried to step forward, reaching out to me but I stopped him. I raised my right palm up as it gave a slight glow. I knew that rain cloud was about to form but with all my might and concentration. I stopped Xanthus and replied, "Stay here Xanthus, stay and continue to doubt my endless love for you. And when your done doubting me, if you ever reach there, find me. I will not be far, for I... I have never doubted you, ever."

Then like a sonic boom effect a white light escaped my palm. That was all I could do really, shine a light like a flashlight, awesome. I took a step back from him as my palm diminished and a little white rain cloud formed and swirled spontaneously above us. I didn't wait for the rain or to see what the cloud would do. I simply turned and briskly walked away from him. I headed for the hut where Hypathia had our supplies. I needed to find Cethios.

Xanthus on the other hand, turned toward Narcissa as he gazed at her with disgust. For he knew that for a brief moment, Narcissa had successfully taken advantage of that miniscule doubt, and had manipulated his mind briefly. He turned away from her and shouted, "Azalea wait! Azalea!"

I was already out of view when he started to run in my direction but, he didn't get very far. He suddenly slammed into something in front of him as he stumbled upon the floor. As he stood he slid his hands over something invisible and cold to the touch. Amazingly enough, my raincloud had turned into a wall of clear ice that now stood in front of Xanthus. Fury engulfed him as he clenched his palms into fists. They glowed a bright red hue as his stone on his stomach burned with intensity. Then with all of his might, he gave one fierce pound on the invisible wall with one of his glowing fists.

Bright white cracks appeared before his eyes as the invisible wall now shattered into millions of enormous chunks of ice and snowflakes. The ice pieces landed on the floor with a thud as they quickly melted. The snowflakes on the other hand slowly sailed to the floor.

Xanthus turned towards Narcissa as she stood there in regret and bewilderment. Her eyes gazed at his glowing palm as they still glowed with an intense ruby hue. It pulsed as Xanthus continued to clench his fists. Still in shock, Narcissa took small steps back as she replied, "Forgive me heir of Trinafin, for my jealousy for your princess. I obviously do not understand the full extent to this story. I underestimated the fate that lies within you both. My place is not here."

She turned as tears fled from her eyes. She quickly galloped away from him. Moments later Xanthus stood there all alone as the suns' rays started to peek over the horizon and warm his face. His palms just barely starting to dim down and fade from his anger. He turned and slowly started to walk towards where Azalea had walked off too. He shoved his hands deep within his pockets in regret as his heart seemed to pound within in his throat. He whispered under his breath, "Oh Azalea, what have I done. I'm so sorry."

The Serpents' Entrance

13

As I reached the hut at the edge of the forest I saw that our supplies were left outside of it for Xanthus and I. Hypathia was in the hut placing some herbs into a small hazel jar. But once she glanced up and our eyes met, I could tell that great concern was upon her. But I wondered what she could be so worried about? I know it wasn't about our trip back inside the castle. I sympathetically asked her, "Is something wrong Hypathia?"

She nodded as she gave a loud gulp. She pushed her hair away from her face as she replied with great concern, "We have found a creature that we believe belongs to you or your friend. He doesn't seem to be feeling quite himself. A true dragon I believe, unable to morph back into his true form."

I gazed upon her face with slight bewilderment. I walked around the small table in the middle of the hut towards the far back. There lying in the corner on some warm blankets was an orange leopard cuddling with its own tail. I gave it one good long look as I realized who I was staring at. As I glanced behind me I saw Xanthus appear into the hut. He slowly walked up to me as his gaze fell upon his poor leopard friend. He sighed, "Oh no Cetus, what happened my dear friend?"

Cetus looked at Xanthus sadly as tears rolled down his furry cheeks. He gave a low whimper as he turned his back on us and rolled towards the wall. Hypathia replied, "We have come to a conclusion that both of his main horns that rest upon his head have been broken off."

I was confused. I remember briefly that in the book that Xanthus gave me, The Legend of the Dragon, I read something about special horns on their head that enable them to morph. I asked, "How do you know that it's his morphing horns that broke? I mean, aren't those horns supposed to be to a point where they're unbreakable? Shouldn't he stay in his dragon form and be the other way around, so that he couldn't transform into his second form?"

Whoa, I think I confused myself! Xanthus though only took in a deep sigh as he bent down to his injured friend. He petted his slowly as he gently stroked his fur. The pain in Xanthus' face spoke a million words, how he hated seeing Cetus this way. He apologized with great remorse to his dragon, "I'm so sorry Cetus, forgive me for leaving you. I shouldn't have just assumed you were going to be alright. I shouldn't have thought that you for sure had the upper paw with Krynton."

Cetus purred softly, "I forgive you, truly it wasn't your fault to begin with. I did have the upper paw against Krynton but, once he was about to fly away we smashed into the side of the mountain and that's when it happened. I was doing so good, you'd be so proud. But, my clumsiness caught up with me. I'm sorry Xanthus, I failed you." Cetus cuddled more with his tail as he scooted more towards the wall.

Xanthus, now sitting on his knees leaned over and hugged his leopard tightly. He whispered to his friend, "No Cetus, you have never failed me. I am very proud of you, for protecting Azalea and me. You are the bravest dragon I've ever known. I am honored to call you my own." Xanthus kissed Cetus softly on the head. Moments passed as he then stood and turned towards me as his eyes glossed over. He whispered softly, "I'm so sorry Azalea, I didn't mean to avoid your words but, for a dragon, when he loses his horns in battle or any other of the sort, for their own safety they morph into their hidden form. That way they can hide sufficiently and protect themselves. But they can't morph back into their dragon form until their horns grow back."

I sighed, "Well how long does that usually take?"

Xanthus shrugged, "It depends on how much was taken off. Sometimes it could end up being permanent."

Hypathia stepped closer as she leaned over and placed some herbs over Cetus, as well as a warm blanket. Hypathia stood and stepped over to Xanthus as she neighed slowly, "Since we found him before the moon vanished from the sky above, we have been giving him some healing herbs with a touch of rosemary in his water. That should quicken his process too, hopefully no longer than a couple of days."

Xanthus turned to Hypathia, to thank her for all that she was doing for his dragon when his eyes truly focused on her face. He froze, she seemed familiar in some way but he couldn't recall. His eyes suddenly widened in remembrance. Of course, he recollected himself and attempted to ask, "Weren't you the one that..."

Hypathia smiled shyly and interrupted him, "That is not of importance right now. Now, you must be on your way to go help your friend. And, try to remove those shackles from your princess. Now, take this bottle of herbs, place it over her heart once a day when her shackles turn a cherry red, only if Cethios is attempting his wrath. It will sting momentarily but, it will melt into her skin. This will allow her to temporarily use her magic before the shackles over turn her magic against her."

Xanthus' hands shook slightly from the anger that festered up within him, knowing she was the centaur that had tortured him not a few hours ago. But, he had to sizzle it down. Now was not the time, and she was helping Cetus. So, after some slight hesitation he took the bottle within his hands. He stared at the bottle as if he was mesmerized by it. Within moments though, he broke his stare as he gazed over to me. I spied him from the corner of my eyes as he stood motionless. I on the other hand, continued on tying another dagger to my ankle when Xanthus slowly made his way over to me. He with took my hands quickly within his warm hands as he gazed into my eyes. My heart fluttered as I gazed into his eyes as they shone with regret and sorrow. He sighed as if coming to realization, "I almost lost you, perhaps more than a handful of times to Cethios' maliciousness, haven't I?"

I nodded slowly with a shrug, "Perhaps a couple…"

He pulled my hands gently closer to him as he dragged his palms slowly over my arms, tenderly pulling me closer to his chest. His arms now embraced me as the warmth of his hands spread over my back and up to the back of my neck, embracing me ever so closer to him. Xanthus leaned into me as a soft moan escaped is lips. The heat of his breath blowing delicately upon the nape of my neck and slowly climbing to me ear had me hypnotized. My breaths deepened as he brushed his soft lips upon mine. His lips curved into mine as his kiss become passionately intense. The vibrating sensation of wanting him closer burned within me as the heat of his passion flowed through my veins. Moments later we parted as my heart raced with madness. He gazed upon my face as he rubbed his thumb over my lips, he seemed surprised and confused, not to mention a bit light headed. He implied, "Your face, it isn't so swelled up anymore. And, your black eye, it's completely gone."

Xanthus slowly brushed his fingertips upon my delicate face. I knew what he had done, I felt his energy flowing into my veins, allowing my body to heal. I honestly felt like I wanted to melt into his arms and stay there, forever more. But of course our moment was interrupted from behind us. Hypathia neighed loudly, "Your journey awaits you. You can take the raft that Denentro and I have quickly built for you both. The stream we have chosen shall lead you directly into the underground of the castle."

We parted and started to pack a few more supplies into small packs of brown rough cloths. And just before we left for the raft, Xanthus walked over to Cetus one last time. Hypathia walked over to him slowly as she placed her palm on his shoulder. She assured him, "There's no need to worry for your friend. Cetus will remain in my care and hopefully within a couple of days or less, he will feel himself once again."

Xanthus raised one of his gorgeous eyebrow and gave Hypathia a solemn look. All she could do was chuckle to herself and bow. He had no choice of course; he had to hope that she would take care of his dragon. Nonetheless, moments later we made our way to a small stream nearby. The raft that Denentro and Hypathia had made for us was floating over the water as it bobbed to and fro. It was the size of a large king size bed as it consisted of six large logs. The wood was smooth to the touch as above it hovered a gigantic green leaf as a couple of vines with flowers on them hung. It served as sort of a ceiling, a protection from the sun. And above that leaf appeared a leaf from the water slides, to conceal us from Cethios and Krynton.

Hypathia gave me a bulky branch to help guide and push along the raft. We quickly jumped onto the raft as we bid farewell to the centaurs. Prince Melancton and his soldiers were there as they bid us farewell and good luck. As we started downstream Prince Melancton shouted over to Xanthus, "Heir of Trinafin, you shall and will always be honored, and welcomed to stay amongst our kind in our village, oh Silvered One."

He bowed and waved good bye as they galloped away back into their city. Moments later once we were out of the view from the city, and sailing down the stream calmly, Xanthus asked, "So, why did Prince Melancton call me, oh Silvered One?"

I smiled to myself as I continued to guide the raft with the branch. I cleared my throat as I turned to face him. I tried not chuckle as I spoke, "Well, during your encounter with Narcissa, she failed to mention something to you of importance. She forgot to mention that you now have an emblem, a tattoo of a piece of a Silver Fern on your back. Permanently embedded onto your skin and within your blood stream, in case you ever encounter the centaurs again. You are actually unable to lie to them, for if you do; your tattoo will burn and will not extinguish its blaze until you reveal them the truth. Now, you can deny them the fact of breathing anything to them, that is your right but, not to lie."

Xanthus frowned as he held onto the vines from the leaf above us. He asked, "Well, I guess that fate has been settled for me whether I wanted it or not. How am I supposed to conceal information from one that is a traitor of their own kind?"

I frowned at his response, "Well honestly, the spell is only really for the one that placed it on you and for the prince of that time, which is Hypathia and Prince Melancton. But honestly, you should know that I have one as well."

And with that being said Xanthus appeared stunned. But within seconds he accepted his fate and composed himself. He seemed to understand as he nodded off to himself smirking. He chuckled, "I should have known, I've seen a piece of a Silver Fern with all sorts of shades of green on your body. If I'm not mistaken, it is above your right butt cheek, am I right?"

My mouth dropped in astonishment. I couldn't believe that he had seen it! It was a bit dark in The Caves of Esmera but, that devious elf. All I could do was shake my head in a small burst of embarrassment. He replied, "I have not forgotten a single detail of that night. I know where my hands and lips were, every ounce of you I have mesmerized. The way your body curved to my touch, the way your skin feels on mine."

Man, are my cheeks getting hot! How intuitive he was. He smirked with contentment; his smugness was getting to his head. I had to diffuse whatever thoughts were turning in his head, we had to stay focused. Of course I would have loved to let myself wander away with him but, that privilege was not available right now. I bit my lip, I had to do something, the tension was rising. I could feel it coming off of Xanthus' skin in sensual waves. I got an idea! I giggled to myself as he continued to eye me. I bent over to the water as I recalled that I do have some sort of advantage to these shackles, my manipulation to water! I am glad I have figured this thing out while I got the chance to, thankfully, perhaps it could come in handy later on. I must try to figure out what else I can manipulate with these forsaken shackles on.

I kept my hand in the water as I swirled my fingers around. I concentrated as hard as I could. Then as my shackles gave a small pressure against my skin, I accomplished my goal! Within my grasp I held a water globe. I stood carefully as it hovered over my palm. I turned and chucked it as it landed right on Xanthus' chest with a splash! I laughed hysterically, that's what he gets for doubting me back there and letting Narcissa get in his head briefly. But before I knew it, splash! I got hit right on the chest as well! Oh, it's on!

And for a brief moment it was as if we had forgotten all of our worries. All of our fears and responsibilities were lost within the mist of time. We played with the water globes free of any costs as we became engulfed in each other's company. We ducked and dodge each other's water globes as suddenly Xanthus knocked me down. He splashed one right on my head as I was now completely drenched with water. Our eyes gazed upon each other as suddenly a perfect moment came for a peaceful kiss.

But of course within seconds, our worry free moment had shattered and came to an abrupt halt as reality caught up with us. Xanthus sat up as I rolled my eyes above me to see what he was staring at. We were just about to enter the castle through this enormous cave, or what was supposed to be a cave. There before us appeared to be the mouth gapped open of a massive anaconda.

The serpents' fangs dripped with yellow ooze as the edges of the mouth seemed to contract to and fro, as if it was breathing and alive. It slowly started to hiss as it opened its deep burgundy eyes to stare at us, briefly. Thankfully once again its eyes were closed. Honestly, the whole thing gave me the chills.

I gulped as we both stood frozen in fear, to stubborn perhaps to admit it, either of us. But as we continued to enter in silent fear, the serpents' appearance continued. The walls of the caves appeared to be the esophagus of an anaconda. It felt so real as a brisk warm breeze past by our skin. Was this a trick to fool trespassers, or was this really a serpents' entry way?

I now stood by Xanthus as I held onto the vines above me. Xanthus still stood in amazement as he whispered, "What kind of entrance are we getting ourselves into?"

All I could do was stare blankly at him. I wasn't sure how to answer him. I knew the centaurs wouldn't lead us down a path they didn't know was accurate. But, all I could do was shrug my shoulders and hope for the best. Everything was going to be alright. I mean, I should keep telling myself that. Right?

The Absorbent Stone

14

The stream that once flowed peacefully under our raft now flowed coarser and wilder. I tied the branch that I had to guide our raft onto the back. It trembled vigorously as it suddenly broke into pieces upon the racing waters. My heart started to pound faster and faster as my breaths deepened within my chest. An icy cool breeze started to pick up and rush past us. The gust became so strong that I was beginning to lose my balance as I got pushed back. I closed and tucked in my wings as much as I could into my skin.

I lifted my arms as I desperately held onto the vines above me. I glanced back to see if Xanthus was doing the same thing and hopefully still there. Thankfully he too was holding on to his dear life! Xanthus shouted, "Do you know where we are going?"

"No! I honestly can say that I don't know!"

"What! I thought you knew!"

I let out a small scream as our raft bashed into a rough patch and as water splashed all over us. I shouted back, "I only know where we will end up in!"

We held on tightly to the vines as we surged down violent rapids. Then strangely enough the rapids grew quiet and calm. We glanced at each other as we laughed nervously. Suddenly Xanthus' expression went blank as a loud rushing sound approached us quickly. Xanthus grinned with sarcasm as he replied, "Should I panic now, or during our descend over the fall?"

I chuckled nervously, "Well, perhaps it's a little fall."

Xanthus frowned at my comment as suddenly we fell. We both screamed as we held on tightly to the only thing we could, the vines above us. We were engulfed in complete darkness as we fell into the oblivious. My body felt almost weightless as it surged down the fall and as my stomach seemed to thrust forward into my throat. I still attempted to keep the vines entwined within my palms, as if that would help. I felt the air rush past my ears as finally, it was over and we hit warm water with a heavy splash.

Within moments we came above the water as Xanthus and I gasped for air. Coincidently we were both faced down on the raft holding onto the front logs as the vines from the ceiling leaf, which wasn't there anymore, were intertwined between our fingers. I turned over to Xanthus as he was now lying on his back taking in deep breaths to control his breathing. I replied breathlessly, "Well, let's look at the bright side, at least the vines held up after the fall."

Xanthus chuckled to himself as he sat up and threw the pieces of the vines into the water. We both stood carefully and glanced around the cave but, that's not what we saw first. Our clothes seemed to desperately cling to our bodies. We laughed at each other as Xanthus only had his sleeves and no shirt and as his pants had now become small shorts. I on the other hand, seemed to have a two-piece dress. Well, my chest was covered and I now owned a very small mini shirt and mini skirt.

Briefly after our good laugh, we glanced around to see specifically where we were. There seemed to be a lot of colorful silk hanging everywhere we turned. We did have to duck our heads a couple of times to avoid the drapery as the raft slowly drifted onward. The silk covered the entire cave as well as the ceiling and walls. Small starfish and shells also hung upon the silk as decoration. Warm steam now flowed just above the water as it swirled around our raft.

Moments later we approach laughter as our raft came to a halt upon some rocks near a shore line. There upon the shore were beautiful mermaids and some fairies chatting amongst themselves. They were all giggling and laughing away deep in their own conversation. Glitter covered most of their faces as did the shells in their hair.

I continued to glimpse upon each face, to make sure no one I knew was with them, when my eyes rested upon this one mermaid. She had curly orange hair that flowed behind her ears. Her hair was all gathered to one side as a glittery blue shell held it all in place. She had clear light blue eyes that somehow reminded me of the morning sky. That was strange, something about her appearance seemed so familiar but, I could not put my finger on it. I had seen her before but, I just couldn't figure out where.

As I shrugged it off one of the other mermaids scream as she saw us. Others gave a small squeal as well until one of the fairies replied loudly, "Ladies don't fright, tis only Azalea, the feathered bird fairy."

263

I gave her a short glare as they all agreed and turned back into their meaningless conversations. Xanthus on the other hand found it a bit humorous. He chuckled, "Not very popular, are we?"

I shook my head, "No, didn't want to be. I avoided this place at all costs but, I did occasionally come to visit…"

Suddenly a mermaid with hair black as midnight and light violet eyes that were a bit slanted, came swimming over to us in a rush splashing about. Her name was Alcina and she was one of my good friends. She is about ten centuries old, still just a child. She had a small pink starfish in her hair as glitter covered that, and as well as her body and fins. As she reached us, she rested her hands upon the raft and replied breathlessly, "Azalea! I'm so pleased to see you! You look, um; well, you've seen better days. Who's this that you brought with you? Can we keep him here, are you in a hurry? Did you really come in through the fall? Wow, you guys are brave…" Alcina turned her gaze towards Xanthus as she started with him and asked, "Do you need help getting to shore, do you swim well? Don't worry it's not very deep from here. But if you'd like, you can hold onto my hand…"

I gave in a deep sigh as I glanced over to Xanthus. I mean, I couldn't explain the energy that she had. All I could do was shrug my shoulders and smile. Xanthus cleared his throat and replied to me, "You know, before I met you, I never had random centaurs or mermaids throwing themselves at me."

I chuckled at his words. We hopped into the water as Alcina swan around us. It wasn't really that deep; it came up to my chest. I released my wings from my back as I gave them a slow stretch in the water, it felt soothing within the warmth. I turned to Alcina just in time, she was taking in another deep breath to reply something but, thankfully I interrupted her, "Alcina, are my old clothes still here where I left them?"

Alcina seemed to ponder as she took a small breath in. She replied, "Um, should be, of course. Would you like for me to go and retrieve them for you?"

"Yes Alcina, I would greatly appreciate it. Oh, and retrieve the second pair as well please, for my friend here."

Alcina smiled widely as she sized Xanthus up with her eyes. She placed her fingers upon her chin as she studied him momentarily, contemplating in her head. She asked, "Do you think they will fit him? He looks a bit more…" Her eyes lingered upon his slender yet muscular arms then traced over his lean yet firm chest.

I interrupted her, "Yes Alcina thank you."

Alcina smiled contently as she lifted herself up and placed her hands upon Xanthus' smooth chest. She replied to him, "I wonder, what's you name oh shiny studded one." With that she jumped up and back flipped into the water.

Xanthus jerked his head back as he asked me confused, "Friend? Shiny studded one?"

I shook my head as I glanced slowly down at his bare chest, gazing upon every ripple of lean muscle within his abs and down to his stone on his belly button, within his navel. It shone a light purple hue. I couldn't help but to laugh at him. Xanthus blushed slightly and pointed to me, "Well I wouldn't be so confident that I'm the only one glowing. You are as well."

Sure enough I glanced down at my stone, it too was releasing a light purple hue. Wow, how embarrassed I felt. Xanthus replied, "So, do you need help swimming to shore, or are you able to manage all by yourself this time?"

I rolled my eyes over to him as he smirked to himself. Of course he had to bring that up. I smiled to him as I suddenly pointed to the other direction with a blank expression. Ha! He fell for my trick as he turned to see what I was pointing at. That's when I had my opportune moment. I jumped up and pushed his head down into the water! Yes! I had another opportune moment as I swan for shore. My goal was to beat him there.

But unfortunately, I wasn't fast enough with my wings. Xanthus caught up as he jumped onto my back, sending me splashing into the water. As I came back up, he helped me regain my footing. We gazed into each other's eyes as we laughed. Xanthus wrapped his arms around me as he leaned in slowly and kissed me, ever so delicately that I felt every inch of his lips on mine. For a brief moment, everything was still in our own enchanted time.

Moments after we parted, we continued to swim up to the shore. As we stood there catching our breaths, we spotted Alcina swimming up to the shoreline. As she reached the water's edge her legs instantly morphed into scaly legs with webbed feet. She was scaled up to her stomach.

Alcina handed us the clothes with a shy smile. As Xanthus with took the clothes from her he gave a slight frown, "Thanks but, these are soaked. It will take hours before they dry and…"

Alcina jumped on a boulder near Xanthus as she reached him and placed her fingertip upon Xanthus top lip. As she let go, she whispered, "Watch." She fumbled into a small seaweed bag that hung over her shoulder. She happily retrieved two small clear see-through stones. She held them between her fingertips as if they were a delicate feather. She handed one to Xanthus then one to me. She turned back to Xanthus and replied, "Once you are out of water in a dry place, place that stone upon your wet clothes."

Xanthus stared at her confused, "Then what?" Alcina giggled as she back flipped off of the boulder and into the water. Confused even more, Xanthus turned to me and replied, "She didn't answer my question. I'm still not understanding what this little rock has to do with drying my clothes."

I laughed at his words as I moved my gaze towards the water. I hoped that Alcina was going to be alright. I took Xanthus by the hand as we walked over to some small holes within the caves' wall. Sapphire silk hung off to the side of the small entrances. They were small rooms to change into your dry clothes after swimming, or before.

Just before I entered a room, I heard from afar Alcina's laughter. Xanthus smiled at me as I replied, "You know, Alcina's parents were killed in an accident off of the streams. Both parents died from a rock slide that landed into the stream where they were. Others were injured but they, they did not survive. Alcina was left all alone on the sandy beach. I found her and brought her here. I know of a small village of merfolk under the castle. I found a nice couple willing to take her as their own, with the help of James of course. I come by to visit her every now and then you know. She is just so full of life and…"

Xanthus grabbed my arms as he tugged me towards him softly. He pushed aside some of my hair behind my ear with his fingertips as he whispered, "You felt sorry for her because she was left without a mother. You didn't want Alcina to feel abandoned like you felt. You didn't want her to end up alone, like you thought you were."

I glanced away from Xanthus as I withdrew in a breath. I mean, what was he trying to get at? Of course I didn't want her to be alone; it wasn't guilt of any kind. I whispered, "I guess we can both relate. We were both left without a mother or a father, left to be raised by others."

I sighed as I with took the small stone from his fingers. I placed it upon the top of the clothes that resided within his other arm. The stone glowed briefly as it echoed a slight sound as it sucked up all of the water and moisture from the clothes. The clothes now remained completely dry as the stone itself seemed to have a blue flow within it.

Xanthus gazed from the clothes up to my eyes, which seemed to grow with more sorrow as the seconds passed by. He whispered softly to me, "Azalea, you know you don't have to keep it in all of the time. You can confide in me. You don't have to be brave every moment that you have."

He with took my hands as he dropped his dry clothes and stone. The water that was being held by the precious stone was now free as it hit the ground. The water splashed all over us as we both chuckled to ourselves. I replied to Xanthus, "What do you want me to do, break down and cry in puddles and explain to you how my world evolves upon this mysterious puzzle called life?"

"No, not just yet but, someday yes. Will it make you feel better?"

"No, not really but..."

Just as Xanthus started to lean closer to me to kiss me, we heard a small giggle nearby. We both turned and saw Alcina off the shore by a small rock, trying to hide. She replied shyly, "Are you guys going to kiss? Kissing is disgusting, it has saliva and germs and..."

I interrupted her, "Alcina, don't you have other things to attend to?"

She frowned as she splashed back into the water. I turned to Xanthus whom was beat red from embarrassment. He replied, "Adorable isn't she?

He bent over and picked up his clothes and the stone. He then went into a changing room, as did I. I quickly dressed myself as I heard Xanthus drop the stone one more time. I laughed as I overheard the water splash all over the room and, as I overheard him curse to himself. I myself carefully dried my clothes with the stone, changed and tied the front laces of my corset as quickly as I could.

Just as I was about to exit the small changing room, I heard some fairies and mermaids shout with enjoyment and amusement. I opened the curtain slowly to see what they were all so happy about. To my horror I heard a familiar voice, which to be honest; I wasn't quite ready to hear. "Good day my beautiful ladies, I am here to grace you with my presence. Please, do ignore me while I watch such enchanting and lovely creatures."

All of the fairies and mermaids flirted and giggled as one fairy flew up behind him and started to rub his shoulders. Cethios dipped his sore feet into the soothing warm water. I concentrated on the fairy who was rubbing him down. Oh no, it was Razyna! Her pink wings glistened in the reflection of the water.

I started to concentrate on how Xanthus and I were going to slip out. Then I heard something even more frightful, someone replied, "Oh Cethios, you just missed Azalea and this tall handsome wingless fairy. Let me tell you, they looked horrid!"

Panic settled in my skin as I quickly dove out of the changing room and hid on the other side of this boulder. I pressed my body against it with all of my might. I glanced over to see where Xanthus was changing. My heart felt as if it was going to pound out of my chest as I saw that it was completely empty! Where could he be? Did he hear or see Cethios? I pressed my ear against the rock to see if I could hear what was going on the other side. I overheard Cethios ask, "Did any of you beautiful ladies see which way they were heading too, or know what direction they went?"

Another voice replied, "Shame on you Cethios, you know we don't pay attention to that feathered freak of nature."

Cethios sighed with disappointment, "What a tragic waste. I now might have to cut my visit short."

I heard mermaids and fairies whine in grief. I then heard Cethios reply, "Wait a minute, what is that?"

I closed my eyes as my heart started to pound within my throat! I heard slow footsteps come closer and closer. I frantically looked around to see that there wasn't anywhere else I could hide! I was going to be found as fear swelled within my heart. Suddenly someone grabbed me from behind and placed their hand over my waist and mouth, preventing me from screaming in horror!

Maze of Doubt

15

Splash! "Ahhh, Cethios!" Phew, a fairy had been pushed into the water as I overheard everyone laughing.

I turned my head up slightly to see Xanthus. One warm arm was tenderly around my waist and the other now held soft fingertips upon my lips shushing me. How was I supposed to know that he was hiding right behind me! I turned my whole body around to face him as he quickly kissed me on the nose. Was he sucking up to me for scaring the living daylights out of me? He whispered, "Follow me, carefully. I think I have found a way out."

We followed a jagged rocky wall until we came to a tight dead end. It was small enough that only one of us could fit at a time as I now stood in front of him. I turned my head towards him as I gave him a blank look. I mean, what were we supposed to do next? But all Xanthus could do was smile with certainty as he commanded, "Now push."

He extended his arms over my head as he started to push. Was he nuts? I whispered back to him, "Xanthus, are you crazy? This is insane. This isn't like the Caves of Esmera back in Trinafin! You can't just push any rock you want out of your way and expect a hall to appear."

Xanthus angrily whispered, "Would you just help me push!"

I grunted as I turned back around and faced the dumb rock. I stared at it furiously. I mean, what do I have to lose, besides my insanity? So, I started to push. I couldn't believe what he was having me do. I was frustrated, why was he so convinced that this was the way out?

Suddenly to my great and utter astonishment, the rock started to budge. As Xanthus and I released our palms off of the wall it slowly opened and reveled a small lavender lit hall. Small colorful bubbles of all sizes seemed to descend from the top of the roof as they floated down everywhere. My mouth gawked open momentarily as I closed it with a pop. This was beyond bewilderment.

We cautiously entered as the rock wall behind us quickly and quietly closed. The walls and ceilings suddenly lit even more as tall mirrors appeared everywhere, except for the ceiling though, that still remained lit a lavender hue. Though, those small bubbles still seemed to appear out of nowhere as they continued to swirl around our every movement. Xanthus remarked with slight enjoyment, "Well, let's look on the bright side of this situation. At least I can see that you look absolutely stunning in that silver dress. It caresses every beautiful curve of yours."

I turned to see a stunned Xanthus with his hands up in the air, as if in defeat. He seemed innocent enough as he slightly blushed. I smiled and shook my head, he was unbelievable. Of course, he would try to lighten the mood. He of course was stunning as well but, I wasn't going to tell him that. He arrogantly already knew it.

We glanced around the room to see that the mirrors surrounded us. They shot straight up to the ceiling. So there was no way I could fly over this to find a way out. Goodness, mirrors were everywhere we turned! I whispered to Xanthus a bit mortified, "Xanthus, where are we?"

Xanthus frowned as concern now covered his once playful expression. He shook his head frustrated, "I don't know but, we better get going. This is starting to feel wrong."

I slowly walked with light footsteps as I extended my arms outward to feel the cool mirrors. I didn't want to bump into them. I was careful, slowly guiding my way with my fingertip, turning every corner of escape that I could. I kept my wings folded upon my back so I wouldn't obstruct Xanthus' view. But somehow, I ended slammed head first into a mirror. I took a step back as pain shot through my face. I placed both of my hands upon my throbbing forehead. Cheese, that was careless of me. How did I accidentally not see that!

Unfortunately, I heard Xanthus burst out in laughter behind me. I turned to face him just in time to see him slam into a clear window glass that somehow manifested between us. His hands automatically shot towards his face as he rubbed his forehead. Horror struck through my veins like electric shock. I gasped, "When did that appear between us?" We instantly placed our palms upon the windowed glass before us, palm to palm. I whispered in panicked, "Xanthus?"

Suddenly his image was slowly diminishing before my faint eyes as my reflection slowly appeared. No, how can this be! My heart started to pound vigorously as I rubbed the mirror in horror. I can't understand what was happening! I pounded on the mirror as my hands shook. I screamed, "Xanthus, Xanthus!"

I felt as if the mirrors were pressing themselves upon my very skin, caving in on my sanity. I had never felt so claustrophobic before, until this very moment! I leaned my back against a mirror as my breaths became heavy, wheezing out. I quickly glanced around to see something, anything else but my reflection gazing horrified back at me! Suddenly and thankfully I heard Xanthus shout, "Azalea, Azalea! Where are you!? Azalea!"

His voiced echoed in fury. I could hear him pounding upon the mirrors, vibrating through the walls. I shouted back, "Xanthus where are you! I can't breathe! I can't seem to move either. This is crazy! Why couldn't we have simply waited by the boulder? We could have figured something else out. We wouldn't be in this madness right now!"

His grunted in anger, "So this reckless situation is my brilliant doing, is it? You are incredibly impossible Azalea. Look, I need you to make your way over to me, I'm sure you are aware that I need not to tell you to be careful. Follow my voice, you can do this!"

I grunted in return, how could he get so irritable so quickly? I shifted my unwilling legs to move. I walked cautiously as I turned to the right and as I followed his muffled cursing. I knew at those times he was slamming into the mirrored walls himself. And eventually, seconds turned to minutes, and minutes seemed to turn into hours. By this time my heart started to pound faster and faster through my chest. Anticipation and fright flooded me with every turn through this horrid maze of mirrors! My nerves were getting the best of me.

I then did something, not very smart I might add but, out of fear and desperation I started to run. I couldn't contain this false calmness any longer! Thud! Thud! Thud! I kept repeatedly slamming into the mirrors as beads of sweat trickled down my temples. Faster and faster I ran and harder I hit those dang walls, until finally out of breath, sore and in doubt, I stopped.

My faced throbbed with immense pain as my ego burned. I no longer heard Xanthus' muffled voice any longer. I leaned on a mirror with my back as I slip down onto the floor. I tried to catch my breath as the pain ached in my chest and vibrated through my entire body. It was with immense difficultly attempting to concentrate on bringing my breaths back to normal.

I glanced up to see those same colorful bubbles aimlessly floating from out of nowhere. I sat there feeling so deserted and depressed. I thought to myself, perhaps if I sit here long enough someone would find me. Even though, I no longer could hear Xanthus. I mean why bother, I would just end up slamming my face on more mirrors!

I continued to sit there as my faith melted into nothingness. But suddenly, as I felt all hope was lost, something rang within my ear. Was I hallucinating it? Was my heart manipulating my mind because I so desperately wanted to hear something? I was malfunctioning, I couldn't possibly be hearing what I thought I was. I jumped in my skin as I hear it once more, almost clear as day, laughter. And not just any kind of laughter, it was that of a child. It became louder and louder, and became closer, ever so closer…

Child of What to Come

16

I looked up to see a child faintly standing just before me. He giggled as he pushed his short brown hair behind his ears. Oddly though, it appeared that he had silver streaks running through his hair. Strange I thought, I have golden streaks in my hair. I was stunned, all I could do was stare at this incredible vision before me. He just stood there, smiling directly at me with his chestnut brown eyes. Something about those eyes seemed so vaguely familiar. Then, he opened his wings.

I was completely awe stuck as I noticed the silver feathers that surrounded his wings. They seemed to let out a small dim white glow. Within his wings were hues of silver and blue as they swirled all around them. He took a step forward and laughed out loud as he extended his delicate hand out towards me. His cute little smile reminded me of Xanthus.

Who was this child and why did he look so much like, me and, Xanthus. I rubbed my eyes and face slowly; perhaps I was hallucinating or something? But when I opened my eyes once again, he was still standing there with his arm extended towards me. I froze momentarily, unable to decide if I should give him my hand. Would it slide through? Was he real? I gazed over to his cute little smile again. I saw so much warmth in it. So then without hesitation, I made my choice.

I slowly reached out and with took his warm little hand. He helped me up as he gave a slight squeeze to my hand. As I stood, I dusted off my dress as he continued to stand there. He smiled with confidence, which gave me a warm sensation within my heart. Just then as I was about to ask him his name he let go of my hand and took off running around a corner laughing with joyfulness. I shouted after him, "Wait!"

I quickly ran after him as I so desperately tried to catch up. I had so many questions to ask. But, oddly enough he seemed to only wait at the end of the mirrored halls, just out of my reach. As soon as I was in arms range, he would disappear and reappear around the next corner.

We zigzagged through the horrible mirrored halls as I realized, he was actually aiding me in finding a way out. I mean, where else could we be going? His laughter though, it seemed to vibrate within the mirrors, and my heart. His laughter only kept getting louder and louder, chuckling with humorous delight with each passing corner.

As I sped up my pace to keep up I took a sharp turn around a corner. And as I did I slammed face first into someone's chest! I fell back onto the floor from the impact. I rubbed my face as I glanced over to see whom I had ran into and whom also was on the floor. It was Xanthus! I shouted out in delight, "Xanthus I found you!"

I couldn't contain myself. I was so exhilarated to see him. Without hesitation I threw myself on top of him. I let out a small shout of joy as he, grunted roughly as I landed on his body. I never thought I could embrace someone with such intensity. His warm arms encircled around my waist, I melted within my skin as he tightly hugged me back. He placed his lips upon my neck kissing me ever so feverishly as I gasped breathlessly, "I actually came to a point in my mind where I thought that I was going to be lost in here forever. That is until this little boy came and…"

Xanthus sat straight up suddenly pushing me with him as I replied those words. He interrupted me, "Hold on a second, you were following a little boy, with silver feathers around his wings too?"

The look of utter incomprehension across Xanthus' face had me confused. I stood slightly on trembling legs as I leaned my back against a mirror to sustain my shaking. I mean, was it possible for us both to be following the same boy? I felt so disoriented, my head seemed like it was throbbing with so many questions.

Suddenly as if answering our question, laughter rang throughout the mirrors around us. That same joyful laugh of the little silver feathered boy. I turned to Xanthus as he stood and with took my hands within his, "Xanthus, do you think he could be, I mean that would be impossible but, perhaps that was, could that have been our future?"

I was rambling, even I was unsure on what to call it. Xanthus on the other hand was probably more confused and conflicted than I was. He shook his head as he took one hand and ran it through his hair. He rubbed the back of his neck slowly as he replied almost hysterical, "You know, I'm not sure if and how that is possible. I'm not sure where we are at this very moment in time but, I don't, I just don't know on what to believe anymore."

Xanthus turned towards the direction that he came from. He griped my hand tightly as we silently continued to make our way through the maze of mirrors. We were both speechless on what had just occurred before us. Was it planned, fate, or just a messed up hallucination that we both wanted to see, or needed to see. Whatever it may be or was, even I didn't want to talk about it. I wasn't sure if this was a weird test of our love or for our devotion for each other.

We both continued on forward as one of Xanthus' hands was stretched out before us, and the other linked within mine. I on the other hand, simply allowed my love to lead as I followed undoubtedly and willingly with him. But moments later I found myself walking in front of Xanthus with both of my arms held out, as he held his right arm around my waist. Our situation had turned and he was allowing me to lead as he followed willingly behind. I felt him give me a small kiss on the top of my head as we continued our silent attempt to escape these mirrors. Finally, as it seemed like hours later of much cautious walking, we came to what appeared to be our exit.

Dark brown rock appeared to finally take over the walls instead of the mirrors. We continued hand in hand as we came to a halt in front of a tall green door that appeared to be made of wavy soft silk. It flowed so peacefully as if a small breeze was flowing gentle through it. As I slowly reached for the door handle Xanthus reached for my hand and replied, "Shall we open it together?"

I smiled and nodded as he gazed into my eyes. Xanthus with took my waist with his left arm and as he entwined his fingers with mine. We both turned the knob and pushed the door slowly together. Strangely it opened with a low creek. And once we took a step in, we were both astonished and in awe at what we saw.

17

The room we entered seemed to be unrealistic. It appeared as if we had entered the bottom of the ocean. Small rare colorful fishes swam all about as they swirled their tiny fins around in groups. Also, within the room itself, were beautiful elaborate corrals that were just about my height. Which of course meant, that I was unable to see over them.

As we stepped forward something lightly brushed against my ankles. I glanced at my feet as I realized that some type of sea weed seemed to cover the entire floor as it swayed with some type of current. It seemed to tickle as we continued to walk on, so I decided to open my wings and fly over it. I did give them a good stretch before we continued. As I glanced back at the floor, I saw that there were many types of sea horses darting in and out of the sea weed, swimming about in their own lost world.

It was all seeming so incredible and peaceful, that is until I looked up. My mouth dropped in horror. I saw black tip sharks swimming about thirty feet above us. I don't think they wouldn't harm us, would they? Just then, as I thought it couldn't get any worse Xanthus replies, "Let's split us."

I turned to him in shock. "What! Are you losing your mind? Do you not recall what just happened to us a few moments ago in the maze? And do you not see the sharks?"

Xanthus moved his gaze upward as he saw the sharks swimming about. He shrugged his shoulders. "Yes, I do see them but, I think we'll be alright."

I murmured with hysteria, "Alright? Alright?" I laughed hysterically; I couldn't help it. Was something else controlling his decision? What had come over him? I cleared my throat, "Xanthus, let me repeat myself. The maze, the sharks." I pointed upward.

But I don't think I was convincing Xanthus because again, he shrugged his shoulders and replied firmly, "Yes, I can clearly see them and I understand the horrendous situation we were in back there. But in regards to the sharks, if we move slowly, perhaps they won't care to notice us. Besides they should only attack if their hungry, and it does not seem that they are. So, just look around for a door or a way out."

Was my mouth open? I swear I could taste dread about to happen. But clearly Xanthus was numb by some degree to venture off on his own. And of course, his smugness would do just that, leave oblivious to my horror filled nerves. He smiled as if assuring me that all was going to be alright as he nodded in return. He then turned and left, walking off and disappearing between the gigantic corals.

I mean, was my expression of anguish not enough for him to realize that his idea was beyond inconceivable? How could he be so much at ease, I was terrified! Alright, so I guess I could perhaps out fly the shark if it came to it, or would I say, out swim them? I shrugged my shoulders and sighed. I carried on slowly, what else could I do? If Xanthus thought it was safe then… Oh who am I kidding those sharks are frightening! Therefore, I decided to stay as close to the corrals as I could and walk rather than fly. I can see from afar if I found a way out anyway.

I had to admit, I started to look around at all of the fishes that were near the corrals. They caught my attention surprisingly fast, and just like that I was distracted. I saw some star fishes, angel fishes, orange spotted filefishes, and much, much more than I can name. And as I continued to glance and walk slowly about, I came to halt in front of this weird looking corral. And just as I stopped a small cubby clown fish swam slowly out of it. It looked so adorable I couldn't help myself. I reached out and slowly petted it above its head. The clown fish let out a small giggle as tiny bubbles escaped its mouth. Suddenly, more clown fish came out of the corral as they swirled around my fingertips. So, I slowly petted them too. I bent over and gave one a little kiss on top of its head. The little fish went from orange to a deep red. Then, more clown fish came out. It was as if I was surrounded by them. They swirled and giggled as they swam all around me.

Just then, a clown fish that appeared to be bigger than the rest of them came swimming slowly up to my right hand. Surprisingly it took my hand within its little fins and started to tug me. I couldn't believe just how powerful and adorable this fishy was. I asked it with a chuckle, "Where are you taking me little one?"

They all cheered lightly as together they started to tug and push me. Well, what else did I have to do, nothing really. I was supposed to find something, but I couldn't recall at this very moment. Oh well, I allowed them to take me wherever it was they wanted to take me.

277

And within moments we came to a halt in front of an enormous dark cherry wooden chest. It had a huge golden lock upon it as green seaweed covered it here and there as well. I stood there in sort of daze of admiration. I wasn't sure what I was going to do but, that same clown fish that started to pull me, sort of answered my question. It came over to me carrying a golden key shaped like the skeleton of a hammerhead shark.

I with took the key from the fish as I became mesmerized by the sight. And as I stood there in a trance, I thought I heard Xanthus shouting something, or perhaps it was my imagination. I wasn't quite sure but, all I heard was noise and not words. But what I didn't realize was that he was actually only a few feet away from me. He was being held back by the arms by one enormously long electric eel. It wrapped its body around Xanthus' arms and waist denying him the pleasure in escaping and preventing him from moving any further. It kept giving him small doses of electric shocks. Xanthus shouted, "Azalea, Azalea what are you doing! Wake up Azalea! Don't!"

I couldn't help it. I felt as if I was in some sort of dreamlike state and didn't want to wake from it, I couldn't wake from it. I slowly walked closer as I knelt down before the chest. I placed the key into the lock as I slowly turned it. As it unlocked the bits of seaweed seemed to disintegrate around the trunk. I opened the chest as a bright yellow light shone from inside. With that, Xanthus ceased in struggling with the eel as it stopped giving him bursts of shocks. Xanthus seemed just as mesmerized by the enchanted sight as I was.

A large lavender globe emerged up from the chest as it hovered in midair. Suddenly an image started to form from within the globe………

There stood an elf woman wearing a blue cloak as she held her infant close to her chest. A fairy woman with a green cloak stood next to her as she too held her infant close. It was an image of Queen Lily and Queen Whistalyn talking together in a low voice. Then you heard Queen Lily reply, "Azalea will become a beautiful fairy, honest and true. And before her coming of age, we shall introduce them to each other, as we have planned. We shall and must meet before that time. I will send a letter to you."

Queen Whistalyn nodded and replied, "Yes, by then Xanthus will be a proper gentleman and faithful. Their love will bond us all and save

278

both of our existing races. With guidance, the errors of our ancestors shall not repeat."

They both embraced each other in an immense hug. Moments later they wished each other safety and fortune as they went their separate ways. It seemed though that the globe was following Queen Lily as she walked through the enchanted jungle. Her pace quickened as she now appeared worried and troubled. She suddenly was startled as a little boy who appeared to be in his early centuries came out from behind some bushes. Queen Lily let out a small sigh as she realized just who it was before her. Queen Lily bent down to the little boy and replied, "Cethios thank goodness it's you. Here, you are a lot faster than I am. Take Azalea to the castle. Take her to the room of which you know I speak of. Go, fly safely with her and take Snowfire with you."

The little boy nodded as he with took Azalea from her and as he embraced her deeply to his chest. A small white dragon slowly flew out from behind Queen Lily. Cethios' eyes widened but he kept still as he nodded with certainty to Queen Lily. The little boy, Cethios asked insecurely, "Are you sure about this? What about you, will you be alright?"

Queen Lily sighed in assurance, "Do not worry about me little one. Now go, and take good care of her. She is your responsibility to look after. Make sure no harm ever comes to her, ever. Now, promise me you'll take care of her no matter what the consequences are, promise me. Promise always."

The little boy Cethios gazed into the queens' eyes as he replied, "I promise. As long as I live, I will protect her with all that I have."

The fairy woman hugged the little boy and kissed her infant on the forehead. She replied almost breathlessly, "Go Cethios, do not fail me."

"I never will. I shall keep."

With that being said the little boy opened his wings and took off as he disappeared with the infant. Queen Lily on the other hand quickly started to run through the jungle towards the castle. But moments later she stopped to catch her breath as she was not accustomed to such tedious running. And within seconds as she turned, there before her standing a few feet away was Zethron.

Queen Lily took her last deep breath in as she stepped forward to him. As she let out her breath she replied softly, "You will never take her life. You are too late; she has already been enchanted by the sorceress herself. And there is nothing that you can do about that. Her future, her destiny and her fate has already been set in stone."

Zethron stepped a bit closer as he raised his nose in the air, disgusted. The edge of his lip curled up in an evil smirk as he sneered, "You of all fairies should know that I always get my way. No matter what anyone does against me. Even if there are certain setbacks but, eventually, I find an alternative. I will succeed and I will have her immortal soul!"

Queen Lily's hands started to glow a dim red as they hung next to her side. She cautioned under her breath, "You'll have to go through me first!"

Just then as she was about to raise her hands to attack, Zethron quickly snapped silver shackles on her wrists and with took her sword. Queen Lily was caught by surprise of his action. Zethron curled his lip as he replied, "With pleasure."

He drove the sword straight into her chest. Queen Lily gasped in shock as all she could do was gaze at her own blood. Queen Lily stared at her hands as they glowed a bright red as suddenly a small black cloud formed above her. The cloud struck bright blue lightning bolts above her head as it slowly started to rain down on her. Queen Lily, started to glow a dim red as her soul and energy was now leaving her. She was dying and there was nothing she could do to save herself.

Zethron smiled contently to himself as Queen Lily now took her last breaths. But just before she vanished with the mist as her appearance was now skeletal, she whispered slowly, "She is, too powerful for you already... The enchantments and magic already flow, within her. She will... Conquer this world... And you."

Zethron raised his nose up as he continued to watch Queen Lily fade into nothing, turning into a memory. But just before she completely vanished, she let out a piercing scream. It forced Zethron to bend over and place his hands tightly over his ears. Then, she was gone, she became a memory. Zethron stood as he gazed at his bloody hands, for her scream gave sight of blood to his ears. Zethron bent over to where the queen had been. He picked up her sword as he smirked with an evil grin. He snickered to himself, "One down, more to go..."

The bubble, in which the images were coming from, suddenly popped and sent a gust of wind outward. White glitter glistened everywhere briefly as it slowly sailed down into the chest. I sat there in shock and in horror at what I had just seen with my own eyes. I wasn't sure whether or not I wanted to believe it. I mean, what was the reasoning behind me seeing this? I wouldn't doubt the fact that Zethron had killed my mother. But, that's not a surprise to me.

As I sat there pondering, it somewhat explained a little why my rude awakenings, that I would have back in Whisperia, would have a fairy being killed by a sword through her chest. I frowned to myself, it was my mother. Would that then mean that, my not so rude awakenings were visions of Xanthus' mother?

I glanced down at the shackles that resided on my wrists. I wondered if these were the same forsaken shackles that were placed on my mother before she was killed. I sighed a desperate moan of grief as tears wanted to so desperately form within my eyes. I choked back a sob.

Suddenly, as if being brought back from a dream, I felt a warm hand upon my shoulder. I wiped away at my eyes, for one golden tear succeeded in escaping. I glanced over to see Xanthus, whom was now sitting by my side. My eyes rested on him as a small smile spread upon my face. His hair was all frizzed and sticking up all over the place as small puffs of smoke escaped the tips. I asked him through a chuckle, "So what happened to you?"

"That eel I tell you, it just wouldn't let go." As humorous as it was my smile faded, I couldn't hold on to it. He replied with concern, "Azalea, will you be alright? I truly am sorry that you were forced to see this. I do not know what I would have done if I saw my mother die before me. But who was that fairy that did that to her? Do you know him?"

I nodded slowly as I took in a deep breath, "Yes, that is the kings' advisor, that was Zethron."

We both sat there speechless but, oddly enough I heard some light sobbing near me. I glanced over to my left as I saw the clown fishes. They were crying and hugging each other. I shook my head; it was horrendous that they too witnessed my mother's death. I turned my glanced over into the chest as I saw my mothers' sword glistening brightly, just lying there ever so innocently. I couldn't believe that the sword I had come to cherish had been the tool that destroyed my mother, and my life.

I glanced around in the chest as I saw that besides my mother's sword and other treasures was a small silver metal sea turtle. It was the size of a hatchling as the shells' patterns were made of mother of pearl stone with silver. I reached over and with took it as I let out a deep sigh. I couldn't believe it. I rubbed my fingertips over the shell as Xanthus asked, "What is that?"

I sighed, "This is called the Silver Truth of Sea. It is made of pure silver with a pearl inlay. The centaurs use these to recall memories on what they have seen before with their very eyes. Their kind are the only ones who know how to work them. I have seen theses in Hypathia's hut plenty of times. Denentro though, explained to me what they are and how they are used. Only those who are worthy among them can use them. As far as I know, only Prince Melancton and Hypathia have used them. They place a memory that they have seen in it and place a spell on it, so only those who they want to share it with can see it, activated by when they come oh so close to it. But if I am correct, once the one who was meant to see it, sees the memory, they are now allowed to use it as well. Preserving the first memory and now able to preserve other memories into it. Confusing I know but, what I am wondering is who saw what had happened?"

Xanthus sat there confused but, he cleared his throat and replied, "If one of the centaurs was there, why didn't he or she do anything to prevent the fate of your mother? Why did they allow it to happen?"

I snorted, "Well, that is what's frustrating of their kind, they do not interfere with anything that does not involve their kind unfortunately. But fortunately, I understand that I was accepted into their kind a long time ago. Obviously after all, all of this happened centuries ago. But I wonder how they got this Silver Truth of Sea here?"

I wondered if that's why Denentro had to leave in such a hurry. But how was he able to get this here? And I wondered if it was even him that left this for me. So many questions and not enough answers, as always.

I stared at its color as I held it carefully within my fingers. I wasn't sure what I was going to use this for but, I shrugged my shoulders and placed it in my inner dress pocket. As I glanced back inside the chest, I saw the bright rubies, sapphires and golden coins surrounding my mothers' sword. I decided that no matter what this swords' history was, the fact of it is, that this is my mothers' sword and it belongs to me.

Moments later we stood, but I bent back down to grab my sword. And as soon as I did though, the ground below us started to tremble, violently I might add. The clown fishes all released low shrieks as they swam away, back into their corral home. I shouted over the rumbling to Xanthus, "Should I put it back?"

Disbelief fell upon Xanthus face as he shouted, "Well it's too late for that!"

I grabbed onto Xanthus' arm as the earth continued to violently tremble. Suddenly the ground below us split open and Xanthus with took both of my arms as we fell into the black oblivious.

18

As soon as we both landed with a hard thud, I was coughing my throat out. All of the dust that surrounded us seemed to clench its fist around us. I glanced up to see the hole we fell through quickly close up. This was certainly a trap. I'm sure it was Cethios that placed the sword in the chest but, did he know about the Silver Truth of Sea? If it was him, why would he want me to see that? Would he want me to believe that he was the boy and that he wouldn't kill me himself? My head was spinning around, I was entirely confused by it all, as well as from the fall.

I guess the only good thing about this was that I had my mothers' sword. Much pride ran through me knowing that, if the memory I saw was correct, she died protecting and she very much loved me. But another question vibrated through me, why doesn't my father or anyone else know about the golden feathers? How could everyone forget that royalty women carry the golden feathers? That was now my new added quest to figure out.

I glanced around, everything still seemed so hazy from the dust as small debris continued to fall from above us. I noticed that we were in a cell big enough for about thirty or so fairies to fit in. Bars surrounded us except for one wall. It was cemented with shackles hanging from it. As I glanced back up to the ceiling I noticed that shackles hung from it too. There was a small wooden bench that was to the far right of us, long enough for four to sit on. As I looked past the bars into the room I noticed something that sent dread into my heart. First, there was spiked object everywhere you looked. Second, there was a fireplace in the way corner with a sword lying not so far away from it. Which meant, that we were in the same dungeon that I was in a couple of days ago. I stood and slowly walked up to the bars as I gave a deep sigh, imprisoned again.

Suddenly we heard some type of noise coming from the other side of the room. A door opened and slammed shut. Xanthus withdrew his sword as I simply stood there. I mean, what could we do? I knew we were helpless behind these bars.

Footsteps started to descend as suddenly Cethios came into view from the stairs. He had an enormous grin on his face as his hands rested in his pockets. He walked up to the cell as he eyed us both with an obnoxious grin spread across his face. He gushed sarcastically, "Oh my Azalea, I knew you couldn't keep yourself from me. I knew you'd come back to the castle for more of my love. And look, I've caught an intruder as well."

Xanthus angrily took steps forward as he placed his sword back to his side, knowing it would be useless to carry it. He replied to Cethios, "Cethios, your fight is with me not Azalea. Remove those shackles that you have so bestowed upon her. They are destroying her and she has nothing to do with this."

Cethios laughed as if Xanthus had replied something hilarious. Cethios answered him, "But you see, it has everything to do with her. Has she not told you the truth on who she truly is?"

I became enraged! He had no right on telling Xanthus, for it was up to me on telling him the truth on what I had recently found out. I was furious with Xanthus when I discovered that he was truly a prince and now, the roles had reversed. But I had only found out just a few days ago. Would he in turn, be upset with me? I stepped forward to Cethios as I replied, "Cethios you two faced deceiver! I haven't had any time nor the proper breath in me to tell him anything of which that I have only just found out myself! Remove these shackles from my skin or so help me I... I..." And with those last words suddenly my breath was taken from me, I felt as if I was being strangled. I glanced down to Cethios right palm as I saw that it was clenched tightly into a fist as it glowed a deep burgundy. I sank onto my knees and onto the floor as I held onto my throat and as my shackles glowed burgundy as well.

Xanthus quickly rushed over to me as all he could do was watch helplessly. I saw him quickly check his pockets as I heard him mumble under his breath, "Hypathia's bottle, no, it's gone." Fear swelled in his eyes for he knew it was useless on any attempts he could think of. He stood and faced Cethios as he burned deeply within his veins with anger. I was almost unconscious as I heard Xanthus demand, "Release her! Are your intentions to kill her? If that may be then take my life instead of hers! Spare hers and I shall spare yours."

Cethios stood there clenching his fist and ignoring Xanthus all together. Cethios was not going to listen to someone who was helpless behind bars. Especially one of the elves he regrettably wanted to destroy. But little did he know that at that very moment something was happening inside of Xanthus. Something was pulsing in his veins that he had never felt before. Something that was suppressed but now, was rushing with mad vengeance through his very skin to escape, a deep kind of magic that now boiled freely in his blood. Xanthus felt this intense warm energy infuse with his inner mind and soul as suddenly, his palms started to glow a bright white hue. He gazed down at his hands as he felt the suddenly urge to release it. And just like that a light emerged from his palms sending a sonic boom wave out towards Cethios. As the light flashed before him Cethios was sent flying across the dungeon and slamming into the wall near the fireplace.

The wall behind Cethios seemed to crack where he had slammed into. And as he landed onto the floor, he laid still briefly unconscious and stunned. Within moments after regaining himself, Cethios carefully stood with his hand upon his head recovering his strength as he shook slightly. He took in deep breaths as anger flooded his very skin and swelled in his expression. He was caught off guard at what Xanthus had done. He was not expecting anything, to say the least, that powerful coming from Xanthus himself.

Cethios cautiously walked back up to the cell as he rubbed the back of his neck slowly with his fingertips. Xanthus on the other hand stood there in complete bewilderment and was utterly confused. He had never before felt that kind of magic within him. He sank onto his knees as he desperately tried to control his unusual heavy breathing and this new uncontrollable magic that festered inside him. Almost numbing his senses this unexplained power surged throughout his veins. And yet, he seemed drained of energy as beads of sweat formed on his brow.

Me on the other hand, as Cethios went flying onto the other side of the dungeon, his grasp was released from upon my neck. I slowly took in deep breaths as I watched Xanthus in disbelief. I was unaware that he was capable of such magic. I stared at him as he simply stared at his own palms in perplexity. My head was pounding as the room slowed its spin. I sat up and placed my hands firmly around my temples as I concentrated on regaining my strength. I glanced back at Xanthus as I whispered, "Are you alright?"

I honestly was afraid he was going to ask me what had happened to him, because I for one could not have explained it. Though he still sat there as if he was searching for answers, as if he was trying to grasp the concept of what had just happened. Finally he turned to me as we both silently helped each other to our feet. And for a brief moment we forgot that Cethios was still there. Xanthus placed his palm upon my cheek as I captured it, holding it within my grasp upon my face. We honestly were utterly about to kiss when Cethios cleared his throat loudly, "Well then, I shall leave you both with this to ponder. The fairy that stands beside you has deceived you. The reason for me not wanting to remove those shackles is simple; they keep her bestowed magic suppressed within her. It imprisons her magic; therefore she is unable to release anything at all from her inner core. And the reason why I must restrain that power is because she is the daughter of Queen Lily, destined queen of Whisperia and destined carrier of one of the stones from The Caves of Esmera. Therefore she contains intoxicating powers from its core. If not for those grateful shackles, she would escape my grasp and go off and find that Prince Xanthus. Whom I figure is still roaming around my castle somewhere as we speak. You see, the prince as well is a carrier of that stone and contains that same significant magic. And once they mate, their souls will forever be combined for all eternity as powerful immortals."

Xanthus' expression shifted from confused to anger as his eyes locked with mine and expressed slight betrayal. Cethios continued, "By the look of your face it truly seems as if she hasn't told you any of this. Perhaps she was keeping it from you as her faithfulness fails you even more, Morpheus."

Xanthus' lower jaw clenched as his nerves and muscles tensed. He continued to stand there without expressing any different emotion. His expression did not falter. In which I was very thankful for, for who knows what he would have done if he had known it was Xanthus that stood before me. I couldn't believe it though, he thought Xanthus was Morpheus! I mean, I know they appear quite similar but, I was very thankful that at this moment he did not know the difference. Xanthus dropped his hand from my face as he turned toward Cethios, placing his own hands within his pockets. Xanthus replied as calmly as he could to Cethios, "And what specifically has Azalea told you."

Cethios snickered as he raised his nose into the air. Something about that gesture reminded me of someone. He replied, "Before or after I had to creatively beat it out of her? Well, I'll tell you what she said after, but you should know of course that it took a while. She thought she was a strong one but, they all end up bending to my will one way or another. Once she gave in she replied that the prince is the carrier of that same enchanted stone. She admitted that she had not mated with anyone, to scared or ashamed to do anything. So, as long as she remains enticingly pure, her immortal soul and magic is still up for grabs."

Xanthus shook his head, "And what makes you think that her magic is up for grabs?"

"Ah, interested are you? Well, have you ever heard of a legend, an elf legend nonetheless, of two nations being united and ruled under a grand king and queen, of course after much bloodshed. After that, their greatness will rule the lands."

Xanthus stepped forward and whispered, "Who hasn't heard of that legend, what's your point?"

Cethios laughed as he ran his fingers through his hair. He cleared his throat, "Well, what they forgot to mention is that, that king and queen will become immortals once they have mate and their magic flees its suppressed cage, sort of speak. But in all honesty, it doesn't matter if they have or have not mated yet, mating with one who is pure is more pleasurable anyway. But, they can never choose unfaithfulness from each other. They must always remain faithful to each other, always, to keep their magic and immortality binding. For if one mates with another, all of that immortality will be lost and transferred into the one that had broken their bond. In which, all of Azalea's immortality as well as the prince of Trinafin, will be transferred to me once I take Azalea. And then I will become unstoppable as your immortal King!"

Xanthus suddenly became outraged and disgusted as he shouted to Cethios, "You're mad! You want to force Azalea's immortality out of her against her very own will by forcing her to lay with you? You selfishly want to take away the immortality and magic that was bestowed upon her and as well as the princes?"

Cethios laughed and shook his head as if in disagreement, "Now you're catching on but, the only thing you have wrong is me forcing Azalea against her own will. Azalea my love, have you not told him about our passionate kiss?"

My mouth automatically dropped open, how could he say such a thing! I turned my gaze towards Xanthus as all he could do was stare at me in disappointment. I was speechless! I mean, we did kiss but, it was only to save my life from when Zethron had driven the sword in me. There was nothing passionate about that, right? I mean, there was no true meaning behind it, was there? I shook my head to rid myself of the doubtful thoughts I had. But a kiss it was nonetheless. So how could I deny it, it was partially true. I don't think I should even admit the small vision I saw when Cethios was kissing me either. That was between Cethios and me.

288

Oh no, how could I even have something to share with Cethios! I was digging myself in a hole as I continued to stand there speechless.

As Xanthus gazed into my eyes I could see them filling up with deep sorrow and emotions of betrayal. Suddenly he turned his gaze from me as he turned back towards Cethios. And Cethios of course found this very amusing, "So much bitter humiliation Azalea, and poor Morpheus, here he thought he caught himself an honest servant. But in reality all he has before him is a deceitful princess who'd rather be with a prince, any prince for that matter, even that Xanthus. Don't worry Azalea, common folk have a tendency of forgiving others very easily. Sad news for that Prince Xanthus too huh, he thought he had something honest and faithful as well."

I balled up my fists at Cethios. How could he say such things, and what's even worse, Xanthus was believing him! I do have to say though, that I did a great job in confusing Cethios on whom I loved, I even have him believing I have emotions for them both. I had kept Xanthus and Morpheus out of danger, for the time being. But after that I turned to Xanthus as I exhaled a deep sigh. Xanthus had now turned away from Cethios as he was staring off into the dungeon. I slowly walked over to him as I replied, "That kiss had many complications behind it. If you just let me explain partially…"

Xanthus turned and glared at me as he whispered under his breath, "Partially? You can't even deny the kiss, can you?"

Tears swelled in my eyes as I choked out, "If I did deny it, I would just be lying to you and to myself. Please, give me the chance to explain…"

I placed my hand upon Xanthus' shoulder, only to have him shrug his shoulder away and push my hand off of him. He whispered with regret and hurt, "Save it for someone who cares Azalea." I stood there speechless as I watched Xanthus turn from me and walk over to the other side of the cell. I felt so horrifying inside, it stung with regret. He didn't even let me explain what I could. Well now that I think about it, perhaps it was a good that I didn't try to explain in front of Cethios. He'd probably turn my words around and against me.

I turned towards Cethios whom had an enormous stupid smirk upon his face. Probably content with himself thinking that he had ruined our relationship and was improving his chances.

Just then the door opened from up the stairs. It closed slowly with a loud bang. I could only hear the footsteps descending down the stairs. I couldn't see who it was nor could I tell. I could only pray it wasn't Zethron. Then a familiar voice rang out, "Cethios? Cethios where have you gone? Ugh, this place is so filthy down here. What are you doing anyway the ball is about to begin."

I glanced surprisingly at Cethios as he closed his eyes. He took in a deep breath as he pinched the bridge of his nose between his forefinger and thumb, attempting to calm the rage that seemed to flow through him momentarily. How dare he! As she came into view I saw her wavy curly hair bouncing all over the place. She was in a beautiful glittery pink ball gown. It made her wings so bright and iridescent. The gown itself was sleeveless for I could see her birthmark shape butterfly on her right shoulder. And once she reached Cethios she planted a big kiss on his lips. He slowly pushed her back by her shoulders carefully as he forced a smile.

She turned around slowly as I replied to her, "Razyna? What do you think are you doing?"

She leaned over to the cell and squinted her eyes as if she had a hard time adjusting her sight to see who stood before her. She replied hesitant at first, "Azalea? Is that you in there?"

Cethios chuckled, "So it seems you two know each other then."

I glared at Cethios as I turned my gaze at Razyna. I spat out through gritted teeth, "Razyna how could you do this? You of all fairies know what type of monstrous fairy he is. Why Razyna?"

She scrunched her nose in as she replied with disgust, "You left him. You turned away from a great opportunity. I was there to pick up where you should have been. I'm not as dumb as you are to walk away from this type of power. Cethios promised me that I shall become his princess. He will share his immortality with me."

My jaw dropped! "Razyna how could you? Do you even hear yourself? He has poisoned your mind and your heart! Do you really think that immortality works that way? How many fairies do you think he has told that too?"

Cethios cleared his throat, "You know I'm standing right here."

I was outraged as I turned my wrath on him, "I don't care Cethios! Keep your black heart away from her! She should not be involved in this and you know it!"

Cethios chuckled, "Oh really, and why don't you ask her yourself. She came looking for me."

I was stunned in utter bewilderment. I turned to her and uttered softly, "No Razyna, tell me this isn't true."

Razyna took a step back from the cell as she slowly brushed her dress off from the invisible dust that was upon it. She took a step closer to Cethios as she linked her arm with his. She replied as if attempting to convince herself, "Cethios loves me. And I mean, truly loves me. You see, the difference between you and me is that I can handle great power. You, you can't! You're pathetic, unwilling, and a terrified unworthy fairy. And that is why you ran from it. Too scared to confront it, you are nothing but an insignificant fairy!"

I stepped back in horror. Who was this fairy before me? Razyna was supposed to be one of my good friends. And now, here before me stood yet another enemy. All I could do was stare hopelessly as I shook my head in disbelief. I sighed, "You keep telling yourself that. I just hope it won't be too late by the time you actually realize the truth as you open your eyes from all the lies that conceal your heart. But for the time being, what a great traitor you have become. I'm sure James would be so proud."

Razyna opened her mouth to speak but no words could escape her. All she could do was stare at me with pride and regret. I wasn't quite sure how much lies Cethios had told her but, he did have her against me. Cethios replied with a smirk, "Come my future princess, the ball awaits us."

As he said those words I glance down and truly notice his attire. He was dressed in a black suit with a black mask that hung from his belt. It was a masquerade ball that they were attending. Why would he hold one now? Just as I was about to ask him about it he turned to Xanthus and I and replied, "Well this has been tremendously enlightening but, I must get going. I shall return in the morning to take you Azalea. And hopefully by then I shall have that prince in my grasp. An elf should be easy to spot tonight, of course him being without wings."

They both laughed in each other's company as they left the dungeon. And as he closed the door behind him, all of the light within the dungeon ceased to exist. Xanthus and I now stood in utter darkness with only a distant dripping of water to accompany us.

Little Lightning Bolt

19

I waited momentarily to see if Xanthus was going to light up an energy globe or even say anything but, he replied nothing. We were honestly in the dark for a good half hour or so. And after much waiting my patience ran out dry. I knew it was going to be up to me to find some type of method of light. Xanthus was too stubborn leaning against the wall somewhere, and probable still upset with me. I for one was not going to stand here all night in darkness.

I closed my eyes and tried to reach down deep inside of myself. I tried to find an opening that secluded my magic, any type of loop hole I could find. I opened my eyes slowly to only see my right palm glowing slightly, then cease. I heard rumbling above me as I glanced up above. It was that darn black cloud as it shot a blue lightning bolt over my head. Moments later, yup, it started to rain down on me. I do though have to admit, it did feel cool against my skin. It was extremely muggy in the dungeon.

I took in a deep breath for I knew I couldn't quit. Perhaps though, if I could manipulate the energy that already exists there, like I can with the water, but instead use the lightning bolt. Maybe just maybe, I could do something with that. I concentrated harder as it poured with great intensity. I was getting drenched but, I could care less. I needed that lightning bolt to get fiercer. I heard the rumble get louder as it vibrated within my ears.

Just then, I found it. I discovered that same bolted up energy that had been locked up since the day I saved James. I felt it flow over inside of me as it burned. Goosebumps swarmed and covered my very skin. And as I glanced back down at my palms I could see and feel that magic awaiting to be released. Then, it stopped raining. I glanced up at the cloud as I raised my hands up within it. I withdrew the blue lightning bolt from it as the cloud itself vanished within the mist. I whispered to the little blue lightning bolt, "Illuminate this room oh delicate lightning bolt, reach every corner of this cell and do not fault."

As it hovered above my palms it slowly raised itself higher above me. Suddenly it zigzagged and stretched itself around the whole top of the cell. It let out a thunderous boom as it glowed brightly. It wasn't much but it was something I was darn proud off. I haven't been able to do anything magical since these shackles had been bestowed upon me. And using the energy from the cloud itself, instead of just manipulating the water, I think was quite clever thinking of me.

I let out a low sigh as I stretched my arms out. I could still feel my magic pulsing to get out but unable to because of the shackles, confined within my very skin. But thankfully, it sizzled down back into my soul. And the humid air was once again pressing itself on my skin as I tried to inhale a deep breath. Small beads of sweat started to form over me as the heat pressed on.

I walked over to Xanthus who simply frowned at me with his arms crossed upon his chest. I for one wasn't going to allow Cethios to dampen our relationship with his manipulating words. I was not going to give up on Xanthus. I whispered the name of my love in a plea, whom continued to lean upon the wall on his shoulder with a frustrating determined frown upon his face, "Xanthus… Xanthus."

He was purposely ignoring me. How infuriating is that? Who likes to be ignored? Xanthus turned around from me as he leaned on his other shoulder, stubborn elf. I grabbed his other shoulder and turned him around so he could face me again. As I did his shoulder slammed into the wall behind him. I thought I pushed him lightly but, it was hard enough that the wall behind him cracked. Xanthus turned to me slightly appalled and astounded. I insisted, "Look, whether you want to hear it or not I'm still going to tell you. Or perhaps better yet, I'll just show you."

I quickly unlaced my front top and pulled the laces from my back. I then threw my corset and shirt at him to get his attention, of course I left my bra on though. I took his hands and placed them on my stomach as I rubbed them all over my side. Once I did that I had gained his attention, he turned in concern and in curiosity. Xanthus bend over slightly as he examined the enormous scar that ran from the middle of my stomach and around towards the middle of my back. His soft warm fingertips glided over my skin as he sent chills down my spine, forcing me to uncontrollable release a soft moan. He also examined the other small scars that swept and protruded across my chest and my back. They were from when Cethios was torturing me for answers. Xanthus replied softly to me with a frown, "Oh Azalea, how did this happen to you?"

"By the fireplace here in this exact dungeon, Zethron tried to kill me with a fired sword. But as soon as he left Cethios saved me the only way he knew how without taking off my shackles. He transferred some of his magic into me so I could close this wound up. Hence the kiss, trust me, there was nothing desirable or passionate about it at all. That was the only way to kept me from vanishing within the mist and fading away like those at the Valley of Melinatha. The other smaller scars are actually from Cethios himself, he humorously made it a game to cut me with his blade whenever I refused to answer any of his questions."

Xanthus stood there running his fingertips over my scars as he whispered with sadness, "Azalea, I'm so sorry. I can't believe I almost lost you. And undeniable enough, yet unbelievable, Cethios saved you."

I with took his fingers as he gazed into my eyes. I replied to him, "Know this, there was nothing that happened between Cethios and me. I love you, and I will not fail my promise that I have vowed to you. Why do you keep doubting me? What must I do for you to know besides me giving you my word?"

Suddenly Xanthus smirked arrogantly as if he had forgiven all that had occurred. His smile sent waves of chills down my core. He raised one of those gorgeous eyebrows and sensually replied, "I know what you can do to convince me so. Tell me, can you recall what promises were made that night in the Caves of Esmera. Do you recall how I made you feel, what you said?"

I let go of his hands as took a step back from him. Of course I remembered what I said, and how tantalizing he had made me feel. Xanthus took a small step towards me with teasing and wanting eyes as I; uncontrollable took another step back from him. Xanthus licked the corner of his top lip smugly and asked, "Azalea, why are you backing away from me?"

"I'm not sure myself. Why are you gazing upon me with those alluring eyes of yours? Are you expecting me to allow you to entice me, here?"

Xanthus lunged a bit towards me as I let out a small shriek and jumped back. Xanthus unbuttoned his shirt and tossed it with my clothes as he replied with humor in his voice, "Are you nervous? I can feel your senses enhancing with lust. You want me, like I want you."

I bumped my back against the wall as my breaths heaved erotically within my chest. I glanced behind me as I was cornered into the wall with nowhere else to go. I slowly raised my gaze towards him as he rested his hands in his pockets. Soft sensual tremors fled my nerves. I whispered through trembling lips, "I am trapped here, vulnerable to your soft touch, your enticing caresses, willing, accepting, anticipating to do your will and..."

With that being said Xanthus lunged towards me as he slammed me into the wall behind us. The wall seemed to crack as Xanthus caressed my skin with his strong hands, kissing my neck, teasing my ear with his lips. I let out a small moan of pleasure as I whispered through heavy breaths, "Is there something you would have me say or are wanting for me to say?"

Through rough breaths Xanthus groaned, "Perhaps you can start by moaning out the name of the one who pleasures you with love, saying my name as you curve to my touch." He pressed himself deeply into me as he kissed me passionately. I ran my fingers over his chest down to his pants, unbuckling his buttons and tugging down on the zipper. As I did he picked me up by my legs as his lips found my chest. Somewhere between that pleasurable moment, he had slammed me down onto the floor with himself on top of me, his lips never leaving my skin. As moments later we continued into desirable love, becoming one. And as we continued our love throughout the night, that little lightning bolt that surrounded the cell seemed to glow ever more brightly.

Enchanted Dungeon

20

I awoke before dawn and quickly got dressed, as did Xanthus. After he was finished, he came over to me to help me tie my laces. But before I placed the corset on, he slowly rubbed his fingers over my skin. I glanced down at my stomach as I surprisingly found that all of the scars were gone, especially the one that Zethron left me. I was astounded that I forgot what I was doing. All I could do was stare at my skin. Xanthus though as if not paying any attention to my reaction, placed my final top part on, my corset, as he started to tie the laces on the back. He whispered within my ear as his lips brushed my ear lobe, "The scars on your back are gone as well."

I turned around to face him as all he could do was smile lovingly and patiently. I asked without thinking it through, "But how could that have happened?"

Xanthus looked at me sarcastically as he grinned from ear to ear and raised one eyebrow up. I sighed and rolled my eyes at him, oh right, of course. I sighed; I am glad to have the scars that were left by my enemies gone. I don't have to live my future in constant reminder with those scars, of theses horrid days.

Just as we finished up, we heard a low bang as the door from the top of the stairs slowly opened. It then closed slowly with another soft bang as it echoed throughout the dungeon. We heard low mumbling from someone but, couldn't really make out just who it was. Suddenly a bright white light engulfed the whole dungeon momentarily. Briefly after that Xanthus shoved me behind him as he withdrew his sword. I did as well. I for one wasn't going to appear to be a coward.

As the footsteps descended quickly down an elf suddenly came into view. Thank goodness, it was Morpheus! Relief came to Xanthus and I as we both sighed out. I laughed almost hysterically, "Morpheus! I am so glad to see you again."

Xanthus and I placed our swords back onto our sides. Xanthus walked up to the cell bars and asked, "Where have you been all this time? Last I saw you; you were jumping about in the room that got blasted open with Azalea in it."

Morpheus chuckled slightly as he tossed us a small loaf of bread each. I eagerly started to chew mine. I was starving. Morpheus shook his head gratefully, "Yeah, I'm so glad you caught her. And as soon as I left the room, which was easier to get out of after Azalea was gone, I ran into this beautiful fairy named Priniza. She helped me hide out for the night. She even conjured up a spell to produce fake wings on me for last night's ball and…"

Xanthus ceased his chewing and he swelled with anger. Oh dear, that was all it took as he snapped, "You went to a ball last night? You went out on amusement, ignoring the purpose on why we are here! Did you even think if we were alright?"

Morpheus stepped back as he frowned and admitted, "Honestly yes, I did think you both would be alright. I knew you would be needing my help eventually. But I didn't know I needed permission from you to enjoy myself momentarily at this ball."

"Enjoy yourself? Morpheus, how could you have this mentality while we are out trying to save ourselves from Cethios? Did you even stop and think what we were dealing with? I'm so glad you can simply forget about me. It's not like I needed your help or anything of that matter!"

I swear if there weren't any bars between them, I am sure they would be on the floor fighting by now at each other's throats. They glared at one other but, Morpheus broke the silence first, "Well at least I am here now, aren't I? Besides the point, if I hadn't been there at the ball, I would have never known where you both were. Cethios kept constantly glancing his shoulder and over to this wall over and over, as if he was reassuring himself or something. If not for that, I would have never figured it out and I would have never found you both!"

I thought Morpheus had a good point as I nodded in agreement with cheeks full of bread. But I had to interrupt them, Xanthus didn't seem like he was going to let it go anytime soon. I gulped the bread down and agreed, "Xanthus, Morpheus is right."

Awe crap, did that just come out of my mouth. Xanthus turned and gazed at me, appalled for me even being on his side. I urged on, "Xanthus I do not mean to offend you. But the important thing is that Morpheus is here now and that he didn't forget about us. Also, Morpheus, I do hope that Priniza still remains faithful to Whisperia. If so, then I am more than happy for you both. But right now, we have to concentrate on escaping."

Morpheus quickly lifted his hand as if he had remembered something. He replied, "Oh also, last night near the end of the ball Cethios had gathered a couple of fairy men. I followed as well; we were all in disguise anyway so I hoped he wouldn't have recognized me. But we met up in this room away from the ball and this other fairy named Zethron…"

Xanthus and I quickly chimed in, "Zethron?"

Xanthus glanced back to me as if expecting me to apologize for some reason. Why, I had completely no clue but nonetheless I shrugged my shoulders as he turned back to Morpheus. He asked him, "Are you sure that was his name?"

Morpheus nodded and continued, "Yes, Zethron and Cethios confirmed that they will strike in battle with the elves of Trinafin, as well as with the rebel fairies against them. The rebel fairies though somehow contacted King Alcander and wanted to join him against Zethron and Cethios. There will be a battle in the Depths of Galligro. I have already sent forth Cetus to inform King Duralos and whatever faithful fairies he has left to join us. And as for Orion, he is on his way to Trinafin to…"

I quickly interrupted Morpheus as his words just hit me, "Wait, Cetus is going to King Duralos? But, would he even believe him or…"

Morpheus raised his right palm up as it glowed. He replied, "He is taking a letter from James and…"

Realization hit Xanthus as he interrupted, "Cetus is flying? Is, is he alright?"

Morpheus nodded and took in a deep breath and continued, "Yes he is alright. He briefly explained to me what Hypathia had done for him and what had happened. He is also going to go gather air support for the battle from Whisperia after he meets with the King. James then also found Snowfire and…"

I felt as if a gust of wind had slapped me in the face. How could I have forgotten about my beloved Snowfire! Last I saw her she was on the ground fighting at The Valley of Melinatha! I just had figured that she was alright and was with James, and that she had left with the elves. I asked Morpheus, "Is Snowfire alright? Where was she?"

"She was in a dungeon on the other side of the castle. She was not harmed; she was quite comfortable in a cage as her snow leopard self. She was very much frightened but, she was alright. She was still able to transform herself into her true dragon form. I think that some of Cethios' fairies found her, and must have not realized just exactly who she was. She is helping Orion now, as they are both on their way to Trinafin."

I gave a low sigh of relief knowing that she was alright. I felt immensely guilty but, it's not like I could have gone looking for her. I was in a dungeon half of the time myself. I mumbled to them both, "So, when are we getting out of this dungeon? We have a war to prepare for and go to."

Xanthus and Morpheus quickly turned their stare towards me. Xanthus was the first to speak as he replied glowering, "We are not going through this again, are we?"

"Xanthus look, you didn't stop me from the last battle. What makes you think that you're going to stop me this time?"

Xanthus glared at me as he hissed through his lips, "I can and will stop you."

I gave a low gulp. I turned my eyes towards Morpheus as he shrugged and turned his glance towards Xanthus. I took in a deep breath assured him, "Look, I am at better use to everyone helping than just sitting on the side waiting hopelessly! You probably will exasperate yourselves anyway attempting to exclude me from the war like last time. So how about this time you don't fight me and just allow me to be there."

Xanthus turned to face Morpheus as Morpheus regretfully admitted, "You know, she does have a point."

Xanthus sighed as he threw his hands at his side. He turned back to face me as he half heartily shouted at me, "Fine! But you are not to leave sight from Morpheus or myself! Azalea so help me, if you get captured from Cethios once more... I can't, I don't know what I would do. I wouldn't know if...."

I walked up to Xanthus as I placed my hands upon his shoulders. He pulled me close as he wrapped his arms tenderly around my waist. He leaned over and rested his head between my neck and shoulders. I sighed, "Xanthus, I am not a newborn. I do not need constant supervision. I can take care of myself. Besides I do not doubt you or Morpheus."

"With those shackles you do need supervision. You are not escaping our sight; do you hear me. Take it or leave it, I can and will send my princess, my love, to Trinafin for safety with Cetus. You are just going to stress yourself even more if you try to leave it."

I buried my face within his chest. I took in a deep breath of his scent, engulfing my senses. Xanthus pushed aside my hair as he brushed the side of my face with his thumb, placing soft kisses upon my head. I nodded without looking into his eyes. What choice did I honestly have? It's not like I was going to wander out on my own. Morpheus impatiently replied, "Great, now that we have that settled, let's find a way out shall we. My enchantment on the door, inside and out, will only last for about an hour or so... I hope."

Xanthus murmured under his breath, "Let's do hope."

Xanthus released me as Morpheus walked over to a small woodened table where some swords laid upon. He with took two of them as he walked back over and handed one to Xanthus. They both walked over to the cell door as they both stabbed their sword into each side of the lock. Morpheus suggested, "Perhaps if we loosen the lock, we can wedge it enough so we can open the door freely."

Xanthus nodded as they both placed one of their feet upon the door. They gripped the handle of the sword tightly within their grasp. Then they flipped sideways in the air in different directions, still holding onto the sword. They both plopped back onto the floor on their feet. I smirked to myself, what was the point in that. Half of the sword was still stuck in the lock of the cell door. The other half was in their hands. As they momentarily pondered Xanthus replied breathlessly, "Alright, let's try something else."

Morpheus nodded as he suggested, "Well, what if we step on it. You know bust it that way?"

"Let's try."

I watched them take a step back, then jump onto the half dull sword. I continued to watch them as they landed onto the floor. Another piece of the swords had broken off and yet a smaller piece of sword still remained wedged in the cell door. I had to admit, this was getting interesting to watch. With much frustration, Morpheus breathlessly replied from the floor, "Well, perhaps I can bend the metal so that you both can escape through it."

They both stood and dusted themselves off. Xanthus asked, "Of course, like a reverse on each side?"

"Yeah, something of the sort." Morpheus held his glowing right palm towards the bars as he replied, "Bars bend to and fro, remove yourselves from this bow." His palm glowed intensely as it released a blue hue. It quickly shone through the bars like a vibrating echo. But before the light could reach the other side, Xanthus quickly raised his right palm up as it glowed a purple hue. The vibrating spell bounced off of Xanthus' palm as it seemed to attack the bars of the dungeon. And within seconds it seemed to send off a sonic boom effect as it knocked over Xanthus and Morpheus. Once the light dimmed off disappointment over took them both as they glanced at the bars.

The dungeon bars, in some parts, were twisted into bow shapes. It wasn't even big enough to slide my leg through. Xanthus and I were still trapped in the cell. I chuckled to myself. Both elves stood with a fresh wave of determination. Xanthus replied to Morpheus, "Well, that was a different approach in thinking, what made you think of the word bow?"

"Honestly that was the first word that came into my head that rhymed with fro! Besides I had to think quickly, I don't see you trying!"

Xanthus frowned as he glanced around the dungeon. They both appeared even more determined than before in escaping. Xanthus replied to Morpheus, "Bring over two more swords." Morpheus quickly ran over to the table and with took two more swords. He came back and gave one to Xanthus. Xanthus gripped tightly upon the handle of the sword within his grasp. He jolted it quickly, and with that it started to glow red. Morpheus quickly did the same. Xanthus replied, "With this sword I do say, turn to fire if you may. Have these bars turn to feather, strip them down from their leather."

The two elves suddenly slashed the bars with the swords. But it didn't seem that the swords did much to the bars. As I gave another glance at their swords it had seemed that they had turned into some type of leather belt. I couldn't help it, I started to laugh. Both of the elves seemed confused by this. As they glanced back down to the leather belts, it quickly turned into a long white feather. Oh how my side hurt with waves of laughter rolling through me. Xanthus on the other hand, who wasn't impressed replied exasperated, "I think I want to cry."

Morpheus on the other hand started to join in with my laughter as he chuckled, "You do have to admit, this is sort of humorous. But, you do

302

realize by now that this dungeon is enchanted. So, whatever we do is completely impractical."

Suddenly their perfect white feathers burst into flames as they quickly released it from their grasp. We all watched the two fiery feathers soar to the ground, then plop and singe away to nothing but a dusty print. They both frowned and turned to me as my fit of laughter continued. By this time, I was sitting on the floor, just about bent over in laughter. The two elves watched me as they waiting patiently for me to finish. Moments later after my humor sizzled away, I chuckled, "Would you like me to try?"

Both of the exhausted elves nodded. I stood and slowly made my way over to the cell door as I glanced up. Sure enough, I saw that the little lightning bolt still remained surrounding the cell with its glow. It didn't glow as brightly as last night but, it still glowed somewhat. I closed my eyes as I opened my wings to their full extent. I flew up a bit as I let my toes gently brush the ground. My hands glowed a dim pink hue as I reached for that hidden magic deep inside that I found last night, and was able to manipulate that lightning bolt. I don't think Zethron or Cethios ever thought about these shackles having a default, a loop hole thankfully. It took me a few minutes but eventually I found it. I overheard rumbling above me, which I'm sure meant that, that black cloud was hovering above me. But thankfully, it didn't rain down.

I opened my eyes and reached up for that lightning bolt. It zigzagged back into that small lightning bolt that I had first started out with. I flew back down as I walked over to the cell lock. I whispered to the little lightning bolt in my hands, "Please unlock this cell right now, I really do not care how."

The little blue lightning bolt zigzagged out of my hands and into the lock. I stood there staring at it as for the moment nothing seemed to be happening. Morpheus mumbled, "Well, that was pointless."

I slowly lifted my eyes to him as I whispered, "Never underestimate the natural magic of the lands. Wait with patience and you shall see."

We continued to wait as I slowly backed away from the door. Moments later small blue shocks of static started to be fusing out of the lock. Larger and larger the sparks grew until it seemed to conquer the entire cell door. Suddenly the lightning seemed to give a static shock throughout the dungeon as the cell door came flying off. It landed on the floor in front of me.

Static clung to everything as my dress stuck to my legs. Not to mention the static in my hair! It was just about standing on ends. I ran my fingers though my hair as small blue static danced around my fingertips. They seemed to infuse within my shackles as they disappeared. The two elves stood awestruck as I replied, "Not completely helpless, am I?"

Xanthus shook his head at me as if he wanted to say something but, rather simply just avoided it. Xanthus and I quickly jumped over the cell door on the floor and made our way out of the dungeons' cell. But it was just in time as for once we were out the cell door jolted up and slammed itself back in place. It made us all jump as it startled us. I for one didn't know it was going to go back on. As I turned back to face Morpheus and Xanthus, they had their arms crossed as they stared at me with smirks on their faces. I simply smiled shyly and shrugged my shoulders, "Well, I didn't say it was going to last. The point is that we are out, right?"

Xanthus rolled his eyes as Morpheus broke out into laughter. I couldn't help myself either, I chuckled a bit too. We all ran up the stairs to leave this horrid place. I never wanted to see this place ever again. Morpheus chanted a few words under his breath as the door lit up. We were now able to open it as he removed his enchantment. Once we pushed our way out, nothing would have prepared us for what we were about to face.

Betrayal or Loyalty

21

We slowly pushed the door open and made our way out. There before us was a hall that seemed to be unoccupied; as if for a couple of centuries. As the door closed behind us, I turned to see that the edges melted away. It appeared as if a plain wall was there before us. I walked ahead of them only to find myself pushing aside some cobwebs that were filled with heavy dust. I mean, how could this have happened. This was impossible, how could this hall become so dusty and deserted in just one day! I mean, there wasn't even any footprints in the dust either, just the ones we were making right now! I turned back to Morpheus confused, "Are you sure the masquerade ball was in here, last night?"

Morpheus' eyes were wide with distraught as he insisted, "Yes I am. Look, up in the ceiling, you can even see the decorations from last night. But, how?"

Suddenly footsteps started to ascend closer to us from the side entrance. We all drew our swords and spun around, prepared to fight. But to our surprise it was only James and Priniza with their swords drawn out as well. I exclaimed, "James!" I ran up to him without hesitation. As soon as I neared him I embraced him, so immensely that I almost knocked him down. But in between his smile he seemed confused and lost. I stepped back from him as I asked, "James, are you alright?"

He nodded but then turned to Morpheus and replied almost hesitantly, "I'm not quite sure. I too was here last night in this hall. It did not appear any sort of the way it is now."

I hung my sword back to my waist as I asked, "Well did everyone come to this masquerade last night? I was not invited."

Xanthus walked up to James as he asked, "I'm not understanding, are you both sure this is the right room?"

Suddenly the curtains from the top windows were pushed aside. It revealed ten soldier fairies, some with their swords drawn and some with their bows extended with arrows pointing right at us. And there amongst them was Cethios with a colossal smirk upon his face, as well as Razyna.

I frowned and shook my head at disbelief that she had betrayed us. I turned to look at our side. We had Morpheus, James, Priniza, Xanthus and myself. Five against twelve really isn't fair. I glanced at Priniza, she was not at all happy with her sister. Her glare could have burned a hole through Razyna's head! Cethios started to clap his hands as he chuckled, "What a great element of surprise don't you think? And look, I finally have the prince here to join us…" Cethios seemed confused as he pointed a finger to Xanthus and then to Morpheus. He replied, "Now that's a good trick I say, I think I can honestly say that I am certain, on who is the prince now. Isn't that right Xanthus? And to think, I did have you within my grasp last night in the dungeon. Huh, and look, here we have the miraculous sword trainer James. Back from the dead are you, didn't I finish you off oh ancient one?"

James smiled at his words as he replied, "Like I've told you before, oh ignorant one, Azalea is stronger and wiser than you have ever thought she was. You doubt her intelligence, that's where your mistake has always been."

Cethios had become full of rage at James' words. I withdrew my sword back up to join everyone else. I turned to James as he simply nodded his head in assurance. And for some reason it was as if I had read his mind, astonishing the things James knows. I'm sure the possibilities were endless with this fairy. I turned my face back towards Cethios as I raised my left palm up. I held it there flat, opened as if I held something within my palm.

I closed my eyes and concentrated with all my might on that little faithful lightning bolt. As I smiled from ear to ear, my palm gave a light pink hue as from my shackles, small blue static lightning bolts formed. Then it combined into a blue lightning globe. It was there, hovering above my palm as if waiting for instructions.

And by the looks of Cethios' face, he was very much in shock. I was very proud of myself, for I now was completely aware on how to manipulate the little lightning bolt, and put it to my use. It was the only magic that I could use with these shackles on, besides manipulating water of course. I turned to James as his eyes revealed all, he couldn't have been prouder of me.

James turned to face Cethios as he too opened his palm up and flat. His palm glowed a low white light briefly. Then there within James' palm formed a fire globe. Within the globe itself, seemed as if burning lava flowing wildly.

306

Xanthus seemed to close his eyes as he bent his neck to and fro. It seemed as if he too was trying to conjure up a fire globe. He opened his eyes and gave a wide grin as he shook within his skin. It was as if he received the chills of some sort. But within moments he too lifted his glowing palm up as a fire globe hovered in the air above it.

Cethios' soldiers appeared disoriented momentarily, but they still stood their ground. Cethios curled his lip in utter rage as he sneered, "Well-well-well, I can see that James' techniques are still being taught here and there. Nonetheless, my soldiers are very well prepared as well."

The tension was stirring quite a bit for it seemed that no one wanted to be the first to break it. But it was quickly broken by Razyna as she flew down towards her sister and gave the first strike. It seemed to throw Priniza off guard as she stumbled back and clashed her sword against her sisters. I threw my lightning globe at Razyna. It hit her with such force that sent her flying off of the ground and into the air about twenty feet high. My lightning globe reverted its course and flung back into my hand, and sizzled back into my shackles. Then, the rest of the soldiers and Cethios flew down too as some arrows were fired.

Xanthus and James quickly set them a blaze with their fire globes as everyone's swords collided with another. I tried to make my way over to Cethios but two enormous fairy soldiers were now clashing their swords against mine. Suddenly the unthinkable happened. One of the soldiers I was fighting stepped back and formed a black energy globe above his palm. He chucked it at me.

I screamed in pain as it hit my skin and burned. The impact also sent me spinning into the air as I pummeled into a nearby wall. As I landed hard onto the floor I tried to quickly regain my strength and focus my eye sight. But my subconscious mind was telling me otherwise. I glanced up to my horror as I saw a soldier running towards me. As I laid on the floor helplessly I could see that his intentions were to drive the sword right into my chest. I waited nervously for him to get closer. And once he did I quickly raised my leg and kicked the sword out of his hands and into the air. I saw my opportune moment as I drove my sword into his chest.

I stood as I caught the other soldiers' sword from the air. I then drove it into the other soldier that was behind me, whom which he thought, would catch me by surprise but in turn I did. For I don't think he saw me kick up the other soldiers' sword into the air and catch it. I withdrew both swords and threw the soldiers sword onto the ground.

I turned to face Priniza and Razyna to see how they were doing but, to my surprise Razyna was now fighting on our side. They both were taking on a huge soldier fairy together as it seemed that they were just about to succeed. It felt good knowing that Razyna was back on our side.

James gained my attention as he called out to me, he threw something to Xanthus, whom threw it to Morpheus, whom in turn threw it to me. I opened my wings and flew up and caught it. It was Trathina's enchanted bow and arrows. I knew I had dropped them when I was sword fighting with Cethios back in The Valley of Melinatha. I flew back down as I placed my sword back onto my side and the case on my back.

I drew out an arrow as I aimed it right at Cethios heart… I froze… Was this how he was meant to die, by my hands? I stood there frozen as I watched Xanthus fighting with Cethios, but I was in an emotional state! I realized to my horror that, I couldn't let go of the arrow. In some strange weird way, my feelings for him deep down were still there. That friendship that burned in my heart centuries ago still somehow remained. I wanted another chance with him, to confront him about what I saw when he kissed me. I needed to know. I didn't want to kill him. I did owe him one for saving my life from Zethron. And this moment would be it. I wouldn't owe him no more.

It seemed as if everything was moving slowly for me to even comprehend the situation. Then for some reason I heard Morpheus within the distant, he was shouting something I couldn't make out. Then as quick as an echo, it all came back to me. I realized just then that Cethios had Xanthus at his will. I glanced over to James as he too was about to fail. I had to choose and fast. And yet once more I just had to save his life.

I let go of the arrow as it moved like a blur into the soldier on top of James. Once the soldier fell the arrow whipped back around into the casing on my back. James took in a deep breath as he bowed his head in thanks. I turned my gaze towards Xanthus.

Suddenly, Xanthus fell to the ground as his heavy breaths seemed to concave in his chest. The unimaginable was about to occur. Cethios pulled his sword back and was about to drive it into Xanthus' chest. And it was already too late for me to retrieve an arrow. I scream out, "Cethios no!"

Suddenly Razyna flew in front of Xanthus as Cethios drove his sword into Razyna's chest. Cethios scrunched his nose in with utter regret as tears instantly swelled in his eyes as the realization hit of what Razyna had done. He sighed heavily as he gazed into the eyes of Razyna, who now choked on her breaths. Suddenly as if an epiphany shook his very nerves, rage replaced his sorrow as he pushed his sword further into her to chest. He then withdrew it and stumbled back on his own feet. Priniza finished a soldier as she turned her gaze towards her sister. She screamed in horror at the sight.

The three remaining soldiers that were left and Cethios suddenly flew up into the air and back to the window where they first came out from. Cethios exclaimed through unwilling breaths, "Much grief goes out to you all, but every young greedy heart finds it doom. I must be off, I cannot linger here any longer and entertain the lot of you. I have a battle to prepare for, to The Depths of Galligro I go. Till another day Azalea."

Deep anger filled me as I saw Razyna now on the floor as Xanthus held on to her hand gently. I quickly made a decision out of rage as I drew an arrow and sent it flying towards Cethios. Of course Cethios smirked to himself as he thought that it wouldn't reach him. But little did he know that the arrow flying towards him was enchanted. Once he realized that the arrow was not going to falter, he grabbed a nearby soldier.

Cethios placed the soldier between him and the arrow. Once the arrow succeeded, it was retrieving itself back to its case, Cethios allowed the soldier fall onto the floor below. Cethios opened his left palm as a dark brown globe formed above his palm. He replied sinisterly, "Two can play at this game Azalea."

Cethios threw the globe at the ground as it seemed to shatter into millions of pieces. He then fled out the window with the remaining soldiers. And within seconds the ground started to shake violently. James quickly flew over to me and took me over to Razyna and Xanthus. James quickly formed a shield over us. His hands glowed a bright white as Morpheus quickly formed one over himself and Priniza.

Pieces of the hall crumbled and fell onto the floor around us as the ground continued to quake. Moments later the violently shaking had stopped. But pieces of the ceiling continued to fall. And after the ceiling had ceased its crumpling, James and Morpheus ceased their shields. The hall now had huge chunks of the ceiling gone, as you were able to see the afternoon sky.

I bent over to Razyna as golden tears slowly fled my eyes. Around us, dim red lights started to shine from the dead bodies as their energy life was leaving them. I turned to Xanthus as I placed my right hand across his shirt as burgundy blood covered across his chest. Xanthus with took my hand and gave it a small squeeze. He whispered, "Cethios' sword did not penetrate me at all but…"

We both glanced over to Razyna as I with took her other hand and held it between my fingers. I cried, "Why Razyna, why would you do such a thing?"

She attempted to laugh but couldn't, all she could do was cough and wheeze. Priniza on the other hand was utterly distraught as she buried her face in Morpheus' arms. Razyna replied softly, "You were right, Cethios last night, Cethios told me about his terrible plans with Zethron and… And with… And… His evil partnership wounds him and can't change him… I couldn't… I don't know why… Please, please forgive me for betraying you, your majesty."

I placed my right hand over her heart as I whispered to her, "Razyna, I have told you, even now I am only Azalea to you. My good friend always and forever. You have never betrayed me, never. But, why did you…"

Razyna turned her head slightly as she faced her sister, she uttered to her, "Priniza, I'm so sorry, forgive me. Continue to keep growing stronger each and every single day…"

Priniza smiled under all of the tears that fled her face. She nodded as she placed her glowing right palm over her heart. Razyna turned her gaze towards me and Xanthus as choked out, "Azalea… I think I would have made a grand protector of the royal family, don't you think?"

I nodded and whispered softly to her, "Razyna, you are a grand protector of the royal family."

Razyna smiled, coughed and slowly turned to Xanthus, "Xanthus… I never had true love before, so then… I shall protect yours."

I bowed my head slightly to her as Xanthus kissed her on the forehead. She smiled as she closed her eyes. Within moments her body started to give off a low red light. She then gently faded into a ghostly figure. Seconds later, nothing laid before us as if she never had existed, she became a memory as we stared at emptiness. I closed my eyes, at least the smile that rested on her delicate face never left, she went in peace.

Morpheus had let go of Priniza as she rushed and threw herself on me. She held me tightly as she silently cried on my shoulder. But strangely enough, I had this feeling as if I was in a dream. As if, I didn't want to come back to reality to face the truth, the truth that Cethios had killed Razyna, and that she was gone, forever.

I gazed over to James whom seemed as if he had just shed a tear and quickly wiped it away. Pain and grief seemed to concave into both of our chests with deep sadness. I know how James was feeling. But, I knew that I had to stay strong for Priniza.

Moment later Xanthus, Priniza and I stood from the dusty ground. Priniza's tears though had now turned into silent hiccups. I replied to her, "You know Priniza, the only thing you can do is take that love that she had for you, and apply it deep into your heart. In which that shall give you even more strength and courage to move ahead with life. We live on braver every single day with them in our hearts, with their memory entwined within our souls."

James walked up to Priniza and me as he embraced us both. As he let go he replied to me, "Azalea my dear, I have watched you grow within the last couple of months, in strength. And I do say that I am proud of you. Also, your ability to speak with the wisdom of your heart has grown with every step that you take."

James bowed his head, as I did back in return. We started to exit the hall in silence, when our moment was shattered. We all reached for our ears as the devastating screeching noise echoed with pain within our ears.

The Truth of Being Doubtful

22

Once the horrendous screeching was over, we all ran for the doors. As we slammed into them and poured out, I noticed that the hall was perfectly intact. I glance back into the ballroom to see it almost destroyed. How strange I thought, how could Cethios' globe only affect the ballroom and not everywhere else? I didn't have much time to ponder it over as James started to run down the hall. He shouted back to us as he continued to run, "Quickly this way! I know a way out of the castle. Let's make hast, I need to glimpse at the creatures that made those shrieks! I have a strong perspective on what they are but, I hope that my mind deceives me!"

We ran down the halls as we turned through multiple corridors. It seemed as if we were running forever! My feet were getting tired and sore. Where was James taking us? I hope James knew where we were heading to.

As I glanced behind me, I saw that Priniza was now flying a couple of feet off of the ground. I knew she was not accustomed on running for so long. Flying was her best way to keep up with us.

Moments later we finally reached a brown brick door with heavy moss almost covering its entirety. James pushed the door slowly as if trying not to get moss on his hands. And once opened we found ourselves being blinded by the suns' heavy rays. You couldn't tell where anything was, all you could see was the bright blinding sun. So, without being able to see, one by one we fell down a steep sandy hill. Except Priniza though, see kept on flying as she followed us slowly down.

I thought James replied that he knew where we were going. But perhaps he was caught off guard and became mislead. So briefly after landing on warm sand and on top of everyone else, I slowly came to my feet and started to dust myself off. Priniza caught up with us as she helped Morpheus to his feet. Xanthus helped James up as he shouted around, "Is everyone alright?"

We all sort of grunted to his question as James glanced back up to the door that still remained open on top of the sandy hill. He rubbed his head slowly as he replied, "Do forgive me, this was not where that door lead to last night. I wonder if perhaps I went out through another door that appeared the exact same. Although, I thought there was only one door of that nature in the castle. How bizarre, I wonder if we ran through a different side of the castle. I'm not quite sure how though…"

I walked up to James as I patted him on the shoulder. Funny though as I did sand fell off of him. I chuckled, "James, in that castle nothing ever seems right. It is its own maze, strong enough to even transfigure your mind, to persuade it that it is something else or somewhere else."

James nodded and smiled at my words. I turned and started to glance around at where exactly we ended up at. A few feet from us were two enormous statues, one of a falcon and the other of an eagle. They seemed to be at least twelve feet high. And between the two was a brick road that seemed to descend into a dirt path. As I followed, the dirt path with my eyes, I noticed that in random order were other different bird statues. They stood facing different direction near trees and in open area.

I cautiously walked over to a statue as I placed my hand upon it. It felt very cool to the touch. Suddenly the stone statue started to make a low rumbling noise. I stepped back as I heard Xanthus grumble over the noise, "Azalea, what did you do now?"

"Oh, so naturally it's my fault!"

We were amazed at what was transfiguring before our very eyes. It was incredible and unbelievable. The statue in front of us was changing, well part of it was. The face was changing into an elf face with long curvy ears. Except the mouth still remained a beak. And it seemed that from the waist up, it was changing into half an elf! The wings though, seemed to be merging with arms. Also, across the front chest seemed to be covered with feathers except the stomach though, perhaps it was a female bird race of some sort.

I glanced to my left as I saw James standing there in completely awe stuck. I asked him, "James, do you know where we are? I have never known that this existed on this side of the city before."

James ran his fingers over his neck slowly as if he was deeply pondering something. Then as if realizing and remembered something, he opened his eyes wide open with excitement. He gasped, "These statues represent the lost civilization, the lost city that belonged to the Cristats. The Cristats used to thrive near this city many centuries and eras ago in peace. I thought their kind became extinct, to tired and depressed to continue to carry on their race. When I was a child, I encountered one. When I whispered the sight of them to my mother she was in awe. She replied to me to take a long glance at them, for they were the last ones in existence and that their race was soon to vanish. It was memorable to glance at something so magnificent, so ancient, one of the civilizations that carried on their race for centuries, before fading away with the others that we only read about now."

I cleared my throat as I asked, "So, what does this statue represent though? Is this truly what they looked like?"

James seemed to smile and frown at my question as if he was unsure on how to react to this news. But as he turned to me, he smiled sadly as if he didn't want to disappoint me. Xanthus turned from the statue and walked up to us as he replied with his hand upon his chin, "I actually read about this recently about a year ago, before Morpheus and I traveled east of Trinafin. The Cristats were a lost civilization of half bird and half elf. Most of the royal ones were hawks though, as for the rest, they were blue and red birds. But somewhere along my reading, it seemed as if they betrayed their own kind. The blue and red Cristats over threw the royal hawk Cristats, if I am to be correct though. Also, if these statues are active, that means…"

His words were lost as the smile on James' face seemed to be growing. James walked up to another statue and placed his hands upon it. It too suddenly rumbled and morphed into a Cristat. James replied with a grin that spread from ear to ear, "That means that this is the correct way to the city of Xylina."

I asked, "Xylina? That's the name of their city?"

James smiled and nodded as he replied, "Yes, she was their first enchantress of their civilization many ages ago when the lands were being created."

Huh, I thought. I asked James, "So, does that mean that mostly all of the cities are named after someone of importance?"

"Yes and no, but, not necessarily, knowledge should not concern us at this very moment in time. Right now, we should be concentrating on those shrieks that we heard earlier. They were slightly similar to those of when I heard them as a child. Also, we must be more concerned with the fact that, if Cethios has befriended them. Therefore, it is imperative that we discover if they are friend or foe."

Xanthus nodded in agreement, "Yes, let's just hope that luck is on our side and does not falter."

As he said his last words, he turned and replied them directly at me. What was he meaning by that? Was he suggesting something that I missed? I crossed my arms across my chest as I asked, "And what is that supposed to mean?"

Xanthus raised one eyebrow up with half a glare as he replied, "Honestly, back there you had a clear shot of Cethios. You didn't release the arrow, you faltered."

"No, I panicked. I thought you would be alright. So I decided to use my arrow wisely, I helped James instead."

"You faltered!"

"I panicked!"

"Azalea you're throwing the point off, you had a clear shot! You did not release your arrow upon Cethios. That action has revealed a lot about your feelings for him. It is actions like these that bring forth doubt in my mind. What am I supposed to do with these deeds that you bring forth upon yourself? In all honestly, it truly breaks my heart having these feeling that you wish to be captured by Cethios. It's like you want to be within his grasp."

I snorted; how could he even dare say something like that to me. Yes, I honestly wanted the chance to talk to Cethios, about what I saw in the short vision that I had about him when we kissed, about a few other things but, that was it! There was nothing else and I certainly did not want to be captured again! Why for, so I could be tortured again? Was he thinking clearly! I took in a deep breath as I gathered up my strength and half exclaimed to him, "I told you, I panicked. You can believe me or not, that is your choice. I am not forcing you to be with me. Just because we are destined does not mean it has to be fulfilled! I have told you once before and never again shall I repeat myself to you, I have chosen you because I love you, take it or leave it. Trust me and stop doubting me. If I didn't love you, don't you think I would be over there with him instead of here fighting with you? You of all people should know that, yes, killing in a battle is required, but never actually wanted! If I can spare a life, I will! I do not wish death upon anyone, even my enemies! The only thing I am regretting is me not being able to convince you, that I love you! Xanthus, you are stubborn to the core, since the day I first met you in the barn. Dismay all of

315

this nonsense or surely you will lose me, but it won't be to Cethios I can guarantee you that!"

And with that I slapped him as hard as I could in the face. Man, did I feel better after doing that! I turned from them and stormed down between some statues. I continued to storm off until I was a good five minutes away from them all. I was so frustrated with Xanthus that I didn't want to be near him at this very moment. I also didn't want him to see me dearly clutching my burning hand. Ouch! I mean, how could he be so thick headed! I wasn't sure if I could ever change his mind about not doubting me anymore. I finally stopped to take in a deep breath as I sat near a statue. Of course, once I leaned on it, it slowly rumbled slightly and morphed into a Cristat.

James turned toward Xanthus and frowned at him in disappointment as he pushed his glasses up. Xanthus shrugged his shoulders in as he asked, "You know her better than I do, am I wrong to think that? She does have something for him, does she not?"

James placed his hand upon Xanthus' shoulder as he sighed, "Come, let's wander off through the ruins, shall we?"

They started to slowly walk through the ruins of statues. Some were missing feet; others heads or some other body part. You could tell that time and nature had taken its toll on the stone. Small cactuses seemed to grow very well here and there, along with some small shrubs. Small birds darted in and out from the small holes of the statues. They had made homes from within the damages of the statues.

Moments later they stopped in front of a huge statue of a hawk. And yes, once Xanthus rested his hand upon it, it too rumbled slightly and morphed into a Cristat. James took in a deep breath as he let it out slowly and started, "I knew Azalea since she was born, per say. She has always kept this vivid imagination within her grasp. Even still today, I can see that spark within her eyes. But that imagination had gotten her in much trouble as she grew, her and Cethios. They were, how do you say, close friends that shared everything at one point. Perhaps Azalea still holds that dear to her heart. You know, when they were younger, they went to the main pool in the oasis near the library and enchanted the water with this substance that they found in the kitchen. It made the water very wiggly and stiff at the same time. They bounced on it for hours." James laughed to himself as Xanthus smiled and shook his head. James continued, "She told the king that they wanted to know how it felt to imagine they had another form other

316

than solid ground below their feet. Took the servants days to get that cleaned up and back to normal. But, the point of it all is that, yes, she does have feeling for Cethios. But they are not the ones that you should fear or dwell on. You know, when they were about four centuries away from their coming of age, Cethios invited Azalea to go with him to Urinia to spend a century there. The king forbade her to go so unfortunately Cethios went without her; there were no hard feeling between them. There were many things that he did without her anyway but, once he returned, he had become something that she feared. He was different and was filled with this darkness that even I could not see where it had come from. He had been manipulated somehow in some way that now, it was as if he was always betraying her. He was evil and he showed it against her. She could not understand any of it. But what you have to understand is that the love that she has and shares with you, shall never be broken or replaced. She loves you and no one else. If she truly did love him, she wouldn't have ran away the night they were going to announce their engagement. She ran because she did not want to marry Cethios, she ran to find love, she ran and found you."

Xanthus sighed as he took in all of the information deep within his mind. How could he be so upset with her, for he too ran to find true love. He ran from the crown and deceived his people and gave it temporarily to Morpheus. In which reminded him as he glanced around for Morpheus. He found him and Priniza gathering what they could find for logs. They were setting up a small fire as they laughed and enjoyed each other's company. He pondered James' words as he watched them. How he desperately wanted to enjoy that ignorant bliss with Azalea, to simply enjoy each other's company and not worry about any of the evil that surrounded them. He closed his eyes and thought of their time when they were in the City of Trinafin. A smile came to his face as he then opened his eyes slowly. James replied, "You know it's because of her intensive panicking and quick decisions that we are all here right now. The reason that you two have met, as well as for Morpheus and Priniza."

Right at that very moment he felt foolish and selfish. How could he have thought that Azalea could feel that way for Cethios? He had placed his own thoughts ahead of him without even discussing them with the fairy that he loves. He truly felt ashamed on how he had treated her.

Suddenly a silver tear escaped Xanthus' eye. He attempted to quickly wipe it away but failed, James had already seen it. James asked curiously, "If I may say, you two have already been together, haven't you?"

Xanthus turned and attempted to appear innocently confused. He was ashamed and did not want the elderly fairy to know of his endeavors with Azalea. But James nudged him in the arm with his elbow and smiled. Xanthus' face slightly blushed as he stuttered and gulped, "Well um, you see we were in a predicament that allowed, um… No-no that not it. You see we were in situation that…" Moments later it had seemed that Xanthus had given up all hopes in concealing the truth. He sighed in defeat, "How can you tell, is it really that obvious?"

James smiled and walked ahead of him a bit. He pointed towards my direction. Xanthus walked up a bit as he saw me softly crying to myself, sitting near a Cristat statue. You could see my golden tears slowly fall from my face as they glistened in the suns' light. James replied softly to Xanthus, "My lady's tears, they give off a golden hue that, no one else can shed. You shed tears with a sliver hue, unless my eyes were playing tricks on me. Although, I am getting old you see, or as Azalea likes to call it, ancient. But as ancient as I am, I know the signs of destined prophets, of love. I know an enchantment when I see one, but then again, not many fairies or elves know what I know, or have seen what I have seen." Xanthus smiled shyly as he knew that James knew about them. He felt sort of embarrassed but, what could he do. James replied with a warm smile, "Why don't you go to her, talk to her. Tell her how you truly feel. You'd be surprised on how understanding and open minded she can be. She is, unexpected. Remember, never underestimate her heart or her mind."

Xanthus nodded and patted James on the back as he made his way over to me. I on the other hand, sat by the statue and wiped my face with my fingertips. I placed my hands upon my knees as I still sat and leaned on the cool statue. I felt so tired, my body ached as well as my heart. How could Xanthus think that I wanted to be in Cethios' grasp? Wouldn't he think that if I did, I wouldn't have these forsaken shackles upon my skin in the first place?

I suddenly saw boots standing in front of me, it was Xanthus. He bent down and sat next to me. I replied without even glancing over to him, "I cannot honestly tell you why I didn't release the arrow. You're right, I faltered. But, not in the way you think I did. I understand that he almost took James life, well, in his eyes he did. I understand that he did take Razyna's life, and if not for her it would have been your life. But, killing him would not make it right, it would not bring her back. Two wrongs don't make a right. Besides, he could have taken my life ages ago but yet, he didn't. And even when Zethron was about to succeed in taking my life, Cethios gave it back to me. He saved me, even though on the outside of his skin there represent evil but, deep down I know the same Cethios that was my dear friend is somewhere trapped inside. But above all and most important is, why can't you trust me with all of your heart, if I have given you all of mine."

As I turned to face him Xanthus gazed deeply into my eyes. And once again, I melted, all of his love glazed over his almond-colored eyes. Then, silver tears formed over his eyes as a couple of them fell over his cheeks. I reached to wipe them away. But Xanthus quickly withdrew my hands within his. He replied, "Azalea no, I am not ashamed that I love you. I am not ashamed that I fear for your life, or that you will leave me, or worse, that your life would be taken by force. I have waited for so long to find someone like you. And now, that I finally have you sometimes it feels as if it is all too good to be true. I love you with all that I have, and it is that- that frightens me. I fear that I will become vulnerable and weak. But in turn what I have not admitted to myself is that, honestly, you have only made me stronger. Stronger in my heart and stronger in my mind. I'm sorry that I have doubted you when truthfully; it is me who has doubted myself. I made a promise to you Azalea, I promised that I will give you my word and all of my will. I promised to be yours to keep forever, if I was allowed to keep you, and you promised. I bound myself to you, as you bounded yourself to me that very first night. I shall never again forget those promises."

Xanthus held my hands tightly within his fingers as his lips kissed them softly. I took in a deep breath as I gazed mesmerized into his warm eyes. He leaned over closer to me as my breaths became heavier. I will never get tired of his kisses. To me each kiss is like the first, slow and oh so tender, focusing on the softness and warmth that spreads through me.

Just as his lips were slowly caressing mine making the heat rise within me, I heard a low cough above us. We ceased the kiss as our gaze moved upward and saw James standing before us. James blushed slightly as he replied, "The sun will be setting upon us soon behind the sandy dunes. We must rest before we charter off towards the Cristats."

He was right, sleeping on the cold damp concrete floor last night was uncomfortable, I'm sure Xanthus would have agreed. We both stood and followed James towards the small campsite that Priniza and Morpheus had made.

Once we arrived, there were two small sand dunes that apparently were our tents. A small fire sat in the middle of them as a small black pot hovered over the blue flames. I turned to Morpheus and asked, "Morpheus, are those tents made of sand?"

He smiled and pointed to Priniza. He gushed, "It was all her idea, brilliant, I think. She told me that a gardener named Beruchium taught her how to enchant the land to make a temporary home for a night or two."

I turned to her as she smiled and replied, "Well, what can I say; Beruchium has been teaching me a bit here and there when I am in the gardens helping out. But don't tell Trathina, she would not allow it, she'd be furious!"

I nodded with a slight smirk upon my face, knowing all too well that hiding things from Trathina was all too common. I walked up to her as I replied, "Priniza, trust me when I tell you that, I will not tell Trathina. I have been seeing James for lessons with the swords long before Trathina allowed me. Your secret is safe with me. Besides, if you didn't spend time with Beruchium, we wouldn't have these amazing tents made of sand right now."

Morpheus laughed, "Well honestly Azalea, we do have tents prepared but it was James' idea not to use them. We wouldn't want to be discovered in the mists of our slumbers. We have no idea how the Cristats will react on having strangers, or trespassers if they think, in their lands."

I turned to James as I asked, "Do you think they are violent creatures?"

James sighed, "Well, I cannot lie to you nor can I give you words of comfort. I am honestly not sure whether they are or are not. They lived in peace many centuries ago but, it all depends if Cethios has gotten to them yet."

I took in a deep breath and gave a slight shiver. I couldn't help it. I was a bit terrified on the thought. I am not sure if we are walking towards our deaths or to our saviors to help battle Cethios and Zethron in their war. I'm going to need lots of rest, especially to find my courage!

I turned as Xanthus handed me a bowl made of stone that was filled with delicious potato soup. I'm sure Priniza enchanted these as well as she seemed to be blushing as I glanced at her. I sat near the fire on a small stone as I gulped the soup down and had seconds. And within a couple of hours of peaceful talking and enjoying our food, the moon and stars became our light. I was certainly very blissful on our small time of peace. I hadn't had that in quite some time. But unfortunately, it did have to come to an end.

Xanthus and Morpheus extinguished the fire and transformed the bowls and utensils back into their true stone form. They cleared up the evidence of ever having anyone there. For in fact, we didn't want to be discovered or worse, captured in our slumber.

Morpheus and James headed for one tent as Priniza went in the other. I nodded to her and told her that I would be joining her momentarily. Xanthus as well, replied to Morpheus and James that he would join them in a few. Xanthus and I wanted to share the stars just once more before we ended our night.

Xanthus and I walked off a bit as we carefully tried not to touch any more statues. James had to enchant the others so they would go back to just being their bird form. He was insightful, and not wanting to take any chances on having the Cristats find out we were within their mist.

Within moments Xanthus stopped and with took me by both hands. He gazed into my eyes as he replied, "Azalea, I understand that you were unaware that you were Queen Lily's daughter, which is until Cethios told you. I am not upset with you. I know that we had not the time. I will go over with Morpheus about what Cethios has told us, and I'm sure somehow James knows. But for tonight all I can say is that, I promise you that one day when this is all over, we will have our time. We will have our peace; we will be together and I will never leave you. You are my love, the one that I have been waiting for, my destined. Without you I am nothing, I am not alive. And unfortunately, I cannot do this anywhere else, and I do not want to wait any longer..."

And with that being said he bent down on one knee. He reached in his pocket and withdrew a small box. He opened his palm as the box suddenly transform into a small emerald crystal dragon. It appeared as if it was one from the chandelier from the castles' main hall in Trinafin. I was in awe as the crystal dragon let out a small mighty roar. It took flight as I took a step back. It slowly flew over to me as it seemed to be carrying something between its tiny claws. I held out my hands as it landed onto my palm. It dropped a ring, and not just any ring, it was the ring that I had admired when Xanthus took me to the City of Trinafin.

The ring was silver as the band was made of ivy vines and leaves. Around it contained four gems, a sapphire, a ruby, an emerald and an opal. It was quite exquisite. I picked it up slowly between my fingertips as I gazed at it with much appreciation. The little crystal dragon flew up as Xanthus whispered to it, "Your journey has been amazing and unforgettable, thank you. You may rejoin your family with honor." The crystal dragon let out another mighty roar as it took off towards the night sky. Then it quickly vanished with a small puff of smoke, as I'm sure it vanished and probably reappeared back in the castle of Trinafin.

Xanthus carefully took the ring from my fingers as he replied, still upon his knee, "Azalea, I love you with all that I have, and all that I am. I promise you my life, my eternal immortal life that I, I want to spend it all with you. Azalea, will you accept these promises, will you marry me and be mine?"

I opened my wings to their full extent as I flew a bit off of the floor. I felt as if I was going to blank out! I found my breath as I replied, "How did you, the ring from Trinafin, when?"

Xanthus chuckled to himself, "Since the day you first saw it, I just knew. My little friend has been keeping it safe for me since that day. Those little dragons are more than just a part of the castles' chandelier, remember that. They can be called forth at any time."

I nodded as I continued to stare at the ring. Within moments Xanthus smiled and replied shyly, "So, your answer is…"

Oh goodness, what have I been thinking of! "Yes, yes I will, of course!"

Xanthus with took my right hand and placed the ring onto my middle finger. He kissed it slowly as he stood. He replied, "To keep wary eyes off for the time being."

I nodded to him as I embraced him. He in turn found my lips with his and kissed me passionately slowly rubbing his warm hands along my back. Moments later as we parted light headedly, we headed off to our sandy tents. We kissed once more and descended into our designated tents as the stars above us seemed to glisten even brighter. It was as if they too had known of the good news below them.

The Questions & the Quest

23

The inside of the tent was just as small as I thought it would be. It was just enough room for Priniza and myself to open our wings to their full extent. We really couldn't stand up all of the way but sitting was alright not to bump our heads.

I knelt down by my pillow as I started to fluff it. From the corner of my eye though, I could see that Priniza was fluffing her pillow too but, after that she started to stare at me. The side of my head started to burn. I turned to her and asked, "Priniza, is there something that you want to ask me?"

She glanced away hesitant as if she wasn't sure whether or not she wanted to begin a conversation. But as she changed her mind she took in a deep breath and asked, as if almost in pain, "How was it like when you went to war? I mean, how did you feel?"

I was uncertain on how to answer her. She already appeared anxious and petrified enough already. I didn't know what and how I should tell her, nothing about a war is comforting or pleasing. I could not lie to her either! I took in a deep breath and exhaled slowly, "Well, it was very... Well I... Honestly, I had to put my fears behind me. I had to step forward with my courage. I am not going to lie, I was overwhelmed with anger and much despair."

"Why were you angry?"

"You see, I felt that we were all fighting for a meaningless purpose. So many lost their lives not even knowing the true meaning on why they were there. They lost their lives because..."

Priniza interrupted angrily, "Because you ran away in the first place like a coward instead of facing your responsibilities like a brave fairy that I thought you were."

My mouth dropped, I was mortified by her reply. That was not fair at all. I took in a deep breath and replied to her, "What would you have done? Would you have condemned your soul, your love life away and betray it? I had a choice yes, but my choice was to run so that I could find true love and find the strength to face Cethios on my own instead of unwilling to even state my own opining. What would you have done? I did not want death to all those innocent soldiers. How do you think I feel knowing that more lives are going to be taken, lives that don't need to be gone. Bloodshed is pointless. All because Cethios and Zethron want to rule all and take my immortality, as well as Xanthus'. Lives will be taken but I can guarantee you that, whether or not I ran that day, they would have taken lives anyway. They will stop at nothing to get what they want. Again I ask, what would you have done? I fight for my freedom as well as for the freedom of my people as well as for the elves. For all of our freedom, so we are free from their evil. Either we are in their grasp or fighting not to be. I fight not to be. What are you fighting for?"

Priniza's eyes filled with tears as they fell effortlessly down her delicate cheeks. I bit my lip slowly, in a bit of regret. Regret for saying some of those things to her. I placed my hand upon her shoulder and comforted her. I sighed in anguish, "Priniza, I'm so sorry. I'm sorry I left both of you behind. I'm sorry that Cethios took the life of your sister."

Priniza took in a deep breath and cleaned her eyes. She reached over and took my hands. She sobbed, "Azalea, I lost her the day you ran away, she betrayed us both. She turned as soon as you left, she ran to Cethios' side the day of ball. She pledged her soul to him. She would tell me all of the evil things that Cethios would tell her, night after night, and she reveled in it. I tried to convince her to leave him and to join me, to escape and try to find you. I wanted to join you and fight by your side. I'm sorry too for my outburst. Forgive me Azalea."

Priniza took in a deep breath, settling her sobs. She finished wiping her eyes. She started to fiddle her fingers as she nervously replied, "Azalea, I don't... I don't think that I can be brave enough like you, fearless enough to fight all of those soldiers. I thought I was going to fall over with just three soldiers that we were fighting back there in the castle of Urinia. I can't imagine fighting all day! I can't go with you to the Depths, I feel useless... I..."

I sighed, "Priniza, I don't expect you to be there during war."

"But, I want to help, I want to help..." Priniza seemed as if her breaths were going to concave in her chest.

I gently squeezed her hands within mine, I tried to calm her down. I quickly thought of something that she could do to help and not be present at the war. Then it hit me! "Priniza I got it! In the morning just before we head out to the city, I want you to go and get help. Go to the City of Magnesio and recruit the centaurs to join us!"

Her eyes sparked with excitement but her expression seemed hesitant. Her eyes darted all around the tent with a new found hope, "I shall not fail you. But, how am I supposed to convince them otherwise. They won't listen to me." I turned my back and plucked two feathers from my wings. I gave a short shriek but quickly shivered it off. I turned back towards Priniza as she seemed completely flabbergasted, "Are you crazy?"

I shook my head as I placed the feathers in her palm. She took them with care and placed them in her dress pocket. I assured her, "Go and run towards the city, make sure you run and not fly Denentro will not be able to hear you if you fly. This is an imperative quest for you. Once you find him…"

She interrupted me, "How will I find him, how do I know it is him?"

"Priniza, he'll find you. Tell him what has happen and tell him we need his kinds' help. Give him those two feathers, he knows what they represent. Tell him the time has come and I call upon him and his kind forth to join and fight for one of their kind. They need to meet us in the Depths of Galligro."

She took in a deep breath as she straightened her back and lifted her chin. Determination swelled within her. She cleared her throat and declared, "Azalea, I… I will not let you down." Courage now filled her eyes as she still shook a bit from nervousness. She smiled at me as she nodded her head. She then turned and laid down into her blankets and snuggled onto her pillow.

I laid onto my pillow and slowly started to close my eyes. I took in a deep breath as I wished I could be in my own room, the room in the castle of Trinafin. I would love to see the stars through the translucent ceiling. I took in a deep breath, and just as sweet slumber almost with took my subconscious mind Priniza whispered, "Azalea, what if I fail?"

I unwillingly opened my eyes and rolled my head to face her. She still seemed wide awake, unfortunately. I yawned, "Priniza, let me tell you something that James once told me. Strength is only the compassion of your mind, in which it conquers over your ability to give back in a physical reaction. He told me that a while ago. And his words were flowing constantly through my mind as Cethios tortured me for information."

325

Priniza's eyes opened wide with horror as she gasped, "Cethios tortured you? Razyna had spoken that he did nothing of that sort to you. Azalea, I'm so sorry that was brought upon you."

I shrugged my shoulders and sighed, "It's over now, it is behind me. I did not surrender to him. I am here now and alive. Let's just get some sleep before dawn approached us. We have much ahead of us and I would love to get some sleep."

Priniza nodded and yawned, "Yes, you are right. Peaceful sleep for one more night sounds incredible, good night Azalea."

I nodded in agreement as Priniza finally roll over and took in a deep breath. I closed my eyes and sighed. Yes, one night of good rest was what I needed, and what I wanted for a long time.

But little did I know, that our peaceful night was going to turn into dreadful horror. Little did we know, that the Cristats knew we were within their lands. Little did we know, that the Cristats were now heading towards us, and within the hours, they would be here, and we would be at their mercy.

Ambush of the Cristats

24

I awoke suddenly from my peaceful slumber as I heard a loud horrific scream from outside of the tent. I shot straight up as I glanced over to see Priniza, whom was now gone. And just before I could react to the situation something pulled my feet. I was dragged out of the tent and ascending high into the cloudless night. I heard another loud scream above me, I had no idea what was going on. From somewhere below me I heard Xanthus shout curses.

I attempted to adjust my eyes quickly to the darkness as our only light was the moon and stars. I felt as if I was being tossed about like some type of rag doll. I could feel sharp claws digging into my wings as fresh warm blood slowly oozed down my back.

Thankfully, within moments dawn approached us as I was now able to clearly see what situation had been bestowed upon us. The Cristats had come to us and were carrying us high above the earth. They carried James, Priniza and me by our wings. As for Morpheus and Xanthus, they were being carried from their backs.

They appeared just like the statues that we saw down below. The males were beautifully red feathered all over except above the torso, where tan skin was exposed. The women Cristats had magnificent tan and red feathers across of their chest, as well as in their short hair. They were all brightly exquisite cardinals. They all had small yellow beaks that stuck out a bit under their nose.

I gazed up to see that the one carrying me was female Cristat, and at the same time I froze. I have to admit, I was in complete admiration for seeing such a creature, yet at the same time horrified. Yet as I stared in blankness, my concentration was brought back as the piercing scream of Priniza shot through my ears.

The Cristat that held Priniza had just dropped her as she fell through the air with her damaged wings. To my horror I witnessed another Cristat catching her by her wings, then flinging her back up to the other Cristat that first held her.

How barbaric, they were playing with her as if she was theirs to toy with. Rage flooded within me. I gathered my courage as Priniza screamed yet again as the Cristat caught her within his claws. I shouted over, "Leave her alone! Pick on someone else who can withstand your insanely barbaric methods!"

Oh dear, I had just realized what my brain had told my lips to say. And though they did stop swinging Priniza around, which was my main objective, the two Cristats started angrily chirping loudly to one another. It sounded absurd within my ears as they spoke in their own language. It was as if I was hearing feisty birds in the morning fighting over the first worm of the day. And yet even though I couldn't understand their language, I knew the extent that I had tremendously upset them.

Of course by my foolish words, the other empty handed Cristat started to fly directly towards me with his claws outstretched. Great, I have obligated myself. Now I have to act out and I must do something. I took in a deep breath and reached up and forcefully tugged on the feathers of the Cristat that had me within her claws. The Cristat screeched out in pain and thankfully had released her grip on my wings, just in time too. The other Cristat that was charging for me slammed into her.

I pummeled towards the ground as I forced myself to open my damaged bloody wings. Pain shot through my entire body but, I knew I couldn't give in to the sting. I reached for my sword that was still tied to my side, thankfully I had been lazy enough to not take it off before I fell asleep last night.

I withdrew my sword and the two Cristats that had clashed together, were flying towards me with their sharp claw outstretched. I waited until they were about the right distance. I clashed my sword against the males' claws as for the other, I just had enough time to slash my sword against her left wing. Instant I was fighting with the two Cristats in midair.

Within the fighting, I succeeded in slashing my sword against the male Cristats' chest but, one succeeded in clawing my left arm. I do have to say that deep down I was proud of myself. I was fighting in horrendous pain in midair and yet, I was still concentrating on my breaths and my timing with my sword. If James was watching, I hope he was proud.

Just as I was about to deliver another blow to the female Cristat, a beautiful sky blue Cristat came flying towards us with immense speed. Thankfully as well, the sun was now peaking over the horizon. The sky blue feathered Cristat, once a couple of feet from us shouted over, "Enough!

You, if you wish to die so be it! But if you do not put down your sword then your companions shall die!"

I glanced around to see that the other Cristats that held Priniza, Morpheus, Xanthus and James were now flying in place as if gracefully awaiting orders. They seemed to be in terrible agony, as Priniza on the other hand seemed as if she couldn't bear anything else much longer. I was in a spot and I didn't know how to correctly answer the Cristat. I didn't want any more harm done to anyone anymore. I quickly pondered my words as I demanded to the sky blue Cristat, "I shall come quietly if you stop this barbaric madness. We are not meaningless creatures and should not be treated nor carried by any means within the claws of these Cristats. Allow us to ride respectfully as equals for the time being as we venture off to wherever it is you unwillingly take us. We have done you no harm."

"And what about my two soldiers that you have neglected to mention that harm has been brought upon?"

I took in a deep breath as I stretched my sword out to her, "Take a look at my companions. It is no more then what your Cristats have done upon our flesh!"

The sky blue feathered female Cristat glanced quickly at the others. She assessed the moment and pondered her thoughts. Thankfully she came to a quick decision. She nodded to her soldiers and shouted, "So be it! We shall allow you and your companions' temporary forgiveness. You all are allow to ride, for now. For this brief moment we shall bare our differences."

I glanced back to see the Cristats released their grasp upon everyone that I cared for. They fell briefly through the air as the Cristats flipped underneath them and caught them onto their backs. A heavy sigh of relief escaped me. This situation could have ended with a horrendously different outcome.

The sky blue Cristat that flew before us shouted over to me, "I am Princess Efterpi, second leader in command of the Cristats. You show much courage for you companions, as well as ignorance! What would you have done if I did not so easily dismay your actions?"

How smug of her. But then again, so was I. I responded, "What actions had we done to deserve such treatment from your soldiers? As I see it, you attacked us first in the mist of our slumbers, completely unaware and unarmed. That is a disgrace, do you not agree? Taking advantage of those who are unprepared? Why the ambush on those who have done no wrong to your kind?"

Efterpi smirk as she bowed in midair and replied arrogantly, "Why, trespassing on sacred lands that are forbidden from all unworthy eyes, such as yourselves. Such a crime is punishable by death. But yet again I still dismay your crimes. And to whom I may ask?"

I turned my gaze towards James who in turn nodded in agreement to the idea that swirled within me. I turned back to face Efterpi as I gave a slight bow. I cautiously replied, "I am Princess Azalea of Whisperia, and my companions and I are not unworthy. If we would have known of your races' existence, and knew that your kind still thrived, instead of hiding within your sacred lands that your ancestors have left behind, then perhaps we would have had a better understanding. We would have not thought that we walked amongst ancient ruins. We would have given enough respect as our kind would have wanted in return."

Efterpi concluded, "To shay."

She then raised a wing up as she chirped loudly to her feathered Cristat soldiers. They in return bowed slightly and started to fly onwards with my companions riding safely upon their backs. And with assumption, they would be heading towards their city. And once they were all a few feet away from hearing, Efterpi flew closer to me and cautioned, "You have spoken with thoughtfulness and wrath. But will your words save you from punishment once we have arrived in my fathers' presence. Nonetheless, I must give you a second chance Princess Azalea, for the time being. Now, I shall be honored to have you ride on me. Shall we go onwards then, and join your companions?"

She took another small bow as she flew directly underneath me. I relieved my wings and closed them. Much tension was released as I landed softly on Efterpi's back. She took off swiftly yet gracefully towards the others, being very careful not to drop me. I was very pleased to see that the other Cristats were flying with much grace and ease and being very careful with the ones that I loved. We soared through the warm morning breeze as we headed towards the unknown within their city of Xylina. Hope and dread filled my nerves as I knew nothing that was expected to come out of this. The only comfort I took in was the glorious sun as it warmed us with its magnificent rays.

Scorching Nest

25

As we neared their city, you could see a vast castle above the tree tops, almost brushing against the edges of the clouds. Surprisingly it was very humid seeing as how much we were high up. Their castle was amongst their city instead of being miles away like Whisperias'. The city and castle appeared to be made up of thick branches and a plethora of leaves. Though, there were a few open ceilings where you could see straight down into the homes of the Cristats. Much feathers stuck out here and there from the walls, it all seemed quite a bit bizarre. You were able to quickly determine which part was the castle, for in comparison to the other buildings surrounding it, this was far superior than the others.

We headed for a clearing that appeared to be their grand hall. The floor was made with thick wooden branches, smooth and flawless as the grain of the wood glistened. It seemed very intricate and unique. I remember Beruchium telling me something once, on manipulating nature to comply with your needs, but this was beyond massive.

Just before we landed in the clearing, the Cristats flipped in midair as we all landed on our hands and knees. And just as quickly as we fell, that's how quickly some other Cristat soldiers tied our hands together with rope. Thankfully it was not behind our backs. They also tied a rope around Priniza, James and my waist, perhaps preventing us from flying off as our wings were smashed against our backs.

I glanced up to see a tall muscular indigo feathered Cristat sitting upon a throne in the middle of the hall. He had small golden feathered surrounding his crown upon his head; this must be the king. Although once I gazed upon his eyes, fear sunk into my skin. I could see the wickedness that rested deep in his beady eyes.

The Cristat king replied to Princess Efterpi in a booming voice, "Well done my daughter, you have captured the enemy that attempted to conceal themselves, underneath our very wings. Tell me Efterpi, do you have the one that calls herself Azalea?"

Princess Efterpi walked up to her father and chirped, "Yes father. Although, she claims herself Princess of Whisperia."

The king seemed to laugh at Princess Efterpi's response. He chirped and laughed until moments later after enjoying himself in his own laughter, he responded, "Just as Prince Cethios warned us she would say. Let us then please Prince Cethios and take her to him unharmed. As for the rest of them, kill them."

As I stood in horror, Xanthus quickly leaped in front of me and replied breathlessly, "No! You will do so to be an honorable king and tell us the reasoning of our sentencing!"

The king raised his wing up and stopped the red feathered Cristat soldiers from taking us all. He chirped to Xanthus, "I am King Aetius! I need not to explain myself to the likes of you. I do not give any reasoning!"

Xanthus kept his ground as he stepped forward and demanded, "But nonetheless you are a king, are you not? And yet, you take orders from one that is not a king; one that does not have higher authority over you, unless I am to be mistaken. These action you are executing incline weakness upon your own kind. Weakness that proves their king cannot make his own judgments."

"Enough!" King Aetius stood from his throne and cautiously approached Xanthus. He glared as Xanthus as he whispered angrily, "I take orders from no one, especially one not worthy of the Cristat name." King Aetius took a couple of steps back and huffed out his chest in a deep breath. He had made his decision. The king shouted to his soldiers, "Take these dreadful creatures from my sight. Take them to the highest Scorching Nest! If Cethios demands Azalea, then he can come forth and claim them all in pieces! We shall not allow this moment to dampen our day of renouncing. This day we will join the others in battle and prove to them just who is the mightier race!"

The Cristats chirped and cheered as they grabbed us from our roped hands with their claws and flew us out of the kings' presence and into the warm air above. As King Aetius and Princess Efterpi descended from our view, you could surely tell that they were arguing about something. Perhaps they were arguing about the kings' decision on what he was doing with us.

Within moments the Cristats released us into a tall deep nest, seemingly just outside of their city. We screamed as we pummeled into the nest on top of each other. As soon as we landed, I quickly stood to see just where the Cristats had gone too. But it seemed that they had vanished within the milky clouds. I turned to everyone and asked worriedly, "Is everyone alright?"

They all seemed to grunt at my question as Morpheus chuckled sarcastically, "Well, on the count that I ironically cushioned everyone's fall, and perhaps on the count of my bruised ribs, or how about perhaps on the…"

Morpheus turned his sore gaze towards me as his expression fell when his eyes met mine. I was not in the mood for his commenting, I had already felt responsibly guilt for everyone's misery. How could I not, everything now a days seemed as if it was the consequence of my first initial decision, when I left Whisperia on the day of the ball. How could I not take a moment to look at all the chaos I have inflicted upon others. How could I not know that truly, I am the one to blame. He continued with a heavy sighed as he lowered his gaze, "Yeah, everyone is alright."

Priniza could barely stand properly. She was not going to be able to take any suffering much longer. I walked over to her as I stifled a gasp that wanted to tear through my lips. Her skin tissue by her shoulders was torn immensely and clotted with dry blood. Hues of deep blue and purple covered the rest of her skin by her shoulder that was not torn. I fought back the burning tears that wanted to stream down my face. I could not allow Priniza to see me shed any tears, I needed to be strong, I needed to show courage.

I turned my gaze towards James, his breaths slowed to an extreme as he laid upon the ground. Xanthus and Morpheus followed my gaze as they too felt the anguish that spread through me as they saw James. They knelt carefully beside him. I hesitated momentarily in joining them. How could I face him? How could I find the strength in me to see him gaze upon me with disappointment? I sighed in realization, I couldn't abandon him now, after all that he has sacrificed for me.

I carefully walked over to him as I too knelt by his side. I placed my tied hands upon his chest as I felt the beats of his heart weakening by the second. I whispered to him, "James, are you alright?"

Tears clouded part of my vision; I honestly don't know how much more of this he can take. His shoulders were severely torn, but not just that, his wings too were shredded from the top like Priniza's. I glanced away as the tears I have been so desperately trying to hold back finally raced down my face.

This was all my fault. If I would have just given in to Cethios, none of this would have happened. I do not want this powerful magic inside of me if the consequence of having it, is only going to hurt the ones that I love.

I stood to get some air and to think things over, and as I did, I short of startled myself. I heard a slight ruckus on my back. Somehow, luck was on my side! Before I had fallen asleep last night, I had left my arrows and my bow on my back, too exhausted to remove them. Oh, the positive that came out of my laziness last night. I glanced to my side to luckily still see that the Cristats had forgot to take my sword.

I quickly rubbed my tied hands upon the blade as I cut the rope off. Once free I withdrew my sword and cut the rope that was around my waist preventing me from opening my wings. As I finished, I cut the rope from Xanthus' tied hands. I handed my sword over to him. While Xanthus worked on freeing the others I knelt back down to James. Heavy guilt continued to swell within me as I sobbed and confessed, "Oh James, I am so sorry for all of this. All of this is my fault. I am so stupid and selfish for thinking that leaving Whisperia in the first place was not going to lead to any real consequences for others. If, if only I had not denied Cethios. If I just let Cethios take me and my magic, only I would have suffered and not anyone else. If then, perhaps, we would not be here, you would not be like this, we could of…"

"We could have been in a worse situation than we are in now. We would have been in an ice-cold cell awaiting our deaths, starved and beaten. Azalea, I would rather be here right now, in this situation with you. We are fighting back, not just simply giving up. I thought I taught you better than to doubt yourself, or of others around you, especially from me." James placed his cold hands upon my cheeks as he wiped my tears away and continued, "I would rather die a thousand deaths by your side. I would rather waste away, knowing that one day you will make your destiny, a destiny that your mother has set off and died for."

Xanthus came by and freed James from his ropes. He took in a deep sigh as he rubbed his delicate hands together slowly. James looked back upon me as he replied softly, "Azalea, I will refuse to have any regrets from you, especially where we are now. Every path is different, some difficult but, the right ones to take. Now, do not allow Xanthus to ever hear those words that you exhaled; it would devastate him. Let us not every speak of this moment of doubt, yes?"

I nodded to him as I leaned over and tenderly embraced him, and as I softly kissed his forehead. I then stood and walked over to Xanthus and Morpheus. I overheard Morpheus reply to Xanthus, "So how exactly are we going to get out of this one? I'm sure there is some type of magic that conceals itself over the top of this nest. They wouldn't leave it that easy, would they?"

Xanthus chuckled, "Well, they did forget that Azalea had her sword and her bow and arrows with her. Surprisingly Azalea herself forgot to take them off last night as she fell asleep, thankfully."

I wasn't sure whether I hinted sarcasm in his voice or not but, I still smiled and bowed my head slightly. I knew being lazy for one night would come in handy.

Priniza walked up to us as a hint of fear glistened in her eyes. She grabbed Morpheus' arm as she gasped, "What do you mean by this one? You mean to say that you have been in situations like this before?"

Xanthus grunted as he crossed his arms across his chest. He glanced between Priniza and myself. He opened his mouth to reply but then chose to close it as he shook his head. Thankfully he had refrained himself from saying whatever it was he was thinking. I'm sure it would have not soothed Priniza's fear. Xanthus then turned and walked away from us with his hands shoved deep within his pockets, attempting to hide his balled fists. Morpheus though, turned to Priniza and hugged her tightly. He assured her, "Do not worry my sweet. I assure you; we are going to figure something out. Everything is going to be alright."

Priniza trembled slightly as Morpheus kissed her softly upon the forehead. I sighed and turned towards James. I wanted to see if he had heard Priniza's words. I wanted to see if perhaps he would be able to give her some of his words of encouragement but, as my eyes laid upon his body I froze. James was unconscious and slightly pale, dread swept over my skin, we have to get out of here and soon.

Xanthus had walked back over to me as he stood right behind me. I couldn't face him at the moment, I knew he felt so distraught and conflicted and I for one could not give him the satisfaction that I was well grounded. Honestly, I felt like I was coming apart. He confirmed my thoughts as he sighed, "How are we going to get out of here Azalea?"

I bit my bottom lip, attempting to prevent it from trembling even more. I didn't know what to say to Xanthus. So, I stepped away from him without turning to glance back at him. I didn't want him to see the doubt and fear that was forming upon my face. I crossed my arms across my chest as I glanced around the nest and concentrated with all that I had left in me. I sighed, just how exactly are we going to get out? This was impossible.

I hung my head in defeat as I placed my palms upon my face. I wanted to scream with all that I had. How could I have let this happen? What choice did we have now but to wait it out. I couldn't concentrate on anything but feeling overwhelmed with anxiety. Suddenly though, warm hands rubbed the gap between my shoulders and neck. I breathed heavily as the gentle yet firm hands massaged my worries away.

As I lowered my hands, I opened my eyes slowly. Out of the corner of my eyes, I saw some of the rope that once bonded us. Then, a great epiphany flowed within my mind, I wasn't completely sure of it yet, but an idea was starting to form.

Without saying a word, I brushed Xanthus' hands off of my neck as I started to gather all of the pieces of rope from the ground. Within moments of me doing so I heard Xanthus chuckle, "Azalea what are you doing? What good are those pieces going to do?"

I shrugged but insisted, "I'm not quite sure, but it's coming together. The idea in my mind, it's forming."

Xanthus continued to chuckle, "I hardly think that an answer to our problem is going to magically fall out of the sky." Once he replied that I stopped and stared up into the sky. It was a brief moment that I thought, well, perhaps the ironic thing would be, that something would fall right out of the sky, and into the nest. But nothing did fall. Xanthus' chuckles were coming in heavier now, almost hysterical, "What are you doing now?"

I glanced back down to meet his eyes as I answered, "Well, being how we're in this ironic situation, I thought perhaps something might just fall in the moment you said that."

I don't think he appreciated my humor as his expression fell and went solemn, "Are you serious Azalea? Do you not comprehend why they call this their Scorching Nest?"

I stared at him blankly, why was he talking to me as if I didn't know the seriousness of the situation? Ignoring him I flew up a bit with one hand extended. Perhaps there was a slight chance that there was nothing there and they had forgotten that too. Our escape would be that much easier.

As I continued slowly flying up my wings ached with tremendous pain. But I couldn't let that agony conquer me, for James' sake. Once almost out my hand had collided with something invisible. I flew and rubbed my hands along all of the edges and the middle. I wanted to assure myself that there wasn't a flaw. As I flew back down to Xanthus, I replied to him almost breathlessly, "Do you think that this ceiling is made from the same clear substance, that was in the room that I stayed in, in Trinafin?"

As quickly as those words escaped my lips, that is how quickly Morpheus turned and headed towards us. He asked with wide eyes, "You were staying in one of the Translucent Rooms?

I shrugged and nodded to him. I guess that was what they were called. Morpheus turned and replied to Xanthus, "Do you realize what this could mean? That very thought could mean our very lives. With that thought we can try to escape instead of..."

"Waiting for death." I added to his words with a shrug.

Morpheus frowned but continued, "Well, not really for death but, if we stay, we will pray for death." He cringed his nose in as I shuttered at his words. I'm not sure I want to wait for something like that. Morpheus took in a deep sigh and continued, "If that's the same consistence, then perhaps we can enchant the pieces of the rope that Azalea has gathered and, perhaps we can make it whole again. Then we can tie it off somewhere in the nest and to one of Azalea's arrows. We can sling shoot the nest across and..."

Xanthus interrupted his enthusiasm, "Well that's a relief Morpheus, if we don't die from the sun, then we can certainly die from the impact of us crashing upon something else! Who knows how high up we are, or if there is anything surrounding the nest."

"It's a chance I am willing to take instead of just sitting here and doing nothing! I am trying something! Why are you so against an idea of mine! Azalea is right; we can't just sit here and wait for death to inherit us all!"

"Don't make it seem like I don't care! I care well enough for the safety of Azalea and us all!"

"Then try to be supportive of my idea of just trying to escape!"

I jolted my eyes between them. It seemed as if they were going to go at each other's throats! I stepped forward between them as I attempted to replied as calmly as I could, "Why are you both acting this way? It's as if you are turning on each other like enemies or something. You're best friends, act like it!" My emotions started to boil as I turned on Xanthus, "And you should be supporting your friends' ideas even if it is ridiculous or not, especially in a situation like this!" Dang, I lost it. I tried to stay calm as well but, man, it was getting sweltering hot in here! I continued on Xanthus as my breaths heaved from my chest, "Look, at least Morpheus is trying to help and think of something, it's some type of attempt. So unless you have a plan other than what Morpheus has come up with, I suggest you be supportive. I on the other hand will be helping him bind the rope together."

I turned my gaze away from him. I couldn't look at him any longer. I headed towards the other side of the nest where the remainder of the pile of rope laid. I glanced back to see if Morpheus was behind me but, he was still standing there glaring at Xanthus. Within moments Morpheus turned his gaze and started heading towards me. Xanthus stood there as he balled his fists up again as they glowed with a red hue.

Moments later Xanthus turned towards James and headed for his side. Priniza on the other hand had already formed a pillow of the feathers that stuck out from the nest around us. James was looking worse, but on the other hand, at least he was a bit awake though. Hopefully he was getting some of his strength back. We needed to get out of here, and fast.

As Morpheus approached me, he smiled enthusiastically, "I want to thank you for standing up for me back there, to Xanthus. I know that took a lot from you."

"Well, I think Xanthus is just feeling a bit overwhelmed right now. I know his thoughts are strong at times but..." I couldn't even finish my sentence, I simply nodded to him. But it seemed as if he knew what I was trying to get at. Xanthus is very strong minded you know. And sometimes he gets carried away in his own world. I would know, once his mind is made up, he's set.

I held up the pieces of rope for Morpheus as he waved his right hand over it as his palm glowed a dim white. The ends of the rope started to dance and swirl together as they intertwined and became one again. I kept glancing over to Morpheus to see if there was anything else he wanted to say to me but, it just seemed as if he was avoiding eye contact. He was

338

becoming nervous as I sat there staring at him. What was he hiding, why did he feel as if he couldn't talk to me? Then, as if he read my thoughts, he cleared his throat and replied without glancing up as we continued to mend the pieces together, "Azalea, honestly, do you comprehend the purpose of the Scorching Nest?"

I shook my head slightly and whispered, "Honestly no, but I refused to allow Xanthus to know that I didn't. I mean, I know that the situation we are in is very serious. But to the extent of the nest no."

Morpheus now trembled as he desperately tried not to drop the other pieces of rope between his fingers. I placed my hands on his to ease his trembling but instead, he took mine within his and he gazed into my eyes with deep fear. He urged, "Azalea, the ceiling from your room in Trinafin is made out of a translucent substance that we enchant to only allow the light of the sun in and not allow anything else in or out. Here though, I'm sure they have reversed and enhanced that enchantment."

I took in a deep breath as I sat back a bit from him and mumbled, "Which means...?"

"Which means, that this substance will allow not only simply the light of the sun in, but also the suns' rays in. So, once the sun reaches high noon, we will scorch, literally. Our flesh will scorch off, and no amount of clothes or weapons will save us."

Okay, now I started to panic. I felt horrible, knowing how Xanthus feels, knowing that he feels helpless for the first time in seriously helping anyone. I think he did lose it for a bit, feeling desperate and aggravated.

Suddenly to my horror, I realized that the sun was minutes away from starting to spew into the nest. I replied to Morpheus with concern, "If we are unable to get out of the nest, how is the rope and arrow supposed to get out?"

"Normally that type of spell only prevents living things from leaving. If we cross our fingers hard enough, we can attempt to sling shoot this nest. You know tip it over, or at least damage it enough for us to escape. Also, if we only brisk by the sun momentarily as we sling shot across, it shouldn't harm us since we aren't sustaining in it."

I took in a deep breath in as I pondered his words and replied, "Morpheus, there's a lot to cross my fingers to."

"Well then pray."

Utter terror consumed my senses as he replied those words. I tried hard now, not to tremble as Morpheus did. I took in deep breaths to calm my nerves but, it didn't seem as if it was helping. As Morpheus finished with the rope, I stood to allow him to tie the rope to the arrow. I then walked over to help Priniza with James as he tried to get to his feet. He stumbled a bit as he just sat back down. I truly hoped that this chapter in his life wasn't the end for him. His fragile body seemed as if it could not stand much longer to anything else.

Moments later Morpheus finished tying the rope around the arrow tightly. Xanthus quickly tied the other end of the rope to the other side of the nest within a large branch. My heart raced as beads of sweat now trickled down my forehead. The nest was heating up fast as the sun approached us. I was praying that this would end up better than what I was truly thinking.

Suddenly as Xanthus yelled over to Morpheus letting him know he had finished his knot; horror filled my very skin. Over on the top of the nest my nightmare was becoming a reality. Rays of sunlight started to gently pour in.

Escape

26

"Hurry Morpheus, hurry!" I shouted over a low vibrating rumble that ascended into the nest with the suns' ray as it poured in slowly. You could feel the intensity becoming stronger and stronger as the rays inched slowly closer to us. Within moments the heat engulfed us all. You suddenly felt sluggish as exhaustion started to take over. Heavy beads of sweat drenched all of our foreheads as our bodies glistened.

James now stood as he leaned on the nest for support. Xanthus shouted something over to Morpheus but, my senses seemed to be shutting and numbing down. I saw Morpheus' hands glow a deep burgundy hue as he stretched the arrow from the bow then shot it out of the nest. Within moments Xanthus pulled the rope towards him hoping it would tighten but, the arrow came flying towards him.

Xanthus picked up the arrow and threw it back towards Morpheus. Morpheus prepared the arrow once more, turned slightly to his left and shot the arrow yet again. And yet once more, to Xanthus' horror as he pulled, the arrow came flying towards him. The second time was not a success.

The suns' rays were now half way into the nest as everything seemed to be moving slowly than ever. I could barely keep my eyes open, this was not good at all. I could tell that both of the elves were getting frustrated to an extreme as Xanthus' palms started to release a dim red hue.

Suddenly the whole nest started to tremble. James and Priniza both fell to the ground on their hands and knees. Over the loud rumble, I wasn't able to make out what Xanthus was shouting over to Morpheus. I wondered even if Morpheus had heard what he had shouted. But suddenly as Morpheus prepared the arrow once more, the arrow became a blaze with bright emerald fire. The flames danced around the arrow as Morpheus shot it once more out of the nest and into the oblivious.

The suns' rays had now cornered us as I noticed Priniza inching her fingertips towards the rays. I gazed at her in horror as I shouted over to her, "What are you doing? Does ignorance rule your decisions!"

I faintly heard her shout back, "I want to know what it feels like!"

Had she gone mad with the heat? What was there to feel? Did she want to feel the pain of her flesh scorching off? I couldn't simply just stand there and allow her to do such a thing. So without hesitation or thinking, I dove towards the ground and knocked her out of the way. But unfortunately, as we pummeled and as I pulled her arm into the shade, my right arm went directly into the suns' rays for a moment. I screamed in agony as the pain shot through my entire body.

As I rolled back into the shade cradling my right arm I heard Xanthus above me shouting over the rumble, "I got it! Hold on!"

Morpheus and Xanthus both tugged on the rope as their hands glowed with a bright burgundy hue. And to our great relief, the suns rays' started to fall back away from us. The two brave elves pulled with all of their might until they couldn't any longer. But this time though, we were practically on top of each other as the nest leaned at an angle.

I turned my gaze towards James. He appeared so fragile almost clinging to life. He met my gaze and smiled delicately as he whispered through his lips, "A thousand deaths I would endure for you, a thousand deaths, I would." As his words escaped his parched lips I glanced back to Morpheus and Xanthus. Xanthus withdrew my sword from his side as he slashed the rope in one swish. My heart and stomach quickly pummeled into my knees as the nest soared off into the untamed air of oblivious.

I desperately tried to hold onto a branch within my left arm, and frantically with all my might, attempted to hold onto James' arm within my sore right arm. I can't let him go, I don't want to let him go. I closed my eyes tightly and held my breath.

The nest had smashed into something as it burst open. I felt my body pummel into something hard as my breaths were taken from my lungs in a whoosh. I heard the shouts of everyone I cared about all around me as we crashed. Finally moments later after much tumbling, I blanked out from the exhaustion, pain and from the impact. I blanked out not really knowing where I was, where I had landed or with whom I had landed with…

The Outcasted

27

My entire body felt limp and numb. It ached so much I didn't even want to open my eyes to see where I had landed. I wanted to stay wherever it was and rest for about a century or two. But alas, I had to get up. As I opened my eyes I found myself mangled between some branches of this enormous tree. The rough bark scraped at my delicate skin as I stirred. I carefully managed to sit up on the thick branch.

I looked around to see if I saw anyone else but to my surprise, I did find someone else, someone I didn't know. There before me I saw a gorgeous elf with eyes of green and blue. His eyes reminded me as if I was hazily looking and the jungle. He too appeared mangled within the branches.

He carefully sat up on the same thick branch that I was sitting upon as he carefully turned his gaze towards me. As his eyes locked within mine, he seemed confused with something. I on the other hand, took a closer look at him. He had wavy dirty blonde hair that was cut short just above his ear that appeared slightly damp. He was a bit muscular with black pants and a white collar shirt. Over that was a black vest buttoned half way up. His sleeves were torn a bit and pushed up past his elbows. He seemed familiar to me, as if from a dream. But I couldn't quite remember, like my memory was clouded or something.

He smiled arrogantly as he pushed himself closer to me. Once situated, he cleared his throat, "Well-well-well, what do we have here? You must be the reason why we were placed in the second nest below, awaiting our turn for the next day. I do regretfully have to say thank you to you, but un-regrettable for your crime. So, what is it that one so enchanting as yourself, could have done?"

My mouth dropped in astonishment. We didn't commit any crime. We, oh my, we! I couldn't believe that for a brief second I had forgotten about the others! I frantically started to gaze around for the others completely ignoring this elf that sat in front of me. Where could they have all fallen too? We couldn't have fallen that far from each other, could we? Were the others still trapped and only I got away? My head started to spin.

The only ones I did find were three other elves above us mangled as well in tree branches. I had to go and look for the others, I just had to!

I guess the elf in front of me noticed that I became frantic. He raised his palms as they glowed slightly with a lime hue. He attempted to soothe me, "Whoa, take it easy. You've escaped, relax, your safe now."

Safe, safe? What about the others! I couldn't linger any longer, I had to find them. But the elf in front of me had other ideas. The light from his palms flickered suddenly. I flinched as the unexpected light caught my eyes. I couldn't help it, I lost my balance and fell off of the branch I was sitting upon. I screamed as I pummeled to the ground far below. I couldn't open my wings. One, they were in so much pain already and two, they would get even more torn from the other branches of the tree.

Suddenly my body jolted as I came to a halt in midair. My whole body glowed a green hue. I glanced up over my shoulder to see that same elf smiling and holding both hands extended out towards me as they glowed brightly. I was slowly floating towards him as my body carefully avoided the other branches. I landed in front of him as I sat down on the same branch. Once I landed softly, he placed his left hand on the branch we were sitting upon. The branch itself started to thicken, smooth and widen.

I gazed back into the elf's' eyes as my heart and mind continued to race. The elf's hands dimmed as he replied softly, "You must've been in something rough, huh?" He paused momentarily and seemed to be analyzing me or something. He asked, "Tell me, I see that you are a fairy but, what's with the feathers? Are you related in some way to the Cristats? Did you offend the…"

"No-no-no…" I gasped. He was moving way to fast with his words. It was making my head pound with all of these questions and accusations. I couldn't help myself, I took in fast short breaths as I glimpsed around to see if I could see anyone. But, the only thing I did see was that the other three elves were now making their way down, towards us. Was this an ambush? Where were the others? I placed my fingers on my temples to attempt to cease the pounding.

I was distraught and the worst part of it all, was that I was alone and powerless with these horrible shackles. Not to mention strength-less! As I placed my hands upon my lap as my breaths slowed, I realized that the first elf was staring at my shackles immensely. I hope he doesn't realize what they are. He sneered in amusement, "Are you a criminal on the run?"

My eyes widened, I couldn't believe he was so enthusiastic with his question. His smile widened as he replied, "Bestowed upon you, are enchanted shackles. Those are very hard to come by. Only those who truly deserve it, become heir to their embrace. Am I wrong, oh powerless one."

I panicked. Would he force me to his advantage? And where in this jungle is Xanthus? How horrible, I probably appear like this defenseless vulnerable fairy to this elf, or what he thought, part Cristat. I gathered all of what was left of my courage and replied, "Of course, you are wrong. Why would you think that these are those you speak of?"

By now the other three elves were sitting next to him as they all glanced at each other and at my shackles. It seemed as if they were contemplating something amongst themselves, nodding as if agreeing with some sort of unspoken agreement. The first elf replied, "Where's the key hole then? Only those enchanted ones, have no key hole. For only magic can unbind them from the one that did the enslaving." A spark of despicable evil gleamed in his eyes. A spark that sent chills running all over my skin. Chills that sent a thought into my subconscious mind that, this elf cannot be trusted. I gave a slight shiver as I slowly backed away from them. But it was only one scoot that I was able to do, I felt the cool bark of the tree against my back. I needed to escape, now! The elf chuckled, "Well then, oh frightened one, my name is Theron, Prince of Yaisla. Behind me to my right is Rowen, to the right of him is Latimer, and to my left is Oleos. We are the Outcasted."

They all smiled and bowed their heads slightly as Theron introduced them. Rowen had orange hair with red streaks flowing through it. His hair appeared wet as it also was cut short right up to his ears and neck, as if in two layers. His eyes were a solid black, as if the dark of the night resided in there. But, covering them were small silver glasses.

Latimer had blonde hair cut short as well up to his ears and neck. His hair too appeared to be wet. But his layers were pushed back behind his ears. He also had a blue feather sticking out from his left ear. His eyes were a swirl of dark blue hues as if I was staring at the sapphire ocean itself.

Oleos had black hair that was only just above his ears. Some of his layers though laid gently upon his forehead. But on the right side of his head were two thick streaks of white hair. His eyes were black as well, as if I was staring at the onyx stone itself.

They all appeared to be a bit muscular from the looks of it. And their clothes, they all seemed to be dressed somewhat the same. They all had white shirts that enhanced their physics, curving around their muscular form ever so gently. Their sleeves were pushed up past their elbows. They had black and gray vests with another vest on top connected with a small silver chain, with black pants.

Theron smiled as he cleared his throat, "Well then, what is your name? We have implied ours, let's not be rude, shall we?"

My breaths started to quicken as my chest betrayed me and heaved with anxiety. I jolted my eyes around in panic. I gulped, should I tell them my name? Or should I just try to quickly escape? Well, it really only took me about a second to come to my conclusion, seeing how I was useless with my wings and powerless. I stuttered, "I... I am... Azalea. My name is Azalea."

Latimer asked, "Are you part Cristat?"

"No, I'm just a fairy."

Oleos chimed in, "From the city of Urinia?"

I turned my gaze towards him in astonishment. How would he know that? I replied, "No, from Whisperia."

Oleos nodded his head back as he replied confused, "I thought that city was deserted. You be awfully quiet up there all by yourself. You know, you never hear anything coming from that city."

What was he talking about being deserted! I shook my head, "That's not true at all! The actual city is above ground within our trees. The castle is a couple of miles away but, I can assure you, it is full of life."

Theron crossed his arms and replied with a smirk, "Then you wouldn't mind taking us there right now, would you?"

Without thinking I blurted out, "I can't go back now!" I quickly shut my mouth with my hands. What was wrong with me? My outburst made all four elves smirk with content. I swear, they are contemplated something.

Then once more, there was that same evil spark in Theron's' eyes. He sneered, "Well then, oh imprisoned one, you are now under the authority of my command; seeing as you have nothing to do or nowhere to go. You will do just that..."

Then it hit me, it was as if all my senses had come back to me. I straightened and fumed, "You of all cannot force me to do what you will. No one rules over me, no one. Not even by force."

Theron leaned forward a bit and lowered his eyes. His hands glowed a light red hue as he replied with a sinister smile, "Wanna bet…"

Panic struck my very skin as I knew at that exact moment, I had to get out. I quickly ducked to my right and grabbed a nearby branch. I then as swiftly as I could, tried with all my might to get down and out of this stupid tree. I knew deep inside that all I had going for me was to run. And perhaps with much despair, try to fly off the ground with my damaged wings. I had to try everything to escape the presence of theses elves.

I glanced up and saw to my terror that, all four elves were coming down just as fast as I was. They climbed down with such speed, like this was some sort of thrill to them, I was disgusted. My heart never pulsed this fast before. It felt as if I was racing with my heart. I tried to take deep breaths to control my breathing but, it seemed impossible. I could only do one of two things, concentrate on climbing down as fast as I could, and concentrate on my breaths so I wouldn't black out!

Moments later, I finally reached the bottom as my feet touched the ground. But I wasn't quick enough. Someone had violently grabbed me from behind around my waist. I wasn't able to see who it was but, I did see a shiny swords' edge blade that now inched from my neck.

The Agreement

28

Latimer had picked me up as he slammed his back against the tree as he still held me tightly around the waist. He held his blade to my throat as he pulled me harder into his chest as the swords edge lightly scraped my delicate skin. Theron laughed sinisterly as he landed on the floor on his feet, right in front of me. Rowen and Oleos quickly landed right behind him on their feet as well. Theron turned to his elf friends and replied with enthusiasm, "Gentleman relax, I saw her first." The other elves laughed as Theron turned back to face me. He smiled shyly as he replied to me, "Thought you'd get away didn't you, especially without magic and, in the company of the fastest tree climbers ever. Please, don't make me laugh."

I struggled a bit as Latimer clenched his grip on my stomach even tighter. Theron seemed to enjoy the fact that I was suffering a bit, the jerk. Theron chuckled to himself as he replied to me yet once more, "Well I do have to say that I do, enjoy the feisty ones the most. Though, it seems to me that you might be a bit more of a challenge for me to break. I do love a challenge."

I grunted, "If you so as place one finger on me, I'll…"

"You'll do what? Glare at me to death?" He continued to smirk to himself as the rest of his elf friends laughed at his remark. I on the other hand was not amused one bit. Theron leaned closer to my ear as he gently dragged his tongue over the rim of my ear. He whispered, "You shall and will do whatever I seem you fit to do. Now, the first thing you can start with is by doing us all a favor and…"

And before Theron could even finish his sentence, a sword appeared, pointing directly under his chin. Theron quickly lifted his head higher as he started to step back slowly. Oleos and Rowen quickly drew their swords with their right hands. As for their left, right above their palms, floating ever so delicately in slight midair, formed a small green globe that seemed to glow with bright intensity. All of this was so sudden I closed my eyes tightly. I focused on situating my nerves, I needed to concentrate on what I needed to do next. But before I could even open them, I heard a familiar voice that made my heart jump out of rhythm. The voice came from behind us as he replied, "If you so much as touch her very skin, by my word I shall have you regret that moment for the rest of your pathetic life."

I opened my eyes and turned my head slightly to the right, Xanthus! I was so relieved to see him as goosebumps crawled over my arms. I turned to my left as I saw Morpheus holding his swords' tip to Latimer's neck. Morpheus replied to Latimer through gritted teeth, "Release her from your worthless grasp. Or I shall proceed and I shall draw your blood."

I could feel Latimer's heart trying to pound right out of his chest as his rhythms quickened. I turned my gaze over to Theron as he chuckled, "Let me take a small guess here, Xanthus, she belongs to you, doesn't she? Of course she would, I mean look at her. She's perfect for you because she's defenseless, therefore, she can't really run away from you, can she? Poor pathetic feathered…"

Xanthus stepped closer as he now rested the tip of his sword right on Theron's neck. Xanthus grunted, "Watch it."

It seemed as all of this merely amused Theron, I was surprised by his reaction to all of this. Theron shrugged his shoulders as he replied with a smile, "Fine, I'm just merely trying to say is, you, as usual, probably lack the courage to love her willing. Am I right?"

Xanthus pushed his sword slightly into Theron's neck, as his skin around the blade now turned a slight pink. Xanthus slightly growled angrily, "Theron, you have always misinterpreted the true definition of love. You know nothing about it, nor honesty for that matter!"

"Xanthus, you are just jealous for the fact that I, I am capable of performing true passion, and that you lack the courage to. Therefore, I had to willingly give that to all of your past loves. Or perhaps I am mistaken, and the true fact is that your lack is just truthfully fear, fear that owns your very skin."

Xanthus glanced over to me and then back to Theron. It seemed as if he was out of breath. What could he have been doing before he got here? Did he too land in a tree or father out pasted all of the trees? Where did he get his sword? Did they travel back to the camp site to get it? My thinking was broken as Xanthus replied to Theron in small breaths, "My life is not, nor has ever been your concern. Not now, not ever! Now release her Theron, or I will swing my blade at you."

I glanced back to Theron as he now became chilled with nervousness. Theron knew he was not able to reach his sword in time. He then laid his eyes upon Morpheus' sword as small beads of blood now trickled down Latimer's delicate neck. Though Latimer still seemed not to be affected but, only his breaths thickened as I felt his chest rise and slowly fall. Theron turned his gaze upon the sword that pressed into his skin as he took in a deep breath and let it out slowly. He rolled his eyes towards Xanthus with a slight glare as he replied softly, "Release her Latimer."

Latimer did as ordered as he removed his grip from around my waist, and lifted the sword off of my neck. I slowly walked around everyone's swords as I made my way next to Morpheus. I glanced around for James and Priniza but, they were nowhere to be seen. Where could they have gone? Did they not make it out of the nest? I turned towards Morpheus as I mumbled, "Where's Priniza and James?"

He in return mumbled, "A Centaur named Denentro took Priniza to a city called Magnesio. As for James..." Morpheus shrugged. Where could James have gone? Did he make it out? Did Denentro find him as well? Well, at least I know for sure he found Priniza. I do hope she wasn't hurt. But if she was, I'm sure Hypathia would take care of her and James if they had him. Though I do hope Priniza hadn't forgotten my feathers that I gave her and what to say. Either way I know she is in the safest place right now; she's with Denentro.

Theron threw his hands up in the air with a shrugged as he retorted, "So what now? You go on your merry way, 'fraid not! You are outnumbered and honestly, out powered. You may be faster with your sword but honestly, with magic, you are out smarted."

Theron twirled his right wrist around as it released a dim green hue. He pointed his index finger down as he took a step back. With that, Xanthus' sword flung out of his hands and dug itself into the ground. Theron's hands grew brighter as he then pointed it to Xanthus chest. With that, Xanthus' feet were taken from him as a vine from the nearest tree twirled itself around one of his ankles. It flung him upside down and into the air.

Xanthus grunted to himself as he formed a blue globe above his right palm and threw it towards Theron. With a sonic boom effect, it pushed Theron into a nearby tree with a hard thud. Xanthus within that moment took out a small dagger from his boot as he cut the vines that

350

smothered his ankle. He slammed into the ground as the leaves around him flew into the air and slowly sailed down.

Both elves grunted in pain as they quickly got to their feet, at the same time. They both formed red energy globes that seemed to contain lava above their palms. They both chucked it at each other as the globes collided with each other in midair. They exploded with a loud blast as heavy black smoke seemed to slowly diminish towards them, it disappeared with the mist that surrounded them.

Theron let out a low whistle, "Xanthus I'm impressed, has this fairy been teaching you new tricks?"

Xanthus shook his head as he replied breathlessly, "No, I just finally caught on to your tricks. But I do say that the old ones are a lot simpler at times." Once those words escaped Xanthus' lips he lunged towards Theron and punched him hard in the face. That sent Theron flying off of his feet and into the ground with a busted nose. Theron quickly lifted his leg as he kicked Xanthus hard behind the knee, knocking him onto the floor as well with a hard thud.

Within moments a loud crash echoed above them as a huge tree branch fell upon them, pinning them both permanently onto the ground. The two elves squirmed in dismay as they both started to punch and kick each other, with whatever they had free. What else could they do?

Well, what they didn't know was that everyone else had already placed their swords down. We all were just there watching them have at it. I for one was in no mood whatsoever. I had had enough of their childish behavior. It was made clear that they seriously weren't going to kill each other.

So, I with took Xanthus' dagger from the ground where he had dropped it, and I saw the unsteady branch above them. I saw my opportune moment and I seized it. I do have to thank Beruchium one day for showing me that. I knew it would come in handy one day. So, I had chucked the dagger just below the spot of the branch where it was at its weakest and, where it had its only support left, and broke it. I caused the immense tree branch to fall ever so coincidently right above them, trapping them there where they laid.

I walked over to the tree first and removed the dagger from within the tree. I turned towards the two elves that were struggling to free themselves from the branch. I leaned over to Theron's side first as I pointed the dagger to his nose. I snapped, "You will do so in answering my questions honestly and correctly, I might add. Then I will remove this log from above you. If you object to my decision, I will and shall remove your ability to smell ever again!"

Theron smirked arrogantly as he slowly licked the corner of his now bleeding mouth. He chuckled within breaths, "Well, if you insist on demanding answers and, are expecting honesty, why don't you ask my cousin first?"

My mouth dropped; I was astounded. My whole plan in my head, just went out the window and went berserk! I couldn't believe that this whole time they were fighting; they knew that they were fighting family! I turned over slowly to the other side of the log as I scrunched my eyes in dismay. As I came to Xanthus, his face was flushed. I couldn't tell if it was from anger or from embarrassment. I sighed, "Alright Xanthus, you go first, explain."

He grunted as he replied through gritted teeth, "Well he started it centuries ago! Just because I was faster and capable of maneuvering better with the swords than he was, he's just, he's just holding an infinite grudge."

Theron shouted from the other side, "Tell her the truth! You cheated!"

"Did not!"

They both continued their attempts to attack each other with their legs. I sat on the edge of the log as I sighed; this was going to be useless. I can see their similarity, stubbornness. There was no way that they were going to come to some type of agreement. I rubbed my forehead as I simply gazed upon the floor. Strange, why were there red and white rose petals on the floor? How did they get here? I didn't see any rose bushes anywhere nearby. Oh well, I shrugged it off. I had other things to stress over. I glanced up, all four elves just stood there as if they knew it was pointless. Oleos replied to me, "You know, as far as I can remember, they have always been like this, insufferable, unbearable..."

Rowen chuckled, "I don't think you are going to get a peace treaty from them. It is simply a waste of your precious time. Especially if you are going to try, you'll just waste away your beauty."

I groaned and glanced back at the two imprisoned elves bickering back and forth with each other. I sighed, what was I going to do? But my thoughts were immediately shattered. A loud piercing screech filled the air as everyone ducked clenching dearly to their ears. I too placed my hands over my ears and closed my eyes tightly, the pain echoed throughout my very skin.

Moments later the noise had ceased, as warmth filled me. I opened my eyes to find that Xanthus had freed himself and was now kneeling besides me, holding onto my ears as well. I turned to him as I gazed into his loving eyes. I sunk into his warm embrace as I buried my face within his neck. It felt so good in my heart, for we hadn't had a moment to ourselves for quite some time.

Of course, though our moment in time was shattered as Theron shouted, "I'm pleased to see that no one forgot about me!"

Xanthus helped me up as he handed me my mothers' sword back, my sword. He replied with a tender smile, "I think this belongs to you."

I with took my sword as he gently rubbed his fingers upon my hand. I blushed, I couldn't help it, his smile and warmth still had that effect on me. Xanthus then went over to the log and lifted it, so that Theron could squeeze out from underneath it. I lifted my sword up to his chest as he stood and leaned on the tree with his back. He took in deep breaths as he turned his gaze over to Xanthus. Xanthus as well with drew his sword and held it to Theron chest. Morpheus withdrew his sword towards the other elves as he kept his back to us.

Theron smirked and replied, "Look, what happened in the past is the past, and it is long gone. Those events now only lie among our memories. What is now is the present, and this very moment is what matters."

I turned to Xanthus whom in turn nodded to me in return. It was as if he knew what I was thinking, even though I really didn't want to say it. So, I took in a deep sigh as I faced back to Theron. I replied to him, "Unfortunately we need your help to get out of here and head towards where the Cristats are heading to, which is war. Which means, we need to get there as fast as we can. My kind, as well as yours are in jeopardy, and we will cease to exist under Cethios and Zethron's rule. My father will be and is in grave danger, as well as your king. You both must put aside your differences of your own spoiled blood. I will not deal with it and neither should you both!"

I glanced towards Xanthus as he shrugged. I continued as I turned back towards Theron, "Both of you need to grow up. I'm sure what's left of the Cristats that have stayed behind have by now noticed that we have all escaped, so our lives are in danger. Would you not help us now? Although, choose your side carefully, or so help me, one of you will see the wrath of anger I can wield with this sword."

Theron sighed as he gazed at my sword and snorted, "Cethios truly exists then huh, you know, all this time I thought he was simply a myth."

Theron looked up as he turned to face Xanthus. He sighed, "Your Azalea has valor within her. I can honestly say, she's not what I expected."

I could see that by that those statement Xanthus appeared confused, as well as I. I wonder if I should ponder on his words but, for the moment I shook them off. I really didn't have much time to ponder anything over really, not with a war on our heels. Xanthus raised his sword higher to Theron's neck as he demanded, "Look, whether or not you believe it, Azalea and I are part of the prophecy that you and I once stumbled upon in the Island of Yaisla. Azalea and I are perhaps the only ones that can somehow stop this meaningless bloodshed. Our fate is challenged by traitors and evil every waking moment of our lives. And if we do not succeed in this prophecy that was laid upon us, our lands, our existence will never see the light of day or peace. We all will live forever in hatred and bloodshed."

Theron took in another deep sigh as he gazed at my shackles. He pointed to them and asked, "And those?"

This was getting aggravating; Theron was being impossibly problematic! I quickly gathered my thoughts as I glared at Theron and angrily snapped, "These shackles we placed upon me by force, by Cethios himself. So he can take my powers against my will, but I will and have put up a fight, forever more. My powers are not up for grabs. Now, if we don't hurry and get to that war before it begins, who knows how many more innocent lives will be taken from this time. So then, what do say? Either you help us, or be dammed!"

I stepped back with anger as I opened my wings to their full extent. They felt so sore but yet so good to extend them out. I could actually feel them slowly start to heal. I did hear the three elves behind me become startled, as well as Theron in front of me. What can I say; I have that effect on others with my wings. And I am glad I still got it. I stepped back and placed my sword back upon my side. It was pointless to try with these

354

Outcasted, either they were going to help or they weren't, and their decision would be made all on their own, not by any other help.

I turned to Xanthus who in turn placed his sword back on his side as well. He with took my hands in between his own as he gently rubbed his soft lips upon them. Goosebumps filled my skin as he gazed into my eyes. He whispered under his breath to me, "I love you; I cannot wait until the day comes when we can both peacefully walk along The Caves of Esmera, and know that we may get lost in time without any worry or dismay. My love for you is truly all yours to keep within your grasp."

I smiled and whispered to him in return, "And there is where I shall keep it."

Xanthus kissed my fingers lightly as he then started kissing my cheeks. A low snorting noise came from behind us. Yes, our moment was ruined yet again. Theron grunted, "Is this what I am going to have to deal with if I do join your side, 'cause I could do without all the mush, really."

Xanthus smiled as he released my grasp and walked towards his cousin. Theron cleared his throat and rolled his eyes mockingly, "This agreement doesn't change anything cousin. Meaning, I still possess more capable magic than you. Don't forget that. Even though you cheat, I guess…"

With that Theron stepped forward to Xanthus and replied with his hand stuck out in front of him, "I forgive you, for now. Will you forgive me?"

Xanthus stood there a bit baffled. He watched Theron smirked to himself with content as if he was still hiding something. But I think for the moment, that was the best we were going to get out of Theron. It seemed as if Xanthus had thought the same. He shrugged his shoulders and reached out and shook his cousins' hand. With that being done, Theron stepped around Xanthus and headed towards his other elf friends. Morpheus in return stepped over closer to us. He whispered to us, "You know I still don't trust him."

Xanthus nodded and agreed, "Well neither do I but, for the time being we need his help, and we need to fly out of here fast. Azalea, you need to watch your back as I will be watching it too. Morpheus, keep your eyes on him at all times."

We both nodded and walked over to the four Outcasted. But before we could even say anything or do anything else, a long piercing screech sent us all to the floor with our hands over our ears. The Cristats were getting closer. And as I stood after the screeching had stopped, I gazed at my hands in horror. Fresh bright blood covered my palms as my ears throbbed with severe pain.

Latimer shouted over the screeches, "We need to head out to The Depths of Galligro! That is where they are heading to now! That is where the war of our century is going to fall! They are calling to each other, gathering and heading out now!"

Morpheus shouted to him, "And how exactly do you know what they are saying!"

"I studied the Cristats and their language from the ancient books from the Island of Yaisla! I actually studied unlike you!"

Oleos shouted to them both, "Would you both quit your yaps? We need to go!"

Xanthus rushed to my side as his expression quickly turned to disappointment. The screeching finally had ended as he took in a deep breath. He shook his head with a disapproved worrisome expression. He mumbled, "Azalea no, what happened now?"

It seemed as if he was saying something else but, there was still a constant ringing within my ears that did not seem to fade. The pounding in my ears was now making my eyes water and my head ache. All I could do was mumble, "My ears…"

Xanthus placed his hands gently over my ears as he kissed my forehead gently with his soft lips. He then dragged his lips down gently towards my left ear as he whispered something lightly in them, but I still was unable to hear his voice. Everything seemed to be moving so slow, so distant.

Rowen shouted over to Theron, "Theron, these trees should conceal us for the time being. But we must get to our griffins on the other side where they are waiting for us. From there we can fly to the Depths. But traveling there, we will be in the open as vulnerable prey. They'll hack us out of the sky!"

Theron shouted over to Morpheus, "Don't you have your dragons? Can't you call them from here? If we have at least one we can subside them with their fire breath or something, just until we reach the Depths of Galligro."

"I can't! They left on our orders to go get help from Whisperia and Trinafin! They are probably at the Depths of Galligro right now awaiting our return!"

Theron grunted and shouted back, "What great master sends their only hope away?"

Morpheus stepped closer to Theron as he shouted, "I took orders from one that is a great leader, from a fairy named James. Don't you dare judge my judgment on those of other minds. I'll tell you what I truly think of your…"

Before Morpheus could say anything else, Rowen shouted to them both, "Enough, we must get going! We have no time for this if we are to truly get away from the eyes of the Cristats!"

Theron nodded to him as he in turn shouted over to Xanthus, "We must get out of here! Is she going to be alright?"

Xanthus nodded to him as he turned and whispered in my ear, as my senses were finally numbing back, "You are going to be alright, I know you can handle this. We must carry on; I know you have the strength to carry on a bit further. We must."

I nodded to him. But before Xanthus could move, I grabbed his shoulders. I just remembered, how could I have forgotten to ask, "Xanthus, do you know where James is."

Xanthus scrunched his face and frowned as he replied in my ear, over the screeches of the Cristats, "No, I honestly thought he was with you."

"We need to look for him Xanthus! He could be anywhere!"

Xanthus grimaced in regret and shook his head, "Azalea, he is probably already ahead of us as we speak, which I ironically truly believe. Or, he is somewhere resting in the lands. It would be better if he gets his rest; I believe that he is okay. You and I both know he can take care of himself; you shouldn't worry. Perhaps Denentro found him, he found us and took Priniza with him."

I stared at his eyes and wondered. James did have a knack for surprisingly being okay but, I honestly wanted to run and look for him. I mean, he was like a father to me, more than my true one at that. But I took in a deep breath and nodded. I knew Xanthus was right, we needed to get out there to the Depths. And I knew that James would have wanted it to be like that. I honestly hoped that I would find James already there.

I took in another breath as I replied in Xanthus' ear, "Let's go."

My ears continued to pound with the pain but, at least they were not ringing. The screeches of the Cristats now seemed to blend into the earth's vibrations as we ran. Thankfully they were ascending into the sky as they flew towards the Depths of Galligro. We ran seemingly, for about an hour. For a good while, I gritted my teeth and flew to give my feet a rest.

We eventually made a stop at this small piece of land that contained thick bushes, but high enough for us to duck under them. As we stopped to rest Xanthus caught sight of my right arm. It was still blistering and covered with dry burgundy blood. It ached and burned with intensity but, I had to push the pain to the back of my mind. I had come to a conclusion a while ago, to deny that knowledge to Xanthus. I didn't want him to think that I was vulnerable and weak. I was already hurting with my ears, wings and left arm from when I fought with the Cristat. I didn't want to add to it! I also didn't want to admit to myself that I was in bad shape. Once again, Xanthus frowned at my arm. He replied between his breaths, "This cannot wait any longer; you are in no condition to carry on. Give me your arm and let me heal you, along with your other wounds."

I shook my head as I replied with deep breaths, "No, I am not weak. I shall not allow you to think of me in that way. I can…"

"If you do not allow me heal you, and refuse, you'll be no use to any of us when we are in battle."

"You, you mean that, you truly mean it? You are not going to force me to stay behind, like the first battle?"

Xanthus shook his head regrettably, "No, that was my first mistake, trying to keep you safe, and look where that got me, you taken from me."

"You can't mean that, you don't think that when Cethios took me, that it was your fault. You can't blame yourself for that; the only one to blame is myself. I should have been more careful with my helmet. I should have been paying attention to my surrounding."

I placed my right palm on his face; it seemed as if tears wanted to pry themselves out of his eyes. But with that, Xanthus grabbed my arm with his right hand and placed his left upon my shoulders and wings where they were shredded from the Cristats. His palms quickly let out a glow of white as it seemed to consume my whole body, as well as his. Pain quickly ran through my head down to my very toes. I was screaming horrendously on the inside so that way no one would be able to hear me.

I closed my eyes and gritted my teeth tightly as I waited for the pain to cease. Moments later I felt Xanthus' cool soft lips caress mine. Slowly my pain diminished to nothing. Xanthus' lips parted from mine, as well as his touch as I opened my eyes slowly. I cautiously opened my wings carefully as I stretched them out to their fullest. Honestly, it felt really good, no pain at all. I mean, I was sore but, no agony. I glanced down at my arms to see that they were completely healed, it was as if nothing had ever happened.

But as I glanced down, I saw Xanthus. He was bent over taking in deep breaths in and out as his hands were upon his knees. I bent over to him as I kissed his forehead. I whispered to him, "That was not necessary, I don't need you becoming weakened because of my foolishness. But nonetheless, thank you my prince, my king."

He gazed up with his almond eyes, still taking in the deep breaths. He smiled and replied in a whisper, "Anything for my future queen, whom I love with everything that I have."

Just as I was about to knock him down and embrace him dearly, a large hawk head poked out from one of the surrounding bushes. I took a step back, and just as I was about to scream, from behind me Rowen placed his hand over my mouth. I glanced around as I saw to my surprise that three more appeared from out of the dense bushes.

Rowen removed his hand from my mouth as he started to pet the creature. I stepped back as the creature stepped forward to reveal its whole. Its head and front legs were that of hawk, as well as its wings. Its body was that of a ferocious healthy lion. The creatures' tail though, was that of a hawk, with the exception of light brown fur covering some of the tail feathers. They were the beautiful creatures that Beruchium had once told me about. I never imagined that I would be able to see one, or be near one for that matter.

The four Outcasted, Rowen, Latimer, Theron and Oleos quickly jumped on one and sat on their backs. Theron replied, "These are our companions, my griffon is Destra. Oleos' is named Arin, Rowen's is Arista, and Latimer's is Dralyn. They are our friends as you have your dragons."

Latimer replied in return, "Each of you may ride with one of us. The Cristats are perhaps already halfway to The Depths of Galligro, and it may take us half of the day to reach it. And, if I'm not mistaken of their language, I overheard the last Cristats reply that there were no slackers. So therefore, we can follow close behind, but, far enough that they won't notice, assumedly."

Morpheus replied, "And we're supposed to trust you that you will take us to the Depths."

Latimer laughed, "You have trust issues. Is it really about me, or is it honestly about your own issues with yourself, get over it! You are in so much denial."

Morpheus shook his head and just as he was about to respond Xanthus shouted to him, "Morpheus we have no choice. We must get to the battle in time before it begins."

Theron laughed, "And do tell cousin, remind me again why we are so willing to help you in this war."

Xanthus stepped forward and withdrew his sword. He pointed it towards Theron as his griffon Destra remained calm. Xanthus cautioned angrily, "Perhaps not this one, but I assure you there will be one. Cethios will definitely make sure of that. Are you going to help me or not cousin? For the last I heard of you, you and your colleges were thrown out of your precious city and were declared as Outcasted! So where does your allegiance lie. Have you not already given me your word, or do you spit upon your own oaths that you make?"

Theron glared at Xanthus; it was as if Theron was hiding something. Or perhaps Theron knew of something that we didn't know. But I didn't like his expression, it meant no good. Theron cleared his throat and smirked to himself. He chuckled sarcastically, "If only you truly knew Xanthus. But yes, I did give you my word for the time being, do not underestimate me and my oaths, I guarantee you that. But yet again, yes, you can trust me that I will help you today. Come, you can ride with me to prove that you can trust me. I'm sure you could merely push me off if you want; you know you are stronger than me in that. As for Azalea, she can go with Latimer. And Morpheus, you can ride with Oleos, since you two were the best of friends back then. So, we must make hast yes? War and fighting awaits us, that is what we are best at are we not? They can't start without us."

Xanthus raised one of his eyebrows as he eyed Theron with uncertainty. It was as if he didn't trust him at all but, I mean again, what choice did we have? Moments later Xanthus placed his sword back upon his side as he grunted to himself. Theron on the other hand seemed content with something.

Unexpectedly as a memory had returned and vanished within me, something about Theron suddenly sparked my subconscious mind. I had seen him before but where? It couldn't have been from a dream, could it? I couldn't shake off the fact that his face, his laughter was familiar in some way. I pondered quickly attempting to retrieve the memory, but nothing else came to my mind. It bothered me because, I felt like it was important to remember but, I simply could not force myself to recall it any longer, I couldn't.

My thoughts were disturbed as Xanthus called out to me, "Azalea!" I turned to him as he mumbled the words, "Be careful, my love."

I nodded as Xanthus climbed up behind Theron. Then with one leap they were off into the sky above us. Then Rowen took off, as well as Oleos with Morpheus sitting behind him. They left in such a blink of an eye I hardly noticed that left was just Latimer, his griffon Dralyn and myself. I sighed as yet again; Xanthus had left me behind to start late in the war. Of course, conveniently, what else could he do right?

I turned and slowly walked up to Latimer with my hands crossed across my chest. I guess you could say I was still holding a grudge against him from when he held that blade to my neck. He didn't even notice that I was upset though! He chuckled ignorantly to my dismay, "Alright, you can ride in front so I can hold on to you. Wouldn't want you falling off with your sore wings and all. Besides, you could also control the flight that way if you want."

I remained there with my arms crossed, I wasn't going to budge. Finally, as if it came to him, he sighed and jumped off of Dralyn. He stood in front of me as he sighed in surrender, "Alright-alright, so we got off on the wrong foot. I do apologize for holding you against your will, and for holding my blade against your neck. Satisfied?"

"No. How am I supposed to trust you, I cannot bend my trust as easily as Xanthus can."

He crossed his arms across his chest as he stood there pondering my words. He started to walk towards Dralyn and back to me as he placed his right hand upon his chin. He paced for a good moment or two when finally, he came to a halt in front of me. He smiled with contentment as he bowed slightly to me. He then stood and placed his left hand behind his back as he placed his right palm over his chest. His right palm glowed a slight indigo hue as he replied, "My allegiance and personal trust used to lie with Theron but, certain circumstances thankfully never allowed for an oath but... Over the past centuries, he has changed. We agreed for a while but, I guess I still went along for the ride even after we disagreed with things. But I now stand before you, and swear my trust, my allegiance, my blood, to you. I shall guard you with my life. Will you accept my life and my word with honesty through blood?"

I frowned and replied cautiously, "How am I supposed to know that you are being honest with me now? And what of Theron?"

"That Azalea, has long been broken by Theron himself. Now, do you Azalea, take me, Latimer, as your guardian of trust, and your life, with respect and honesty between us both, as long as we breathe on these lands?"

I pondered his question and his statements. I mean, how am I supposed to really trust him. Now a days you can't tell who is a friend, and who is a traitor. Though, he did seem truly honorable. And yet, something about this seemed familiar... I eyed him carefully as I wondered, "Alright, I do. But, are you promising me this?"

Latimer nodded, stuck out his hand and assured, "Through my word and blood."

My eyes widened momentarily, what in the world did he mean by that? I shook it off though, I mean, it couldn't be anything serious. Could it? Ugh, I had to shake it off; we needed to catch up with the others before Xanthus thought something was wrong. So, I did what I never thought I would do, I made a pack with him. I stuck out my right hand to shake his.

But the unthinkable occurred. He quickly took a dagger out from his left side holster with his left hand. He sliced my right palm open as he threw the dagger onto the floor as he then grabbed my arm. This all happened within brief moments, before I could even retrieve my arm back in pain or even scream. His right palm now glowed a sage green hue as the dagger on the floor quickly shot straight into the air and sliced him across his right palm. The dagger then fell back into the floor as it dug itself half into the ground. He grabbed my bloody right palm with his glowing and bloody right palm, and squeezed it.

Agony filled my lungs and nerves; I wanted to scream as I saw bright burgundy blood dripping onto the dagger and smearing over its handle. My heart raced with immense intensity as small tremors shook my core. Icy pain spread throughout my whole arm. Within moments he glanced over to me and smiled. What the hell was he so happy about! If I wasn't in so much pain, I would stick him in the face!

I glanced back down to gaze upon the blood that seeped from our palms and onto the dagger but, I noticed something was different. The blood that once was there was now transforming into a mesmerizing ivy plant. It grew with a sudden pace as it stretched its vines up and wrapped itself around both of our right hands. By now the pain ceased and amusement with took me.

I watched in curiosity as it twisted and wrapped its vines and leaves around my right hand and, as well as Latimer's. It then split into two and started to swirl up and around our arms. The vines and leaves of the ivy plant now only existed around our arms as it continued to travel up upon our upper arms encircled it. Then before I could become more amused, the ivy started to form a burning sensation over my delicate skin, upon my upper arm only. It slowed and stopped as it melted into our arms.

Moments later, Latimer ceased in squeezing my hand and released it. I rubbed my palm as I glanced at it bewildered. It appeared as if it had never been sliced open by Latimer's dagger! This was unbelievable. I started to rub my upper arm as more perplexity covered my very skin in small bumps. There encircling all around my upper right arm was a unique tattoo of a brightly exquisite ivy plant with many shades of green. Latimer too had one coiled around his upper arm as well.

I stroked it gently with my fingertips as it felt very cool to the touch. I took in a deep breath and let it out slowly as I tried to take all of this in. I gazed up to see Latimer taking in deep breaths and rubbing his upper arm as well. I replied to him, sort of breathless, "How, why?"

Latimer took in a deep breath as his gaze locked with mine. He chuckled momentarily, "Well, if I told you I wanted to make a Blood Oath with you, would you have of refused, or taken it?" I stretched my right arm behind me as I stretched it with my right wing. Latimer smirked to himself as he replied, "Do you trust me now that my commitment is sworn upon you, in a Blood Oath?"

I didn't know how to respond to him. I was sort of still amazed at this but yet again, was it truly necessary? I shook my head confused and replied, "I'm not sure I would have doubted you in the first place but, I mean, I guess there was some doubt in trust. I don't trust Theron and..."

Latimer interrupted me quickly, "I'm not Theron, please Azalea, I'm not him. Does me not swearing on oath to you through blood... I mean, is this not enough for you to believe... Do you comprehend the immense power behind a Blood Oath?"

I couldn't stand the sorrow and longing in his eyes any longer. I could tell he was not like the others at that exact moment. He was truly sincere about what he just did. I apologized, "Latimer look, I'm sorry. I take great honor in... Well, I'm honored that you swore your oath to me, of all others, me. I respect that, and you. But please do tell me, explain to me what this Blood Oath is, for it is new to me. I have no knowledge of this."

Latimer thankfully was pleased with my apology as his face flushed with excitement once again. He replied with enthusiasm, "Well, it is a binding oath that is unbreakable, only to be released by an ancient one or an Immortal. It is a binding vow through the Eternal Spirits. This tattoo represents our promise to one another. I promised to guard your life, with my life. Also, if I am ever dishonest with you, that tattoo will let you know. It will sting momentarily to inform you of my dishonesty or disloyalty, and me as well. But if I lie to you, my tattoo will scorch my skin, same goes for you."

I pondered his words as I nodded and replied, "So, if I am to understand this, if you lie to me, my tattoo will sting and your will scorch your skin, and likewise for me. So, we are bound to each other?"

Latimer nodded and slightly flushed, "Yes, is that alright?"

"Well, like you said, you are my guard. A guard I can trust, a friend, one I can count on with my life. But I do have one question? When these Blood Oaths are performed, I understand now how they become binding but, what happens if I or you break it? Also, is it always ivy vines?"

Latimer chuckled, "No, they are not always ivy vines. It is up to the Eternal Spirits to create a representation of the oath that was created.

Amazingly they chose a great symbol. The ivy plant is an evergreen plant, it represents eternity and strong friendships. An ivy plant also represents life and immortality. Also, to answer your other question, if ever the oath was ever truly and completely broken, whom ever breaks it, loses a century of their life. Almost instantly, their bodies will turn to death form, until that century is over. But during that century, the other can then go forth and find the traitor if they so choose, and end their life. The tattoo will cease, and the oath ends, obviously."

"That's harsh don't you think?"

Latimer shrugged his shoulders, "That's' the trust I have in you, I noticed it in your eyes Azalea since the moment our eyes met. You are different than anyone I have ever met. Xanthus must be really lucky to be with someone so pure. Which is why I decided to guard you and befriend you. This is my destiny; I just know it." Latimer took one more bow as I stepped forward and embraced him, catching him off guard. It felt so reassuring that I can bestow my trust in him, as my right-hand guard, and as a friend. I'll tell him one day, but I'm sure he already knows.

After that, he jumped on Dralyn as I flew up and sat in front of him. And as soon as I closed my wings, the griffin leaped into the air. Just as simple as that we were already soaring through the buttery clouds. I knew in the back of my mind that in all reality it was going to happen just like that. But I guess I supposed that perhaps it wouldn't be. I couldn't even take in a deep breath when the pitfall feeling landed in the bottom of my stomach.

As Dralyn took a dive down I tensed up and tried to hold on to my dear life. I couldn't help it, what can I say, I screamed in fright. I would say, slight fright, but who am I kidding, I was mortified. I screamed so loud that it rang throughout the magnificent sky above us. I heard Latimer shout, "Azalea, you're going to break my arm off! It's alright, relax, I will not let you fall!" I sank into his chest as the dips and climbs made me feel even more nauseated. And of course, moment later, Latimer understood. He bellowed out in laughter, "Wait a minute, am I understanding this correctly, a fairy afraid of heights? This is priceless!" His laughter echoed within my ears as I clamped my mouth shut.

I felt completely humiliated. Oh well, better he knows now about it than later. But this time, bravely enough, I kept my eyes opened. I wanted to see the grand view, what can I say, I've never seen this side of the lands before.

And curiously enough, I wondered if Dralyn was the fastest of the other griffins because in no time, we caught up with the others. And with much regrettable dread, moments later the horrendous sight of the Cristats appeared not so far in front of us. I cringed at their sight as the slight sound of their screeches brushed against my ears. But on the good note, they never suspected us right behind their trail.

Hours later as the sun started to descend into the west, my nerves started to shake and my stomach sank to my knees. The view of the Depths of Galligro started to slightly come into view. It was incredible as the suns' rays, reds and oranges, bounced off of the rocks.

Instantly though, the nauseating emotional pain struck my heart and my head. I knew at that exact moment my subconscious mind was preparing itself for yet another blood filled and unnecessary war. And as everything inside of me screamed to escape, I knew deep down that I couldn't. I had to face it, I had to face Cethios. I needed to fight for everything and everyone I cared for. And I knew that within the coming hours, the treacherous and agonizing screams would swell in my ears, and burn within my soul.

The Depths of Galligro

30

I reached for my ears as the Cristats started to screech in a high piercing noise. I clenched onto them tightly, I didn't want them to start bleeding again from their sharp calls. Oddly as it seemed their calls were as if they were distressed or something. But yet they still remained in their formation. I wondered what would be disturbing them so?

Within moments my question was answered. Nearly twenty feet above them appeared the images of fierce dragons. They flew so gracefully at top speed above them. They soared as if they were dancing upon the clouds with the air around them that smothered their wings.

But strangely enough, the Cristats did nothing that appeared as if they were going to attack them. I wondered why? Had Cethios given them strict orders? Or did they simply know they would be out strengthened? As I pondered these questions I could feel Latimer's grasp tighten around my waist as the dragons approached us. Then suddenly within the realization of recognizing the dragons, joy sank into my heart. I turned and shouted over the rustling wind to Latimer, "It's alright! I know those dragons!"

Latimer's grasp still did not loosen as I stared at Cetus and Orion soar towards us. And as they were within some distance, I saw Morpheus and Xanthus leap off of the griffons as Orion and Cetus dove towards their friends. Once they each landed on their dragon, they flipped around and continued to fly safely next to the griffons.

Just before doubt could seep into my mind I saw another glistening dragon speeding towards Latimer and me. It was whom I had so desperately waited to see, my best friend, Snowfire. I held back the tears that so painfully wanted to escape. I wanted to cry out in sadness, for missing her so, and in joy for finally seeing her. I had so much to tell her since last I had her by my side. Which oddly enough was the last battle we were at, the battle at the Valley of Melinatha. But alas, I knew now was not the time to dwell on it. Latimer replied into my ear before I too jumped off, "Please be careful Azalea, I just know this war is going to be vigorous. Take care of yourself. I'll be beside you when I can, if I can find you. Conceal yourself from him, you must!"

I nodded and embraced him. For a moment I was confused by his words. For I thought, if he was talking about Cethios, why then would Theron say that he thought Cethios was a myth? Well, I knew there was more to it but, I couldn't wait any longer to be reunited with Snowfire. I'm sure it was nothing.

As I released Latimer from my grasp, and his grasp upon me, I held my breath, opened my wings, and jumped off into the free open air around us. I dove head first as I saw Snowfire below me. I spun around and closed my wings as I landed on her with a soft thud. As soon as I did, I hugged whatever it was I could hug of her, which was just about only a small piece of her neck. I had never in my life been that long, without her by my side. "Snowfire! I'm so glad you are alright! I am so sorry for ever abandoning you in the Valley. Where have you been all this time?"

She shot a blue fire bolt out of her snout as she replied, "Some of Cethios' fairies found me after you were captured, while I was in Urinia. I tried to find you but, I was ambushed while I was in my snow leopard form. I tried with all of my might to escape but, Cethios has become more powerful than I can ever imagine. Especially Zethron, he's madder than ever! They are both so corrupt with evil I've never seen anything like that before! But thankfully James and Kaya found me. James told me to go to King Duralos after I went to Trinafin with Orion and explain everything. He also wanted me to recruit every possible fairy that still remained on our side. James assured me that you would be alright, that he would find you. So, right at this moment, both kings are side by side going to fight against Cethios' and Zethron's fairies and elves. Who knew they had so many followers. But that doesn't matter, what's important is that we reach our side before the sun touches the earth. Oddly enough they all have agreed none would strike till then."

I sighed and pondered her words. I wonder if it was frightening for King Duralos when Snowfire approached him as her dragon form. But I'm sure Cetus got to him first. Then, as I pondered deeper I realized what Snowfire had replied. I asked, "Snowfire, what exactly did you tell King Duralos? I must confess, there is something that I need to tell you, it's important, it's about my real father, about King Duralos…"

As I took in a deep breath to tell Snowfire the rest, and the truth, she sort of shivered. She turned her massive head slightly towards me. The sadness in her eyes made me stop on what I was about to reply. She in turn replied shyly, "Azalea, before you tell me, there is something that I must confess to you. Something I'm sure I could have told you long ago but, if I did it would of complicated things for you. Something that James promised me not to tell you, and much more but, only until the time was right. For now I can only tell you to trust me, that secrets will be revel to you when the time is right, but... Azalea, please do not be angry with me, I gave my word as a dragon to James not to... You're going to have to take it up with him later but... Azalea, I know that King Duralos has always been your true father. I was there when your mother, when Falin, placed the enchantment on you and Xanthus. When your destiny was set I made many oaths that day, many I shall never forget."

I felt a stab into my heart, I felt so betrayed. "All this time you have known about me, about my father, and yet, you remained silent through it all, since that day in Trinafin? And yet, even then you still did not tell me?"

Snowfire spewed red hot flames above us as it warmed the air even more around us. You could tell she was upset. She fumed, "I couldn't tell you, I swore to James before I even got a chance to really know you, or know what was important! I literally swore as soon as I broke out of my shell! I would have told you everything, I wanted to tell you, so many times!"

My head was spinning; I guess it wasn't her fault anyway. I couldn't blame her, I just couldn't but, all I could say was if James was alright, he was going to get an earful from me. There was really too much going on right now for me to even be upset at Snowfire, too much running through my subconscious mind. I took in a deep breath. I guess what was important right now was to get to the Depths of Galligro as fast as we could, and to stop Cethios and Zethron. "Snowfire, I will not hold anything against you, but promise me this, any new information that you hear or stumble across, anything..."

"Azalea I swear! I will tell you right away, I promise it to you. I shall never again make vows to hold anything from you!"

I hugged her yet again as I kept myself there upon her soft scales. I wanted to just stay there in relaxation forever. I didn't want to fight; I didn't want to do anything. What I really wanted to do was stay in the arms of Xanthus forever, safe.

Moments passed us as I finally decided to look up and see my surrounding. There below us and all around us, was the enormous Depths of Galligro. It was a breath taking sight, tall valleys formed of red rocks that glistened in the suns' rays. It was all so incredible but yet, there was no sign of life anywhere. And even with its beauty present, there was still the presence of many battles here. The crimson colors within the stone and rock gave presence of bloodshed and anxiety. The dry cracks within the land seemed to be yearning, awaiting the moist blood and life of those whom did not deserve death. Yet through it all, here we are within its marvel.

We were now approaching the vast amount of warriors that formed on the south side of the Depths and as well as from the north. Within the north side were fairies, elves with some dragons in the air and of course, the Cristats in the air as well. Within the south were some fairies, elves, dragons in the air and some on land. And now our new friends upon their griffons. Also which surprised me; I saw some unicorns within the south in our mist. I wonder if they were here avenging their prince, my friend, Prince Mirage. Surely they would be able to kill many with just one blow. Also who would want to kill a pure unicorn? Whoever did would be forever cursed. But yet unfortunately, I could name one who would kill them or shall I say did. Hopefully the purifying mist is upon and with the unicorns, for I fear the thought that I could be wrong. I hoped there weren't any in this war prepared to destroy them.

And as I looked closer, warmth overwhelmed my heart as I saw who else had accompanied us on the south. It was the centaurs. I was proud that they could make it. And I wasn't surprised at how fast they got there. They were the fastest creature I could think of. They liked to say that they run with the echo of a whisper. Which I with took as that they could run with the speed of lightning. And, I am glad to say that I am very thankful and grateful that they came to our aid, to my aid to fight with us. And hopefully, Priniza stayed behind with Hypathia. I knew Priniza did not have the strength for this.

As we finally landed safely on the south side, we landed near some huge auburn tents, just about an hour before the sun set aside us. I jumped off of Snowfire as I took a deep stretch. Snowfire morphed into her snow leopard form as she replied, "Thought you might want to clean up a bit, before we head out to the front lines."

I nodded to her, "Yeah just a bit. Perhaps I can find some change of clothes as well."

One tent that stood before me had its flaps wide open. Inside it contained a stone table with a fairy gentleman standing behind it. He was handing out a purple smoothie within a small stone cup. I went up and took one thankfully from him. It was delicious and revitalizing, it tasted just like the one from the previous battle. But as I gazed at the stone cup, I wondered, what was I supposed to do with this one? Fortunately before I was able to reply anything to anyone, my cup transformed itself into a small pebble. Cool, I thought. I took the pebble with me as I exited out of the tent, then dropped it nearby. I found another tent that was giving out clothes. That was weird I thought.

As I neared it I was in shock to find an elf woman handing out clothes and armor. She was giving out brown pants, black loose button tops, silver plated chest plates and silver helmets. Another elf woman was taking in the dresses and shrinking them. She placed them in a large ivory trunk with pearls on it. I couldn't believe my eyes. Women elves and fairies were getting prepared to fight in a war! They shouldn't be here, me of all but, I was. One elf woman with a green velvet dress and chocolate curly hair approached me and replied, "Hurry up my dear, pick up a change, gather some armor and find an empty tent, we haven't got much time before the sun touches the earth."

Before she had a chance to set off I grasped her arm gently and asked her, "But why all this? War is for men, women shouldn't…"

She placed her hands delicately upon my arms as she quickly interrupted me, "No my dear, I correct you. War is for the brave, for the strong who have a desire and want to fight for their freedom, those who want to fight alongside their loved ones. We will not and shall not stay at home and twiddle our fingers and hope that our loved ones return. No, we will be here, we live with them and we will die with them, if it comes to that. Besides, if we stay at home and our love ones don't return, we are already dead on the inside. No my dear, we belong here."

With that she turned and hurried along on her way. I stood there as golden tears freely fell from my eyes. There was nothing that I could do to change her mind, or any of their minds for that matter. There were so many of them, and yet, she was right. I would not dare leave Xanthus alone; this wasn't his fight to begin with… Well at the very beginning it wasn't, but now, it was all of our fight.

Before I could continue to dwell on the thought Snowfire caught my attention. She yelled over to me. She had already gathered some clothes and some armor for me and had an empty tent available. I ran over to her as quickly as I could without even thinking, and ran inside the tent to change. I quickly tried to conjure up something pointless. I undressed just as the little black rain cloud appeared. I quickly bathed in it. Oh well, might as well use it right?

I changed into the clean fresh clothes and ran out to Snowfire. As I stepped out to her, she was already morphed into a white horse. Snowfire had body armor on herself and a helmet and breast plate for me to wear, she was prepared. I placed the helmet upon my head, and the breast plate over my chest as I jumped onto her back. We raced through the other warriors as we now neared the front lines. Suddenly before we did Snowfire came to a halt. I asked, "What is it?"

There a few feet ahead of me was King Duralos. I stared at my father as I fought back the tears that so desperately wanted to escape. He sat there on a magnificent ivory unicorn with armor upon it. He sat there patiently with his sword on his side, and there within his hands was the flag of the fairies. He held it up with great pride. It was a beautiful flag with sapphire and golden trimming along the edges and within it. And in the middle was a moon and a sun, merges together as one, with beautiful indigo fairy wings extended outward from the merged sun and moon. Also, small gold and cerulean stars surrounded it all within.

King Duralos turned slightly as his eyes widen as they rested upon me. I jumped off of Snowfire as I took the helmet off of my head and my breast plate off. He dismounted his unicorn as he dug the flag pole into the parched earth. I couldn't help it, I ran to him. I ran to him like I have always dreamed I would when I found my true parents. Who knew he was right in front of me all this time.

As we collided, I embraced him as tightly as I possibly could. It was an embrace I never felt before, warm, caring, regretful and joyful. It warmed my heart knowing that he too finally knew the truth, after all of this time. I wanted to shout to the world that before me, was my father, that before him was his daughter, I was his daughter. I wanted to tell him how I saw my own mother die, how Zethron had betrayed us all, how Queen Lily, my mother, loved us all. But yet, all these words were stuck in the back of my throat, unable to escape the madness of this all.

As we finally parted I gazed into the swelling eyes of my father as he replied to me, "Azalea, my beloved daughter, forgive me. Forgive me for all that I have done to you, for all that you had to go through because I, was in denial through it all. The signs were there, there were so many but yet, I choose to ignore them all. I choose to dwell on my sadness, on my regret, on the thought that I was alone. I loved your mother dearly. Queen lily would have been so proud of her daughter… I am proud of my daughter."

We embraced yet once more as it pained me knowing that I had to eventually release this grasp that I had on him. From behind us though Snowfire neighed softly, "Your highness…"

We parted as King Duralos went past me and embraced Snowfire by the neck. Snowfire purred softly as it sent pure vibrations into my heart, it soothed me. I'm sure it soothed King Duralos' heart as well. He turned back towards me and replied, "James told me, about an hour ago that I would be able to find you here and…"

My heart stopped at those words. And without thinking I interrupted him, "James, you've seen him, you spoke with him? Recently? Where is he, is he alright? Why didn't he… After the Scorching Nest I…"

King Duralos raised his right palm up as it glowed a dim white. He silenced me as he just pointed up into the sky above us. I moved my gaze up towards the sky where many soldiers were on their dragons. And there in the mist of all of that chaos I spotted James on Kaya. A warm smile came to me as for the moment I knew he was safe, and out of the Cristats' grasp. How had he survived the fall from the nest, I do not know nor do I care, as long as he had the strength to fight and was prepared for yet another horrendous battle.

As I gazed back down, I saw that my father, King Duralos, was back upon his unicorn holding our flag. He held that fairy flag with such pride, it honestly put a bit more courage into my heart.

I looked back into the sky towards the north as I saw the Cristats soaring around practicing their attack moves. I moved my gaze towards the south above me, as I saw the dragons simply diving in and out of the buttery clouds, as if dancing in ambush maneuvers, as well as the four griffons. I gazed back down as I turned to Snowfire. I ran my fingers through her mane as I asked softly, "So, where is it that we shall fight this time? In the air, or on land?"

"Everyone we know is in the air, except…"

"Except my father." I sighed and took one last peaceful glance at everyone I cared about. I stopped at Xanthus and Cetus, my heart was with them. For I did turn and gazed off towards Cethios and his dragon Krynton. Krynton let out a loud bellowing roar as red and blue flames spewed out of his throat. It's not that I was afraid to face Krynton or Cethios but rather, I wanted to fight next to King Duralos, next to my father. I answered, "Well Snowfire, we shall fight on land... I will fight besides my father."

And with that I placed my armor back on and jumped upon Snowfire as we quickly headed for the front lines, and just in time. For when we reached the front, the sun started to brush the earth. And within moments of that, the trumpets began to sound off. They echoed within the Depths of Galligro, they echoed within my soul.

Death

31

The sun continued to touch the earth with its belly as the horns continued to blow vigorously in the breeze. The south had already started to charge as we were immediately greeted by millions of flying arrows. There were so many, they seemed to cover the stars above that just started to wake and glow. Luckily many of us had shields that protected us; some thankfully hid behind others shields.

As we too sent arrows into the darkening sky, we charged onward. Within moments we collided with a heavy clash, and those same agonizing screams that haunted my nightmares, once more echoed within my ears. The moans of death stabbed my heart. It was a horrific sight. I simply tried to concentrate on the fairy or elf in front of me that tried to take me down. That was all I really could do.

Before long, red and blue energy globes were flying between us, knocking fairies and elves to the ground defenseless. Above us, the Cristats and the dragons collided with such force that it seemed to produce its own thunderstorm. Feathers and scales flew within the air as each tried to conquer the other. The griffons were doing great though, as luck seemed to be on their side.

As the night smothered the land our light had vanquished within the Depths of Galligro besides the milky way up above. But between the constant fire from the dragons' throat, and the consistency of the energy globes flying around us, it seemed as if time was everlasting in dusk. Hours pasted as it merely seemed like only moments. Strike after slash and slash after scream, just seemed to drag on, never ending.

Since my second fight, I had been fighting on foot. To Snowfire's regret, I was knocked off suddenly and she was needed in the air as her dragon form. And truly unfortunate, Snowfire and I were separated yet again in battle. Fear crawled up my skin for I thought I would never see her again, but I had to push that thought far out of my subconscious mind. All I could do was hope, for I knew she was fighting with all of her might.

Sometime after midnight, I gazed into the sky to thankfully see that the Cristats were retreating back towards Xylina. I could just barely see that King Aetius was discussing something with Cetus and Xanthus. I was

376

exhilarated to see that the dragons had won, we had won. Briefly after that, Xanthus and the others started to descend to help the others. Once they landed, all of the dragons, including Snowfire, took off into the air to take refuge in the cliffs that surrounded us. I'm sure they wanted to recover; they had just fought in a horrendous battle. They also looked a bit torn up, they needed the rest.

I continued to fight as just then, the sight and thought hit me. I didn't even recognize whom was whom anymore. Who was on whose side? Both races were just hacking at one another, this was madness! I couldn't tell who Cethios' men were anymore. Was I fighting one of my own on my side? This was and is a useless bloodshed! This was pointless! Innocent lives were being taken away with hatred, but from what? WHY!

Hours later I heard extensive arguing and shouts from somewhere behind me. I turned and found Cethios fighting Xanthus and Theron. Both elves were so desperately trying to take down their enemy fairy. Cethios was just too fast; his unbeatable title and luck still followed him.

I fought a few more men, merely knocking them down injuring them is more like it, I wasn't trying to kill anyone anymore. As I neared them I heard Xanthus shout to Cethios, "Do you truly not comprehend all of the innocent lives you have and are destroying? Just surrender so your fairies can coexist with one other and live in peace! Your selfishness has caused meaningless hatred and madness amongst others!"

Cethios released a sinister laugh as he continued to battle with them. He shouted, "They fight on their own free will. Your pathetic race will not conquer our superior kind. Do you want to know the true story behind elves? Elves are just meaningless worthless fairies that were banished from the Eternal Spirits; their ability to fly was taken from them. In a curse, so they could crawl upon the dirt in shame!"

Xanthus and Theron swung harder with more force as Cethios merely continued to laugh in between strikes. He snorted, "This war will cease if you simply give up what is rightfully mine. Deliver me Azalea, then I'll ponder the thought on letting you and your disgusting race live and to tell the tale... The tale of your powerful Immortal King Cethios and his sadistic Princess Azalea!"

With that being said, uncontrollable rage festered within me. I saw my opportune moment and I jumped in to join the fight. It paid off waiting, as I was able to slash Cethios across the right arm as I faced him. He grunted in agony as he inclined back and withdrew another sword from the ground, that still stuck out from a lifeless fairy's' chest. We were all three now trying to take down Cethios. We all took small steps forward as Cethios took small steps back.

Beads of sweat trickled down my forehead and back. I was burning up in this helmet! I couldn't breathe properly anymore; I had to throw this thing off! So, I had to take the regretful chance, I took it off and threw it somewhere aside me. The cool air brushed its hands through my hair and over my face. It felt sensational. I was wearing that horrible thing throughout this whole battle.

I turned and faced Xanthus who seemed to fill with extreme disappointed and fury. And within seconds, Cethios saw it was me. He suddenly laughed out loud as if the sight of me humored him. This was not good; perhaps I should have kept that thing on. Cethios continued to laugh as it echoed within my ears, and as we continued our attempts in bringing Cethios down. But as usual Cethios was just too difficult and unbeatable. Cethios continued to laughed as he replied through chuckles, "Ah Azalea, there you are my sweet, I knew you would find me. I'm so glad you can finally join us. I thought it was you under that thing you choose to disguise yourself with. But my darling love, you forget to remember one small detail… I still own you!"

Those words seemed to burn deep down into Xanthus' ears than mine. Xanthus allowed those words to anger him, and it enraged his fighting. But I remembered James' words as they whispered through my subconscious, 'when you fight with anger, you shall and will always be defeated. Anger will not conquer your goals.'

I took deep breaths and patiently studied Cethios' blocks and blows. I concentrated on his balance and his patterns. I noticed that with his left he blocked Xanthus' hits as he flicked his wrist to block me. During that he would quickly twisted his right wrist to block Theron's, and then in between that he would strike.

I calculated and I was patient, I held my sword in midair momentarily. Then just as I was about to strike, I saw my opportune moment and I swung low as Cethios blocked Xanthus' and Theron's hits. I think Cethios caught on but was not fast enough to react in time. Cethios jumped up in midair and back flipped about a foot away from us.

As we all stood still from the shock of his flip, we all took that moment to take in some deep breaths. I on the other hand, during my breaths, was smirking to Cethios. Cethios dropped his left sword in

378

complete shock as he placed his left palm upon his stomach. He turned pale as he realized and saw that burgundy blood appeared on his fingertips. It wasn't a deep wound but, yes, I broke his skin. He gazed down as he tightly gripped his sword. His right palmed glowed a deep ruby hue.

Suddenly without warning, both of my hands gripped my sword as I dug it into the ground below me. My shackles had become extremely heavy as I was forced in complete stillness. I gave a low shriek, how could I forget my shackles! I was unable to move my feet or my hands; I was petrified in stillness from his magic. I tried to free myself, but it was useless as of course I was unsuccessful. But was he just going to leave me here vulnerable in the open?

I glanced up to see that Cethios, Theron and Xanthus had continued in fighting with their swords. You could see that truly they were all very exhausted. I shouted over to Cethios, "You coward! Are you afraid that I will defeat you?"

Cethios laughed once more as he replied, "You will regret the moment that you decided to decline me, that day that you left with that pathetic Mirage! Now, the blood of your beloved elf, will reside in your hands!"

Suddenly Cethios quickly spun around and slid under Xanthus. Seeing that move before from me, Xanthus quickly turned around to attack Cethios. But he was not quick enough, fatigue had caught up with him…

Cethios had driven his sword right into Xanthus' chest, right into his heart. Cethios formed a silver energy globe in his right palm as he quickly chucked it at Theron. That globe had knocked him over, sending him truly far out into the distance, into the oblivious. Horror filled Xanthus as a single silver tear rolled down his right cheek. Cethios scrunched his nose in as he tilted his head and replied smugly to Xanthus, "You shall rejoin your precious mother soon. And do not worry your highness, I shall take care of your beloved Azalea how I see fit."

With that Cethios reached out and stuck his left hand under the top of Xanthus' shirt. He with took Xanthus' necklace, breaking the chain off of his neck. Cethios placed it into his pocket and withdrew his sword from Xanthus' chest as he took a step back, which allowed Xanthus to helplessly fall onto the ground. And as I finally was able to see what had happened to my beloved, I screamed…

I screamed with everything that I had inside me. I struggled with everything I had; I desperately tried to reach any type of magic within me. Though as I continued I failed, I couldn't concentrate enough to conjure anything with the lightning bolt or with water. I was only able to produce that little black cloud. But as the golden tears flowed freely down my face, the little black rain cloud swelled and grew. My screams echoed throughout the Depths but yet, I felt as if no one was able to hear them. "Xanthus NO! No- XANTHUS!" As my body shook with rage and with sadness, there was nothing I could do, I was completely helpless. All I could do was merely watch my beloved Xanthus slowly smile at me, whisper softly that he always loved me, and watch him slowly close his eyes as he took his last breath. Xanthus' body collapsed upon the ground.

Cethios came up by my side and spat out, "You have no one to blame but yourself. As I've told you before, you will be mine, and I shall and will have you." He turned as his eyes laid upon the lifeless body of Xanthus. He whispered, "So unexpected, but grand indeed."

And with that being said Cethios released his high pitched whistle for Krynton. Within a blink of an eye, Krynton was there as he landed with a thunderous boom. Cethios jumped onto his dragons' back as he replied, "Don't you dare think for a second that I am going to leave you here. We are both heading off to my private castle, to the Castle of Vigoro. And we will finish our business there. We have much to discuss in such little time."

And with that he grabbed me by the waist and with took me onto Krynton. He took me away from my love. What was left of my heart, I left it there with Xanthus. And as I saw my love beloved shrink from my sight I screamed once more as my soul was torn into pieces. My screams vibrated thorough out the Depths... The Depths of Galligro...

Little did I know that- that little black rain cloud that hovered over me, when I so desperately tried to conjure something, anything to save my love, it had stayed there increasing in size. Doubling massively as the rain cloud thundered with large indigo and violet lightning bolts webbing all upon the sky.

Moment later the earth shook, shook with such massive force that all those that were still left alive in the Depths of Galligro, good or bad, stopped in mid battle with each other and fell to the ground, upon their knees.

Rain of Renewing

32

The earth below the soldiers kept with a steady quake. Elves fell to their knees while fairies flew above the trembling earth. Some fairies did help some elves by holding them up, preventing them from being tossed about from the earths vibrations. And just before the suns' rays touched the Depths of Galligro, all of the lifeless bodies started to release a dim red glow and reveal a ghostly skeletal figure. Their energy life was leaving their bodies, as for their bodies themselves, they were diminishing and disintegrating within the mornings mist becoming only a memory.

Suddenly within all of the commotion Morpheus stumbled upon his best friends' body. He cried out in agony and in horror as he realized just whom it was. But despite how hard he shouted for help, no one was able to hear his cries over the rumble. Morpheus laid there desperately clutching his friends' body, hoping that he would not disappear within the red mist of all of the other disappearing bodies.

Suddenly, as a few more lights continued to go off of the lifeless bodies that remained, the ground ceased in shaking. Within moments it started to rain. At first it poured with such intensity that those who stood next to you were invisible. It poured with force momentarily as it then slowly calmed and vanished. My rain cloud had finally disappeared, leaving only a mist surrounding the Depths.

But within a couple of minutes, those still breathing had realized that there was this new rain that started to fall. This was certainly not your ordinary rain. This rain was from the heavens above and not that of water. And as this new rain had finally reached the earth, those alive were able to see that it was that of red and white rose petals. And within moments the gentle rays' from the glorious sun now poured in and illuminated the rose petals as they sailed down ever so gracefully to the ground.

All the fairies and elves stood and were baffled and confused as they gazed upon the falling petals. Morpheus, whom still laid on the ground clutching his dear friend, refusing the thought that he too would diminish, also became confused. Though not on the thought of the petals that now surrounded him, but on the fact that his best friend Xanthus, was still in his grasp. Morpheus placed his ear upon his friends' chest, nothing... He moved his ear and held it above his lips, hoping to hear breathing, but nothing came...

Xanthus was laying there lifeless without any color upon his skin, eyes closed without a heartbeat, dead. But yet Morpheus thought, why was he still within his grasp? Why had he not vanished as all of the other soldiers that had died? Many thoughts crossed his mind as he sat up and gazed at his friend. Suddenly within the distance someone cried out, "This rain is that of an immortal life! The heavens above us are renewing an immortal soul! There is an immortal amongst us!"

More and more elves and fairies continued on repeating those words as petals continuous fell upon the ground. But, what were they meaning by immortal life? Who was immortal? Morpheus thoughts were racing as he glanced back down upon Xanthus' pale face.

Then with a blink of an eye Morpheus' heart began to race as color flooded Xanthus' face. Morpheus lightly pressed upon his friends' chest as he examined the wound. Where there was once a deep hole from the sword that was driven through his chest, was no more. His chest was whole once again.

Heavy breaths increased in Morpheus' lungs as he pressed the back of his palm to Xanthus' forehead, miraculously he felt warmth. The impossible and incredible abruptly occurred, Xanthus opened his eyes slowly and took in a slow deep breath. A large cheer exploded and engulfed Xanthus and Morpheus.

Xanthus clenched his chest as he broke out into a soft laughter as he teased his elf friend, "Did I miss something?"

Xanthus carefully sat up as he gazed at those who now stood before him, those he recognized and those he didn't. Morpheus of course continued on sitting next to him, whom appeared pale at face, as if he had seen a spirit from the beyond. James walked over and stood next to the two elves as he simply appeared as if he was waiting for him to wake, with his arms crossed across his chest. Theron and his friends were upon the many other faces of elves and fairies that simply smiled with bewilderment and amazement.

And as Xanthus carefully stood, with the help of Morpheus, the cheering had silenced. As Xanthus gazed around with astonishment he saw before him, that those who were near him, as well as the four griffons and some dragons, were all bowing before him. Even Morpheus now bowed before him. Xanthus' mouth dropped, he was overwhelmed by the fact that now, every elf and fairy had removed their helmets and were upon one knee.

Moments passed as one by one, dragons, elves and fairies, stood and started to make their own way home. A single silver tear escaped Xanthus' eyes as he gazed at the event that occurred before him. Fairies and elves alike were all patting each other on the shoulder and helping each other along their way. Some shook hands as others hugged, peace was coming, peace was in their hearts. Xanthus took in a deep breath as his heart struck knowing that this horrendous bloodshed battle was over. He also was in awe as he noticed all of the rose petals on the ground.

Then, somewhere from a distance he heard someone exclaim, "Hail to the prophecy of the future king and queen of the new era! May history never repeat itself within these Depths of Galligro! May they never taste the blood of hatred ever again! May the new king and queen fulfill and complete their destined paths! May they bring peace upon this land and unite us all!"

All Xanthus could do was stand there speechless as he watched the Depths of Galligro empty. Moments later as if waking up out of a trance he turned to face his friends, old and new. Morpheus smiled proudly at his friend as he asked, "So future king of unity, where to now?"

Xanthus sighed and glanced around. He took in a deep breath as he let it out slowly running his sore fingers over his face, then through his hair. He replied with a smirk, "So, who will come forth and join me on this next journey? Know this though before you decide, I will not stop until I have Azalea in my arms and Cethios is destroyed. I do not know how vigorous or painful this new excursion will be? Who will join me? My blood is boiling with this new energy inside me and I, I will and shall not be stopped. Determination flows over my very skin."

Without skipping a beat Morpheus stepped forward and replied, "I will. For I will never again leave your side in doubt, not this time. No uncertainty conquers over within my mind. And you'd be proud, I didn't even get a speech from James."

Xanthus nodded as James came forward and patted Morpheus on the shoulder. James bowed slightly and then replied to Xanthus, "This moment in time, I cannot. I must venture out against my own vengeance. But I guarantee you that we shall meet once again along the way. I just hope that my bids are not too late to take upon. Our paths are unwinding and my secrets will soon be revealed, so I must make hast to finish my promise that I made many, many centuries ago. For if not, my part of my time in this puzzling prophecy will ceased to exist. And I would have failed everyone."

With that James bowed once again and started to make his way with Kaya, as her wolf form by his side. But before he took any more steps Xanthus shouted over to him, "James, before you go, please, where do I head towards to find the Castle of Vigoro?"

James turned towards Xanthus confused and astonished. He walked back up to Xanthus as he just stood there in silence momentarily. Without any words James reached into his pocket and withdrew an envelope that appeared to be folded many times. He gave it to Xanthus, hesitant at first but nonetheless, Xanthus grasped with in his fingertips. James reached out and folded his hands gently upon Xanthus', which clenched onto the envelope tightly. Tears seemed to be filling within James' eyes as he sadly gazed upon Xanthus. Finally James replied softly, "I'm surprised that even in death your hearing was just as great as my own. Xanthus, follow that letter, I know you will understand it. I have few words for you, for I must sincerely must make hast and be on my way. Xanthus... They are heading to my fathers' castle."

With that he quickly turned and headed off out of the Depths of Galligro with Kaya by his side. Xanthus turned towards Morpheus as he too realized that he seemed confused by James' words, but then again, when were they not. All they knew was that this Vigoro had his own castle, and why didn't they know about this? And most importantly was, they now knew that this Vigoro was James' father.

All of his other elf friends gazed between Xanthus and Theron, as if awaiting their response. Theron was the first to speak. He placed his sword back upon his side as he replied with amusement, "Well cousin, this has been tremendously entertaining thus far. Therefore, I cannot leave you at the beginning of this new adventure. Besides you probably need help reading that letter that your fairy friend has given you. I'm sure my brains can help you there. And who knows, perhaps you'll need my greatness in magic too. So we don't mind, are you up for our company?"

Xanthus nodded in agreement, "You are welcomed to join us."

Theron's friends all agreed as well. And with that, they all started to head towards their griffons to await their next steps.

Xanthus turned towards Morpheus as he replied, "First, we find Orion, Cetus and Snowfire. Then we take off quickly to Trinafin to restock and gather more supplies. Lastly after that, we read this letter, find the Castle of Vigoro, and bring Azalea home. Somewhere within that we find and destroy Cethios. After that, Azalea will be free."

They both agreed and started to head towards the cliffs where some dragons had taken refuge to heal after their battle with the Cristats. Where their dragons were and Snowfire. They left with determination and with hope as their new journey awaited them. For who knew how long or vigorous this next one would be…

And now I must leave you before we venture off into the lands unknown within the Islands of Yaisla and the Castle of Vigoro. While to some, the lands are a mystery, but to one other, it is home. What dark secrets does this castle contain? What shall be revealed along the path?

I leave you once more as we head off to yet one more adventure that will and shall reveal all. Especially one marked as destiny, and another that was united in the same but unique way. A journey in which all questions reveal themselves, even those that should have never been told.

Is this last quest ensured by the prophecy of peace, the completion of the prophecy once for-told? Or is this the beginning of more evil and betrayals that are to come along the paths of both Princess Azalea and Prince Xanthus. Will their love survive this horrendous path of time? Or will it be marked as a Forbidden Fairytale, never to be told again…

Islands of Yaisla

The Beginning

1

It had been hours since Cethios had last seen Queen Lily. She had made him promise her on keeping baby Azalea safe. So he was taking her to the castle of Whisperia, taking her to his private quarters. No one knew where his room resided within the castle, only him and him alone. Cethios knew he could keep baby Azalea safe there until Queen Lily had returned.

He glanced back over his right shoulder as he giggled to himself. He was the fastest flyer ever born in all of Whisperia and Urinia. And Queen Lily had sent with him a white baby dragon that was named Snowfire. But it seemed he had lost it along the way. It didn't seem to bother him that he had lost it though, for honestly the dragon slightly frightened him.

Hours later after much tedious flying Cethios arrived within the gardens of the castle. He slowly flew down and landed in the main water fountain. The cool water soothed his feet as he took in deep breaths to ease his sore lungs. He slowly gazed over to the hovering globes that were dimly lit. They gave off a soft blue light that gave the gardens such a peaceful appearance, and it soothed his heart.

Just as he was about to take off he heard something rustling a few feet in front of him within the shrubs, almost violently. He quickly withdrew his small sword that was given to him as a gift, a gift from his sword trainer, James. Cethios held the sword out in front of him tightly within his grasp as he bravely shouted, "Who goes there? Show yourself! Or face the wrath of Cethios, the knowledgeable of the swords."

A tall dark brown skinned fairy, with curly hair and dark green eyes stepped forward. His wings quickly changed hues with the colors of emeralds and cobalt as he slowly made his way over to Cethios. His wings were so desperately attempting to blend into his background environment. At once Cethios took in a huge sigh of relief as he saw the fairy. Cethios replied with a chuckle, "Oh Beruchium, thank goodness it's only you. I've been practicing my moves. And I don't want to unleash them just yet. I'm still perfecting them. Although, what are you doing out so late? Is everything alright?"

Beruchium stepped closer to the fountain as deep concern filled his eyes. He replied with a hush voice, "The Eternal Spirits of this earth have spoken of a terrible incident, a terrible involving that has taken place. But I'm ashamed for there was nothing I could have done to prevent what has fallen on those out there. But I can do something upon you and your chosen that you hold so dear. I can give you something to protect you both from this night and for the days to come. Do you agree to this... this simple spell of protection? A small nod is all I need."

Cethios stood there as he pondered on if he should agree to it or not. What was the risk of this simple spell of protection? He kept a tense grip on baby Azalea and his sword. He thought quickly as he came to a conclusion. Azalea and he could benefit greatly from this.

He placed his sword back onto his hip holder. He snuggled baby Azalea closer to his chest as he flew up out of the water fountain and landed just a few feet from Beruchium. Cethios bowed his head in agreeance, "I trust you with my life as Azalea will learn to trust you as well. She is mine to protect and mine to keep. Do as you wish upon us."

Within a blink of an eye Beruchium darted into the herbal section of the gardens. You could hear him vigorously fumbling between the plants and tearing leaves apart with his fingertips. Briefly after about a few moments Beruchium came back over to Cethios and baby Azalea. There within his grasp were two tiny glass bottles. Inside them were some green and lavender herb pieces that seemed to tumble upon each other as they released a dim glow. Upon the neck of the bottle was thin hemp rope that was tied tightly upon it. The hemp looped and formed a necklace as well. And the bottle itself also seemed to be corked tightly with that same hemp rope. Beruchium quickly replied breathlessly, "Take these; I shall place it upon your neck as a symbol of my protection, using the help of the Eternal Spirits. Wear it upon your neck at all times. Do not dare to take it off before the herbs vanish. For if you do, the spell will cease as it would represent that you no longer need them. But if you wish, you may come back after they are empty within a century or so, and I shall remove them from your neck and I will refill it for you. It will not cease if I am the one to remove them and fill them. That is if you wish young Cethios."

Cethios nodded and replied with a smile, "Of course Beruchium, anything to protect my baby Azalea. And I shall have you refill them for us. There would be no reason not to."

Beruchium proudly placed the necklaces upon them, one on Cethios and the other upon baby Azalea's neck. After Beruchium bowed and whispered, "Now go, quickly young Cethios to your quarters and rest for the night, before more sadness falls upon this earth tonight."

Cethios was a bit confused by his words, what sadness had fallen on this night? He had baby Azalea with him and surely Queen Lily would arrive soon to retrieve her. He shrugged his shoulders slightly and nodded with a smile. He then took off towards the castles' side entrance and entered through a small window that lead to the kitchens. Once he snuck in he flew towards the ceiling and started to zigzag through the castle halls. He quickly flew all the way towards the north end of the castle with great speed. And moments later he entered an abandoned hallway filled with white marble statues of miniature dragons. They were all around the size of small leopard cubs.

He entered hesitantly at first as small cobwebs swayed gently from above the statues. No one ever entered those halls anymore, hence all the silky cobwebs, no one cared to clean them. For dragons were said to be long extinct and now, those statues were meaningless. They were the very least of their concerns. But now that Cethios himself had seen an existing one with his very eyes and flew a bit with one, his stomach swirled into a knot. He wondered how Queen Lily had come to have one and why she had sent it with him.

He shrugged his shoulders with a sigh; thankfully he had lost it within the jungles of Whisperia. It couldn't keep up with his lightning bolt speed. But he now knew that they truly existed and honestly, the one that had flown with him had frightened him slightly. But yet, in his heart he knew he couldn't let that fear grow, because deep down dragons fascinated him. That was why the entrance to his private chambers was in these halls. He had always felt an admiration towards them. And now, he was not going to allow that admiration to become fear or hatred. In fact, thinking more of it, it made him curious, curious on the thought if there were any more alive. Perhaps one day, he could have one of his very own to cherish.

About half an hour later after slowly walking through the forgotten halls he arrived at a dead end. There before him stood a dark granite stone dragon that was bigger than the others. This one stood on its hind legs and was about six feet high. Its dark marble carving appeared to be that of onyx. It had its wings spread out with its mouth wide opened, revealing rows of sharp fangs.

Cethios stood there intimidated slightly. Normally he wouldn't second guess himself but once again, after seeing one alive he just had to stop momentarily. He took a deep breath and gathered his courage. Cethios slowly flew up towards its face, he is just around five centuries old and not that tall just yet. He reached into the dragons' mouth. He wrapped his warm fingers around the dragons' cool stone tongue and pulled.

Once he pulled the tongue the statue started to tremble slightly. The dragon seemed to come to life as it silently blinked its eyes and flapped his marbled wings forward. Suddenly as if triggering a reaction a door that appeared to be made of molting lava revealed itself to the left of the dragon. It bubbled and flowed smoothly downward as steam escaped the edges of the door.

Cethios smiled at the sight as he extended his hand forward towards the boiling lava. He pushed his way through as his hand appeared to melt and burn. But yet, he continued to move forward with a confident smile. He pushed his whole body through as he and baby Azalea seemed to melt within it.

Once they vanished within the lava, the dragon pulled its wings back and closed the secret opening. There next to the dragon was no trace of an entrance ever being there. And on the other side of the secret door Cethios smirked to himself as he and baby Azalea were unharmed and perfectly safe. He glanced down and whispered to her, "See Azalea, things aren't always what they seem. We'll be safe here, but right now we must rest and sleep for the remainder of the night. I'm exhausted as I'm sure you are as well."

As Cethios gazed up a comforting grin spread upon his face. His room was simple and he liked it that way. The floor consisted of cool white sand with palm trees that seemed to sprout miscellaneously around the room. He had two dressers that were made of bamboo and a canopy bed with green leaves dropping over the sides. And the best part was the ceiling. It appeared as if the evening sky was upon it, with soft clouds passing by. It all was Cethios' tranquil getaway. To the far right of the room was a small waterfall. The water fell from auburn stones and poured into a small pond. Within the pond swam a couple of baby sea turtles. They jumped in and out enthusiastically once Cethios walked in. They were ecstatic to see him.

Cethios walked over to his bed and placed baby Azalea in the center of it. He then walked up to his tallest dresser. He turned one of the knobs as it opened like a door with all of the front drawers still attached. He walked in and disappeared within it. You could hear him fumbling about as moments later he came walking out in his sleeping clothes and with blankets floating behind him. The door of drawers closed behind him as he spun around and opened the bottom drawer. He withdrew a small hourglass of sand and a small bottle of milk. He closed the drawer and walked over to the bed as the floating blankets followed behind him. He withdrew them from the air and placed them on the bed next to baby Azalea.

Just as he was about to lay next to her four pink butterflies started to fly away from baby Azalea. They had just changed her into a fresh clean diaper and a new pair of warm clothes for the night. Cethios bowed and whispered, "I will see you early in the morning, my thanks are to you."

Cethios gave baby Azalea the bottle of milk as she took it happily. He lay next to her as he unfolded the blankets and covered himself and baby Azalea snuggly. Cethios took the hourglass and placed it gently upon his forehead. He closed his eyes and whispered, "Shatter the stars upon this night, I say this with all my might." He opened his eyes as the hourglass floated out of his hands and flew towards the ceiling. As it reached half way it took speed as it suddenly shattered upon the ceiling. But yet the shattered pieces spread quickly upon the ceiling consuming its entirety. And as the glass and sand spread the sky turned dark as the night sky and twinkling stars came into view.

Cethios smirked to himself as he turned to baby Azalea, who in turn had already finished her bottle and was now sleeping peacefully. He turned back and closed his eyes as he too soon fell fast asleep with a smirk upon his face. This he knew was one of his best nights ever. This to Cethios was the beginning of a new friendship he had always wanted. Someone he can share everything with. He knew great times were on their way, fun times with Azalea. But little did he know what the future truly held for them both.

Cethios woke just before the sky in his room mimicked the approaching sun. Dim lighting slowly filled his room. He took a long stretch as he slowly flew out of his bed. He flew over to his dresser as he opened it and walked in. Moments passed as he finally came out dressed for the day. Floating behind him was a small tray filled with slices of orange cake, fruit, and a small cup of juice and a bottle of warm milk.

He walked over to the bed as he carefully sat upon it. He withdrew the bottle from the tray and gently gave it to baby Azalea, as she now was wide awake and hungry. She took it with her little hands and quickly started to gulp it down. Cethios smiled to himself as he softly replied to her, "I was anticipating your arrival. I was hoping Queen Lily would let me have you for a while, I was prepared princess. But I still have a very busy day ahead of me. After breakfast I must go do my chores for the morning. Then I have class with Beruchium. But I'll be here for lunch! After I do have lessons with James, and I'll be back for dinner, and then we can play! I can tell you all about it! I can even show you some of my moves. But also, I'll have to make a stop in the kitchens to pick up some more food for us. Trajean is preparing your bottles. Some even have a bit of cinnamon and rice to help you get stronger. Oh princess, we're going to have a great week together! That is until Queen Lily comes back, or requests you."

After they happily ate, baby Azalea was changed by some butterflies as Cethios gazed away. He walked over to his dresser as he opened one of the drawers. He with took a small hourglass filled with sugar and sand. He closed the drawer and walked over to the bed as he whispered to the hourglass, "While I'm away, shine down from the sky. For the only thing my princess can do is lie. Entertain her for the day and make her laugh, keep her warm and safe for she is all I have." He opened his palm as the hourglass slowly rose from his hand. It slowly rose over baby Azalea as it shattered on its own combustion and transformed into eight bright blue stars. As they hovered and moved they emitted soft sparkling glitter. They slowly swirled and danced around baby Azalea as she giggled with delight.

Content and knowing that the stars would watch over her, Cethios slowly left the room to attend his daily errands. He also knew that if baby Azalea needed anything, that the pink butterflies would take care of her. They never failed him and he knew they wouldn't fail baby Azalea.

And although Cethios was happier than ever, on the other side of the castle was another fairy that wasn't quite as content with life. A fairy whose intentions were filled with treacherous evil and hatred; a fairy whom particularly spent his entire night searching for baby Azalea. A fairy named Zethron.

Keep

2

Zethron entered the gardens of Whisperia exhausted. He had been desperately searching the surrounding jungles for the baby princess, Azalea. He had searched everywhere high and low thinking that Queen Lily would have hidden her somewhere near the castle. But where could she have hidden her? She wouldn't have had time to place her anywhere else. He even spent hour's un-enchanting sections of the jungle, thinking that perhaps she had hidden her with enchantments. But atlas no, he was unsuccessful.

He rubbed his temples slowly as he deeply pondered on the whereabouts of the baby princess. According to Trathina, Queen Lily's plans were to arrive with baby Azalea right after the enchantment was complete. She was not going to be taking any detour routes. But what was Queen Lily doing alone when he reached her? Perhaps someone else has already found the baby princess.

Zethron grunted to himself as he realized that was a foolish thought to ponder over. Who else could have out run him or out flown him? He rubbed his hands gently over his face and through his hair. He should go and check with Trathina before he continues his search. But then he thought, if Trathina had already found princess Azalea and she did not come and get him sooner, she was going to be in a heap of misfortune. Rage filled his veins momentarily. That knowledge would have saved him from the all night searching he had just accomplished.

He grunted to himself once more, he was stubborn at times and he knew it. And his stubbornness was the reason why he is currently in the situation that he is in at this moment. He forcefully shoved his hands in his pockets with a heavy sigh as he began to make his way towards the castle. Within moments of his walking he spied someone out of the corner of his eyes. It was Cethios. He was prancing happily towards the green houses. Zethron wondered to himself, what could he be so damn happy about so early in the morning? So, Zethron swiftly made his way over to him and asked, "Cethios, what motivates your steps so early this morning?"

Cethios sucked in a deep breath, he was about to reveal to Zethron exactly why he was such in a great mood, but before any information escaped his lungs he spotted Beruchium. Beruchium appeared extremely stressed as his wings continuously blended in with his surroundings. He slowly shook his head and pointed to his lips. Cethios thought, why would he not tell everyone about the great news of baby Azalea within his quarters? Was the news not worthy of sharing? But, he trusted Beruchium and quickly reorganized his thoughts. Instead he enthusiastically replied in just about one breath, "Why, it being such a beautiful morning with the surrounding mist of the early sun's rays. They gently grace us with their presence today and they are not hidden behind the feathers of the clouds. Today and this very morning I get to spend it with Beruchium as we learn about the species of roses that sing sweet melodies only when the sun's rays get to dance upon the…" Cethios spoke very fast.

This was abundantly overwhelming for Zethron. It was seriously too early in the morning for him to deal with this type of enthusiasm. Zethron scrunched his nose in and interrupted him, "Yes-yes that sounds amusing to your sort. Let me ask you, have you seen Queen Lily recently? Have you seen anything that she could have possessed so dear?"

Cethios placed his right hand gently upon his chin as if he was sincerely pondering his question. Beruchium didn't want him to reply anything of the sort about baby Azalea to Zethron. He was sure Beruchium would explain everything to him later. It must be very important for him not breathe a word of her to anyone. So he made his decision quickly. If it was important to Beruchium then it was important to him.

Cethios continued his playful pondering as he suddenly raised his little pointer finger in the air; as if coming to some sort of conclusion. Zethron's eyes lit up, but Cethios changed his mind and shook his head and continued to place his fingers ever so carefully back upon his chin. Zethron grunted to himself, he was in no mood to play his games today. Zethron replied cautiously through his teeth, "Well? Do you have anything to tell me that is worth having me waste my valuable time in standing here and wait upon your incompetence?"

A massive grin spread upon Cethios' face. He nodded with delight and replied joyfully, "Well now that you mention it, yes, yes I did. I saw Queen Lily last night heading to the other side of the gardens, towards the far north on the other side of the castle walls."

Zethron released an evil grin that spread through his lips. Zethron whispered under his breath, "Yes of course, clever. Why didn't I think of that?"

And with that Zethron took off towards the north side of the gardens. It would take him half of the day to finally reach the end, if he was walking and carefully searching, and the other half of the day returning back. Cethios nodded to himself happily as he was proud of himself for tricking Zethron. And honestly, Zethron would now be gone all day. Cethios didn't mind having Zethron out of sight, his company wasn't the pleasurable type anyway.

And once Zethron was completely gone Cethios chuckled to himself. Moments later Beruchium stepped out of his concealed location and walked up next to his little friend. He rested his left palm upon Cethios' shoulder. Fully aware that Beruchium was aside him, Cethios asked, "Beruchium, why was it so important that Zethron knew not of me having baby Azalea? She is mine and not of his concern anyway. Why does he want her?"

Beruchium bent down and gazed into the eyes of Cethios with much sadness and grief. Cethios frowned and asked with deep concern, "Is everything alright? Did I do something wrong?"

Beruchium slowly shook his head as he gently rubbed his fingertips over his wet eyes, "No, you did nothing of the sort wrong. What you just did was worth baby Azalea's life as well as your own."

Cethios seemed confused by Beruchium's words, he asked, "I don't understand, why would Zethron…" But before he could finish his own question he dazed off into the sky above him. He was confused within his heart. Why would Zethron want to hurt him or his baby Azalea? What would be worth more than their own lives?

Poor Cethios continued to ponder many thoughts, but thankfully they were interrupted when Beruchium whispered, "Cethios, would you make me a promise?"

Cethios' attention was pulled as he turned back to Beruchium slowly as if he was still attempting to piece together a riddle. Cethios wiped his eyes ever so carefully, "Of course Beruchium, will it be about me and my baby Azalea?"

Beruchium nodded slowly and whispered, "Yes it is, but you must follow these instructions to the precise. You cannot falter, do you understand? If we do falter, our world will become chaos once more. Instructions you must stay on. James and I will help you keep."

Cethios nodded and replied very seriously, "I made a promise to Queen Lily to keep baby Azalea safe, and that is what I intended to do. She is mine... mine to keep."

Beruchium took in a slow deep breath with contentment, "One week, keep her safe and hidden within your secret quarters. One week keep that secret no matter what you hear you must speak of nothing. James and I will help you keep after that. You must not breathe any of this. For one week she does not exist, do you understand? Will you keep this promise?"

Cethios nodded with great pride as he whispered under his breath, "Yes... I will always keep."

The Mission

3

Cethios kept his promise and he kept baby Azalea hidden from everyone for one week. He stayed with her as he kept her company, played with her and brought her warm milk. But he did have the butterflies change and entertain her while he was gone during the day. They didn't talk very much to him. It seemed the older you got the feistier they would become with you, oh well. All he cared about was that the butterflies were very polite and friendly to baby Azalea and that was all that mattered.

During that week Cethios grew more concerned with each and every single day that passed. Weird things were happening and everyone was acting so strange. One of the most inexplicable things that worried him was that he still hadn't heard from Queen Lily or had seen her. He was concerned about her. Where could she be that would keep her from baby Azalea? He hoped that she was alright and just tending to some important things before she came for her infant. He wouldn't want anything to fall upon the Queen. It would break his heart if he never saw her again.

Another peculiar thing was that James and Beruchium were being very mysterious and disappearing for hours at a time, once it was all day! Then they would reappear as if they were there the whole time but, they were breathless. And the worst of it all was that whenever he saw Zethron, he appeared more nerve wreaked every single time. Everyone just seemed strange, even his mother and King Duralos were acting very mysterious.

On the last day of the week, in the evening after he had his lesson with the swords, James waited until everyone had left. He then cautiously walked up to Cethios. He slipped a small rolled up parchment into his bag. James whispered to him, "The parchment will not open and reveal itself until you are well hidden in your quarters, and only by your touch. Follow the instructions to their precise. Do not allow yourself to be followed. Make no stops until you are there, now go quickly before my whispers are carried to unwelcoming ears."

And with that being said Cethios took off into the air and flew out of the room in a blink of an eye. Cethios couldn't help but smirk to himself, for when he dashed out, he slammed into James' door, converting them from sliding doors to swinging ones. The only regret Cethios had was not being able to see James' face when he did that. He was sure though that once he reentered James would have him fix them. Or perhaps he would have him do extra training.

Within moments Cethios entered his room. It did not take him long as he was positive no one spotted him upon the ceiling zigzagging to his quarters. Once he entered, he spotted baby Azalea sitting propped up upon some indigo pillows on the floor. She was sitting near his small waterfall clapping and giggling. She was watching his baby sea turtle, they were pretending to be acrobats in the pond. And it looked as if two were sitting out as they sat next to baby Azalea clapping their fins for their friends as well. A warm smile spread upon his face as he knew his baby Azalea was well taken care of and content.

Cethios walked carefully over to his bed, he didn't want to disturb baby Azalea's enjoyment. He plopped on his bed as he reached into his bag. He took out the parchment that James had given him. He balanced it upon his fingertips as the parchment started to glow a dim white. It slowly opened itself as Cethios allowed it to unravel and lay flat upon his bed. He began to read, "Once the moon reaches its highest peak within its sky, that is when you must make hast. Take Princess Azalea with you and fly to the king and queens' bedroom, you know of which I speak of. For they both have a couple of quarters that reside within these castle walls. The one near the main kitchen is the direct one I speak off. Wrap Princess Azalea in that same blanket that she first had when she was given to you by Queen Lily. Once you both leave your quarters, do not allow yourself to be seen by anyone's eyes, even mine. You must be invisible and blend in within your environment like I have taught you. Secrecy is your main defense upon this very night, both of your lives depend on it. Once inside enchant the doors with the spell I once taught you, to only allow the one you want, which shall be the king, to pass through with the Eternal Spirits of Fire. I believe in you, you can master it. Once in the room place Princess Azalea in the center of the bed and conceal yourself. The King will not be long to enter. Once he finds her, he will leave with her to one of his secret quarters, we are sure of it. Do not worry, she will be alright. I am positive those butterflies will follow her and keep her safe... Once he is gone, make hast to your hidden quarters for the remainder of the night. In the morning continue your regular routine. Tell no one of this act you are about to embark upon. This event must never leave your lips, until the timing is right. If you accept this, which I know you will, place this parchment upon your skin and allow it to melt within your skin as an acceptance to this promise you are making. And I will make a promise to you, one day when the timing is right and you are at an acceptance of your own life, I will reveal to you your true father. This is a promise for you to keep, and a promise I shall keep... James"

Cethios smiled widely, for he very much anticipated on the day when he was finally able to know who his true father was. It was always kept from him, for they told him it was for his own safety. But he wondered for his own security, that perhaps he was an explorer and was probably out on a grand adventure and would one day return to him. But for now honestly he was truly content not knowing.

He rolled up the parchment carefully and rolled up his left pant leg. He placed the rolled up parchment upon his skin as it quickly started to melt and absorb into his leg. It stung momentarily as Cethios gritted his teeth. But it was all over within a few moments and the pain was gone. Now, there upon the side of his left leg was a tattoo of a blue moon with a lock upon the edge of it. It symbolized his promise of the secret he needed to keep, about this night he was going to embark upon.

Cethios took in a deep breath and let it out with a slow sigh. He rubbed his leg gently with his fingers and closed his eyes momentarily. He took in another deep breath as he jumped off of the bed and walked over to his dresser. He with took a bottle of milk from the bottom drawer for baby Azalea. He gave it to her gently as she took it and gulped it down happily. He picked her up and placed her upon his bed as she started to drift away into a peaceful slumber. But before she was completely asleep two exceptional intricate pink butterflies appeared, shooed Cethios away and started to change baby Azalea into fresh clothes for the night and into a clean diaper.

In the meantime, Cethios went over to his dresser once more. But this time he turned the knob and opened the drawers like a door again. He walked into it and disappeared within it. Within a few moments he walked out with a fresh pair of clothes, an hourglass, a towel and a bar of soap hovering behind him. He wanted to start getting ready for the nights adventure.

He glanced over to see how baby Azalea was doing, and he found her sound asleep with a warm smile upon her face. As well as the two butterflies, they were sleeping next to her upon the pillow. Well, at least the butterflies where there to keep her company while he bathed. But before he went over to the small pond he went over to one of the posts of the bed. He pulled on one of the strings as a curtain gracefully fell over the canopy bed. He didn't want to take any chances just in case baby Azalea woke up.

Once he was by his pond he leaned over and replied to his sea turtles, "Give me about an hour, half of that time to change and bathe and the other half as the pond refreshes from the soap."

They all nodded and disappeared deep down within the pond. Once they were gone he quickly undressed, with took the bar of soap still hovering in the air, and slipped into the pond. Moments later as he finished his bath, he dried himself and changed. He with took the hourglass from the air. He whispered to it, "Wake us when the moon is high, do not let the time go by. High in the east is where it shall be, wake us then so we can see." The hourglass slowly lifted off of his palm as it suddenly flew towards the ceiling with intensive speed. It shattered upon the ceiling as the pieces scattered all upon it darkening the sky and turning into millions of twinkling stars. Cethios smiled to himself as he mumbled under his breath, "I shall never grow tired of that."

He carefully laid upon the bed next to baby Azalea. He didn't want to wake her. He stretched one blanket over him as he then stretched another upon baby Azalea. He fell fast asleep next to her. For he knew he needed his rest for within the middle of the night he was going to wake and go on a mission; a mission to get baby Azalea safely to the king and queens' bedroom.

Truth

4

Cethios awoke just before the moon rose above the east, its highest peak. His hour glass did no fail him. He prepared a bottle for baby Azalea and whispered the location to some of the butterflies there, of where baby Azalea was going to be at in the morning after they changed her. Even though he was sure that they would know, he still told them otherwise. The butterflies quickly disappeared as soon as baby Azalea was comfortable in her brown cloth blanket that her mother had so lovingly wrapped her in, so many days ago.

Cethios carefully pick up baby Azalea, whom was now awake, and held her close to his chest. They left the quarters as baby Azalea waved goodbye to her baby sea turtle friends, as they too waved farewell.

Baby Azalea clung on dearly to Cethios' chest as he flew up. He didn't go all the way up to the ceiling, but he did fly up to only allow his toes to gently brush the cool marble floor. As he made his way down the corridor that contained the miniature dragons baby Azalea stared curiously at them. For she had thought she had seen one before. But she couldn't quite remember so. For the days before she was with Cethios were quickly diminishing within her subconscious mind.

She started to ponder about the baby sea turtles and how much she'd miss them. She giggled to herself a bit out loud as she thought about their tricks. And as soon as she did Cethios stopped and leaned upon the wall. He placed his fingertip softly upon his lips as he whispered to baby Azalea, "No-no baby Azalea, we must be unseen and unheard. We must be quite until we reach the other side of the castle. Understand my Azalea."

Baby Azalea stared with her big chestnut brown eyes into his. She nodded gently and laid her head upon his shoulder. Cethios held her close as he continued to cautiously fly towards the other side of the enormous castle. It was becoming very time consuming as Cethios had to cautiously peer around every corner to make sure no one was there before he could continue. He quickly changed his route as he started to head towards the main castles' kitchens. He was planning on taking a short cut through there, that would speed up their quest and in no time, they would reach the king and queens' bedroom.

He entered slowly cautiously pushing one of the swinging doors, but he came to an abrupt halt as he heard voices within one of the rooms nearby. He quietly landed on his feet as he took in a deep breath of air. The voices could be in the room that they needed to travel through next. He needed to quickly think of his next move, they could not be seen nor heard. He closed his wings and carefully walked up to one of the island counters and hid behind it.

He suddenly realized that the voices were coming from the grand eating room. But who would be awake at this moment? He listened closely as within moments he recognized the voices, it was Trathina and Zethron. Why were they awake at this late hour? And what was so important that they had to discuss right now? Well, whatever it was Zethron did not seem quite content. But he couldn't help to wonder, what would the kings' advisor want with the Queens' main maiden?

Cethios' concern grew more intense as he had promised that no one was going to find out about him and baby Azalea. He had promised he would stop at nothing on his quest. But this was the only way that was the quickest to the king and queens' quarters. He would lose precious time if he turned back now!

Cethios' eyes swelled with tears as a few fell down his cheeks. He couldn't help but feel like he was failing his quest, failing his promise to keep. He gazed down into baby Azalea's eyes. What was he going to do? He felt hopeless as he kissed her upon the forehead. But to his surprise he saw baby Azalea smiling. Cethios slowly took in another deep breath as he whispered to her, "Princess Azalea, we are in grave danger at this moment. We are in danger of getting caught. You are not safe, and I don't know what to do. This is the only way I know that is the quickest, we can't go back now."

Once those words escaped Cethios' lips, baby Azalea silently giggled. She pressed herself into Cethios, stretched out her little arms and embraced him. Baby Azalea held on tightly to his shirt as she giggled quietly once more.

Cethios was confused. What was she so happy about? Here they were, near danger of being caught and she seemed delighted. Was he losing it? He seriously thought he was going to go insane. But then something distracted his thoughts, something extraordinary. He now seriously thought he was losing it.

Right before his very eyes, he and baby Azalea were disappearing! Were his eyes deceiving him? Was he seeing this correctly? He wasn't sure anymore but he continued to gaze upon baby Azalea and his arms as they continued to disappear. And as baby Azalea continued to silently giggle, Cethios realized that it was her that was making them disappear.

Finally, a smile came upon Cethios face as he whispered to her, "Princess Azalea, you already are full of surprises. This is absolutely amazing." Moments later they were completely invisible. Then, with baby Azalea tightly in his arms, he headed for the eating room…..

Zethron paced back and forth by the head seat of the eating table. And Trathina stood near him with her arms crossed upon her chest, with a frown upon her delicate face. Trathina replied to him as her eyes followed his pace, "What shall you have me do Zethron? Your anger and your impatience brought us to where we are now. No queen, no princess, no Immortality, no nothing what-so-ever! I told you to wait for me, and what did you do? Do you see what you have done?"

Zethron quickly turned and stopped to face her. He kept his hands behind his back as he sneered, "I couldn't help it, I was not going to just sit and wait like your pet, until you arrived with Queen Lily and Princess Azalea. So I left, and to my utter astonishment I found Queen Lily. And do you want to know what sent my rage a flame? How about the fact that first, I found her alone with no princess baby. And secondly, that you weren't with her! You didn't go to the ceremony, which means you didn't go into the Caves of Esmera! Heavens know we'll never find those caves. And even if by some miracle we do find the entrance we will not be allowed in by Esmera's spirit! How in the world do you expect this Immortality to happen for us without any of that knowledge?"

Trathina threw her hands in the air and whispered, "First of all keep your voice down; you don't want to wake those of which we don't want to know. Secondly, she left without me. What was I supposed to do, head off into the oblivious? I wouldn't even know where to begin without her. I was at the location I was supposed to meet her at and I was even there waiting for her earlier than the time she gave me to be there. I waited there all night for her, until you showed up. And then you told me what you've done! And then, you suggested that we needed to split up and find baby Azalea. But truthfully in all reality, all you had to do was be patient! Together we could have come up with something else! You didn't have to go and kill her! I did not want death upon her. She, she… she was my friend."

Suddenly somewhere within the enormous eating room, like a whisper of an echo a small gasp was heard. Zethron and Trathina both were confused as they gazed around the room. They were positive that they were completely alone in the room, so what could have made that noise? Zethron continued to gaze around the rooms' entirety with much caution. He slowly began to walk around the room as quietly as he could as he whispered over to Trathina, "Well, she would have just been in the way, sooner or later, death was coming her way regardless."

By now, silent tears flooded Trathina's eyes and streamed down her face. For truly, she did not want any harm to come to her friend. Even though she had betrayed her, she still cared for her. She now was filled with much regret and sadness as she had realized with much guilt, that choosing to side with Zethron was wrong. She felt ashamed of herself; she should have been a better friend, honest and faithful. Perhaps then, Queen Lily would still be alive and her infant would not be missing.

At once Zethron stopped his slow footsteps as if he had heard something near him. It was as if he was trying to concentrate on it. He suddenly appeared confused and frustrated as he started to make his way back towards Trathina. He stopped near her as he sneered with a whisper, "So, what has Cethios been up to these days? Why has he been so mischievous lately and where does his quarters reside? The truth this time, where is he right at this moment?"

Trathina tried to calm and silent her hiccups as she wiped her face with her sleeve. Without glancing at Zethron she sobbed, "What? Who? I'm not sure what you mean?"

Zethron stepped closer to her as their eyes now locked. He raised his nose up as he glared at Trathina with discuss. He angrily hissed through his teeth, "Where is he? Where is your son Cethios!"

The Discovery

5

As Cethios reached the king and queens' bedroom he placed baby Azalea gently on the bed. And although he couldn't see her just yet, baby Azalea was already fast asleep with a smile upon her little face. And as Cethios released his grasp from her, they both slowly reappeared. Cethios carefully lay next to baby Azalea, for he didn't want to wake her. He also didn't want her to see him as tears flooded and fell down his cheeks.

How could this have happened? How could Queen Lily be dead? He cared so much for her; it was as if she was his mother and not that betrayer Trathina. But only if he was there, he thought. Perhaps he could have helped Queen Lily. Perhaps then she'd still be alive.

After a few moments had past, Cethios wiped his eyes and gathered up all of his courage. His mother had a lot of explaining to do. But right now at this very moment of time, he had a promise to keep. He sat up from the bed and leaned over and kissed baby Azalea on the forehead. He whispered to her, "I promised Queen Lily I would protect you with all that I have. I promised her I would not fail. But today I make my own promise to you. I promise I shall do everything that I can to keep you alive. I will never allow Zethron to take your life, ever."

Cethios kissed her once more upon the forehead as he closed his eyes and rubbed his nose upon hers. Baby Azalea lifted her chin slightly as if returning the snuggle as once more a smile spread upon her face in her slumber. He slowly hopped off of the bed and quickly realized that there was a rolled up parchment upon it, next to baby Azalea. He with took it carefully and began to read, "Do not allow yourself to forget about that door." Cethios dropped the parchment and quickly ran up to the door. He knelt right in front of it as he placed both of his palms upon the door above his head. He sat there momentarily as he took in deep breaths. Both of his palms began to glow a bright red. They glowed brighter and brighter until suddenly, they were a blaze. Crimson flames danced upon his fingers as Cethios remained still.

Within seconds small fireflies emerged from the flames as they danced in harmony upon the door. Millions seemed to swarm the door and emerge from his fingers. Once the door was covered in flames, Cethios'

405

fingers sizzled down to nothing. Cethios raised his head and released his grasp upon the door. He cautiously stood and took a step back from the door as he watched the fireflies dance in rhythm upon it. He took in a deep breath as he rubbed his fingers together. He released a small whistle from his lips as the fireflies seemed to stop on command. They all glowed with anticipation as if waiting for orders. Cethios took in another deep breath as he whispered through his teeth, "Spirits of Eternal Fire, I have called upon you to do my desire. Protect the one who resides inside, only King Duralos shall you confide. Deflect the rest with your might power, I allow you to make them cower. And once this task is done oh Spirits of Eternal Fire, I thank you so you may retire. You are free to return to your earths wonder."

Once his words ended and his enchantment was complete, the fireflies swarmed once more around the door until it became a blaze. It filled the room with mild heat until moments later the fireflies melted within the door to nothing. Cethios stood there briefly until it had all vanished. He cautiously stretched out his left palm as he could feel the warmth coming out from the door. A smile came forth upon his face; he had mastered the enchantment as the eternal fire swelled inside. It wasn't so easy to manipulate the natural elements of this earth. And he was very proud of himself that he was able to accomplish this one enchantment.

Cethios quickly walked back to the parchment that he had dropped earlier. He picked it up once more and continued reading, "Once again follow these words to their exact precise, as this parchment will over rule the other that was first sent to you. Due to the recent events that have taken forth this night, you will be doing things a bit differently this very moment in time and for the following week that we are about to enter in... As much as this is going to upset you, you will not be able to stay with Princess Azalea until King Duralos arrives. The butterflies will be transporting you to your quarters, as soon as you finish this letter. They have been given strict orders from Beruchium to stay, protect and take care of Princess Azalea. Do not worry about her, she will be safe. You must trust us. Have faith, the necklace that you allowed Beruchium to place upon you and Princess Azalea will keep both of you safe from any harm or evil... Furthermore, you must not return to your regular tasks in the morning. You must as others will say, disappear for at least a week. You must remain in your quarters for the time being. Do not allow yourself to worry; the butterflies will bring you anything you would like to eat. This is for your safety as well, due to recent events. Do not allow yourself to wander; do not attempt to go looking for Princess Azalea either. Trust us, she will be out of harm's way, she will be with her father... Then, before we enter the

406

final day of the week, before the suns' rays touch the earths' surface, meet me in the sword swinging room. Once again as that morning arrives, do not allow any wandering eyes to see or hear you. Enter quietly; I will know when you arrive within my quarters... I do apologize for so much, you will understand one day, I assure you. And yet once more, allow this parchment to melt into your skin on the exact location where you had the other parchment melt into. It shall renew and as well add to the other first parchment. Of course, this is all onto you if you agree to everything within this parchment. I promise you, this will all settle down for some ages, peace is coming one day, centuries and centuries from now, but hopefully one day, if all goes well, I promise you, it will be here... Your Sword Trainer and Mentor, James"

Cethios rolled up the parchment and held it within his fingertips. So many promises that he had to keep, swirled within his subconscious mind. Whatever happened to those peaceful days? Those days of ignorance bliss within the castle seemed as if they were ages ago now. He closed his eyes and took in deep breaths. He started to feel dizzy and a bit nauseated.

Perhaps he had much on his shoulders, and James did promise that Princess Azalea would be safe. He thought, a week's time would be enough for him to relax and settle his own thoughts. Perhaps he could finally use that journal James gave him once. He could write some of this down, about these past days. It could help clear his thoughts.

After a few moments longer of more pondering he sat upon the bed's edge and lifted his left pant leg. He placed the rolled up parchment onto his skin where the tattoo of the moon and lock was. The parchment quickly melted into Cethios' skin as he gritted his teeth. He clenched his eyes as the pain stung briefly, then resided to nothing. Cethios opened his eyes slowly as he gazed down upon his leg. There upon it was now a tattoo of a moon and a sun that was merged together as one, with one lock on the bottom corner of it, as well as another lock above it in the other corner.

He let out a small sigh as he released his pant leg and turned towards his baby Azalea. He didn't want to abandon her but, he trusted James. And he was right; she would be with her father. He could not be so selfish; baby Azalea needs King Duralos as he needs her. Without a mother, it was going to be difficult for her. He knows how it feels to only be with one parent, for he doesn't know who his father is. They related in that sort of way, missing one parent.

x

407

Cethios leaned over and kissed baby Azalea on the forehead. He softly whispered to her, "I will see you soon, my baby Azalea. You will be safe here, and your father will be here soon. And I promise you, we will be together again." Moments after those words escaped his lips, a variety of different colored butterflies began to appear within small wisps of blue smoke. Within minutes there were about thirty of them fluttering about in the room. Cethios smiled as about ten of them landed near baby Azalea and seemed to be getting comfortable for the night. He felt comfort knowing that he wasn't leaving her completely alone. The others fluttered by Cethios as if waiting for permissions.

Cethios stepped forward and bowed a bit to them. He took one more glance at baby Azalea and turned back to face the butterflies. He sighed, "Alright, I am ready to be transported to my quarters."

They swarmed around him, faster and faster they flew until they were just a blur of sapphire hue. Then as if just a memory, Cethios and the blur of butterflies slowly diminished to nothing. Within seconds, they were gone and baby Azalea was alone in the king and queens' quarters with the other ten butterflies.

An hour went by as they all slept peacefully. But as if awoken by a startle, the butterflies were awake. They all flew up towards one of the canopy post and quickly blended in with it. It was as if they weren't even there, but they still kept a watchful eye towards the door, and at Princess Azalea.

The door suddenly glowed a crimson hue and quickly melted into the ground; the Spirits of Eternal Fire had done their task. They were now retiring back within the elements of the earth. The door knob slowly turned and the door creaked open. Slowly a shadow figure entered the room; King Duralos stepped in with much sadness and grief.

For the past few nights, he had been wandering the gardens in hopes of perhaps finding his beloved wife. He thought, just maybe, just maybe, he would find her wandering the gardens. Perhaps she had lost her way in their vast beauty. But alas, every night he found nothing but just the echoes of her laughter within the gentle breeze and within his subconscious mind. It flowed within his heart, falling down as tears upon the soft earth. His hopes in finding her were diminishing, as tonight marked his last night in searching for his love, for his Queen, his wife Lily.

King Duralos closed the door behind him with a heavy sigh. And as he stepped towards his bed he froze. There upon his bed was a baby sound asleep, an innocent baby that had many of Queen Lily's' features. He stood there staring at her as if she was now his reason for moving forward. He didn't know how she got here in his room but, he was very grateful she was safe.

After a few moments passed he finally regained the strength to take a step forward. He walked up to the bed and carefully picked up the baby. He held her close to his chest, close to his heart. He kissed her softly upon the forehead as tears fell down his delicate cheeks. He whispered to her, "My beloved child, I have no doubt in my mind to whom you belong to. Therefore I have no regret on giving you the name your mother would have wanted to give you. Queen Lily would have named you Azalea, that was her middle name, as well as your great grandmother. And that my dear is what I shall name you. Unfortunately I cannot keep you just yet. Without a mother I cannot claim you. And if you are here without her, then I can only come to one conclusion on the fate of my wife. So, what shall we do?"

King Duralos continued to ponder as he walked around to the other side of his bed with baby Azalea. He reached over to the top post and tapped on the wood. He replied, "Spirits of Eternal Earth, form a cradle for my child of birth. Keep her safe throughout her nights, always grow with her for she has your rights. Royal blood is what she's filled with, so bend to her will- for she is not a myth." Once those words escaped his lips, the wood post from his bed started to twist and crack. The wood seemed as if it was growing its own limb with the bark curving around the bottom of it. It then started to form a small cradle that was still attached to the post. As it formed green vines started to sprout from it as the vines twirled on the top forming small decorative designs. And within a few moments a swinging cradle, still attached to the post, hung ready to be used.

King Duralos stood there studying it momentarily before he placed baby Azalea within it. He walked up to it and plucked one leaf out from its vine as he whispered under his breath, "Softness for my child." He placed it on the inside of the cradle, took a step back and waited. It began to enlarge in size and form little white cotton balls upon it. Suddenly it made a small poof noise as it exploded in softness. The inside of the cradle was now filled with smooth white fabric. King Duralos stepped back up to it once more and placed his hand upon it, testing it for his beloved baby. Then as if satisfied, he gently placed baby Azalea inside the cradle as he kissed her once more upon the forehead.

King Duralos sat on his bed as he gazed at his daughter sleeping peacefully. He took in a deep breath and placed his hands gently upon his chin. He whispered to her, "What are we going to do?" He sat there pondering so therefore he could keep his child with him in the castle before she receives her wings. Then as if he had an idea he whispered to her once more, "I got it, yes-yes. I shall hold an adoption week, and within that week you shall receive your wings. You seem right of age, that perhaps on that first day you shall receive them. Then, we will be able to be together once they all see your mother's exquisite wings. But first I shall ask all of the servants about you, yes-yes. And after they see your wings, I shall keep you, I will keep you safe within the walls of our castle. You are my daughter, my Princess Azalea."

The Enchantment

6

Many things occurred during the following week. The most dreadful was that no one spoke of Queen Lily any longer. There was the disappearance of the young Cethios. James, Zethron and Trathina's behavior continued to be very mischievous, as they too all had their own secrets. Even the gardener Beruchium and the head chef Trajean all had a part within it all. And if that wasn't enough, all of the servants within the castle were oblivious to the events that were occurring around them due to the fact that they were busy preparing for the adoption week to come, of baby Azalea.

Many fairies from Whisperia and even those from Urinia were stopping by and taking early glances at baby Azalea and the festivities to come. Some were even taking up temporary residency as guests in the castle; only the ones that were deeply interested in adopting her. And although they were granted permission from the king to stay, he himself was not at all concerned. For he knew once baby Azalea received her wings, she was his to keep.

Before the sun's rays brushed upon the land at the end of the week, Cethios cautiously entered the sword swinging room. He glanced around and found it completely empty. He slowly made his way in as he carefully slid the door shut. He walked over to a small table on the far right as he sat down to wait for James.

But he didn't have to wait for long. Within the mirror, the one right across from him, started to form a blue mist upon the reflection. Then to the far left of him where the reflection of the entry door was, James casually walked out. Cethios turned to the actual door to see nothing, James was only walking around in the reflection of the room, within the mirrors. James continued to walk around till he neared the mist. He walked into it and slowly emerged from the mirror and into the room; and as soon as he did the mist in the reflection slowly disappeared.

As James walked up to the table, Cethios took note of James' attire. Cethios was concerned, it seemed as if James was going into battle. But why would he be dressed in that sort of way? What was he planning on doing tonight? Was there something going on that he was missing? James

411

stopped in front of him, "Thank you Cethios for keeping your promises. I know this past week and the week before were a bit frustrating and difficult for you. And truly I say to you, age is just a number. For your acceptance and knowledge is much grander than anyone else your age. Now, I am at an understanding that you are well aware that Zethron killed Queen Lily. I was told you heard it yourself from his own lips. Was I informed correctly?"

Cethios slowly nodded as he opened his mouth to ask how he had known but, James answered for him before he could reply anything, "Yes, the butterflies told Beruchium which in turn, he implied it to me." Cethios nodded and closed his mouth as he gazed into James eyes. He waited patiently for him to continue. James nodded as he sighed and replied in just about one breath, "Yes now allow me to explain something to you that I know you will understand. But can you promise me, before I release my words to you about what is going to take place on this evening that will change the very lives and memories of mostly all, that you will keep this a sincere secret. That is until the timing is right. "

Cethios stood and walked closer to James. He withdrew his sword and gently placed the blade to his forehead, he pointed it to the ground afterwards. Cethios replied with great pride, "You have my word oh great mentor. You are my reasoning for my wisdom and strength."

At that very moment James had never been more proud of Cethios, his pupil, his successor. In return, James did the same as he gently placed his blade to his forehead then pointed it to the ground, having it cross on top of Cethios' sword. Moments passed as they nodded their heads in acceptance and then placed their swords back upon their hip. James replied to Cethios, "Now, since we became aware of King Duralos' plan of holding an adoption week, our plans have changed slightly. In turn, it actually helped us prolong and convince the mind of one we needed to. Now, after our moment your mother is going to enter my quarters, after being allowed by the Eternal Spirits of Earth. You and Trathina are going to travel to the city by foot at a breath pace; for if your steps quicken, your traveling's will go noticed. Once there, you both will stay hidden for the night until dawn breaks tomorrow. The promise I am wanting from you, is for you not to breath a word of anything that has happen since the day Queen Lily ask you to meet her within the Jungles of Whisperia, since the day you laid your eyes upon princess Azalea; all the way until tomorrows' day break. As well as you knowing that Azalea is princess to Queen Lily, she will be known to you only as baby Azalea. None of this until the timing is right; you shall only reveal this to Azalea. She will understand, and you will know when it is right to show her. Show her with the help of the Eternal Spirits, she will understand."

James stared at Cethios as he nodded in understanding. Cethios whispered to James, "I shall, it shall be as if my memory has vanished from these past events."

James seemed amused as he replied, "That is exactly the idea! Trathina has bravely convinced Zethron that tonight, once all of the high fairies from Urinia and Whisperia are within the Grand Hall, is the night he is going to cast one of his grand enchantments that will blind all of their memories about the golden wings being Heredity of Royalty. He will cast the spell once Azalea is in the process of receiving her wings, which we are certain she will receive tonight. And although the spell will not affect royal blood, baby Azalea is too young to remember anything. And as for King Duralos, well, he's too far in denial at the moment, I do not think he would go against anything that will eventually allow him to keep his daughter." By this time James now started to pace as he continued, "Trathina and a couple of other servants have already been removing paintings and statues within the city and castle that imply anything of golden feathers upon the royalty of women fairies. And the king does not deny any action of this at all. As I reply again, he is in a state within his subconscious mind that, he cares not of that or anything else, but to simply keep his daughter Azalea within his loving arms."

James slowed his pace as his hands now rested behind his back. He continued but lowered his voice, "But as fate will have it, I have been able to conjure up another spell to twist with Zethron's enchantment that will lift the original enchantment from everyone's memory once Queen Whistalyn wakes from her slumber. But the only default to this is that she must survive this day, even if she stays slumbering for a time, she will wake when Zethron's poison has vanished. Otherwise we will have failed and it will not succeed."

Cethios stood there taking in all of James' words as he pondered them carefully. Cethios whispered with much concern, "So when this enchantment flows over the lands, me and my mother will be safe? As well as baby Azalea?"

James took in a deep breath as he rubbed the back of his neck slowly with a heavy sigh. He gazed towards the door as if reassuring himself of something. He gazed back towards Cethios as he answered, "Yes, we have already enchanted one of the servants to appear and

413

acknowledge herself as Trathina. She will be replacing your mother for the day until day breaks tomorrow. Therefore you and your mother will be safe from the enchantment. For our beliefs were confirmed. Zethron wants Trathina to place baby Azalea into the crib at the head throne tonight. Zethron wants Trathina to lose the memory of the golden feathers as well, but we know the true Trathina will not. And once the sun touches the earth in the morning, the servant that has been enchanted will appear herself once more and have no recollection of what she did. And as for baby Azalea, do not worry about her for now. She still has the necklace you allowed Beruchium to place on her, she will be out of the way from evils eye. And King Duralos has not let her out of his sight, and I don't think he will any time soon."

Without missing a beat Cethios added, "What about you and Beruchium, and Trajean? Will you all be safe as well? I don't think I can bear anymore sadness if anything falls upon others that I truly care about. James, you promise me that you'll be alright. James?"

James stared in the swelling eyes of Cethios as he gently placed his hand upon his shoulder. Cethios cared so much for his friends, and he did not want them to follow the same fate as Queen Lily. He could not bear to lose anyone else within his heart.

James bent over and embraced Cethios momentarily as he too embraced James in return. Moments later James stood and wiped a tear quickly from his eye before Cethios could have a glimpse. James replied to him, "Worry not about us Cethios. We will be within the city's safe haven before Zethron's enchantment can over take our memory."

A few tears fled Cethios' eyes, but he too quickly wiped them away. He did not want James to think he was weak. But in reality, to James, tears are a sign of bravery and of acceptance. Cethios whispered over his sobs, "James, I shall keep all of my promises and I too shall attempt to forget these terrible days, even though in my heart I know they existed. And I shall reveal this only to Azalea when the timing is right. The Eternal Spirits of Fire can assist me in the enchantment. Azalea will see these events through my eyes."

Cethios bowed towards James, as he too bowed towards him as a sign of their respect for each other, and acceptance of their promises. For James too had a promise to keep to Cethios, to one day reveal his true father.

Moments later Trathina entered the sword swinging room cautiously as she appeared under much stress. Once inside she closed the door while it slowly transformed into a boulder. She turned and placed her right palm upon the boulder as she whispered to it, "Thank you."

The door seemed to slowly vibrate as it morphed back into the same old sliding door. And once Trathina turned her face back around, tears fell down her delicate face. Then without a doubt, Cethios ran into her arms. They embraced each other tightly within their loving arms. Without glancing up Trathina replied to her son, "I know I shall never be forgiven for all the things that I have done wrong, especially my betrayal. But, come my son, I shall explain everything tonight. And tonight we both shall mourn one so great, our Queen and our beloved friend, Lily. Forgive me my son; I was very wrong for wanting something that was never mine to take upon. I love you so much. Come, we make hast before we are found and our doing goes wrong. We will be able to see the enchantment from where we will be hiding. And once day breaks, we shall return anew."

Cethios gazed into his mothers' eyes as delicate tears fell freely. He whispered to her, "Yes, we do have much to discuss, but most importantly, I forgive you mother. I love you too..."

From deep within the City of Whisperia in a hidden hut high above the tree tops sat Cethios and Trathina. They gazed towards the castle as the stars above them lit their faces. They sat there embracing each other within a warm blanket discussing all of the recent events. They warmed themselves as well with some orange tea given to them by Trajean.

Suddenly as the moon reached its highest peak, it began to fill with darkness as it glowed with a black hue. Once the moon was engulfed with this darkness, an enormous purple lightning bolt struck across the sky above where the castle stood. Bright light engulfed that whole area as Cethios and Trathina watched from a safe distance. Then within moments it had all vanished, as if nothing had ever touched the sky or the moon at all. Zethron's enchantment with James' had been casted and set.

Cethios snuggled his face into his mothers' neck and whispered, "It is done. Once we enter the castle I promise I shall not tell anyone that you are my mother. I will tell no one about the recent events that have fallen upon any of us, especially about Queen Lily. I shall keep my promises I have made to everyone. I promise I will keep."

Such heavy burdens were placed upon many that night, heavy burdens that were never forgotten, especially for the young and brave Cethios.

****

Fire

7

I awoke suddenly very alert and drenched in sweat, gross. It was just about pitch black, wherever I was, but there was a soft strand of moonlight that gently entered somewhere to my far left. Perhaps there was a bay window nearby. Hopefully it was open because I felt as if I was on fire! Why was I burning up so?

As I continued to rest on my back, wherever I was, my head swirled with confusion. It was very strange, all of those dreams. They all felt so real; too real. Was my subconscious mind melting in this horrible heat? Was I hallucinating within my own dreams? I wonder, did what I just dream, could that have been true? Did Cethios truly go through all of that with me? Was this another piece of my puzzled life? Honestly I wouldn't doubt it, nothing now a days surprised me anymore.

I rubbed my fingertips gently over my eyes. My golden tears were sliding down the side of my face and into my hair. Even though there could be a chance that those dreams could have been fake, they still dug deep within my heart. I felt so overwhelmed with sorrow and despair. I honestly don't know how much more of this I can take.

Then, other thoughts hit me. Was Xanthus truly gone? I know we mated, so therefore that would have made us Immortals, right? But, because I have these shackles on, would that have kept him from his Immortality as well? I wasn't sure anymore what could be or what couldn't be. All I know was that I saw Cethios drive his sword into Xanthus. I know I saw Xanthus fall. But how would this Immortality work?

My heart grieved as it was torn with the thought that Xanthus could very well be dead. But deep within my subconscious mind, somehow I knew he was alright. So then what was it? What do I believe in? And why was it so bloody hot in here! My brain swirled within my head as the room seemed to be spinning with it. It didn't help that my skin was still on fire! Wow! Why wasn't I cooling off?

I grunted to myself as I sat up slowly to see if that would alleviate some of the dizziness, my hands flying to the side of my face. But unfortunately the spinning continued as I placed my hands upon my forehead. Suddenly to my horror I realized something, I wasn't alone.

417

Small breaths came from my left, I glanced over slowly, there sleeping upon his stomach was Cethios.

My heart stopped. What did this mean? Did we sleep together? Was I that knock out that I felt nothing! Oh no, did we? I mean, if we did, what would that mean for Xanthus and I? Does that mean Cethios is now Immortal? Did Xanthus have time to heal after Cethios drove his sword into him, if he was Immortal, before Cethios took it from me by force?

So many more questions swirled around my mind. I think, no… I can't think anymore. I felt like my brain was going to ooze out of my ears from this heat. Goodness, I could probably start a fire with my fingertips!

Still with my hands upon my face, I gazed over to my right. Damn, the bed was pushed up against a wall. I glanced over to the end of my feet, more wall. I turned my head around to glance behind me, crap more wall. Was this bed shoved within a nook or something? My only escape was over Cethios himself! Did I really want to trample over him to escape? I pondered, that would be intriguing. I could try to squish him as I rolled over him, perhaps sock him in the eye even. But no, I don't think it would be worth waking him.

Honestly, I could very well be completely powerless. And besides, I don't think I would make it very far. I can't go anywhere with this head spinning out of control. I probably would make it over Cethios, wake him, and fall onto the floor with a loud thud with my luck. So unfortunately to my utter horror, I did the only thing I could do for the time being, I gritted my teeth and laid back down. I hated this, but what could I do? I was feeling so miserable and hot; I don't think I could physically do anything. I did not have any strength left in me to even try to escape.

As I moved my left arm over my head my elbow brushed against Cethios' skin. It sent good shivers down my spine; his skin was very cool to the touch. I turned onto my side as I faced him. Should I do it, do I even dare? Unfortunately I'm sure my body would thank me one day. I physically couldn't help it. I regretfully snuggled into his cool body.

I sighed in slight contentment. It did feel very relieving as his cool skin soothed my fire. My head even seemed to be slowing down in spin. Then before I knew it Cethios' arm was resting upon my back and my face now smothered into his neck. I took in a deep breath and let out a slow sigh. I was insane for doing this.

I hated it, I gritted my teeth as my body singed down and my subconscious mind drifted away back into a heavy slumber. And as I fell deeper into that slumber, I thought I felt Cethios kiss my forehead. And I thought I heard him whisper gently as he brushed his lips upon my ear, "Azalea... I love you. I promise to always keep."

Then, darkness overwhelmed me as I fell deeper into my subconscious dreams.

Determination

8

I awoke surprisingly very alert as I sat straight up and gazed over to my left. Cethios was not there anymore. I know it couldn't have been a dream. The fire was all too real last night. Everything felt very real. And yet even though it seemed as if I knew more to my puzzled life, strong questions still swirled ever so effortlessly around my subconscious mind. But I could deal with that, I can't deal with the pain; pain within my heart of wondering if my Xanthus was truly gone forever.

I slowly turn as I now sat on the side of the bed. I glanced down at my wrists and ankles. Damn, the shackles were still there embracing my skin. So what does that mean for me? Did I still contain magic within me? I shook it off as I grunted lowly. Did it truly matter anymore? I rubbed my eyes with my fingertips; I didn't want to think of anything anymore. Right now I wanted to concentrate on where exactly I was, if I wanted to get out and how to actually get out if I decided to do just that.

I stood and gave a long stretch of my arms, legs and wings. And as I gazed around I realized that there was good news right away. I wasn't in a dungeon or chained to the wall or anything of that sort. It actually was quite warm and inviting where I was. It seemed as if I was in a study or a small library, an ancient one at that. Upon the walls were books of all sizes and colors. They also looked as if they were bound with different kinds of leather. Some had much dust on them while others were laid wide open in the shelves, as if someone didn't want to lose their page or something. The books and shelves covered basically the entire room all the way up to the ceiling.

To my far right were two enormous bay windows with a large stone balcony on the outside. They were wide open as the green and tan silk curtains swayed with the gentle inviting breeze. Between the two bay windows was an enormous cherry wooden desk. On the counter were a couple of blue leathered books that were open and piled upon each other. Some of the pages seemed very fragile as small finger prints smudged the dust on the edges of them. Someone was doing some intensive research.

There were also two chairs that seemed to be made of that same cherry wood. Although the wood seemed twisted in some areas of the legs and back of the chairs, they still appeared quite comfortable. There also was a brown pillow that covered the entire seat.

Weird, I thought. Why would Cethios bring me here and leave with the windows wide open? He obviously wasn't in the room right now. So perhaps he thought I'd just jump out, because honestly that's what I felt like doing. But if not, I'm sure there was a spell to prevent me from escaping that way. I'm positive he wouldn't just leave it that easy for me.

As I started to make my way over to the windows, to humor myself in hoping that they weren't enchanted, I stopped midway in my tracks. Something was not right, I gazed to the floor to see what felt sensational below my feet. It was soft tall green grass. Weird but, nothing seemed to surprise me right now. I bent down and brushed it with my fingertips. It was healthy green grass and I wasn't imagining it. I sighed; perhaps I'll lay on it later. The breeze from the window was just a bit more tempting right now.

I stood back up and continued my way over to the windows. I pushed the silky curtain aside as I felt the warm air smoothing it's fingertips upon my skin. Goosebumps covered my skin, it was soothing. I closed my eyes and took it all in. And yet, even though my mind was overwhelmed and screaming inside, my soul took in a sweet sigh of relief.

And before I got carried away in the moment, I slowly stretched my hands forwards. Yup, they stopped on this hard substance that perhaps was the same from the translucent room in Trinafin. Oh Trinafin, how I missed the castle and the city. I even missed the castle in Whisperia, my home.

I grunted as I opened my eyes and walked over to the door. Locked of course and I'm sure enchanted as well. Then I simply stood there staring at the door. It had happened, depression had over taken me. It was starting to sink and dwell in my heart and my very soul. Truly, I wasn't motivated to carry on anymore.

Then what I had been so desperately trying to hold back with all my might came crashing forward like a raging river. It was all of my questions that swirled within my subconscious mind. The questions that made me feel as if the room was spinning out of control.

Was Xanthus alive or dead? We were supposed to be Immortals but with my shackles being on, would that prevent Xanthus from inhabiting his magic too? And yet perhaps if he was alive, was he not an Immortal anymore. For last night when I awoke with Cethios by my side, I was convinced that he did take me against my will. I can't remember anything though. All I can remember are all of those dreams, the dreams that had me seeing everything through Cethios' eyes.

Was that all real or just made up? But yet, if Cethios did take me, why would I still have my shackles on? And yet, if he didn't take me, then what in the world was he doing by my side last night? And if he didn't take me last night, when was he going to come back and attempt to take me? Would he keep me here in this room of peace as his prisoner?

Whoa, I think part of my brain just melted through my eyes. Oh wait no, it was just more tears. I quickly wiped them as I tried to refocus my energy in keeping all of those questions back inside towards the back of my subconscious mind. But one more question quickly escaped. I'm sure once Cethios takes me, or if he did, he'd surly kill Xanthus once he was not Immortal any longer.

I pressed my fingertips upon my forehead. I couldn't even slightly think of Xanthus ever fading away into the mist of just a memory. I pressed harder; perhaps I could push that right out of my head. But then something strange started to swirl inside with my subconscious mind.

At first it was sort of fuzzy as if, it was not part of my thinking but wanted to be. A vision began to move forward. It was as if my memory was swirling together colors and wanted to create something but could not. Then after much more concentration it came to me. It was James in the sword swinging room, he was saying something to me but I couldn't make it out. I closed my eyes and concentrated even more.

Then it came to me like an echo of a whisper, I heard James words, 'Follow the voice inside you that speaks the truth. Trust what you see within your eyes and your heart.'

Of course! James' prediction of words that he first spoke to me on the day of my last training with him; how his words followed me so. Another one emerged as I remembered more of his words, 'Your magic is greater than you see content with, dig deep into your mind to find your utopia for there it shall be.'

That's it! Greater than I see fit! All I needed to do was dig deep and there was where I found it, the magic that allowed me to manipulate water and that little lightning bolt. My magic is still there. Xanthus is still alive! That is what the voice inside me is speaking, no doubt whatsoever

422

now! Even though with my eyes I saw Xanthus' life get taken away, with what my heart sees is that he is still alive!

My body singed with this new emotion. How could I ever doubt myself or forget about James' words for that matter. I gazed around the room looking for something. Even if Cethios did take me last night I wasn't going to give up my fight. I will not surrender and stay here as his prisoner!

I continued to gaze around the room a bit more motivated this time. But all I could see were books, parchments, a huge desk, a folding wall, a bed, a sword… wait-wait, what? No, I couldn't believe it! There wedged between the wall and the bed was my sword. Was I imagining it? Did Cethios forget that it was with me or did he simply forget it there? I know he wouldn't have left it purposely.

It didn't matter, I ran to it. I took it within my grasp and sighed out in relief. As I gazed back down to where my sword was I found to my surprise a pair of clean clothes. There was a royal blue dress with golden lace and some crystal sequins on it, and matching under garments. That's weird I thought. Was he attempting to suck up to me?

I grunted to myself. I hope I was not taking a bribe or something but, I was sort of all grungy. And after waking up last night in all of my sweat, I think my body would thank me if I did clean up. I don't think it would hurt if I did take it. Well, this was an easy decision.

I scooped it up and ran over to the folding wall. I got out of my war clothes and tried to conjure up something meaningless. Thankfully that faithful little black rain cloud formed and rained on me. I don't think I was ever so happy to see it, unless I needed to wash in it. Truthfully, it was relaxing to finally be clean once again. And after I showered I dried within the warm air and quickly stepped into the clothes. I do have to say though that it felt smooth like silk, but cool against my skin like cotton. If Cethios wanted to suck up to me… no, this still wouldn't work. The dress felt sensational but it was just a change of clothes, that's it.

As I finished I thought to myself, I should at least head over to the windows to see if I could try to find where Cethios had me this time. Perhaps I could spot something that I knew or maybe I could see someone that could help me.

But before I could continue in my thoughts, something distracted me, footsteps. They were coming closer to the room and were fast approaching. Well, I for one wasn't going to stand here and appear helpless. I withdrew my sword that I had hung from my side. And as quietly as I could I ran to the door. I stood next to it and raised my sword high above my head.

I just got this crazy idea. First I could careless anymore about Cethios. He was nothing to me… nothing. I had made up my mind. Secondly, I was going to hit him by surprise, at like his legs or something. Yes, that sounds good. He'll have no choice but to remove the shackles so therefore I could save his life. Hopefully he'll come without his sword. Then I'll heal him to a point, knock him out of his subconscious mind and make a run for it. Yes, this plan was sounding better by the second. I'll run for it and find Xanthus. Together we could fight Cethios and Zethron.

Nothing can go wrong. Nothing is going to change my mind. I had a plan and I was sticking to it. It was fool proof! I would not be stopped for anything! Determination flowed through my veins. I was taking Cethios out, yes. He for one would not and could not change my mind. I was stopping at nothing…

Surrender

9

The door knob slowly started to turn. I could hear Cethios' heavy breaths from the other side of the door. Why did he sound as if he was out of breath? What did he do, run here? Why was he running anyway, was he in a hurry or something? Or perhaps he was running from someone.

No, no-no-no. I was not doing this to myself. I shook my head to get those thoughts out of my subconscious mind. I could care less what he was doing. I had made up my mind. I was taking him out and I was going to stop at nothing. No distractions. I gripped my sword even tighter between my fingers.

James words suddenly flowed within my ears... 'Trust those whom you think least of, when the timing is right and calls for it'. Oh James' words, how they followed me. But perhaps those words were not meant for Cethios... or were they?

No, again I shook my head and waited patiently as the moment finally arrived. The door slowly swung open and Cethios stepped in. And that's when I made my mistake; I gazed upon his eyes and froze. I couldn't help it, I was in utter shock. What I was seeing with my very own two eyes seemed unreal. I froze at the sight at something I had never seen before. Here before me was the turn around, I was caught off guard. So, I did the unthinkable, I lowered my sword.

Here standing in front me was Cethios, tears falling from his eyes and down his cheeks. I shook my head slightly. My plan had gone right out the window with the breeze. I have no idea what had come over me. Here I was determined to stop at nothing a few moments ago, and now, I was frozen and confused on what I should do next. Standing in my presence was not the evil vicious man I grew to loath. But yet, now before me stood the old Cethios that I once knew and trusted. The Cethios I cared about once before many centuries ago.

Soft tears continued to fall from his sore eyes as he raised his glowing white palms up. It was if he was surrendering to me. Why though? Did he have some type of epiphany or something? Should I even take the chance to ask and risk perhaps even my life? He whispered through his lips, "Azalea, I cannot go on like this any longer. I do not have the will power to carry all of this anymore. I want nothing to do with any of it. Azalea, please listen to my words of forgiveness, my words of sincerity, of regret. I need your help and I cannot fight this on my own any longer, or death will surely come to me swiftly. My heart and soul ache with the sorrow and darkness of this earth that I cannot set free. Azalea..."

I'm sure my eyes balls were pressing out of my skull at this very moment. I could feel them doing just that. I mean, what was going on here? Who was this fairy standing before me? Was he being serious, did he really need me? Should I trust him? I feared for my heart, for I did not know what was the right thing to do? I mean, I trusted him once and look where that led me.

I just subconsciously realized that I was not breathing as I sucked in a deep breath of air and held it. What can I say, I was in utter astonishment! But as I quickly let out that breath I gazed around the room. There wasn't anything in here for torturing. There wasn't anything in this room that symbolized death. There was only that warm breeze from the window and the books that covered this room. If he were to go back on his word, what would he do? Would he attack me with a book or something? Would he take me from this comforting room and take me to a dungeon?

Before I could go any further with my thoughts Cethios interrupted them and whispered, "Azalea please, I cannot go on any further with all of this. It's eating away at my soul. I promise you, no more lies. I surrender to you... I surrender all to you. I swear to you Azalea I will answer anything you ask of me. I promise Azalea on my life, I will set you free. I will free you... after I tell you everything. Azalea, I surrender to your will."

This time as I took in my deep breath, I let it out slowly. I stared at his tears as they continued to slowly flow down his face ever so freely. I made my choice as I placed my sword back onto my side. I just hope that it wasn't a bad choice, again. But I still stood there motionless as I continued to take in deep breaths. I felt a bit queasy on my decision, I had no idea on what to expect from Cethios anymore.

I wasn't sure if Cethios caught on that I was confused in my decision. But he continued to stand there with his hands up in surrender. Then to my surprise I found myself regrettably saying to him, "Alright Cethios... I'm listening."

We both surrendered to each other in that very moment as suddenly Cethios lunged towards me and embraced me. He hugged me tightly within his arms as more silent tears fell from his soft cheeks.

The Outburst

10

It seemed like forever for Cethios to finally calm down. He was having some sort of nervous breakdown or something. His breaths were heavy as his chest heaved in and out. I thought he was going to spontaneous combust or something. But finally, I was able to get him to sit near the desk in that twisted cherry wooden chair. I positioned the other chair right in front of him so therefore I could still keep an eye on him. I was not taking any chances this time. I also sat in a way so that I can easily withdraw my sword if I needed it. I didn't want to take the chance of not being able to access it.

As Cethios made himself comfortable, he was still taking in slow deep breaths. I rolled my eyes over to him, "Alright Cethios, begin."

Cethios slowly raised his eyes until they locked with mine. He whispered through his soft lips, "Prepare yourself Azalea. There is a lot that you are going to take in, in such little time that we have. I assure you; your head will spin."

I grunted as I crossed my arms across my chest. Who was he to tell me what I can and cannot handle. I frowned, "Cethios, I am not a child that needs to be taken care of. I can take care of myself just fine."

Cethios raised his nose up and smirked, "You can take care of yourself all your own you say? Really Azalea, must I repeat myself to you as I once told you in the dungeons of Urinia?"

Did he really have to remind me of that moment? I was not going to play any of his games. I reached over and gripped the handle of my sword with my right hand as I kept my gaze on Cethios. He seemed to have caught on as he raised his hands up as if in surrender. His palms glowed slightly as he replied, "I mean you no more harm Azalea honestly. I just meant that I don't want to overwhelm you with so much information. I know you can handle yourself just fine. But truly there is no need for your mothers' sword. I am the one without a sword here trusting you."

What a way to turn it around huh? He really just made me look like the bad fairy. And although I hated to admit it, he had a good point. I still continued to grip my sword though. I wasn't going to give him the

427

thought that I wouldn't strike at him. I gritted my teeth and replied, "The things you have put me through Cethios, it is to my own great amazement that I am even trust your actions or anything that you have to say. But yet, here I am right? I'm sitting across from the fairy that once told me to trust him. And as those words escaped from your lips, was it not an hour past that you had me at your mercy in tears and in blood? Forgiveness and understanding is an understatement for you Cethios. Besides, what you are about to do is just explain yourself right? They are just words, right? I think I can handle words thrown in my face from you."

Cethios placed his hands down as he closed his eyes and stretched his neck. It seemed as if he was deeply fighting with his own subconscious mind as he scrunched his eyes together. And as he ran his fingers over his face and through his onyx-colored hair, his breaths once more seemed to take a toll on his chest. I watched him for about a few minutes as once again sadness overcame his face. I sighed to myself as I remembered that I did decide not to take his life and give him a chance. Regrettably I let go of my sword and placed my hands upon my lap as I waited for Cethios to gather himself once more.

Moments later as if satisfied with himself he locked his eyes with mine as he gently brushed his tongue against the side of his bottom lip. He whispered, "Alright, let us begin with…"

But before he could go any further an image came to my subconscious mind that I could not ignore. And for some reason, I need to ask for my own comfort. I interrupted him, "I want you to do something for me before you begin. It's really to comfort my thoughts right at this moment."

Cethios shrugged his shoulders, "Sure, apparently we seem to have all day."

I gazed down onto his legs as I asked, "Lift your pant leg." Cethios irritably grunted as he lifted his right pant leg to reveal nothing upon his skin. I shook my head unsatisfied, "No… your left pant leg."

Cethios mumbled under his breath, "Picky." He lifted his left pant leg and turned his leg slightly as there upon his skin was a tattoo of a sun and a moon merged together as one as a lock appeared on one corner of it and on the other corner was another lock. At that very moment I realized that I needed to close my mouth. It somehow dropped open in slight shock. I guess some part of my brain was satisfied although I couldn't quite yet piece it together. And as I lifted my eyes to meet with Cethios' gaze, it seemed as if he was smug about it. He replied through his teeth, "Satisfied?"

I nodded. I guess I was. Not really sure on what though? But within seconds Cethios stretched his neck and leaned in closer to me. I could almost feel his breath upon my skin as he replied, "Well then, now that your curiosity is out of the way, let's start from the beginning, shall we? Last night I performed an enchantment on the both of us, with the help of the Eternal Spirits of Fire. The enchantment enhanced my memories, only those memories in which I choose mind you. It transformed them into a dream and projected them from my subconscious mind to yours. I have never performed that spell until last night, and I believe it was quite successful. Do you remember the dreams completely that you had last night, other than remembering my tattoo?"

I broke my gaze from Cethios' eyes as I stared down at my palms. Shoot, they began to glisten, I couldn't help it. Curse my natural instincts. I admit it, I became nervous on two things. One was remembering that Cethios was sleeping and snuggling with me all of last night. And two, was the thought that I was sharing the same dreams with Cethios. It is very unique and intimate to share one's dreams. And even more personal and almost sensual, that they were coming from Cethios himself.

I gazed back into his penetrating and mesmerizing eyes, their light brown color with a tint of green in the middle had me almost holding my breath as he smiled at me. Which of course made me even more nervous and almost feeling light headed. I hate to admit that honestly Cethios is more than easy on the eyes, he's attractively handsome. I couldn't help but blush. Curse his good looks, I wanted to break our gaze but found myself unable to. So, I gathered my courage and replied, "Of course, I remember it all very vividly. But was any of it even real or true?"

Cethios slightly scowled, "Need I to show you my tattoo once more? Or is that not enough proof for you."

The dreams were coming back to me as I continued to stare at Cethios' gorgeous face. Although, I wanted him to answer my question and not just flash me his leg again. And yet, how am I supposed to know that remembering his tattoo was not just a part of me remembering a vision when we were younger. Perhaps I saw it there long ago, who knows what my brains thinks now a days. So, I shook my head in disagreement as Cethios grunted in frustration to my response. He replied with a sigh, "Yes Azalea, everything is real. From the day I took you from Queen Lily and

429

made a promise to her; to the days that I made promises to James and to Beruchium. And finally, to the day I watched Zethron and James enchant the city to forget about Queen Lily and the golden wings being hereditary."

I stared at him as I watched his smile fade to sadness. I asked, "But why the big spell though? Why would Zethron go through all of that effort just to have everyone forget that I was a princess? And just for in the end for you to take my Immortality and for you to be king? How would that benefit him?"

Cethios shook his head with frustration, "That's one of the many pieces that are missing from my own puzzle. For what he truly wants is your Immortality. I just don't know what it's got to do with me getting it first though. Zethron is truly twisted to the core. Everything that he wants and everything that he does never makes any sense."

I pondered for a bit, it was very odd to have Cethios take it from me when in reality, Zethron wanted it for himself. It was all very confusing. But before I could carry my thoughts forward, I had to ask, "In the memories that I saw, why did you keep calling me your baby Azalea?"

That hypnotic smile came back onto Cethios' face as oddly enough it soothed my heart. Cethios half chuckled, "Because you were and still are to this very day. Although you are not a baby anymore, you are mine to keep. You are my best friend Azalea, no matter what has happened in the past and what lies before us in the future."

My cheeks burned! Why did he have to go and say it like that? Curse my hormones for making me blush. I mean, what in the world was going on here! It was his smile; yes, it was only that. That was the only thing making me blush. I ran my own fingers through my brown and golden streaked hair as I took in a deep breath. I mean, seriously what was going on. What effects did the enchantment that Cethios did on me have? Why was I feeling this way? I wonder if he performed any other spells on me with these so-called Eternal Spirits. I was pretty out of it, who knows what happened! I think he was sucking up to me. Yes, that's it. So, if he was trying to get on my good side, it wasn't going to happen. Then the worst thought hit me. "Cethios, tell me honestly. Did you take me last night?"

Cethios smirked to himself as he gazed down at his fingers. He slowly massaged them upon each other as if he was debating on telling me the truth or not. I repeated myself almost irritably, "Cethios, did you or not?"

He slowly raised his eyes until they locked with mine once again. His smile sent goose bumps running all over my skin. He raised one eye brow up as he replied smugly, "Would you have wanted me too?"

I frowned at him. Really? What was he trying to get at? Was he attempting to have me confess that I wanted him or something of the sort? I think not! I mean don't get me wrong, for some strange reason I was finding myself very attractive to him but, I'm sure it was just the lighting or something. There was nothing more in my heart for Cethios than friendship at that. Nothing could compare for my deep admiration and love for Xanthus.

Suddenly Xanthus' smile swept across my mind like a gentle whisper. Oh how I wish I could feel his soft lips upon mine once more. I closed my eyes and tried to hold onto that thought. But the horrible memory of him falling with death pushed ahead of my thoughts. I gripped the seat as I dug my fingertips into the chair.

I opened my eyes to see Cethios still gazing at me sensually. It took all my effort to contain the rage that wanted to burst through my skin and punch Cethios in the face. So, I took in another deep breath as I tried to comfort my aching heart.

But I started something so I must finish it. I gazed over into Cethios' eyes as they locked yet again, "Cethios don't flatter yourself. The only one I would ever share my love with is Xanthus. Now answer my question truthfully, do not make me regret the decision on allowing you to explain yourself."

Cethios' smirk slowly faded to a sneer, "Relax Azalea, it's a no. I did not take you last night. The only thing that I did do to you last night was share my sights and perhaps a slight caress here and there. But the enchantment that I performed did require me to sleep next to you. And of course, your body had a physical reaction to the magic of the Eternal Spirits of Fire."

My mouth dropped as I realized his last words. "Is that why my skin was feeling as if it was being set on fire? I was melting last night!"

Cethios began laughing at my comment as he wiped his left eye. Great, did he think I was joking? I seriously felt as if I was made of fire. I wasn't trying to make him laugh but it seemed as if I was amusing him. After Cethios saw that I was not laughing in return he cleared his throat, "The Eternal Spirits of Fire requires some acceptance from the soul of the one being enchanted on and on the one using their magic. If I remember correctly, you were very accepting to it last night. And by the way, I also had a physical reaction to it as well, it wasn't just you."

I stared at him as I was completely confused. I remember nothing before the dreaming last night, nothing. How could I have been so accepting to something like that? But then as if Cethios was reading my mind he answered with an embarrassed shrug, "You were a bit out of it I admit, you were actually at one point calling me Xanthus. So, I sort of went with it and asked for your permission to enchant your soul to share my subconscious mind and you accepted."

Once again, my jaw dropped as I exhaled all of the air within my lungs. How could he do such a thing? Did he think he had the right to do so? I re-crossed my arms tightly across my chest as I asked in frustration, "You manipulated me in thinking you were Xanthus?"

"No, absolutely not! You allowed yourself to think that. I did nothing of the sort but simply ask for your permission. Besides, I was well aware that we both were going to have a reaction to it. I just wasn't sure on how much we were going to be affected. You know, it was not just you who suffered last night. I made a promise and I kept to it, I showed you even though I knew the consequences. You forget that my skin was ice cold. I went into a death form while you were inside my subconscious mind. I was your counter weigh for your heat. I was freezing last night. I suffered just as well as you. How easily you forget that."

Oh, I guess I did forget that. Man, once again I hated to admit that he was right. I do remember last night Cethios feeling so cold, and how it made me singe down by touching his skin. I wonder if I warmed him. I asked, "Why would that be? Why would our bodies have that effect?"

Cethios broke his stare with me as he gazed down. He gripped the arms of the chair as he replied through his teeth, "I guess the spirits have some sense of humor or something of the sort."

As I watched him stir in his chair my gaze suddenly went behind him as I watched the curtains sway back and forth. It was as if they were inviting me to join them in a dance. So, as I spaced out, I thought about the dreams last night. I thought about his thoughts, and of all the things he went through by himself. I sighed; I wasn't the only one fighting a battle here; realizing that made me feel so much worst. Great, now I have more guilt for wanting to beat him up.

As my gaze came back into his eyes, I saw that they were filled with much regret and sadness. It was like I actually wanted to embrace him and tell him it was going to be alright. I grunted to myself. I hated having so many mixed emotions all in one moment. I was driving myself crazy. Especially because it was about a fairy that I once cared about, then loathed, and now...

Cethios cleared his throat as he took in a deep breath, "Yes well, shall I continue or shall I let you ponder on things some more?"

I shook my head. I stared at Cethios as it seemed as if he was struggling with something. And yet somehow, I think this was all making sense. I scooted a bit towards him as I placed my hands gently upon his. He seemed to cringe slightly at my touch but it didn't matter to me. "Cethios, thank you for sharing what you've been through and my beginning, sort of speak, with me. I appreciate it. But, do you truly know what Zethron's plan is through all of this? Please be honest if you do know."

I sat back away from him once more as I saw him grit his teeth and reply, "Like I said, I can tell you everything. But that is the only thing I don't know. That is my quest that I am trying to figure out myself." I pondered quickly on it as he continued to stare at me with tension. He relaxed a bit as he whispered through his lips, "Azalea, I wanted to tell you everything about those days on numerous occasions but, I swore I wouldn't until the timing was right."

I had to ask, "How did you know this time was right?"

Cethios shook his head with slight disappointment, "Because our lives depend on knowing the truth now. If you had never left Whisperia the day of the ball, I would have shown you that night."

I couldn't stop my mind from wandering as I unintentionally asked, "Would you have married me?"

Cethios' lips curled slightly, "I'm not sure how far I would have gone to keep up the rouse but, I knew you were destined for someone else."

I nodded and blushed slightly. The odd thought of the slight chance of being married to Cethios had me pressing my fingers upon my forehead. My life could had been so different in so many ways. So many little things had such a huge impact and effect. I shook my head and dropped my hands as I cleared of my throat, "Please, carry on."

Cethios finally let go of the chair as he stared at his fingertips. It was as if they were numb or something. He rubbed his thumbs against his fingers as he took another deep breath. He let it out in a whoosh as he turned his gaze back towards me and continued, "Alright, with the beginning out of the way, let's continue. So Zethron convinced the king that I was the true Prince of Urinia, and that we were meant to be or something of the sort. Not sure why myself, I think Zethron thought you wouldn't put up a fight. He should have known better though; you are the daughter of Queen Lily. But I was given orders. And the night of the ball, when you left, I honestly did not know or want Zethron to kill Mirage. You know that right?"

As I gazed into his eyes they seemed to swell with tears. I sighed. I had to tell him the truth. I had to return the favor of him being truthful to me. "Honestly no. Why would Mirage's death be difficult for you? You killed Razyna and per say James as well."

Cethios gripped the chair tightly as suddenly he stood and kicked the chair from under him. He grunted as he ran his fingers through his hair as he screamed, "This burden is killing me! It's eating away at my soul and my heart, you don't understand! I was given strict orders to stop anyone who gets in my way! Azalea, I have been so desperately trying to secretly save you; despite all of my orders. I've somehow been able to maneuver around them just for you. It's always been just for you!"

Cethios lunged forward towards me as he gripped the arms of my chair as I leaned all the way back into it. He continued shouting, "Don't you see, I have known all of it! Everything from the day you decided to run away with Mirage. I knew he was going to try to save you. I wasn't one hundred percent sure you would actually leave. So, I sent forth Krynton to try to lure another dragon near the castle before the ball started so you would see it, to motivate you to run! But who knew it was actually going to be Xanthus' dragon Cetus! And I knew you'd be there to fight in the war at The Valley of Melinatha. I had to find you before Zethron or Theron did, I just had too! And then when I finally did find you, here you were prancing along within the valley. I was so enraged when I found you! You could have ruined everything! Did you know Zethron and Theron were actually out there within the valley looking for you! You were so careless! Do you know what could have happened if they found you first! And then after that, I had to torture you in Urinia on direct orders! Do you think I wanted to do all of those things to you? It was killing me that I was hurting you! But I have been successful on prolonging on actually taking you. Don't you think I would have taken you by force anytime I wanted too? The day you escaped with Morpheus, he unlocked the hand print with his own blood, damn it Azalea I knew! I knew he was already in that damn room, why it took him so long, I don't know? Was he waiting for me to be naked? Who knows! I knew who was who; I had to play ignorant because Theron was on my case! But I did know that Xanthus was already circling the castle with Cetus. I knew he was out there! But then I was given orders after you escaped with Xanthus to burn your soul, they hoped he'd bring you back. But I was hoping you'd reach Hypathia in time. Then, Denentro told me you were going through the serpent entrance, and he gave me the Silver Truth of Sea from Prince Melancton! And I knew you were there in the stupid cave, Delphina told me she saw you enter! And I was hoping you'd find The Sea Room where your mothers' sword was with the Silver Truth of Sea. I knew you'd take it, and once you did, I rigged it so I can find you myself in that dungeon and not Theron or Zethron! Oh! And I knew it was Xanthus in there with you, I had to get him angry to release his inner magic! Who knew it would actually work! And then I held that stupid ball so Morpheus and James can hear Zethron's plan themselves on the war in the Depths of Galligro. I somehow was able to convince Zethron that we were recruiting more soldiers that night. Then the next day I didn't know Razyna was going to jump in front of Xanthus! She was so stupid for doing that, I was angry with her, angry! Out of stupidity perhaps I actually thought she'd be safe with me! But I already knew Xanthus was Immortal; my orders were to kill him! Oh! I knew he'd be just fine! But I had stupid orders! Then, you just had to get caught by the Cristats didn't you, didn't you! That made it even worse for me! You don't think that I don't suffer under Zethron's wrath myself! Theron and his Outcasted went after you but failed when he found out that Xanthus was still alive! I had to kill him in the Depths of Galligro to buy me some time with you, I knew he'd be just fine, he's Immortal! But Theron and Zethron didn't know that, they didn't know you two had already slept together! And then I had to get his necklace once I stabbed him, I had too! That day in the castle of Urinia in the dungeon before Zethron stabbed you with the sword, when I held the crystal to your jewel on your stomach, I convinced him that if it glowed, you were still pure! I obviously lied! It actually meant that you were already an Immortal! For the love of all creations Azalea, I knew it all!"

Suddenly I placed my hands upon Cethios face as I shut him up. Whoa, I had to catch my breath and I wasn't even the one shouting. Now that was way too much information all at once. I sat there in shock staring straight into his eyes. I seriously was trying to process all of that. I don't think I even blinked. Did my heart stop? Crap, I forgot how to breathe.

I finally took in a deep breath as I suddenly became dizzy and light headed. Lack of oxygen, I'm sure. I felt like I was on a fierce dragon ride and wanted to get off. But as I took in another deep breath I asked, "Cethios, you've been doing all of this to protect me? I mean, back at the castle of Urinia when I saw the Silver Truth of Sea and when I saw a boy that took me and made a promise to my mother, heck, I didn't realize it was you. I don't think my brain put that all together then. And wait, you've been doing all of this with Theron? So that actually means that he's on Zethron's side? And I thought I heard him say once that he thought you were made up? So, was that his cover up? And also, why has Denentro been helping you?"

I let go of Cethios' face as he first fell onto his knees, then to the ground on his back. Deep breaths concaved within his chest as he flushed a crimson hue within his cheeks. He replied within breaths, "Denentro is my friend too, about a century before you were born. I too have been accepted into their kind. They don't know the extent of my treachery but, I was actually surprised to see them at the Depths. But Denentro has been helping me through it all willingly. But that is not all of it. Before I answer your questions Azalea, remember that century that we planned a trip to Urinia for our grand adventure and you were unable to go?"

I nodded slowly. I remember that century very clearly. For when he came back, he was a changed fairy. A fairy filled with evil and hatred. That was when I took off our matching necklaces. I didn't know they were protective necklaces. I was so enraged with the fairy he had become, I wanted nothing to share with him. Cethios continued, "Azalea, I'm so sorry. I shouldn't have left without you. That century that I spent there in Urinia, that century I met Theron. That century, I made a Blood-Oath with him."

Once those words escaped his delicate lips, I understood. But before I could ponder on it, he stood and took off his shirt. He turned and knelt on the floor in front of me with his back facing me. There a few inches down from his neck upon his back, were what appeared to be thorns digging within his skin. They stretched from one corner of his back to the other side. The tattoo itself seemed as if it was actually real. It appeared as if it was painfully digging into his skin.

I couldn't help it; curiosity or stupidity over took me. I reached out for it. I wanted to touch it; I wanted to run my fingertips slowly over it. And as I caressed his tattoo with my fingers, Cethios shuttered as he sighed and rubbed his neck with his hands. His tattoo seemed as if it was on fire.

It burned my fingers as I gently followed the thorns. How was this possible, my ivy plant tattoo on my arm wasn't painfully burning my skin. But then again, I wasn't fighting against it either.

Cethios was so tense, I'm sure he was under a lot stress. Part of me understood him now. Part of me wanted to reassure him that it was all going to be alright. And before I knew it, I found myself on the ground near him gently rubbing his back with my fingertips. He turned around and our eyes locked and for some reason, I couldn't help it, I replied softly, "Cethios, I'm so sorry this was brought upon you. I could have... I should have been..."

He reached for my face as he brushed his fingers softly upon my cheek. I closed my eyes as I felt his nose gently brush across mine. Oh my goodness! What was I thinking? Was I seriously that out of it that I didn't realize what I was doing or what was going on? I felt Cethios' hands upon my back as he gave me a small squeeze. I felt his warm breath within my ear as it sent slight sensual shivers up my spine. He whispered, "Oh Azalea, if only this was a different time, if only we were in a different situation. This... us... we could have been..."

I reached out and wrapped my arms delicately around him too. I think by having this time to ponder, I thought of all the things Cethios has done for me. How truly he has been there for me, protecting me against Zethron, and Theron. He'd been there helping me along the way, the best way he knew how against his Blood-Oath. I whispered to Cethios, "When we kissed in the dungeons of Urinia, the vision that I saw, the sadness that I felt, the question that I wanted you to answer, I know how you became this monster you chose not truly to be. Cethios, I do comprehend what I saw. I didn't know it at first but I do now. And when I saw Theron in person for the first time, something sparked in my subconscious mind then, because I have seen him before. I saw him in the vision, I heard his laughter. I saw what and how it all happened, I saw your Blood-Oath."

Cethios sighed, "It was our oath, for me to follow direct orders, to follow every word he tells me to do. And he falsely promised that it wouldn't be anything more than what was needed for me to do. How foolish I was. He replied to me that if I did this, he would tell me who my true father was. Oh Azalea, I was so impatient and unwilling to wait for James to tell me. If only I knew truly then what Theron was, I would have never complied. I was so naive. I didn't know that he too has his own Blood-Oath, with Zethron."

We parted as I gasped. I continued to hold onto his hands though as everything was unraveling so fast. I didn't want to let go for some reason. Yet, I felt that if I did, I would fall. I would fall into this black oblivious and never return to this land. I don't think I can keep up with any of this much longer. Cethios raised his palm as he softly cupped my cheek, the warmth from his hand soothed my skin. His lips parted slowly as he replied softly, "Azalea, allow me to get something out before we go any further. There is something I've always wanted to do, and do properly. Just once, I promise."

Cethios seemed hesitant at first as he leaned closer to me. He cautiously leaned over as if waiting for me to stop him, but all I could do was stare at his slightly quivering lips. And so, Cethios gently placed his soft lips upon mine, kissing me gently and softly. His lips caressed mine as the sensation sent waves of regrettable pleasure through me. He groaned inwardly slightly as his other hand found the back of my neck. I vibrated with some sort of weird energy as I wanted to end the kiss and yet, I wanted more. My mind reeled as my hands found his hair. Our kiss intensified slightly as his tongue brushed against mine. We parted momentarily to catch our breaths as a moan escaped my lips as Cethios' arms wrapped tightly around my waist bringing me closer to him. We were on our knees now, pressed firmly together as his lips found my neck. This triggered something within me as suddenly I began to hear rumble above me.

Thankfully before our foolishness could take us any further it began to pour on us. It rained down on us with such great intensity, we were soaked in seconds. As we parted, we laughed, I guess we couldn't help it, it felt good. Moments later the rain slowed and stopped. That little black rain cloud disappeared with the breeze, and we were left with nothing but our soaked clothes and the memory of that little black rain cloud. Cethios cupped my face as he slowly rubbed his thumb over my lips. He replied breathlessly, "Azalea, I regret nothing and I am not ashamed for kissing you. But this will be our last kiss, ever. Do not worry that I will try to seduce you or over take you by force, because I refuse to do that to you. We cannot be, I know that. But know this; I will always fight for your freedom Azalea. I do love you, but I know you, and you belong with Xanthus."

I nodded as I cupped both of my hands upon his face and replied, "Perhaps in another life time, but I am destined to Xanthus, and that is where I want to be."

We embraced each other and stayed there for a few more moments enjoying the peace and understanding of each other. I nuzzled my face within his wet neck, this was the Cethios I always wanted. The fairy I can place my trust on, my Cethios was finally back. So when we parted we helped each other up. We scooted our chairs a bit closer and sat back down as we already started to dry. It was a bit humid and I'm sure my hair was already starting to frizz a bit. But oh well. I took in a deep breath as I replied to Cethios, "Alright, back to where we left off. So, you are somehow getting Zethron's evil through Theron from the Blood-Oath. Do you know what Zethron and Theron's oath is?"

Cethios ran his fingers through his wet hair as water dripped down his neck. He shook his head. "No, I wish I knew. That would help out immensely though. But, Zethron basically hands out what he wants to be done. One order Theron has me on, is to do what Zethron commands upon; which basically has me running about. But that is not even the tip of it. Azalea, the main point is that by now, Theron knows that Xanthus is Immortal; which means Zethron knows he is Immortal. So know this, Zethron forced Theron not to take you, because he wanted me to do it. But now, since Theron knows I failed, he will try to prove to Zethron that he is more loyal than I. Which means Theron probably is already on his way here to finish Zethron's orders. Theron will take you himself by force. And trust me; I cannot stop him for I am on his orders. Azalea forgive me, I have failed you. I just couldn't... I can't. How can I allow anyone to do that to you... I mean..."

Whoa, and just like that, Cethios was stressed out again. He was not going to relax. I reached over for his fingers as I replied, "Cethios, I will do everything I can to help you the best way I can. You've done everything you could for me; allow me to return the favor. But before I do I want to get one thing straight. I understand you were always following orders; I get that but... why did you try to kill James? After all that he has done for you, you couldn't figure out a way to go around that?"

Cethios stood and started to pace, and quickly. He was pondering something as he kept his hands behind his back. I watched him pace, I guess I was trying to come up with something myself. None of this was going to magically disappear, it would be nice but honestly it wouldn't. I closed my eyes to think some more, I couldn't keep watching him pace it was getting me dizzy. There was already a small path in the grass from his pacing.

As I opened my eyes, Cethios lunged towards me once more as he caught himself by holding onto the arms of my chair. He was still standing as he replied, "Seriously Azalea, don't you know? Must I always have to explain things to you?"

He stood back up and stared at me in slight disbelief. It was if he was studying my reaction. I probably appeared beyond help as once again, my mouth hung slightly slacked open as I shrugged. As I closed my mouth, I clenched my jaw slightly. I mean, I hated admitting that I was honestly missing something. I quickly gathered my thoughts but came up with nothing. I cleared my throat, "I'm sorry Cethios, I don't know what you are talking about."

Cethios took another step back frowning as he crossed his arm across his chest. He sighed, "I actually thought that you'd figure this one out on your own. Or, I thought that he would have told you. He trusts you more than he does me."

Ok, now I was becoming frustrated. I stood and opened my wings to their fullest. I flew up a bit as our eyes locked. I shouted, "Would you just tell me! I haven't got the slightest clue Cethios!"

He lifted his hands and placed them carefully upon my shoulders, slightly pushing me down forcing me to land upon the ground. His expression fell with slight sadness as he replied softly, "Azalea... James is Immortal."

Loop Hole

11

My mouth dropped as I fell back into my chair with a soft thud. I was in complete and utter disbelief. I mean, I don't understand how that could be? Why wouldn't he tell me, did he not trust me? How was it that Cethios knew and I didn't?

So many questions swirled within my subconscious mind, it was almost numbing. So, it was about an hour or so of Cethios simply pacing in front of me. He was probably allowing me to take everything in and process, I'm sure he needed the time as well. Somewhere within that hour he had managed to find cups of water and sweet bread for us to eat. Finally, Cethios crossed his arms over his chest and cleared his throat, I guess my time was up. Either that or his throat was severely dry. Cethios whispered through his lips, "Azalea."

I slowly moved my gaze towards him until they finally met his eyes. I was able to finally speak after what seemed like eternity. As I opened my mouth, I stumbled out the first words that wanted to come out first, "So James is, Immortal? How? And most importantly, why didn't he tell me?"

For the first time ever, I was upset with James. How could he have not told me! I could have understood, I think. I wouldn't have told anyone, I'm sure. And why did Cethios know and not me? Once again Cethios cleared his throat. Cethios stepped closer as he knelt in front of the chair, I sat in. He gently took my hands within his, "Azalea, please do not be angry with James. Allow me to tell you that, I honestly stumbled upon this information on my own. He did not whisper a word to me. But, that day before the ball began, I was given orders to find James and kill him before anything had started. I was to dispose of him before he could have the chance on reaching you. They were afraid he would try and stop you from accepting me at the ball. They were afraid he would interfere with their plans. But as much as I was unwilling to do the task, I had no choice but to follow orders. But little did they know that he was going to survive. Only I knew he'd be alright. Well, besides you now."

Cethios stopped and seemed to ponder something as he dazed off into the oblivious. He continued to hold onto my fingers as he twiddled them within his. He was deep in thought so I didn't think to stop him. But suddenly a huge smile flooded his face as he asked, "Azalea, do you remember when you went back to your room that day before the ball; that day that you thought I killed James."

I stared into his eyes as I mumbled through my lips, "Of course I do, I remember it as if it was yesterday. You had red and white rose petals covering my entire floor. I had to tiptoe around them because I was afraid I'd slip on one. I actually though you went nuts with it."

"That was the point Azalea. When an Immortal renews, the gates of Immortality open and petals fall from the sky wherever their body lies. So, I went crazy with petals all over the place so Zethron would not figure it out. I even dropped some on my way to your room and here and there within the castle. And if he did stumble upon it I wanted him to think that it was just me making a mess everywhere."

The thought suddenly hit me. I remember seeing red and white rose petals on the floor near us by the City of Xylina, when Xanthus and Theron were still arguing with each other. I didn't think nothing of it them, but now, that just meant that his life renewed because he didn't survive the fall.

Of course, suddenly Cethios broke my thoughts from wandering as his smile faded slightly and he replied, "But you know what? When I saw James running about in Urinia, I saw that he had a thick scar upon his neck where I slashed my sword. That was very odd I thought. Immortals don't have scars when they completely renew. Which means someone disrupted his renewal and saved him." He paused and turned his gaze away from me as he quickly pondered. And as he turned back towards me he squeezed my hands a bit tighter. He understood completely, "Oh Azalea, it was you wasn't it? That explains why he kept gazing towards the wall. Oh Azalea I understand now, he saw you spying. He saw you standing there, watching us. Oh man, nothing hides from that fairy, I tell you." He stood and began to pace on his now pressed path in the grass. As he paced, he kept one hand on his chin and the other upon his back. He turned towards me suddenly. I think he pieced it all together. Man, I hate how easy it is for him to figure things out. "Azalea, I think James actually allowed or perhaps wanted for you to see something extreme that night. He needed you to see, he needed you to get angry. It had to be dramatic so therefore you could release your magic, as I did to Xanthus in the dungeon. That's why I ticked him off, so that way his magic could be freed. Oh Azalea, don't you see, that's why you can manipulate the energy from the shackles themselves, which no other fairy has ever done before. Your powers are already freed. Don't you see, James had you see so you could do just that. And your new immense power prevented him from his renewal. You thought he was truly dying and you saved him."

I probably looked beyond confused, because Cethios frowned and threw his hands up in the air giving up. He grunted, "You know that lightning globe that you chucked at me in the ballroom; which actually was a big shocker for me that you figured it out. But that day in the Depths of Galligro when you thought I took Xanthus' life; you enlarged and enhanced that little black rain cloud, that forms above you, into a violent thunderstorm. You manipulated it and actually left it there until we were out of view, I'm sure of it."

If there was a face for an utterly shocked fairy, I would be doing it right now. I mean, slowly but surely this was all making sense. I wasn't sure how but it actually was. It was all falling into place like fog lifting on a muggy morning.

I briefly placed my hands upon my face as I rubbed my cheeks slowly. Suddenly, I let them both fall into my lap. I screamed slightly, it all suddenly made sense. I can manipulate that lightning bolt that I somehow figured out how to use and the water globes as well. It all now made sense to me. Oh man, all this new knowledge juggled within my subconscious mind. I took in heavy breaths as my head seemed as if it was going to spin off. Oh my, the overload.

I suddenly felt Cethios' warm fingers upon my back as he massaged my neck and soothed my tension. My head sagged forward slightly as I relaxed into the massage. Without lifting my head, I replied to him, "So how is it that you know that James is Immortal?"

Cethios sighed as he continued to gently rub my back, "Well as hard as it is to believe, James has chosen me to be his successor. Even though he thinks I went wrong somehow. I never told him about my Blood-Oath. It's my mistake and my burden, not his. And one day, I will explain it all to him. And I know he'll be disappointed but, he'll forgive me. And he'd probably would say that this all went according to fate and he wouldn't want to change it any other way but... he deserves to hear the truth. And when I am ready, which is soon I feel, I will tell him. And yet, even after all that I have been through; I still come here to one of his old quarters to think and to study. And as strange as this sounds, I actually stumbled upon one of his old journals. And as much as I knew it was wrong, I read it.

That's how I found out. The room that we are in right now, no one knows how to enter it, just James and I. He showed me before you were born. I believe he wanted me to find out about him."

Well, I guess I could give Cethios that one. Although the next time I see James, he was going to hear it from me. And as much as I wanted to just sit here and think about all of this, I knew we had to carry on. I grunted, "Alright then, so what do we do now?"

I heard Cethios take in a deep breath and he slowly let it out, "Well, first I actually need your help on a couple of things."

I knew it, I knew he would want something from me. I sighed, "What specifically do you need me for?"

I heard him gulp and take in another deep breath. It was as if he was preparing himself. He replied slowly, "Well, first I need an Immortal to forgive me for killing a pure Immortal, whose life cannot renew, Mirage. Because yet, even though I did not slay him, I was still caught in the Blood Rain of Immortal Life. My heart and my soul ache until the very day I am forgiven. Ironically, sort of already an Immortal myself, unable to die, but cursed. If I am ever stabbed per say in the heart, I will stay in that death form, choking out my every word for eternity. I am cursed never to live my true life ever again. But I need to be truly forgiven to heal and renew, for my heart and soul yearn to be free."

I grunted almost smugly, "So, what does that have anything to do with me?"

Cethios sighed as he continued to rub my back gently almost sensually. Was he trying to suck up to me or what? It did feel relaxing but, that was it, nothing more than just relaxing. He continued, "Well, only an Immortal can forgive and free, and only an Immortal can release a Blood-Oath without its consequences. I need, and want to be free of Theron and Zethron."

I lifted my head as I turned back to see him. Cethios stepped back as if he was waiting for me to explode or something. That wasn't my intention but, I was getting angered. He raised his hands up as they glowed a dim white; it was if he was surrendering. I asked, "Let me get this straight. You want me to forgive you and free you, since I am an Immortal." Cethios nodded shyly as he cringed a bit as if he was expecting me to yell at him. I continued, "Why didn't you simply ask James to do all of that for you in the first place?"

Cethios shrugged, "I didn't believe he would. But I have faith in you."

Now I exploded. I stood from my chair as I flew up and around towards him. I shoved my hands at his chest as I shouted, "Then release me!"

Cethios took a step back as he almost whimpered, "Well there's a slight problem to that. Sort of a step back per say."

What was he talking about? How could that be? Ugh, this was really frustrating. I flew forward to get closer to him as his back slammed into the wall of books behind him. "Cethios! Take these off!"

He matched my shouting as he threw his hands up, "I can't!"

"Why not? I promise Cethios I will help you! Just take these things off!"

"That's not it, I can't! Only the one who placed them upon you can release you from their grasp! And that was... That was Zethron."

I closed my wings and fell upon the floor onto my knees, I'm doomed. I was surly going to be taken. And the worst part of it was that I would probably die from slow torture. Zethron killed my mother without a doubt. And there wouldn't be any reason that would stop him from killing me. The truth of it all was that Zethron would never release me from these shackles. Once again, I'm doomed. But before I could continue on with my thoughts Cethios whispered, "But there is a loop hole to that."

I lifted my head towards him as I too whispered, "And what is that?"

A smirk came upon his face as he replied, "Remember when Xanthus took you to the markets in Trinafin..."

I didn't even allow him to finish as I stood and interrupted him, "Cethios I know you were there. King Alcander told me that you wrote to him telling him that you found me in their city. I'm sure you probably stalked us. But what does that have to do with me becoming free?"

Cethios frowned, "Would you allow me to finish without interruption? I have a point you know."

I frowned and shrugged my shoulders. I don't remember anything that would be of importance there. So I replied with a sarcastic smile, "Go ahead Cethios, prove me wrong. I remember that day very clearly, what about it?"

"Well, it wasn't just me in the city that day following you until you took off on that dragon. It was me and Delphina."

Great, I was confused all over again. "Who are you talking about?"

Cethios smirked to himself as he gazed down at his feet. He seemed to kick some invisible rock or something as he replied shyly, "I'll share with you a piece of my puzzle if you promise not to breathe a word."

I nodded and whispered, "Nothing shall escape these lips."

Cethios smirked as he gazed back up to me, "Well James and Falin are Immortals, husband and wife of air and sea. They both can enchant only one other of their kind to unite with the Eternal Spirits and become Immortal. And they can unite other kinds that are not of their own if need be. That is if the other Ancient Ones cannot fulfill that. And the reason why they can do that is because they were the first that were united by the Eternal Spirits themselves. James and Falin are called The Ancient Ones. I read a little about them from one of James' journals. I believe there were six of them. I'm not sure myself what happened to the others but, going back to the main subject. I heard that Falin was the one that enchanted you and Xanthus, air and land. And from what I understand is that the last unity failed, many centuries ago. Although I'm not sure if it was the second chosen ones or if it was the actual Ancient Ones that failed at that. But, James and Falin have decided to enchant another unity of their kind to join them of air and sea, like them, since they are Ancient Ones apparently ready to retire all responsibilities. And actually, for air and sea, it is me and Delphina who are destined. Delphina is James and Falin's daughter. We are their successors. We have been keeping our relationship a secret for our safety for quite some time now. Our enchantment to unite has been placed on hold, until all of this is over."

I opened my mouth to reply something but I changed my mind and closed it with a pop. I should allow him to finish. I mean, I think I was still in shock to the fact that James is actually an Ancient One. Who knew all this time that I called him that, that I was actually right! Cethios smiled and continued, "Yes well, that's my own story to go off in. But change of subject and back to the point. That day…"

My thoughts burst through my mind and I couldn't help but interrupt him, "Wait, how could you live with yourself? Didn't you sleep with Razyna and all those other fairies in Whisperia and even Urinia! Do you really think you can be faithful to your Delphina once this is all over? If this ever does get over."

Cethios frowned. "Really Azalea? I can't believe you think so little of me. Truth be told, Razyna ended up in Theron's chambers multiple times in the middle of the night. She always figured it was me in there. And of course, by day break Theron was gone into a different chamber so, she never even knew. And, all those other fairies in Whisperia and Urinia, really Azalea? Theron's evil flows within me yes; it does cloud my actions most of the time but, beside the point. I never went all the way and slept with any of them. Kissing a few here and there to keep up with the rouse is hardly called unfaithful. Besides, thankfully Delphina is very understanding. She knows who and what I was and am. She knows I can't help it, much. Besides, our love is at stake if I act otherwise. But honestly Azalea, truthfully, I have been faithful to my Delphina. So, may I continue or do you have something else to accuse me of?"

I shook my head. Alright I'll try not to interrupt him anymore. Cethios walked past me as he headed over to the bed. He took his boots off and sat there upon the bed momentarily with his arms upon his legs. He was taking in deep breaths as he began to rub his neck with his right hand, as his palm glowed a slight purple. It was intriguing to watch him as he soothed himself.

And for some strange reason, I yearned to be by his side. I wanted to help smoother his pain with my fingertips but, I kept my ground and refused my legs the freedom to move. I stayed where I was supposed to be. Moments later he replied, "That day Delphina purposely set out to find you and Xanthus. She was given the task to find you both, and make it seem as if you two had won these necklaces. You see, Zethron made the mistake by giving me those shackles and wanting me to keep them for him until we had you. So Delphina and I created a key, with the help of the Eternal Spirits, which will actually unlock the shackles without having the one who placed them there present. We formed this key and then split it, and created necklaces. We had successfully hidden the key in plain sight, but invisible and unknowing to Zethron. We had the perfect…"

I had suddenly put it all together as I remembered the one thing that did stand out from my time in the City of Trinafin. I interrupted him as I shouted, "I knew it! I knew she looked familiar! She has James' eyes and

Falin's hair! I've seen Falin in the painting, the one that is concealing one of my mother's chambers. That orange hair, she is the girl from the market! And I saw her in the caves when we entered the castle of Urinia through that entrance! Oh! I remember what she said about the necklaces! Cethios, she said that when we place them together, they would unlock anything that our hearts desire! The necklaces are the key! I get it!"

I was so excited I forgot how to walk. I flew over to him and landed right in front of him. I startled him with my quick reaction. Cethios smiled as he stood. He slowly started to reach towards my face. It seemed as if he was going to kiss me once again as he leaned forward. But I quickly reached for my necklace that was upon my neck and took it off. I shoved it hard upon his chest. He took a slight step back as it seemed like I stunned him. Now, I don't know what he was thinking but, as much as my hormones were shouting yes, my heart was shouting no. I replied to Cethios almost breathlessly, "Here, take it! Xanthus has the other one. All we need to do is…" The sadness in Cethios eyes made me stop in midsentence. "What? Cethios what is it?"

Cethios sucked in a deep breath as if preparing himself for my anger. He swallowed loudly as he replied, "I actually took it from his neck, when I stabbed him in the Depths. But…"

"But what Cethios? Where is Xanthus' necklace?"

He stared at me as tears seemed to swell in his eyes. He replied softly, "I accidently dropped it on our way here."

I couldn't contain my rage any longer. The only thing that could have set me free was lost somewhere, who knows where? I mean, how would of you felt? So, I lost it. "You did what! How could you! The only thing that led to my freedom is now lost forever!"

Cethios raised his glowing white palms in surrender as I instantly smacked them. He was frustrating me even more when he did that. He frowned at my reaction as he attempted to replied as calmly as he could, "I couldn't balance myself, hold onto you, hold on to Krynton and concentrate on not dropping the necklace while Krynton is flying at high speed. And you didn't help either as you kept struggling about."

"So, then it's my fault that you dropped it!"

"Better it than you, right?"

Was he crazy? "No! You should have dropped me instead! Because honestly, I am dead without it! What's the point of my survival without my freedom! I'd rather die from a great fall than have Zethron kill me himself!"

I felt like I wanted to tear him to shreds. But once again, I knew I had to listen to my brains rather than my emotions. I had to relax. Besides, me beating him up would not help any of us. Perhaps make me feel better at first but in the end, I'm sure I would feel terrible when I was done.

I realized that I was still flying as my nose was basically touching his. I flew back a bit to get some distance between us. I didn't need Cethios trying to kiss me again. That is the last thing I need right now. But Cethios surprised me as he stepped forward and embraced me. He hugged me tightly as he whispered gently in my ear, softly brushing his lips upon the edges of my ear lobe, "We will fight forever if we have to. And I'll look for the other necklace for all eternity until I have it. If I could I would poof myself from here to there. I will always..."

That's it! A brilliant idea had just come to me. So naturally, I hugged him tighter in return, he grunted slightly as perhaps I embraced him a bit too hard. I huffed out in excitement, "Cethios that's it, poof! What a genius idea! Poof!"

I think I confused him and perhaps frightened him too. He slowly pushed me back as he held onto my shoulders. He gazed at me with much concern as he replied, "Azalea, have you permanently lost it?"

No, I didn't lose it. I wasn't going nuts; it was a perfect idea! I laughed as I let go of Cethios and flew over to the balcony. I stopped and landed in front of the translucent enchantment. I took in a deep breath and closed my eyes and concentrated. I had a brilliant idea; it was fool proof! This time I would stick to my plan, because this was going to work. That little chandelier dragon from Trinafin was going to save my life.

I stood there with my eyes closed thinking of that little chandelier dragon. I was trying to visualize it within my mind. I honestly did not know how or what I should be doing to call upon it. I remembered Xanthus telling me that we can but, he never told me how. I mean, should I call for it out loud? If it is out loud, what do I say? How should I say it?

As I continued to stand there concentrating and pondering, I heard a muffled laugh behind me. I ignored him. I took in deep breaths and slowed my breathing to relax a little more. I focused on the gentle breeze as it pushed its fingers through my hair, tossing it here and there. I felt the heat smoother itself against my cool skin, it was sensational. I concentrated some more.

Another muffled laugh, this time a bit louder, then the question, "Azalea, what are you doing? Are you kidding me right now? You can't be serious?"

Without opening my eyes I replied to him as I stretched my wings out and my arms forward with my palms up, "I am calling forth the crystal dragon from the chandelier. I am in need of its services."

There was a pause, then more questions, "Azalea have you lost your mind? We need to be leaving right now to go out there, not just standing about! We need to go looking for that key before night fall. Theron would surely be here by then. Azalea are you listening to me right now? Azalea!"

"Shush Cethios!" Oh yeah, I just did. I needed to do this and him interrupting my thoughts was not helping me.

I heard Cethios grunt to himself as he started cursing under his breath. He began to pace, I could hear his footsteps upon the grass. After a few moments he stopped and replied, "Azalea, do you know why I am unbeatable?"

At this I stopped and turned to face him. It seemed as if he was glaring at me. Now, what on earth could I have done to upset him? I responded to his question, "No Cethios, I don't know why you are unbeatable. But what has that got to do with our situation right now."

"Think about it Azalea, did you not pay attention to James' teachings. I am unbeatable because when I fight, I fight with courage. I do not allow that to fail me. You see, if you fight in your own anger you will be defeated, therefore I do not allow it to inherit and dwell into my actions. I do not allow it to consume my soul, for if I do, I would fail."

I crossed my arms and frowned, surely he had a good point to this. "So what is the moral to your story?"

Cethios stepped closer to me as he whispered through his teeth, "Which means I cannot fight in anger. And by you being so foolish right now, you are angering me to the core. Which means, I will not be able to fight off Theron once he gets here. I will not be able to save my life and protect yours."

"Then don't get angered and trust me." I turned from him and continued to close my eyes and concentrate. Then somewhere behind me I heard a crash of things falling to the ground, and much cursing. Shish, he was losing it. But I had faith, I believed in that chandelier dragon. I couldn't lose my focus. It was going to come. I just know it!

As a few moments passed us, Cethios grew quiet, finally. But suddenly I felt Cethios brush past me as I heard him mumble something under his breath. I felt a gush of heavy heat rush past me, followed by the gentle breeze again. Cethios wrapped one of his arms around my waist, slightly jerking me into his side. He brushed his lips around the outer edge of my ear as he whispered, "There, I removed the translucent wall. So feel free to jump over without flight. I will be doing so in just a few moments myself since we are just waiting here so carelessly for death. It would make Theron and Zethron's job a lot more difficult if we are already done with. You know, you could at least..."

My patience ran out as I turned to face him. Whoa, I wasn't thinking how close his face was to mine as I collided with his forehead. The thud seemed to echo in my ears as I naturally reached for my face and as he released me. Ugh, I hope this wasn't going to leave a bruise. "Cethios, would you just have some faith in me! I can't do this if you don't give me the chance. Trust me, only a royal blood can do this, hence why I am concentrating! And with all of your discouraging cursing, you are distracting me! I know the chandelier dragon can do this!"

The look on Cethios face was priceless. He was in utter shock and in astonishment. Perhaps he was in shocked at my outburst. He quickly changed his facial features as he appeared smug. What was his issue, was he glad that I knocked my face into his? He smirked and replied, "So my Azalea, would you be a dear and describe this crystal chandelier dragon to me?"

You know, he was going to drive me nuts calling me that. And I don't think that Xanthus would be too keen on that. But I shrugged it off for now as I took in a deep breath and straightened up. I thought to myself, perhaps he was mocking me somehow but, I took this opportunity to relax. Perhaps I can get him to calm down enough for me to concentrate a bit more. And as I ran my fingertips over my hair I replied as smoothly as possible, "Well, they are the size of your fist per say. And they are made of this exquisite crystal that you can enchant. And they come in many different colors. Like…"

"Green."

I stared at him confused as he interrupted me. Seriously? I took a deep breath as I continued, "Yes, they could be green. And the unique thing about them is that in the middle, in the inside of the crystal dragon is a…"

"A diamond of ravishing color?"

Okay, now what was he doing? I crossed my arms across my chest as I paused. I frowned at him as he continued to smirk with his hands in his pockets. Ugh, he was so full of himself. If only I could reach over and grab a book, I would beat him with it. But I think I would be afraid of damaging the book. And just before I could say or do anything else I heard a faint roar right next to my left ear. I jolted a bit as it startled me at first. I quickly turned towards the sound as there in front of me was a green crystal chandelier dragon. It was flapping its little wings in harmony with the gentle breeze that was swaying it.

I took in a deep breath and held up my right palm as it softly landed upon it. It let out another low roar as it turned its gaze towards Cethios. It growled at him as I gently patted its little head. I turned towards Cethios and whispered over to him, "Perhaps you should take a step back."

Cethios grunted, "Why? It's not like that thing is actually going to hurt me."

452

"Perhaps not but you are disturbing its feelings. They are not keen on those who are disbelieving in them and who are not…"

Cethios raised his palms up as they glowed white. He took a couple of steps back and stared intensely as I turned my attention back to the crystal dragon upon my palm. It sat there patiently waiting for me. I whispered to it, "Hello my delicate yet strong friend. Thank you so much for coming all this way to help me. I am in need of your help."

I reached for my necklace but it wasn't there. And before I had the chance to panic, I saw the crystal dragon turn its head and hiss. Cethios was near me, he was handing me the necklace as it swung gentle in his grip. I nodded and took it from him. And although I was trying to be brave, Cethios appeared as if he had given up on all hope. The sadness upon him was unbearable to look at. I tore my gaze from him and closed my eyes tightly. I wanted to comfort him, to embrace him; I wanted to tell him that we were not doomed and that we were going to succeed. But I had to focus on my crystal dragon friend.

I opened my eyes and held up the necklace as I whispered back to the little dragon, "I am looking for the other one that looks exactly like this. My friend over there has lost it along our way from the Depths of Galligro, to where we are now. Do you think you would be able to accept this task, and try to retrieve us that necklace as quickly as possible. It is important that your quest be successful. Do you accept this challenge?"

The crystal dragon bent its head low as if it was bowing at me. It then let out one more roar as it took flight off of my palm. It soared gracefully out of the balcony window as it suddenly vanished with a small puff of black smoke.

I took in a deep breath and exhaled it slowly as I walked out onto the balcony and into the sunlight. I closed my eyes and allowed the warm air to smoother my skin. It felt good as I pondered over all of the recent information that Cethios had replied to me. And as I pondered I suddenly became aware of my feeling for him. But not in that passionate way, I actually felt a bit sad for Cethios. He had pretended to hate me because secretly he had been trying to save me all along. What a burden to carry all this time.

And this whole time Cethios still remained as James' successor, even though James thinks that Cethios went mad. Well, like Cethios said, he would tell James the truth. James deserves the truth. And as weird as it is to think about, the one good thing that Cethios did succeed in is somehow always knowing things like James.

But he made one mistake though; he trusted Theron and allowed himself to foolishly do a Blood-Oath with him. And all that time Cethios had been given the thought that he was going to be told, just who exactly was his true father. But no, he had been lied to and was betrayed.

I opened my eyes as I stared out into the jungles below me. Weird. I do not recognize any of those. Just exactly where did Cethios have me? Where was I? But before I could carry those thoughts I heard Cethios behind me. I replied to him, "You know what Cethios; I will do everything I can to help you find your true father. I will remove that evil that binds you to Theron in that Blood-Oath. And I will forgive you so you can free your soul from the cursed Blood Rain of Mirage. And we will defeat Theron and Zethron, somehow. But we will."

Cethios placed his palm gently upon my shoulder as he replied, "I will release you from those shackles Azalea I promise. I will free you. I promised to keep, and I intend on keeping that promise, forever."

We both stood there staring off into the jungles as we pondered with our brief silence. But of course, being with Cethios, that means it doesn't last very long. He cleared his throat and replied, "Are you sure you can trust that crystal dragon Azalea? I don't doubt you but, certainly we are relying our very lives on that little crystal dragon and that thought. The thought that, that crystal dragon will find the necklace before night fall and bring it to us."

I sighed as I continued to stare off into the distance. I couldn't bear to gaze upon his face, it pained me so. So without turning my gaze I reached for his hand upon my shoulder with my right hand and gave it a small squeeze. "As much as I trust that Xanthus is coming for me, I trust that crystal dragon. It will succeed, I just know it. Have faith Cethios."

I heard Cethios mumble something under his breath as he tugged upon my right hand. I turned around to face him as he still kept my hand within his. He was twirling the ring that resided upon my middle finger. I couldn't help it, I blushed in embarrassment. And of course that amused Cethios as he replied with a chuckle, "So, that elf has already proposed to you huh?" He continued to rub my fingers and twirl the ring around my finger as he bent over and slowly kissed my palms. His eyes meet mine briefly but then he turned them somewhere off into the distance. It seemed as if he was going to reply something but, he stopped in mid thought as if he was caught off guard. He gently released my fingers, as his jaw dropped in astonishment. What was it that had him confused and shocked so quickly? I turned to face the jungles to see if I could see what he was lost in.

An enormous grin from ear to ear spread upon my face. Warmth filled my inner core as something far off twinkled in the distance. Whatever this thing was, it had incredible glistening rainbows shooting from all around it, as if the sun's rays were caught within a dance around it. The colors swirled so iridescently I was in complete awe. It was coming closer and closer at top speed. Without removing my gaze from this thing that approached us I replied to Cethios, "Cethios, your words are genuine to the core right?"

He chuckled, "Every one of them Azalea, every single word."

My breath was taken from me as I replied with an exhale, "Well then... Prepare yourself to set me free..."

****

The Ruins

13

James pushed the tangled vines aside from his view as he ventured deeper into the jungle. He was hoping the ruins were just a few more moments away, for the excruciating heat was starting to press down on him. Heavy beads of sweat drenched his forehead and the back of his neck as moisture clung to him. He was positive just a further more deep breaths and he would be alright to continue on without stopping. The Ruins of Yaisla were tucked away so well behind greenery, that if he hadn't been there before, he would completely overlook it. But without a doubt he knew he was getting closer as he now paced his footsteps with his breathing.

The ruins were that of an ancient castle that once stood with massive integrity and honor. During its reign at one point a long time ago, it contained vast rooms of many varieties that there was no need to go anywhere else. It had so much life and laughter within its walls which could last a life time. But in the end, it had become just a memory, a symbol of the last blood war centuries ago. They were ruins of a grand castle that was of his birth place that he once cherished; the castle of his mother.

As James pressed on with more determination with every step, he hoped that he would reach his destination before Zethron did. For he had caught word along the way by a passing soldier, that Zethron had discovered the hidden location of where Queen Whistalyn slept. And that Zethron was probably there as he spoke. But he didn't know what to believe.

But of course for centuries Queen Whistalyn slept under the death spell that was once placed upon her by Zethron and James. And although Zethron's first arrow was to kill her, James sent out another to try to alter and help over time, heal her of that evil in her slumber. And now Queen Whistalyn still slept undisturbed as her own body fought off that evil, until the right day came for her to wake. In which case was any day now.

Much worry filled James as he had no doubt that by now, the enchantments that he had placed to hide Queen Whistalyn, had now diminished to nothing. She would be vulnerable to travelers passing by if they found her hidden location. Time was running out and he had to hurry.

During the end of the battle at the Depths of Galligro, he had lost sight of Zethron, so James was worried that he had gone off to a head start.

As James continued his horrendous pace his surrounding had finally become familiar to his ancient eyes. The jungle around him thickened as he now had to squeeze ever so gently between the trees. He seemed so graceful as he danced around the vines, making sure he himself did not get tangled in their grasp. Suddenly his breaths were taking a toll upon his chest; his constant effort to not stop had caught up with him. He bent over and placed his hands upon his knees as he attempted to focus. He concentrated on settling his heart beats as they effortlessly thumped loudly within his ears.

Within moments he stood and quickly realized just where he had stopped for his rest. A smile came upon his lips as he extended his right palm out towards some vines that seemed clumped together upon an enormous tree. The vines started to sway as if a gentle breeze was passing through them. But James knew all too well that it wasn't a breeze, for it was too dense for any soft wind to pass through. Suddenly the vines gentle sway converted to quivering. Within moments small lime bulbs quickly formed and transformed into bright buttery flowers with a tan bulb in the center. Once the flowers bloomed the vines continued their gentle sway in the false breeze.

James reached out with his left hand towards one of the flowers as he gently stroked its petals four times. The flower seemed to giggle with delight as it detached itself from the vine. It slowly glided through the air and landed upon James' left palm. He moved his right index finger slowly towards the flower, fully aware of the flowers true intentions. The flowers' petals suddenly became sharp as a knife as it pricked his finger.

James continued to stand still as the flower carefully collected two drops of blood from his fingertip. The flower swirled it around within its petals until it melted within its core. Once complete the petal froze, as it slowly began to morph into a burgundy rose. Once finished it bowed to James as if accepting him. James bowed his head in return and at once gently placed the flower back upon the vine from where it first detached itself from. Like a wave from the ocean, all of the other flowers upon the vines morphed into red roses. And although patience wasn't really on James' mind, he waited until the vines swayed apart revealing a stone door. A sigh of relief brushed against James' soul as the first step to get to Queen Whistalyn was still under its oath. There was no sign that anyone had entered here… so far.

As he brushed his fingertips upon the cold stone, it slowly opened to reveal a ceiling less hall. And at once he quickly stepped in and closed the stone door quietly behind him. Inside were giant white marble pillars that seemed to stretch into the fluff of the clouds above. Below him laid a broken stone pathway with tall emerald weeds peeking through. And at once he started to jog through it as his footsteps echoed between the ivory walls. He had no worry on any other type of trap within these walls. For he himself was the one who placed them there in the first place. And within this hall, there were no enchantment.

A little over half an hour, he finally came to a halt in front of a room that had a stone balcony facing outward towards him. James stood underneath it and jumped up to reach it, as he proceeded to climb it. As he jumped over the stone banister he landed near four throne chairs drenched in velvet jade fabric. The middle two thrones though were much larger than the outer two.

He closed his eyes and briefly touched the fabric with his fingertips. A warm smile came to his lips as the memories of his childhood touched his subconscious mind. For after much time had passed him he was finally home. But unfortunately he could not stay for long. He was there on a mission, on a task that he could not fail at. He opened his eyes and continued on, he could not dwell on the memories of ancient times at this time of rush.

There behind the throne chairs was a wall draped with velvet sapphire fabric that he gently pushed aside. There upon that wall was a wooden door that appeared fragile to the touch. He reached out ever so carefully and pushed it open.

James stepped into a large circular room. Once he entered the room, it became lit with candles that hung in midair upside down at almost eye level. The white candles surrounded the rooms' entirety as they glowed brightly. Below the candles were another set of candles that were upright and lit as well. Wax slowly fell and rose between them as if keeping their consistency.

The orange flames kept dancing upon their wick as James continued slowly into the room. The circular room itself seemed to be made up of about twenty white doors. The doors themselves were about two feet apart and made out of soft white feathers. The feathers themselves seemed to glisten under the glow of the candles.

As James reached the center of the room the door he entered from slowly closed with a bang leaving him alone in the room with only the candles brightly glowing. James closed his eyes once more, only this time concentrating upon the feathery doors. He outstretched his right palm as it glowed with a burgundy hue. He began to step forward and carefully maneuver around the candles. He was gently brushing his palm upon each door as he circled the room.

Once finished he stepped back upon the center of the room and sat upon the floor. He remained motionless with his eyes closed within his meditating position. He remained that way with his palm resting up upon his knees.

Suddenly his left palm started to glow with the same hue as his right palm. They glowed brighter until both of his palms were a fiery red. And once his palms were intensely glowing, the flames upon the candles slowly drifted away from their wick. They floated around the room and towards James. Within moments the flames started to swirls around him as their speed gracefully increased.

James' palms intensified as they glowed brighter and brighter, until both of his palms were suddenly a blaze. Within moments of that a bright light pulsed through the room and halted abruptly as the swirling flames stopped still as if frozen in time.

James' palms ceased their flames as he finally opened his eyes. He turned his head slightly as if waiting for something. There was a sharp crack behind him. He stood cautiously and turned to face the door. But this door was not of delicate feathers any longer, this door was on fire. The orange flames danced as if calling forth to him, as if inviting him to dance along.

He carefully walked over to the door as he pushed aside the weightless orange flames, as if they were dust particles within the air. He stood in front of the door as the heat from the flames soothed his skin. He whispered to the flames, "If I am truly a liar, go ahead and set me on fire. But flame of Eternal might, today we will set things right. I ask of you to open this door, so that I may enter through the floor. For that day is near, for all to be revealed."

Suddenly the floor started to rumble as James flew up a bit to prevent himself from jolting around in the quake. Stone stairs now formed and circled downward into a darkness hole below him. Moments later the quake ceased and James landed back onto the ground. James stared into the darkness as he pondered his thoughts. He was afraid of this, no lighting, one small default in his planning.

He gazed upon the room as he raced through his thoughts. He ended up staring at the flames that were frozen in time simply hovering in place in midair. He frowned, of course, how could he have let that slip his subconscious mind? He leaned over to a hovering flame and whispered to it, "Shall we, if you don't mind."

Like a gust of wind, all of the flames shot down the stairs and lit the way as they seemed to stop a few feet apart at a time. James smiled to himself as he quickly started to make his way down the stairs. After about what seemed like an eternity of steps he reached yet another white feathered door. But this time he seemed hesitant on touching it or approaching it too close.

He stretched his right palm towards it, but quickly pulled his arm back. James closed his eyes and took in a deep breath. He just had to continue on, lives depended on him. He opened his eyes with more determination as he held his breathe and brushed his fingertips upon the feathers. He crunched his eyes shut as he waited. Moments passed and nothing had changed. He opened his eyes cautiously as he let out his breathe in a whoosh. He relaxed and ran his fingers over the feathered door once more. Nothing happened as he sighed in relief. He leaned over and rested his palms and his forehead upon the feathered door. He whispered under his breathe, almost hysterical, "Thank the heavens. My sisters' beloved has not been here."

He slowly opened the door and stepped in cautiously. At once he was within a room that had cathedral ceilings made of that clear translucent, viewing the grand sky above. Inside it seemed as if he had walked into an ancient secluded jungle. And there in the middle of it all, with a single strand of sunlight falling ever so gracefully upon her, was Queen Whistalyn. She was sleeping peacefully next to an enormous blue dragon with silver hue around the edges of its scales. She of course was being guarded by her husbands' dragon, Atrigo.

****

Trust

14

Xanthus stood at the very edge of the Gardens of Vinalin. He faced towards the south where the ocean would lie, staring out as if he could see it. Staring towards where he and Azalea had become one in the Cave of Esmera. And his heart burned with intensity, not knowing if his beloved Azalea would be alive or not at that very moment. He knew that he and Azalea were Immortals but, with her having those forsaken shackles on he knew she was helpless; everyone knew she was helpless.

A single tear fled his sore eyes as he quickly wiped it away. He did not want anyone to see that he was weak within his soul. And as moments passed him by, Rowen slowly walked up to him and stood by his side. Rowen stared off into the jungle as he carefully pushed his silver glasses up his nose and as he crossed his arms across his chest. He took in a deep breath as he replied over to Xanthus, "You know, there is no shame in shedding a few tears for the ones that you love."

Xanthus grunted as he rubbed his hands almost forcefully over his face and through his dark brown hair. He whispered through his soft lips, "I cannot. Crying is a sign of weakness, which I am not. I cannot be."

Rowen chuckled as he now turned slightly towards Xanthus. He replied in humor, "No Xanthus, the Eternal Spirits would actually call that strength. For tears is our souls' courage pouring out from our heart."

Xanthus turned towards Rowen as he raised an eyebrow confused, "Come on Rowen, your starting to sound like James. And that fairy hardly ever makes any sense at all." Xanthus turned from him as he gazed down towards his hands. He was fumbling two golden feathers between his fingertips. He stared at them and sighed, "Rowen, may I ask you something and confide in you momentarily?"

Rowen frowned at his question. "Xanthus when have you not been able to trust me? You use to always trust me before. Just because you left the classes within the islands and our Outcasted per say, that does not mean that our alliance was left there. I may follow your cousin Theron around but, that doesn't mean that I agree with most of his actions and thoughts." Xanthus nodded as he continued to fumble Azalea's feathers around within his fingertips. Suddenly Rowen placed his hands upon Xanthus', stopping him from his continuous fumbling of the feathers. Rowen replied as he let go of his hands, "Xanthus honestly, what is on your mind?"

Xanthus ran his fingers through his hair once more as he replied still staring at the feathers within his palm, "I feel hopeless Rowen. I do not fear on the idea, because I know Cethios is going to take Azalea this time. Who knows, I'm sure by now her Immortality and mine are already gone and in Cethios. And yet, I wonder if Azalea will stumble into a down fall and not want me anymore after that. I wonder; am I fighting a war that is unbeatable? Am I just prolonging the inevitable? What if the Eternal Spirits were wrong? What if Azalea was meant for someone else and not me? Perhaps I am understanding this all wrong. But I can't help but feel so lost. I honestly feel so… so ashamed for losing Azalea again. And I am confused on what truly is the right thing to do next."

Xanthus chuckled seeming as if his mind had been lost, "You know, as confusing as James is, is it weird that I am longing for his twisted words of wisdom right now."

Rowen ran a hand through his orange hair with red streaks as he took in a deep sigh. He too was confused and was unsure of the right words to say to his dear friend. But the only thing he can do is be honest. Rowen replied, "I don't know what words of comfort I can give you but, what I can tell you is what I do know. While in one of our free studies I've done, I came upon this book. And let me tell you that book was fragile to the core but, the Eternal Spirits that we live with share our wanting to combine in unity. Our own kinds are actually the ones that choose who we become Immortals with. The Eternal Spirits do not choose, we do, they only give the ones we select Immortality. That is our unity with them. In return to keep peace amongst us all, we unite air, water and earth with fairies, mermaids and elves. This has been tradition since the lands were created by them when we all first began. If we do not unite, there is war and hatred between the races that were not united. Example, you and Azalea unite earth and air. The last Immortals evidentially failed that, hence the war. And only a certain type of Immortal knowledgeable of the Eternal Spirits can perform that enchantment. And if I read correctly, I believe it can only be done on infants, I could be wrong though. But, we all know how rare it is to actually conceive a child. But as you saw at the Depths, peace is coming. Peace is amongst us because you and Azalea were chosen by your parents to lead this new unity. Peace is here because you both fight for that. And yes, if you do fail, if Cethios takes Azalea, we need to find a new unity of air and earth. And who knows how long it will be until then. And honestly, you need to give Azalea more credit than what you think. I may not know her to an extent but, I see it in her eyes, she is a fighter Xanthus."

When Rowen finished he stared off into the jungle as silence flowed within the air around them. The breeze pushed softly past them as it flowed with warmth. Rowen took short glanced at Xanthus but, he seemed as if he was lost in his own thoughts. Rowen sighed as he let his hands fall to his side. He replied to Xanthus softly, "Xanthus, for what it's worth, I think you should still be determined as all to bring the one that you love back within your arms. Taken or not, she loves you and that alone should thrive in your heart. Immortality or not, she belongs with you and not Cethios. I've seen the way she looks at you, and you need to make sure you get to her. Late or not at least you get to her."

Xanthus finally turned his gaze towards Rowen as he replied with a heavy sigh, "It's not that I doubt my love for her, it's just, I'm afraid of the state she will be in when I do find her. Or even if she would want me anymore."

Suddenly both Xanthus' hair and Rowen's flew forward in a gust of smoke. And as both of the elves turned, there was Cetus, sitting calmly behind them. Xanthus crossed his arms across his chest as he replied to his dragon, "And how long have you been sitting there?"

Cetus seemed to laugh a bit as he replied with another puff of smoke, "Long enough to know that we need to get you to Azalea, and fast. You don't do so well alone."

Xanthus shook his head as he replied to Cetus, "Thanks for that valuable information Cetus. Besides that point, what brings you here?"

Cetus stretched out his neck towards the castle then back towards them. "Your father, King Alcander, wishes your presence as well as Rowen's. He wishes to speak to you all before we head out tonight."

Xanthus nodded and whispered to his dragon friend, "Thank you Cetus, we are on our way."

And with that Cetus nodded and took off into the air. Rowen on the other hand turned towards Xanthus and patted him upon the shoulder. He too started to head towards the castle. Now, Xanthus stood there alone as he continued to hold on to Azalea's feathers. He closed his eyes and took in a deep breath as his thoughts settled. He just wanted everything to be calm like it was in the beginning, before the first war of the fairies and the elves. He wanted Azalea in his loving embrace, to hold her tightly against his chest, to caress her smooth skin, to kiss her softly upon the lips. But unfortunately he knew that was impossible at this very moment. And as he opened his eyes he took in a deep breath.

He will see to it, that one day he and Azalea will have their peaceful moments again. He was determined to do so. He wanted to always see that smile upon Azalea's face. And he was going to save her; he was going to be there for her.

He opened his palm and allowed the feathers to lift with the breeze and soar up into the air. He slowly dragged his tongue softly upon the corner of his lip as he whispered, "I'm coming for you Azalea, hang in there my love. No matter what, I'll move mountains if I have to, but I am coming."

The Orders

15

Xanthus walked into the castle through the grand hall. He gazed up to see the crystal chandelier made of the little colorful enchanted crystal dragons. They were all darting about twirling around each other lost in their own bliss. Suddenly one of the little chandelier dragons disappeared with a puff of smoke.

Xanthus stopped and stared at the crystal dragons. Did he just see what he thought he just saw or were his eyes playing tricks on him? If he did see one go, where would it be traveling too? Weird he thought. He shook his head and continued on his way. He was a bit distressed to concentrate on those crystal chandelier dragons. For they were about to enter midday and yet, here they were still in Trinafin. If he could of, he would have left after he had awoken from being renewed in the Depths but, his father had held him back about a day or so.

Moments later he pushed aside a tall wooden door as he entered the main ballroom of the castle. Inside was Morpheus, who seemed to be glaring at Theron, was standing next to Rowen and Latimer. And on the other side was Theron and Oleos. Oleos seemed to be standing next to Theron just to keep some kind of peace but, he kept his arms crossed upon his chest as if putting up with the arrangement. And King Alcander was sitting in his throne at the head of the ballroom as bright red suede fabric drenching the back wall.

And although the sun was shining brightly through the windows, the gloom on King Alcander's face sent chills over Xanthus' skin. There was something wrong about him these past few days, he just didn't know what. He wanted to ask his father really but, his own thoughts were elsewhere. Xanthus just knew that his father was alright and in no real danger. King Alcander knew how to take care of himself. So he shook off the thought that something just might be wrong. And once Xanthus stood next to Morpheus, King Alcander cleared his throat and began, "I have gathered you all here in great importance. I have collected my thoughts these past few days and I have come to a grand decision. A conclusion really, but I have orders for you all to follow, especially for you Xanthus and Morpheus."

Once those words escaped King Alcander's lips, Xanthus balled up his fists and took in a deep breath. What on earth could be more important than saving his love, Xanthus thought. The king knew the importance of him leaving and going to save his Azalea. What on earth could be swirling within his father's subconscious mind at this exact moment? Xanthus took in deep breaths to ease his reaction as he replied as calmly as he could, "Father, I have been patiently waiting for your words, thinking I was going to get words of wisdom, not words of orders. I cannot follow any at this time of hast. I need to find Azalea before she is taken and…"

King Alcander raised his right palm up as it glowed in a dim white hue. He interrupted, "My son, there are other situations that are of more importance than your Azalea."

Xanthus' mouth dropped in utter shock. Was he being serious right now? Who was this king that stood before him, not his father that's for sure. His father would not easily dismay a prophecy like it is nothing. And as Xanthus continued his quick pondering, he became enraged. And as calmly as he could and with much positive authority, he replied to King Alcander, "Father, I will not be doing anything else but going off and saving Azalea, saving our destiny with this land. Saving the prophecy my mother bestowed upon me many ages ago. You of all should know that you cannot force me to go against my wish."

Immediately King Alcander flushed red and stood as he shouted, "I am still king upon the land you reside in and your father! Your will is to your obligations, which is king in waiting, which therefore you must still abide by my orders until the day you start to reign. So, with a difficult heart I forbid you from going to Azalea until your orders are complete!"

Xanthus' fists began to glow a dim red as he took a step forward. But Morpheus quickly with took his arm and held him back, stopping him from doing something he'd probably regret later on. And from the other side of the room Theron chuckled to himself as he crossed his arms casually across his chest. Morpheus and Xanthus both turned towards him with a glare. Theron's smile faded once his eyes meet Xanthus. Theron replied with a slight chuckle, "Honestly I mean no disrespect here. But I am sure the king has his reasoning's behind having you not go and be with Azalea. Let us give him some credit don't you think Xanthus. He is our king you know."

Xanthus' fists glowed a bit brighter as he attempted to take a step forward towards Theron. But this time Rowen stepped in front of him as he placed his glowing white hands upon Xanthus chest. Rowen shook his head as he quickly let go of Xanthus and dimmed his hands. He whispered to him as he shook his head once more, "Xanthus do not be so foolish in acting in ways you will regret later on in your life. Be wise and think upon your actions before you act on your angers behalf."

At that Xanthus took a step back and gazed over to Theron. His blood burned as he saw Theron smirking and chuckling to himself as if laughing at some sort of secret joke. Xanthus replied over to his cousin Theron, "If you are a part of this Theron so help me I will…"

Theron raised his palms up as they glowed a dim turquois as he interrupted, "Please cousin, do not humor me, for laughter is simply my weakness on this day. Besides, your fathers' words are his own free will and not that of my own. Why would a king consult with me or even follow my advice, especially him being your father."

King Alcander interrupted then both as he spoke one word, "Xanthus." Xanthus turned back around to face his father as his fists dimmed in glow. His father continued, "Xanthus allow me to explain my reasoning before your anger clouds your judgment as it always seems to. I have received word that your mothers' resting tomb is being disturbed by someone or something. You and Morpheus must go to her and see to it that no harm comes her way."

Xanthus was confused by his father's words as he quickly asked, "But I thought my mothers' tomb was here, within Trinafin's castle. Where else would it be?"

King Alcander took in a deep breath as he sat back down seeming exhausted. And in Xanthus' eyes for some reason, his father seemed to be becoming paler. But then again, perhaps he was just getting upset with the news. And without thinking, Morpheus replied, "So you have been lying to Xanthus all this time?"

By now Theron couldn't hold it in any longer; he started to laugh out loud a bit. He rested his palms upon his hips as if to steady himself but once again, his laughter dimmed as he glanced over to Xanthus. Theron replied with a chuckle, "Oh and that's not all my dear uncle has been lying about. Go ahead uncle."

At this Xanthus became enraged and tried to lunge at Theron. But Rowen, Morpheus and now Latimer all attempted to restrain Xanthus as his fists were just about in flames. Xanthus hissed through his teeth at Theron,

"Don't you dare talk to my father in that manner. How in all hell do you know what my father lies about? You have no right to even be here Outcasted! And… and, what in all hell are you laughing about! So help me I will go over there and…"

King Alcander cleared his throat loudly as at once, Xanthus stopped struggling and stopped in midsentence. Xanthus turned toward King Alcander confused as the king replied with much sadness, "Xanthus, I admit it, I have lied to you on the whereabouts of your mothers' resting tomb, but only in sheer protection for her life. But recent events have set you along another temporary path. I am not forbidding you from going to Azalea. I know she can fend for herself until you arrive. But your mother still lives, and she needs you right now. For if she wakes, I need for you to deliver a message to her from me, and to keep her safe. Unfortunately for the sake of my elves, I cannot leave and go to her. And you must take Morpheus with you as well."

At that Morpheus stepped forward and replied to the king, "Your highness if I may. There is no doubt that I wouldn't join Xanthus on this incredible journey but, why do you say I must?"

King Alcander took in a deep breath as he waited momentarily before allowing any words to escape his lips. It was as if he was debating on if he wanted to release the words, he so desperately held onto all these centuries. But within another breath and without a doubt he replied, "That's because she needs to see you Morpheus, she needs to see you in person. For she would not believe Xanthus by his words, but with her own eyes she will. Tell her that I always truly loved her and that I honestly never meant to hurt her. And that one day, she and I will be together again."

At this Xanthus stepped closer to his father. He was now even more confused than ever. Xanthus asked, "Father, what is all of this about?"

King Alcander gazed at Xanthus as tears began to swell in his delicate eyes. He replied to his son, "These next words are actually meant for Morpheus…" By this time Morpheus now stood next to Xanthus as King Alcander continued, "Morpheus… Nylina is your true mother."

Morpheus chuckled as if hysterical as he replied, "Your highness I already know that she is."

King Alcander took in another deep breath as he closed his eyes and replied, "Yes but, it is about your father."

"What... About... My father..." Morpheus replied with slow deep breaths.

Then King Alcander replied softly with his eyes still closed, "I'm your father Morpheus."

King Alcander opened his eyes slowly and carefully to find both Morpheus and Xanthus staring off into the oblivious in shock. It seemed as if they were both made of stone as they stood there. And as King Alcander stared off to see the other elves, they too were in shock. The only one that seemed smug with the new news was Theron. It seemed as if he had already known and was waiting patiently for everyone else. But it seemed like moments later that Morpheus had regained some part of his subconscious when he replied softly, "But the letters, they all implied that my father was off on theses grand adventures in the sea and in other lands. The letters stated that he couldn't make it to be here, to watch me grow and that he desperately wished he could embrace his son and..."

At this, even though King Alcander appeared fragile, he jumped off of his throne and ran to his other son, Morpheus. He embraced him as if he had never seen him before. He embraced him just how he always wanted to. As King Alcander continued to hold onto his son he replied a bit muffled upon Morpheus' shoulder, "Forgive me Morpheus, forgive me my son. But you must know that I loved them both. I loved Nylina and Whistalyn, and still do. I couldn't abandon one when I adored both. I was young then, I couldn't send Nylina away when I was arranged to marry Whistalyn. I guess in the end they both knew but denied themselves the truth because they too loved me. But I should have told them, but in truth how could I? They were best friends. And I was foolish and selfish; I didn't want to lose either of them. But you and Xanthus are my sons. And yet I tell you that I am not one to look up to, I guarantee you that. But believe me when I tell you that I love you both, and I did write those letters to you in truth. I did have those adventures, at one point in my life, before I became king. I did go off with Atrigo. And I did too run from the crown to find love like your brother Xanthus. And that's when I found Nylina. I didn't know I was already destined for another when I returned; and I sure for one did not know that they were so close. But truly, forgive me for not telling you sooner, I only have myself to blame. My words of wisdom though have never faltered, but only the truth of myself. But my reign is almost over, then you and I, if you wish, we can take one of those grand adventures out in the sea with our dragons like I promised you."

A few more moments passed them all before Morpheus and King Alcander parted their embrace. They gazed over to Xanthus, whom still seemed to be in utter shock. But King Alcander waited patiently for Xanthus' words. He was afraid that Xanthus would deny him, seeing that he was unfaithful to his mother. And he didn't blame him. The king knew that being faithful meant everything to Xanthus. But King Alcander was prepared for his furry and he waited for it.

Moments later after much pondering, Xanthus turned to gaze into his fathers' eyes. It pained Xanthus knowing that his father had betrayed his mother. And yet the king had also betrayed Nylina's trust. And yet, who was Xanthus to judge the elf that he knew as his father. He was his reason for living. And as far as he can remember, King Alcander had raised them both, he and Morpheus, as his sons. Xanthus couldn't remember a time when he wasn't there for them.

So therefore, to Xanthus the title of his father was that, a father and a king. He could not pass judgment on his father that he loved dearly. But the kings' title as husband, that was onto Nylina and Whistalyn. That would be their judgment and not his. King Alcander's love was his weakness. And Xanthus knew all about that, for Azalea was his weakness. He would do anything for her. But in reality, what he didn't know was that like his mother, love was actually strength. For love gives you strength to achieve the impossible and overcome your fears for the one that you cherish so dearly.

Xanthus turned his gazed upon both Morpheus and his father. He replied softly, "Well then, in truth there is only one misfortune to this…"

Morpheus and King Alcander gazed at each other, then back over to Xanthus waiting for his respond. But impatiently King Alcander whispered to Xanthus, "And what specifically is that my son?"

Xanthus took in a deep breath as he gazed over to the head throne. Something had caught his eye but he quickly shrugged it off. He glanced back over to his father and to Morpheus as he replied, "The misfortune to Morpheus. Morpheus… You too are cousins with Theron."

A smile came upon Morpheus face as Theron shouted in dismay, "You know I am standing right here." And when no one replied to his outburst he replied a bit louder, "Well besides your great news dear uncle, why have you gathered us all here? I know it wasn't to hear this. Come now, what orders do you have for us?"

King Alcander took a step back and carefully eyed Theron. While Theron on the other hand once again had a smug grin upon his face. It was as if he had already known what was needed to be said. So, King Alcander cleared his throat and replied without taking his gaze off of Theron, "Yes well, early this morning we received a few letters from my brother, King Zyren. He is ill and is requesting the presence of Oleos, and wishes him to return to the main island and to his side at once."

With that being said, Latimer, Rowen and Oleos all gazed at each other with confused expressions. First, they thought they were casted out centuries ago, unable to take upon permanent residence on the main island. And second, why would the king want Oleos? Wouldn't he want his son Theron to be there? Oleos turned towards Theron as he asked, "Theron, I don't understand. Why would your father want me instead of you? Theron? Theron!"

Finally, King Alcander broke his gaze with Theron as he went back to sit upon his throne. Xanthus caught their gazes as now his thoughts were abrupt. Something was going on and he wasn't sure whether or not he completely believed Theron. But what could Xanthus say that Theron won't deny? He was up to no good and somehow, it involved his father.

Theron suddenly turned to Oleos as he with took an envelope from his inner pocket of his vest. He handed it to Oleos. Theron replied to him smugly, "Here, this belongs to you. I actually arrived a bit earlier here this morning and caught the servant that brought the letters. The first envelope I received was addressed to me simply stating that there were other envelopes that would be addressed to Oleos and King Alcander. It seems my dear father wants you by his side for some certain situations. No matter, I wouldn't have gone if he did call me forth. Perhaps that is why he is asking for you Oleos. He knows you will leap to his call."

At this Oleos crunched his eyes in dismay. He was not thrilled on how Theron replied his last words. But nonetheless he took the envelope and quickly removed the seal, opened it and read it. As his eyes skimmed the parchment as he replied, "Alright, and who says I'm going? Honestly Theron, it should be you not I."

As Oleos' eyes left the parchment King Alcander replied, "Oleos, King Zyren, my brother wishes you there by his side. That is an honor and a request made by a king. Go and seek his wisdom and spend every moment you can before he passes. Here, take this secured parchment. Give it to him as soon as you see him. I have already given him my peace."

Oleos bowed and went over to King Alcander and with took the parchment. Theron cautiously glared at the king and stared at the parchment as if he wasn't approving. But what was he to do? Oleos placed the parchment in his inner pocket with the envelope and walked up to Xanthus. Oleos briefly placed his right palm upon Xanthus' shoulder as he replied, "Truly who knows when we'll meet again. But I guarantee you we will. And have faith Xanthus, you will be with Azalea sooner than you think and you will find her. Keep your eyes open and take care."

At his last words he quickly glared over to Theron and back to Xanthus. And Xanthus knew just what he was meaning by. And with that Oleos left the hall with hast. And once Oleos was out of sight King Alcander replied, "Now Xanthus, my last orders are for you to give Theron the letter that James gave you, while the rest of you go with Xanthus to find Queen Whistalyn's tomb. And Theron will find Azalea and bring her back here and…"

Xanthus did not allow his father to finish as he shouted with anger, "Absolutely not!" Xanthus continued as his fists began to glow a dim red hue once again, "The love of my life is not going to be in the hands of an Outcasted! Especially that of Theron!"

Theron on the other hand smirked and replied calmly, "An order is an order Xanthus. Your father, your king has made his decision and there is no going against it."

Xanthus grunted, "Damn you Theron! You can go to hell!"

Theron smiled and chuckled, "Been there thanks, got kicked out for selling frozen creams."

Xanthus took a step forward, but this time no one stood in his way. And at this Theron's eyes widen as he seemed to take a small step back. But before Xanthus could start anything King Alcander shouted, "Xanthus, do not allow your stubbornness to cloud your thoughts! Your mother needs you and you must make hast! I trust that Theron is going to bring her back safely. Besides, Cethios will be looking for you and not Theron. Cethios would least expect it. And Theron can slip in without much notice; he is cunning, swift and with few obstacles. And once Azalea gets to you, you may both finish whatever tasks you desire. Now, that is my ruling. Give Theron that letter and let us begin these quests!"

Xanthus seemed hesitant and before he could react and give the envelope containing James letters to Theron, Latimer quickly replied, "Well as for me I will be joining Theron on his quest. I will also see to it that Azalea comes home safely. Here Xanthus, I will take the envelope and keep it safe. I will keep both safe."

At once Xanthus knew the meaning behind Latimer's quick outburst. And without skipping another beat Latimer continued as he turned towards King Alcander, "That is, if it is alright with you your highness. I do truly wish to join Theron. We can both enter unseen."

And without thinking the king replied naturally, "Certainly, I see no objective to that request."

Theron's face was priceless. He was in complete and utter dismay as his jaw dropped down. All of the other elves had grins from ear to ear. And at once Xanthus gladly and willing turned over the envelope to Latimer. And as Latimer neared Xanthus, Xanthus whispered to him, "Thank you for your quick judgments. I was doomed to give this up either or, and I am glad it is with you rather than him. But Latimer, keep her safe. Guard her with all that you have."

Latimer smirked to his words as he in returned whispered, "You have no idea on the extent of that. But, I will."

Xanthus still confused on his words, shrugged it off and handed over the envelope to Latimer. And at once Theron glared at Latimer. If looks could kill, Latimer would be nothing but dust particles by now. Rowen cleared his throat and replied to the king, "Your highness, although I am to honorably join Xanthus and Morpheus, where are we actually heading to? Are we as well to follow a letter or a map?"

As if seeming to remember, King Alcander reached over to his shoe and seemed to withdraw a small piece of parchment, which seemed to be made of leather from his sock. He stood and went over to Xanthus. He handed him the parchment as he replied with great concern, "Follow these words to its precise. There are many enchantments that will lead you astray to another if you do not follow it precisely. Hence if you do wander, the meaning of this map is worthless."

The king turned to everyone else as he replied loudly, "Now, go everyone and accomplish each quest successfully. And may the Eternal Spirits guide you with your hast."

And with those last words being said, they all bowed towards the king and exited the hall as quickly as they could. They were all striving to reach their destined quest. Especially Xanthus, for he wanted to quickly finish his first task so he may take off to his Azalea.

And within moments King Alcander stood alone by his throne. And as the silence passed by, King Alcander took in slow deep breaths. And yet suddenly all of the color drained from his face. He knew the inevitable was coming. He closed his eyes and took in one more peaceful deep breath. And as he opened them, a fairy suddenly stepped out from behind the velvety curtains. This fairy clapped his hands slowly with a grin upon his face.

King Alcander knew his time had come to face this perpetrator once more. The king knew he could no longer linger as he slowly turned around to face this fairy. And as he did, he took one step back, and there, slowly making his way over to him was Zethron.

Frozen Soul

16

King Alcander slowly turned as he faced Zethron. Truthfully the king was mortified to his core but, he remained as courageous as he could. Zethron on the other hand smiled as if he was being amused. He replied with a chuckle, "Miraculous how one reacts when their own life is at risk, wouldn't you agree?"

King Alcander took in a deep breath as he replied with confidence, "I have done what you have asked me to do. Now, keep your promise and give me the antidote with the words for the enchantment."

Immediately after those words escape his lips, the king fell to the floor upon his knees as he held onto his right wrist. King Alcander gazed upon his wrist as his veins pulsed with an icy blue hue. The king gasped for breaths as he replied through his trembling lips, "What kind of enchantments do you will with your hands?"

Zethron casually walked around the king with his hands resting within his pockets, as if amused that the king was suffering slowly. He stopped and bent down near the king as he whispered within his ear, "I will that magic of ancient times; ancient magic that is filled with the dark elements if you know what I mean. Pity actually, for I'm sure you don't. No matter, the point is that I get my way. And I always get my way. And don't worry about your queen. She shall die quickly, unlike yourself."

Zethron stood as he smirked arrogantly. He was proud of himself for accomplishing what he thought was going to be difficult. He was able to access the king of elves, poison him, and get valuable information from him as well.

Zethron withdrew a small green vial with a small parchment tied to it from his pocket. He twiddled it within his fingertips carelessly. Zethron took one step back from the king as he gazed upon his now icy blue skin. It seemed as if the king was being frozen from the inside out. And as Zethron saw this he chuckled to himself. He simply opened his palm and allowed the vial to fall from his fingertips onto the floor below. The vial shattered with a loud crash as the green liquid flowed freely.

King Alcander gasped through his chilled blue lips as he now shivered uncontrollable. He seemed to reach for it desperately but couldn't, for his muscles had given out in strength and were not allowing him the freedom to move. Zethron chuckled a bit louder, "Well then, I really must be off. Don't worry, once I gain your kingdom I'll make sure to it that your elves endure the same kindness you showed me. And don't worry about your sons either. They will endure their justice once I get to them. Farwell your highness, it is a pleasure to see you kneel before your true king before you perish." Zethron stared at King Alcander's body as now silver mist escaped his delicate lips with every breath. And with that Zethron left chucking to himself as he left the grand hall. He left King Alcander half frozen in death kneeling upon the ground.

Moments had pasted by as it seemed like King Alcander was on his last breath when someone had barged in through the front doors. The doors crashed against the walls as Nylina came rushing over to King Alcander. She ran to his side as she fell upon her knees near him. She hovered her right palm over the shattered vial. Her palm glowed with a lavender hue as she concentrated with all of her might on the pieces upon the floor. And within moments the green liquid, being dry at one point, now flowed freely under her enchantment. The glass pieces immediately morphed themselves back to the original vial with the green liquid inside as well.

Now Nylina held the vial within her fingers as if it had never had been broken. She uncorked it and carefully tilted King Alcander's frozen neck back. She slowly poured the liquid over the kings' delicate lips and down his throat. Once she finished she untied the hemp rope from the vial that held the tiny parchment. Nylina unrolled it quickly and read through it. She nodded to herself as she replied loudly with trembling lips, "Sugar from the leaves of might, release this one from your frozen bite. Oh spirit from Eternal Earth, free this elf for what it's worth, I call upon thee to do my will, please I beg of you, let this be fulfilled."

As Nylina tightly held onto the little parchment, she prayed. She had nothing else to do but trust her faith that something was going to happen. Someone was going to help the elf that she loved so dearly. For she knew deep down that this enchantment was not just any ordinary one. It was an enchantment that used the ancient magical elements of the earth; magic that wields the Eternal Spirits. And not just anyone knew or was allowed to call forth upon them. They wouldn't allow just anyone to manipulate them. And there was always a consequence to those who seek their wisdom and their magic.

As Nylina gazed upon the elf that she loved so dearly, her fear became realization. So she started to weep. King Alcander now knelt completely frozen before her as his face stared off into the oblivious. Nylina gently placed her hands upon his as her tears continued to flow down her delicate face. But her thoughts were quickly disrupted by light footsteps that ascended towards her.

Suddenly a tall elf looking woman with long curly orange hair came into view. She appeared very beautiful and fragile all at once as her jade dress flowed like silk behind her. And as the woman approached them, all Nylina could do was stare through her weary eyes.

The woman bent over and placed her hands upon King Alcander's cheeks as she closed her eyes. She opened them with a grin as she gazed over to Nylina. She replied to her, "May I? We haven't much time before he is completely lost."

Nylina nodded and stood from the kings' side. She took a step back as she gazed upon the woman. And as if remembering, something familiar about this woman sparked within Nylina's deep subconscious mind. She seemed familiar but Nylina couldn't quite make the connection just yet.

The woman knelt in front of King Alcander as she placed her hands upon his. She took in a deep breath then let it out in a whoosh. She replied in a firm voice, "Sugar from the frozen leaf of might, release this elf from your bite. Spirit of Eternal Earth, free this elf for it is worth. I call upon thee to do my will, I ask thee, allow this to be fulfilled."

And as soon as the last words left her lips a brisk wind started to swirl around the woman and King Alcander. And as both of their hair flew upward, suddenly color and warmth started to swell within King Alcander. And within a blink of an eye the small wind twister that swirled around them now contained snow flurries. Faster and faster the twister spun until all of a sudden it exploded through the whole grand hall. It abruptly ended as about a foot of snow engulfed the whole grand hall.

The elf looking woman continued holding the kings' hands as he took in his first deep breath and breathed slowly. King Alcander blinked his eyes sluggishly as if recovering from a deep slumber. And once he seemed fully recovered he smiled shyly at the elf looking woman. The king replied, "And to whom do I give my eternal thanks too?"

Ignoring the kings' words, Nylina bent over and embraced her love, her king. They all sat there momentarily as small puddles of water now appeared within the grand hall. For the humidity of the day had quickly melted all of the snow. And as they stood, together they helped each other to their feet. Nylina reached over and embraced the elf looking woman. She replied within her embrace, "Truly I thank you. You are a grand elf indeed. But before you make hast, if you are about to, just who exactly are you? I have seen you before, but where? And how did you know to come here?"

The elf looking woman chuckled as they parted. She bowed her head in respect as she pushed her hair ever so carefully behind her ears. The woman gazed at them both as she replied softly, "So many questions all at once, which one do I answer first? Nonetheless though, you have a right to know the truth. But for this moment I first tell you that my name is Delphina. I am daughter of two Ancient Ones, the Enchantress Falin and the Mighty James. I am actually a mermaid and no other form. And although I do have my fathers' skin, I do resemble my mother quite so. I think that is where you find me familiar in your eyes. You remember my mother and not truly me. And also, I knew it was of great importance to find you, because Cethios sent me here. He told me that I would be greatly needed. And by the looks of it, I am glad I made hast."

With that being said King Alcander's eyes grew wide with curiosity as he slowly replied, "Ancient Ones? I actually thought that they had died out, myth even. And Cethios, why would he concern himself with anyone but himself."

Delphina placed her arm around King Alcander as if holding him up as she giggled, "Your highness come, allow me to enlighten you more than what you already know. Allow me to expand your knowledge into greatness. Come, let us discuss who truly are your enemies and who are your true allies."

King Alcander stuttered, "But-but… My sons', they are b-both in grave d-danger."

Delphina giggled a bit more as if the king was amusing her. She shook her head as she ran her fingers lightly through her hair. She replied, "No your highness, I'm sure your Immortal son can take care of himself just fine. And as for the other, he will be safe within the presence of another that can wield the Eternal Spirits."

Without realizing it, these words escaped the kings' lips in a whisper, "Immortal, my son? Eternal Spirits?"

Delphina and Nylina both helped King Alcander out towards the Gardens of Vinalin to finally hear the truth of their true enemies and their true allies. And as they entered the gardens, the suns' gentle rays warmed their hearts with the new hope of their new coming future.

****

Frustration

17

Xanthus stood in a circular room with multiply white feathered doors as half of his clothes were burnt and singed off here and there. Morpheus stood next to him as both of his palms seemed to be severely bandaged with white cloth. And Rowen sat in the middle of the room with his eyes closed as he took in slow deep breaths. He was concentrating on the candle flames that swirled around them. They swirled in a quick blur as Morpheus and Xanthus attempted to stand completely still. Suddenly Rowen seemed as if his whole body was a flame. Xanthus half angrily shouted over to Morpheus, "Seriously this is nuts!"

Rowen continued his meditation as suddenly the flames cease and a bright white light gulfed them all. The sudden light startled the two standing elves as they fell upon the floor onto their backs. And just after that, Morpheus lifted his head to gaze over to Rowen. He saw that he was back to normal and simply sitting still in his meditating position. Morpheus turned his head towards Xanthus, whom still remained on the ground taking in deep breaths trying with all his might to control his frustration. Morpheus replied to him, "Xanthus, honestly I'm not sure how much more of this madness I can take."

Xanthus nodded and replied within breaths, "Agreed brother."

As Xanthus sat up his face fell in shock. One of the feathered doors that were right behind Rowen was crackling about with heavy flames. And as soon as Rowen heard this he opened his eyes with a grin from ear to ear. He replied calmly, "Well, this has been easy enough."

Xanthus and Morpheus both grunted as they stood wearily. Morpheus replied to Rowen, "Easy for you to say. You didn't have those flowers prick the crap out of your fingers."

Xanthus chimed in, "Let's not forget these flames before you got them under control."

Rowen chuckled to himself as he replied, "Hey, I can't help the humor of the Eternal Spirits. I can wield them but not completely control their passion. I do have their acceptance but not authority over them."

Xanthus rolled his eyes as he shrugged and pushed aside the now frozen orange flames within the air. He replied, "Now what Rowen? I am not going to be the guinea pig attempting to go through that door."

Rowen stood and turned to face the blazing door. He placed his fingertips ever so carefully upon his chin as he replied, "This one might be a bit more challenging. Xanthus, what does the next riddle say about this?"

Xanthus grunted as he reached for his pocket and withdrew the parchment. He read it out loud, "The element that embraces your blood will revel upon one of nature's clouds. Have the words escape your lips within a whisper to open something upon which you pass through. And enter through which you walk upon with your bare soles. And do not allow yourself to gain the mind of one that is not filled of kindness."

Xanthus looked up and frowned at Morpheus, who in turn shrugged his shoulders and replied, "Well at least we've made it this far, right?"

Xanthus grunted as he turned back to gaze upon the parchment. He replied with frustration, "Alright Rowen, what the hell does it mean to open something which you pass through and enter through which you walk upon with your bare soles? Are we supposed to open something with our feet? Seriously Rowen, I truly believe James was the one that somehow got this parchment to my father."

Morpheus stepped forward and asked, "How do you know it was James that gave it to him?"

Xanthus turned towards Morpheus with a sarcastic expression and replied, "Who else does this sound like? Besides, I think I made some sort of connection. Last I spoke with James at the Depths he told me that we were heading to his fathers' castle, which was where we were first heading to, where Azalea is. And thankfully I was able to study that map before I surrendered it to Latimer. And that island is next to us where we are now. And both islands are below the main Island of Yaisla. These two islands are somewhat similar so the connections could be there. Who else could it be? Perhaps these ruins we are in now were from his mothers' old castle. The Ruins of Yaisla, perhaps?"

Morpheus appeared confused but still nodded in agreement. Rowen on the other hand asked Xanthus, "And this is the fairy that you so desperately wanted words of wisdom from?"

481

Xanthus frowned as sadness overcame him momentarily as he whispered, "Unfortunately at that time I did."

Morpheus saw the sadness that overwhelmed Xanthus and it ached him knowing that his brother was hurting. So he quickly replied to drift his brothers' thoughts, "Alright then, being frustrated with this next riddle is not going to help us solve it or get us to where we are supposed to be. Patience is what got us through the other riddles, right?"

Xanthus replied through his teeth, "Barley."

Morpheus nodded slightly to his comment but he continued, "Alright, so we obviously need to open a door. But which door would it be that includes using our bare soles?"

They all pondered as Xanthus took one more glance at the parchment. He rolled his eyes as he replied to the other elves, "I think this last one is meant not to be pondered over much. It's an entry way through the ground, some kind of stairway perhaps."

Rowen nodded as he closed his eyes and placed his fingertips lightly upon his temples. And as he opened his mouth to speak Morpheus leaned over to him and whispered sarcastically, "Remember to be filled with kindness."

Rowen opened his eyes and glanced over to Morpheus who was smirking. Rowen frowned and shook his head as he once more closed his eyes. He pondered momentarily as he took a deep breath and replied, "Spirits of Eternal Earth, break ground and give birth, to these hidden steps below, so that we may go, and save the life of our Queen... Please"

As Rowen opened his eyes he saw Xanthus smirking with his hands folded across his chest. Rowen shrugged his shoulders as he asked, "What?"

Xanthus grunted with a chuckle, "Did that even make sense to you?"

Rowen ran his fingers through his hair as he replied with frustration, "Well let's see you try at this whole Eternal Spirit thing."

Xanthus chuckled and as he was about to reply, the ground below them began to shake. The three elves were jolted about momentarily as the quake abruptly ended within a few moments. Suddenly before them, three stairways appeared and seemed to curve downward into darkness. Once they saw this, all three elves frowned. Morpheus was the first to respond as he crossed his hands upon his chest, "Right then, do we split up or choose one to follow? Either way they all appear to lead to our doom."

Without missing a beat Xanthus replied, "We'll split up. I'll go first, Rowen take the next and Morpheus take the last one. Hopefully we'll meet at the same location. If not, come back up the steps and take the next staircase. According to the parchment this is the last enchantment before we arrive to my mothers' tomb."

Rowen nodded and started to descend down the staircase but Morpheus grunted and replied, "Seriously, why do I have to take the last one?"

Rowen stopped and glanced between the two brothers as he snapped his fingers. And as he did about five flames darted down the staircase lighting his way. And as he started to make his way down the stairs he shouted over, "The faster we get to Queen Whistalyn the faster we can protect her. And the faster we can leave and start our next task."

And with that Rowen was gone as the flames followed him down. Left in the room was Morpheus and Xanthus as they stared blankly at each other. Morpheus was the first to break the silence, "You know, if I were to snap my fingers, I'd probably just get ambushed by these little stubborn flames."

Xanthus chuckled momentarily but then as if realizing something, his face fell with sadness. He replied with sternness, "Rowen is right, we must make hast. The faster we find my mother, the faster we can finish this. Then I can finally make my way to Azalea."

Morpheus stared at Xanthus as if surprised by his words. He replied to his brother, "Xanthus, you say that as if you care not for your mother, none at all. Why is that, do you not love her?"

Xanthus took in a deep breath as he let it out slowly. Morpheus had his passionate moments. Rare they were but, right now he was having one. Xanthus seemed to deeply ponder his brothers' words. And before the time could carry on Xanthus withdrew his sword and faced down the steps. He knew he would regret these next words, but it was how he truly felt at this moment in time. And without glancing up Xanthus replied, "Honestly, it's not like I can actually do anything for her. For all we know, we could arrive to an empty tomb as death has already taken her. I do not keep my hopes high for her. Yes I do love her for she is my mother but, I have

<704> 483
</704>

already mourned her death a long time ago. I have let her go. It is Azalea's life that I do not wish to mourn. And truthfully, my mother's path is no longer with mine. It should have been my father coming to aid her; he should be coming for his love. Love is worth more than a crowns duty. And I should have been looking for my love, not foolishly looking for one whose path has already been chosen."

And with that he snapped his fingers as about ten little flames darted forward lighting his path. Without gazing up, Xanthus started his way down the staircases with the little flames following behind. And within moments Morpheus was left alone in the chamber. He stood there as if waiting for something. But as nothing but time past him he eventually threw up his hands in the air and sighed, "Great."

He turned towards the darkness of the stairs as he crunched his eyes tightly shut and snapped his fingers. Suddenly warmth briefly passed him as the smell of burning cotton reached his nose. And as he opened his eyes slowly he gazed down to his clothes. Sure enough there were little burnt holes within his shirt and pants. He frowned as he gazed down the steps and saw the flames innocently floating in the air, as if they never had done anything wrong. He shook his head in dismay and made his way down the steps to the unknown as the flames followed him lighting his path.

But in truth only one staircase would successfully lead the way to the Queens' tomb, without any distraction. Only one would arrive just in time for Queen Whistalyn. Only one elf would be followed down to the queens' tomb…

Queen Whistalyn

18

Xanthus placed his sword within his side holster as he pushed aside a feathered door. And as he stepped in admiration with took his heart. There before him was a beautiful ancient jungle. The room was filled with that of old ferns and ancient maples that he once read about, in the history books named 'Ancient Times in Trinafin'. The bark on some trees seemed as if they overlapped each other with small bubbles upon them. They seemed to grow and shrink slowly as if the trees themselves were taking in the sweet air. While the bark of other trees appeared as if it they were made of tough dragon skin. Such miracle it must be, to be here within this secluded time.

And in the middle of this wonder was a small clearing, with an alter that seemed to be made of velvety black fur. Surrounding that alter was white roses that bloomed with intense pride. They overwhelmed Xanthus' soul, for he thought they would only bloom that wide in the presence of unicorns. And surely he doubted that some would be in here, instead of the free jungle outside of this room. And there above the alter, lying in what appeared to be sweet slumber, was Queen Whistalyn his mother. She appeared just like she did in his dim memory, beautiful and peaceful.

And to no surprise near the queens' side, knelt James. He seemed to be muttering something very quickly as his hands glowed a deep lavender hue. And at that very moment Xanthus knew his mother was in no harm as he sighed a breath of relief.

Xanthus stretched his neck up for relaxation as he gazed into sky above him. He noticed that there was a translucent ceiling as the fluffy clouds peacefully rolled by. But there seemed to be this one piece of sky that seemed odd. And as Xanthus squinted his sight he realized that there diving in and out of the buttery clouds was a blue dragon soaring about. Xanthus whispered under his breath, "Oh Atrigo, so this is where you've been all these centuries."

Xanthus shook his head as he smiled to himself. He had just solved the mystery on where the kings' dragon had gone. Atrigo had been here, protecting the queen.

Xanthus gazed over to where his mother and James were as he began to slowly make his way over. But as he was about fifteen feet away a fierce wind with a thousand leaves rushed upward and stopped his path. It quickly flew towards him as the leaves began to swirl around his body. He took a step back as he was surprised with this outcome. Why would there be something like this here? Especially a few feet away from his mother and with James being here.

Xanthus reached forward to push the leaves aside but instantly regretted his decision. His fingertips were sliced by the edges of the leaves as he quickly drew his hand back. He held his hand dearly to his chest as it throbbed with pain. He concentrated on subsiding the slices on his hand to close as drips of blood fell upon the floor. And to his horror he realized that the sharp leaves were tightening their spin around him. Xanthus tried to quickly think of a solution but his concentration was thrown off by the rushing wind that gushed by his ears.

Xanthus gazed towards James as he realized that he had not moved from his mothers' side and that his palms were getting brighter. He needed to gain James' attention and fast. If James could just see that it was him, then he would help stop theses razor leaves of might. Xanthus shouted, "James! James, it's me Xanthus! James help!"

A leaf quickly sliced his face as his cheek burned with intensity. Xanthus took in a deep breath and grunted in frustration. Why couldn't James hear him? Was the winds gust just as loud out there as it was within it?

A few more leaves sliced his arms as he now held onto his breath. His bleeding arms and cheek were beginning to make him feel a bit dizzy as the wind rushed by him, disabling his balance. Was he done for? Was he still Immortal? If he was, could it be as painful as the first time his life was taken and had renewed? Two more leaves sliced his chest as the leaves increased in speed. And at that moment, Xanthus came to a realization on his true feelings buried deep within him. He whispered under his breath, "Truly mother I love you. Forgive me for being so foolish and not showing more respect and determination to find you sooner than this."

Xanthus closed his eyes and took in a deep breath as he waited for the inevitable to occur. But the wheezing by his ears suddenly stopped. Could he have died already? Was this really the end for him without pain? And as curiosity with took Xanthus' thoughts he opened his eyes. As he did he saw a few things, one was that the leaves had stopped spinning around him. They now simply hung in midair and spun slowly where they had stopped. And two, was that his mother was now staring at him with a soft smile upon her face.

A rush of happiness overwhelmed Xanthus as the spinning leaves suddenly seemed to explode as they flew in all directions. Two leaves flew past James as the back of his neck was sliced slightly. His hands dimmed in glow and then ceased. James reached for his neck as he spun around. His eyes widened as he saw who had disturbed his concentration. He stood and replied in shock, "Xanthus, what in all names are you doing here? It is dangerous for you to be here! You should be out looking for Azalea, protecting the prophecy!" James' eyes narrowed as he glimpsed at the parchment within Xanthus' fingers. James replied with concern, "My map, where did you get it? I thought I last left that within my chambers... No, Cethios..."

James eyes fell upon the map once more as his eyes widen with fear. It seemed as if he had pieced something else together. And Xanthus' thoughts were correct. It was James' map but, it wasn't him who gave it to his father. It just had to of been Cethios then, or even Zethron himself, but how? Perhaps his father was in real danger before they left him. Xanthus grunted to himself, for in truth there wasn't anything he could do for his father right at this moment. Right then and there he was hoping that he would be alright. He hoped that when he returned, he would find his father in good health. And he comforted his own thoughts by relying on the fact that his father was a wise elf. And he knew that his father was a courageous elf who knew how to take care of himself.

James spun around and took Queen Whistalyn's hand as he replied with deep concern, "Your majesty, forgive me but with this recent knowledge the unimaginable that I have feared has occurred. This enchantment that resides within you is still too powerful for me to cure, I need more time and I am afraid we no longer have that here in this sanctuary. Your life still connects with that of the first enchantment and yet, the weight of it is, is that we need your life to sustain till just a few more moments. And we must make hast before the worst occurs."

Queen Whistalyn's gaze never left that of Xanthus' as tears fled her eyes. She replied to Xanthus, "My son, forgive me for failing you. I have not been there to protect you, to guide you along your way. Do not be angry at me, for truly it is my own actions that have led me to not be there for you. And I do regret that fact; perhaps if I had fought harder, or had become wiser, I would have not been here in this tomb. But do know that if there could have been any other way, I would have not left you."

With that Xanthus rushed to her side and embraced her as he whispered through a sob, "No mother, you have never done anything wrong. How could I be upset with the elf that brought me life, and brought me to Azalea."

And as Xanthus sat up he saw his mothers' grand smile. He wiped Queen Whistalyn's tears from her face as she replied, "So you have fulfilled your destiny. Is she as beautiful as her mother? Is she filled with honesty and peace? And most importantly, do you love each other?"

Xanthus smiled and gazed upon the bravest elf he had ever met, his mother, who sacrificed even her own life so her sons' destiny could be fulfilled. He nodded and whispered to her, "Yes, we have fulfilled our destiny. And she is beautiful beyond all amazing things that I have ever laid my eyes upon, except for you. And yes, we love each other dearly."

Queen Whistalyn sighed and placed her right palm upon her sons' cheek as she whispered back, "Cherish her always. Protect that in which has been bestowed upon you."

Just then James interrupted as he with took the queens' left hand within his, "Please my lady we must make hast. Zethron might already be on his way, or worse."

At that Xanthus turned to James in shock. Xanthus asked, "James, why would he be on his way here? Why is he after my mother?"

James turned to him as he stood and pointed to the map as he replied, "Because of that. I made that centuries ago, unfortunately my memory isn't as grand as remembering spells. But I made that to remind myself how to get here. But I only have disappointment in myself. You see, I had given my old quarters and that map to Cethios centuries ago for safe keeping in case he needed anything or needed to find his way here. But that was before evil had with taken his soul. Xanthus you must understand that I trusted him once. Believe it or not, Cethios is my successor."

At that Xanthus took a few steps back in disbelief and in utter disappointment. How could James say that Cethios is his successor? Perhaps his hearing confused the information and he heard James wrong.

Perhaps there was a mistake. Xanthus replied slowly, "Cethios is your what?"

James spoke up just a bit as he replied, "Cethios is my successor." With that Xanthus' palms burst into flames as James took in a deep breath and took a cautious step back. James raised his palms up as they glowed a dim white. James replied, "Xanthus, there is a lot to this story that you do not comprehend. It is more intertwined than you know."

Xanthus glared at James as anger burned within him. Then as calmly as he could, so he wouldn't lose it in front of his mother, Xanthus replied, "Tell me the truth, are you truly on his side? I can't believe it James, all this time, all this time! After all that you have done for us, after all that you have said to me, I trusted you. I can't believe that even after all of this; he still is going to replace you? Does Azalea know any of this?"

James took a deep breath as he replied sternly, "Xanthus do not allow yourself to ponder on the thought that I have betrayed you. You have to understand that…"

Then Xanthus lost it, "I have not to understand anything that you reply since you are not one to trust any longer! How could you do this to Azalea, to me! I should just…"

Suddenly Xanthus' outburst was disrupted by small giggles that came from his side. He turned to see his mother laughing and wiping her left eyes softly with her fingertips. As calmly as he could her replied to his mother, "What is it mother? What amuses you so?"

Queen Whistalyn continued as she now wiped her right eye. She reached for her son as she extended her right hand towards his. Xanthus' palms ceased in their flames as he with took his mothers' hand carefully. The queen replied to her son, "Xanthus, you have my anger." A soft smile came upon Xanthus face as she continued, "Xanthus listen, James has his reasoning's for doing the things that he does. He has not betrayed you nor will he ever, it isn't in his nature. James is the wisest of us all. Trust me, he will explain himself in due time, to those who deserve to hear the truth of what has come upon us all. And only if you are willing to intake the knowledge he so carefully shares."

Xanthus chuckled as he replied, "Oh mother, you are starting to sound like him."

The queen nodded off towards James as she whispered through her delicate lips, "I had the honor of his teachings once long ago. If wisdom is what you seek, then he is whom you shall see. For what your mind craves is the truth of what your eyes see, and not always is that a pleasure. So then trust in the words that escape through his lips, for that knowledge will one day be the savior of us all."

Xanthus took a step back from his mother as he stared at her in amazement. And at that Queen Whistalyn sat up carefully with the help of James. And with that Xanthus bowed to his mother and towards James as he replied to them both, "It is obvious that I have a lot to learn. I'm sorry James, I do not doubt you, confused and frustrated but, without a doubt I accept your word."

The queen replied to him, "Yes, with acceptance and with an open mind you will understand."

Xanthus nodded and went over to his mothers' side as he too helped her up. And although she seemed to be very fragile, she had a sturdy grip as she with took Xanthus' arm to steady herself. And as she leaned onto James for support they slowly made their way from the open tomb. And as James tried desperately to move her along they came to a halt in just a few feet. And as James and Xanthus' eyes were on Queen Whistalyn her eyes were ahead of her, and they wondered why she had stopped.

Suddenly the queens' palms glowed a burgundy hue as small flames danced around her knuckles. And as James and Xanthus gazed forwards as well they too saw what had stopped her. Within seconds Xanthus' palms were a flame as James withdrew his sword.

There out of the shadows stepped out Zethron with a smirk upon his face. He held his sword proudly within his right hand out towards them. As above his left palm hovered a silver tinted energy globe, awaiting its command.

Eternal Spirit

19

Zethron smirked to himself as he arrogantly raised his nose into the air. He turned his gaze towards the sky as he saw that Atrigo was fiercely making his way down towards them. Zethron turned his gaze back towards the two elves and the fairy as he replied smoothly, "Dragons are honestly the lands most powerful creatures, but truth be told, they are extremely ignorant."

Zethron push his palm upward as the silver globe quickly flew towards the translucent ceiling. And of course, Zethron's globe got there first. Once it hit the translucent ceiling, black cracks began to form within it as the dark magic quickly spread all over. The cracks themselves started to release shadowy lightning bolts as one struck Atrigo.

It shocked him as the mighty Atrigo released a horrifying roar in torture. Within moments Atrigo fell unconscious to the earth below within the Jungles of Yaisla as the lightning bolt freed him. Soon after that the lightning bolt whipped the air as if wanting to claim its next victim.

Seconds later Zethron smirked as he replied arrogantly, "Now, I always get my way. And I purposely came here specifically for Queen Whistalyn. And I am not leaving without her life." Zethron took in a deep breath as he held it briefly. He let it out slowly as he seemed to ponder on the words he was about to release. He gazed upon those who stood in front of him. Zethron replied softly to them, "Before we go any further, I do have to thank Cethios for giving the map to King Alcander. And I did thank the king so generously for giving Xanthus the map. For without Xanthus and the other foolish elves, I would have never been able to translate those foolish riddles. So in turn, I shall have to thank you Xanthus, for leading me straight to the Queen."

Xanthus bit his bottom lip in frustration as he knew the horrible truth, the truth that he had actually lead Zethron to his mother. But he was not going to let her go without a fight, one he was dearly hoping he would win. He stepped in front of his mother as he replied through his gritted teeth, "You will not touch her."

Zethron chuckled as if Xanthus had told him a humorous joke of some kind. But within moments Zethron replied through laughter, "My dear boy, I don't need to touch her. I just need her dead."

By this James stepped in front of both of the elves as he now held his sword towards Zethron. James replied sternly, "This ends now Zethron. You shall not take any more lives."

Zethron chuckled once more, "You still alive old fairy? Well, it seems as if Cethios never truly killed you off. Perhaps his sword faltered in a way that just missed your soul. No matter, his life will soon come to an end, just like yours."

James gritted his teeth as he spit out, "Over my dead body."

Zethron casually shrugged his shoulders and calmly replied with a sigh, "Alright then."

Suddenly Zethron lunged forward and collided his sword with James' as blue sparks burst out of the metal blades. They fought with agility and strength as each tried to overthrow the other. And with each blow James successfully had begun to push Zethron farther away from Xanthus and Queen Whistalyn. For James was attempting to do everything within his will power to get Zethron away from them, even if it meant using all of his strength at once. And James knew all too well that if you do such a thing, failure was sure to come, eventually. But that didn't matter, what mattered was giving the queen and her son a chance to escape.

And within moments of watching James and Zethron fighting, Xanthus' realization hit as he withdrew his sword finally coming to his senses. But James quickly shouted to him, "No Xanthus! Take your mother and make hast from here! Go now!"

And with that being said, Zethron's tactics changed and were now simply to overthrow James and to quickly make his way over to the queen. But that seemed impossible, for James was preventing him from succeeding. And as Zethron watched the Queen and her son make their way towards their freedom, his own rage over powered his soul. Zethron had lost control of himself, just like that day when his anger over powered his own emotions and he instantly killed Queen Lily. His anger flowed within his veins like a swift mist as suddenly he collided his sword with such force against James' that, it sent James soaring high within the air.

Zethron released an evil sinister laugh as he forcefully dug his sword into the ground in front of himself. He held his palms up at shoulder length as suddenly a black lightning bolt from the ceiling shot down in front of him. At once the ceilings bolt of lightning had turned its vengeance inside as it struck multiple bolts in front of the door that lead out from the room. It trapped Queen Whistalyn and Xanthus as they fell to the ground onto their backs as the force of the bolt surprised them.

Black lightning continued to whip the air around them as some now struck all around Zethron. And within seconds from that, Zethron began to hover off of the ground as his feet gently brushed the earth. The lightning started to seem as if it was emitting from Zethron himself as the ground began to shake violently. Chunks of the earth fell into the oblivious as James flew a bit off of the ground. He quickly flew towards the two elves but a black lightning bolt struck his left wing, damaging his ability to fly.

James pummeled to the ground as he landed on his hands and one knee. He gazed up towards the two elves as his heart just about stopped in horror. From the darkness of the earth he saw that something had begun to emerge from a hole that formed from the quake. And that something rose up in front of Xanthus and Queen Whistalyn as they still remained upon the ground. And it wasn't just anything that was emerging up, the soft whisper of the name escaped James' lips, "An Eternal Spirit."

Suddenly as if realizing the extreme of the situation, James shouted over to Zethron, "No Zethron! Cease this madness! You do not understand what you are condemning! Zethron stop the calling! Zethron!"

There before Queen Whistalyn and Xanthus was what appeared to be an elf woman with fair skin. Her eyes were black and pit less with heavy purple circles underneath them, as if peaceful sleep had never embraced her.

She had long black hair that flowed as if a wind circled around her. This elf woman grinned as she revealed three razor sharp teeth on each side of her mouth. The sharp teeth were each a different width and length. And she wore a black silk dress that flowed effortlessly upon her. She hovered within the air about a foot off of the ground as her pit less eyes seemed to stare off into the distance.

Suddenly a faint scream escaped through her lips. And once this began, many things followed. One, Queen Whistalyn lunged over to her son and placed her hands forcefully upon his ears. Two, Zethron ceased the quake and ceased the lightning bolts. He quickly flew over to James as he

493

drove his sword straight into his chest, into his heart. And as he withdrew it he shouted to James, "This time, there's no failure in your death old one!"

The Eternal Spirits' scream began to increase in sound as Zethron turned to gaze upon her. And there behind the Eternal Spirit jumped out a black unicorn as it leaped and sped towards Zethron. Once it was about a foot away from him, Zethron flew up and landed upon the unicorns back. They both took off towards the jungles of the back room and disappeared within it. And just like that he had escaped and was gone.

The Eternal Spirits' scream grew louder and louder until it vibrated over their very skin and into their souls. And within moments James was lost in death, but in process of renewing. Xanthus was still in shock upon the ground as his mother dearly held onto his ears. And as for Queen Whistalyn, her body was already disintegrating on the inside due to the Eternal Spirits' scream.

The Eternal Spirit continued her screams until she seemed that she couldn't continue any longer, she ceased her screams. And once relaxed, she casually turned her gaze towards the two elves upon the floor as if amused with herself. She smiled as she slowly hovered over to them. She bent down as she stared into the eyes of Queen Whistalyn. The Eternal Spirit seemed confused momentarily, as if trying to remember a thought of long ago. The Eternal Spirit reached out and gently brushed the queen cheek with her long icy fingers as it sent cold chills over the queens' arms. The Eternal Spirit replied gently to her, "Could my eyes deceive me? Could it truly be the queen of the elves herself? The one who fights with as much passion and integrity as an Ancient One? Whistalyn is it?"

The queen nodded as she continued to bravely hold onto her sons' ears. The Eternal Spirit continued, "You have shown us such bravery within your era. Even here now choosing your sons' life yet once more over your own. We are pleased with your efforts and we have come to a grand decision that we hardly ever do. A rare gift I offer you today, to live forever in our world and give you the opportunity to forever watch over your children and so forth beyond. And to guide them and help them in ways you never thought possible, as an Eternal Spirit yourself."

Queen Whistalyn, now seeing that the Eternal Spirit was not going to release her deadly scream, slowly removed her hands from her sons' ears. Queen Whistalyn stared into the empty pits of the Eternal Spirit as she slowly took in deep breaths. The queen knew her time was up as her lungs desperately clung to whatever was left of their health. The queen quickly gathered her thoughts as she bravely replied to the Eternal Spirit, "I shall accept your rare gift with gracious thanks. But if I may so ask for one request, give me your permission to leave this world after sun set. Once the sun has vanished for this day, I shall go willingly and enter into yours."

The Eternal Spirit seemed to ponder the queens' words. She nodded and replied softly to her, "Certainly I may give you your request; it is a great honor to have someone such as yourself join us."

She turned her empty eyes towards Xanthus as she suddenly seemed confused. She turned her head towards him as she leaned closer to him. Almost touching noses, she smiled and replied, "Well isn't that something you don't see every day. It seems as if we have two Immortals within our mist in this moment of time. And not just any Immortals do we have. In front of me I see the son of a chosen one from the grand Whistalyn. Yes, I see now. And yet a few feet from you lies an Ancient One, one whom I chose myself ages ago that started this all. Yes young Immortal, I assure you, you will learn our ways." Suddenly she seemed to look up as another smile spread across her face. She replied, "And here comes one that is knowledgeable of our ways. He shall teach you."

Xanthus turned around to see Rowen descending down some stairs near the edge of the jungle. The stairs that he came down from were made of vines that whipped in front of him with each step, as if catching him before he falls. Xanthus turned back towards the Eternal Spirit as he replied to her, "And so he shall become my mentor."

The Eternal Spirit nodded as she then slowly vanished like the mist in the early morning. Xanthus watched as if memorized by her, but once she was completely gone he sat and turned towards his mother and with took her right hand within his. Queen Whistalyn laid upon the floor as deep breaths concaved within her chest. She seemed to be in great agony with each breath as tears swelled within Xanthus' eyes. He could not bear to watch his mother like this and worst of all, he was truly helpless. There was nothing he could do to save his mother. He whispered to her as tears now fell freely from his face, "Mother, I do not understand, where are you going? Are you truly leaving me? I cannot bear to lose you again."

Queen Whistalyn smiled faintly as she replied weakly, "No my son, I am never going to leave you again. The place where I am going is a place where I can forever be with you. I can forever keep watch and protect you and those you love."

495

By this time James was now on the other side of Queen Whistalyn holding her delicate hand. He replied to her softly, "Your highness, sunset is yet moments away so your suffering will be brief. I am so sorry I have failed you. Forgive me my queen, for I did not save your life at all."

Whistalyn took in a slow deep breath as she whispered, "No James, you are my king, you rule above me and I am just your pupil. Your apologies mean nothing to me because you have not failed me. You have only succeeded in helping me keep the prophecy. And if not for Zethron's foolishness in attempting to kill us with an Eternal Spirit, I would have never had this opportunity that has been blessed upon my soul. And as this day ends, Zethron's enchantment will diminish and we will have succeeded in breaking it. Truly James, and my son, do not weep for me, for I will join the Eternal Spirits and now I can always be with my loved ones. And I can help whenever you both ask, as well as for Azalea."

The Queen turned herself slightly towards Xanthus as she whispered specifically to him, "Xanthus, I'll always be with you. I am never leaving you again. I have always loved you. Always cherish Azalea, love her and protect her. Protect your love... because if you do not... we shall repeat history in blood shed... do not allow this to come to pass. That is why we are all here in the first place. Xanthus my son... I love you so much..."

Xanthus placed his right palm upon his mothers' cheek as he whispered to her, "And I love you mother. I promise to protect the prophecy. You shall not go in vain. I promise mother, to protect everything that is Azalea's and mine."

And with that Queen Whistalyn's hair suddenly began to turn black, from the roots to their tips. Her skin became paler than snow as she closed her eyes briefly then opened them. Darkness had quickly overcame them as they appeared pit less and cold. And as she smiled three razor sharp teeth formed within her left and right top sides. She smiled and slowly vanished like a morning mist fading away within the sunlight as the stars above them shone brightly.

And just like that she was gone, leaving both Xanthus and James kneeling down to nothing, leaving both Immortals staring off into the oblivious.

The Entrances of the Elements

20

Rowen now stood next to James and Xanthus as his arms hung upon his side. He sighed, "I'm so sorry I arrived too late to be of any help to anyone. My passage led me down a chamber of vines. And unfortunately, the vines did not allow me to return the way I had entered from. Therefore, I had no choice but to fight them and go amongst them. It took me ages but eventually I was able to bend them to my will with some enchantments. But…"

James stood as he brushed two white rose petals off of his shoulder. He gazed at Rowen as he smiled weakly, and whispered, "Queen Whistalyn was beyond rescue since the day Zethron chose to destroy her. There was nothing any of us could do to save her. And actually, to her benefit she is now in a world where she will enjoy her eternity and her new powers, and use them with greatness."

Xanthus stood and wiped his face gently with his fingertips as he turned towards James. He replied cautiously and firmly, "Which reminds me James; you have some explaining to do. Oh Ancient One."

As Xanthus replied his last words Rowen turned to him in shock as he replied, "Are you kidding me?"

Rowen turned towards as James crossed his arms across his chest as if in disappointed with Xanthus. Xanthus replied smugly, "Am I wrong James? You cannot deny it. I saw the rose petals upon you and I did not hear wrong from the Eternal Spirit. I know your knowledge is more than you lead us to believe. Why have you been hiding this from us? Don't you think this information could have been useful for us to know then? Does Azalea know who you truly are?"

James crunched his face in as if he was deeply concentrating on his words. It seems as if he was contemplating with himself. James cleared his throat and replied firmly, "Yes, what you assume is true. I am an Ancient One and I do doubt that you knowing of me would have helped any of you. Why, it could have even put you more in harm's way by actually knowing. And do not doubt me, for I will explain myself in due time. Azalea does not know, but I'm sure she has the mentality to comprehend my reasoning now. She was too young to understand anything then. But at this very moment we must make hast and capture what truly is important right now. We must preserve your fate and not allow it to crumble. We must make hast to find Azalea and get out of here before any more lives are lost."

As Rowen nodded, he gazed around as he quickly added, "And find Morpheus."

James frowned as he replied, "He too is here? Then who went to find Azalea?"

At this Xanthus glared out into the jungle as he replied, "My father insisted on Morpheus joining us. He explained that my mother needed to see him for herself so she would know the truth of him being my half-brother, and him and Nylina. And to answer your question, Theron went for Azalea, with Latimer."

James eyes widen as he replied, "Theron did? We must hurry then."

It was as if James had read Xanthus' mind as he too felt the worry on not trusting his cousin. And so, with hast they began to head towards the back of the jungles within the room hoping for another way out. For the entrance where they had come in from was completely destroyed. And thankfully within a few moments of charting through the vines, leaves and trees they came to a halt in a clearing with what seemed to be four doors.

The doors at first seemed to form a line as they were about five feet apart. But once they stepped closer, they could see that they were spaced out in distance by about three feet. The closest door to them was that made of pure water as you could see through it. Small colorful fishes and drifts of seahorses from all variety swam about; as if in their own peaceful bliss. The second door seemed to be made of misty air as small green leaves swirled within it in a circular motion. The third was made of a grey stone that had small animal carvings upon it as they glowed in a silver tinted light. And the final door was made of blue and green flames as they swayed ever so gracefully to its own musical rhythm. And there before them stood the Entrances of the Elements.

Once they all took in the vision of each door, Xanthus threw his hands up in desperation, he grunted, "Seriously, for the love of all spirits! James, do you know what this is? I can't believe this, can't there ever be a simple way in or out of this forsaken place?"

Rowen chuckled at his outburst as he replied, "Come on Xanthus, if I remember you used to love these islands when we were younger. We'd get lost within them for days camping out in different locations learning so much."

Xanthus crossed his arms across his chest as he frowned and replied sternly through his teeth, "Yes, I do remember, those days everything was so carefree. But now a days my life and the life of Azalea's are constantly at stake. And I need to make hast and find her before she gets taken or killed. I don't even have that map James gave me to find her on the other island!"

At that James turned to him confused as he quickly asked, "Xanthus, where is the map of my fathers' castle?"

Rowen actually answered him as Xanthus simply stood there becoming frustrated and angered with his own thoughts, "Theron has it."

James bit his bottom lip slowly as he replied, "Well then, thankfully you both now have something better."

Xanthus gazed over to James whom in turn was standing there smiling enthusiastically. Xanthus lifted his palm as he hit his head with it. He replied, "Of course, how could I have over looked it. We have you James."

With that Xanthus now seemed a bit more motivated as he neared the doors. He gazed between them studying them as he replied to Rowen and James, "Alright, which door will lead us out."

James seemed to stumble a bit as he turned his focus on the doors. He placed his right palm upon his chin as he replied softly, "You know, I can't remember."

Xanthus threw his hands up within the air once more as he turned from them both. And as he did, he quickly found a swords' tip right in front of his face almost touching his nose. He heard a breathless shout, "Oh crap, I found you! My mistake Xanthus I can't see anything since those forsaken flowers exploded their pollen."

Morpheus lowered his sword but couldn't seem to put it back upon his leather loop that hung from his belt. Xanthus filled with concern as he saw his brothers' eyes. They were swollen and almost closed as a bright red rash covered his surrounding eye area with small lavender bumps within. His actual eye color was black with a scarlet tint to them.

Xanthus slowly with took the sword from Morpheus' hands as he placed it upon his brothers' side. Xanthus reached over and cupped his brothers' face within his hands. With deep concern Xanthus asked, "Morpheus, what in the world did you get yourself into? All you had to do was cautiously make your way down here."

Morpheus replied as he blinked his eyes slowly, "Well that's easier said than done. After I descended down the steps, I entered this room that seemed to be made out of these types of bushes. Although each bush had these small purple balls that cover their entirety just about. And past these bushes on the other side was an open door that led to this room that we are in now. So, I figured all I had to do was make my way safely across, and I thought I'd be alright. And…"

James took a step closer to Morpheus as he interrupted him and replied, "But you did not, did you? Curiosity with took your subconscious mind didn't it."

Morpheus nodded glumly, "I couldn't help myself; they looked intriguing and harmless at first. And I was basically already out which was easy enough. Then, I figured it wouldn't hurt to just touch one innocent puff ball."

James sighed, "In the midst of a place of serenity that one thinks is what seems to be peaceful, the mind wanders from its safe haven and forgets to be cautious."

Xanthus and Rowen turned and frowned at James as he in turn simply smiled and shrugged his shoulders. Rowen leaned over to Xanthus as he whispered to him, "You know, I think he purposely likes to confuse others with his words."

Xanthus chuckled as he replied to him in a low voice, "I think he can't help it actually."

They chuckled as Morpheus continued, "Yes well, I plucked one unfortunately and all of a sudden like some type of reaction they all started to explode. They seemed to release this mist that was inevitable to avoid. So unfortunately, I did the first thought that crossed my mind, I ran for the door."

Rowen asked sarcastically, "Did you make it?"

Morpheus frowned as he replied, "Obviously I made it out but not without being harmed in the process."

Xanthus shrugged his shoulders as he turned towards James and asked, "There has to be something we can do for him, right?"

James pushed up his glasses with his index finger and sighed. He stepped up to Morpheus as he with took his face within his palms. James asked, "Are you completely with no sight or is your vision with a slight blur?"

Morpheus took in a deep breath as he sighed, "No, not complete lost but using the word slight is an understatement, it's all severely blurred. I can see some sort of figures. I noticed Xanthus only when I was realized it was him, thankfully he has his own unique stance really. But I really didn't know what I would have done if it wasn't. I guess just swing and hope for the best."

James continued to study Morpheus' face until he seemed satisfied with his observant. As he let go of his face he replied, "We are going to have to bandage them up. And honestly, we are going to have to send you back with bed rest. Those puffs are actually my doing. I set them there thinking that Zethron would be coming in from that entrance. I never thought that he would actually follow someone else in the right way but…"

Xanthus interrupted him as he replied, "So now what? We have to simply send him away?"

Morpheus seemed to sniff as tears started to swell in his swollen eyes. He replied softly, "No, there has to be another remedy other than simply bed rest. I can't leave, I am not abandoning Xanthus. I have to help him find Azalea."

At this Xanthus embraced his brother as he replied to him, "Morpheus, you have been the bravest elf I know, and you have never failed in helping me, and you are not abandoning me. But I cannot take care of you while I am trying to search for Azalea. You need to heal yourself properly. And once you are healed, make hast and find your way back."

Morpheus nodded as he released his brother. James replied with confidence, "Morpheus, we will be heading northeast from here. We will be in the island that lies directly south of the main Island of Yaisla. You will be heading to the main island, and stay in the north until you are healed."

Morpheus seemed confused as he replied, "But… There is nothing worth in the South Island but an old abandoned castle and…"

501

James quickly interrupted, "And that is where you will find us. Looks can be deceiving."

Morpheus nodded as he started to wipe at his face with a blue handkerchief that he with took from his pocket. And at once James took it within his own hands as he wrapped it around Morpheus' eyes and tied it. James replied, "This will help ease the pain. It will also give your eyes the ease to heal quickly without the light affecting them. That way it will only take a few days to heal. Rather than months."

Morpheus grabbed James' arms as he replied, "Wait, Rowen is your griffin still here circling the islands' beaches? Or did she go off with the dragons to Maliko Island? If she is, can she take me to the Castle of Yaisla? I'll keep Oleos company and it'll give us a chance to catch up. Also, that way I'm only a day or two away and not days away!"

Rowen turned to Xanthus awaiting for his reply to Morpheus question. But in turn Xanthus turned to James for his reply. James sighed, "I think that would be a wise decision. Come, I will explain some things to you all as we make our way out to find Atrigo. Hopefully he's not too much wounded, that way he can take off to Maliko Island before any of Yaisla's enchantments affect him. And then we head towards my fathers' castle. Hopefully we will find Zethron there before he destroys anyone else."

Xanthus placed his arm around Morpheus' shoulder as Morpheus did too for support. They faced towards the doors once again as Xanthus sighed and asked James, "Right, which door should we take then?"

James slowly paced pasted each door, studying it carefully. He stepped up behind Rowen as he gave him a slight nudge towards the door in flames. James replied, "It's that one, I'm sure of it."

Rowen stepped closer to the door a bit unsure as he turned his gaze back around towards James. Rowen's palms began to glow a slight blue hue as he raised them up towards the door. He asked, "So why am I going first if you are so sure that it is this door in particular."

James smiled and replied, "Well, I am only about ninety nine percent sure."

Rowen turned back towards the door as he took in a deep breath. He whispered to himself, "Well that's comforting." And with another deep breath he replied, "Alright, here we go."

Rowen reached for the door with his glowing blue hands. He pushed opened the door that they all were hoping would lead them to the free jungles up above.

****

Indestructible

21

Theron and Latimer arrived early morning within the island that lies directly below the main Island of Yaisla. They landed near the top north of that island as they mounted off of their griffins. They bid them farewell as their griffons headed for Maliko Island. For the atmospheric aura that surrounded that specific island prevented the griffons and the dragons from remaining within their mist.

Both of the elves traveled in peace following the map inland. And as mid-day neared they arrived near a castle that seemed to be covered in roses and thick ivy. The castle seemed to be enormous as it stood seemingly to blend in with nature itself. The walls of the castle were made of stone that appeared to be made from tree bark and massive banana leaves. And although the castle appeared to be extremely fragile, it was quite resilient to nature's fury. The castle has held up for centuries undisturbed by the damage of the elements, and it wasn't ever going to give up its fight and become ruins. No, it was always going to stand mighty and exquisite.

They reached an open area that was once an exquisite garden. Empty pots, patched of dirt and grass seemed to flow upon the stone pathways. There were also small areas of wild flowers that sprouted untamed that lead towards two massive doors of the castle.

Theron and Latimer stopped and began to gaze around to see just where they were. Latimer withdrew the map from his pocket as he started to study it once more. Theron, seeming a bit nervous, suddenly cleared his throat as he gently pushed upon a large pot. He replied casually, "Latimer, how about you allow me to gaze over that parchment? Perhaps I can make out an easier path for us. I could see something that you may have over looked?"

Latimer quickly folded the parchment and placed it within his pocket. He turned and faced Theron as he replied sarcastically, "Yeah right Theron. When I give you this map personally in the hand, that will be the day my arms fall off. So honestly, I don't think so. Besides, my trust in you has diminished ages ago. We are going to head straight to Azalea to help her, free her and get back to Xanthus."

Latimer's words struck Theron as he filled with frustration and anger. Unconsciously he replied under his breath, "That can be arranged."

Latimer's response was not the one Theron was anticipating on. Latimer turned from Theron as he started to cautiously make his way through the abandoned garden and over to the massive castle doors. Theron followed with a bit of distance as he quickly pondered. He needed to actually find Cethios first, before Latimer did. And if he has not taken Azalea, then he needed to. He needed to prove to Zethron that he was worthy, that he was better than Cethios. And once he took Azalea, he was going to kill Cethios.

Theron had come to a conclusion, he was going to take Latimer out of his way. Besides, the more Theron thought about it, the more he liked the idea of killing Latimer; he never liked him anyway.

Theron paced himself quickly to catch up to Latimer as he now was walking directly behind him. Theron withdrew his sword as quietly as he could. He raised his sword high above him. Latimer sensing that something was not right, stopped briefly and spun around to face Theron. Theron, without hesitation, struck him across the chest. The blow sent Latimer stumbling back a bit as he clung to his chest. Latimer was in complete shock, never had he thought that Theron would try to kill him.

Theron took a step back as he gazed upon Latimer. He was waiting patiently for the blood to start seeping through Latimer's shirt and chest but, nothing was spilling out. The only thing that he noticed upon Latimer was that his vest and shirt were slashed and torn where he had struck him. And to both of their utter astonishment Latimer was completely unharmed. Latimer ran his fingers over his chest to feel where the skin should have been torn to shreds. But nothing, his skin was unscratched.

And within these few moments that Latimer had, he quickly tried to piece everything together. First, why was Theron trying to dispose of him? And secondly, why was he not dead? A blow like that should have killed him. He should have been upon the floor bleeding to death instantly.

Theron as well quickly gathered his thoughts as he could think of nothing other than to try once more. He swung his sword across Latimer's chest and then swung it with all his might across his neck. But Latimer, naturally, raised his arms up as he blocked part of it. Latimer was thrown back once more. And as he regained his balance he ran his fingers over his arms, and around his neck, nothing. No broken skin, no blood, no pain, nothing.

Both elves simply stood there staring at each other as they took in deep breaths in exasperation. Suddenly Theron angrily shouted within breaths, "Why in all hell can't I kill you!"

Latimer's eyes widen as he shouted back, "Why do you want to kill me Theron? Is it because I won't give you the bloody map!"

Theron crunched in his nose as he placed his sword back upon his side. Evidentially he can't kill Latimer with it so, might as well put it away. Theron replied, "Oh Latimer, it's so much more than that. But first, yes, just give me the damn map."

Latimer quickly responded, "No. Why do you want it anyway? Together we are going to find Azalea whether you carry it or I."

Theron placed his hands upon his hips as he took in more deep breath. He was going to have to tell him the truth, unfortunately. He replied a bit calmer, "Because I need to find Cethios first. Because I need to know if he has already taken Azalea. Because if not, than I need to do it."

And without thinking Latimer shouted, "Theron No! What do you think you are doing! How could you betray your own cousin, turn your back on you own Outcasted! We trusted you, we followed you!"

Theron threw his hands up in the air as he replied exasperated, "Exactly, that was all in the past! You yourself said you don't trust me anymore! Besides, how can you be so naïve? Remember ages ago when Xanthus stumbled upon an ancient hidden library at the Castle of Yaisla, within the gardens far eastward."

Latimer shrugged his shoulder as he replied, "Sort of, I remember Xanthus complaining that the books were written in some sort of ancient language. And that you both found a library the size of a small pantry. But, I thought that you and Xanthus sealed it back up. Besides, what does that have to do with anything that is going on now?"

"Everything! It has everything to do with now! Since that day I found out quite a few things about Xanthus. I learned that he was different than the rest of us, I saw that gem upon his navel. And I found an ancient magical book, the ones that write themselves about our history and the future. I read quite a few interesting things. And you know what, I too want to be a part of something unique, to be a part of history. I want my name in those magical books. I stumbled upon one story in particular that actually told about the legends and I did more research. I reopened that ancient library to study more myself and somehow I stumbled upon Zethron, fate brought me to him."

Latimer stumbled back a bit as he raised his right hand and smacked his forehead. He shouted, "Fate! This is all madness Theron! Madness! You need to drop this! Theron you must! This is bigger than you and I."

Theron started to pace as he placed his hands behind his back. He replied, "Well that's just it. I don't want to drop it, I can't. I want to be a part of that bigger sense. Besides, Zethron promised me my share of the prophecy. He promised me that I will be in those history legends. He promised me! Do you even know who he truly is? I couldn't pass up this opportunity. So..." Theron stopped pacing as he now stood about five feet from Latimer. Theron replied softly, "So I did a Blood-Oath with him. All I have to do is follow him without question, do what he asks and I will have my part, perhaps even Immortality."

Latimer stood there speechless as he was in utter disbelief. Words were meaningless on how he felt at that exact moment. What could he say to Theron anyway? He had done a Blood-Oath with the worst enemy ever. There was no redemption or safety for Theron. He truly was already lost.

Theron's eyes suddenly widened in shock as he pointed to Latimer's arm. He shouted to him, "What the hell is that!" Latimer followed Theron's gaze as he now stared at his right arm. There upon his upper arm was the ivy plant that coiled around, his own Blood-Oath with Azalea. Theron shouted, "Is that what I think it is? You... you did a Blood-Oath? With who?"

Latimer now stepped forward with confidence as he replied, "Oh you should talk Theron. Don't judge me. You're the one who has a Blood-Oath with the demon from the underworld himself!"

And out of instant reaction and fury, Theron punched Latimer in the face with all of his might. And to both of their surprise, Latimer fell back upon the ground. And as Latimer sat up he placed his hands upon his nose to suppress the pain and the blood that slowly flowed out. A massive grin spread upon Theron's face as he replied through his teeth, "Well-well-well, not completely indestructible are we?"

Latimer quickly stood and withdrew his sword as he took a step back. Theron laughed hysterically, "Oh Latimer, do you honestly think you

507

can defeat me with a measly sword. Please... Don't you realize that I am within my own element, within the lands of my ancestry."

With that Theron's palms glowed a slight green hue as vines shot out from a nearby bush. The vines twisted themselves around Latimer's wrist and legs. It forced him to drop his sword as it flipped him sideways. More vines sprawled out and tangled around him as they lifted him about five feet off of the ground. They kept him sideways as if he simply laid twisted upon the vines. Another vine swirled upon his sword as it lifted it up. His sword now was tangled about one foot from his reach, as if taunting him.

Theron stepped up to Latimer as he reached over and withdrew the folded parchment from his pocket. Theron replied with pride, "Thanks, I'll make sure to say hello to Azalea for you."

Theron turned from him. And just before he took off towards the castle, Latimer shouted, "You told Xanthus you had a truce! You promised him after we got out of the scorching nest! Does that not matter to you, or just your bloody oaths!"

Theron turned and stepped close to Latimer as they were just about eye to eye. Theron replied smugly, "You should talk. Besides I had to go with it. What choice did I really have at that moment; Cethios' plan had gone wrong. We were supposed to find Azalea alone with the Cristats. We weren't supposed to find her with Xanthus and Morpheus. But we improvised; in the end we got Azalea away from Xanthus at the Depths. And, we have Xanthus out of our way as he looks for his dear mother. This leaves us free to Azalea's Immortality; whether it is Cethios that takes it or me."

Latimer replied through his teeth, "If you so as touch one hair on her body I'll..."

And before he could finish what he was about to say, Theron punched him with all that he had in the face; knocking Latimer unconscious. Theron turned from him as he rolled his neck around. He opened the parchment calmly with a smile. And as he studied it he whispered to himself, "Immortality here I come."

****

Uncontrollable

22

Cethios and I had just pummeled onto the ground basically on top of each other as I took in slow deep breaths. We had just fallen out of a door that had a hidden drop as we entered it. We fell to our doom as we landed upon white sand that was thankfully extremely soft to the touch. I glanced up, about twenty feet above us, as the door that we pummeled out of closed with a loud bang and disappeared. I grunted as I pushed Cethios' legs off of my chest. I was going to have a bruise there later, I just know it.

I sighed a breath of relief as yet again we had managed to escape Theron. The last couple of days had been exhausting, mentally and physically. One, we were trying to evade Theron, which was becoming more intense every time we met. He was bound to get us soon or later if we don't escape this castle of madness. That was the next thing; this castle was out of control! It seemed as if every time we entered through a new door it simply led us to another room of chaos. This was insane, were we ever going to escape?

I mean, we should have just flown down from the balcony of James' old quarters. But no, we didn't. But I do have to say, there is one good thing out of this so far, I was free. I no longer had those forsaken shackles upon my wrists and ankles. Cethios and I had destroyed them, for good. And the keys that unlocked the shackles had turned to one, and I kept it, hung upon my neck tucked into my dress. Who knows; perhaps one day it would come in handy.

Having my magic accessible once again was a relief, except for one thing; my magic was uncontrollable. I'm not sure what has happen to me but, this power that I have seems like it is too much for me to handle at times. I wonder if Xanthus is having this problem too. It's weird though. But the stranger thing is that Cethios is actually trying to help me tame it, to keep it under control.

As I sat up I started to rub my arms and legs, they were extremely sore. I sighed, well perhaps somehow I'll be able to gain muscle strength out of this. Perhaps is the key word.

As Cethios sat up next to me he suddenly opened his wings. He fluttered them briefly as sand flew all over me. Great, more sand in places that I didn't want to think of. You know, I do have to admit that having that little black ran cloud was convenient. I got accustom to washing up in it when I needed to. I could just conjure one up if I really need it. But the last time I did that, a day ago, let's just say we both really got washed up.

I gazed at my fingertips as I rubbed them slowly together. And suddenly Cethios' fingers came into my view as he began to massage them. I gazed up at him as he simply smiled shyly. I grunted softly, "Cethios this has been so frustrating, how can you tolerate me or even be so understanding. Even though it is my magic, it's frustrating me; I think I'm annoyed with myself. It's like this magic just wants to burst through my fingertips and yet, when it does, nothing but madness escapes them. And this chamber after weird chamber is not helping me relax either."

Cethios smirked as he let go of my fingers and stood. He took a few steps from me as he turned to face this new room. It seemed like we were in some sort of desert with no beginning or end. Nothing but a bright fake setting sun and sand! I was going to lose it soon. As Cethios casually placed his hands within his pockets he replied, "Well, if or when I get my Immortality, I would want you to be just as patience with me as I am to you."

"So you're only being nice to me because you want me to be nice to you?"

Cethios turned to face me as he frowned and replied, "Azalea, it's not like that and you know it. Do not manipulate my words against me."

I was becoming really stressed out. I ran the base of my palms upon my forehead and grunted, "So, do you want to camp out in this room for the coming evening or do you want to keep searching? This room doesn't seem to have any food or a resting area though."

Cethios chuckled as he gazed around the room, "Already wanting more snuggle time from me huh Azalea? Well, I know you can't keep your hands off of my skin but, we do need to keep looking. This room does not seem suitable for camping out for slumber."

I sighed, he still had his moments of arrogant charisma, which was frustrating at times. But at least he wasn't smug or rude anymore, especially at night when we slept next to each other. It was mostly, to keep ourselves warm and to keep an eye out for one another in case Theron or one of his soldiers found us. Sometimes though, in the middle of the night, deep depression would fill my core. He would find me silently crying due to the weight of everything falling upon our shoulders. Thankfully, he would simply hold me within his arms, wipe my tears away and reassure me that everything was going to be alright, and that we were going to make it out alive. I was grateful that he didn't bring it up during the day or make fun of me for it. He truly was showing his characteristics of his old true faithful self, when our friendship was at its strongest.

I shook my head slightly, I needed to clear my thoughts of frustration. I needed to vent out somehow. Suddenly I had a crazy idea. I picked up some sand as my right palm glowed. I formed a small sand globe as I chucked it at Cethios. I ended up hitting him in the leg with it. He chuckled, "Two can play that game."

And before I even had the chance to get up, a sand globe was coming straight for my face. Thankfully with my quick reflexes, I raised my glowing beige palms up to block it. And what do you know; the sand globe actually bounced off of my hands and went straight for Cethios. It smashed upon his chest as it seemed to explode with intensity as sand engulfed his entire body. I laugh instantly, I couldn't help it. The sand clung to him like static as the pieces seemed to actually vibrate. I managed to reply through a chuckle, "Whoops, sorry Cethios. I think I am going to ban myself from magic for a while."

Cethios tried to dust himself off but for some reason with every brush the sand seemed to multiply. The sand bits also seemed to be turning into fluffs of cotton with a small popping noise every time one turned. I laughed, I couldn't help it. Right before my eyes, Cethios was turning into a big ball of cotton. And before I realized it Cethios was standing there with his hands upon his hips, frowning. My laughter subsided into chuckles as Cethios replied, "I would appreciate a little help here. I have no doubt that this was your doing."

I chuckled to him, "Seriously Cethios, I really don't know what I was thinking that would have caused this. You can't do anything about it? I mean, are you sure you want me to try?"

Cethios dropped his hands as small cotton balls flew off of him. The pieces soared to the ground as they turned back into sand. Cethios replied slowly, "Azalea, don't you think I would have done something by now if I could. You know that my magic is no match for yours."

I stood still chuckling a bit as I dusted my dress off. I lifted my right hand out towards him as my palm glowed a light blue. Before I

511

started, I replied to him, "Alright, you asked for it, brace yourself." I closed my eyes and concentrated on the little white balls of cotton upon Cethios.

Cethios whispered, "Concentrate Azalea, focus on what you are trying to accomplish."

I took in a deep breath and slowly let it out. Alright, here goes. I concentrated on diminishing the balls of cotton back to sand form. I thought perhaps if the blue static sizzled away above us, perhaps the sand can fall off. Perhaps a little wind to encourage the sand to blow off of him. Well, that was it. I thought on that, I dwelled on it.

It seemed like a few moments had gone by of peace and serenity. That is until I heard Cethios' shouts. Do I really want to open my eyes? Do I want to see what creation I had done this time? I hesitated on opening them. But I heard Cethios shout my name. I was afraid to see what I had done but, Cethios shouted my name once more. And he sounded like he was in danger.

I opened my eyes and immediately I was in awe of myself. For one, I was floating ever so gracefully upon my stomach as warm air gently pushed me upwards and back down slowly. I do admit that I had my wings opened, for it did feel exhilarating. It was like I was flying but, without the nauseating feeling within my stomach of everything blurring by.

I became aware of what was around me. I admit I was mortified a bit. Surrounding me were two small twisters that twirled beside me, as if dancing with the rhythms of my breaths. Towards the top were bright blue and purple lightning bolts that shot and stretched across the ceiling. And there almost reaching the bolts within one of the twisters was Cethios. And I noticed that his wings were closed tightly upon his back. I shouted to him, "Cethios open your wings!"

"Don't you think I would if I could Azalea!"

Well I was just suggesting it; although, the wind was pretty intense. And as Cethios neared the bolts once again he shouted in horror. Alright, breathe. Breathe. I closed my wings as I instantly shot straight towards the ceiling. And as soon as I neared Cethios I opened them to steady myself. I shouted over to him, "Cethios, reach for my hands!"

"Seriously! That's what you got!"

"Yes! I'm trying not to panic and cause a bigger chaos, I am trying to stay calm and I am trying to save you. So just go with it!"

Cethios kept getting tossed about as he spun away from me and back. I closed my wings a bit more as I flew up a bit higher within the air drifts that passed around the twisters. It seemed as if I could only go up or down, I couldn't go forward or backwards, which was frustrating. And of course I myself almost reached the top lightning bolts as well.

I stretched my arms as I tried to reach for Cethios. And just as I was about to succeed, Cethios was shot across into the other twister of sand and wind. Great, how was I supposed to reach him now? The wind gusts weren't allowing me to turn as well. I was stuck facing away from him as I heard him shout out again. Alright, breathe. Concentrate.

I crunched my arms in and patiently waited. He just had to be tossed back towards the other twister, hopefully. And if that did happen, then I would take that chance and attempt to pick him out of the other wind gust and into the one I was in. And luckily for me, within a few moments I heard his shouts near me. I reached up and thankfully I had gotten a hold of him as we both reached for each other's arms. Pain shot through my arms as I tugged on him and brought him closer to me. We held onto each other's arms as we continued to float between both twisters spinning around us. Cethios shouted, "Well?"

I smiled a bit as I shouted back, "Well at least you're in here now with me then out there being tossed about within the twisters."

Cethios did not find this humorous. He frowned as he shouted, "And…"

I thought about it for a second as my humor was still with me. I shouted back, "And the balls of cotton are gone!"

Cethios seemed to turn red as he shouted back over the wind gusts, "No! Not that! I meant that you are now going to stop this scene before us and finally get us out of this castle!"

"Cethios are you serious? I can't do anything without exploding it into complete madness!"

Cethios seemed to close his eyes momentarily. It seemed as if he was pondering something. I really hope he was reconsidering. Perhaps this time he could try to manipulate my magic and not have it turn worst. He opened his eyes as he shouted over the gusts, "Alright Azalea, this is what you are going to do! You are going to concentrate on exactly what you want. Forget about everything else around us. Simple focus on what you want!"

"What I want! What I want!" I laughed hysterically. I think I finally lost it. If it wasn't for the wind blowing all around us and in my face, tears would have fallen. I rubbed my face upon my arms as I shouted, "I want all of this madness to stop! I want to escape from these castle walls! I don't want to be imprisoned here any longer! I just want to be outside in the free air!"

And strangely enough, with those words that escaped from my soul the two sand twisters that spun around us split in two. Now four sand twisters spun around us as the lightning bolts grew thicker and louder. Three bolts struck the ground as they remained there vibrating with intensity as if creating a wall around us all. It seemed as if the ground below us started to quake as it cracked open to reveal darkness.

Suddenly the lightning bolts became thicker and one by one, the sand twisters pummeled down into the darkness. And just before the last one pummeled, the lightning bolts vanished with one sonic boom effect. Then, the last twister seemed to follow the others down into the opening. And just as Cethios and I were slowly soaring down, the last sand twister seemed to whip its tail back up to us. It wrapped around our bodies as it took us with it towards the black abyss. And as we both held tightly to each other we pummeled down into the darkness with the twister. Not knowing where we'd end up, again.

Captured

23

As we pummeled into the darkness, blurred shades of emerald and violet passed us. It was a bit difficult to focus on anything as the sand twister continued to spin around us. And after what seemed like forever, I had come to realize that the twister was actually guarding and guiding us somewhere. Strange I thought, did my words actually work? Were we finally being lead out? Well, I didn't want to jinx it if it was doing just that. So as nauseating as it was I continued to attempt to focus on the blurred colors passing us by.

And yet again, moment later after my thoughts were stirred, we pummeled to the ground on top of each other. Pain shot through my body as Cethios landed on top of me. You'd think I'd be accustomed to it by now, but I wasn't. I pushed Cethios' legs off of my chest as I gazed up. And wait... could it be? Was I hallucinating? Were my eyes deceiving me? No, I wasn't losing it. There before me, was the true open sky with white puffs of clouds here and there. I rolled my gaze a bit further up until I saw it, the sun!

I started to laugh with excitement and I'm sure with a bit of hysteria. I never thought I would miss the glorious sun and the free open sky. Oh! I couldn't wait to see the marvelous stars. It's weird how you really don't know how much you appreciate the little things, until it is taken away from you. If I could hug the sky, I would. I closed my eyes as I placed my hands behind my head.

I concentrated very little and morphed my dress into black slacks with a white button up shirt and a blue vest. That was the only great thing I was able to perfect throughout my lost days with Cethios, my wardrobe thankfully. I took in a deep breath as I enjoyed the breeze passing by my sore skin. I bathed momentarily in the suns' warmth, it was soothing. I could lie here until sunset. Well, perhaps a bit after so I could dwell in the stars' presence.

But of course, peaceful moments are rare at this time. Especially right now, us being who we are and where we are. And before I knew it I heard muffles to my left. And before I was able to open my eyes, I felt a cool blade upon my neck. Awesome, just what I need right now. I cautiously opened my eyes to see a soldier fairy, one whom I did not recognize.

I looked to my left as I saw Cethios upon his knees with his hands tied behind his back. Cethios seemed out of breath as his sword laid in front of him as two elf soldiers had their swords' tips upon his neck. The look upon Cethios' face was clearly readable to me. He was beyond angry as he slightly shook his head. I'm sure he was implying for me not to say anything and to keep my mouth shut. But I did what I thought was needed. I turned my gaze back towards the fairy soldier that had his swords' tip upon my neck. And as smoothly as I could I asked, "Dear young sir, what have I done to deserve such a welcoming like this?"

The soldier seemed more nervous than anything else as he kept swaying from one foot to the other. His brown owl colored wings were open and fluttering a bit, which gave him away that he was more unease than ever. It seemed as if he was debating with himself whether he wanted to strike at me or not. He shifted his gaze between the other two elf soldiers, Cethios and me. A few more wrenching moments passed by as of course, I got tired of waiting. So I asked once more, "So, am I allowed to get up or am I simply going to stay here on the ground?"

The soldier lifted his sword from my neck as I was given room to stand. But he still kept his sword pointing at me. He then, not sure why because I was standing about two feet from him, shouted, "I know who you are! You both are the traitors of the fairies! Theron has warned us about you and we have been skillfully trained to defeat both of you! I have already sent forth a message to Theron our king. And he should be here momentarily to deal with you, prisoners! And you feathered one, don't you dare reach for your sword. Just because you are an intriguing and exquisite fairy does not mean that I will not wield my sword at you!"

I couldn't help myself, I smiled shyly. It's not every day I get complimented you know, even though if it is the enemy that replied it. So, for some reason I had the need to reassure my ears. I guess, I just wanted to know if what I heard was right. You can't blame a fairy for wondering. But like I said, I couldn't help it. I took a step back as I replied softly, "You think I am exquisite?"

The fairy soldier lifted his sword a bit higher as he took a step forward; the blade now resting upon my chest. Cethios replied through his teeth, "If you so as harm her with your sword, you shall regret the moment you wielded it."

I turned slightly towards Cethios as he gave a quick glance at my wrists and shook his head. What was he implying? I slowly moved my gaze down as to my surprise; I saw what appeared to be shackles upon my wrists. But they seemed to be poorly painted on or something. It would be convincing from a quick glance but not if you stared at them directly. You couldn't see my ankles so I'm sure there wasn't any there. But by the time I took in another breath, I knew why Cethios had done what he did upon me; for my safety.

Suddenly I heard scuffled footsteps behind me as I took in another deep breath to control myself from exploding my magic upon everyone here. I do admit though I was a bit afraid to turn around as I saw the look upon Cethios' face. For at that exact moment I knew it was Theron who was behind me. And honestly, I had to face him sooner or later so, my running was over. I gulped, loudly unfortunately as I turned slowly to face Theron. Once our eyes meet I replied softly, "Theron, you don't have to do this. Do not betray us. Zethron will not keep the promises that he has made to you. You can change, you can help us escape. And I can help you. If you just…"

His laughter cut off my words as my instant reaction made me take a few steps back. And instantly, I regretted it. Sharp pain spread like fire within my lower back. I slowly stepped forward as I felt a cold sword tip slid out from my back. My breaths wanted to become heavy but I tried to deny my lungs that pleasure. And then it happened, my head began to slightly spin as I felt blood slowly drip down my back.

Within my ears I could hear Cethios struggling about. I turned and gazed over to him as I saw that about seven elves were now attempting to hold him down as he kicked their heels and rammed others to the ground. But shortly after they over powered him, they quickly tied him to a massive tree. And as he continued to struggle he shouted over to the fairy soldier behind me, "Your life will come to an end, I guarantee it!"

The soldier behind me chuckled and replied, "My life today will not end, yours on the other hand, will. Besides, she backed into my sword on her own accord. I simply held it where it was. Technically I never wielded it at her, did I?"

Cethios continued to struggle as he watched me fall onto my knees. I'm sure I'd be alright. I was just a bit dizzy that's all. It was just the feeling of my blood seeping onto my back and oozing slowly over my skin that had me a bit nauseated. What I really needed to do was seal my wound. It wasn't deep I could feel it. But as I gazed back over to Cethios he shook his head once again. Why didn't he want me to use my magic? I mean, I know it was out of control right now but, it would actually be helpful blasting everyone away. But like I told him before, I trusted him with all my life now. And I wasn't sure what he planning but, by the look of things we weren't doing so well.

Theron chuckled as he walked over to Cethios. Cethios glared at him as his breaths heaved in his chest. To this Theron seemed amused as he replied to him, "Amazing how actually studying you has come in handy. Thankfully I have trained these soldiers on the element of surprise rather than that in combat. And finally after all of these days of evading me, I have caught you ever so effortlessly. And let's face the facts; you are helpless and weak without your sword and there is nothing that you can do to help your precious Azalea. You're pathetic! I don't see why Zethron had you in higher command. Sure Zethron told me that you are unbeatable in strength with your sword, and that you would always win in battles. Perhaps that is one of the reasons why you were his right hand. But like I just said, you were at his right. Not anymore, after he hears about this, how you betrayed us and chose to fight with Azalea rather than take her for yourself. No matter, the job will get done one way or another, and I'll have the pleasure in taking her myself by force. I have the upper hand now not you. Look at yourself, you are worthless. And you know what, I honestly wanted to defeat you in a true fight, not like this, a fish in a shallow pool. But oh well, I'll take anything for the moment. Precise mentality wins over ignorant strength. Therefore, I win."

And with that Theron stepped back and with took Cethios sword from the ground. He stared at it momentarily as if contemplating something within him. He nodded his head as if making his decision. He turned and quickly drove the sword straight into Cethios' chest as if regretting nothing. Theron then pulled it out slowly, as he wanted Cethios to suffer. Theron was enjoying watching Cethios' attempts to take in slow breaths as his chest caved inward. And as blood dripped from the sword, Theron tossed it upon the ground in front of me. Theron replied under his breath arrogantly, "Here's the sword of your pathetic unbeatable prince."

Chills ran over my spine as a wave of horror shook my core. I screamed, "No! Theron what have you done!"

My blood boiled as I felt my magic wanting to burst through my skin. Magic sizzled between my fingertips as if waiting for their command. And just as I was about to stand my eyes met Cethios'. He shook his head slightly. Wait what, did I see him correctly? Why was he doing this, did he truly want to die? My eye sight was already becoming slightly blurred! What if I passed out, then where would we both be? Dead, that for sure. Well I wasn't going to just wait for Cethios' plan to work, whatever that might be. But before I could react, the fairy soldier behind me forcefully picked me up by my arms. I heard Theron whisper to himself, "Immortality here I come."

I gazed over to Cethios as he attempted to take in deep breaths. I could tell he was trying to stay alive as the other soldiers were now walking away from Cethios and walking up ahead. And as the soldier fairy began to drag me along I shouted over to Theron, "Wait! Theron wait! I'll go quietly. I swear I won't fight you. I'll even make your task a pleasurable one. I'll give you what is rightfully yours if, you allow me to do just one thing before we go. Theron please!"

At this Theron stopped as well as the other soldiers. Theron turned around and walked up to me as he replied to the fairy soldier holding me, "Alright then, Demik let her go."

As he did, part of me regretted it as I fell upon my hands and knees. I was becoming weaker and if I was going to do something, now would be the right moment. Theron bent over as he rested his hands upon his knees. He whispered to me, "Well then, you have my attention oh love slave of mine, what is this one thing you ask of?"

I stared into Theron's mesmerizing green and blue eyes as I replied through my breaths, "I want to kiss Cethios… just once before he vanishes into nothing, that way, I have something to remember him by. One simple kiss, a kiss to a fairy whose life is about to cease into a memory."

Theron stood and gazed over to Cethios as his body began to give off a slight red glow. He chuckled as he extended his arm out to me. I honestly wanted to rip his arm off and beat him with it but, I needed to remain calm. And since I didn't really have my own strength, I reached over and with took his hand. Immediately he lifted me up as he pressed his body upon mine. He pressed upon my back as my legs trembled from the pain that shot through my spine. I gasped for air as he leaned me over a bit and slowly dragged his tongue over my neck and up to the rim of my ear. He whispered within it, "If there is any trickery here to your obsessive kiss, I guarantee you; I will leave you begging for death to inherit your soul once I take you."

As he let me go I stumbled a bit as I quickly opened my wings to their full extent so I could catch my balance. Theron took a few steps back as I startled him a bit. Good. I'm glad I still have that effect on others with my wings. And hopefully, my plan works before I black out and it's too late. And as the soldiers started to walk off a bit more, Theron replied to me, "Make it quick, I would like to have this Immortality before I face Xanthus again."

Those words made me forget how to breathe as I froze. What did he mean by face him again? Did Xanthus already know he was a traitor? Was he nearby? Oh crap, focus, focus; one thing at a time. I nodded to Theron as he spun around and started to walk over to his soldier. Great, privacy! I spun around slowly to see Cethios, perhaps on his last breaths as he glowed a bit. I stumbled over to him as I landed upon his chest. I grabbed his shoulders as I lifted myself up. We gazed into each other eyes as I replied softly to him, "And what in all creation were you thinking if I did not come to your rescue? Did you even have a plan or are you wanting to die?"

As he whispered my name, I knew I had to act fast. I'll yell at him later. I leaned into him and placed my lips gently upon his. I caressed his lips tenderly with mine as I took my magic to new heights. I poured some of my magic into him so he could heal his wound as I healed myself as well. One of my hands had found the back of his neck as the other ran through his hair. My simple kiss had become an unintentional and momentarily passionate one. And as we parted Cethios carefully brushed his tongue under my top lip. He unintentionally gasped out a soft moaned as he quickly bit his bottom lip. He shut his eyes and shook his head slightly, he whispered, "Sorry, instant reaction."

I stared at him, his body no longer glowed red with death. He now was glowing a soft white hue. It was as if he was emitting his own light of some kind, I knew he was infused temporarily with my magic. I placed my hands upon his face as I chuckled a bit, he was though red in the cheeks. I whispered to him, "Is the unbeatable Cethios blushing?"

Cethios chuckled as he took in some new deep breaths, he opened his eyes as he replied with a smirk, "No, it's simply your magic vibrating through my core and within my veins. It has nothing to do with the kiss. Besides, is this truly how you currently feel?"

I placed my forehead upon his chin, "Truly, it is for the current moment. My senses are heightened everything feels more pronounced, do you know what I mean?"

Cethios chuckled as the blush in his cheeks reddened, "Yeah, I understand completely. A simple kiss can instantly enhance your hormones spontaneously out of control."

I laugh quietly, "I can't wait to get this magic under control and for it to sizzle down."

Cethios nudged my forehead with his chin as he whispered, "Azalea, perhaps it's just a bit out of control because it was trapped for some time within you because of the shackles."

I grumbled, "I sure hope so."

I lifted my head as our eyes meet once more, and with that Cethios tilted his head and pressed his lips gently upon mine once more. I pushed myself off of him as I frowned. I placed my hands lightly upon my hips as he chuckled, "Had to get one more in there, can't blame a fairy for trying."

I shook my head as I stepped back from Cethios. He was insufferable and yet, I don't think I could live without him anymore. I gazed at him, looking him over as he attempted to free his arms. The rope that had him tied to the tree was not very well knotted. I asked, "Do you think you can manage to get yourself out? Or, do you want me to help you before I head over to Theron."

Cethios chuckled, "Azalea, I temporarily have some of your magic. What can possibly go wrong?"

"Lots."

We both chuckled a bit. And before I began to head out I replied to Cethios, "Don't forget about me."

I turned from him, as I started to go. But I heard Cethios faintly say, "I never have Azalea, and I never will."

Within a few moments I came into view of Theron. I did my best performance to act as if I was blacking out and stumbling about. I had to continue the rouse that I still was injured slightly and not at all feeling well. And just as I reached him, with my clumsy luck, I tripped over a stupid tree root. Luckily for me, Theron caught me and believed that I had finally collapsed. He pulled me over his shoulder as we began heading towards

521

that frustrating and annoying castle again. Oh well, I guess I can try to look on the bright side. Hopefully Xanthus would be nearby, hopefully I'd be able to see him soon. Hopefully he was alright…

The Debate

24

Theron continued to walk carefully as I remained relaxed upon his shoulders. I cautiously opened my eyes here and there as I noticed that we were walking by these heavy bricked walls that were covered in moss. It seemed as if the walls surrounded us as we continued to step through broken ones. I felt a bit overwhelmed as it seemed that we were going through some type of maze. If it was up to me I would simply fly over it, but that's just me. If I really want to, I could just pretend to wake up and fly away from Theron and the other soldiers but, two things. One, there was a fairy soldier among the elf soldiers and he would surely follow me. And two, I wanted to see if Theron would take me to Xanthus, or at least somewhere near him.

After what seemed like forever we neared these huge glass stained doors. And once we entered the castle I was able to see the design upon the glass more clearly. Within the designed glass was a massive lime colored dragon with two heads. Each head had enormous horns with spikes descending down the back of the neck. Its body was that of a fierce scaly lion with wings of a feathery eagle. Below it was a city that appeared to be within the treetops. It was a city that seemed quite familiar to me, a city that resembled that of the fairies, the City of Whisperia. I shivered; I wondered if that design was just that, a design within the stained glass. Or perhaps it was depicting something that once was. I couldn't help it; I shivered once more upon the thought. And hopefully Theron did not notice my shudders.

We continued to head farther and farther into the castle as we passed through many corridors. Strange to say that at one point, I myself seemed to get lost as the corridors all appeared the same. And one by one, the soldiers began to slowly fall back as they stood with their backs upon the wall. And in no time we neared this wooden door that had holes within it. And within the holes were clumps of raw blue and violet gems. It was as if they were trying to excavate the door or something. I wonder what it precisely meant.

Theron replied to the last soldier that happened to be the fairy, "Demik, I'll take it from here. Stand guard at the foot of this hall and do not allow anyone to pass. Although inform me immediately once Zethron arrives."

Demik bowed and took a couple of steps backwards, as if not wanting to turn his back upon Theron. I wouldn't blame him, I wouldn't either. He stopped as he stood with his back upon the wall and gazed off into the distance. Once satisfied, Theron spun around as I heard him fumble around within his pocket. He opened the door as it squeaked with high intensity. Chills ran down my spine as I tried with much concentration not to quiver at the noise.

Once we entered, the door behind us shut just as loudly as it opened. Theron began heading down this magnificent hall. The walls were vibrating with bright colorful silk that seemed to sway and flow downward towards the ground. Bright turquoise light seems to swirl behind the silk as I quickly became memorized with its beauty. Hummingbirds suddenly started to dart about between the two walls as my trance continued to overwhelm my heart.

Moments later we passed through this enormous archway that was made out of water droplets that contained small silver and rosy beads swirling within it. It was quite breath taking seeing them hover in place to form this archway and not blend together as one massive water tunnel. As confusing and frustrating that this castle is, it still does not cease in amazing me.

Once we passed the archway we entered a circular silvery stone room. Theron immediately placed me gently upon this sinfully soft bed. I sighed a breath of relaxation as I pretended to open my eyes slowly for the first time since I pretended to pass out, outside of the castle. Theron carefully pushed strands of hair off of my face as he brushed the back of his fingers upon my cheek. His fingers dragged ever so tenderly down my neck and down my arms. He rolled my hand over so my palm was facing up. He gently stroked my palm and my fingers with his. He stared at our hands as if he was having some sort of sentimental longing deep inside him. I was not expecting this, he seemed saddened by something. Curiosity filled me, I had to ask, "Theron? What is in your thoughts right now?"

Theron's lips twitched as if he wanted to smile but couldn't. He reached over and lifted my shirt slightly revealing the stone within my navel. He brushed his fingers over it as he sighed, "You know, before Xanthus was so successfully chosen by my Aunt Whistalyn, it was I that was meant for the unity? It should have been you and me as the destined ones, not you and Xanthus."

What was he talking about? Was this even remotely true? It couldn't be. This has to be a mind trap, he was just attempting to get inside my subconscious mind. I huffed, "I don't believe you. Xanthus and I were bound together long ago. We both have gems upon our navels, binding us together and symbolizing our love for one another. This was foretold by the prophecy…"

Theron interrupted me, "Yeah well, the prophecy did not state the names of those that were to be united, that is until the enchantment was complete. Xanthus couldn't read the text completely, but I could. It also stated that before the elf child was to be chosen, it stated that of the two heirs of the elf kings only the strongest of the two would be the rightful chosen one. It should have been me."

Theron gazed up and stared at me as our eyes locked. There was much grief and resentment within his eyes. It made sense why Theron felt like he had to defeat Xanthus in just about everything they did. Theron felt like it should have been him.

I broke my gaze with Theron as I stared down at our hands as he continued to stroke my palm with his fingertips. I was not going to allow his manipulation to work on me. I need to end this conversation and get out and find Xanthus. I asked, "Theron, is that why you have a grudge with Xanthus, because he was chosen and not you. You both couldn't have known at such an infant age. Xanthus was chosen by his mother, it was not his fault."

At this Theron stood from the bed and began to pace with his hands behind his back. He seemed lost within his own thoughts as he paced. And as I watched him I propped myself up upon my elbows. As he paced he muttered, "My father once expressed the truth to me that there was a trial between Xanthus and I, before one of us was chosen. And somehow Xanthus had bested me. He always has bested me, but no longer. I am the wisest in strategy and the strongest in magic. I just recently bested the unbeatable Cethios, and killed him. I am soon to inherit Immortality. And soon I will finally defeat and destroy my selfish cousin. Yes, Zethron will be very much pleased once he hears of all the recent successes I have achieved. I will inherit it all, I will become the invincible Immortal King Theron."

Alright, I can't stand to hear Theron talk like this any longer, especially of what he just implied about Xanthus. I asked as calmly as I could so I wouldn't anger him, "Theron, do you know where Xanthus is? Where is it that I can find him?"

He didn't pause in pacing as he mumbled, "My cousin matters not anymore. I have defeated him and he is where he belongs. He finally is getting what he deserves."

I sat up impatiently as rage began to boil inside me. I replied irritably, "Theron what have you done? Where is Xanthus?"

He ignored me as he continued to mumble, "Once I am Immortal I will rid myself of Zethron's Blood-Oath. Zethron will then bend to my will, let see how he likes it. I will destroy all of those foolish elves that chose not to follow me. I will…"

Enough was enough. I left the bed as I was now flying about a foot off of the ground hovering in midair. I wanted to see Theron at eye level as I waited for him to turn into me. I took him by surprise as he took a step back. I shouted, "What have you done with Xanthus! Where is he Theron!"

Theron seemed oddly calm as he lifted his nose up in arrogance. "Why do you care about someone who is so weak. You shouldn't waste your precious time with someone like that, someone who is withering away in his own grave. Why… you should have someone who is powerful enough to defeat his enemies, someone who can pleasure the one that he loves successfully. Join me Azalea, I can give you everything and more. I can give you satisfaction beyond your imaginable dreams."

I think not. I grunted, "There is nothing you can give me that I want, you could never satisfy me. Xanthus is the better elf than you. I will never join you."

Crap, bad choice of words. Theron took a step back as he glared at me. He snorted with anger, "You are just like Xanthus, pathetic and worthless. I was a fool to believe that a stupid fairy such as yourself would be wise enough to be my queen."

Before I knew it, Theron had quickly withdrawn his sword as he forcefully swung it at my chest. The blow flung me across the room as I back flipped within the air and landed upon the ground upon my hands and one knee. My instant reaction had me reaching for my chest automatically.

I gazed at my shaky palm expecting to see blood. And oddly enough, and thankfully, I saw nothing. I felt immensely sore but no blood seeped out. Weird, a blow like that would have surely injured me and have me at my weakest, long enough for Theron to take me before my last breaths even began.

I carefully stood still clinging to my sore chest as and gazed over to Theron. He simply stood there taking in deep breaths as his anger was surging through him. He replied furiously, "I'm going to get your Immortality tonight! Once I am finished with you, you are going to the dungeon with Xanthus. You both can rot in there forever! And there is nothing you can do about that!"

He chose the wrong set of words. I replied with a smile, "Wanna bet..." And with me replying that Theron laughed, he was so sure of himself. I gazed around for my sword as I saw it upon Theron side. He must have taken it off of me and placed it upon his side when he was carrying me through the maze. Alright, I took in a deep breath and concentrated. I extended my right hand outward as my palm glowed a dim blue. I whispered to myself, "Rightful sword within my grasp."

My sword upon Theron's hip glowed briefly as it boomeranged from his side and flung towards me. My swords' handle landed ever so carefully within my grasp. I couldn't help it, a smile spread across my face. You know, I can get this magic under control. This is a great feeling, the feeling of almost having my own body back to myself again. I shook slightly as chills ran through my core. And instantly the fake shackles upon my wrists faded away as if soft clouds were upon them and vaporized.

The look upon Theron's face was priceless, he was in utter shock. His eyes widened with fear as he took yet another step back from me. He stuttered, "No... This, this cannot be! Only Zethron can free you! How is this possible! No! I cannot fail!"

I quickly gazed down to see my now whole pendant. It was a key that unlocked the shackles that were once upon my wrists and ankles; a key that was once two but is now one. This key pendant will unlock anything that my heart desires, which represents the heart of Xanthus and I as one; and of our faith in each other. And as I gazed back up, my eyes locked with Theron's as I replied, "One last chance Theron, you don't have to do this. I can help you, I can free you from Zethron. You can change."

Theron took one last long look upon my wrists as he took in a deep breath. He grunted, "I'll take my own chances." He lunged for me as I stopped his blade upon mine. He collided it quickly with mine as blue sparks seemed to explode with each intense clang. He was fiercely attempting to knock me down. He took another swing as I back flipped upon the bed. And that was when I realized that he was seriously attempting to kill me. And not only that, he was fighting with all his might in anger. And that was his first mistake.

I blocked his next blow as I flipped over him and landed behind him. We fought a bit more as all I did was continuously block his moves. I mean, I couldn't fight him. I didn't want to kill him. Enemy or not, he still is Xanthus' cousin. And after a few more blows that he sent my way, he finally seemed to be worn out. Theron was trying to situate his breaths as heavy beads of sweat clung to his forehead and to his chest. He wiped his forehead with his sleeve as he replied breathlessly, "You're not going to fight back are you?"

I shook my head and replied through breaths, "No, I am not going to fight back with the intensions of killing you. But I am not going to allow you to kill me or knock me out."

Theron placed his free hand upon the side of his stomach as he gasped for more air. He replied breathlessly, "Even though I killed Cethios."

I chuckled. I couldn't help it, but I had to tell him the truth. Sooner or later he would have found out. So I replied, "No, you didn't kill him. I made sure of that."

Theron took in another deep breath as he threw his free hand in the air, "Great, so now what?"

I shrugged, "You could surrender."

Theron laughed as he took in more breaths as he now steadied himself. He was preparing himself to fight me once again. Well, what else did I have to do at that moment. I could over power him but, I'm not sure if I have my magic under control just yet. So, I simply shrugged my shoulders and pushed my sleeves a bit higher up to get better mobility. Once I did Theron's face fell in shock as he simply tossed his sword towards me upon the ground. I was a bit confused. I gazed upon his sword, then back to him as I asked, "And what made you change your mind just now? I know you didn't have an epiphany."

Theron glared at me as he stepped closer. He stopped just as I laid my swords' tip upon his neck. He frowned, "Seriously Azalea, we both know that you will not allow harm to come to me. So do us both a favor and put it away."

I wanted to punch him in the face for his arrogant comment. But he was right. I grunted as I moved my sword from his neck and placed it back upon the holster on my side. I asked, "So are you going to explain to me what made you change your mind?"

Theron stepped closer as he pointed to my right arm. He slowly traced the leaf patterns of my tattoo with his fingertips. It sent chills up my arm and through my spine as he gazed into my eyes. He asked softly as his breaths slowed, "Do you want to explain to me your Blood-Oath with Latimer?"

I took a step back from him as I crossed my arms upon my chest. I replied to him, "Sure, as soon as you first explain to me the Blood-Oath that you have with Zethron."

Theron raised his eyebrow, and at that brief moment I saw the resemblance of Xanthus in him. He too crossed his arms as he replied, "Toshay Azalea."

After a few moments of silence, I gave in. I wasn't one to wait. I dropped my arms and replied, "Alright Theron look, I just want to know where Xanthus is. I don't care what side you end up on. I just want to find Xanthus and be with him so we can take out Zethron. So, whether you decide to help us or not that's fine, that's on your conscious, not mine. But you are going to have to move out of my way."

Theron seemed to ponder my words as a huge grin appeared upon his face. He took a couple of steps back from me as he replied with a smirk, "Fine, have it your way. I'll help you with one of those requests. But, I'll truly deny you the other. And I guarantee you Azalea... mark my words, I will have your Immortality one day."

And with that being said Theron formed a blue energy globe upon his right palm. It hovered there momentarily as I realized that I couldn't take any more steps back, for the bed was right behind me. I froze; I guess I sort of waited to see what he would do. Would he send me to Xanthus? Would he try to kill me again?

The blue globe vibrated with every breath Theron released. His eyes of green and blue stung my heart as they filled with tears. And that was the true moment when I knew, that truth be told, he was fighting the Blood-Oath with Zethron. There was some goodness in him, somewhere. And just as I was about to reply words of wisdom to Theron, he tossed the energy globe onto the ground near me. It split the floor open as I immediately fell down as a powerful gust of wind pushed me into the oblivious. It was inevitable; I couldn't even open my wings or grab on to anything to stop myself from falling into it. The only thing I could do was scream as I fell deeper into the black abyss.

The Events

25

I landed upon a rough hard surface that seemed to tear into my wings and back. I gazed up as my vision blurred in and out of focus. I wanted to say that I actually blacked out for a bit. But once I gained a bit of my sight back I started to gaze around slowly. I noticed a couple of things. I was in a cavern of some sort, perhaps a type of dungeon. To my left were what seemed to be dark wet tunnels. And to my right were bright bars that lit up the cavern as they vibrated immensely. Above me were spiked rocks that slowly dripped water from their tips and... wait a moment... there was a familiar face. But I couldn't quite tell just who it was; my vision was still a bit blurred. A familiar voice cried out, "Azalea? Crap! It is Azalea! Are you alright? Did Cethios or Theron hurt you, did one of them take you? I swear on our oath I'll kill them both! Rowen come quick, it is Azalea!"

I tried to move but, it was as if my muscles were not allowing me the privilege to use my strength. I felt so weak and disorientated. I suddenly felt cool hands upon me as they carried me. They laid me upon something that seemed so comfortable and soft. If I could lay here for a day or so and rest, I would.

My hearing ringed in and out as I heard two voices arguing about. Thankfully by this time I at least knew that one of the voices was Rowen. I wasn't quite sure just yet who the other was. He sounded familiar but it didn't quite come to me. Why was I so out of it? Was I really injured that badly? I mean, I just fell with the gust when Theron sent me here. Was it really that big of a fall?

After it seemed like an eternity, my subconscious mind finally allowed me to come to. I was able to focus my sight as I saw that to my far right was Rowen. He seemed angered as he paced with one hand behind his back and the other upon his forehead. I turned my gaze closer to me as I saw someone hovering over me. Once I recognized him I wanted to jump for joy but, my body didn't quite allow me to just yet. I replied as best as I could, "Latimer..."

Instantly he bent over and embraced me. Ouch. Pain and soreness still swelled within my skin. I managed to reply, "Not so tight Latimer. What is going on here? What happened?"

Latimer carefully helped me stand as I realized that I was lying on a handmade cot made of stone and shirts. How long have they been down here? Truly what did I miss? And before I could ponder on it, Rowen was at my side carefully embracing me. He whispered, "Azalea, you have no idea how astonished, grateful and relieved we are to see you. We thought you were never going to wake."

At this I became a bit more alert. I still clung to Latimer's arm to balance myself as I took a good look at them. They both looked a bit rough. Once again, how long have they been down here? How long have I been down here? So I asked, "How long have you both been here? How come you haven't escaped yet? Where are the others? Where is Xanthus?"

Their faces seemed grim, as if, someone had died. And as their faces revealed something out of my nightmares, my breaths became heavy. I clung to my chest as pain struck at my heart. I began to feel the cavern spin but before I knew it Latimer had grabbed me by my shoulders. I thought he was going to steady me but instead, he shook me a bit as he replied, quite loudly in my face, "Azalea no! Do not allow yourself to believe that Xanthus is dead, do you hear me! Do not place yourself in the state of mind that he is in right now. Even though we might have failed, we can still escape and fight. We can still survive, we have each other."

With that I opened my wings to their full extent, painfully I might add, as the two elves jumped back. I startled them a bit as I replied sternly, "What happened? Where are we? And would someone please just tell me where Xanthus is?"

Latimer seemed a bit dazed as he stepped over to the cot and sat down with his hands upon his lap. Rowen on the other hand had taken a step back as he took in a deep breath. He let it out slowly as he gazed at his feet and shoved his hands within his pockets. And without lifting his head Rowen rolled his gaze up towards me as he replied, "Alright, here goes. After you were taken by Cethios, Xanthus' life was renewed. He is Immortal as you are, or were or whatever. We headed back to Trinafin to regroup but, King Alcander had other plans. We believe forced is more like it though. So Morpheus, Xanthus and myself headed to save Queen Whistalyn; while Latimer and Theron headed to find you. Oleos was sent back to the main island to be with King Zyren for his last breaths. We were unsuccessful in saving Queen Whistalyn but found James. Morpheus got himself wounded but is alright. He is at the main Island of Yaisla; hopefully he made it out of harm's way and is in safety. Once we exited we headed here and attempted to find you, with James' help thankfully. But we ended up finding Latimer here tangled up in a bunch of vines. And then, James quickly abandoned us. He said he had unfinished business to attend to that needed his urgent abilities, whatever that meant. But, Zethron found us first, a little confused to find Xanthus alive but nonetheless, even with the three of us, we were no match for Zethron. He was way too powerful beyond what we've ever encountered. He imprisoned us here after literally a days' worth of battle with him. He left us here in this enchanted cavern dungeon that blocks all of our magic, even Xanthus himself. Theron came down to visit us, we had a few choice words for him, and he had some powerful words for us as well, more for Xanthus really. Overall, we have been here a couple of days, not quite sure on how many that is anymore, our food rations are slimming down to nothing. But, there are a few tunnels that lead to other abandoned caverns but, after fumbling in pitch black darkness we found that this was the only way out. Although there is this tunnel that leads to the only cavern dungeon with a bared window high up and…"

Rowen allowed his hands drop as he slowly made his way over to me. He whisper, "And that is where you will also find Xanthus. The first day or so of being in here we tried to escape. But every attempt we tried, we failed at it. We couldn't conjure anything. And these bars are like lightning bolts enslaving us in. Xanthus and Latimer got shocked a couple of times and got thrown back."

"That was painful." Latimer chimed in.

I turned to him and smiled at him. If I could reassure him that everything was going to be alright I would but, I was getting to a point where I myself wasn't so sure anymore. I turned back to Rowen as he continued, "After that, Xanthus became basically mute. He attempted a couple of enchantments in the other caverns but, nothing. Only in the last cavern where the bared window is, is where he stays now. He repeats words to himself sometimes. He repeats that the stars are brighter if he tries. Azalea, it's like he has lost all sense in life. It is like his mind is gone. And when you fell through, we shouted to him that you were here but, we heard nothing from him. We didn't want to abandon you being the state you were in. We know he is there but, we just don't know what to do anymore. Theron betrayed us, which actually came to no surprise. Xanthus is gone without will or hope. We are nothing but dying rats here in this cavern. And… and it feels like we have failed… like we are doomed."

Rowen's breaths seemed faint as I walked over to him and placed my right palm upon his cheek. He reached for my palm as he held it there and closed his eyes. Two tears rolled down his face as he tried to settle his breathing. I sighed a bit as I truly had no idea on what I could say at this moment to Rowen. I didn't want to believe him but, how could I feel any more positive when the truth is right in front of us. We were helpless, but I couldn't allow any of them to see that. I needed to be brave. I needed to keep some kind of faith within my soul. And as Rowen opened his watery eyes I gazed into them and replied, "It is going to be alright. We are all going to get out of here. I have not been taken and my shackles are now gone, so there is still hope. Now, point me to which tunnel I need to take to reach Xanthus."

Rowen released my hand as he pointed to the tunnel to my far left. I took in a deep breath, gathered my courage and started to make my way over to the entrance. And just before I entered it, Latimer stood in my way. He placed his palm upon my shoulder as he whispered, "Azalea, I am your protector, through my blood I made an oath to you. And I do take it seriously; I shall do everything in my will to protect you, even if it is from Xanthus himself. Now I trust him but, the state that his mind is in right now, I am not so sure of him myself anymore. I'm not saying that he will try to hurt you but, well just be careful alright. Give a shout if you need help of any sort and I will come instantly to your side. I will be standing here awaiting if you need me. And also before you go Azalea; remember we are here without magic. I just don't want you to rely on your magic and forget that we are helpless. Also, one more thing, it does get truly dark within the tunnel before you reach the cavern itself. Do be careful."

I reached for his hand as I removed it from my shoulder and held it momentarily. I nodded to him as I released his palm. I whispered to him, "Latimer, he is my Xanthus. Nothing can change that, not even he himself."

Latimer bowed his head slightly as he stepped aside, allowing me to enter the tunnel. I slowly started to make my way into it as I lightly brushed my fingertips upon the cool wet cavern wall. I embraced the darkness as it quickly wrapped around me. And as I walked ever so carefully onward, I prepared myself in finally facing my love, my Xanthus. My nerves were on edge as I yearned to finally see him again, to finally touch his warm skin. I wanted to run into the cavern and embrace him with everything that I had. I didn't want to believe that he was truly lost. I couldn't allow myself to think that, I won't. But no matter what has come to him, he still is my Xanthus, my love. My Xanthus...

The Extraordinary Night and the Stars

26

I felt as if I was walking around in this dark tunnel, for what seemed like forever. I wonder how far this tunnel leads down. Was I going the right way or did I miss a turn or something? Either way, my feet were sore and my clothes clung to my body with the wetness of this humidity. Drips from the ceiling, I'm hoping, kept falling down my back which kept startling me.

Finally moonlight began to drift towards me as the cavern came into view. Once I entered I saw that there were about five enormous boulders facing in a circle. They were each a different size as carvings covered their entirety. The carvings were that of different plants, dragons, and what looked like stars. Normally I would be intrigued to run my hands over them and study them but, I desperately wanted to find Xanthus. It has been too long since I last saw my love.

I gazed to my far left as I saw that about fifty feet above the boulders was a window with bars made of stone. The window was as wide as a baby dragon, about ten feet wide and high. I could fly up there and see if I could squeeze between the bars but, I'm sure up close they would be to close together to attempt anything. But you were able to see the enchanting moon and stars. And yet, they seemed to glow brighter with every step I took closer to them, weird.

I made my way around the boulders looking for Xanthus. I passed the first two, nothing. I passed the third and fourth, nothing. Of course, Xanthus would be with the last boulder, the boulder closest to the stars. I took in a deep breath and made my way around the last boulder. And sure enough, Xanthus was there. And as my eyes laid upon him, my heart shuddered.

Xanthus sat upon the floor with his back upon the boulder. His legs and arms laid in front of him as his eyes seemed strained and weary. He had a bit more stubble upon his face, more than what he would usually have. And his clothes were drenched with the humidity, as I'm sure mine were as well. And as I got closer I could tell that Xanthus was dazing off staring into a dark corner of the cavern. I softly replied to him, "Xanthus? Xanthus my love, it's me... It's Azalea."

I stepped closer and knelt beside him. I tenderly wrapped my left fingers around his as he barely moved. I inched closer to him as I placed my right palm upon his cheek. I brought my lips near his ear as I whispered gently, "Xanthus, I'm here. It's me Azalea."

At this Xanthus slowly turned and met my gaze with his warm intoxicating brown eyes. I can't describe the joy that overwhelmed my heart, my soul. And yet, the sadness within his eyes made me sigh in despair. Suddenly my soul leaped as a small smile broke across his face. He whispered, "The Ancient Eternal Spirits have found mercy upon my condemned soul, my mother has helped. Here in this hell, they have granted me the chance to see my beloved Azalea just once more. I shall remember this hallucination forever as a gift. They have allowed me the extra sin of imagining Azalea's gentle embrace. Would it be too much to ask for; if I ask my hallucination for a kiss?"

How can I deny him? I leaned over and gently wrapped my lips upon his as I ran my fingers through his smooth brown hair. He carefully bit my bottom lip as soft tremor flooded through my core. And as we continued our passionate kiss, Xanthus began caressing my back with his cool hands, gently running his fingertips upon my wings. Chills ran over my spine as we parted and exhaled with a soft sigh. I replied with a breath, "Xanthus, I am not a hallucination of your subconscious mind. This is real, I am real. Xanthus, whatever deep abyss your mind has taken you in, you need to come back from it. Come back to me please."

Xanthus chuckled lightly as he traced his fingers across my jaw line, then over my bottom lip, "What a thing to see, my hallucination is begging, and for what? To come back to a reality where I have to admit to myself again that I am a failure? Theron and Zethron are right, I was unable to save my mother, I could not save Azalea from being taken and killed, and I cannot even help my friends escape. I'm a pathetic worthless fool who is going to die in these lost caverns. For all I know we are already dead, and this is my personal hell for failing to protect the prophecy."

I pressed my forehead onto the side of his face. Latimer was right, he was in some sort of helpless state of mind. I don't think anything I say will be able to change his mind. I was beginning to feel a bit hopeless for Xanthus. This was not fair, Xanthus did not deserve to feel this way. I can't believe they would lie to Xanthus and make him believe all those horrible lies about me.

I closed my eyes and released a heavy sigh as Xanthus placed a cool hand upon my cheek. Xanthus chuckled lightly once more, "Look at that, I'm even granted the chance to feel my beloved Azalea, to feel her lips, to feel her skin, her warmth…"

I sat up slightly as I crawled onto his lap, straddling him as I gently placed my hands upon his cheeks. I locked my gaze with his as he wrapped his arms around my waist. I replied, "I am not dead Xanthus, nor have I been taken. You have been lied to, you are not pathetic nor worthless. You are my Xanthus, and you are faithful, courageous and true."

Xanthus shook his head slightly out of my hands as a silver tear escaped his eye. He grumbled, "Theron is right, it should have been him and not I for the prophecy. He is the better elf."

I cupped his face once more as I lifted his chin forcing him to gaze into my eyes. I snorted, "Absolutely not, you are the better elf. You are filled with pure love while Theron is filled with pure hatred. I do not doubt you, and I never will. You were chosen just like I was, we are destined for each other. There is no one else I would rather share my love with. You are meant for me."

I leaned over and placed my lips urgently on his. If I couldn't convince him with my words, then I would convince him with my love. My lips traveled form his lips, to his ear lobe, to his neck. I kissed every inch of him that I could. And within moments Xanthus began placing his lips upon my skin, at first ever so carefully, almost hesitant. But as soon as my first soft pleasurable moan escaped my lips he seemed to come too as he feverishly began continuing our love further. And just like that, my ordinary night had turned extraordinary…

Hours later, once Xanthus had fallen asleep, I flew up towards the window and with took a stone bar between my fingers. I stared out and gazed at the twinkling stars above me. Xanthus was right; they did look amazing and ever so brighter than usual. They seemed to be pulsing with some sort of unique energy, as if calling me somehow, somewhat mesmerizing to watch.

I broke my gaze with the stars as I glanced over to Xanthus, whom seemed so at peace now as he slept. And unfortunately I couldn't help but feel desperately ashamed that perhaps Xanthus was right, we had lost. Here we were in a dark murky cavern, dungeon of hell is more like it, which had us without magic and helpless in escaping. We were sitting bait, and as hard as I tried to come up with something, I couldn't think of anything.

And I'm sure by this coming morning; Zethron would be here to surly take my Immortality and destroy us all.

I buried my face in my hands as the negativity sank in deeper into my heart. My breaths became heavy as I turned back towards the stars, as if they had the answers I was seeking. And yet, once my eyes met the shining stars, there was a voice, an epiphany inside my subconscious mind that spoke quite clearly. James' words flowed effortlessly, 'Remember reach for the stars above you, for they too conceal energy, and always reach deep inside yourself.'

Holy Crap! I couldn't believe it! How could I have been so foolish in forgetting James' words. They have always followed me so, what difference would this situation be from the others. When I finally see him again, I'm going to give him the biggest hug ever! Even though I was still slightly upset at him for not telling me he was Immortal.

I flew up a bit higher as I was being extremely careful not to bump into the spikes hanging down from the ceiling. I leaned into the bars as much as I could as I stretched out both arms. It was so interesting to know that the stars themselves knew that we shared some sort of connection. That's why they were and are shinning so bright! Xanthus noticed it, but couldn't figure it out. Thankfully I did, and just in time too for it appeared that the sun was making its way to the surface.

I closed my eyes and reached high above me. I concentrated with everything I had, I had to. I concentrated on the energy deep within me and on the energy that the stars emitted. I inhaled deep breaths, I tried to absorb it. And although for a brief moment it felt like hopeless efforts, a new surge of energy began to swell within my fingertips. It felt sensational as I opened my eyes. And as I did, astonishment overwhelmed my soul at that very moment.

Tiny glittering stars began coming in from a strand of remaining moonlight that flowed into the cavern. They swirled ever so carefully around my fingers as they emitted sparkling colorful glitter. They continued to flow downward as they now swirled within my hair and around my wings. And within moments they filled the cavern with their sparkling light. They darted around the cavern as they began to swirl out into the tunnel.

I turned back around to see that there were no more stars coming in through the window, so I flew down and started to follow them slowly. They continued to swirl out into the tunnel as I turned and glanced back over to Xanthus. He still slept peacefully, and I did not want to disturb him. I sighed as I pondered on his sanity. Who knows if he truly is lost or not, I can't make that decision for him. It has to be up to him to come back. It has to be his own will. And although he had given up his hope, I knew I couldn't, for both of our sakes.

I quickly flew over to Xanthus and bent down and kissed him upon the lips softly. He remained motionless as I whispered, "Please do come back to me Xanthus, I love you."

I stood and took in a deep breath, my decision was made. I was going to follow the stars and see just where they were heading to on their own. So, as I follow the remaining stars that were left down the tunnel, courage flow within me. And hopefully, that courage would never leave my soul again.

Underestimated

27

As I made my way through the tunnel, I realized that these were no ordinary cavern walls. And I appreciated the darkness when I traveled through it the first time. It was extremely eerie to see all the carvings in the stone that seemed as if someone or something, was trying to escape the walls itself. It sent chills through my spine knowing that I was once touching them with my fingertips, quite disturbing.

Finally after it seem like forever, again, I reached the main cavern entrance as I started to hear shouts. I quickly exited the tunnel as my eyes fell upon the two elves. And once I saw them, I could not contain my laughter. I chuckled as I saw the glittering stars dance around Latimer and Rowen. They both tried with all of their might to swat them or maneuver around them. But every attempt failed, the stars were just too fast for them. Latimer caught my glance as he shouted over, "Azalea what is going on! Is this somehow your doing?"

I shouted back, still chuckling, "Technically it's all thanks to James but, yes it is me! I simply did what I did not know I was able to do until I remembered that I could."

I think I dumfounded Latimer as he gazed at me with his mouth slightly open. I think he thought that I had lost it as I continued to chuckle. How could I not? I wanted to jump about and shout in excitement! And then, I remembered my purpose in calling them, the bars of the dungeon. I had to act quickly before they disappeared and my chance was lost.

I rushed over to the bars as I stopped about two feet away from them. They still vibrated with intensity as their glow pulsed upon my skin. I closed my eyes and whispered, "Stars of mighty power, consume these bars within this hour. Destroy the magic that imprisons us, and morph it into useless dust. Give us the chance to be free, for I can see that you agree. Release us from this forsaken room, before you return to your precious moon. I say these words with all my might, as I thank you for being our saving light."

A low vibrating hum began to form and grow swiftly behind me. The other two elves shouted but I kept my concentration. I opened my eyes slowly as I stared at the bars. They continued to vibrate as the stars began to swirl around my body and fingers. I denied myself the thought of becoming frightened as I saw that my skin started to give off a slight glow that matched the stars. Small blue lightning bolts emerge from the bars as they sizzled into the tiny stars.

The once tiny stars began to enlarge as the lightning bolts continued to enter them. And as I became hypnotized by their enchantment, I could still slightly hear Latimer and Rowen shouting my name. But I did not want to move for fear that this would all go away. The feeling of the magic ruffling through my hair and sweeping across my skin was intoxicating.

Suddenly like a sonic boom effect the stars exploded into millions of glittery pieces as they rushed back out the way they came in. The gust knocked me off of my feet as I fell onto the ground. Immediately though I sat up. I wanted to gaze upon the bars to see if anything had happen upon them. And as the cavern still seemed lit from some type of far off light, the bars vibrated no more with magic that withheld them. Heavy breaths concaved in my chest as I became overwhelmed with my thoughts. I had to grab the bars to see if they were powerless, if they were I had to try my magic. And perhaps then escape. Yes, that would be grand. And if not, I had to continue to try something else. I couldn't give up; I refused to allow that emotion to ever dwell within my soul again.

I stood as I slowly reached for the bars. Latimer shouted, "Azalea no! You'll be blown over!"

As much as I regrettably knew the consequence for touching the bars, I had to see if the stars had done what I had set them out to accomplish. I extended my fingers and with took the bars within them. I waited, nothing. I reached over with my left and with took another bar, nothing. I sighed out a gasp of relief. I seriously needed to thank James; truly he is the best mentor ever.

Suddenly I jumped slightly as Rowen startled me as he whispered within my ear, "Azalea, you truly are underestimated, you're unexpected. The obstacles that you have overcome are truly worth that of a grand queen."

I turned towards Rowen as I smiled shyly. And just as I was about to reply to him we heard a loud explosion far off from the other side of the bars. Rowen and Latimer withdrew their swords as they stood one on each side of me. I stood back a bit from the bars as I opened my wings to their full extent. I raised my right palm as it glowed a slight ivory hue. I was planning on fighting with my power instead of my sword. And with much pleasure, I can finally say that I have my magic under my control.

We waited as the footsteps quickly approached us. Then with a huge sigh of relief I saw Cethios sprinting around the corner. And as our eyes met he shouted with satisfaction, "Azalea!"

I couldn't help it. I instantly shouted with contentment, "Cethios!"

The joy in my voice was distinct, and it was true. I was ecstatic in seeing him. Immediately Cethios raised his right palm towards the bars as he whispered something under his breath. Bright emerald light emerged from his palm as it shot onto the bars, and within moments they melted to nothing.

Without hesitation I ran to Cethios and jumped into his arms. Laughter and relief escaped my lips as Cethios embraced me in return. I closed my wings as I let him go. I replied to him, "How? How was it that you found me?"

Cethios' expression instantly fell in grief as he gazed off behind me. I spun around to see that Xanthus was slowly making his way over to us. And he didn't seem so content. I attempted to stand in front of Cethios but he stepped aside as if waiting for judgment. And as Xanthus was about arm's length from me, I raised both of my palms up as I replied to my love, "Xanthus wait, this is not what you think."

Xanthus stopped as he smiled smugly at me and replied, "Azalea, I've expressed to you that I shall never forget our promise, and I intent to always keep that. I gave you my word as you gave me yours; a promise to belong to one another, to be faithful and honest with the other. And I will listen to your explanation. I do not fear that you have betrayed me or our love. I will allow you to explain. But first…"

And before he could finish his sentence he quickly stepped aside me and punched Cethios hard in the face, sending him flying upon the floor and landing with a heavy thud. I was in utter shock as Xanthus then calmly turned back towards me as he shrugged his shoulder and replied smoothly, "Alright, now you may explain."

A cheer arose from Rowen as he shouted, "Yes, Xanthus is back!"

I frowned at them both as I went over and helped Cethios up. I replied to Xanthus, "Cethios is not our enemy, nor was he ever. He was under a Blood-Oath with your traitorous cousin Theron. He is actually here to help us and honestly, if not for him I would have been taken by now or worst, dead. He is the reason why I am alive. This punch of yours was not needed."

Xanthus shrugged as he replied, "Fair enough, I simply thought I could take out my momentary rage on his arrogant face for all of the things that he has put me through. Sure I'm grateful for him keeping you safe, if that's what you want to call it. But that does not dismiss all of the other evil that he has done."

I stepped closer to Xanthus as I replied a bit louder to him, "That was not his fault. Your cousin has a Blood-Oath with Zethron himself, which in turn, transferred some of that sinister darkness to Cethios."

"That still doesn't mean that he couldn't fight it! And why the hell did he allow himself the stupidity to do a Blood-Oath with Theron!"

I inched closer as I continued shouting back at Xanthus, "He had his reasoning's for the Blood-Oath. But beside the point Xanthus, he couldn't go completely against it! I am sure you are well aware of the consequences of going against a Blood-Oath! He'd be dead right now if he did, we'd all be dead!"

"Azalea, that is not an excuse, there are multiple ways to maneuver around Blood-Oaths!"

"And don't you think he was doing just that!"

By now Xanthus' fists were on fire as our faces were mere inches from another, almost touching our noses together. And before we began our argument once more, a slight cough startled us. And as Xanthus and I turned, we saw that Cethios was standing there with his arms crossed lightly upon his chest. He smirked as he took in a deep breath and replied smugly, "It does come to great satisfaction to see you both arguing, especially over me, but we really need to get moving. We need to get out of here, now."

With that Xanthus turned back towards me momentarily. He shook his head slightly frustrated as he quickly turned back around towards Cethios as he punched him once again quite forcefully in the face. And once again, Cethios tumbled onto the floor. I shouted to Xanthus, "What was that for!"

Xanthus smiled as if he had done nothing wrong. He shrugged his shoulders and replied smoothly, "I just thought I could get one more in. He did in his eyes, kill me in the Depths you know."

I threw my hands up in the air. "I know Xanthus! That was merely for show, he knew you were already Immortal!"

Xanthus raised that one gorgeous eyebrow of his as he replied softly, "Still hurt."

I grunted. Xanthus was being stubborn to the core. And within moments Cethios stood as he wiped the side of his lip with his sleeve. Cethios glared at Xanthus as he replied, "Seriously, one more punch and I will not be holding back for Azalea's sake. Azalea is my best friend and you are just going to have to get over that. She loves you truly I know that. But trust me, there is nothing no one can do or say to change that, except you. So watch it."

Xanthus glared at Cethios as he knew he was right. Partially, I wouldn't leave Xanthus but I let Cethios run with the idea. Perhaps that could persuade Xanthus to calm down. Xanthus took a step towards Cethios as Cethios lifted his chin a bit as if egging him on to punch him. Xanthus replied through his teeth, "Fine, then what do you suggest we do now."

Cethios gazed over to me as did Xanthus. I stood there as I gazed at both of them. It was a no brainer but it seemed as if neither of them wanted to make the decision. I turned to face Latimer and Rowen but they were no help either. They too were glaring at Cethios. So as I turned back to face Cethios and Xanthus, I replied, "Like Cethios implied, we get out of here."

Xanthus turned slightly to see Cethios slightly gloating at my comment, but when his gaze met Xanthus' his smugness fell. Cethios cleared his throat, "Right, this way to the gardens then."

Xanthus stepped back a bit as he suggested to Cethios, "You first."

Cethios rolled his eyes as he replied, "Look, I'm not going to stab you in the back if that's what you're thinking."

Xanthus snorted as he glared and whispered, "Didn't stop you before, did it?"

I grunted, this was going to take a while to smoother over. I hope when it came down to having each other's back, they wouldn't be so stubborn. I frowned as I grabbed Xanthus' arm and pulled him to face me. "Look Xanthus, I promise that Cethios will explain himself later but, you trust me right?"

Xanthus' glare finally left Cethios as his eyes met mine. And at that exact moment, it seemed as if he was truly gazing upon me from the longest of times. Sadness and relief fell upon his face as his eyes seemed to swell. He reached out and placed his palm gently upon my cheek, stroking the bottom of my lips slightly with his thumb. Xanthus whispered, "Azalea, I trust you with everything that I got."

Xanthus leaned in closer as his eyes stared at my lips. He brought my face closer to his as he gently placed his forehead to mine. I whispered, "If you trust me, then believe me when I say that Cethios would not bring harm against our lives. Trust him as you do me."

Xanthus gently pulled me in for a soft, passionate kiss. His kiss left me breathless. He smirked, satisfied with himself that he could manipulate me so easily. He cleared his throat and replied smugly to Cethios, "Lead the way Cethios."

Cethios nodded and started to make his way over to the left of the cavern as I follow him, with Latimer beside me. Xanthus walked with a quick pace behind us with Rowen. I don't believe he was so quick to trust Cethios so simply. Rowen caught on as he nudged Xanthus and whispered to him, "Xanthus I know you, you can't be serious in trusting Cethios so effortlessly, can you? Azalea can't surely guarantee us that he will be so trustworthy. Are you sure she isn't being manipulated by him? I don't like this Xanthus, I do not agree with this at all."

Xanthus sighed as they paced to keep up to us. He whispered over to Rowen, "I do not want to trust Cethios, but I have faith in Azalea. Therefore that leads me no choice, so yes I'm trusting Cethios. Besides, you're the one that told me not to underestimate Azalea. She knows what she is doing, she is not one to be fooled or manipulated. And to be honest, I choose to no longer underestimate her."

Rowen nodded as he replied, "Alright, let's just assume then that he will not betray us."

They both caught up with the rest of us as we made our way out of the caverns and into the gardens above. But little did we know what waited for us within the gardens. Little did we know that our final battle was just moments away.

Epic Failure

28

In no time, we reached the Gardens of Vigoro. Thankfully, Cethios had spent the whole day yesterday and the night enchanting the halls. That way we can make an easy escape from this castle of madness. And as soon as we stepped out, the warm sun greeted us. And as everyone rushed forward, I stopped to close my eyes to have a brief moment with my surrounding environment. I allowed the suns' rays to penetrate my skin and warm my soul. Such a peaceful moment I had. I wish it would last longer than just a few moments, perhaps forever.

I stretched my arms up a bit as suddenly I felt a warm embrace around my waist. I opened my eyes to see Xanthus as all of his rough appearance was washed away. He was his old self again, I'm sure as soon as we stepped out he enchanted himself and gave himself a cleanup and a magical shave. He still had a bit of stubble just the way I liked it. But instead of a smile he appeared worried. "What is it Xanthus?"

Xanthus' face filled with frustrated as he replied softly, "If we don't make it out of here together, again, I want you to know that I will always come for you. No matter how long it takes me, know that I will forever come for you."

"Xanthus I…"

He pressed his fingertips tenderly upon my lips softly as he replied, "Please, allow me to get this out before we go on."

I nodded as I with took his fingers within my hands. I waited patiently as Xanthus seemed to be taking in slow breaths and pondering a bit. He gazed so lovingly into my eyes; my heart simply melted. He was so heavenly to gaze upon. He took a deep breath and continued, "I know you will fight your way back too; I know you love me. But I want you to know that I will never give up on searching for you, ever. I will search the world, under rocks and in between walls if I have to, just so I can have you back in my arms again. Immortal or not, it's you that I care for. And together we can do anything to defeat Zethron. I know we can, if we are together. Not alone, together we can do this."

I turned my gaze from him as I fumbled around with his fingers. This was going to be difficult but, I had to be truthful with my love. So as I gazed back into his eyes I whispered to him, "I have to tell you something too. When I arrived here in the Castle of Vigoro with Cethios, he had to show me the truth about our past. And Cethios and I... Well, we shared a few moments of..."

Xanthus pressed his fingers upon my lips once more but this time he closed his eyes as he took in a frustrated breath. He grunted slightly, "Azalea, honestly, do you love him more than I?

I took Xanthus' fingers off of my lips as I softly answered him, "No I do not."

Xanthus sighed still keeping his eyes closed, "Would you rather be with him than I?"

Without hesitation I answered him, "No Xanthus. It's you that I love. It's you who I want."

With that Xanthus opened his eyes and gently placed his lips upon mine cupping my chin slightly. As we parted, he gently lifted my face as he sighed, "Then I do not need to hear anything that has pasted between the two of you. I do not need another reason to go and collide my fist into his face. We shall leave it at that. As long as nothing of the sort ever passes again, you are mine and I am yours, I do not share what is mine and neither should you. I love you Azalea."

I leaned towards him as I felt his gentle breath upon my lips. I brushed them softly with mine. And just as I was about to caress my lips upon his once more, a firm cough stopped me. I turned my gaze towards my right as I saw that Cethios was standing there with a disappointed look. He crossed his arms upon his chest as he replied, "If you two are going to be pausing every so often to discuss your love for each other, then we should just place a sign over our foreheads that says, free to Zethron, take at will."

And before I could argue with him, Xanthus quickly replied, "You are right, we need to keep moving."

Xanthus began to make his way over to the other two elves when he stopped. He spun around and faced us as he seemed confused. I didn't want to tell him that he really did just agree with Cethios; because by Cethios gloating alone, that revealed all. And just before Xanthus could

547

reply, Cethios quickly made his way over to Latimer and Rowen as if wanting to avoid any regrettable words from Xanthus. I chuckled to myself as I walked over and grabbed Xanthus by the arm and tugged on him a bit.

We started to make our way through the ruins of the once beautiful garden from Vigoro's ancient castle. And before we knew it the sun was already rising high above us as we continued onward. We passed this marvelous water fountain, which perhaps was once used for reflecting. Its blue rustic stone seemed grainy as it still glimmered like glittery flakes as the suns' gentle rays fell upon it. I wanted to rest briefly by it but, we continued to cautiously make our way past it. I knew resting was not an option at this very moment. And honestly, I didn't want to say anything being the only female here. I didn't want to seem that I was weak. So I kept my mouth shut and continued up with my strength to push forward.

As we continued upon the pebbled pathway as we pasted ruined greenhouses with shrubbery shooting out from here and there. We even passed a few fruit trees along the way as we plucked some to satisfy out hunger. We passed gardens of stones and statues that were covered in morning glories and other unfamiliar ivies. Old shattered pots seemed just about everywhere as we continued on. And as it reached about an hour past high noon, we finally stopped to catch our breaths.

I took off my shoes as I gently lowered my feet within this marvelous water fountain. It still had about an inch of water within it as it sparkled within the sun. It felt sensational upon my skin as it relaxed my sore feet. I wonder if perhaps this fountain was used for reflecting ones thoughts. I gazed around the fountain to get a better look as I noticed that the rustic sapphire stone seemed grainy. But it still glittered like... wait a minute...

I quickly stood and jumped out of the fountain as I quickly placed my shoes back on. I began to pace about as I really gathered my thoughts upon our surrounding area. My heart raced with my steps. I heard Latimer shout over to me, "Azalea what is going on? Are you alright? Is the heat coming upon your subconscious mind in a hallucination?"

Whispers escaped my lips as I continued to pace about from each corner of our surrounding, "No... No this isn't right." I stopped in mid pace as I replied a bit louder to them, "We've been circling."

Rowen sat on the edge of a ruined stone bench as he replied to me, "Azalea, I would have noticed. It is impossible to be circling when we are using the sun as a navigation; as well as the winds from this land. Azalea, you appear mortified. Are you sure you're alright? I believe you should rest for a bit."

I wasn't going to agree with them, something was not right. I withdrew my sword as I held my left palm up as it glowed a dim lavender hue. I realized that I was standing about twenty feet from the others as ruble surround us here and there. Everything around us seemed to give off a mesmerizing hum, like it was purposely enchanting us to become oblivious. I shook my head as I tried to focus on my true surroundings.

Cethios eyed me cautiously as he made his way over to me with his hands up in surrender. What was he thinking, that I was going to attack him? Was he thinking that I'd go crazy on him? I was not losing it. Cethios replied softly, "Azalea, relax. Everything is alright right now. We are ways from the castle and out of harm's way for the moment."

I glanced over to the others as they all had taken a seat next to Rowen. Xanthus replied with a frown to Latimer and Rowen, "I believe the heat is getting to her. I've never seen her so distressed like this before. Perhaps we should rest here momentarily. I know she's been through much and she does need to rest. Although, let's allow Cethios to attempt to calm her first. If we're lucky, perhaps she'll take a swing at him or two."

They chuckled amongst themselves, but I was not amused. Cethios continued to step closer as he gazed at me with much concern. I gulped as I replied to him in a soft whisper, "Cethios, how long have you known Zethron."

Cethios chuckled slightly with a shrug, "Long enough."

I gripped my sword tighter within my fingers as I replied to him within breaths, "Take a long hard glance around you. Does this seem real to you? Is any of this real? What is your heart telling you?" As he glanced around, I continue to whisper to him, "It's too late isn't it? We are too late."

And as Cethios really began to gaze around his face fell. I could tell he immediately tensed up as he withdrew his sword. He slowly walked backwards as he made his way over to me. He placed his back gently upon mine as he replied sternly, "Know this Azalea, I'll forever protect you. And I have no doubt that you'd do the same for me. So, remember, keep your eyes focused. Breathe slow breaths. Sword fighting is a graceful dance of determination and not anger."

I nodded as he continued, "Pace yourself, focus. Each move is a concentration of the mind. Determine your motivation ahead of time."

Latimer snorted a chuckle, "Awesome, now we have two that have lost it with the heat."

I ignored Latimer as I stared off into our surrounding. I quickly gazed over to Xanthus as I locked my gaze with his. I hope he could see that this was all a rouse. I hope he see the seriousness within my expression. And to my relief his expression suddenly fell with grief as he nodded, he understood. He quickly stood and withdrew his sword preparing himself for a fight. Rowen grunted, "Oh no Xanthus, not you too."

Suddenly my breaths were taken from me, and at that exact moment, I knew Zethron was here. Suddenly the ivy that clung to the nearby ruins quickly shot up and spun around Latimer, Rowen and Xanthus. It wrapped around their waist, arms and legs, immobilizing them in strength. And for Latimer and Rowen, they were trapped upon the stone benches that they sat upon. As for Xanthus, the ivy trapped him in his stance. Small leaves emerged from the ivy as it wrapped around their hands. It enclosed their fingers into a fist, preventing them from opening their hands and using magic.

Xanthus' fists became a flame as the leaves turned red and started to crisp. But just before you would think the leaves would disintegrate, they formed sharp thorns. The thorns dung into Xanthus' fists as his palms cease in their flame. Small drips of blood fell freely upon the ground from his fists as his face fell in disappointment. Xanthus grunted in slight agony as he was suddenly hoisted about two feet off of the ground by the vines. Latimer and Rowen as well were hoisted up from their seats into the air.

Chills covered my skin as I heard the sinister laugh of Zethron. And within moments Zethron stepped out from behind a stone pillar. He walked up to the elves as he replied through his chuckles, "Now what do we have here? Are these the three elves I defeated with ease a few days ago? Did you enjoy being defeated so much that you found a way to escape my dungeon in the caverns? Well, let's not allow your imprisonment to go to waste shall we, I created those caverns just for you. I was going to allow you to make your tombs within them. But since you insist, I can have you suffer in agony once more with torture before I send you back. But before I do just that, do either of you want to tell me where I may find that forsaken Azalea?"

Neither of them replied a word or glanced over towards where Cethios and I were standing. I'm sure Xanthus would have wanted me to run but, I wasn't running away any longer. I stepped a bit forward as Cethios stepped beside me. I shouted over to Zethron, "Zethron, my running ends now! If you want my Immortality, you're just going to have to come get it yourself."

Utter despair fell upon Xanthus' face as he whispered under his breath, "No Azalea… run."

I shouted over, "No! I'm not running any longer!"

Zethron chuckled as he turned towards me. He replied ever so calmly, "Azalea my sweet, are you prepared to face me yourself? Do you really believe that you can defeat me? Why, your own mother could not stop me. What makes you think that you can. And look, you have the pathetic pitiful Cethios at your side. I knew I should have just disposed of you myself centuries ago. Oh well, better late than never. I guess I can just kill you both now."

Suddenly James stepped out from our far right with his sword at hand as he shouted over to Zethron, "Not this time Zethron. Your era has come to an end."

Zethron took a step back as he seemed confused. He casually placed his hands within his pockets as he replied, "I stabbed you myself. How is it that you keep appearing out of nowhere? Did you bargain with the Eternal Spirits yourself, or have you been killing unicorns like I have to stay alive?"

James stepped closer and replied with humor, "I will gladly share with you my secret, if you explain yourself to Cethios first."

Zethron chuckled and shrugged, "Why, he needs not an explanation. He just needs death to inherit his soul."

"Suite yourself Zethron."

James shouted over to Cethios without taking his eyes off of Zethron, "Cethios, remember that promise I swore to you ages ago!"

At this Cethios turned his body slightly towards James as he continued to keep his sword pointing towards Zethron. Zethron on the other hand did not seem amused as he glared at James. James shouted at Zethron,

"Once more Zethron, I'm not asking you! Tell Cethios your plans. Tell your son your doings!"

I froze as I spaced out in astonishment and in horror. I couldn't believe the words that escaped James' lips. I wonder if anyone else had caught that. And as I turned to see Cethios, he had the same expression upon his face as I probably did. And instantly, Cethios had dropped his sword upon the ground. The next words escaped Cethios throat dryly, "Why? Why have you had me endure all of this? And yet through this all, I am your son? Is this true?"

Cethios stepped a bit forward as I quickly grabbed his arm and pulled him back. I whispered to him, "No Cethios, this doesn't change the thought of who he truly is."

Cethios turned his gaze from Zethron to me, then back to Zethron. He replied with deep breaths, "Why? Just answer me that. I have a right to know!"

Zethron raised his nose within the air as he seemed disgusted to even look upon Cethios. He shrugged slightly and replied, "Alright. I'll fall in for the moment before I destroy you all. I am an Ancient One, original of the six that first began this forsaken unity. The others I could careless who they were but, I was destined with an elf. Her name was Urinia. But after many centuries had passed, there came an era where I fell in love, with another. I foolishly fell in love with Trathina. And at once the day her and I acted on behave of that love, after our act, I lost my Immortality, and she gained it. But months later when Cethios was born, she lost that Immortality by giving birth. I pleaded with the Eternal Spirits to grant me my Immortality back but there was no convincing them, unless I paid a price. I would need to convince my son on doing the same adultery I did, upon a new unity, upon my same form of unity of elf and fairy. He would inherit their Immortality, then I'd have to kill my only son so I can therefore inherit my Immortality back. And the new Immortality of Cethios, once he gained it, would not work upon my hands, giving me the freedom of killing him as an Immortal. And if not that way, then I would have to stab the hearts of the two new destined ones at the same time with one stab; which is impossible. So, I decided to go with the first option. That one was a bit more rewarding."

Cethios, almost in tears replied, "So loving me was not an option? You simply decided to rid yourself of the one who reminded you each and every single day of your life, that you are incapable of true faithfulness and that you failed your first love. You failed your own prophecy."

Zethron's lips curled as he replied through his teeth, "Watch it boy."

Cethios gently pushed me aside as he stepped closer to Zethron. He replied to him, "So convincing me, that it should have been me and not Theron was all part of your plan? It was never going to be Theron, was it?"

At this Zethron chuckled and replied, "No foolish boy. I thought it would motivate you a bit, knowing that you had feelings for the feathered fairy. And that you desperately despised Theron."

"So where did you get that stone that I so carefully convinced you that if I held it to Azalea's stone, and when it glowed, it represented that she was still pure, pure enough for me to still take her Immortality."

Zethron frowned as he quickly withdrew the stone from his pocket. He threw it into the fountain as he replied grumbly, "It was once a part of me, until that day I was with Trathina. After that day it fell off and merely became a stone."

Zethron took in a deep breath as he continued, "Well then, I guess I'm going to have to go with my second option."

And before anyone could react, Zethron withdrew his hands from his pockets as both of his hands glowed a bright charcoal hue. He waived them within the air as I was instantly pushed by a gust of wind. I shot through the air as I landed upon Xanthus as my back pressed into his chest. I turned my head to my right to see Xanthus as I saw the fear in his eyes for the first time. And the more that Xanthus struggled in attempting to free himself, more blood flowed upon the floor as the thorns dug deeper into his knuckles.

And I realized to my horror, that I was unable to move any of my muscles in my body. I was petrified! I thought, was this the moment that Xanthus' life and mine ended? I leaned my head back slightly as I pushed against Zethron's magic. I whispered within Xanthus' ear, "At least I will be with you in the afterlife, wherever that may be."

A single silver shimmering tear fell from Xanthus' eye. It rolled down his cheek as I allowed my head to face forward, to face Zethron. But thankfully what I saw brought a jump back into my heart. James was fiercely fighting with Zethron. Although I couldn't tell who had the upper hand because they were both fighting vigorously. And there standing further away from them, was Cethios. He stood there, frozen with the thought that all this time his father had been Zethron. He kept whispering under his breath the words father and Zethron. I couldn't imagine what was going on within his thoughts; he must be torn in two.

And although I knew it was awful, I still needed Cethios to snap out of it. If we had a chance in defeating Zethron in a sword fight, it would be Cethios himself, he was unbeatable. And I needed him to realize just where he was and what he needed to do before James lost his will. I shouted over to Cethios, "Cethios! Cethios wake up! You need to get out of whatever trance you are in! Cethios! Cethios I need you!"

My shouts seemed pointless as it seemed as if I was shouting to a stone sculpture. He wasn't moving at all. And as I turned my gaze over to James and Zethron, my heart stopped as epic failure filled my soul. Zethron released a sinister laugh as he stabbed his sword deep into the chest of James. Zethron replied with a breathless chuckle, "So, how many unicorns have you killed to live yourself? And I am not asking, I'm telling you to tell me. Unless that is, you would rather wait until after I take the Immortality of Xanthus and Azalea."

James stumbled a bit as he landed upon his knees upon the ground. Slight blood oozed from the side of his trembling lips. He withdrew Zethron's sword from out of his chest as he threw it with all that he could towards Cethios. Whom still was frozen. Zethron stepped up to James as he took James' own sword from his fingers. Zethron's lips curled as he replied, "Fool, do you truly think that my son Cethios has enough will power to kill me?"

James chuckled a bit as he replied through a cough, "Yes... Yes I do."

At once Zethron spun around to face Cethios with James' sword in hand. And as he did, he unintentionally stabbed Cethios within his side. As Cethios himself drove a sword into Zethron's chest and into his heart. And it wasn't just any sword that pierced Zethron, it was his own sword.

Zethron sneered as he dug the sword more into Cethios. He pulled it out swiftly as he watched his own son fall upon the floor. Zethron chuckled a bit as he pulled his own sword from out of his chest and tossed it upon the ground as he still kept James' sword within his hands. He replied, "Foolish boy, I'm sure by now you've been forgiven for the death of

Mirage by Azalea. So, your heart actually beats now. Well, not for long anyway. But I am cursed! My heart does not beat as a normal fool!"

And with that he spun around and turned towards Xanthus and I as we hung defenseless in midair. And just as he pulled his arm back to drive the sword within our chest, James began to laugh. That of course stopped Zethron in mid strike. Zethron turned to him as he replied in a frustrated hiss, "What is it that brings you to laughter?"

James attempted to take in a deep breath but couldn't. You could tell that he was trying with all his might to stay conscious. He replied through a soft whisper, "Go ahead, I beg of you, strike at them with all that you have. You have nothing and no one to stop you. But… would you like for me to tell you my secret, before… or after you strike at them?"

Was James being serious! I was in utter shock, oh, if you could only see the look upon my face. It would not have been pleasant. How could he gamble our lives within his own plans? If he even had a plan! But strangely, Zethron allowed his hands to fall towards his hips as he chuckled, "Humor me."

James gathered all of his strength and ever so carefully stood. He dearly clung onto his chest the best that he could. He stared into the eyes of Zethron as he smiled and replied calmly, "I… I am James… The Ancient One of uniting air and water as one. I am… an Immortal with Falin, the sorcerous of the ocean; hand chosen by the Eternal Spirits. I James hear by release you from your Blood-Oath with the elf Theron. And… and I hear by truly forgive you for the deaths of the unicorns Mirage, Violet, Trinafin and Midnight. I forgive you for the deaths of Queen Lily and Queen Whistalyn; and for the death of your beloved wife Urinia… My sister."

Zethron's face fell with utter despair as his eyes widened with great fear. Fear I have never seen before, fear of epic failure. Zethron clung to his chest as now, his heart jumped with life, but unfortunately with all the damage of his past, and with recent events, it was unable to give him what he wanted, life. Zethron fell to his knees as the vines freed the three elves and as the enchantment lifted off of me. We all stumbled a bit as we continued to stand in shock as fresh blood seeped through his clothes. His body immediately began to give off a dim red glow as his energy of life was leaving him.

And within moments Zethron appeared skeletal as his last words escaped his lips as he gazed over to Cethios, "Forgive me of my jealousy, and my greed, my son. Truly, I wish I could have just been satisfied with simply being a great father to you; to my son Cethios."

Cethios smiled through his agony as he choked out, "You just became one."

And with a smile upon his face, Zethron's skeletal figure vanished with the mist. I turned and glanced at James, whom now laid still upon the earth. And I just knew he'd be alright; his life was renewing. I turned and rushed over to Cethios whom now was flat upon his back upon the ground as blood freely spread underneath him. I knelt beside him as I gazed over into Xanthus' eyes as deep sincerity filled them. Then as if reading my thoughts, he simply shook his head and whispered, "Go ahead... save him."

With an enormous grin upon my face, I turned to Cethios as I leaned over close to his lips. He smirked and replied in short breaths, "You know... I have to be honest, his quick decision to forgive you earlier surprised me. I didn't think he would let it go so effortlessly. But this... Right now, I am going to enjoy the most, because Xanthus has no choice but to watch. This is so going to tick him off."

I frowned at him, "Don't bet on it, he's bigger than that."

Cethios coughed but half chuckled out, "We'll see about that..."

I rolled my eyes as I leaned closer and gently pressed my lips upon his, kissing him. He wrapped his warm hands upon my back as I transferred some of my magic to him so he could heal himself. Cethios was going to be so full headed after this; especially after I heard Xanthus loudly grunting in disapproval with much colorful cursing under his breath near us. And all Cethios could do was arrogantly hold me tighter upon his chest.

Finally

29

I opened my eyes to see warmth and color fill my room, in Whisperia, as the suns' rays poured in. I leaned over to my right as I nuzzled my face into Snowfire's neck as she purred softly. She was still sleeping peacefully as last night's chat probably exhausted her. We were up pretty late as we caught up with everything we had wanted to say to each other. I had explained everything that had happen to me since the day I was taken from the Depths of Galligro. I told her the truth about Cethios, about his Blood-Oath and true side in which he was always on. The news surprisingly caught her a bit off guard. She knew something didn't smell right about him but she never knew that it could have been that.

In turn she told me about her adventure on Maliko's Island. She informed me that Maliko was an Ancient Dragon that was banished to the far southeast Islands of Yaisla, and why he was banished in the first place. She told me the history of her ancestors and why dragons are not allowed on any other island other than Maliko's and the main Island of Yaisla. That explained why she had not attempted to save me once Cethios brought me to Vigoro's Castle. She also explained how Krynton had told them that he truly never wanted to be evil and how he transferred over from Zethron's evil to pure goodness once again.

After a long, well deserved stretch I carefully got out of bed so I wouldn't wake Snowfire. I walked over to my night stand where a silver goblet with raspberries had been left for me. A small smile came upon my face as I thought of yesterday morning when I finally arrived back home to Whisperia. Trathina was waiting for me with tears in her eyes. I rushed to her as I embraced her dearly as I knew what she truly went through to protect her son Cethios and me.

I placed my right palm upon the goblet as I closed my eyes. I was about to prepare myself on transforming my berries into a smoothie when my thoughts were interrupted. Snowfire purred, "Do you really think that is wise of you to do right now since you have not mastered that of the simplest spells? Complex magic yes you have, but simple ones no, not quite yet. Your magic is days away from being one hundred percent yours; since it was enchanted within your skin. And I for one do not need or want berries all over me. You especially do not need berries all over your wedding dress either."

I sighed as I realized that Snowfire was right. Even though I was able to control my magic to a point, the little things always seemed to go over what I wanted. And as I turned towards my folding wall I gazed upon my wedding gown that hung upon it. It was an exquisite ivory gown with open silver laces upon the back that was going to revel my entire back basically. Crystals, sequins, and tiny shells with pearls flowed from the mid front, to the side and down in spirals. It had small slits upon the right of it that revealed layers of beautiful fabric. It was that of different honey colored laces that flowed freely as some crystal beads clung in small dangles around the edges of it.

A soft knock came to the door as my thoughts were disrupted. I responded, "Enter."

An older servant came in and bowed slightly as she carried a sliver tray with honey cake and juice. I would like to add that I missed Trajean's honey cake; it was rather enjoyably sweet to devour it once again. How I truly missed this place.

The servant placed the tray upon my bed as she turned towards me and replied with a smile, "Breakfast my lady. And if I may say, it is a great pleasure to finally gain my memory back of your mother. It was an honor serving her as it is now an honor serving her daughter."

I bowed slightly as I replied to her, "The honor has been mine. Being able to hear all of the exquisite stories about her kindness, wisdom and bravery from everyone, since that spell has been lifted has only been a great joy to my heart. Thank you."

The servant bowed her head gentle as she exited my room. And just after her Priniza came in wearing an exquisite honey colored silk dress. Laces covered her front and back as small crystals dangled from her back in a swirl. Her dress alone was a days' work for our crafters as more lace flowed from the bottom of her dress.

Priniza took one look at me and chuckled as she replied, "Trathina warned me that I'd find you unprepared. You do know that we are already heading out to the gazebo, before the sun reaches half noon. Although I am sure everyone is already there."

I yawned as I stretched once more, "Well, they can't start without me."

Priniza frowned slightly as she shook her head and as from behind her swirled out about twenty brilliantly colored butterflies. Each carried pins and crystals as I walked over to my dresser and sat down on my cushioned stool. Immediately the butterflies began to work upon my hair. They brushed and swirled pieces together as they also added the small crystals into my still slightly damp hair.

What can I say, I just had to go back to the room of no existence last night and see the seahorses Sunbloom and Lavender again. They didn't keep me long as I quickly bathed in my mothers' personal bathing chamber. I promised them that I would come back and visit again. But they did tell me a few stories as I dried off and changed.

And this time as I entered my mother's chamber, I knew just how to get pasted the painting. And although Falin was not in it this time, the unicorns were still there jumping about. And as strange as this sounds there were now four unicorns as one resembled Mirage. I definitely have to look further into that. And I know it is going to be fun searching as all of the locked up chambers from the castle have been opened. Who knew we had so many different rooms in here, especially all of the libraries and small oasis.

As I turned my head slightly around I saw that Priniza walked over to my bed and began to make it. She replied almost under her breath, "Sorry, old habit."

Once she finished she sat upon it as Snowfire curled up near her feet. As I turned to face her a few butterflies screamed in slight anger. You know, as annoying as these butterflies were, I missed them. Priniza and I both chuckled momentarily as they continued working upon my hair. I chuckled slightly as I gazed back over to Priniza and replied, "Priniza, you do not need to apologize. I do believe I will be doing a few chores myself out of habit. But, it is the ease and relaxation of accomplishing even the simplest of things. It is quite divine both physically and mentally to not be running about thinking that we're all going to die any moment. Truly, I cannot wait to begin my responsibilities and my new adventure of life with Xanthus."

Priniza sighed in a deep breath as she brushed off the invisible folds in her dress. She gazed at the butterflies fluttering about as a few started to leave and new ones arrived to start upon my natural face touch ups. She chuckled momentarily at them as if lost in her own world. But, she stared off into the oblivious behind me as she sighed once more. She turned her eyes to me as they filled with concern. She replied softly, "I do say, this is all so new to me as well, more me than you, you were actually a privileged servant. I was merely a servant, and now, I am treated like royalty. It is quite a bizarre feeling, being called Princess of Trinafin. It just will take time to become accustomed to it, you know. I am so fortunate, blessed and blissfully in love with Morpheus. I'll get used to the title eventually."

We chuckled as the butterflies seemed to be almost finished with their work. And as our laughter dulled Priniza took in a deep breath once more and asked, "Azalea? May I ask you a concerning question?"

I didn't hesitate in responding, "Of course, anything. What is on your mind?"

Priniza pondered her question briefly, then asked with a quick huff, "Are you worried about Theron? Are you not afraid that he will come for you?"

I stood carefully and made my way over to the side of the bed as I sat next to her. The butterflies followed as well, not very happy mind you. I replied thoughtfully, "You know, I am hoping that with Zethron's Blood-Oath gone Theron will have time to gather his thoughts and hopefully make wiser decision. Xanthus and I have discussed looking for him within a century or two. But, who know, only time will tell and only time will heal."

Priniza took my hands into hers as she replied sarcastically, "And you have Xanthus and Latimer there to protect you."

I chuckled, "No, I can protect myself, thank you very much. They are there for moral support if I need it."

We both leaned over bumping our shoulders with each other as we chuckled. And as we did the high pitched squeals of the butterflies made us laugh even more. "No-No-No-No! You smudge our masterpiece! No-No!"

*****

I inhaled deep breaths as I walked through a tunnel of scarlet roses and sweet white lilies. They seemed to wave in excitement as I passed with James, as he walked me towards the clearing. My father insisted on having James walk me down. For this day would not have been, if James was not there to guide me through it all. And my father seemed content with it being James.

Of course James did not deny the honor, as in his eyes, I too was his daughter. You can say James raised me rather than my true father. And I do not blame my father for not ever truly being there for me, I knew his reasoning for not getting too close. We did have the chance of having time together out in the gardens talking about many things. And even though it was great to catch up, there was still more to learn and much more moments that we will be able to now enjoy.

And yet, I think it is right for James to walk me down, after all of the things we had gone through together. I would not have wanted it any other way. And I too am glad that James and I were able to catch up, for he had a lot of explaining to do.

After the tunnel we entered the familiar clearing as it welcomed me once again with sweet aromas, and a loud cheer from a crowd. Familiar faces old and new surrounded us and the gazebo. Elves, fairies, centaurs, unicorns, mermaids and Cristats' were all here on this memorable afternoon.

Mermaids swirled in and out of the pond that surrounded the gazebo. They twirled in beautiful mesmerizing dances as I noticed that Alcina was among them. She appeared much older as glitter and starfishes clung to her black hair in a stunning do. And as I gazed right above them, I saw a few dragons mirroring their dance ever so gracefully within the free sky.

And among the dragons within a dance were Snowfire, Cetus, Orion, Krynton, Kaya and Atrigo. With them as well were Dralyn, Arin and Arista, the three griffons as they too danced gracefully.

As James and I continued on our way towards the gazebo we pasted Princess Efterpi as she bowed slightly. Denentro and Hypathia stood proudly next to her as they too bowed slightly as they continued to throw pink rose petals within the air. The rose petals seemed to take their own flight once they were released. They soared slowly all around everyone as they twisted in their own dance.

Oleos, the new King of Yaisla, stood hand in hand with another enchanting elf as she smiled and waved elegantly. Next to them also waving enthusiastically was Rowen as he too held the hand of another. She was a beautiful fairy with light brown skin and wings of green and tan. She appeared familiar as her green eyes revealed all, Beruchium's daughter Gardenia. And of course next to her was Beruchium, who seemed to be cheering the loudest with King Duralos and Trathina. Trajean was even there smiling and clapping as well.

A bit ahead right before the gazebo was King Alcander with Nylina in his arms as they waved with the crowd. And just before we neared the stone steps to enter the gazebo James whispered over to me, "Look over to your right, whom do you see upon the ground with her new earth, healthier as ever because of you."

And as I did I saw my favorite little blue rose that loved to tell me great stories of ancient times before fairies came to this land. Last I saw of her I had planted her in another pot because she was ill. I waved slightly as my little blue rose friend waved back happily with her petals. James whispered once more, "Beruchium brought her here. She insisted on seeing you wed today."

Joy filled me as I turned and carefully stepped upon the stone steps. Some mermaids waved their hands as the water that fell upon the gazebo and down onto the pond opened like a curtain. That allowed James and I to pass through without us getting drenched by the waterfall.

As I walked in I was in awe at the beauty that filled the gazebo. Exquisite flowers hung on the vines in rows as hummingbirds danced about emitting colorful glitter as they swirled between flowers. And there at the head of the gazebo was the Enchantress of the Mermaids, Falin. She looked just as lovely as she did when I first saw her within the painting waving about.

To her left were Cethios and Delphina who were already waiting hand in hand, as they too were going to wed. And on Falin's right side was Xanthus, looking ever so handsome. He was smiling shyly and waiting patiently for me. About a foot from Xanthus was his brother Morpheus and his future wife, Priniza. And of course, a few steps back from them was Latimer, my friend, my protector.

James walked me over to Xanthus whom in turn with took my hands gently into his. James stepped back and walked over next to his wife, Falin. Falin ran her fingers through her hair as she cleared her throat. She replied softly, "On this beautiful morning we are here to unite two in marriage as Xanthus presents himself to wed Azalea. And Cethios, whom presents himself here today to wed Delphina. My husband and I will also be enchanting Cethios and Delphina with the gift of Immortality to reign as the new unity of air and water. Take note though, Immortals can only perform this enchantment on infants. But because James and I are Ancient Immortals, only we can perform this on both infants and adults. And only two Immortals of the same unity can exist at a time. For the one who is trying to cast the Immortality enchantment on infants, creating a third unity of the same, their enchantment will not work. Therefore, if Cethios and Delphina try to enchant others on air and water; their magic will not allow them to. But Xanthus and Azalea on the other hand will be. And it is because they are the only ones that exist in uniting air and land. But only on one other, and only on infants of their choosing, will their magic work upon. Now, confused? All is forgiven. Moving on!"

Falin pushed her hair back as two star fish seemed to emerge from the side of the gazebo. They walked ever so gracefully as they each carried one stone. The stones sparkled as I realized that they appeared just like the gems from The Caves of Esmera. The starfish were mesmerizing to watch as it appeared that with each step they gracefully twisted their heads from side to side. It was as if they were enjoying their own dance. As they reached Falin, she bent over and carefully with took the stones from them as she threw kisses at each starfish. She stood back up and replied, "Now, these stones that I hold within my delicate hands were hand chosen by Cethios and Delphina. And by choosing one, I will be switching the ones that you choose for yourself, and I will be giving it to the other. This symbolizes your desire for each other and your bond as one, one in unity."

Falin turned and handed a stone to James. He walked over to his daughter and softly kissed her upon the forehead. He then placed the stone gently upon her forehead with his left hand as he took his right hand and placed it upon her stomach. James closed his eyes as he started to softly mumble words. Delphina closed her eyes as they both suddenly began to lightly glow an aqua hue. And once that happened, Falin walked over to Cethios as she too did the same to him.

Moments passed as the glowing ceased and as the stone vanished from Falin's and James' fingertips. I could only guess that the gems were now within Cethios' and Delphina's navel, just like mine and Xanthus'. My thoughts were confirmed as Cethios took a small step back. He lifted his shirt as sure enough, there upon his stomach, upon his belly button was a gem glowing a light blue hue. He ran his fingers over it as he shivered. He looked up to Falin as he asked, "So, is that it?"

Falin frowned as James chuckled to himself. James replied to Cethios, "And what was it you were expecting?"

Cethios shrugged as I rolled my eyes and turned to Xanthus. I smiled shyly as Xanthus locked his eyes with mine. Chills ran over my skin as my heart melted. If only I could reach over and plant my lips upon his, I would. But I knew I couldn't just yet. His warm fingers twirled into mine sending my soul soaring. Xanthus leaned over as he kissed my nose softly as he whispered, "Thought I could sneak one in before our vows."

I chuckled and blushed slightly as I am sure, that was just the first of many to come. I could not wait to finally wed Xanthus, to bind ourselves not just in our prophecy but in holy matrimony. A vow that is shared between two that love each other with everything they have. A vow for better or worse, in sickness and in heath, for all the hardships and the good, a journey an adventure, that I will never take alone, a shared path that would last an eternity.

The actual ceremony lasted quite a while as my toes became numb. But nonetheless, it was the most memorable and breathtaking ceremony ever. And in the end when I finally kissed Xanthus, it seemed as if time itself had come to a standstill. The hummingbirds hum went silent, the rustle of the wind between the flowers ceased. As well as the water falling from the fall froze as Xanthus and I finally had our carefree moment to enjoy our passionate kiss as husband and wife.

Once we parted time carried on as the roar of the cheers, from everyone outside of the gazebo, echoed louder than the waterfall itself. We all exited the gazebo as the mermaids pushed the water from the fall aside with their magic. Xanthus carried me out and over the pebbled stone path with ease.

After, we all continued the celebration within the city of Trinafin with a feast for all to enjoy, and just before the sun set under the earth and upon our day, Cethios, Delphina, Xanthus and I joined James and Falin near the Waterfalls of Aqualyn. We went there to bid them farewell as they were about to venture of into their own adventure within the ocean, in the underwater City of Oceanna. I came to bid my final farewell to James. And although I knew he was going to leave for quite a few centuries, I knew that one day we would meet again.

James' Farewell

30

"James, truly, how long will you be in the City of Oceanna? Will I ever see you again before you return?"

James gently wiped the golden tears that fled my eye with his right hand. I couldn't hold my tears in any longer. I honestly did not want him to leave me. I wanted him to stay longer, more than just the few days of peace that we had. I wanted more of his words of wisdom, I wanted to grow more like him.

James placed both of his palms upon my face as two more sparkling tears fell. James wiped them away yet once more as a warm smile spread upon his face. He replied, "I must join my other world with my Falin. But just in case, you may follow our daughter. She knows the enchantments that are needed to visit us. Do not worry Azalea; we will see each other again sooner than you are lead to believe. Perhaps not for a while but, when the time comes, I will be here for you."

I embraced him with all that I had. I snuggled my face into his chest as I took in deep breaths. I know I am brave enough to fight evil now, but not brave enough to see my mentor leave. It was if he was taking a piece of my heart with him. And as we parted, James, as if reading my mind asked, "Now before I leave, I know there is a question you have been holding back on asking me. Now is the time to ask Azalea, before it buries deep within your subconscious mind."

I nodded and asked softly, "I do have just one; it is not of doubt but, just out of curiosity. Why was it that you so easily dismayed Xanthus' life and mine when Zethron was going to deliver his final blow? Were you not afraid that Zethron would have chosen to have you explain your secret after he slayed us? Xanthus and I were helpless. I had nothing to defend myself with, if he did strike at us."

James seemed to ponder my questions as he looked over to Xanthus, whom was surprisingly enjoying Cethios' company, while Falin said her goodbyes to Delphina. A warm smile spread upon James' face to see then finally getting along so well. He sighed as he turned back to meet my gaze. He pushed up his glasses gently as he replied, "Walk with me upon these pebbles, yes?"

I chuckled a bit, "James, you need not to ask me. You know I would."

As we walked James took in a deep breath and slowly began, "You know, some things in this world are mysterious and wondrous all on their own. And yet, even though we attempt to analyze what seems to be confusing, sometimes the answer is just to be amazed at what lies before you. Therefore we respect it, and take caution over it with the faith that perhaps one day we will understand it. You then carry your knowledge of what you have learned from it, and apply it to what might come at you with the respect that you first received from it."

I smiled as I shook my head. There was no stopping James' advice of words. To this of course, James laughed. I stopped as I placed one hand upon my hip as I asked, "Meaning…"

James' laughter ceased to a chuckle as he replied, "Meaning, not everything can be explained. Some wonders are exquisite because they are just that, a mystery. Azalea, what I am trying to say is that I myself do not know the extent of this new unity that you and Latimer have made. You, already an Immortal, made a Blood-Oath with one that is not. And somehow this new unity brought a challenge to the Eternal Spirits. If Latimer was to be your protector, then he needed to be much more of what he was already capable of. Therefore, the Blood-Oath made Latimer some type of new Immortal. And the both of you now have some new extent of Immortality since it is an oath shared by blood. I had the privilege to see an extent of this new unity at the Depths of Galligro. But I myself did not know what had fallen upon him. During the battle, neither sword nor arrow wielded by anger or hatred could harm him. But, when he so clumsily fell upon a sword himself, he bleed slightly but then healed rather quickly. I do not believe Latimer knew much on what was going on then, with his new unity that he made with you. But, I was able to catch a glimpse of his tattoo when we meet up with him, when he was caught in those vines from Theron. He explained a bit of what had occurred between him and Theron. So, when Zethron had you at his will, I glimpsed the exact tattoo upon your arm. And it brought humor to me, knowing at that exact moment that Zethron's sword would have failed to penetrate your heart. Seeing as you were now a barrier between Zethron and Xanthus."

You know what, for the first time, in a very long time, I completely understood. I shook my head as I chuckled, "So that is why you were so willing in having Zethron strike at us. You knew his blow would be pointless and cause us no harm."

James smiled and nodded. I stared of into the ocean as I pondered his words, how wise and patient he was. I sighed as I took in slow deep breaths and inhaled the salty air. The breeze felt intoxicating as it pushed its hands through my hair. And as I closed my eyes briefly a new question popped within my mind. I replied, "I wonder if that is why Theron surrendered his sword to me once he spotted my tattoo. Do you think he completely understood it at that moment?"

James shrugged, "Perhaps he figured it out before I did."

I chuckled, "Wow James, your ancientness is catching up to you. I can't believe Theron figured it out before you."

James crossed his arms upon his chest as he chuckled, "Well, perhaps this new unity is for the simple minded."

We both chuckled a bit as we started to head back towards the others. And before we reached them I asked James, "James, do you think we'll see Theron again? I mean, do you think he has changed?"

James stopped near a boulder just a few feet away from the others as he replied, "I guarantee you will definitely see him again, in due time. And no, I do not believe he has changed. He might be free from his Blood-Oath but, he has always had his own bit of darkness within his heart. I'm afraid my dear, that is another quest you and the others will have to embark upon, without me."

I huffed a breath out as I leaned upon the boulder with frustrating thoughts. I'll have to discuss this with Xanthus, Cethios and Delphina soon. And as I pondered, another question popped within my mind. James of course seemed to have picked up on it as he replied, "Another question my dear?"

"Just one more I swear. So, who were the other Ancient Ones?"

James placed his hands within his pockets as he sighed once more, "Well, Esmera is for water, she is the most humorous mermaid I know. And Magnesio is for land, the elf king, although he has permanently given his land to the Centaurs. His castle is wondrous, hidden ever so cleverly within the trees. But don't worry Azalea, you will meet them one day. They both actually live in the adjacent castle in Oceanna, seeing is how Esmera is Falin's cousin and best friend. And of course Zethron was air and Urinia was land, an elf."

I had to ask, "How was she your sister if you are a fairy and she an elf?"

James chuckled, "My mother was Queen Yaisla an elf, and my father was King Vigoro, he was a fairy, they were the first of their kind to fall in love with another not of their own. They both had us, twins. Not identical mind you. But we were hand chosen by the Eternal Spirits to be destined Ancient Ones. You see, you have to understand that before there were any chosen Ancient Ones or any Unities there was much blood shed over these lands, never ceasing in war to conquer the other. Our first ancestors became Eternal Spirits and came up with a prophecy to bind the races together. Only with this Unity will peace flood the earth."

I nodded as I couldn't help myself yet again, I walked closer to James as I embraced him once more. I whispered within his ear, "I can't say I won't miss you."

Once we parted we joined the others for a bit longer as we then, bid farewell to James and Falin, just as the stars began to glow. Delphina and Cethios too said their goodbyes as well, as they headed off with Krynton to Urinia, for a century or two.

Xanthus and I picked a soft sandy shore as we gazed upon the moon and the stars above us. We walked hand in hand enjoying each other's company and the peace. Xanthus was the first to ask, "Well then, would my bride care to join me in a blissful night, in the Caves of Esmera?"

I smirked; I knew what he was meaning by. I chuckled and replied, "Of course, I'd join you anywhere my husband."

Xanthus picked me up and deeply kissed me as he spun me around. I have to admit, I got a bit dizzy. We both laughed as he placed me down carefully. And as our laughter calmed Xanthus kissed me passionately, yet softly once again, as we had another peaceful moment just to ourselves. And as we parted he gently brushed his fingertips over my cheeks and through my hair. He couldn't help himself, he once again brushed his lips over mine sighing a deep warm breath over them. Chills embraced me as he whispered softly, "So my Azalea, is this your Forbidden Fairytale that you so desperately wanted?"

I shook my head with a smug smile as Xanthus gazed into my eyes. I replied, "No, it's one better than that."

Xanthus began placing tender kisses softly upon my jaw line and neck. Oh how I will never grow tire of his lips. We began making our way to the Caves of Esmera, back to where our unity became one. And as our laughter rang out within the waterfalls, we kept each other close, embracing every peaceful moment we had.

And so ends my first cluster of journals of my Forbidden Fairytale. Treasure them forever, and always keep them close within your heart. And perhaps one day you just might discover my other journals, or of those of others. Farewell for now, from one that still lives hidden among you,

Your treasured fairy…

Azalea…

Character Guide

Fairies:
Azalea – Princess of Whisperia
Cethios – Prince of Urinia
James – Ancient One, Sword Trainer
Zethron – Ancient One, Cethios' father
Queen Lily – Queen of Whisperia, Azalea's mother
King Duralos – King of Whisperia, Azalea's father
Trathina – Head Maid
Beruchium – Head Gardener
Trajean – Head Cook
Razyna – Twin of Priniza
Priniza – Princess of Trathina, Twin of Razyna
Fendric - Soldier
Kaleen - Servant
Demik - Soldier
Gardenia – Beruchium's daughter
King Vigoro – King of Islands of Yaisla, James' father

Elves:
Xanthus – Prince of Trathina
Morpheus – Prince of Trathina, Xanthus' half brother
Queen Whistalyn – Queen of Trathina, Xanthus' mother
King Alcander – King of Trathina, Xanthus' father
Nylina – Head Maid, Morpheus' mother
Theron – Outcasted, Prince of Islands of Yaisla, Xanthus' cousin
Latimer – Outcasted, Azalea's Protector
Rowen – Outcasted
Oleos – Outcasted, New King of Islands of Yaisla
King Zyren – King of Islands of Yaisla
Urinia – Ancient One, James' twin sister, Zethron's wife
Queen Yaisla – Queen of Islands of Yaisla, James' mother
Magnesio – Ancient One

Mermaids:
Falin – Ancient One, Delphina's mother, James' wife
Delphina – Princess of Urinia, James' daughter, Cethios' wife
Alcina – Friend
Esmera – Ancient One

Centaurs:
Denentro - Friend
Hypathia – Herbalist
Melancton – Prince of Magnesio
Narcissa – Princess of Magnesio, Melancton's daughter
Dragons:
Snowfire – Azalea's
Cetus – Xanthus'
Orion – Morpheus'
Krynton – Cethios'
Kaya – James'
Atrigo – King Alcander's
Maliko – Ancient Dragon

Griffons:
Destra – Theron's
Dralyn – Latimer's
Arin – Oleas'
Arista – Rowen's

Unicorns:
Mirage
Violet
Trinafin
Midnight

Sea Horses:
Lavender
Sunbloom

Cristats:
Efterpi – Princess of Xylina
King Aetius – King of Xylina

Places:
City of Whisperia – Fairies
City of Urinia – Fairies
City of Trinafin – Elves
City of Magnesio – Centaurs
The Great Plains of Oasia
The Valley of Melinatha
Waterfalls of Aqualyn
Caves of Esmera
Gardens of Vinalin - Elves
The Great River of Anusuma
City of Xylina – Cristats
Islands of Yaisla – Elves
City of Oceanna – Mermaids
Castle of Vigoro - Fairies
Ruins of Yaisla – Elves

Hello Reader

If you want to be up to date with my projects and more, please visit,
Facebook: YPCreations84
Instagram: yanet_platt
Goodreads: YanetPlatt